CROOKED RIVER BURNING

MARK WINEGARDNER

CROOKED
RIVER
BURNING

HARCOURT, INC.

New York   San Diego   London

www.harcourt.com

This is a work of fiction. Names, characters, and incidents,
such as Dorothy Fuldheim's interview with Lou Groza, are either products
of the author's imagination or are used fictitiously for verisimilitude.

Library of Congress Cataloging-in-Publication Data
Winegardner, Mark, 1961–
Crooked river burning/Mark Winegardner.—1st ed.
        p.   cm.
ISBN 0-15-100294-0
1. Cleveland (Ohio)—Fiction.   I. Title.
PS3573.I528 C7 2000
813'.54—dc21   00-031951

Text set in Monotype Sabon
Designed by Trina Stahl

First edition
A C E G I K J H F D B

Printed in the United States of America

This book is a love song to J.
and the grand, misunderstood city she came from

CONTENTS

ACKNOWLEDGMENTS

For support in the writing of this book,
the author would like to thank the Corporation of Yaddo,
the Ragdale Foundation, the Ohio Arts Council,
Florida State University, the Black Dog Café,
and Carl and Carol Keske.

Cleveland, city of light, city of magic.
Cleveland, city of light, you're callin' me.
Cleveland, even now I can remember
'Cause the Cuyahoga River
Goes smokin' through my dreams.
                    —Randy Newman, "Burn On"

History would be a wonderful thing—if it were only true.
                    —Leo Tolstoy

"We're going to burn you."
                    —Marilyn Sheppard's murderer

PART ONE

∾

THE BIRTHPLACE OF
ROCK AND ROLL
The Sixth City: 1948–1952

— I —

NINETEEN YEARS LATER, excerpts of David Zielinsky's truncated telling of what happened that day—July 14, 1948—would be broadcast on two of what were then three network news broadcasts. In his opinion (the opinion of a man whose great love was Anne O'Connor, a woman whose great love was being on TV), you can't get more truncated than the nightly news. But that's an opinion he won't have for a while yet.

Here's the deal.

David Zielinsky was fourteen years old and did not want to go with Uncle Stan for a drive into the city. He and two buddies were supposed to ride their bikes to Brookside Pool, where they'd heard there was a redheaded lifeguard who for a buck fifty would take guys into the woods behind the zoo and let them see her pubes. Doubtful. Still, it was worth riding over there and seeing what you could maybe turn your lawn-mowing money into. What he turned his money into instead was a better investment. But like anything of consequence, it happened by accident.

You'd have thought he'd want to go. David grew up eight miles from downtown Cleveland—his first four years in his parents' bungalow in Old Brooklyn, the last ten with his mother's sister, Betty, and (since the war ended) his Uncle Stan, in the house next door, identical but for the shutters, the furnishings, and the state of repair. In his fourteen years, David had crossed the Cuyahoga River only for school field trips, Christmas shopping, or Indians games—never, as far as he can remember, in a car. The streetcar was how you went, when you went, which was seldom.

And so: on a hot, gray Wednesday in July, David had finished mowing his lawn and the lawn of his father's house, and was putting away the mower when Uncle Stan, who worked downtown and was never home during the day, pulled into the drive in his week-old car, a yellow 1949 Willys Jeepster. It looked like the result of a night of gin-provoked coitus between a runtish moving van and a ragtop Studebaker and was, David thought, the worst match of car to driver ever to hit the American road. Uncle Stan had been a Chicago cop, the short young balding one in that famous picture placing the cuffs on Capone, then Eliot Ness had brought him to Cleveland as one of his Untouchables here, then Stan went to war and did things that Aunt Betty said

[3]

he couldn't talk about so don't ask, then he came home and opened a one-man detective business and accepted the obligation of raising his nephew, his wife's sister's half-orphaned kid. A man like this, David thought, should drive a four-door Ford.

"Shower up, ace." Despite the threat of lake-effect rain, Stan got out and began, with due American efficiency, to put down the car's cream-colored top. "I'm buying you lunch."

Stan was the kind of man it was hard to question. David felt brave asking where.

"Downtown," said Stan. "We're meeting someone. Maybe get a haircut, too, if you get a move on." He stroked his neatly trimmed silver mustache, took off his hat, and ran his hands over his friar's fringe of hair. "Both of us. I'll get you back here in plenty of time." By which he meant David's paper route, the afternoon *Cleveland Press*.

"Where downtown?" David was, he knew, pushing his luck.

"Place on Short Vincent."

"Who are we meeting?" David asked, already sure.

"It's a surprise," Uncle Stan said, which, to David's mind, cinched it: they were going to see David's father, Mike, a Short Vincent regular, who every couple weeks swung by the house next door to get his mail or sleep one off. Mikey Z. David hadn't spoken to him in months.

David had of course never been to Short Vincent Street. It wasn't a place you took a kid.

Aunt Betty called hello. She was on the front porch, reading *Beowulf* (she'd been taking night school classes for as long as David could remember, toward a degree in no one knew what). Stan smiled and went to kiss her, and David heard them chortle like kids going steady.

Then Stan returned to his car. "You still here?"

"I am," David said. "Listen, you want me to move back over there?" He pointed to his father's house, where David had not lived since he was four, and his mother left for Hollywood and drowned soon thereafter, and to which he did not even have a key. "I will if you want."

"What?" Stan furrowed his brow, shook his head. "Where'd you come up with that? Did you think that was what I meant?"

"Maybe." No.

They regarded one another with resolute puzzlement. David was an all-elbows beanpole in cutoffs and Keds. Stan Lychak was a compact, guarded man who hadn't wanted children and seemed never to have been one. Once, for a trip to Euclid Beach Park, Stan wore brogans and a fat tie.

"Well?" Stan resumed the ministrations needed to transform his nutty car. "Shake a leg."

Going anywhere with Stan was like taking a school field trip. He was the sort of man who stopped at roadside markers and read them aloud. On the drive up Pearl Road, he tuned in a recorded broadcast of the Cleveland Orchestra, identifying each piece on the program. At each stoplight, he had to turn the radio down; as he got under way again, he'd turn it back up, overtaxing the tinny dashboard speaker. "Ah, *Finlandia*," Stan said. Pearl became West 25th. "By the Finnish composer Jean Sibelius. Pride of the Finns."

As if David cared.

"Born I believe in 1865," Stan said at the next light. "Still living. Sadly neglected these days."

"Great."

"Yes," Stan insisted. "Great."

"Did I say he wasn't?" Yes. Though you had to be impressed by a guy who was practically a hundred years old.

The light at the west-side foot of the Lorain-Carnegie Bridge turned green. Ramrod stiff behind the wheel, Uncle Stan adjusted his hat for the up-coming wind, put his car into gear, and began the slow ascent up and over the Cuyahoga.

Flanking the road, on each corner of the bridge, were mammoth sandstone pylons, each carved into the shape of an impassive art deco angel, each clutching what looked like a large toy to its breast: the one on the left a stagecoach, on the right a car, what looked like a 1930 Dodge. Stan pointed and, over the scratchy music and howling wind, yelled, "The Guardians of Traffic!"

David felt a pressure on his chest, which might have just been the wind off the lake and down the Cuyahoga Valley but felt like more. Everything, everywhere, was large and possible. The limitless lake shimmering in the haze to the north. Closer, on Whiskey Island, were mountains of gravel and salt, and those monster-movie-insect Huletts that loaded and unloaded the freighters. And to the right, to the south! As far as the eye can see stretched a crooked valley: a tenebrous wonderland carpeted with smokestacks and tank farms, drawbridges, ore trains, and every stippled color of smoke and fire you could imagine.

Would you *look* at all the bridges! A Tinkertoy exposition of drawbridges, cranking every which way, spinning and lifting, rotating and tilting, pitching and yawing: right, left; up, down.

Halfway across the mile-long bridge, with nothing above him but the sky, David threw back his head and let the wind throttle his face. Even the *sky* looked too large to fit where the sky used to go!

Uncle Stan, hat securely in place, tapped him on the arm and winked. "Nice view, eh?"

David could only nod.

Before them loomed two more sandstone angels, the one on the left holding a steam engine, the one on the right a dump truck. Beyond the bridge was a hobbled mess of truck docks and sooty brick food warehouses, and beyond that: Terminal Tower!

The tallest building in the world, if you don't count New York City, and let's not. Fifty-two craggy, greenish, wedding-cake stories, rising and tapering toward the turreted spire. On top, an American flag. Below that, a Cleveland Indians flag.

Could it be a mistake? Isn't this an off-day, the day after the All-Star Game?

"Indians flag," shouted Uncle Stan, pointing. "They fly it anytime the Indians're home."

"No fooling."

"What?"

"Nothing."

Only as they were about to reach the eastern side, as bridge became road, did David think to look back at the river they'd crossed: the Cuyahoga, clotted with black freighters, kinked as a great beast's spilled intestine, glowing green and yellow.

It was a beautiful damn thing.

⟍⟋

UNCLE STAN PULLED into a parking lot just as the sun broke out and the orchestra played the brassy last bars of *Finlandia*. Stan shut off the car, turned the key, and they sat listening to the applause. The radio went to commercial. All Stan said was "outstanding." All David could think to say was "yeah." David asked if Stan wanted help putting the top up. Stan assessed the sky. "No," he said. "I'll risk it."

The Indians were in first. Cleveland was no one's idea of a joke. An ex-cop felt OK about leaving his new car unlocked. The sun shone.

At least until you turned the corner onto Short Vincent, that dark 485-foot-long glorified alley.

"I thought it'd be bigger," David said.

"That," said Uncle Stan, "is how it usually goes."

Doormen and bellboys milled around under the canopy of the alarmingly medium-sized Hollenden Hotel. The two main restaurants, Kornman's and the Theatrical, were normal-sized, with nondescript facades. There were no elephants or famous movie stars or flagpole sitters or presidential motorcades; nothing that local lore or David's father had led him to expect. Just a 485-foot one-way street, westbound.

Stan checked his watch. They were of course early. "In here." He held open the door to Ciccia's Barbershop. "Let's get our ears lowered."

David and his uncle took the last two seats, underneath a cobwebby moose head sporting an Indians cap (black, red bill, wishbone C, no Wahoo). On the television set was a floor fight in Philly, over a civil rights plank in the Dems' platform.

In the middle of a workday, Ciccia's was full of cigar smoke and men, and the talk was full of what you'd think. Baseball. Mock despair over women. Lies about fish. The word on what's what in City Hall, who's bent and straight at the CPD. The things the *Press,* the *News,* and the *Plain Dealer* knew about but wouldn't print. The skinny from the touts and sharps about today's sure things. *Plus* the guy in the next barber chair could be anybody. Bill Veeck, say.

"Mr. Veeck," said the barber. "You're next."

David, the only kid in the place, stared as the Indians' owner, a young, curly-haired, sunburned ex-Marine, grappled with his metal crutches—he had a wooden leg—and, still chuckling over one of his own jokes, climbed into the chair. In 1948, to own the Indians was to own Cleveland. Give a snake-oil salesman single-malt scotch to sell instead, and, as David's father would say, the world lines up to suck his dick.

"What about it, Billy?" called a monstrously fat man in a derby. "How long can it last?"

Already, David was thinking how he'd tell the story to his buddies in Old Brooklyn. He reached into his pocket, but there was nothing for Veeck to sign. Just some change and a comb.

"Should be a hell of a race," said Veeck. "Come out and see. Bring your wives."

"Shoes ain't got a wife," somebody said.

"Don't need one," Shoes said. "I got yours."

There was talk of who might catch Cleveland—the A's, the Red Sox, the evil Yankees. Someone asked Veeck about the Satchel Paige stunt.

"It's no stunt, fellas. That fucking guy can still pitch. Come out and see."

"That nigger's fifty years old if he's a day," someone said.

Just outside the screen door to Ciccia's was a shoe shine stand, where two old black men worked. No white man, then, would have thought to lower his voice because of them. In less than twenty years, any white man would have.

"That *Negro*," said Veeck, and he paused to let his point sink in, "might be the best pitcher who ever lived. Not the best Negro: the best, period. When we tried him out, Boudreau felt like some of you fellas do." Lou Boudreau was the player/manager, a thirty-year-old shortstop leading the league in hitting. "Then I had Satch pitch to him. That, as Satch put it, was when Mr. Boudreau found religion."

The men laughed. David wanted to join in the conversation, wanted to ask Mr. Veeck for free tickets, an autograph, a real American League baseball. But he couldn't. He remained a kid in the corner, undetected.

"I'd have done it earlier," Veeck said. "Back in '44 I tried to buy the Phillies. Wanted to release all those sorry bastards and hire a Negro all-star team."

"What happened?"

Startled, David realized it was Uncle Stan who asked. Stan, as far as David knew, didn't follow sports. The eyes of Ciccia's were, for a moment, on David, but nobody said anything.

"I got blackballed," Veeck said. "No sale." The barber was finishing: the green tonic, the powder. He was the fastest barber David had ever seen. "It kills me," Veeck said, "that Brooklyn got Jackie Robinson up last year those few weeks before I got Doby, but that's baseball. They'd've never let *me* do it. Had to be one of the old boys, and it had to be in New York, see, for publicity reasons."

As Veeck got out of the chair, Ciccia's broke into laughter and applause. At first David thought it was for Veeck, but the men were facing the door. There—dressed in white shoes, a houndstooth suit, a cigar in one hand, a stack of handbills in the other—stood David's father.

David knew it. Gee, what a surprise.

"If you'll excuse my French," Mike Zielinsky said, "fuck you all." He bowed. He was a tall, broad-shouldered, pie-faced man. "It was a fucking joke, OK? I meant it as a fucking *joke*."

As Veeck left, Mike shook hands with him (David, agog: *My father knows Bill Veeck?* then angry: *My father knows Bill Veeck—and I don't?*) and began to pass out the leaflets, thrusting them with his palm against people's chests, and did not notice his son or his brother-in-law. Stan, poker-faced, didn't move. On television Eric Sevareid talked to angry white Texans.

"Next," said the barber.

"Everybody's heard, right?" said the fat man. "Mikey Z's big moment at the City Club?"

"Fuck you, OK?"

"Our esteemed colleague and candidate for the state senate of the great state of Ohio—"

"I mean it, Shoes."

Candidate for what? David thought. *Is this just somebody who* looks *like my father?*

"—he gets asked by one of those ladies from the League of Dame Voters—"

"Women, Shoes."

"—what his position is on the Taft-Hartley Bill, and he says..." Shoes stood up and milked the moment. "Get this, he—"

"I said I already paid it," Mike said. "Satisfied? I didn't hear her so good, you fat fuck. So fuck you."

Someone helpfully pointed out that Mike had initially said he'd meant it as a joke.

"That's right," Mike said. "What's your point?"

"Joke, my ass," Shoes said. "No sale."

The Short Vincent regulars were loving this, cheering, egging on, laughing, jostling.

"I said *next,*" said the barber. "Somebody better park his heinie in my chair or I'm chasin' you bums outta here and going home with one of your lonely wives."

Stan stood, then motioned for David to go first.

"I'll be damned," said Mike, noticing them. "Hiya, guys! What brings you down here?"

"We're meeting someone," said Stan. "For lunch."

They *weren't* there to meet David's father?

"I need some lunch myself," Mike said. "Fellas, this handsome mug here is my boy!"

David sat in the barber chair.

"I see the resemblance," Shoes said. "Looks just like me."

Mike Zielinsky winked at David and Stan, then spun around and swung. His fist connected with the side of the fat man's head, making a sound like a rib roast falling on linoleum, sending Shoes's derby flying and Shoes himself back down into his chair.

"Christ." Shoes rubbed his face, no more fazed than if he'd been slapped. "Touchy, touchy."

"Not in front of my boy," Mike said. "Show some respect."

The barber tied the apron behind David's neck. Mike retrieved the derby and handed it back to Shoes. Stan stood in the middle of the floor, hands thrust coolly into his pockets, shaking his head.

"How's he want it?" the barber asked. Stan started to answer.

"Flattop," David blurted.

Mike shrugged. "Flattop's good," he said. "How's tricks, Stanley?"

"Can't complain. Keepin' busy."

"I guess a guy like you would be. Oh, hey," Mike snickered, "nice car you bought. Guess they saw *you* comin', huh?"

How long had it been since David had talked to his father? Two months? Three?

The barber's hands fluttered around David's head. Hair flew. Every few seconds he would grip David's head with his left hand, like a greengrocer palming a melon.

Stan said that Mike ought to drive the Jeepster sometime, and told about how he'd gone right to the factory in Toledo to pick it up. This set off a flurry of stories. New cars were just getting easy to come by. Everyone had just bought one or was about to. David wanted to ask about that state senate thing. He wanted to ask who they were there to have lunch with, if not his father. But he was stuck in the chair. He couldn't even bring himself to tell the barber the apron string was too tight.

The barber finished and spun David around to face the mirror. "Great," David said, because it was. A perfect flattop.

"Hard to believe," someone said, "Mikey Z's got a kid. How old's your kid, Mikey?"

"Old enough to whip your ass," David's father said.

"Yes, Mike," said Uncle Stan. "How old do you think he is?"

David had never received an on-time birthday present from his father.

"Shut up," said Mike. "I know what you're up to, so just shut up. Frank!" he said to the barber, "keep his thing on and give the boy a shave, willya?" He wadded up one of his own handbills and tossed it at Stan. "He's old enough for a shave, right?"

Stan caught it, then looked as if he couldn't decide whether to throw it back or dispose of it properly. Instead, he unwadded it, smoothed it. "Right,

Mike. You know," he said, reading the flyer, "I had no idea you were a man of such standing in our community."

"There's a lot you don't know, Stanley. Frank? Shave the boy already."

The barber looked over to Stan.

David had in fact been thinking he was close to ready to start shaving. "Come to think of it," David said, trying to deepen his voice, "I could really go for a shave."

As soon as he said it, he'd have given ten bucks not to have. All the men laughed, even Stan. Everyone but the barber. He pressed a foot pedal and pulled a lever; the next thing David knew he had a hot towel on his face and let out a yelp. The men laughed some more. David could hear the barber working the strop. The barber snatched off the towel. David squinted into the fluorescent tubes above. The barber slathered David's face with hot shaving cream from a feather-soft brush.

The straight razor started scraping David's long face. The barber pressed down harder now than with the haircut. His breath smelled of cloves. David closed his eyes. Then the barber slapped David's cheeks with Skin Bracer and he was snapped back up into the whorl of the smoky room. The barber cracked the apron like a bullwhip. He nudged David out of the chair. "Next."

⚬

IN CLEVELAND, ELIOT Ness busted hundreds of bent cops and racketeers. He was a drinking buddy of the newspaper swells; they were his unpaid press agents. It couldn't last forever. The mob put pressure on all the right people. A new mayor wanted to appoint his own top cop. And a city as Catholic as Cleveland lost patience with the twice-divorced, thrice-married Ness. He was out. During the war, he opted not for intelligence, as Stan had, but a civilian post, in charge of fighting the spread of V.D. After that, Ness sunk all his money (a modest sum) into an import-export business that went quickly bankrupt. The Eliot Ness who walked into the Theatrical that day was forty-five, ten years shy of TV fame (by which time he'd be dead), a hollow-cheeked man in a once-fashionable suit, who last year had allowed the Republicans to draft him as a mayoral candidate. Ness's personal charisma hadn't translated from barroom tables to the podium at the City Club, where he'd been a nervous wreck. Even Stan (in fairness, he voted straight Democrat his whole life) didn't vote for his old boss.

It was Ness—not Mikey Z, who could lead even while in tow—whom they'd come to meet.

They were seated away from the bar, upstairs, in a dark room with velour chairs, flocked wallpaper, and countless signed glossies of actors and singers David didn't recognize. In the center of the table was a jar of pickled eggs and a bowl of kosher pickles. From downstairs there drifted the sound of jazz on the jukebox and a din of male voices.

As they waited for Ness, Mike called the waiters by name and ordered two Rob Roys and a Roy Rogers. Stan drank ice water, his Rob Roy untouched and sweating on the table, and listened to David and Mike talk baseball. David could quote statistics and do a passably nasal impression of Indians' broadcaster Jimmy Dudley. His father was the sort of man who played sports but when it came to talking about the pros just faked it.

"Christ, you're getting big." Mike was six eggs, ten pickles, and two Rob Roys into it. "Gonna be bigger'n the old man."

"I haven't grown an inch in over a year," David said. Already this year he'd grown three.

"Fill out," Mike said, "and next summer I'll get you a job." He winked. "A *man's* job, down on the loading docks."

Stan was shaking his head.

"What?" Mike asked.

"Nothing," said Stan. "It's not my place."

"What's not your place?"

"Nothing, OK? Drop it."

David did not call his father *Dad*. He didn't have the nerve to call him *Mike*. He didn't call him anything. He had to have eye contact. Now, when he got it, he said, "I have a question."

"Shoot, Sherlock." Mike was amused. "I'm an open book."

"Yeah, a road atlas," said Stan. "Or a comic book."

The Uncle Stan that David knew was not a wiseass. David looked at him. Then back at Mike. "You're running for state senate?"

Mike waved a paw at his son. "Just for show. The muckety-mucks in the union think it'd do us good to run somebody in the primary. Politics." Mike said *politics* the way you'd say it if there were a cat turd under your nose. "I don't suppose that makes sense to a kid, huh?"

"I'm not five years old." David frowned. "I'm not a moron."

Mike grinned. "I guess not. What it is," Mike said, "is I'm doing a job for the union. Helping out people who know people, see, which then helps me help out the little guy." He popped another egg, whole, into his mouth, and, mouth full, said, "It's complicated, kiddo."

Mike did not call David by name, either.

From downstairs came the sound of a wailing trumpet and the faint edges of an argument over *nigger music*. Twenty years later, David would purchase a copy of this very Louis Armstrong record. Twenty years after that, he'd replace the worn-out record with a compact disc. But now, he had no clue or even, in this respect, a desire for one.

"Eliot!" Stan stood, extending his arm, then using it to pull Ness into a manly back-slapping embrace.

Mike Zielinsky sat back in his chair. "Sic transit," he muttered, "gloria fucking mundi."

Excuse your Latin, too, David thought.

"Excuse me?" Ness said. He had an alarmingly soft voice. Almost girlish.

"Nothin'," Mike said. "Just thinkin'."

"This is my brother-in-law, Mike Zielinsky."

Ness smiled wanly. "Pleased. Have we met?"

"Maybe," Mike said. "I think we shook hands after you spoke at the union last year." He tapped the Teamster pin on his lapel. "I'm assistant treasurer of one of the locals."

"Huh," Ness said.

"This is my nephew, David," Stan said. "David, Eliot Ness."

"Your uncle's told me a lot about you, David."

"Thanks." *Thanks?* Well, what else do you say to that?

"Sorry I'm late," Ness said. "I thought you'd be downstairs."

"Forget about it," Stan said. But nothing galled Stan more than lateness.

Ness sat down and ordered a Gund beer. Everyone ordered steak sandwiches.

Ness wasn't famous enough for David's friends to be impressed. The first time David would brag about having met him came a week after the 1959 Desilu Playhouse television debut of *The Untouchables*. Once Ness was fictionalized, he seemed real, and that gave David a story to tell. The more he told it, the more he relied upon its own past tellings than the superseded facts of what really happened. David would give his listeners the impression he'd felt like a boy who touched the cape of Superman. In his mind's eye David, like his audience, would see Robert Stack or Kevin Costner, not Eliot Ness—a tired-looking man who swapped cop-talk stories with Stan while David's father ate and drank too much and kept oddly quiet.

Then the bill came.

Ness grabbed it from the waiter's hand, and the men began to argue over it. Ness wouldn't relent. He had the bill; David thought he'd won. Mike went to the men's room downstairs. When the waiter told Ness and Stan that the gentleman had already taken care of it, they bickered for another forever. Peace was achieved only when Mike allowed as how he'd let them buy him another Rob Roy. Stan, still nursing his first drink, slipped the waiter a five and ordered another round.

"So, Stan," Ness said, "how's business? Being your own boss and all that?"

"It's all right," Stan said. "Boring. But after the war, boring suits me fine."

They all agreed to this, although Stan was the only one who'd been in the military. Mike, even though his sister-in-law was raising David, had used David to stay out of the service.

"Stan, I was wondering," Ness said, "what I mean to say is, I'd regard it as a favor if you could put me on the payroll." He paused, cleared his throat. "For about sixty a week."

"Put you on the payroll?" Stan asked.

Ness nodded.

"Which would mean what?"

Ness grinned—a sheepish grin, a boy's attempt to charm his way out of something. A silence settled over the men. Ness's grin faded gruesomely. The three men all seemed to try not to look one another in the eye. A waiter came by. Mike bought Ness another drink.

Stan checked his watch, shifted his weight in his chair. "The thing is, Eliot—"

"I understand."

"—as things are, you know, I just hired a secretary—"

"Really."

"—and I've got enough business to keep *me* busy, but I—"

"Don't say another word," Ness said. "Don't worry about it. I thought I'd ask, is all."

Mike Zielinsky sat his drink down, too hard.

"You know, Mr. Eliot Ness," Mike said, "if you're looking to be on a payroll"—and here he jabbed a finger at his own breastbone—"I might have a payroll you can be on."

Ness looked at him, still, it seemed, trying to place him. "You would, huh?"

"Mike," Uncle Stan said. "For god's sake."

"What?"

Stan started to say something, then looked at David and stopped himself.

That, apparently, was enough time for Ness finally to place Mikey Z. "I appreciate the offer," Ness said. "I do. But I still have some other avenues I'd like to explore first."

"Fine," Mike said. "Whatever you say." He stared across the dining room and said something under his breath that everyone let go and David thought sounded like *Mr. Bigshot.*

The Rob Roys and the beer came. Into the breach of another squirmy silence, Stan mentioned that he had a new car. Did Ness want to go see it? It was just around the corner. Maybe take it for a spin down by the lake?

"You gotta see this car," Mike said, "to believe it. What's a private dick doing in a car like that?"

Stan said he didn't do stakeout work, and anyway what's it to Mike? "Whattaya say, Eliot?" Stan was trying too hard, which David had never seen him do.

Ness looked shifty-eyed now, like he wanted to go—which David did, too. But Ness said, "Sure, why not."

"My paper route," David blurted. "What time is it? I have to go do—"

It was almost three. "Take the streetcar," Stan said. "You got time."

Could Stan really be suggesting that David risk running late?

"I'll give you a ride, kiddo," Mike said. "I got nowhere to be until later."

"No," David said, too quickly. "I have time. I'd rather."

"Sheesh." His father showily sniffed his armpits. "Usually, people like me. Y'know?"

The whole scene felt to David like a glimpse of something he shouldn't have seen.

"I like the streetcar," David said, though he didn't, particularly. "I've taken it alone a million times." Hardly ever. But he had done it. It was 1948. Children rode bikes and streetcars alone to distances that would soon be unthinkable.

David got up and shook hands manfully with the overfirm grips of Mr. Ness and Uncle Stan. His father gave him a quick hug. David stiffened. Mike laughed and called David *little man.*

⌒⌒

How much of history—personal, national, cultural—*does* happen by whim and accident? Half? Three-quarters? All of it? In a story, people want to know why a person does a thing. In their own lives, not a day goes by when they don't do a thing they can't explain.

David Zielinsky walked out of the Theatrical and onto Short Vincent, left onto East Sixth, right onto Euclid Avenue, heading to Terminal Tower, where he intended to take the streetcar home, heave rubber-banded newspapers onto stoops all over Old Brooklyn, eat the dinner Aunt Betty would serve, and after that meet up with his buddies and see if that redheaded life-guard was still over at Brookside, if she even existed, and be home by dark.

Instead, as he waited for the light at Public Square to turn green, he looked fifty-three stories up in the air and saw the Indians flag flapping in the wind above the crags of Terminal Tower. The light turned, but David started walking the other way, toward Lake Erie, the north coast of the United States of America. His legs seemed to know where he was going before he admitted it to himself: he's going to the game. A night game, sure, but why the hell not? He was fourteen years old, practically a man.

Outside the stadium, he found a phone, called his friend Carl, his usual sub, and asked if he'd do the paper route for the usual buck. Carl said sure without even asking why. David bought a ticket. It would be over an hour until the gates opened. David walked down to the oily lakeshore and sat there running his hands over and over his smooth face. He watched the Huletts at the mouth of the river, unloading ore, loading salt on Whiskey Island.

Only then did he even stop to think about who the Indians were playing. He looked at the ticket. *Indians v. Brooklyn? We're playing a National League team?* Last month they'd played Brooklyn in Brooklyn, an exhibition game for some sob-sister operation. This probably had to do with that. Probably won't be ten thousand people there.

A part of him knew that he'd get in trouble for staying out late like this and not telling anyone. A part of him thought maybe not. The biggest part of him, which he did not for a moment understand, didn't care.

൭൧

WHEN THE GATES opened, David was more or less the first one in. He bought a pencil and a scorecard (he always keeps score; one day these score-cards will fill a four-drawer file cabinet in his law office). He emerged from the tunnel to the first glimpse of green field, a heart-shock of loveliness, and seventy-two thousand empty seats, and the hand-operated scoreboard, and the oversize American flag thrashing high above the bleachers.

But the best part were those men, the '48 Indians. David took a seat near third, to watch them take batting practice. Mitchell, Doby, Keltner, Gordon, Hegan: the names and faces of heroes who will dance in David's head for the rest of his life. He was fourteen and the Indians were in first; no other team will ever hit balls as far, field as well, run as gracefully, throw as hard, get along so well, or look better in crisp white Cleveland uniforms.

Enthralled by the choreography of men taking their places at the plate, of outfielders shagging fungoes, and infielders gobbling up short-hop grounders,

David hardly noticed the stadium fill. Only twelve thousand advance tickets were sold; paid attendance was 64,877. By the time an usher told David he'd have to move now and go find his real seat (fourth row, upper deck, up the first-base line), the place was packed: all walk-up sales, all black.

Well, not *all*. But as David made his way up the ramps to his seat it looked that way. Black faces everywhere, men, women, and children. But mostly men: thousands of dapper men. More black faces in one place than a kid from the West Side had seen in his life up to then. His seat was on the aisle, next to a stocky white-haired Negro in a porkpie hat, waving a Brooklyn Dodgers pennant.

"Hello," David said. "Are you from New York City?"

Reasonable question, right? The man looked at David like he was crazy. "No," he said. "Are you?"

"No."

That was all they said to each other for a while.

Then things got strange. The lights came on (though they weren't yet needed), the game began, Brooklyn came to bat, and the crowd was rooting for . . . *Brooklyn?* How could this be?

Later David would stress how he felt, being for the first time in his life a minority. That wasn't what he felt. He was unmoored by all those Clevelanders rooting for the Dodgers.

Reese, the Dodgers' shortstop, led off the game with a bunt. Hegan threw off his mask, bare-handed the ball, and gunned it to first. David leaped from his seat, shouting. But all Hegan's great play got was polite applause. David was the only person in his section on his feet.

Like a kid in math class who'd yelled to be called on and then gave a rockhead answer, David hung his head and sat down. As he bent over his scorecard and recorded Reese's out—2–3, with a tiny star next to it so he'd remember it was a great play—the old man to his right jumped up and so did everyone else, and Cleveland Municipal Stadium rocked.

"Now batting, number 42, the second baseman, Jackie Robinson. Robinson."

Oh, David thought. *So that's it.*

They stayed on their feet through Robinson's whole at-bat. David stood up, too. But no one, he thought, was going to make him root against Cleveland.

Robinson hit the ball. The crowd roared, but it was just a routine fly ball to Doby.

To Doby! David wanted to yell. The first Negro in the American League, weeks after Jackie. Everywhere Doby went last year he was the first. No matter. Jackie was The First. That, and the addition of Roy Campanella, a second Negro before most teams had one, made Brooklyn black America's team—even, to David's horror, in Cleveland. Even *Clevelanders* respect a thing that happens in New York more than they do a thing that happens here. The Midwest's boosterism is just a cloak for its self-loathing. A midwesterner who accomplishes much will soon feel the suspicious glare of the neighbors: *If you're so good,* the glare says, *why are you still here?* At the time, all David could have said was that you're not supposed to root against your home team. He didn't understand, as the man beside him did, the range of what *home* can mean.

All this said, let's not lose sight of the fact that it was a splendid baseball game.

In the bottom of the fourth, Cleveland scored first, when Doby doubled and Boudreau knocked him in. David doesn't remember it this way, but the crowd did cheer for Doby. Brooklyn tied it in the fifth. Cleveland came back in the bottom of the inning with two more, on Mitchell's blast to right-center, a long double that missed going out by this much.

The old Negro man looked over at David's scorecard. "Robinson leads off the sixth," he asked.

The man had a slight southern-sounding accent and it took David a moment to realize it was a question, not a statement. "Right," David said.

"The name's McNabb." The man extended his hand. "You keep a nice scorecard."

"Thanks." David didn't think to introduce himself. By the time he realized it was rude, he was afraid to say anything for fear of calling attention to his rudeness.

"Pinch-hitting for the second baseman, number 11, Eddie Miksis. Miksis."

This caught the crowd off-guard; it took awhile for the boos to mount. *What'd they expect,* David thought. *It's an exhibition.* The starters on both teams were getting lifted. David figured that this would get the crowd back where it belonged, behind Cleveland. But Miksis singled, then went to third on a single. Campanella came to the plate, and the crowd stood for him, and he singled in both runners, tying the score 3–3.

David got up to go home. It was nine o'clock. The sun was setting. Light blazed from towers atop the stadium roof. By now his aunt would be worried and his uncle would be mad. Still, David stopped to pee. While he was packed into the stifling, reeking room, waiting to wriggle forward to the long porcelain trough, the pause got to him. Despite everything, and to hell with the consequences, David was not the kind of guy who left a tie game.

From a pay phone, he called home. He cupped his hand around the mouthpiece, in case the crowd cheered. His story would be that he was out collecting for his paper route. Only when the phone rang and rang and no one answered did David remember: *Beowulf*. Betty had class. Stan must be working late. There was a chance David could leave now and beat them both home. Maybe he could even stay for one more inning.

By the time he made his way back to his seat, it was the top of the seventh.

Abruptly, a bizarre hush came over the crowd: sixty-four thousand people grown collectively silent. The silence hung thick in the lake air. David couldn't for the life of him figure out what was happening. Finally, he screwed up his courage and asked Mr. McNabb. The man thwocked David backhand on the breastbone. He pointed to the bull pen. "Satch."

As David will remember it, at that exact moment Cleveland Municipal Stadium erupted into a thunderclap of applause.

Satchel Paige had not warmed up. He just materialized. He made his jangly, loose-limbed, ageless, unflappable way to the mound, more slowly than you'd think a man could walk.

The crowd was on its feet. Paige had pitched in Cleveland scores of times, usually in League Park against the Negro League Buckeyes, but he'd also pitched *for* Cleveland: a whole year for the '32 Cleveland Cubs (the day Joe McNabb moved north, his brother celebrated by taking him out to League Park for a game between the Cubs and the Pittsburgh Crawfords), plus a one-inning relief stint last week for the Indians, a debut that wasn't advertised in the *Call & Post* and thus seen by maybe forty Negroes in the stands.

Now there were more than forty thousand.

Everything changed. A tide had turned. The world was a different place.

Paige struck out the first batter, and the crowd got louder. Next up was the pitcher. Paige toyed with him, throwing blooper pitches and curveballs in the dirt, and the crowd laughed and that was his second K, jack.

Next, Tommy Brown, batting for Reese. (Not letting the facts get in the way of a good story, or maybe just forgetting to check his old scorecard, David will later say that this was Jackie, Paige's old Kansas City teammate, who got the call Paige thought should have been his.)

Here comes a pea at the knees. Yessir!

Look out: reet-peteet heat. For*get* it!

Paige got the ball back from Hegan. *He* was laughing now, and in pure human joy wound up like a whirlybird and reared back and gave that big leg kick so all the batter could have seen were the spikes on Satch's huge shoe, and . . .

[19]

Freeze.

The hesitation pitch.

Swi-i-i-ing! and a miss.

The word you're looking for, David, is *deafening*.

Joe McNabb hollered what sounded to David like *Family!* Might have been *Finally*. He and the boy looked at each other, jumping up and down and laughing, and they did what came naturally, which was to throw their arms around one another and hug each other so hard it hurt.

"Jesus!" said McNabb. "Sweet *Jesus!*"

David was crying. He was crying! Tears ran down his cheeks and he didn't care or know why. "Go-o-o-o-o-o!" he screamed, "INDIANS!"

McNabb threw back his head and gave a war whoop.

☙

PAIGE PITCHED A perfect eighth, too: two easy grounders to short and a pop-up he caught himself. He was relieved in the ninth by the knuckleballer Gene Bearden—a war hero in the midst of one of baseball's charmed one-year-wonder seasons—who pitched three more shutout innings and won when Hegan knocked in Gordon in the bottom of the eleventh.

The next day Paige earned his first win, in relief in Philly against the A's. David, grounded for two weeks, listened to the game on a console radio he'd rebuilt himself and played so softly in the dark no one could hear. That day's mail brought his copy of the *Sporting News*, in which an editorial called Paige's signing a circus stunt. The commissioner should put a stop to it, it said, and force Cleveland back to the real business of trying to win a pennant. Paige went 6–1 for the season. The team finished the season tied for first (and then won a one-game play-off against the Red Sox); signing Paige was what won the Indians that pennant.

Later that summer *Ebony* ran a story calling Cleveland the best place in America for a Negro to live.

David never found out for sure about the lifeguard at Brookside Pool, though he would always have a thing about redheaded women. He never saw Joe McNabb again. He never saw Eliot Ness again. He didn't see his father again for months.

But that summer night, a day that in truth (though not in fact) was Satchel Paige's first day in a Cleveland uniform, David Zielinsky left the ballpark happy, surrounded by a sea of black faces, knowing he was in trouble for being so late (he would in fact barely beat his aunt and uncle home) but feeling so much a part of something bigger and better than himself that he didn't care.

David swept up West Third to Public Square and into Terminal Tower, where he stood in line for a westbound streetcar.

He got a window seat. He tried to see his face in the filthy glass, to see if he looked different, shaven, but it was too smudged to see.

The car left the bright street and dipped into a steep tunnel at what seemed excessive speed, swaying and rocking as they hurtled downward. David, white-knuckled, eyed the concrete wall of the tunnel, a finger's-length away. Nothing was wrong, he knew; this was how it always was, that feeling that maybe the brakes are gone and it's a runaway train.

At the bottom of the incline the streetcar made a sharp turn, and the steel wheels pressed against the rails with a shriek. *Business as usual,* David thought. He was right, but it didn't feel that way.

Then the scary part: the car emerged into the open muggy darkness of the Memorial Bridge subway deck, with nothing more than an iron railing keeping the car from plunging off. It was a full moon. David could see the Cuyahoga, two hundred feet below. The ride was less scary if you looked straight ahead. But he couldn't stop looking at that glowing yellow river.

Not, at least, until the car disappeared into the dark tunnel on the other side, twisting and straining to pull the boy safely back to street level, where he'd transfer to the bus that would, for now, take him straight home.

— 2 —

AT THE NOON bell, Anne O'Connor handed her books to an obliging friend (Anne had a talent for acquiring these people), bolted from her desk (three back, by the window, fourth period, eighth-grade English, hawk-nosed Mr. Keagle, Tennyson), ran down the hall (against the rules, unladylike), and burst through the double back doors of the school. She was a green-eyed, coltish, red-haired, Irish Catholic beauty, a year ahead in school, with that spooky knowingness that blazes from twelve-year-old girls. She leaped across the flagstones and down the steps, juked past the drained-for-the-winter fountain, and, her uniform skirt whipping in the wind, cut across the lush green hockey field (also against the rules), toward home.

Anne was a boarding student, but home was only eight big Shaker Heights blocks away.

She kept running, along the sidewalks that cut hems into the wide lawns, across Shaker Lakes on a footbridge you'd have to be from there to know about, cutting through a construction site (a mother-in-law cottage), waving merrily to laconic carpenters. She was a runner, though this was not a thing a girl was encouraged to be. She was a diver, too; a good one. She loved anything with speed, sensation, blur. It was a gray day, warm for Cleveland.

Anne didn't often go home but had been there yesterday—or, rather, went home to go to mass and to Game Five of the World Series with her father and her youngest older brother, Patrick, home from Notre Dame for the weekend. (The boys all went to Notre Dame. The oldest, John, twenty-eight and estranged from the family, was a housepainter/screenwriter in Anaheim. Steven, the smiling cornet-playing fullback, volunteered for the war midway through sophomore year and was shot down over the Pacific. His letterman jacket was awarded posthumously. His room upstairs was repainted, refurnished, and converted to a guest room.) Thomas J. O'Connor, reigning political boss of Cuyahoga County for years (ascending to power *after* one undistinguished term as Cleveland's mayor), was also part-owner of the Indians (that, and much of Cleveland). He had a block of tickets hard by the first-base line.

It seemed so perfect yesterday! The Indians led the Boston Braves three games to one; one win away. On the mound was our ace, Bob Feller, that homely, smiling war hero from Iowa. How could we lose? (Feller lost Game One only because the ump blew the call: *everyone* could see that Boudreau tagged Masi out.) Cleveland Municipal Stadium was full: 86,288 people, biggest crowd *ever* to see a baseball game! Spending a sunny fall day with 86,288 hopeful people is to feel laced into the warp of history. It's not good if you have to go to the bathroom, true, especially if you're a girl. But by then Feller had been shelled, the Braves were up 11–5, life itself felt deflated, and Anne's father snuck her into the press box and guarded the unlockable door as she entered the unmarked (it was understood) men's room.

Now, today, from under the grape arbor at the back of her yard, Anne emerged to find the party in full swing, already spilled out onto the lawn. She hurried past the periphery (a cheaply dressed clutch of the also-inviteds: disc jockeys, accountants, and newspaper swells—people who literally or figuratively worked for Tom O'Connor) and then, closer to the house, past a swarm of the usual highball-swilling rich people, when she literally ran into Carrie and Edith Van Sweringen, the wizened, reclusive old ladies who lived in the mansion next door. Both old women toppled backward in choreographed perfection and landed on their behinds in the soft shady ground under a massive elm. They wore identical organdy dresses.

"Oh!" Anne said. "Excuse me! I'm so sorry."

"Haste makes waste," Edith said.

"You wit," Carrie said to her sister.

"Don't start," Edith said.

"Who's starting?"

"Lemon."

Carrie looked at her, blankly.

"Bob Lemon, the pitcher," Edith said. "The young man who used to be an outfielder. He's starting for us."

"Oh for the love of pete." Carrie made a sour face.

Anne stood over them, frozen, trying to get a word in. "Are you all right?" Anne asked.

"*I* am," Edith said. "Sister, however, is a southpaw."

"Sister never gets tired of that one," said Carrie.

When Anne didn't react, Edith explained. "Right-handed, all right," she said, squinting up at Anne. "Left-handed, all left."

"Lord," Carrie said, eyes heavenward, "take me now." Edith laughed.

Anne helped them to their feet and into a pair of Adirondack chairs. They were the surviving spinster sisters of Oris P. and Mantis J. Van Sweringen, the visionary bachelors whose money and big dreams brought about the modern Cleveland: Terminal Tower, Public Square, the rail line that made Shaker Heights possible, and, for good measure, Shaker Heights, too. The women knew her mother's family (whose money originated in paint and explosives), and Anne had lived next door to them all her life. But until now she'd never talked to them, never done more than exchange waves from across the expanse of their lawns.

"Let's start over with this, young lady," said Edith. They looked up at her and, in unison, said, "Hello, dear." They raised their cocktail glasses—Gibsons. Though Anne didn't know, then, what they were called. She learned years later, when a man with a cocktail onion in his drink told her she was fired, and all she could think to say was, *What do you call that drink?*

"Your mother insisted we come," said Carrie. "Why not? We do love ball."

"You know," said Edith, "she's the very image of her mother at that age."

"Can you even imagine," Carrie said, "being that age?"

"Sister, you never *were* that age." But they both cackled at this.

Anne, to the sisters' visible disappointment, said she would be back, and excused herself.

She hurried across the wooden covering of the half-drained pool, across the patio, through the back-flung rear doors, and into the formal living room, where Patrick—a reserve flanker at Notre Dame, home for yesterday's Series game, risking expulsion from the team by cutting school and staying home to watch today's—was setting up the family's second television set, the biggest money can buy. The O'Connors might have been the first family in the county with a second television. The Cleveland TV station that will, for the first time west of the Appalachians, broadcast the World Series was another part of Tom O'Connor's part-owned empire.

"Hiya, Babe," Patrick called, flat on his back, attaching wires to the back of the Emerson while a dozen-odd of the younger party guests watched, transfixed. Everyone in her family called her Babe, and no one else. "Mom's—," Patrick said.

"Upstairs with a migraine." Anne rolled her eyes. Natch.

"And Dad is—"

"Onstage." Double natch.

Patrick smiled and then winced as he did; he had a shiner, suffered in the one and only play he'd participated in during Saturday's victory over Navy. The O'Connors bruised easily.

"Don't electrocute yourself," Anne said. "It'll short out the house. We'll miss the game."

"Fresh kid," Patrick said.

Onstage meant the echoey, vault-ceilinged, oak-paneled dining room, where Boss Tom was fond of hauling out a cut-glass bowl the size of the witches' cauldron in a lavish production of *Macbeth*, setting it on their oak groaning board (a legacy of Anne's mother's old-money roots), and mixing a Caesar salad. Servants ferried plates of cut meats and vegetables from the kitchen, and Tom O'Connor punctuated his ceremonious pouring and stirring with toasts, jokes, bows, and gossip. The other television set had been dragged in there.

"'Oh!' says the drunk fellow," said Tom O'Connor. "'I thought you said *busy ditch.*'"

His guests roared.

"Babe!" he called, setting down the old fraternity paddle he used for a stirrer and reaching out to embrace his daughter. "You're late!" He smelled exquisitely of cigars and the best oaky bourbon. "Ladies and gentlemen," he said, bowing, "I give you, my lovely daughter, Anne."

Anne blushed.

"Guess we can't say you never gave us anything, Boss." It was one of Tom's aides.

"Just for that," said Anne's father, "I'm giving you your pink slip."

Big yuks.

"The Babe here will sing the national anthem for us," her father said. "A capella. We'll turn down the radio and the television set. Wait'll you hear her."

Though this was news to Anne, she did not consider demurring, or that her father was joking.

"To my lovely daughter!" Tom O'Connor said, raising his amber-filled glass.

"And her all-boy orchestra," called a county commissioner.

"Long may they wave!" called a congressman.

The big hard room was filled with mayors, state reps, county commissioners, lawyers, businessmen, bankers, newspaper publishers, and their wives. All these sad ornamental women!

"Babe, get a drink," her father said, sprinkling diced hard-boiled eggs into his beloved, leafy miasma, "and make your own toast."

As if by magic, a Negro hand gave Anne a fizzing glass of Cotton Club ginger ale. She took it, stood on a chair, and raising her glass heavenward, toward the chandelier that her mother had commissioned from a shop in the Italian Alps after seeing one just like it in a Paris hotel, said, "To Daddy's Cleveland Indians—and ours, too!"

"To Bob Lemon," some mayor shouted.

"Scalp the Braves!" said a scion of industry, a big bald sweating man who then went into a war whoop. Many others joined in. "We give-um heap big headache."

Political correctness will not arrive for forty years. You think Chief Wahoo is bad *now*, get a load of the vicious, big-nosed red-faced thing they used in the '40s.

The conversation turned to baseball minutiae. On the television, with the sound down, was a flickering test pattern. It, too, had an Indian on it. Like most Clevelanders, Anne assumed this was because of the baseball team. Television was too new for people to know it was the same pattern everywhere.

She stood at the right hand of her father, beaming, soaking up attention along with the cigar smoke, hoping her mother would never come downstairs, rehearsing the national anthem in her head. She was rich, smart, and pretty. She knew what a thing it was to be rich, smart, and pretty. Since nearly everyone she went to school with was also rich and smart, Anne knew that what mattered most was pretty. Also, she had good posture.

Food filled the groaning board: fried chicken and cold cuts and potatoes and a relish tray as big around as a truck tire. On the porch of the old carriage house out back, caterers had set up a concession stand: roasted peanuts, hot dogs, and a keg of Gund beer, brought here by the brewery owner himself.

Conversation had turned, admiringly, to that already famous photograph that ran in all three Cleveland newspapers and in almost every paper in America, too, of Saturday's Cleveland heroes, the white and sweaty Gromek and the black and sweaty Doby, hugging each other.

"That's why we're here," proclaimed Tom O'Connor. "Because Bill Veeck had the sense and goodwill to hire those wonderful Negroes." He poured a dishful of capers into the salad and grabbed his bourbon. "To Larry Doby, Satchel Paige, and the cause of brotherhood!"

Suddenly, all eyes in the room were on the four people in the corner, the only Negro party guests, whom Anne had not noticed until now: John Holly and his wife and William O. Walker and his wife. They were by far the most formally dressed people there. Walker, editor of the *Call & Post,* the Negro newspaper, wore a tuxedo. At noon! Holly, a tiny and extremely black man with pomaded hair, ran a group called the Future Outlook League, which organized Negro boycotts against segregated businesses. The four Negroes forced smiles, avoided eye contact with the all-Negro serving staff, and drank a hearty toast to brotherhood.

STILL IN HER school uniform, Anne O'Connor again stood on a dining-room chair. She clutched in her sweaty right fist the napkin on which, as everyone else was eating, she'd scribbled the lyrics. She'd had a tough time with this (try it; at *perilous night* you get ahead of yourself and wonder what comes next, *ramparts, rockets,* or *bombs*) and had looked in her father's library for something with all the lyrics written down. No go. She went through three napkins before settling on the version she now clutched and hoped not to need. In tandem, the volume on both television sets was extinguished. One of the deejays, the skinny vulgarian who did *Request Review,* presumed to dash up and introduce her. Alan Freed. This brought grins from the half-drunk guests, but Anne saw the look her father shot the guy.

Anne opened her mouth and, in her trained, silvery soprano, began to sing.

No one sang along.

Boozy adults smiled, too-wide and indulgent. Two lines in, she's got them. The girl can *sing.* She looked over the heads of all these people, toward the idea of a person in the last row.

As she got to *the twilight's last gleaming,* though, at the foot of the staircase, right where Anne was looking, was Sarah O'Connor. Her (dyed) brick-red hair was wild and her eyes (heavy on the mascara, which she didn't usually use) were unhappy as ever. No lipstick. She finger-waved. Anne glanced at her brother. Patrick hadn't noticed anything; that's Patrick for you.

"Through broad stripes and bright stars," Anne sang, eyes on her mother now, and paused. Anne was getting it wrong. Sarah rolled her eyes. "In the perilous night."

Anne paused again.

"In the . . . ," she sang. "Oe'r the ramparts we watched."

Another dead pause. Sarah looked angry, or at least pained, and was mouthing some obstreperous, stage-motherly cue that Anne couldn't see from here. Anne would have looked at the cheat sheet, but that would only call more attention to her gaffe.

She soldiered on: "Were so gallantly streaming."

People mumblingly joined in. The house was abuzz with botched patriotism.

Sarah, who had a contralto so full it could have risen above anyone's and everyone's, remained sotto voce. She was giving cues. She was, in Anne's eyes, a mean, sallow-cheeked scarecrow mime. Exactly what anyone else was doing, Anne couldn't have said.

Finally, Anne felt the tears on her cheeks, which had been there for who knows how long. She looked up at that big Italian chandelier. She closed her eyes. Someone took her hand. She knew without looking that it was her father. The volume came up on one television set, but it was too late to get back in sync with the Marine Band–accompanied singer in Boston.

The party guests tried to help out this hapless, defeated twelve-year-old, and so kept babbling the hapless, defeated anthem forward.

Anne swallowed; she took in a full breath.

"O'er the la-and of the freeeeeeeeee..."

Eyes closed, she held that note, and held it and held it and held it, until no one else was singing and she started to hear applause, and she held the note a little longer, took it a little higher, and the applause got louder, and the pressure on her held hand got more firm. Anne imagined she heard her mother shouting, too, along with everyone else.

Anne breathed.

"...and the ho-o-o-o-ome," she sang.

She opened her eyes. "...of the..."

And here she paused, faux dramatically, then winked, then broke into a fabulous smile.

"India-a-a-a-ns!"

The party guests broke into laughter and applause; more than one person nudged the person next to him and said, how clever, substituting *home of the Indians* for *home of the brave* at a ballgame being played in the home of the Braves—Midwesterners, moved to explication.

"Ladies and gentlemen, the lovely *Anne O'Connor!*" Freed shouted. "*Anne O'Connor!* LIVE! from Shaker Heights! Give her a hand!" Though of course everybody already was.

Anne hopped off the chair and into her father's arms. He kissed her on the crown of her head. "C'mon, everybody!" he said. "'S'more to eat! Don't let all this food go to waste!"

Anne ducked outside before her mother could come up to her and say something, though her mother wasn't the sort who did that. Anne was just playing it safe. From a distance, she watched Sarah O'Connor walk through the party, sizing up the food, running an index finger over the surfaces of the bunting and balloons, shaking hands with people as if her own house were a world filled with novelty. Anne swung by the carriage house to get a hot dog and another ginger ale, then went back inside, through the French doors to the living room.

The television screen was small and the party guests in front of it were many. Anne couldn't see. But she was small and thin, which helped her wriggle through the others, plus she was the host's daughter and had just given a performance, which gave Anne just enough (very) local fame to create a berth she could squeeze through. Before she knew it she was up front, near Patrick and his friends, who had a habit of mussing her hair, a habit she had noticed, lately, felt different. She caught something in some of their eyes. Today, for instance, a younger friend of Patrick's—a junior at St. Ignatius—offered her a seat on the floor beside him, an unobstructed view. She knew she was pretty, though boys don't realize that knowing this and being confident about it are different matters entirely. Anne sat, ate, drank. As she did, her elbow would graze the hard softness of the St. Ignatius boy's flank.

The game began. For a couple innings, there was no score.

§

WHEN ANNE HEARD from the dining room the syncopated slap-*slap,* she never would have guessed what it was that had happened.

At first she was only idly curious. It was, after all, unlike them both: Sarah O'Connor walked up to her husband, tapped him on the shoulder of his tailored suit, threw a drink in his face, and slapped him, hard. In return (a reflex, he'd claim), Tom O'Connor slapped his wife, harder. She fell to the floor, crumpling like a bad actress doing a death scene. That was what Patrick said, later. He was in the dining room, on a dessert run.

In the living room, people craned their necks to see. At first, after the slaps, it was quiet. Then you could hear scuffling feet and people saying, "Hey, hey, *hey!*" Only when she heard her father's voice saying over and over he was sorry did Anne even get up. By then, though, the mayor of Cleveland stood in the doorway. He was a wide man with silver hair and wire-rimmed glasses; the lakefront airport that opened last year would one day bear his name. "It's nothing, people," he said. And that was that. A moment later, the third inning began.

Patrick intercepted Anne. "C'mon, Babe," he whispered, turning her around by the shoulder. "People are looking."

People are looking? But did what she think happened just happen? It did. She knew it, she had to know why, and yet she found herself doing what she was raised to do. She could hardly believe she was doing what she was raised to do. People were looking, it was true.

Anne allowed Patrick to lead her back to her seat, and she tried not to look at the boy from St. Ignatius, who was trying not to look at her, either. She kept her eyes on the television set, where Dale Mitchell doubled and Boudreau, the shortstop/manager, doubled him in and Cleveland took a 1–0 lead, and just like that the party turned back into a party. After the inning, Anne said she wanted some dessert, too, and slipped away to look for her father.

He was in the dining room, looking like nothing had happened, except for the red blotch on his cheek. He was a public man, working the room, putting his arms around other public men. Apparently, nobody was talking about the thing. He caught Anne's eye and frowned, slightly. He shook his head, quickly, slightly. Then he winked.

Winked!

Something inside of Anne fell and churned. On the outside, though, she nodded, kept walking toward the desserts, and did not let on. The last thing she wanted was dessert, but she took a piece of cake (in the shape of Chief Wahoo; half the head was gone), and she did not let on. She went outside, around the corner of the house, and tossed the cake in a thicket of pampered japonicas. The front door would be open; she could go in that way and sneak upstairs to her mother's bedroom. It would be locked, but Anne could talk to her through it.

But then she got to the northeast corner of the house, and there her mother was, standing with two women her age (late forties; old!). They were all smoking. Only Sarah had a drink, a cup of beer. Beer? Yes, beer. In a cup. The blotch on Sarah's cheek was no redder than the one on Tom's and was, if anything, smaller. The mascara (applied, it now occurred to Anne, to make for a more dramatic mad scene) was smudged, half wiped-off.

One of the women—a birdy creature in a winged red hat—saw Anne and grabbed Sarah by the bicep. "Well, if you ask me," said the other woman, hatless and stocky, with copper-blond hair and a clutch purse. Then she saw Anne, too. They all fell silent and looked at her.

"Babe." Her mother dropped her half-smoked cigarette on the lawn and stamped it out. Crazy, as if Anne didn't know she smoked. Sarah's hands were shaking.

"Mother."

"A triumphant piece of salvaging, darling."

Anne swallowed. She had no idea what her mother was talking about. She wanted to ask but couldn't find the words. Anne couldn't believe it. That *never* happened.

"The anthem," Sarah said. " 'Home of the Indians.' Very clever."

The other two women smiled, but no one laughed.

"Triumphant." Sarah grasped her left wrist with her right hand and tapped her foot to the beat of a fast song that wasn't playing anywhere. The other women looked at Anne as if they expected her to perform another trick. Or burst into flames. Or leave.

It was only about three, but it was getting cold. Rain was called for; lake effect, always worse and more erratic here on the East Side. Anne looked away, across the back lawn. The Van Sweringen sisters were still on those Adirondacks under the elm, where Anne had left them. They were eating. Anne's guess was that someone had served them.

"Of course, you might have rehearsed," said Sarah. "Haven't I always told you . . ." She stopped herself. She sipped from the beer cup, grimaced, sipped again. "Well, it's a bad habit."

Anne would have liked to fight back, but she was stuck. The best she could have done was to say that her father had given her no notice. Until this moment, Anne wouldn't have even considered criticizing her father, not to *her*. Now, Anne didn't know what to think. She'd give anything to ask, but somehow she can't. Funny how often the thing you want the most is the thing you just can't ask for. Then you want it more! Then you *really* can't ask for it.

Also, in truth, Anne did not like to rehearse. "Yeah," she said. "I know."

"Is there a score," the hatless woman said, so flatly it was clear there wasn't a thing in the world she was less curious about.

"One to nothing," Anne said. "Us."

"Well," Sarah said. "Hooray for our side." Another sip of beer.

The other two women averted their eyes, the way you do when you are at someone's house and she gets a phone call. Sarah kept eye contact with Anne. Anne thought her mother was about to tell her something, something worth telling. She had that look.

But nobody said anything, until Anne shrugged and said she should get back to the party and her mother nodded. "You better," she agreed. She leaned toward her daughter, as if to give a kiss. Anne flinched. Beer spilled. Sarah's lips stopped short of Anne's cheek. "Don't go back to school," Sarah whispered, "without saying good-bye."

∽

WHEN SHE CRUISED back into the living room and heard that the Braves had somehow tied the game 1–1, Anne knew she needed to leave. That, and the way all the women were touching her shoulder, taking her hand, asking how she was doing, as if *she* had been slapped. Before she got all the way back to Patrick and that ropy-muscled, Aqua Velva'd St. Ignatius boy, Anne stopped. She had to get out of there—pdq.

All season Anne had noticed a strange thing. The games she watched, on television or in person, the Indians usually lost. And so Anne would go to the ladies' room at the stadium or would, here, go for a swim. When her parents weren't around, she'd sneak into their bedroom upstairs and onto their balcony and go diving off it, flying over seven feet of cement patio and into the deep end. At school she'd leave the lounge (the television set there had been donated by Anne's father's station) and go do her homework. When she returned from the ladies' room, or when she was tired of swimming, or when her parents came home, or when she finished her algebra, she'd come back to the game and the Indians would be ahead. Yesterday, if she'd just gone to pee sooner, everything might have been OK. She knew this was a thing people would laugh at, but she really *believed* that a change in her own viewing affected the players.

Well, not *really*. Just a silly superstition. Not her fault. She's Catholic. So, OK, the truth: she *did* believe.

Anne can't go upstairs. Her path was blocked by her mother in one direction, her father in the other. But she can't stay, can't bear to watch, couldn't bear the guilt if she did.

The heck with it. She'd go back to school. By now it would be over, school. She had friends she could talk to about impossible parents and who wouldn't think she was churlish to complain, given all her advantages.

With the Braves coming to bat in the bottom of the fifth, Anne stood on the worn spruce-wood decking of the pool cover and looked around, calculating which way she could go so that no one would notice.

By now she could taste the coming rain, the metal-on-a-filling zing of ozone.

She walked backward, away from the house. On the west lawn, the Hollys and the Walkers were walking away from the house, too, in what seemed like a hurry, toward their cars. How strange. Why would the Walkers and the Hollys leave the party, and their chance to watch the game? (Both the Walkers and the Hollys had television sets at home. This wasn't why they were leaving.) Maybe they had the same superstition as Anne?

The Negroes' cars were parked next to each other: a white Cadillac and a Studebaker Silver Hawk. Anne was surprised they had such nice cars, but then caught herself, felt bad, and blamed it on the fact that she didn't go to school with Negroes (she'd signed a futile petition demanding her school admit some). The only ones she knew were maids and cooks (every day these women rode predawn buses from Hough, from Glenville, from Collinwood, up Cedar Hill at dawn, to Shaker Heights; Anne couldn't have said where any of them lived). She hated herself for this. Somehow this must be her mother's fault, too.

Whereupon she ran into the Van Sweringen sisters—again literally, tripping over her own feet and bumping off one sweatered vanilla-smelling hollow-boned old lady and into the other, spilling their drinks. This time, though, it was Anne who fell.

Carrie and Edith were (this is the only word for it) giggling.

Carrie: "We have to stop running into..."

Edith: "...each other like this."

They each extended a hand to Anne. As Anne rose, the sisters tipped forward. For a second Anne thought she was going to pull them down. But equilibrium prevailed.

"All these years," Edith said, "we've watched you growing up and only now we..."

"...bump into you," said Carrie.

"Sorry," said Anne.

"Don't give it a second thought," said Carrie. "Sister doesn't get out of people's way as spryly as she should."

"As for Sister," said Edith, "she has forever been in *somebody's* way."

"The game's on," Anne said. Maybe this hadn't occurred to them; they'd been out here the whole time. "If you're interested. It's on the television sets, inside."

"Bah," said Carrie.

"It will never replace radio," said Edith. "Television."

"We tried watching for an inning there," said Carrie. "That little screen defeated us. Who can see anything on that little screen?"

There was a radio on the porch of the carriage house, but you couldn't hear it from here.

"There's a radio over there," said Anne.

"Well, of course there is," said Edith.

But they didn't move. They'd said they were baseball fans and seemed, earlier, to know some of the players and care about who won. Now, though, they stood in Anne's yard, grinning like mental patients, regarding her, sizing her up. Though no one had even asked, a Negro placed a newly made Gibson in each lady's hand. Neither sister looked at him.

"We have excellent hearing, dear," Edith said to Anne.

"Like dogs," said Carrie.

Anne did not see how they could possibly hear that radio and presumed that they were pulling her leg. "Excuse me again," Anne said. "But I really have to be going."

"Do you know who Charles Dickens is?" Edith blurted.

Anne frowned, startled. "Pardon me?"

"Charles Dickens. The famous British writer."

"As if," said Carrie, "to avoid confusion with Charles Dickens, the little-known Chinese pawnbroker?"

"I read *David Copperfield*," said Anne, which wasn't exactly true. She'd been assigned to read it and had read some of it, but mostly faked it enough to get an A on the test.

"Oh, that's a *good* one," said Edith. "It's between that, *Oliver Twist, Little Dorrit,* and the one about the life of Jesus for my favorite."

"What my sister is so clumsily trying to ask," said Carrie, "is if you would like to see the Charles Dickens Room in our home."

"Thank you," said Anne. "I would, but I have to be getting back," she said, "to school."

"Of course you do," said Edith.

The sisters eyed Anne with raised drawn-on eyebrows, as if they hadn't heard her gracefully decline their invitation, as if they were still waiting for her to respond.

Anne had never been in the Van Sweringens' house. Even Halloweens, she didn't stop there. She looked across the vast lawn at what you could see of that brick hip-roofed federal-style house, shrouded in gone-wild yew trees, thickets of untrimmed box elders, and scores of doomed chestnuts (blight will kill them all within two years) and elms (Dutch elm; twenty-five years away). That cupola, the archway that spanned the second-floor balcony, the long windows that ringed the third floor, the five-car garage (once a livery) that you can't see from here and that Anne knew about only because she sometimes used a path behind it to cut through on the way to the Colony, the movie house at Shaker Square.

Some mysteries dog you with cat-killing curiosity. Others, right under your nose, you can get so used to knowing absolute bupkis about that you don't stop to wonder.

Upon such epiphanies (made more grandiose in retrospect) are journalists made.

What was there to do, now, but accept?

ୠୠ

THEY WENT THROUGH the front oak doors, twice as tall as any of them. As they did, a cheer rose from Anne's house. Who goes into their own house through the front doors?

"Oh, dear," said Edith. "We must have missed something."

What they missed was Joe Gordon's towering home run to center. Indians 2, Braves 1.

Carrie hurried past two ancient, identical collies, each sitting on the marble floor of the cathedral-ceilinged entry hall, to the huge radio in the front parlor and snapped it on. Immediately she started muttering at the radio, slapping it, grumbling. The dogs watched the old ladies but didn't bark, didn't move anything but their heads until Edith patted them and said that they were good boys. "This is Romulus," she said. "And this is Remus. Boys, this is Anne."

"They're not twins," called Carrie. "Only brothers."

"Despite their names," Edith explained.

Anne bent over to pet them; each dog licked her once on the wrist and stopped. She had no idea the Van Sweringens had dogs. All the times she'd cut through their yard, she'd never heard dogs bark. She couldn't remember ever seeing them out for a walk or peeing in the yard.

The radio crackled, warming up. The parlor was filled with leather furniture, Shaker legs, all of which, to Anne, looked new. The walls were a gallery-overload color-blast of painting: a Stuart Davis, three John Marins, a Reginald Marsh, two O'Keeffes. No servants in sight, but the house smelled bleachy-clean. No must, no dust, nothing like what Anne would have thought. She was twelve. All four of her grandparents died before she was born; her ideas about old people came from the movies.

"Try the one in the living room," said Edith. "It's newer."

Anne could hear more shouting from next door, which apparently Carrie could hear, too. Frowning, she made a doddering, purposeful beeline toward the back of the house.

"Sister," Edith whispered to Anne, "loves that old radio. But it's slower than she is and a devil on tubes."

"I heard that!" Carrie called.

"Like dogs." Edith pointed to her own right ear.

The living room, as big as the one at Anne's house, looked like it was in the middle of being painted except that there was no paint smell. The ceiling was half repainted. The only furniture was a sheet-draped davenport, three wooden folding chairs, a card table with a hatbox-sized plastic radio on it, and, in the far corner, two A-frame white doghouses.

"Excuse the mess," said Carrie.

"It's a long story," said Edith.

Both radios, here and back in the living room, came up in sync: "... two runs, two hits, and two men left," said the trademark nasal voice of Jimmy

Dudley, "and we go to the bottom of the sixth with the score, Cleveland 3, Boston 1. And now this word from *Chesssssterfield!*"

The two women hugged each other and then gave brittle hugs to Anne, too, and sat stiffly down at the table.

"I wonder how those runs scored," said Carrie.

Edith narrowed her lips and shook her head, as if this grim question was outside human ken. "Please, dear," she said to Anne, motioning to the empty chair.

Anne obeyed.

"Oh, for heaven's sake!" Carrie said. "The Dickens Room! Aren't we the fools?"

Edith burst out laughing. "Aren't we!"

"Don't you think we're fools?" said Carrie.

Anne shook her head. "I forgot, too."

"We don't have to see it," said Edith, "if you don't want to."

"Sister," Carrie said, "don't make her beg. Simply show it to her. There is no need to subject this nice young lady to the inexhaustible mother lode of your self-doubts."

Edith frowned. "'Mother lode'?"

"Yes." Carrie raised one faux eyebrow, impressively. "Pun intended."

"I would like to see it," Anne said. *Or at least get on with it.*

"So you would," said Edith. The women rose and motioned for Anne to go first. She did, but she didn't know where she was going. "Up there," said Carrie when Anne turned away from the wide oak staircase. They waited, again, for her to lead.

She did, but felt cruel to get to the top so much faster than the sisters. "Right or left?"

"Left," said Edith.

"And up," Carrie said. She was not out of breath. "One more flight." There was a radio on a stand in the stairwell landing, and Carrie turned this one on, too.

Romulus and Remus followed them in tandem, a hairy rear guard trailing six feet behind.

"Through the ballroom," called Edith. "All the way, to the far northeast corner."

The ballroom?

Anne emerged at the top of the stairs, to exactly that: a full, grand, ghostly ballroom, spanning what looked to be the entirety of the third floor. The floor, waxed to a high sheen, sported in its center an inlay in the shape of a "V" with a red-white-and-blue Ohio flag in the middle. On the far wall was a bandstand, empty save for two clef-decorated music stands and a battered bottle-green baby buggy. Against the near wall was a hearth as wide as a stadium gate. Above it hung a portrait of a magnificently bearded Union soldier.

"Our father," said Carrie, "in full romanticized regalia."

"He was wounded at the Battle of Spottsylvania," said Edith.

"Yes, well," said Carrie.

"He was," insisted Edith.

The sisters did not turn on any lights. Outside the long windows, the sky was storm-dark.

"Those are our brothers," Carrie said, pointing to the life-size portraits hanging on the west wall. "The short, nervous-looking one is our younger brother Mantis James. M. J. is the practical one. The stout one is Oris Paxton. O. P. is the idea man, the one who could talk."

In this dark, empty, echoey place, Anne was unnerved by the present tense.

"They built this house," Edith said, "and we all lived here together until they built the house out in Hunting Valley and moved out there."

"Things were never the same after that," said Carrie.

⌇

THE DICKENS ROOM had been set up in the Hunting Valley home. When the stock market crashed and J. P. Morgan foreclosed, the Vans auctioned off that estate. M. J. died a few months later at age fifty-four, of high blood pressure and the flu. A heartbroken O. P. wandered the earth for eleven months after that and, at fifty-seven, died in his sleep in a private car on a Nickel Plate train to New York. But before all that, Carrie and Edith spirited the contents of the Dickens Room to this paneled, one-windowed study in the corner of the ballroom, crammed with first editions of Dickens's books, portraits of Dickens, a square turned-leg oak stool with a caned top that came from Dickens's own estate sale, the elm and yew desk chair that Dickens had used when he was editor of the *London Daily News,* and a life jacket from the *Constitution,* the steamship that took Dickens across Lake Erie and up the Cuyahoga, where, on April 25, 1842, he docked, went ashore, and, in remarks published in *American Notes,* invented the Cleveland joke.

Carrie turned on a new console radio, the only twentieth-century thing in the room.

"Baseball," Edith pronounced, "is a game best suited for the radio."

"I dislike television," said Carrie. "But it is the future. That much is clear."

Edith dismissed her.

"You know," Carrie said, "for some reason, O. P. and M. J. never could abide baseball. It was our interest in the game, you know, that motivated them to purchase the team."

"Don't listen to her," Edith said. "They never spent a nickel on our say-so."

"Your brothers owned the Indians?" Anne said.

"Part-owned, like your father," Edith said. "Nothing gold can stay."

"They must have really loved Charles Dickens," Anne volunteered.

"In theory, yes," said Edith. "O. P. and M. J. never read any of Dickens's books."

"Except *American Notes*," said Carrie.

"M. J. started *Oliver Twist*," said Edith, "but it defeated him."

On the radio, it was the bottom of the seventh. Bob Lemon mowed down the bottom of the Braves order. Dudley could hardly contain himself.

"Our brothers' favorite authors," said Carrie, "were Rand and McNally."

The sisters laughed. Anne smiled and nodded. We're headed to the top of the eighth.

"They loved maps," explained Edith, giving Anne a solicitous pat on the shoulder.

"They read Westerns, too," said Carrie. "But business was their pleasure."

"They went to the little motion picture house in Chagrin Falls," said Edith.

"And M. J. smoked and rode horseback," Carrie said.

"Until O. P. expressed his displeasure with the former," Edith pointed out, "and M. J. broke his arm doing the latter."

The Braves brought in their ace lefty, Warren Spahn. The sisters fell silent. "We have the lead," Anne said. "It's not like he can take any runs away."

Cleveland scored again and seemed to have the game in hand. Next door someone set off a string of firecrackers. Anne thought she should be going.

"M. J. made the snowballs," said Edith, "and O. P. threw them. They never married."

Carrie gave her a dirty look.

Anne was about to leave, but the bottom of the eighth started and, in the face of her own superstition, she couldn't bear to miss anything.

The Braves loaded the bases. One out. She needed to leave. She, *Anne O'Connor*, listening to the radio in someone else's weird attic, was dooming the Cleveland Indians.

"I think," Edith said, "they should bring in that charming old Negro. Paige."

"Do *something*," said Carrie, bent over and chastising the radio. The collies started to bark. "Hush, you." And they did.

It wasn't Paige but the knuckleballing Gene Bearden who came in, a twenty-eight-year-old rookie because of the war. He won twenty games, including the game that clinched the pennant and a shutout in Game Three of the Series.

"This is fate," Carrie said. "This is the young man who should be there."

"I agree," said Edith. "An inspired choice!"

Bearden got a pop fly, but then that evil Masi (who really was out on the pickoff play in Game One, which cost Cleveland the game) doubled, knocking in two. Indians 4, Braves 3.

"I need to go," Anne said.

"The powder room is around the corner," Edith said.

Anne lacked the nerve to correct her. Outside, it began to rain. Distant thunder was causing the radio to crackle. And just like that, Bearden got a grounder to end the inning.

Next door the party erupted. Anne and the Van Sweringens stood and looked out the window. The rain had driven everyone inside. Shredded napkins were being thrown about the living room. People jumping around in there, like a boiling pot.

Anne, to save face, used the little bathroom around the corner. Inside the medicine cabinet: syrup of ipecac, a bottle of porcelain repair, a straight razor, a bottle of warm Carling beer, and a two-cent postage stamp.

The ninth began. Spahn set Cleveland down in order.

"...and this is what it's all about, Cleveland," said Jimmy Dudley, through the static. Suddenly, he was calm. "Three more outs to go, and Cleveland is the champion of the world." He said it so calmly, Anne thought, it was like he somehow knew it wasn't going to happen.

Carrie cleared her throat. "Let me tell you something, young lady."

"It was my idea, Sister," said Edith.

"Very well."

Anne thought she'd done something wrong. Or worse, that they were going to present a version of the blunt speech her mother gave a year ago about becoming a woman.

On the radio was a commercial for Sealtest ice cream.

"Cleveland is doomed to apocalypse," said Edith, apropos of nothing, as far as Anne could tell, "because there's no one like our brothers around with a vision for its future."

"The Rockefellers," Carrie said, "are all gone from Cleveland."

Anne's mother was a Rockefeller cousin twice removed. Anne did not point this out.

"Tom L. Johnson, gone. Burr Gongwer, gone."

"With all due respect to your father, of course," said Carrie.

"Of course," said Edith.

Anne shrugged.

Bearden walked the first batter. For the Braves, the winning run came to the plate.

Carrie Van Sweringen offered Anne a swig of her Gibson.

"Carrie," Edith admonished.

"What's the white thing?" Anne could barely stand to listen to the game.

Carrie frowned. "It is, I remind you, Sister, a festive day. That's a cocktail onion."

Anne took a bitter sip and tried not to make a face.

Edith turned to Anne. "All those men of vision—"

"Gone to Lake View Cemetery," Carrie interrupted. "Food for the worms."

Edith laughed. "They'll get you, too, dear."

"I'm afraid not," Carrie said. "I'm sorry to disappoint, but I have decided to live forever."

"Can I have the cocktail onion?" Anne asked.

"Of course, dear."

The onion was not bad. Not bad at all.

Just then, the Braves batter, trying to bunt, popped up. The Indians catcher, steady Jim Hegan, snared it and fired to first. Double play!

Anne leaped to her feet, screaming, jumping up and down. The two old ladies looked on and smiled, as if Anne were doing a perfect job of celebrating for the three of them. They did not tell her to be ladylike. She gave an Indian war whoop, and the sisters laughed, applauded, and leaned closer yet to the radio.

Next door the O'Connor lawn was awash in hugging and delirious white people.

One more out to go. At the plate was pesky Tommy Holmes. Bearden threw him a knuckler, and he swung at the first pitch and . . .

And nothing! Nothing! Lazy fly ball. Bob Kennedy camped under it.

He's got it! He's got it! The Cleveland Indians are the champions of the world!

Cleveland is the champion of the world!

Anne and the two women embraced. Edith, trembling with laughter, crossed the ballroom to the bandstand, where she put a 78 of an especially sprightly waltz on the crank Victrola. Carrie and Edith met under the chandelier and, in celebration, danced, like a slower-moving version of a man and a woman in a movie. From the bandstand, the collies watched.

"I have to go," Anne said. The ladies didn't offer to show her out. All they did was wave.

Outside, the rain stopped.

Anne's head was swimming, and so, now, were most of the party guests: literally, fully clothed, in the cold, brackish water left in the O'Connors' pool. The cover had been cast aside. Most of those not in the pool were running through the yard, full tilt, in circles, headed nowhere. As Anne crossed the lawn, she saw the beginnings of a modest fireworks display.

Anne went to find her father, who was in the pool, laughing that great braying laugh. Her mother was in the pool, too. Somehow, her mother had gotten excited enough to jump in the pool—or had been thrown in and did not object. Laughing and filthy with green water, Sarah O'Connor found her husband and they embraced, and Tom O'Connor hoisted her to his shoulders. Both of them were laughing like Anne had never seen them laugh. Her mother was waving, at everyone and nobody. She whipped her arms around like a madwoman. Her big fat husband clutched her calves. They were at the center of everything, and they were beaming.

֍

THE PARTY DID not end until the fireworks did, which happened when Patrick blew his thumb off. Even that was not enough to ruin the day. It wasn't his whole thumb, and it was the left one, which a right-handed person doesn't use that much.

The next morning the team's train pulled into Union Terminal, underneath Terminal Tower. The players were greeted by tens of thousands of crazed Clevelanders, pushed into city buses, and driven up Euclid Avenue, flanked by a quarter million more crazed Clevelanders. Children were excused from school to be there. The lead car of the parade had Lou Boudreau and his wife, Della, and Bill Veeck in back, Mayor Thomas Burke in front, Tom O'Connor behind the wheel. It was, after all, his car. In some ways it was his city, too, then.

Later that night—at least as Anne would remember it, and perhaps she's right—Edith Van Sweringen died in her sleep. A month later, so did her sister, Carrie.

Years later, when the city was on fire, or when the river was on fire, or even when the flames that licked the city and the river that bisects it were only figurative, Anne O'Connor would remember that day. She'd think of those two oracular old ladies who lived in the mansion next door and the only day she ever talked to them. She'd think of her parents, letting go of their differences so they could hold on to each other, so they could bounce like happy, filthy children in a half-drained pool. Cleveland was champion of the world! In comparison, everything from that day forward seemed doomed, in decline, and irretrievable—or, at least, smaller.

Everything but TV.

LOCAL HEROES

ᖇᎧ

First in a Series: Blues for the Moondog

March 1952

SEVEN MINUTES AFTER eleven, Alan Freed makes his entrance. Leo Mintz is sitting on a metal stool in the corner of that glorified phone booth music studio, dressed in a shiny gray suit, tapping on his wristwatch, fiddling with his thick black eyeglass frames, and looking like his big fat heart might blow up from worry. *Welcome to radio,* Freed thinks. *Welcome to the Moondog House! You bought it, but I made it!* Eight minutes to air: forever, if you're a pro, if this is your life. Tiny Grimes is supposed to be here, too, an in-studio guest to help hawk tomorrow's Moondog Coronation Ball, the biggest thing like it anybody's ever seen—a *dance,* at the fucking *Cleveland Arena,* can you believe it?—which Freed is scared about, too, but scared in that light-your-nerves-on-fire way he loves, loves more every night. Tiny's not here. Is Freed happy about this? He is not. Does Freed look concerned? He does not. Freed gives Mintz a wink. Mintz again taps his watch. Freed forms his hands into make-believe six-shooters and points them at Mintz and fires off a dozen make-believe rounds, then throws back his head and, even before he gets on the air, lets fly with his level-best Moondog howl.

In the adjoining news studio, the rheumy old newspaper hack who comes in at ten and eleven to do local news knocks on the glass and frowns. Freed laughs, flips the guy off. It's not like Freed's baying could've been picked up in there. The mike's off; it's the tail end of the eleven o'clock ABC news from New York, last feed of the day, filled with volcanoes in the Philippines, Italians fighting with Yugoslavians about where to draw their borders, and some senator who today compared Joseph McCarthy to Hitler. Blah, blah, blah. *Nobody's listening,* Freed thinks, *but my people.* In general, his people are not now nor have they ever been Yugoslavian.

Freed sticks his head in the studio. His studio. He is twenty-nine, skinny, wavy-haired, and weasel-faced. "Got the wax, Leo?"

Mintz points to the box in front of the mike. "All you need 'n' then some. Listen—"

"Right back," Freed says. Plenty of time to pee and grab the telegrams and to pluck some records he feels like playing, just to bust Leo's balls a little, show Leo he doesn't own him.

His mail slot is so stuffed with telegrams Western Union should give him a cut. By now he's accustomed to the nigger-lover ones. In truth, those are a smaller part of the whole every day. Today almost everything is a fan letter or a request. *Now* he's getting somewhere. All the dues he's paid. All the times people counted Alan Freed out. Well, fuck *everybody!*

A fistful of 45s in one hand, attaché case in the other, telegrams tucked under one arm, Freed rushes through the Mintz-held-open studio door, slides behind the mike, sets his things down, and slaps on the headphones. The old guy hits the 11:15 time check. Freed opens the attaché case and pulls out his cowbell, a battered telephone book, and a bottle of Erin Brew beer. On the other turntable, Freed cues up "Moondog Symphony." Then he takes off the record Mintz cued, the new Varetta Dillard single, and puts on the Dominoes' "Sixty-Minute Man."

Mintz lets this defiance go. He grins. "Six thousand," Mintz says.

He claps Freed on the shoulder. Freed looks at him, stunned. They've sold *six thousand tickets?* Not even in Freed's wildest. He's plugged the show and plugged the show, with prideful lack of shame. But Mintz nods. "Six thousand tickets," he says. "Nine thousand bucks." He chuckles. Their overhead is about a grand. Freed starts to say something, but he hears his cue.

"And, now. It is time," says the old guy, like he's at a wake and introducing the family's drunkest, most flatulent uncle, "you . . . hep. Cats," pronouncing it like a foreign word, that fuck. "For the, ahem, Moon. Dog. House."

Always that *ahem.* Every night. Fuck *ahem!*

Drop the needle. On the air!

Freed howls along with that novelty record he uses to start the show, screaming along with that corny barking dog. "All right, Moondog," he says, as if to the dog. "Get in there, kid. Howl it out, buddy!"

Freed doesn't let this go on as long as usual. Big show tonight. Mintz hands him a note, scrawled on the back of a Record Rendezvous business card: *Tmrw—2,000 more tix 4 sale—$1.50 adv, $1.75 @ door.*

Freed nods. Freed leans into the mike.

"Hello, everybody, how're y'all tonight? This is Alan Freed, the old *king of the Moondoggers!* Welcome to the *Moooooooooondog House!*" Freed clangs the hundred-proof bejesus out of that cowbell. "It's the night before my crowning! The night before my own coronation! Tomorrow night, at the Cleveland Arena, and you'll hear it all *live* right here on WJW, right here on the Moondog House! You heard me right, Moondoggers: It . . . is . . . a . . . sell-out! And I owe it all to you, to all of the gang out in the Moondog kingdom. Now here's one of the bands we'll be bringing you tomorrow, one of the bands who'll be swinging you tomorrow: the Dominoes, Federal Records, with their number-one smash hit record, 'Sixty-Minute Man.' Go, Lovin' Dan! Hey, hey, hey, play, *go-o-o-o-o-o!*"

Freed cuts off his mike, for a change. As he and Mintz hug each other manfully and jump up and down in that cramped studio, shouting, "We did it," what's broadcast to the subjects of the Moondog kingdom—young Negroes throughout the Cuyahoga River watershed, plus fringe Moondoggers like the racy, cigarette-smoking girls at a certain private school on the East Side, listening after lights-out, and isolated white boys on the West Side who are about to graduate from high school and volunteer to serve their country in the Korean War—is the sound of Billy Brown, the Dominoes' deep-voiced bass player, who is not the group's usual lead singer (churchy tenor Clyde McPhatter is), proclaiming that he is called Lovin' Dan and sharing with us his habit of rocking and rolling the girls all night long: fifteen minutes of kissin', fifteen of teasin', fifteen of squeezin', and the euphemistic but impressive fifteen of blowin' his top.

൭൬

ALL THOSE YEARS: working podunk markets (Youngstown, Akron), then doing well enough to make Cleveland stations sit up and notice but getting screwed because of a no-compete clause in your contract. Moving to Philly, actually *moving,* for what you thought was a job but was really just an interview. Didn't even tell the wife the truth about that one. The first wife, who's since taken your two kids and moved to Florida. (How long has it

[45]

been since you've seen them? Three years, Moondog. Three years.) Then there was that stupid Alan Freed School of Broadcasting you started up with your brother; it closed down before the first class finished. How about that afternoon movie-host gig on Cleveland TV with that fucking puppet? Even *this* job started out as a classical program that only dope-fiend longhairs and old-lady insomniacs listened to.

Eight months ago there you were, down at Mullins Saloon, where you went every night after your shift, and Leo Mintz—another Mullins regular, owns a big record shop nearby, at the edge of what's becoming a Negro neighborhood—started razzing you about all the people who weren't listening to you play Beethoven records.

"I'll buy you a radio show," Mintz said, "if you'll play nothing but rhythm and blues."

"Are you nuts?" you said. "Those are race records."

"Not anymore," Mintz said. "Rhythm and blues. They changed the name."

Well, *you* knew that. That wasn't exactly your point.

"Radio's dead," you said.

But Mintz got you into the store, didn't he? Got you in a listening booth with platters by LaVern Baker and Dinah Washington, plus, *wow*, all those honking sax guys: Cleanhead Vinson! Big Jay McNeely! Bull Moose Jackson! It hit you: there's nothing on the radio anymore that kids can dance to. What's a guy and his gal supposed to do with records like "Come on-a My House" or "Goodnight, Irene"? Credit where credit is due: this part you got, right away.

You agreed to be Leo's employee. Galls you, right? Later, you will tell this story and therefore lie (the essential truth of storytelling, even if you stick to the facts: especially then). At first the party line was that Mintz saw white kids coming into Record Rendezvous and buying rhythm-and-blues hits, realized the music's wider appeal, and set out to facilitate that. Good one. Kind of garbles the cause-effect thing. Later you'll finesse the part where the show (and you with it) was bought and paid for by Mintz and a friend of a friend of his at Erin Brew (the Phonograph Merchants Association and the Teamster local the brewery needed to get the beer delivered were run by the same guys, some of whom you and Mintz drank with at Mullins). You'll leave out the part about all the stray folded fifties that came in from the record-company reps (you're right; everyone *was* doing it; you really did play the music you liked; we know).

Reality is, you made it. You made you. Whose idea was it to keep the mike open and hoot and holler and ring that cowbell and pound along on that phone book like a dope-addled hepcat bongoman? Yours. Whose idea was it to call the thing *Moondog House* and make up a community of in-the-know listeners called Moondoggers? Yours. Whose idea was it to stage dances in halls all over the signal area, which cross-promoted everything: the dancers listened to the show and the listeners came to the dances, and you could plug both at each, each at both, and the money that came in was cash, cash, cash? Let's just say that was you, too. Mintz would claim otherwise, but, yeah, Alan, you're right: fuck him. Who needs Leo Mintz? He'd say that you do. You'd say *did;* past tense. History, it would seem, needs only you. You're given credit for giving rock and roll its name, and why? Because, first, *you* gave you credit. What about those schoolmarmish, fact-wielding cranks who say it isn't so? Fuck them, too. We're with you, Moondog.

೦೧

"So, folks, take a tip from the ol' king and give it a try," Freed says, sticking his finger in the empty beer bottle and making a sound uncannily like popping a top, "and your very first sip will tell you: here's true beer flavor that can't be beat. Enjoy the finest! Save money! Always ask for Erin Brew."

It's half-past midnight. Mintz is gone, off bending an elbow at Mullins. Tiny Grimes never showed. Freed's in the studio alone.

"Tomorrow night, at the Cleveland Arena, at the Moondog Coronation Ball, the Most Terrible Ball of Them All! Tomorrow, when you buy one of those two thousand tickets we're putting on sale or use the tickets you already bought, step lively right up to the bar there and get yourself a cold, delicious Erin Brew. Or if you can't make it and you stay home and listen to the Moondog Coronation Ball *live,* right here on WJW, the *Moondog House,* dancin' and tearin' it up right in your own living room, be sure to have a nice supply of the finest, best-value beer there is, right there, handy, cold, in your icebox."

Sometimes the wife (#2 in a series) complains about him coming home late, booze on his breath. *She* should try doing all these live beer commercials without drinking any. Can't be done.

"Why wait? How about it, folks? Right now! Pop the cap off a bottle and *live it up!* You deserve it. You do! Drink an ice-cold Erin Brew with me," Freed says, making gulping sounds into the mike, "as we enjoy your favorite blues and rhythm records. Wherever you are in the ol' Moondog kingdom, you'll hear 'em all!"

All anyone in the kingdom hears that night, though, are the four acts who are performing tomorrow night at the Cleveland Arena: Paul Williams and the Hucklebuckers, Varetta Dillard, the Dominoes, and the local-hero dance-hall heavyweights, Tiny Grimes and His Rockin' Highlanders. Grimes, a protégé of Charlie Christian, once led a jazz band that featured a kid sax player named Charlie Parker. Now he leads a group of Negroes in kilts. Crazy!

"Now here's Paul Williams and the Hucklebuckers, Savoy Records, and, hoo boy, just listen: pickin' up that tenor horn and blowin' it strong. Here's 'Rock and Roll'!"

Freed sends the song out to a dozen-odd names from the telegrams, and he pounds on that phone book. "Here we go. Hey, hey, hey! Hey, ho, go, ho, play, hey, hey!"

Freed believes! It's a corny act, he knows. But he's sincere. If he wasn't, they'd know. If he wasn't, he could never have sold out the biggest venue in the state of Ohio for, let's face it, some bands who are hardly the Count Basie Orchestra. It's him, Freed, who—

There's a knock on the studio window.

Freed jumps, his heart knocks against his ribs, and, on the air, he says *shit.*

Tiny Grimes waves. Smiles like nothing's wrong. He's got some kid with him who looks sort of like an Arab. Tiny is the rare Tiny who is not a large fat man. He's just a few years older than Freed but shiny-headed bald. As for Freed: just look at that nonreceding head of curly hair!

Freed goes on with some *hey-hey*s and *ho-ho*s, to cover up the *shit,* but then he abruptly dials down the turntable. "Ladies and gentlemen, Moondoggers all, we interrupt that crazy, rollin' thing to bring you a special treat." He waves Tiny into the studio, and he comes, bringing his uncased guitar, and the Arab/Negro kid comes in with him, though there's no room.

"As promised," Freed says, "and the ol' king of the Moondoggers keeps his promises, we have here, live, in the studio, in the Moondog House, the one and only Tiny Grimes!"

All Freed has is the one desk-affixed microphone. Grimes leans into it. "Hello, Moondog kingdom. This here's Tiny Grimes, and I got with me my chauffeur, a young orphan fella from right here in Cleveland, who it's my pleasure to announce will also be joining us onstage at the dance tomorrow as our new singer. This here's Jay Hawkins."

Hawkins says hello and starts to say more, but Freed takes the mike back. It's his show. "That's great, Tiny. You've mostly been known for your instrumental hits, 'Rock the House,' 'Annie Laurie'; we know 'em and we love 'em! I've been playin' 'em all the livelong night!"

"We do appreciate it," says Grimes. "Boss."

Is this a dig? Sarcasm? Freed asks Grimes about playing with Charlie Parker.

"Parker played with me" is all Grimes will say about that. He is awkwardly trying to put his guitar on, and there's just not room. The bustle is, Freed knows, being picked up on the air.

"How'd you fellas come to be known as the Rockin' Highlanders, Tiny?"

"My family's all from Scotland," Grimes deadpans, and the Hawkins kid screams. For a skinny, baby-faced kid, he has an otherworldly deep voice, even screaming.

"That's great, Tiny," Freed says.

"It's on account of old Tiny's cheap as a Scotsman," Hawkins pipes in.

"But, really—," says Freed.

"It's on account of Tiny likes his scotch whiskey," Hawkins says, and he and Tiny both laugh like hell. Tiny is a giggler.

"That's great, Tiny," Freed says. "Of course, it's no match for good old Erin Brew. Tell me, Tiny, how does it feel to be a part of the *sold-out Moondog Coronation Ball!* The biggest dance in the history of the state of Ohio!"

"Feels great, kid," Grimes says. "This here'll be our new record, first since we found out my driver here could sing. It comes out I'm not sure when. Before too long, I expect."

"That's great," Freed says. He has not done a lot of live interviews.

Grimes plays and the kid sings. He's a shouter, not bad, though he won't make anyone forget Wynonie Harris. Freed has to stand aside. It kills him not to be able to pound along on the phone book. He does ring the cowbell. The lone voice mike is inadequate for a trying-too-hard kid singer, an unamped acoustic guitar, and a well-meaning white guy clang-thunking his little bell, and what goes out over the air is muddy, overmodulated. It's pushing one o'clock, early Friday morning in Cleveland, Ohio. No one calls in to complain.

⌒⌒

THE SHIFT ENDS and the station signs off, and Freed invites Grimes and Hawkins to go have a drink. Tensions have waned, aided by news of the big crowd Freed has whipped up for the Rockin' Highlanders to play to, and everybody seems to be getting to like everybody. "I'll buy you some of that scotch you like," Freed says. "Top shelf."

He really is a good guy, Freed. Everybody's pal. Lifetime, he's bought more drinks for others than others have bought for him, which must figure in heaven's calculus *somewhere,* right? They pull on their coats and leave the station, a cold knifing wind off Lake Erie at their backs, over which Hawkins tries to tell a joke about a male monkey and a male lion stranded on a desert island and the monkey's quixotic, ultimately successful attempt to get the lion to let the monkey fuck him. And so it was, distracted by the cold and a half-heard joke and, earlier, by the adrenaline jolt of what a big damn triumph he was about to have, that it didn't occur to Freed that these gentlemen, Grimes and Hawkins, would quite probably be the first Negroes ever to cross the threshold of Mullins Saloon. This, even though since Freed's show has caught on, maybe a third of the songs on the jukebox are rhythm-and-blues records, including one by Grimes himself.

By this time they are inside. The place grows sort of quiet, and every eye in the place is drawn to Freed and the Negroes. Hawkins whispers, "Uh-oh."

There is no music on the jukebox.

Freed greets the bartender by name.

Then Mintz appears from the back room. "Tiny!" he calls.

He lumbers across the room and inflicts upon the flinching guitarist a bear hug. Most of the people in the bar go back to what they were doing. They've certainly seen Leo Mintz hug people before. He's a hugger, Mintz.

"Did Alan tell you?"

Grimes allowed as how he did.

"Who sells out the Cleveland Arena for a *dance,* huh?" says Mintz.

"Apparently," says Grimes, "we do."

"This man drinks free all night," Mintz says to the bartender. "This your new singer?"

Grimes introduces Hawkins.

"This boy drinks free all night, too," says Mintz.

"I was already buying for them," says Freed.

"White folks arguin' over who buys me drinks," Grimes says, "I'm doin' somethin' right."

Hawkins: Jesus, what a booming laugh the kid has! Contagious, too. Everyone in the bar is smiling along with him. About then, someone has the wherewithal to punch up Grimes's "Midnight Special" on the jukebox.

"C'mon," says Mintz. "Got some people I want you to meet."

Freed, Grimes, and Hawkins follow Mintz to the back room, where Freed has only occasionally been. Today he's greeted with a cheer. It's just a room with two pool tables and an octagonal poker table. Against the far wall is a long table with a row of telephones on it. All those phones, but Freed never sees anyone using any of them.

There are ten or so guys back there, most flanked by much younger women in evening gowns. The only people Freed knows already are Mikey Z—a Mullins regular, loud enough in the back that the front-of-the-bar regulars know him, too—and Lew Platt, the promoter Mintz called in when Freed got the wacky idea that the logical next step from dances in jerkwaters like Lorain and Elyria would be Cleveland Arena, a hockey rink, where they'd need three times more people than ever before just to break even. Too big for Mintz. Lew Platt's been doing major-hall shows from here to New York for twenty years—circuses, political conventions, religious revivals, title fights. Mintz introduces Freed, Grimes, and Hawkins to everyone. Freed shakes hands with and accepts congrats from these slitty-eyed, paunchy, loudly dressed men. Seems many of them are getting a cut of tomorrow's show. No one has told Freed about any of this. His first thoughts are how this might affect what *he's* getting.

Hawkins and Grimes wind up at a table with Platt and Mintz and a couple other guys. The two musicians keep looking around, over their shoulders and otherwise, as if this is some kind of joke that's about to go south on them.

Mikey Z asks Freed if he wants to shoot pool. Freed claims to be terrible. Mikey Z tousles Freed's wiry hair and accuses him of trying to hustle a hustler. Freed says, "Really, I have no talent for it," and big Mikey Z slaps Freed on the back, harder than would have been necessary, and laughs.

"No money," he says. "Just a game, sport. When I tell my son I shot pool with Alan Freed, I'll be a hero. My nutty kid, head fulla bees, never misses your show. Can you imagine?"

Why is that unimaginable? Well, Freed knows. But he has white listeners. He does! He balls his hands into fists. Mikey Z is the kind of popular footballer-type that's been giving skinny Alan Freed the business all of Alan Freed's life. Is Freed going to stand for it anymore? No. He clears his throat. He'll use his wits.

But he can't think of anything good.

"Tell me his name," Freed says. "I'll see to it your son's got two tickets for tomorrow."

Mikey Z laughs. "Right," he says. "Sure. Rack 'em, Al."

No one calls him Al, and he's not sure why the offer of tickets is funny. Still, he racks the balls, as told. Mikey Z spots him the break. The condescension in this is clear, but Freed lets it go. He breaks, sinks nothing. Mikey Z runs the table. The end.

Mikey Z buys Freed a drink (Rob Roy, no cherry).

Hawkins apparently says the wrong thing to somebody's woman and there are words, but cooler heads prevail and Hawkins and Grimes are allowed to leave. This is all Freed knows about that. Freed only gets the gist of what has happened.

∽

You closed the place. And why not? You kept trying to buy drinks, and people kept getting to the bartender before you did. All you spent was your change, dumped into the jukebox to play the music that was your ticket, the music for which you *were* the ticket. Go ahead, Freed. Hoist another one; you've got plenty to celebrate.

You stood, alone, in the men's room, the last of your jukebox selections floating back to you there, in the back of the bar, and you got a look at yourself. Your mouth looked wrecked from holding a smile too long. You were getting the first flap of a double chin. Your eyes looked like two cherries in a glass of buttermilk.

You did have a conscience.

You toweled off your face and went and caught Mintz before he left and pulled him aside, in a booth by the front door. "I don't know if I like being in business," you said, "with these people."

"You want to stage a show like the one we want to stage," Mintz said, "in a place like the place we want to stage it, which I remind you was your idea, well . . ." Mintz shrugged, palms up.

"Are these people," you whispered, "mobsters?"

Mintz laughed. *At* you. "Freed," he said, "you naive spo-dee-o-dee."

He called you this because Mintz did not swear. But you both knew that *spo-dee-o-dee,* from Stick McGhee's immortal hit, "Drinkin' Wine Spo-Dee-o-Dee," really meant *motherfucker.* Also, he called you this because you *were* a naive spo-dee-o-dee.

"You think it's so simple?" Mintz asked. "'*Mobsters,*'" he said, mocking you. "It's not simple, like that," Mintz said. "Let me tell you a story."

You let him.

When he first started Record Rendezvous—first record shop in the world (he claimed) where you could browse through the records and pick what you

[52]

wanted instead of having to ask some clerk for it—three fellows came in the store and asked him, would he like them to have the contract for washing his storefront windows. No thanks, Mintz said. I do 'em myself. You don't understand, they said. We really think you should give us the contract. They just looked at him. He thought they were neighborhood punks. He thought the thing to do was stand up to them.

Next day the windows were all smashed. Nothing was stolen. The punks stayed parked out front, keeping guard until Mintz came to open the store. He got their license plate, called the cops. An officer came out, had Mintz fill out a report, and that was the last he heard from the cops. Mintz called around to glaziers, all over the city; when he gave them his name and address, every one of them said he was busy, try someone else. Everybody listed in the phone book was a member of the glazier's union (and whattaya think happened to a nonunion glazier right after he got listed?). But Mintz—young, dumb, and stubborn—found a place in Canton that would sell him the glass. He borrowed a panel truck, got the glass, brought it back, glazed the window himself, him and a clerk. Then he stayed in the store all night to keep guard. Nothing happened. He thought he had the system beat (though what was he going to do, stay in the store every night?). Next day all's well until late afternoon, busiest time of day. Three different punks came in, picked a fight with each other, swearing and shouting, driving away customers. That night someone shot out all the glass with a tommy gun and this time didn't stay to keep guard. Store was picked clean. Mintz called his insurance man, who said that Mintz's policy had been canceled. You declined your insurance, the guy said. I got the report right in front of me.

"You see?" Mintz said.

You said you didn't.

"You don't *want* to see," Mintz said. "Next day I signed up with the Cuyahoga Window Cleaning Company, which wasn't all that expensive, and within twenty-four hours my insurance guy, just a different kind of insurance after all, stops by with a claim check. His mistake. See?" Mintz said. "It's all connected."

You didn't like the way that sounded. You were twenty-nine years old, a baby.

"I don't want to get involved with anything crooked," you said.

Mintz slapped you, hard. Even drunk as you were, this hurt like hell. Mintz had a better right than anyone would have guessed.

"I'm *not* crooked," Mintz said, "and Lew Platt is as honest as the day is long. But. You want to do big things, you need to understand: people take an interest in big things. Many people. Which is not to say that *those* people are bad people, or that they're crooked, 'cause, really, they're not. Understand?"

You didn't say anything. Mintz started to slap you again, but you intercepted it.

"Youth," said Mintz. "Reflexes. Good for you." He took off his eyeglasses and cleaned them with a handkerchief. "Look," Mintz said. "I'll put it to you this way. Someone has to supply the records for jukeboxes. Lucky for me it's me. Each record, I make a tiny profit, but I make good on volume. Without that, I got no money for your little radio show, and none of what's about to happen tomorrow stands a ghost of a chance."

You want to leave, but you can't. For a change, you shut up and listen.

"How do you think a man gets the business of stocking jukeboxes?"

You shrug.

"What do you think would happen," Mintz said, "if you tried to get into jukeboxes, or cigarette machines, or pinball, anything like that, if you went up to Mr. Mullins and told him your machines were better and would cost him less?"

You got it.

"Things just are the way they are," Mintz said. "I didn't make them that way and neither did you, and there's not a daggone thing either one of us can do about it. That doesn't make you dishonest, you stupid so-and-so. It makes you a grown man, getting by in America."

He patted your hand, softly, like a disappointed lover. He offered to call you a cab. You said no thanks, but he couldn't resist. *"You're a cab!"* he shouted, and you left.

You drove home, who knows how.

You dragged yourself up the stairs to that apartment in Shaker Heights and dove into bed, and the wife let it go, said nothing about when you got home or how you smelled when you got there. Halfway through breakfast, at noon the next day, you thought, finally, to share with her the news of what a big day you were about to have, what a big man she was married to. She knew about the show but had no idea how much money was involved. She kissed your sallow face. She listened while you talked about how you thought maybe you could stage one of these shows a month. She listened, squirming happily in your breakfast nook, as you tallied up some pie-in-the-sky per annum guesstimate. She watched you get *entirely* full of yourself; she let you, and you were ungrateful. You told her nothing about the people in the back room at Mullins (you'd already made yourself forget). What an H-bomb of ego you set off at breakfast that morning! She went with you that afternoon

[54]

as you bought two pricey suits. She did not object when on a whim—a *whim!*—you swung by the Cadillac dealership on Prospect Avenue and traded in your perfectly good Chevy on a shiny black Fleetwood you neither needed nor could yet afford.

∞

TIME FOR ALAN Freed to climb history's stage and hit his mark.

That's more or less what he's thinking, listening to a radio show from the Indians spring training facility in Tucson, sipping an Erin Brew, and piloting his new, money-smelling, creatively financed car westward on Euclid Avenue. He's wearing a white sport coat, open-collared black shirt, jazzy houndstooth slacks. He is a white hepcat. *Yasss!* He looks in his rearview mirror, not at where he's come from but at himself. He smiles at that good-time rockin' spo-dee-o-dee, shoots that handsome devil a wink. Right before Freed left, Mintz called and said they'd sold another twenty-five hundred tickets. Alan Freed—self-made small-town boy—has himself a public. Live it up!

Long before he gets to the Cleveland Arena, he sees the crowd. It's nine, an hour before show time; already they're lined up for blocks. He marvels at all these majestically dressed Negroes: broad-brimmed hats and smaller sharper ones and long dashing overcoats. Great bouffant hairdos, defying the wind and glimmering like jewelry in the streetlights of Euclid Avenue.

Freed beeps his horn at them, *his* Moondoggers. No one reacts, as far as he can see. He's just a voice on the radio to them. He rolls down the window and howls. He thinks he hears a small cheer go up.

Behind the arena, at the mouth of the private lot, the guard calls him *Mr. Freed*.

Inside, backstage (none of the bands have arrived), Freed shakes hands with an unctuous, lisping VP from Savoy Records, home to most of tonight's bill. A real handshake, not a bill-palmer. Freed breezes past well-wishers to the bunting-draped bandstand. There's Mintz, across the arena floor.

"Alan!" Mintz waddle-runs across the covered-up hockey rink, laughing like a mental patient, his hand outstretched the whole way. Freed hops down from the bandstand but otherwise lets Mintz come to him. The handshake, upon arrival, melts into a bear hug. "Ready?" Mintz has a nose full of gin blossoms; they shine.

"Ready, Freddy," Freed says.

They weave their arms around each other's shoulders, walking to the lobby abreast like little-boy fishing buddies.

When they get there, though, Freed stops in his tracks. People are flattened against the glass front doors, pounding and yelling and waving whiskey bottles.

"Hey, kid." Mintz elbows Freed. "You're a star. Keep smiling."

Mintz gives the security guards a nod.

The doors open, just two of them. Hundreds of ticketed Moondoggers pour through this human funnel, a zillion-footed roiling blur of arms and elbows and furs and liquor-breath and pomade and perfume and bubble gum and jostling shoulders and quilted skirts and pheromones and clicking high heels and black skin and brown skin and less-brown skin. Freed and Mintz do smile, and they welcome the onrushing crush, glad-handing and amazed.

"This is just the folks with tickets," Mintz says. "Get a load of that." He gestures with his head toward the box office; the line stretches into the darkness farther than the eye can see. "We're gonna break the attendance record here."

Freed is sweating, like crazy, but keeps smiling, shaking hands, asking people's names. He asks the younger ones what high schools they go to, though of course the answers will nearly always be Central High or John Hay.

By the time they get a security guard to escort them through an underground tunnel to a makeshift radio booth in the corner of the arena, the floor is jam-packed. The air is a haze of cigarette and marijuana smoke. In the Moondoggers' rush to get in, most did not check their coats or hats. The heat! Must be twenty degrees hotter, just like that. Below the dance floor, under the insulating straw, hockey ice begins to melt. Freed is drenched with sweat. Should have brought a spare shirt.

Freed pulls up a seat in the booth. The engineer the station sent is a one-thumbed kid named Patrick, son of one of the station's owners. "All set," Patrick says.

"What do you make of all this?" Freed asks.

Patrick shrugs. "Looks fun," he says. "Good turnout."

Freed looks out over the full floor and filling seats. Later, there will be police reports of a stabbing, newspaper reports of brazen hepcats jabbing heroin needles into their arms. Freed sees nothing like this. From where he stands, he sees happy kids, happy because Freed made them that way. Every time out, the Moondog kingdom gets bigger, younger, and a little bit whiter.

☙❧

A HALF HOUR to air Mintz gets a tip that the cops have sent fourteen squad cars for crowd control and the fire marshal has been called. He closes the box office. Moments later the mass of people waiting outside—ten thousand eager-to-be-entertained Moondoggers—storms the front doors, shattering the glass, rushing in, trampling everything in its path.

This is what Freed is told. He's pacing beside the stage door, waiting for Paul Williams and the Hucklebuckers to arrive—willing, for the sake of peace, to put them on now, before the radio feed starts. The lisping Savoy VP introduces Freed to Varetta Dillard, who turns out to be a seventeen-year-old crippled girl, hardly the package Freed imagined that big sexy voice came in. "*She* could go on first," says the VP. "She's a natural!" She looks down in girlish mortification. *This crowd'll chew that kid up,* Freed thinks. The Hucklebuckers are road dogs; stick with Plan A.

The Savoy VP's shirt is apple green and unwet.

"What size shirt you wear?" Freed asks. Flummoxed, the guy answers. "Close enough," Freed says. "Give it to me." Guess what? He does! Can you believe it? Alan Freed can have anything he wants.

Finally a customized hearse pulls up bearing all nine Hucklebuckers. No time to chew them out. Freed shakes hands with all the fellows, shows them briskly to the stage.

No stage lights. It's just a bandstand. The house public address system. Thirteen years from now (which is how long it will take Freed to drink himself to a disgraced and heartsick death), a sock hop at the most forlorn junior high gym in Utah would have a better setup.

When Freed takes the stand, grabbing the microphone with the hand that's not toting an ice-cold bottle of Erin Brew, the crowd—there is no other right word for this—roars. Adrenaline and adulation wash over him, through him, like a current, and put a coppery taste in his mouth, and make him feel like he is flying.

Freed eyes Patrick, back in the broadcast booth in the corner, who gives him a thumb-up.

"Hello, everybody, how're y'all tonight?"

Judging from the applause, they are most fine.

"This is Alan Freed, the ol' *king of the Moondoggers!* Welcome to the *sold-out Cleveland Arena...*"

Woo-hoo! Who among us is unthrilled to be part of a sellout?

"...and the *Mooooooooooondog House!*"

The crowd bays along. Behind Freed, Paul Williams and the Hucklebuckers take their places. They are a miniorchestra: drums, bass, guitar, piano, three saxes, two singers.

"We're all *live* on WJW Radio, right now!" Freed shouts. "Let 'em hear you howl so loud, even the Moondoggers without radios can hear you!"

Freed goes on like this for a while, but the din is so loud hardly anyone in the arena hears him. That sound system couldn't have blown the roof off a house of cards.

"Now, as I promised," Freed says, "here's those international sensations, with such hits as 'Do the Hucklebuck,' 'He Knows How to Hucklebuck,' and the brand-new 'Even Grandma Hucklebucks,' let's give a big Moondog Coronation Ball welcome to my very good friends *Paul Williams and the Hucklebuckers!*"

At the front of the bandstand, Williams and the other two saxophonists blow a wailing, throaty A-sharp, then as one, rock back on their heels, a cue to their bandmates: they all rip into "Do the Hucklebuck." Freed remains onstage, clapping his hands and bobbing his head (Freed has impeccable rhythm) and semidancing. Williams frowns at him. Freed doesn't notice.

What Freed does notice is that almost no one else is dancing. Except in a few tiny pockets of space, where people have backed off to make room for the ball's most twirling and athletic couples, the crowd is too tightly packed. Even onstage, with enough room to dance, Freed finds it tough. No stage monitors. What he hears has been ricocheted off the unforgiving cement reaches of the arena, suffused with human screams and syncopated with the steady tinkling of unseen breaking glass (wine bottles? doors?). The Hucklebuckers are pros, with rehearsed dance steps even, but they can't be hearing themselves, either.

Faraway though the haze, Freed sees what seems like a body flying splaylimbed from the balcony to the floor. Jumped? Thrown? His imagination? He's again sweating badly.

The Hucklebuckers play "Do the Hucklebuck" for what seems like a long version of forever, but when they finally stop Freed realizes it was a medley of all the Hucklebuck songs. Paul Williams, an elegant pigeon-toed man in one of those tan, hugely baggy suits that (sadly, from Freed's perspective) you have to be a Negro to wear, comes to the mike and says some things to the crowd that Freed can't make out, a joke, it appears. *This is going out over the air,* Freed thinks, and slips offstage to go to the booth and see what he's responsible for.

The apple-green shirt is now as sweat-drenched as his own shirt had been.

Backstage, shielded from view by a threadbare velvet curtain, the other musicians have materialized and, along with a lot of people who know somebody, have made quick work of the buffet table and the giant washtub formerly filled with Erin Brew. A fat man in a red suit offers Freed a marijuana cigarette. Freed wades past well-wishers, winking and elbowing his way back to the broadcast booth. It's maybe forty feet away, but at this rate it'll take all night. Billy Ward, the Dominoes' pomaded and dictatorial leader, stops him. Ward shouts in his ear that they won't go on unless their fee is doubled, seeing as how the turnout is so big.

"Take it up with Mr. Mintz," says Freed, "or Mr. Platt. I'm an employee, same as you."

Ward asks where these gentlemen might be. Freed says he has no idea, and breaks away.

Finally Freed makes it back to the kid in the booth. "How's it sound?"

"OK, Mr. Freed." Patrick starts using technical mumbo jumbo that makes Freed think the kid has no idea how it sounds. Onstage the Hucklebuckers seem to be covering Wynonie Harris's "All She Wants to Do Is Rock," the inspirational tale of a woman who wishes to hucklebuck with her man *all night long!*

"Throw it back to the station after this song," Freed says.

As Freed leaves the booth, a pack of uniformed, nightstick-bearing Cleveland cops comes through the stage door and start storm-troopering their way to the stage. Freed squirms through the crowd. *Maybe,* he allows himself to hope, *these cops are just here for extra security.*

When the cops get to the bandstand, they stop. Freed is relieved, until one of the cops points at him. They are waiting for him. He arrives, swallows hard, and says, "Yes, I'm Alan Freed."

"We closed down your bar here," says the bullnecked police captain in charge.

"Not my bar," Freed says. "I'm just an employee, a hired hand, just like the musical acts."

"You need to announce we closed down your bar, ten minutes ago, and for good." The bullnecked cop, Freed notices, has greasy smudges all over his face. Two of the other cops, same thing. Turns out, it's hastily wiped-off blackface. They've come directly from the annual police department minstrel show, all proceeds to charity.

"One of our sponsors," Freed thinks to say, "is Erin Brew."

"Yeah, so?" says the bullnecked amateur minstrel.

"This is a live broadcast. Part of what they're paying for is live onstage commercials."

"I wouldn't advise that."

Paul Williams shoots a what-gives look over at Freed and the cops. Freed puts up his index finger. *One more song?* He mouths, *Please?*

Williams nods.

Freed tells the cops he'll be right back, then rushes backstage to see if Tiny Grimes will round up his band and go on. The kilted Grimes and the undershirt-clad Savoy rep are sitting on the decimated buffet table, smoking black Cuban cigars thick as baby-arms. On the floor beneath them, swaddled in a painting tarp, Jay Hawkins sleeps. Grimes gets up. He'll do what he can.

Bullneck is turning sort of red.

Freed really needs to pee.

Freed makes it back to the cop-filled wings. The Hucklebuckers finish and Freed bounds onstage, requesting further applause. The crowd obliges. Freed turns toward the booth; the telltale on-air lightbulb goes dark. In front of his big, adoring crowd, the offstage threats recede. Freed feels tall, loved, and big-dicked.

Bullneck approaches. Freed motions him back.

"Ladies and gentlemen," Freed says, "as you may have noticed, for the good of everyone, it's been necessary," he says, bracing himself, "to close the bar."

They boo. His Moondog kingdom! The faces closest to him are contorted into frowns. He's losing them. He can feel it. This is no crowd. It's a mob.

Behind him come the Rockin' Highlanders. The only one without a kilt is Hawkins, who's dressed in a purple satin jumpsuit and a voluminous yellow cape. Hawkins takes a position inches behind Freed, eyes closed, arms messianically outstretched, as still as a mannequin.

"Heh, heh, heh," Freed says.

But Hawkins stays put.

There is more booing.

"How 'bout it, Moondoggers?" Freed says, regaining composure. "Are you having a rockin' good time?" He vamps like this for a while, fending off mounting jeers. Again and again he looks over his shoulder for the on-air lightbulb to come back on. No go. "Live radio," says Freed. "Heh, heh, heh." The light still does not go on.

"Kid?" he says, trying to see through the haze. "Patrick?"

Fumes of wine and sweat rise toward the rafters in near-visible sheets. Before him, the Moondog kingdom lurches, sways, shoves; the stage is moving. From a tunnel to his right comes a cluster of ax-toting white firemen. To his left, the cops push kids away from the stage. Behind him, the Rockin' Highlanders fling profanities. Jay Hawkins remains motionless.

A glance to the booth. Still, there is no light.

What choice does Freed have? Live feed or no, the show must go on.

"From *Cleveland, Ohio! The sixth largest city in the United States of*

America!" He is yelling into this piss-poor mike so loud he can taste blood in his throat. "The Moondog Coronation Ball is proud to present *Tiny Grimes and His Rockin' Highlanders!*"

Jay Hawkins bursts alive, seizes the mike, *scre-e-e-e-e-e-e-e-ams!* For Hawkins, as for no one else, this mike *rocks!* Even against a rising tide of apocalypse Hawkins gets *heard!*

Freed runs offstage. But he is stopped, caught in the extremely literal arms of the law. "Don't move," Bullneck yells.

It is unclear if Hawkins is singing words or harnessing the deep, booming, in-tongues voices of the world's twenty-one most powerful pagan gods. The muscles in the kid's face draw back into an otherworldly grimace. The veins in his sweaty neck jut like ropes. His cape whips behind him in a wind that comes from Freed cannot imagine where.

Bullneck pokes Freed in the rib, yells in his ear: "That's it. We're shutting you down, nigger lover! You're going to jail."

Freed goes weak in the knees. Onstage, Hawkins is a terrifying, croaking dervish. Behind him, swinging kilted Negroes flail at their musical instruments. Young women scream. Freed can still taste blood. He feels on his thin biceps the grips of at least three police officers.

Suddenly, there's a loud *pop.* The music dies. From stage right come the firemen. Jay Hawkins keeps singing into the killed mike. Bullneck runs onstage, wrestles it from him. Hawkins lets go and stands back, as dazed and docile as a child shaken awake from a nightmare. A fireman takes the mike from Bullneck, gives a signal to god knows whom, and power to the stage is restored. "By order of the city fire marshal," he says, pausing with portentousness you have to be in public safety all your life to love this much, "this event is deemed closed. Please walk, do not run, walk, toward the nearest exit."

He repeats this last sentence over and over. As he does, mayhem ensues. The cops let go of Freed to attend to the shouting, bottle-hurling mob. Freed falls to his hands and knees, crawls to the back of the stage, and ducks behind the curtain. Backstage is as crazy as anyplace. Freed disappears into the maw of what was once his kingdom, and he is swallowed up as cleanly as the next sweaty spo-dee-o-dee. He goes for refuge to the place he knows will have him. The booth. Patrick's there, all apologies, yammering about what the people back at the station had told him. Freed tells him to go the fuck home.

For some reason, Freed doesn't need to pee anymore. He sits down, on the floor, underneath the console. He lowers his head to his bended knees.

Quietly, Freed weeps.

There it is, kids. History's first rock concert. *Live,* from Cleveland. Thanks for coming!

՟

Two hours later, when the reporters found you, still in that radio booth, you blurted your third denial of the evening. You're just an employee. Same as the musical acts. You blamed the cops for overreacting. Somewhere, a cock crowed.

The next day Cleveland police and fire officials sought warrants for your arrest. You violated fire laws, they said. You deliberately oversold the hall.

That night you brought the wife with you to the studio, for support, and took to the air. You did not play "Moondog Symphony." All that ever has mattered to you, you said, is bringing your listeners the best in blues and rhythms. You made it clear that nothing that happened was your fault. You bragged about not skipping town. You told your listeners you loved them. You cried out over the abuse and blame you received in the local papers. If you'd been the promoter, you said, you'd refund the purchase price of everyone's ticket. You were just an employee. Still, you wanted to set things right. No place is big enough to hold a dance for the Moondoggers. But you promised to make amends, with a reserved-seat show, free to all Coronation Ball ticket holders. This whole matter calls, you said, for an expression of love and understanding. You asked your listeners to call the switchboard and tell the operator *I'm with the Moondog.* If they're not, tell the operator that. If they're not with you, you said, you'll leave the air.

We're with you, Moondog!

People who knew people took care of, y'know, things. No charges were filed against you.

You never staged the promised concert. You got bigger and bigger, and the cigarette-smoking private school girls and the soulful lonely West Side boys about to join the navy were joined in the Moondog kingdom by more white kids every day, and all was forgiven.

A year later, coming home from Mullins, you fell asleep and wrapped that Cadillac around a tree. The skin was ripped off your face. Your lung was punctured. Your liver was (further) damaged. You were expected to die.

You lived. You took 260 stitches and underwent surgery galore, plastic and otherwise, and you lived. Two months later you resumed broadcasting, from the breakfast nook of your apartment. You had a falling-out with Mintz. But soon thereafter, people who knew people wanted you in New York, to hawk your kind of music there. Some crank street poet who called

[62]

himself Moondog sued you, so you dropped that name and began your incessant use of the term *rock and roll*.

You lived. You invented rock-and-roll radio. You made movies. For a while there, your kids even lived with you. You staged all *kinds* of rock concerts, all up and down the eastern seaboard. You jettisoned wife #2 for the younger, blonder wife #3. You were rich. You were famous.

(The less said about the payola scandal, the better. You go to New York, you get what you get. Nothing that happened was your fault. The last record you were allowed to spin was "Shimmy Shimmy, Ko-Ko-Bop." Into an open mike, you sang along with the first verse: *"Sittin' in a native hut / All alone and blue / Sittin' in a native hut / Wonderin' what to do."* You'd already been fired. Midsong, you walked out. You didn't die for another five years, a technicality. Age: forty-two. Let's call it natural causes.)

You lived.

You died.

For the record, all of the following is incontrovertibly true[1]: Alan Freed named rock and roll, in Cleveland, Ohio, in 1951. In 1952 he staged the first rock concert. Cleveland is the rock-and-roll capital of the world.

---

[1] None of it is factual.

—— 3 ——

LATE ONE MIDSUMMER afternoon in 1952, a sparsely peopled ferryboat chugged out of Sandusky, north into the choppy brownness of Lake Erie toward Kelley's Island: a thirty-two-minute trip this ferry made four times each summer day and—except when the lake lay frozen—twice every other. On deck, leaning against the starboard rail, lost in indistinct daydreams about love and ambition, was a tall, narrow-shouldered young man named David Zielinsky. The island, from here, was a green hump on the horizon. Behind the ferry, from mainland Ohio, came first a whine, then a buzz, then, as David noticed it, a roar: a twenty-foot spruce-wood speedboat, filthy with chrome, coming at the ferry like a lit rocket. The boat was filled with bottle-wielding merrymakers, laughing (it seemed) at the ferry and the ferried. It grew closer. The ferry sounded its horn, a *basso profundo* bleat that startled the bejabbers out of David. The speedboat turned, taking a line parallel to the ferry. As the fast, shiny boat drew near, there, lying across its prow, facing the sun, wrapped in a jade maillot bathing suit and wearing big sunglasses, was the most beautiful girl David had ever seen. Her head lay in a nest of curly blond-tinged auburn hair. Her skin was oiled, tanned, and unfreckled. Against it, a thousand beads of water glistened. The nipples of her small breasts were apocalyptically hard.

She turned over and was gone. She, and the boat upon which she so magnificently rode.

As he watched it zoom away, ahead of the stolid ferry, around the east end of the island and out of sight, David felt like the hand of a malicious god had somehow reached inside his steaming thorax and, in its cold fist, given his every organ a squeeze.

There goes everything in this life that I will never have.

He returned to the backseat of his uncle's car, that ugly, mint-condition 1949 yellow Willys Jeepster. Its top was down. His aunt and his uncle saw the ashen look on David's face and asked if he was OK. He said he just needed some sleep. Long week at the docks. The worst stuff this week: grain (the hottest, the dustiest, you can't breathe, you itch for days) and cowhides (maggots everywhere). He lay down. He closed his eyes. After a while Aunt Betty started singing along with a sappy song on the radio—the sort of music that Stan, who preferred anything classical, disliked most. Through a sneak's squint, David peeked at him. The wisp of a smile played across his strong-jawed cop face. The ferry drew close to shore. Betty excused herself to go powder her nose. Softly, Stan chuckled.

David closed his eyes tight. Then and there, he resolved that he would, before going off to war, end things with his fiancée. Irene. Irene Hrudka. She was a happy, medium-height, large-breasted girl, and smart, too (she'd finished sixth in their class, just ahead of David). She was without question the sort of girl who'd make a fellow a good wife. But he just couldn't. Poor Irene. That, for weeks now, was how he'd thought of her, as if it were her name: *Poor Irene*.

∽

DAVID HAD SOUGHT an appointment to the United States Naval Academy. He shared this ambition with friends, teachers, neighbors, priests: everyone. Of the 102 hopeful young men in his congressional district who took the qualifying civil-service exam, David was one of eleven who passed. His interview with the congressman went well (they talked sports). David was an A student, class vice president three years running, with a letter in track (the mile) and two in basketball (he was a fine backup center). His debate-team honors included a merit-based trip to a contest in Washington, D.C.—near Annapolis: an omen. He was so certain of his bright, regimented future that on New Year's Day of this year, when he and Irene, his steady girl since sophomore year, finally got the opportunity and nerve to perform the marital act, David spontaneously proposed. Poor Irene, lying naked and surprised in her grandparents' bed (they wintered in Florida), burst into tears. David withdrew. Irene shook her head, reached around, placed her fingertips against his hipbones and guided him back. Then she said yes. The next day he took one of the few mementos he had of his dead mother—a sapphire ring, set with four tiny diamond chips; not her engagement or wedding ring, but it was nice—and gave it to Irene, whom it fit. She broke into tears again. Though she wore the ring on her left hand, they kept the engagement secret. If asked, they denied it. Her right hand was bigger, they said, that's all.

A week later came the shameful news of David's rejection. He read and obsessively reread the letter from his congressman, as if that might change something. He couldn't believe it. He'd done everything everyone told him to do.

"That right there was your fucking mistake, kid," his father told him. Mike Zielinsky said this with his mouth full, in the break room at the docks. He was a big believer in the rules being for suckers. David, raised by his father's sister-in-law and her straight-arrow husband, hated to believe this. But he was starting to. Anyone who sees what-all goes on at a loading dock will drift toward the case-hardened pragmatics that idealists call cynicism.

A couple of years back, his father sold the house next door to Betty and Stan's and took a two-room suite in a hotel downtown. David rarely saw him, until this summer. After Annapolis fell through, David had enlisted in the navy anyway. Irene bravely supported his decision. When David reported to the induction center, he requested submarine training, which felt right and came with hazardous-duty pay. There was a six-week wait for this. He spent the first five weeks on the docks (his usual summer job was at Stan's detective agency, doing courier work to law firms). Most days his father, a union official, came by the docks with a bag of food. When David got to the break room, there he'd be, eating and making jokes. Mostly, his father kept talking to the real dockworkers. But David got to spend a few profane, chatty hours with his father. This seemed like a good thing to have done, before going off to Korea to fight the spread of Communism.

David would spend his last week as a civilian, though, fishing with his uncle and staying in a rented cabin here on Kelley's. Irene—who'd let her parents talk her out of becoming a doctor and had started nursing school—would cut her Friday classes and come later in the week.

When the ferry docked, Stan was in a hurry to get to the cabin and get situated, but Aunt Betty said she was famished. Stan said he'd feel better if he could just find the cabin, which he'd rented from an agency and had not seen. They could drop off their things and then see what there was in the way of restaurants. Stan was driving and thus got his way. They kept quarreling, though, and the drive around the wooded, rocky island wasn't as pleasant as it might have been. Finally they found it. It was no cabin. It was a forty-by-eight house trailer, a mile inland from the common dock where their rented boat was, set off from the road in a woods infested with ticks, chiggers, and bats. As the Jeepster bounced up the rocky drive, Betty—who'd brought along a straw bag full of novels from the Old Brooklyn Public Library and had envisioned herself spending this week in a white Adirondack chair smack in the middle of a long sloping lakeside lawn—caught sight of the place and said only, "This *can't* be it."

In response, Stan said only, "Give it a chance."

David cleared his throat and volunteered that he, too, was hungry.

Stan shot him a look. David shrugged. Stan took a deep breath.

They unloaded the Jeepster in silence. The trailer smelled of fish and coffee-farts. It had one bedroom. David would have to sleep on a saggy plaid foldout. They set their things among the wobbly-legged furniture, grunted and said *hmm,* opened the windows, and left.

The main road made a loop around the island. Stan—who'd been to other of the Erie islands, but not Kelley's—took the long way to the island's only town-part, which was, it turned out, right by the ferry dock. One block, ringed by a general store, an arcade, two bars, a hamburg joint, a seafood shack, and, right on the corner, a fancy place. The Lychaks and David went to the seafood shack. They all ordered walleye. Stan and David had beer. Betty had iced tea. Once Betty ate her first few bites, she sighed and said she felt a world better and apologized for being short, earlier. Stan said, no, it was he who should be sorry. David stared out the window, across the road and to the lake. Darkness was starting to fall.

Then, before him, on the backseat of a bicycle built for two, rode the boat-girl.

She wore a baggy white turtleneck sweater and tan Bermuda shorts. Her legs were tautly muscled. She was barefoot. The wind blew her hair back. David had a lump in his throat, and otherwise. The bicycle ran the stop sign and kept going, leaning acrobatically into the curves of the winding lake road. David never saw who was on the first seat. *Was* there anyone?

"Someone looks like he's seen a ghost," Betty said.

"What?" David said.

"Dreamer," said Stan. He reached out and, in a gesture he'd unconsciously borrowed from the kind of men he used to arrest, patted David's cheek. "Never lose that."

"What?" David said.

※

THE GIRL ON the boat and on back of the bicycle built for two was Anne O'Connor, naturally. She was sixteen. Unless you looked her right in the face, which wasn't the first place David Zielinsky looked, you'd never think she was that young. This was not only because she was pretty. Her very *carriage* bespoke adulthood.

That *carriage* is the right word tells you a lot right there.

That was the summer her brother John came back from California to help her mother refurbish Ashcroft, the family's Victorian home on Kelley's

Island, which, following the demise of this dowager and that, Sarah O'Connor had inherited. She moved in, taking with her the contents of her painting studio, steamer trunks full of clothing, of china, of books, plus a loyal old cook and a wolfhound puppy named Virginia. John was thirty-one and had spent the last ten years painting houses and trying to act in or write for the movies. In two different John Wayne movies—one a Western, one a war movie—he appeared briefly and pretended to get shot dead. He received money for writing movies that were never made. Once he had a three-month stint at a studio, in a cottage two down from Dorothy Parker's. Mostly he painted. When Sarah called him to ask if he might come home, just for the summer, John shocked her and agreed. He brought his friend Kenneth with him. Kenneth was a Negro. Though he was the only one on the island (not including servants), this, as far as Anne could see, made no difference to anyone.

All summer Anne spent weekdays with her father in Shaker Heights (because of diving practice and meets, but also to go to deb-class dances and to perform with Cleveland-bound friends the time-sucking nothings of teenagery) and weekends at Ashcroft. She was shuttled back and forth on that Chris-Craft by Kenneth, who was a charming daredevil. Sometimes she brought a friend, though she was careful about this. The lake was smelly, the island quiet, and the houses on it dowdy. Her friends would make sport of this, whereupon Anne would reconsider them as friends. More often, the others on the boat were friends of John's. Kenneth and John were the sort of people able to conjure friends from thin air.

This particular weekend, John was gutting the third floor, making it into a painting studio. He was up there with a sledgehammer, pulverizing plaster and drinking mint juleps. He and Kenneth had made friends with some college boys from good families over at Middle Bass Island. They were helping out, willing to be paid in liquor and food.

"Babe!" John called. "Kenneth! Boys, this is Anne. If you touch her, you'll be killed."

The college boys laughed.

"Intriguing use of the passive voice," said Kenneth. He was as brawny as John.

"Killed." John swung the sledgehammer, reducing a beam to splinters.

"Oh, John," she said, secretly thrilled. "Cut it out."

John was handsome: black-haired like their father, with a shiny black beard. The air was filled with dust. The wolfhound puppy, supposedly their mother's, greeted Anne only when John gave the signal. When John wasn't around, Virginia chewed everything. When he was, she was as obedient as a show dog.

Kenneth did no renovations. Back in Los Angeles, Kenneth taught high school English. He was also writing a novel. Sarah had given him her husband's study here at Ashcroft. The novel was a tragic story of the friendship between two college football players.

Unmindful of John's showy threat, a boy named Chet, a freshman at Harvard, was the one on the front of the bicycle built for two. He was a big, blond horny brute.

For dinner the cook served fresh walleye *(quelle coincidence!)*. After, as the light drained from the day, they played badminton. Anne was a terrific player: quick-wristed, devious with eye-fakes. She tattooed one fratboy after another. Chet lost to her twice. When he watched her play the others, he had that look. He was *such* a boy; they all were. At sixteen, she already had them all dead to rights.

From the porch John and Kenneth watched and cheered her on. Sarah played Britten records on a new hi-fi, powerful enough to be heard out here, and sat in a white Adirondack in the middle of her sloping lakeside lawn, drinking herself blind, mortifying her daughter with the occasional cheer. Finally John could take it no longer. He stepped up and, in a game lit by lights mounted to the porch and the flagpole, beat Anne, bad. She got only four points. She was tired and sweaty. "I haven't played in ten years, Babe," he said.

"Yeah," she said. "Right."

"Seriously."

Chet stood behind her. He cleared his throat and asked if she wanted to go to the arcade and get a pop. John said that they had plenty of soda right here, thanks.

"He doesn't speak for me," Anne said. "Let's go. We'll walk."

"John!" said Sarah. "You go with her."

"Leave her be, Mother."

At this, Kenneth both arched an eyebrow and clucked his disapproval. He was the most conservative Negro it had been John's pleasure to know.

∾

DAVID WAS CLOBBERING his uncle at table tennis when Anne walked in with four of the college boys and a plain-jane girl (who'd have seemed less plain if her name weren't Jane), who lived two houses down from Ashcroft and whom Anne had, on the way over, thought it prudent to enlist. In addition to table tennis, the arcade offered three battered pinball machines, a paint-peeling fortune-telling scale, a billiards table, a jukebox, and a soda fountain.

"How delightfully quaint!" Chet said, in a dumb English accent. He used his own voice to call the place a dump.

Already Anne wanted to ditch this joker. She'd traveled all over Europe and knew people of means and influence; she disliked people who could not take pleasure in life's humble joints.

Playing on the jukebox was the new Varetta Dillard song, "Easy, Easy Baby." The sound of it made Anne glance at David. Had to be him—not the man with the silver mustache and definitely not the old lady at the soda fountain—who'd played this.

"Eleven serving point," said Uncle Stan. Then, "Twelve serving point."

David loved his uncle but would've given anything, right then, not to be playing with an old man. *Is it me,* he thought, *or did the redheaded girl just give me a look?*

"Thirteen serving point."

David met her eyes. She pointed at the jukebox and raised her eyebrows. David nodded.

"Fourteen serving point."

She smiled, nodding in approval.

"Fifteen serving point."

She mouthed, *Good song.*

"Sixteen, point."

David felt in his pocket, checking for more dimes for the jukebox. The girl returned to her friends. They took all the stools at the soda fountain.

"Seventeen serving point." Uncle Stan was sweating and breathing hard. He set down his paddle and wiped his hands on his fringe of hair. "How 'bout that, eh?"

The guys started playing pool. The girls were invited to play and had declined and were being razzed for it. Chet went to the jukebox and, grimacing at what he called nigger music, punched up what turned out to be a string of top-of-the-pops piffle.

"Eighteen, point!" Stan laughed, too loud. People looked. "My game's coming *around.*"

David couldn't help staring at the boat-girl's hair, now pulled back and tied. But he could see it the way it was on the boat and on the bicycle—wild, ablaze, beyond pretty—just as plainly as if that were the way it was now. She made him feel like his clothes were too small.

"Nineteen, point."

David shook his head, like a dog with an ear itch. *Focus.*

He slammed the ball so hard he cracked it.

"Game," he said.

Stan nodded grimly. David and Stan had been playing for an hour. At first it had been a kick to see the young bulldog come out in his uncle, a flailing, pugnacious side of him he kept mostly hidden. But David had, until this game, beaten him by at least ten points every time. To play him again just seemed cruel. Also, they were no longer the only people in the place.

"Well?" Stan nodded toward the pool table, which was what David had suggested they do after this game but which the newcomers had taken over. He bounced the cracked ball, a sickening sound. "One more?"

David shrugged. "We'd have to get a new ball." Why he didn't just say *no*, who knows.

Stan went to ask the woman at the soda fountain for a new ball.

He came back both with it and, to David's horror and wonderment, the two girls.

The boys at the pool table glared.

"May we play doubles with you?" said Anne.

"Great!" David said. "I mean, that'd be, you know, fine." This was no game for doubles. Either it's no game at all or else people argue.

They introduced themselves. "Anne with an *e*," she said. "Never *Annie*." She shuddered. "Never ever."

Jane nodded toward the men, but Anne shook hands. "Girls against boys?" Anne said.

"Great!" David said.

Anne saw David flinch, like he hated himself for saying the wrong thing. Really, it was just adorable!

The game began.

For quite a while, there was no score.

Finally, after an impossible string of polite hits, the girls scored the first point.

"So," David said, "are you guys from here?"

"Nobody's *from* here," Anne said.

"That's not true," Jane said. "A few people are."

"Very few," Anne said.

David's uncle seemed to be intent on the game and not saying anything.

"We're from Cleveland, actually," Anne said.

"No kidding!" said David, as if that weren't the most likely place.

From the pool table, Chet, in falsetto, said, "*No kidding!*" David's voice was not high.

"We're from Cleveland, too," David said, a touch deeper than he might have.

The men went up 6–4, and the serve came back to Anne and Jane.

"East or west?" David said.

"East Side," said Anne.

"Shaker Heights," piped up Jane, though Anne wished she wouldn't have.

"Oh," David said.

"What about you?" Anne said.

"West Side. Old Brooklyn. By the zoo, kind of. Probably you never heard of it."

"Sure I have," said Anne, lying. If you gave her a million bucks, she couldn't have named ten West Side neighborhoods. Not that she needed a million bucks.

"Everyone's been to the zoo," Jane said.

"What high school?" Anne asked.

"Rhodes," he said.

"Never heard of it," she blurted, and then would have given anything not to have.

Points slowly accrued. The conversation stalled. The gap between Shaker Heights and Old Brooklyn lay on the table, as unattractive as the decorous, lobbing game they were playing.

It was 15–all.

"What school do you guys go to?" David finally said.

"Jane and I will be sophomores at Vassar," Anne said. This was true, of Jane. Jane let this pass; she was a let-pass kind of girl. David seemed oblivious both to the lie and to Vassar. Anne thought maybe he'd never *heard* of Vassar, which somehow thrilled her. "And you?"

"He's joining the navy," said the uncle. It was the first thing he'd said, other than the score, since the soda fountain, when he said doubles sounded fine; let's see what my nephew says. "He ships out a week from Monday. Submarine training."

David didn't say anything.

Was he trying to be a taciturn hero about the whole thing? Or was he just embarrassed his uncle said this? Saying this had made the uncle swell up with pride. And the way the uncle said it, too: what love! You could tell that the uncle wasn't that kind of guy. Made you look twice at David, that he could make a gruff-looking man like his uncle feel like that.

The boys at the pool table sang "Anchors Aweigh."

Jane lobbed a ball to David's side.

He smashed it.

It hit the table, caromed off Jane's large forehead, and back to David, who snatched it and flipped it to Anne. "Your serve," he said. "Game point."

Her ears grew hot. She reached back for her good serve, an unreturnable thing that looked like a rifle shot.

It missed the end of the table by a quarter inch.

"Game," said David. "Us."

But she'd sent her message. He was looking at her in a different way now. It did not seem to her the way boys always looked at her, or the way her father's friends looked at her (in hallways, outside bathrooms, in quiet corners of the kitchen, places she could no longer go alone when there were drunken men around; she feared there was something wrong with her that brought this on). David looked at her in a way that was interested. Not *at* her, but at *her*. There's a difference. A man who knows the difference knows women.

"Singles," she said.

"Definitely." He was biting his upper lip, just a little. "Singles."

Now the real game began.

♾

DAVID HAD PLAYED quite a bit at CYO. Anne could beat all comers at the table in her school's game room. David was a purely defensive player, unflustered by her power/spin game. Everything: back-to-her, back-to-her, back-to-her. Made you nuts. But you had to admire it, Anne thought, in a boy playing a girl, watched mostly by other boys. She'd occasionally lob him something, to provoke him into aggression he couldn't control. Nothing doing.

As for David, he stopped thinking how beautiful this girl was; what interested him was the game itself and how she played it. He got more and more lost in it, placing and doinking whatever she slammed. He had her running all over her side of the table, which ordinarily would mean that he was killing her. He was not. Anne won their first game, David the second: both went to deuce.

The arcade lady said their half hour was up. David thrust his hand in his pocket.

"That's it for me," said Stan. "Time for this beekeeper to kick the ol' mulberry bush."

As David gave the woman her quarter, Stan stood there frowning. Anne couldn't figure out what this was about. David knew. *Poor Irene.* At the moment, this bothered David only insofar as it made him worry about what it would make his uncle do, or say.

"It's such a nice night out," Stan finally said. "I think I'll walk."

David said, no, he'd walk, that'd be fine. His uncle said, really, it's just a mile, he could use the fresh air. He made a big show of tossing David the keys to the Jeepster. At home David seldom drove this (the first option was always Betty's well-kept blue Ford). "See you, sport." This was Stan's way of saying, *Inflict so much as a scratch on my car and I'll kill you twice.*

Chet asked if he could play the winner of the next game.

"No," Anne said flatly. She didn't even look at him.

As she and David started their next game, she allowed herself to peek. Chet was huddled in the corner with two of his pals. The third sat next to Jane at the soda fountain. Halfway through the game, Jane told Anne they were leaving.

"Bye," Anne said.

Jane waited three more points. Her new beau kept checking his watch.

"I thought you said you were leaving," Anne said.

Jane gave her an eyes-wide, don't-play-stupid look.

"Do what you want," Anne said. David was walloping her. "I'm sort of busy."

They left. At game point Chet and his buddies came up to say they wanted to go, too.

David took the point and won, 21–12.

Teeth bared, Anne reached around and grabbed a savage fistful of Chet's shirt. "Go," she ordered. "Leave me the . . . shit alone."

Anne swore poorly. They laughed at her. One of them called her *potty-mouth.*

"You heard what the lady said," David said. He'd never been in a situation like this. His ideas of what to do came 100 percent from the movies.

"*The lady,*" Chet said, falsetto. The boys cracked up. They all took turns saying *the lady.* All this time, Anne still had hold of Chet's shirt front.

"I'd like to know," she said, "how you assheads think you're getting home. It'll be a long swim." She let him go. "Killed," she said. "Remember?"

Killed? David had no idea what she was talking about. "C'mon," he said. "This is nuts."

On cue, all three of them snapped to attention. Then they broke up laughing, again, and waved off David and Anne, as if they were beneath attention, and left.

"Another game?" David said.

"Definitely," she said.

She asked him to wait a sec, though, and went to the jukebox and looked to see if they had more Moondogger records. Only a few. She punched them all up.

The games were too intense, now, for them to talk during them. In relative silence, it became her turn to trounce him. He took it with grace.

"How'd you start listening to this music?" David asked afterward.

"I don't know," she said. "Sort of gradually."

"Yeah," he said. "Me, too."

The song now playing was "Lawdy Miss Clawdy."

"Hey, hey, play, hey, hey, go," chanted Anne. She drummed her hands on the table. She did a great Alan Freed. David felt like a light inside him had for the first time been flipped brilliantly on. "Hey, ho!" Anne shouted. "Play, go, ho!"

You'd think that now would be a good time for them to compare notes and find out they'd both been at the Moondog Coronation Ball. Anne could tell about how she broke curfew to go. David could say that's nothing, he got in free, on tickets from Alan Freed himself. They could have their first argument over whether the crowd was 1 percent white (Anne's estimate) or 10 (David's). They could compare notes on what it felt like to be in the minority, for a change. At minimum, they could talk about when the concert was shut down and the stampede broke out. But here's the funny thing: right now, months after the world's first rock concert, it's still not that. For now, it's just a Friday night that ended disappointingly.

What David and Anne did is, they danced.

Anne had learned to dance at deb class, in party dresses and mary janes, paired with rich boys in white gloves, blue blazers, and bad moods. Everything was programmed. This was nothing like that. David had, at Aunt Betty's insistence, gone to Arthur Murray's in anticipation of his prom date with Irene. This was nothing like that. In heartfelt imitation of the Negroes they'd seen dancing at the Cleveland Arena, Anne and David made it up as they went.

David couldn't believe he was dancing with this vision. As his hand touched hers or grazed the small of her back, or as her hair brushed against his forearm, he got lost. Further. Farther. Lost.

Anne couldn't believe she was dancing with a public school boy from the West Side, who was about to become a slim, handsome, boyish sailor in a pressed blue uniform. This would have provoked her crowd at school to new heights of teenaged-girl/woman scoffery. She didn't care.

The song ended. It was the last of her selections. They were sweating. It was a hotter night than either of them had thought.

"Another?" David said.

"Dance," she asked. "Or game?"

"I don't care," he said.

Anne looked at the Cotton Club "Less Sweet" Ginger Ale wall clock. It was pushing eleven. "I don't know," she said. "Maybe I . . ."

"Fine," he said. He did not want to push his luck.

"David?" she said.

It made something in him move, hearing her say his name.

"Would you," she said. "Well," she said. "Drive me home?" She only lived a few hundred yards away. But the uncle had made such a thing of his car that she was curious.

Naturally, David agreed.

They returned the paddles and ball and waved a merry good-bye to the lady at the soda fountain. "Come back," she commanded. She did not return the wave.

The night was riddled with stars.

As the wooden screen door banged against the frame, out popped Chet and his buddies. Before David knew what was happening, one got on all fours behind him, Chet shoved David, and David fell hard on the sidewalk, smacking his head against a tin downspout.

The boys reeked of whiskey.

"Get up," Chet said.

David already was. "C'mon, guys," he said. "This is nuts."

Anne felt nailed to the spot. Every right thing she could think to do felt wrong. Go home and get John? Wrong. Come in on David's side? Not if she really liked him. Wrong. Tell them off for fighting over her? Right, but something about the fighting felt too good, so: wrong.

Chet kept shoving David, now without assistance. David kept backing up, but only a little at a time. "You think you're a big man, huh?" Chet said.

David didn't shove back, but now braced himself and stood his ground. "Go away."

"Ooo," said Chet, "I'm scared."

The buddies guffawed.

"You have bad manners," David said. "You should be ashamed."

"Ooo!" Chet said. "*You should be so-o-o-o ashamed.*"

"Nice meeting you." David turned his back on them and placed his hand lightly on Anne's shoulder, and they walked briskly to the Jeepster and he opened the door for her. She didn't think this was going to work, but she turned her back on them, too, and got in.

It was a *terrific* car! She'd never seen anything like it. A convertible with the hug-me-I'm-ugly charm of a basset hound. She *loved* it! She had to get one.

Only when David got around to the driver's side did he see that the windshield had been soaped. The air had been let out of the driver's-side tires.

David got in. A hurled egg smacked into the hood of the car.

"That's it," he said, and something in him snapped. He excused himself and bent over in front of Anne's knees and unlocked the glove box and, in one fluid motion, reached into it, grabbed his uncle's old service revolver, felt its balanced heft in the meat of his hand, leaned across Anne and out the passenger side, closed one eye, and fired.

The bullet clanged through a stop sign above their heads. Chet and his drunk friends ran like hell.

"You're crazy!" Anne said. A compliment.

Already, David was suitably abashed. "Jesus," he said. He put the gun away. He locked the glove box. "Sorry."

"Thank god you missed 'em," she said. Her heart raced. God, she loved it when her heart raced. "Don't be sorry," she said. *A gun!*

"I meant to miss," he said. Stan had, for sport, taken David to target ranges, but in truth he wasn't much of a shot.

Curiosity-seekers from the restaurants were wandering into the street now.

"It was three boys," Anne called. "They went thataway."

David, despite himself, laughed. Despite the state of this hallowed car, he laughed.

"What?" she said. Her heart would just not slow down.

He reached out, took her by the cheek, and kissed her. It was a soft kiss.

"My god," she said.

"I don't know what—"

"Shut up," she said. "Whatever you're about to say, don't say it."

"Right," he said.

They both sat back, grinning.

A gun! America. The beautiful.

There *were* gawkers and passersby. They were older and, to a person, married. They knew what it was when they saw what they saw. Hard to see a kiss like that on a starry summer night and not be so nostalgic you could drop-kick your heart from here to mainland Ohio. Later that evening, a statistically unlikely percentage of these people enjoyed robust sexual relations.

First, though, they saw the state of the Jeepster and asked if David and Anne needed help. David said, well, maybe, and he borrowed a bucket of soapy water and a rag from one of the restaurants, a tire pump from a man who had one in the trunk of his car. Years from now, David and Anne will argue about whether or not that man was dressed in a scoutmaster's uniform.

◌◌

"AREN'T YOU SCARED, though?" she said. It was now their third slow lap around the island. Anne kept thinking she should tell him it's OK to stop, somewhere. With the top down and the breeze off the lake, it was cold. The heater was on, but it was still cold. Also it was late.

He shrugged.

"C'mon," she said. "My brother never said he was scared, but he got killed. He *should* have been scared. Maybe if—"

"You can't think like that," said David. "You can *maybe-if* yourself screwy."

She wanted to argue. She bit her tongue, literally, and counted to ten. She did not want to argue about Steven. Also lurking in there were years of etiquette and deb classes, about how to talk to boys and how they think.

On the lap before this, she'd brought up the subject of Steven, the biggest, strongest, best-looking brother, who earned his football letter at Notre Dame and wanted to pack up his cornet, go to California, and join the jazz scene there, but instead took Boss Tom's advice, joined the air force, became a fighter pilot, and had his plane shot down by the Japanese. This, Anne was certain, destroyed her family. Just this summer she'd decided: it all came back to Steven.

David had been going on and on, belaboring the folly of speculation.

"But all that aside," she said. *Pause. Make eye contact. Smile to reassure him.* "Aren't you scared?"

"Very," he blurted. "I am." He sat up straighter. "To be honest."

"Yes, be honest," she said. "Always. No matter what else you do with me, be honest."

In a flash, Anne thought of her lie about Vassar. David thought about Poor Irene. Both, triggered by *no matter what else you do with me,* were shocked to think maybe the answer to that could be spread out over more than tonight, more than this week. Who knows how long?

[78]

Their specific takes on *do with me* diverged along cleanly cleaved gender lines.

"Right," he said. "I will. Promise me the same," he said.

"I will," she said. "I promise."

It was never like this with Irene. It was never like this with any of the boys Anne had dated (at least two of them seriously, she'd thought at the time). Anne and David were having a night in which the talk just flowed and flowed, and they were able to talk about everything, and everything they talked about seemed interesting and alive, and they both felt understood.

"Pick a star," he said. "Any star. Make a wish."

"OK," she said. "Got it." She couldn't believe how corny this was. More so, she couldn't believe how much she loved this, despite and because of how corny it was.

"Me, too," he said.

"I wished we could talk all night," she said. "But if we're going to make a go of that, you better take me home."

She imagined she could still feel his soft lips against her cheek.

"Right," he said. "Of course, your wish won't come true if you say it."

"We can talk at home," she said. "Once we're there and on the porch, nobody's going to stop us or get mad or anything."

But when David pulled the Jeepster into the O'Connors' long lake-gravel drive, both Sarah and John were on the porch, sipping brandy. Virginia the wolfhound puppy barked like mad. Upstairs, the light in Boss Tom's study was lit. Kenneth was at the typewriter.

David couldn't believe it. This was the sort of house you'd drive by and wonder what you and yours have done wrong that you'll never have a place like this. His skin tingled in the night air. This girl *lived* here. She'd show him what it was like, inside.

The car pulled even with the porch. Anne slowly shook her head.

"Do you know what time it is, Babe?" said John. "*Hush* you," he said, and the dog stopped barking and sat down.

Babe? thought David.

"Midnight," Anne said. It was closer to one, she knew. "Who died and made you Boss?"

"Ha-ha," said John.

Everyone caught the allusion but poor David, who hadn't yet learned whose daughter he was sitting in the Jeepster with. If he had, it wouldn't have meant anything. He didn't know there *was* a political boss of Cuyahoga County. If you're surprised to learn that someone this naive can grow up to become city councilman in a place as grand as Cleveland, you may not understand the United States of America and/or what it is to be an eighteen-year-old boy.

"Who's your young man?" asked Sarah.

"Where's Chet?" John was certainly more drunk than Sarah. Less practice.

"Who's your young man?" said Sarah, though Anne heard her the first time.

Anne could have killed them. What's David going to think of her now, with these fey, snifter-wielding freaks as relatives? Chet and his pals were harmless compared to this. But she did what she'd been trained to, which was to get out of the car and wait for David to escort her to the porch (he was several beats slow to do this), and introduce everyone properly.

At the sound of the word *Zielinsky,* Anne was sure she saw her mother wince.

When the introductions were complete, Anne gave her mother and her big brother a could-I-have-a-minute-here look.

"Get in the house, young lady," Sarah said. "Young man, this is hardly an auspicious debut. I don't think you have the first idea—"

"Good night, David," Anne said. She curtsied, a reflex she immediately was mortified by.

"OK," David said.

"Come by tomorrow!" she called. "If you can."

"She will not be permitted to go anywhere tomorrow," Sarah O'Connor called. She and Anne began squabbling like feral cats. Ashcroft's big oak door slammed shut.

John was still on the porch. The huge puppy had jumped up on the porch swing and rolled onto its back. "Did you by any chance see those other boys?" he said. "Chet, Tad, Pete, and Nelson? They were counting on us for a ride back to Put-in-Bay."

David shook his head. "Sorry," he said.

"All right," said John. "Well..." He shrugged. "Life, huh?"

"Yeah," said David.

"Want a brandy?" John said. He was scratching the dog's belly.

"No, sir," David said. "No, thank you. I'm not much of a drinker."

John nodded, thoughtfully, as if he should have known. "Do you know how to plaster?"

"No," David said. *What?*

"I'll teach you," John said. "We'll see you tomorrow, about noon, say?"

"OK," said David. "Noon." He got in the Jeepster. He turned on the heat, full blast, and drove across the island to the rented house trailer. Betty and Stan had left a light on for him. David tugged the trailer door closed. He tried to be quiet while he pulled out the foldout bed (like being at a movie and trying to open a bag of licorice slowly). No stirring from the back bedroom. On the formica kitchen counter was an empty bottle of wine, a brand from here on the island. Bloodsucking flies pinged off the trailer's small screened windows.

David kicked off his penny loafers (he used dimes, to be different) and lay down to sleep, fully clothed, covered by a chenille blanket Aunt Betty had set out. His heart raced. The last enchanted thing he thought, again and again, as he was drifting off, was this: *She curtsied!*

❦

CHET, TAD, PETE, and Nelson had wound up back at Jane's house. Her parents weren't coming up until next weekend. Everyone drank quite a bit more whiskey, Jane included. It was Nelson, in what started out as a joke, who brought up the idea of swinging. Y'know? *Swinging.* He was balky in describing this, though he got his point across. Everyone was laughing and having a good time. Jane couldn't believe her luck; all this attention. What fun! Eventually, she felt like she had the first time she jumped off a high dive. Just like that, with the exact same thrill as that (*go!*), she agreed. But after the first one (Tad), she panicked. He had finished and gone out in the hall, where the others were whispering and politely waiting, and, in those few moments alone in the dark, she got her wits about her. *Look at yourself!* She still had on her blouse, her brassiere (unclasped, but by her; Tad never touched her breasts), and her socks. All that was missing were her shoes, skirt, and panties. She had not been a virgin, though neither had she done anything like this before. Who had? She wanted to scream and get dressed and throw them out and drink black coffee and wonder what the hell she had been thinking.

But she did not say anything. She hardly moved. She went along. Chet. Nelson. Pete. Pete stopped in the middle and—who knows why?—rolled her over and jammed his thing in her bottom. Only Pete kissed her, though. "You're so pretty," he said. Jammed in, wrong. Done, he kissed her shoulder blades. "Thank you," he said. "That was fun." She didn't say anything.

Jane took a long shower, put on clean clothes (a sweater of her father's, some threadbare flannel slacks of her own), and went out on the porch, in a rocking chair that had belonged to her great-grandmother, staring at the dark lake. It hurt, that chair. The boys, actual blushes lingering on their faces, sat in the kitchen, sipping her father's beer and playing a quiet game of

[81]

euchre. They didn't talk about what had happened. They tried to be nice to Jane, but all they got in return was silence. They stopped trying. Finally, she went back upstairs. At dawn the boys went down to the dock, swiped her father's sloop, and sailed it back to Middle Bass. When they got there, they bashed holes in its hull and sank it.

Jane never spoke a word of this to anyone, except, the following weekend, to take the blame for the boat. She must not have tied it up right, she confessed. Her father started to beat her. Her mother said her father's name, softly, and he stopped. Jane's father forgave her; Jane forgave him. That fall she went back to Vassar and began seeing a shy young man from Columbia. She soon found herself pregnant. They married. The boy became a banker. Chet became a tenured professor of religion at a university in one of America's rectangular states. Nelson joined his father's insurance concern. Tad became an oncologist. Pete, much later, hanged himself from a cross-beam in his wife's parents' mountain house (who knows why?). Jane and the banker have three grown children and are, at this writing, still married, albeit unhappily. Though when it comes to other people's marriages, who can say? The end.

☙

FIRST DAY OUT and a person couldn't have asked for a better fishing day: warm but not too, cloudy but not too, and no one else around (two ore carriers in the distance). Up at first light and out on the lake—in a leaky rented boat, powered by an outboard motor, a prewar Johnson—Stan caught two walleyes, not to mention a handful of throwbacks, before David even felt awake enough to ask for more coffee. His only contribution was to take an old cottage cheese container and every few minutes bail the standing, worm-smelling water.

To fish with Stan was to cultivate grand, monastic realms of manly silence. Hard to believe how long the man could go without saying something, or how, once you got as used to this as David was, that silence becomes so articulate.

There was never a morning David appreciated this more. Or loved his uncle more for it.

That's not to say looks weren't exchanged. Stan wore green-lensed sunglasses, but David could feel the looks. All morning he kept waiting for something from his uncle. Disapproval, probably. But David wouldn't have been surprised if Stan talked about being a man, the code of men, and what men know of men that they don't say to women or criticize in other men.

Irene will understand. She's lucky. She won't have to wait for me to come back from the war. She and I, it was just habit, not love. She deserves better, David thought, managing both self-loathing and self-congratulation, *than the likes of me.*

They trolled through the shady perimeter of a cove west of the island. After a while Stan opened up the motor and turned the boat north. They bobbed through open water for a few miles and left the United States, to try their luck in the waters near Pelee Island.

David felt entirely outside himself. A couple days ago, his life felt salvaged from the shame of the unproffered Annapolis commission. He'd do the honorable, logical next things: serve his country, come back, marry his high school sweetheart (the first, only girl he'd "been" with), start a family, and go into business either with his uncle or his father. One day, he'd take over for one of them. That choice had seemed like his last big unmade decision.

Ka-boom: one magical, maybe-he-dreamed-it day and David was launched into the delightful terror of seeing that his life could go any which way.

The Willys was good as new. With any luck, they'd get back to Cleveland before Stan thought to look at his gun. David could filch a bullet from the arsenal in the basement. No one would be the wiser.

I shot a gun over the heads of assholes! David watched his unloved bobber, shaking his head in disbelief. *The girl on the boat is real, and she likes me!*

David looked at his watch. Seven-thirty-five. Four and one-half hours until he could go to Anne O'Connor's house. Less than. Two hundred sixty-five minutes.

"OK," said Stan. "Fine. I can take a hint." He started up the sputtering motor.

"I didn't mean—"

"Did I ever tell you," he said, "about how your aunt and I came to begin courting?"

"No," David said. He had no idea. "Something to do with Chicago, right?"

He nodded, turning the boat toward Kelley's. "I was seeing someone else at the time," he said, "which is a part of this story I'd rather not get into."

Most of Uncle Stan's stories, if they were about him and not history or geography or the fine arts, were full of such parts.

David waited for Stan to continue. The boat kept going and going. Somewhere at about this time, they reentered American waters. Stan kept chewing on his lower lip.

"She was at Mundelein College," he finally said. "Your aunt. I'm Chicago, born and raised, but I never heard of the place. A priest at Mundelein was a friend of Eliot's"—meaning Ness—"and he had Eliot there to give a talk. I was so used to going places with Eliot and having all the women go for him, see."

Stan pointed at the floor of the boat. David employed the cottage-cheese container.

"Well, your aunt was serving punch at the reception afterward. I'd already had two cups of it and hadn't noticed her," he said. "Don't tell her that," he said. "Anyway, I'm waiting for Eliot to...y'know, decide..." He stopped. "Well, several were talking to him. Not that..." He stopped again. "This isn't about Eliot. Point is, I'm killing time, and I go back for thirds on the punch. Your aunt spills it on me. On purpose. She denies this." He shrugged. "I looked up and saw her. Really saw her. Those eyes of your aunt's, y'know?" He cleared his throat. The sun shone on his face; he was sunburned. "She handed me a napkin. The rest is history."

Silence settled on them again, for the better part of the ride back to Kelley's.

Irene's the lucky one. Irene will understand.

David had no idea exactly where Stan came down on yesterday. Finally, he just broke down and asked. "Uncle Stan? What..."

But he could not find the words. His uncle just watched him stammer.

"The thing I was wondering, is..." Couldn't do it.

"This isn't my strong suit," said Stan. "As you know." He licked his lips. "Cigar?"

"Um, OK," David said. This was a new one.

Stan killed the engine. They lit up. "Fella at work," he said. "Twins."

"Great," David said.

They drifted.

"I know you don't feel like this," said Stan.

"Like what?"

"Like what I'm about to say," said his uncle. "Don't take this wrong. But you have no idea how young you are, or what that means."

"You're right," David said, too quickly. He hadn't meant to be glib.

This is crazy, he thought. *I just met this girl, Anne. It's only the novelty of it. Irene, that's different. Irene is a more mature situation.*

"Look." Stan frowned. "I won't bore you with a 'when I was your age' speech. Although maybe I already did."

"No," said David. "You didn't."

"OK," said Stan. "Good."

They smoked, for a long time. Caught fish flopped in the full wire basket. Dilettantish sleepyheads were just now taking their boats out. David and Stan looked upon them, pitiless.

I won't go to Anne's. She's probably grounded anyway. Irene, that's different. What was I thinking?

Finally, Stan restarted the engine. As they neared the dock, he let out a deep breath. "This is ridiculous," he said. "I'm sorry."

"Sorry for what?" David said.

"Thank you," he said. He let out another long breath. "David," he said. "I—" He started to laugh, though not exactly. He hit himself on the thigh.

"I know," David said.

"Like a son," said his uncle.

"Understood," said David. "Say no more."

As they docked, David imagined that small impulsive kiss. He thought of losing to her in Ping-Pong. He closed his eyes and saw her curtsy. He kept them closed and saw her in that jade bathing suit, across the prow of that speedboat.

○○

"CALDONIA!" SCREAMED ANNE. "*Caldonia!*" Eyes closed, fists clenched, pumping her arms in the front parlor. "*What makes yo' big head so hard?*"

"Enough," Kenneth said, "with this primitive stuff! I mean, *really!*" He stood at the top of the stairs, hands on his hips, stamping one foot, a gesture Anne had heretofore seen performed only in the movies. "People are *trying* to get work done."

"Sorry," she said.

"What you're trying to prove," he said, "with this music, is anybody's guess."

"Sorry." The record finished.

"*Thank* you," he said, and went back to work. He was on a roll, it seemed.

It wasn't Kenneth she was trying to piss off. Her mother was outside, reading the final pages of a biography (*Myron T. Herrick, Friend of France*, by Col. T. Bentley Mott), close enough to the house, Anne hoped, to be annoyed. Anne would have thought Kenneth would like the *Moondog House* music. But he hated it. Thought it set the race back, traipsing out images of sexual wolfishness, sluttiness, and alcoholism. Kenneth was big bands and classical, all the way.

If she were arguing with either of her parents, Anne would have jutted out an insolent hip and thrown back her hair and said that as far as she can tell, wolfishness, sluttiness, and liquor *do* uplift the spirit. But it was Kenneth, in most things an ally, and so she did not know what to say except that she was sorry and would try to keep it down.

Anne turned off the hi-fi and turned on the news. She listened for news about Korea. Strange, David going off to war, instead of her. She wanted to be a war correspondent. What's more exciting than to go where life is horrible and violent, to stand in front of rubble with a microphone in your hand and let the world know all there is to know? She'd told this to her teachers at school. No life for a woman, they said. But she had an in! Her father's part-owned radio and TV stations. She hadn't yet found the nerve to tell her father. Lately, after years of being his favorite, a chilliness had fallen upon them. They no longer conspire together against her mother. They no longer hug. They no longer kiss.

Who cares? Here's what she cared about, then: what will David look like in uniform? A tall sailor, in a blue uniform. She imagined getting pictures of him, or letters, posted from those guttural-sounding Korean towns. Earlier this morning she'd snuck into the study, before Kenneth went to work, and looked at Korea on the globe and in the *Encyclopedia Britannica* (chief exports: sardine meal and lightbulbs; favorite sport: stone fighting).

"He'll be here," John said. He'd come downstairs on a Pepsi-Cola break, his tennis shirt and chinos spattered with plaster. "Stroke of noon. Trust me."

"You're the same person," she said, "who told me not to trust anyone who says *trust me*."

"My point exactly," he said. "If I can't—"

"Besides," she said. "What makes you think I'm worried about that . . . boy?"

"Right," he said. "Of course." He'd told the cook to expect a guest for lunch, and also that Kenneth and he would be taking lunch in the study.

Her mother kept reading, reading, reading. If it weren't for her turning the pages and sipping the tea John brought her, she might be taken for dead.

A girl can dream.

They had not spoken that morning. Nothing about the threats of being grounded, which Anne was already disregarding.

In the portico the grandfather clock (which had in fact belonged to Sarah O'Connor's grandfather) started to strike twelve.

No sign of the keen yellow Jeepster.

It finished tolling the hour. He still was not there.

She wanted to take more pleasure, of course, in John being wrong.

I despise my life, she thought.

∽

BETTY LYCHAK WANTED to go to lunch at the fancy surfy-turfy place. It was her plan to tell David things about his mother. Betty's big sister, Joan. Things that might not make David's father seem the only villain in the fairytale-gone-wrong that resulted in Joan going to Hollywood and drowning in the surf off Santa Monica, cause undetermined.

They went.

Her husband and David talked about the Cleveland Indians. They talked about the navy, and they talked about fishing. The food was pricey and undercooked. That's how it is, Betty thought, in resort areas. She kept waiting for an opening. As they finished, she decided merely to plunge into this. She took a breath to start.

"Can I meet you guys later?" David asked. "I want to, I mean, I need to, you know—"

"Say no more," Stan said.

It was of course a given the boy would not pay the bill.

He was a boy! She'd raised him like her own and never missed his basketball games (though she disliked sports), and now he was going off to war. Still a boy! Practically yesterday she was teaching him to read. Practically yesterday she was the den mother of his Scout troop, teaching him to make a picture of an Indian chief by gluing macaroni to cardboard and painting the macaroni with bright tempera paints. Mary, mother of Jesus, now and in this, my hour of need, you of all people should see that sending this boy to war is *wrong.*

"Where are you going?" Betty said. "How will you get there without a car?"

David started to answer. Her husband interrupted him.

"Betty," Stan said.

And so Betty watched David leave. His clothes did not fit. When did he get so tall?

∽

NEAR TWO-THIRTY, after sitting for a long time on that famous rock on the harbor shore, the one with Iroquois pictograms on it, David finally sauntered up the O'Connors' lake-gravel drive. He wore a green short-sleeved shirt and chinos. Sarah O'Connor—sitting in the shade of a front-yard oak, smoking

[87]

a holdered cigarette, done with the biography and onto an Edna Ferber novel—glanced at him over the top rim of her sunglasses but did not otherwise move. From inside Ashcroft came the sound of the barking wolfhound. Anne came bounding down the front steps, then seemed to catch herself. She walked a few slow steps toward David. He gave her a small, stiff wave. She stopped. She didn't wave back. She waited for him to get closer.

"Your mother said you couldn't go anywhere today," he said, softly, though Sarah was across the lawn from them, out of earshot. "The way I figured it, that didn't keep me from coming by. To see you. Here."

"She's not my *boss*," Anne said. "She's hardly even my mother. She pretends to be motherly when she thinks other people expect it of her."

"Oh," David said. "Hmm."

"You didn't have to come by," she said.

"Are you kidding?" he said. "I wanted to. But I sort of came up here to fish with my uncle, so that's where I've been," he said. "With my uncle. Fishing."

"Oh," she said. "Are you thirsty? Do you want something to eat or anything?"

"Not really," he said.

They both stood with their hands stiffly at their sides.

"Your, uh, brother," he said, "said something about needing help with a plastering job."

"He was kidding," she said. "He's a jerk."

They sat on the porch. She took a seat in a ladder-back rocker. David took the swing. Before long they reclaimed the rhythm of the night before, laughing and talking like people who'd been waiting a long time to talk like this. David accepted a cold Pepsi, which Anne gave him in a bottle with a straw in it. They exchanged autobiographical ephemera. They listened as if they might someday be tested, as if this were their new favorite subject.

"I *thought* I heard voices," John said.

He appeared on the threshold of Ashcroft, looking as if he'd stood near a vat of plaster that had been exploded. On his left, looking up at him worshipfully, was the dog. "Holy Moses, is it hot up there," he said. "On the third floor." He opened a can of beer with a church key that said ¡ACAPULCO! on it: a relic from the O'Connors' final fully intact family vacation, all four kids and both parents, in a cliffside resort called Las Brisas where the help took guests down to the beach in pink Jeeps. Several movie stars were also there. Anne was three years old.

"That's where I'm working, the third floor," he said to David. "I sure could use a hand."

"We're busy," Anne said.

John said he was at a stage where some help would be a godsend. He promised he'd only borrow her boyfriend here for a little while. Neither Anne nor David corrected him. David allowed himself to be led upstairs by Anne's brother and was soon sweating and learning to plaster. Like most home-improvement matters, this is hard work that's easy to learn to do, with the right tools. There's a gap between doing it and doing it well, but David did fine.

Then John had him paint. The ceiling, which John had plastered yesterday and was now ready. With a brush.

David went along. He did not complain. He got plaster and ceiling paint all over what had just a few weeks ago been school clothes.

Anne kept bringing her brother more beer and David more straw-penetrated Pepsi-Cola (a fresh straw with each of five successive bottles).

She sat on a stool in the corner and watched them work. They talked about nothing—baseball, weather, R&B music (which John also liked, though he said not to mention that to Kenneth), and what fish Uncle Stan had caught and expected David to come to the trailer and eat, cornmeal-breaded and fried. David left out the part about the trailer. Anne dragged up a radio and another electric fan. No good music; she settled for WDOK, the Indians-Senators game.

For weeks John had been drafting strangers to help him work on the house. But this was different. Anne presumed that David hadn't been around many houses like this and yet here he was, in one, and what happens? He gets put to work, like a common laborer.

David felt no such slight. He was getting in good with other members of the family. Even the dog liked him. This was among the few shreds of fatherly advice he'd gotten from his father. *Get in good with the family.*

Downstairs, Anne's mother came in and turned on the radio receiver of the hi-fi, loud enough so you could hear it all the way up here. It was Sibelius, much played in this, the summer of the Helsinki Olympics. The typing in the room below them stopped.

"*Cocktail hour!*" shouted Kenneth.

"Shift's over," John said.

⁓

DAVID ACCEPTED JOHN'S offer of a change of clothes. He took a shower, too, though managed only to get the worst of the paint and plaster off him. What a huge bathroom! Marble everywhere. Wood everywhere. Paintings, in the john! But these people had no pumice soap.

He came down, cleaner, and was offered anything he wanted to drink. He thought he should take something. But Anne didn't and so he didn't.

"My uncle," he volunteered to Sarah O'Connor, "is a huge admirer of Jean Sibelius."

"Oh, yes?" Sarah couldn't have given him a more withering look if he'd just farted.

"Um, yes," David said. "Pride of the Finns."

"Your uncle's Finnish?" she said.

She and a lady friend were going to what promised to be a laughably amateurish light-opera performance in Port Clinton. Sarah was already dressed for it.

"No," David said. "I think Sibelius is."

"Kidding," Sarah said. Most people, when they kid, they smile. Her, no.

"Can you stay for dinner?" Kenneth said. "I stuck my head in the kitchen. The cook's outdoing herself." He said what she was making. It was foreign.

David was ready for anything. Something with the head still on, or served raw. A creature David knew to be food but had never eaten: squid, alligator, dung beetle, moose, lobster. Anything that drew him closer to the wrought-iron, high-ceilinged world where these people lived.

"I'd love to," David said. "But I can't." Killed him. But he really couldn't. Neither was this the kind of girl you could invite to come eat fried fish at a rented trailer.

Anne wondered why he didn't invite her to come eat his uncle's fried fish. What bliss, to get away from her sorry family and go to some cozy cabin, where the people are nice and normal and real and have earned what they have. But she couldn't possibly invite herself.

David apologized up one side and down the other and asked if maybe, possibly, he could meet up with Anne somewhere, later tonight, say at eight, at the arcade?

"It's a date," Anne said.

The sound of this! Gave her the whim-whams, like that elevator in the hotel in Florence that fell three stories before the brake caught it and everything was more than fine.

⁊

THAT NIGHT THEY met at the arcade and played more Ping-Pong (Anne was starting to win most of the games) and shot some pool (nine ball) and went for a walk along the lakeshore, with each dark step swinging their arms infinitesimally closer and closer, until their hands brushed, brushed again, and, finally, with a pang of big-time, two-way triumph, they found their fingers intertwined. Damp. Warm. Tight.

Later, they will each have sexual liaisons aplenty—grunting, sweaty, hairy intercourse, complete with orgasms and fresh towels—that will deliver not a sliver of the jolt of this nonerogenous hand-holding. This is the final time either of them will get that feeling.

Anne squeezed David's hand. David squeezed hers. They gave each other a series of rapid little squeezes. Together, they laughed.

At Anne's door that night, unobserved as far as either of them could tell, they had their first real kiss. It was soft and tentative and it took a long time and neither of them were any good at it. "Wow," Anne said. "Yeah," David said, "wow." Then they did it again, no better than the first time, and made vague promises about tomorrow and said good night.

∾

NEXT DAY, SAME drill. John—very drunk, tossing a tennis ball across the lawn for the amusement of the frantically retrieving dog—watched them pull out of the drive, in the yellow Jeepster with its top down, and said, "So long, Gatsby! So long, Daisy!" They passed the big dead elm at the bottom of the drive. Anne yelled back at her brother to *shut up!* David had never read the book. "It was a mean thing to say," Anne explained. "Leave it at that." At the end of the night, their kissing improved some.

∾

KENNETH WAS NOT a morning person. But Anne (being Anne) got her way, and there he was, eight o'clock and piloting the devil out of that Chris-Craft, his thermos of coffee already half empty. On the seat behind him, David and Anne sat together, holding hands. Anne wore capri pants she'd borrowed from Jane.

They were going to Cedar Point, on the shore of Lake Erie. Where Knute Rockne, Anne's father's coach at Notre Dame, worked as a lifeguard one summer and, on the beach, invented the forward pass. Home of the Blue Streak, that impossibly high wooden roller coaster.

"Five sharp," Kenneth said when he let them off at the park pier.

What a thing it is, to be young, slim, and tanned, and to turn, on a summer Monday, to a person whose kisses are new to you (when really you're supposed to be back in Shaker Heights at diving practice or out fishing with your uncle and preparing to go to war) and, as the chain brake catches and click-clacks the roller-coaster cars toward the crest of that first big hill, to feel the tip of your tongue against the taffy-tasting tip of the other person's tongue, and to finish that kiss, with a look on your face like you've just come up from a sea dive, right before your car, the last one on the coaster, reaches the top and fires you into the sweet hurtle of artificial peril.

They rode it and rode it and rode it and rode it and rode it and rode it.

All day Anne kept trying to pay for things—rides, concessions, Skee-Ball, miniature golf, *something*—and David kept looking at her like she was nuts. She'd have given anything to be a poor girl, to think that this had only to do with him being the boy and her the girl.

Later they went swimming.

She didn't wear the maillot but rather her diving suit—high-necked and navy blue, with her swim club's patch centered on her bosom. Yesterday, as David affixed striped wallpaper to her mother's studio, he looked out the window, three stories below, on the indifferently tended lawn, and saw Anne in yet *another* bathing suit—a low-cut flowery one with an attached tulle skirt. Where David came from, girls didn't have a wardrobe of bathing suits. His aunt had been wearing the same dull blue one for as long as he could remember.

He noticed that Anne had bruises on her arms. "Are you OK?" he said.

"It's from the roller coaster. Sorry. People in my family bruise easily."

"Don't be sorry," David said.

Anne and David entered the brown lake together, running and holding hands. They swam out to the far rope. It was still shallow enough to stand. They embraced and, underwater, began to grope each other. She ran her hands over his back. He slipped one hand in the armhole of her suit and, for a respectful moment, held her warm wet bare breast. She looked him fiercely in the eyes. She whispered his name. She wrapped her arms around his neck and her legs around his hips, and they kissed some more.

It was long after five. Kenneth had been at the pier but then caught sight of Anne's red hair and drove over to the rope buoy at the edge of the swimming area. He cut the engine, stuck his fingers in the corners of his mouth, and whistled so loud everybody looked.

"Shit," Anne said.

David was liking it, her cussing. At this, too, she was getting better.

They hurried into the bathhouse to get separately naked (the thought, the thought!) and to wash off the oily film of the lake and get dressed. The other beachgoers kept staring at Kenneth. He was the only Negro around.

༄

ANNE WENT TO the general store in the morning to buy a journal. Nothing said *Journal* on it. Just *Diary*. The small ones said *Autographs*. How girly. What she bought said *Log*. It was for fishermen. She bought this while David was fishing. She also bought a fountain pen.

She was not the sort of young woman to begin a thing like this with cheesy preliminaries. She got home, locked herself in her room, sat at the little rolltop desk that John had refinished last week, sat down, and boom: *Love is about the chance to be someone else,* she wrote. *Love is about getting a glimpse of a fully formed life—one's own—down a path belonging to and/or discovered by someone else.* That was what she'd been thinking for a while, those two sentences, and why she'd bought the journal. She stared out the window for a long time. Then she wrote, *Love is profound narcissism that feels like profound selflessness. Also the converse.* She paused again. With meticulous crosshatches, she X'd out those last two sentences. *This is not a fairy tale,* she wrote, *but its opposite. I've been raised to think of myself as some stupid princess. I'm not some stupid princess. I don't have to live the life everyone expects.*

༄

WHAT WAS DAVID supposed to do, borrow the Jeepster one morning and take the first ferry to Sandusky and drive all the way back to Old Brooklyn and find Irene and take her to the nearest malt shop and tell her she was a swell kid, but he didn't want her to have to wait for him? Then what? Listen to her cry and get mad, cry and tell him he doesn't deserve her, cry and ask for explanations that don't exist? Then what? Get slapped? Watch her storm out? Then decide whether to follow her and calm her down or just go. Either way, eventually, as soon as possible, go. He could have come back to Kelley's later that day.

Sure, sure, sure.

There are so many good plans a sanctimonious armchair historian/swain can retrofit to a place, a time, a person, a situation, and say here's what should have been done. If you're in the middle of a thing like that yourself, it's 100 to 1 *you'd* actually do it. So pipe down.

Plus which, without such dumbass human error, we'd have little love, scant science, no history whatsoever, and fewer stories.

Thank you.

❦

DAVID AND ANNE spent another afternoon and evening—the hottest ones so far—together back on Kelley's, working on the house and then, late afternoon, going for a swim at one of the abandoned rock quarries in the middle of the island. David borrowed a baggy pair of John's trunks. Kenneth and John went along. Anne knew a place where there was a cliff fifty feet high and, below, water so deep she'd never been able to find the bottom. She'd had her eyes on this place from the time they arrived. But for quite a while, in water colder than you'd think, they swam in a bright, open part of the quarry, diving off a puny ledge. David was a jumper. With Anne's each dull front dive, she became more aware of the etiquette-class brainwashing.

Eventually everyone took a break, stretching out on the sun-warmed limestone. John had brought a sweating, tinfoil-covered stoneware pitcher (circa 1870) full of Sea Breezes. John and Kenneth had been drinking for a while. Neither said anything when Anne and David had some, too. John had, after all, brought four glasses.

"These are really nice glasses," David said.

The glasses weren't crystal or anything particularly fancy, but in a flash Anne saw how pretentious this must look to David, and blushed, and, on instinct, said, "Thank you."

"You're welcome," David said, swirling his drink, studying it.

"Don't mind John," Kenneth said. "He can't take paper cups like ordinary people would."

"Ordinary people," John said, and affected a stage shiver.

Anne stood. She was less woozy than she'd feared. It wasn't like she never *drank* before. Without telling anyone what she was doing, she made her way up the lip of the quarry, toward the cliff. By the time the three men were moved, inevitably, to protectiveness, she was already there. This is, she thought, one *hell* of a lot higher than she'd figured. She did feel a bit dizzy. Hard to know if it was vertigo or booze.

She could hear John shouting *Babe,* Kenneth and David shouting *Anne.*

She thought, for inspiration, of Mrs. Pat McCormick, the great diving champion from Ohio State, who'd put on an exhibition at the diving camp Anne attended last summer. Anne closed her eyes and thought of the Olympic Games that, as she stood there, were going on in Helsinki. She'd been looking forward for months to watching these on television, looking forward most of all to watching Mrs. Pat McCormick dive for gold. Now, for a *boy,* she's here instead, on Kelley's Island, where her stupid mother refuses to have a TV.

Insane.

She opened her eyes. It was her earliest childhood memory, those Acapulco cliff divers. She held back a smile. She raised her arms. This wasn't much higher than a platform dive.

She threw herself off the cliff, into nothing more ambitious than a one-and-a-half.

From below, David Zielinsky watched her, in the sky, bring her lovely face swiftly near the knees of her impossibly straight legs, as if to kiss, spinning, all the way around and then opening up and falling, falling, spear-straight, toes pointed, toward the dark water.

The last few, horrible feet: it *was* higher than a platform dive, and her legs drifted over behind her; she hit the water with a sickening, simultaneous *whoosh-thwack.*

David dove in, swimming toward her as fast as he could, which was not fast. Despite a panic of unpretty strokes toward the spot where he'd seen her last, he was no more than a quarter of the way there when, at that exact same spot, she surfaced.

"*Yes!*" she yelled, triumphant. Then: "*Shit.*" The backs of her legs burned.

She saw David swimming toward her. Probably, she would have gotten mad at him, but she caught sight first of something floating in the water behind him, then of John and Kenneth convulsed in laughter, then of the chinawhite domes of David's bare buttocks.

"Hey!" she said. "Buddy-boy! Hey, pal-o'-mine!" she said. "Lose something?"

The look on his face! Her legs were numb. Within the hour they'd bruise so badly she'd look like she'd been flogged. But the swift justice of the punishment meted out (to he who presumed to rescue *her*), and how hard this made her laugh: *that,* at first, was what hurt.

৩৩

ANNE CALLED HER father and told him she'd be staying at Kelley's for the rest of the week, this time missing not just diving practice but an invitational meet and a deb class dance.

"Who is he?" he said. She could hear the disappointment in his voice: strange, since he never attended her diving meets.

"'*He*'?" Anne said. "What do you mean, '*he*'?"

Jane mouthed, *I told you.* She'd come over that morning and, after nodding gravely and accepting the story about how Anne's calves got so bruised, was won over on the subject of rhythm and blues. Now Jane sat next to Anne, shuffling cards at the Chippendale kitchen table. The cook was doing the lunch dishes. David would be here any minute.

"What else could it be?" Tom O'Connor said. "You and your mother—"

"I'm not going to talk to you about her," said Anne. "Or vice versa." Anymore, it wasn't much better with him.

"So?" he said. "Then what is it?"

"Helping John with the house," she said. "Seeing my friends here. You know. Goofing off. Girl things."

"'*Goofing off*'? C'mon, Babe. It's your old dad you're talking to here. Who is he?"

She could hardly breathe. "Nobody!" she said. "Can't I just have one week in my stupid life when I don't have to do some stupid activity or study some stupid book or display my *poise* at some stupid place for some stupid people? Can't I just be a normal teenaged girl for one stupid week?"

"'*A normal teenaged girl*'?" he said. "Christ, how you talk." He sighed. "Well," he said, "if it's OK with your mother..."

"How *you* talk!" she said, meaning not the *Christ* part of course but the *your mother* part. This got a chuckle out of the old man and allowed them to hang up on good terms.

Her father, as always, had not asked about John. He knew only vaguely about Kenneth. Anne avoided the subject as assiduously as the next O'Connor. Midwestern Catholics believe that a thing you don't talk about is a thing dispatched to the dank subbasement of oblivion.

Jane had obligingly dealt out the cards for double solitaire. "I can't believe," she said, "that David still thinks you're my age."

"I can't believe I'm *not* your age," said Anne. "And anyway, I told him I'm a year ahead in school, which is true. I can't believe *you're* your age. Double solitaire? For pete's sake."

Pete made Jane think of the other night. She dug her nails unobtrusively into her thigh. "He'll be mad when he finds out he's robbing the cradle," Jane said. "What do *you* want to play?"

Anne had no idea. She hated cards.

"There's a lot about love you need to learn," Jane said.

"Who called it *love*?" asked Anne. "Who used that word? Did I? No. I did not."

"You didn't have to," Jane said. "You might as well have."

"You're such a *girl*," Anne said. "Do you know what I mean?"

Suddenly Jane looked like she would cry. Somehow, this made Anne bloodthirsty.

"You're going to wind up just like your *mother*," Anne said. She hardly knew Jane's mother, but this was not the point. "My god, Jane, it's the 1950s. Wake up."

Jane kept looking like she would cry and kept not crying.

The doorbell rang.

Virginia the wolfie raced clumsily down two flights of stairs, barking like mad. She could hear John descending, too. Right above them, Kenneth yelled for quiet, please.

"Go home, Jane," Anne said. "I have things to do. *Sit.*" Jane nodded and rose, to do as she was told. Anne half expected her to sit. God knows the dog wasn't going to. This damn puppy was a galloping one-owner bitch.

Anne got to the door to greet David before her brother did. She had a big day planned. When she threw open the door, though, he was standing there with a funny look on his face.

"I've got good news and bad news," he said.

"What's the good?"

"I've got a big day planned. All kinds of stuff for us to do."

"So do I, actually. What're your plans? Wait, what's the bad?"

He winced. "My aunt and uncle," he said. "They're going with us on the first part of it. Sightseeing stuff. It was the only way I could get the car, for later."

"Sounds great," she said. That was it? That was the bad news? "I've been dying to meet . . . Hey, you know Jane, right? Jane was just leaving."

David said hello, but Jane breezed past them and kept going, down the porch steps and cutting across the Ashcroft lawn, head down and wordless.

That was when, with parallel pangs of terror, David and Anne noticed that Sarah O'Connor had left her Adirondack chair, set aside her novel, snuffed out her cigarette, gone to the Willys, and was standing near the driver's side, chatting with Uncle Stan and Aunt Betty.

"*Sit*," John said. Virginia sat. "David! My cheeky helper! Have you ever felled a tree?"

David blushed. He hadn't, he said, but he'd be willing to help. Anne was surprised *he* hadn't sat on command.

"That dead elm," John said, pointing. "It's gotta go."

"John! I *told* you," Anne said. "We have plans. So, good-bye."

John shrugged. "Your loss. Bye, kids. Don't do anything I wouldn't!"

"Who'd want to," Anne said.

John stayed on the porch, going on like that and waving like a cartoon character.

"Don't mind him," Anne said to Aunt Betty and Uncle Stan. "He's the village idiot."

To Anne, her mother looked every inch the snobbish harridan. To David, his aunt and uncle looked every inch the provincial bumpkins.

All unmade introductions were exchanged. Anne radiated charm (again the training kicked in), but everyone else looked like they'd lunched on bad clams. Betty said it was nice to finally meet David's new (and here her lips grew sphincter-tight) *friend*. Sarah, forged by the same training she'd secured for Anne, had reached an age when she felt too tired to bother. It felt good to be rude. Furthermore, what grown man would choose to drive a vehicle like *that*?

Sarah claimed it was nice to have met them. She walked away, calling for the cook to bring her a half-carafe of chilled white wine.

"Quite a house you got here," said Stan, backing out of the driveway, when it would have been easier just to drive around. He made a comment about the gravel drive.

"It's *better* than paved," David quickly said, meaning (but not saying) *more expensive*.

"It's lovely," said Betty, sore enough about the rented trailer to fail to suppress her envy. "The house, the driveway, the grounds, the trees, the shrubbery. Everything. When I dream of a house, this is the kind of a house I dream of."

"What's your dad do?" Stan snapped.

David wanted to die. "It's been in their family for years, Uncle Stan."

Now Anne wanted to die. "My father is in business," she said, "and also an attorney."

"Huh," Stan said.

Betty just kept going on and on about the beauty of the house. Finally, Anne cleared her throat and asked, as politely as humanly possible, where they were going.

"Those glacial grooves," Betty said. "I've heard so much about them. You've probably seen those grooves a million times, though."

"Anyone who comes here should certainly see the grooves," Anne said. "Actually, it's been awhile since I've been up there. When you can go anytime, sometimes you don't."

"How true," said Betty. "We live near the zoo. I haven't gone since... heavens, since we had David's eighth birthday party there."

We live near the zoo. David balled his hands into fists.

"After the grooves," he said, "how about taking the noon ferry over to Put-in-Bay? That's what I was thinking."

"Great," said Anne. "Perfect."

At least David changed the subject fast enough to keep Betty from telling the part about how, at that birthday party, he'd snuck off and got caught behind the lizard house, kissing Karolyn Znidarsic, who sat next to him in practically every class, K–12, and grew up to be Rhodes High homecoming queen, a girl David had for years considered out of his league.

Anne reached over and gave David's thigh a lightning-quick squeeze and did not look at him but out the window, smiling like a person who'd just gotten away with something.

When a girl like Karolyn Znidarsic seems like nothing...damn. Words fail.

◦Ϲ

THE GLACIAL GROOVES were a few hundred yards of exposed limestone, striated with veiny rock stripes: a gorge about twenty feet deep that would have stretched to the horizon, except that quarrymen had cut away a good mile of it. A ten-story cliff marked the end of the cutting. Even so, the grooves are the largest found in the United States. Which is great. But you look at them awhile and think, *Well, there they are. Glacial grooves. Let's go.*

The glaciers themselves, David thought, *must have gone through here faster than Uncle Stan.* He read every educational sign aloud. These were about more than glaciers. The state park people, while they had you, felt compelled to slip in lessons about flora, fauna, and Indians.

"Sorry," David said.

"For what?" Anne said.

Her hair, the smell of it, the light in that red hair. Her face, stippled with sunlight from the canopy of oak trees above. The way she carried that lithe body. Her teeth. The way she put up with all this. The way he felt toward her, his heartbreak every time he got a glimpse of those bruises peeking out from under the back hem of her sundress. How smart she was.

I love you, he thought.

"Looks like we might miss the ferry," David said.

"Forget it," Anne said. "Look at them."

He stifled the urge to apologize again.

"Isn't it great?" she said. "I could watch them forever. They still love each other. How long have they been married?"

David had no idea.

"You're lucky," she said. "That's a great thing to get to see, as you're growing up."

Like the day, the East Side–West Side thing lay breached and beached between them; Anne and David were stunned silent.

Finally Anne broke through it, summoning the courage to ask a thing she'd been wanting to ask. "I was wondering," she said, "why it is that you live with your aunt and uncle?"

"I told you. My mother died."

"And not your father, I mean."

David shrugged. "My father travels a lot," he said. "For work."

"Right," Anne said, nodding. "You don't have to do it right now," she said, "but sometime, will you tell me what happened? With your mother?"

"Absolutely," David said. But that was all he said.

৩১৩

STAN REFUSED TO speed, and as a result they drove right up to the dock and had the honor of watching the ferry pull away. "What the hey," Stan said. "It's a bit cramped, but why don't we just take the fishing boat over?"

"Terrific," Anne said.

All the way to Middle Bass Island—squeezed together on that boat, with David bailing water—Aunt Betty kept giving David these looks. This he could definitely have done without.

৩১৩

PUT-IN-BAY was the town part of Middle Bass. Once exclusive, it had since the war slouched toward becoming a vacationland for Toledoans. Still, it had arcades, amusements, and carnival rides around its town square, plus souvenir stores, candy shoppes (not shops), and a slew of gimmicky bars. The longest one in Ohio. The roundest. A block apart. Tell your friends.

The four of them wandered together through all but the bars. It was Betty who looked around, furrowed her brow, and said that she'd heard about the Erie islands wineries, but where were they? (At the time, on the four islands, there were ten, all but three pretty small.) Stan and David both ventured guesses. Anne, sighing, stuck her head in a fudge shoppe and asked. Thus empowered, they walked straight to the closest one: a one-story cement

[100]

building, painted the color of sand. Looked like a family-owned tool-and-die shop.

Stan paid for everyone's tour. At the stroke of three, joined by a tottering retirement-home group, they were exposed to a prideful description of the local soil, a glimpse of distant family-tended grape arbors, a cavalcade of pressers, casks, bungholes, bottling nozzles, corking devices: all of it suffered through so as to earn samples of sugary wine, served in paper cups. Happy bees swarmed near the lidless steel trash cans.

"*This* one's good," said Betty. They were, after all, on vacation. Live it up! Stan got the sampler so they all could have a sip of everything. David had told them Anne was a college girl; nobody thought anything of her taking part. Except on other grounds.

"Ordinary people," David said, tapping the rim of his paper cup.

"I'm sorry about that," said Anne.

"I'm just joking," David said.

Stan bought a bottle each of the two varieties Betty liked best, plus two other bottles to give as business-related gifts. David bought a bottle, too. He had the giddy thought that he and Anne could open this fifty summers from now—in a new century!—and toast a life well lived.

They walked back into town.

"We can't come to Put-in-Bay," Anne said, "without going up in the Perry Monument. It's a must."

"The Perry Monument?" said Betty.

"That big tower," Anne said, in a nice way.

You could see that tower from almost anyplace on any of the islands. Only then did David realize: except for two years in Chicago, his aunt had lived her whole life in Cleveland and hardly gone anywhere, not even here. Even he'd been up in the Perry Monument before.

"I'm not sure that's my sort of thing," said Betty. "Do you know what claustrophobia is?" she said to Anne. "I have that, and also to some degree a fear of heights." She was looking longingly, though, at the tower at the end of the island.

"We could take the stairs," said David. "I think there's stairs."

"I'm afraid," said Betty, "that it's been too long a day for that. And also too much wine. You young people go, if that's what you want to do."

"We don't have to," said Anne. "It was just a suggestion."

Betty nodded. Stan studied the toe of his brogan. "Go," Betty said.

"It's OK," said Anne. "I've been there before."

"I imagine you've been all over," Betty said.

"Come *on*," David said, taking Anne's arm. "We won't be long," he said.

The line was short. They took the next elevator car up. David apologized and said wine made his aunt loopy. Other than that, they rose in silence to the top of the monument, your usual phallic stone spire, this one commemorating the last battle fought in Ohio waters, Commodore Perry's successful efforts in the War of 1812 to make Lake Erie free and safe for all Americans.

On the observation deck, they held hands. First time all day. There were other people up there, but Anne and David couldn't have told you this. They kissed, a long in-public kiss.

"You can see Cleveland from here," Anne said.

"Where?" asked David.

"You used to be able to," she said. "What haze," she said. "Jeez."

"Still." David looked out over the lake and the adjoining green islands. "It's beautiful." He swallowed. "Like your eyes." He felt like a dork. But he'd been honest with her.

On cue, Anne looked into David's eyes. Then she crossed hers, and they cracked up.

❧

Lies on top of lies, lies compounded and squared, drawn and quartered, sautéed and simmered, served piping *hot!*

What is it about love that ascends so well from the smoldering peat of lies?

So well, in fact, that a person looking back on those rare loves rigged for the long haul will lie to himself: forgetting, denying the lies told to set that love asail. Excuses made. Other suitors spurned. Versions of one's self invented on the spot, debuted for the sake of another, and stuck to, in a pallid, nervous version of forever after.

❧

"Your dad," said Uncle Stan, "he wouldn't by any chance be *Thomas* O'Connor?"

"Yes," Anne said. "Do you know him?"

The rented boat drew near the pier. David willed it closer.

"*The* Thomas O'Connor, right?" Stan said. "Used to be mayor?"

"Just for a term is all," she said.

"I don't really know your dad," said Stan. "I know a lot of people who know him."

"Like me," Anne said, clearly trying to make a joke of this. No one laughed. "What I mean is," she said, "you know me, and I—"

"I got it," said Stan.

I could almost throw a baseball that far, David thought. *We're that close.*

"I hope your friend can join us for dinner," said Betty.

"I'd be delighted, Mrs. Lychak."

"Dinner out, right?" said David.

"We have that fish," said Betty.

"Walleye," said Stan.

"We have that walleye," said Betty. "It's not getting any fresher."

"Yeah, but Anne and I sort of had plans to go out," said David.

Anne looked at him.

"I'd rather go out," David said.

"Go, then," said Betty. "You and your friend go do what you'd *rather*."

"Help me tie up," said Stan.

I'm causing this, Anne thought. "I'd be delighted, Mr. and Mrs. Lychak. Fish sounds great. Walleye is a favorite of mine."

They docked the boat and rode in the Jeepster to the trailer in the woods. Already, two hours before sundown, it was dark enough in the forest that the rustle of bat wings had begun. It was also a time of frenzy for the chiggers and bloodsucking flies, thus requiring the fish to be fried inside the hot, smelly trailer. Eaten there, too, on a flimsy foldout table. Anne volunteered to help cook but was told, "No, sit, get comfortable." *Not a chance in hell of that,* David thought. She *looked* comfortable, though, and kept saying how cute the trailer was. David thought this more than fair. But he could see it was not sitting well with his aunt.

Betty served everything (corn on the cob, tomatoes, Jell-O imbued with celery and fruit cocktail) on paper plates. Stan, who'd gone to take a shower, emerged shaven and stinking of Aqua Velva. He opened one of his bottles of varietal wine and poured it into jelly glasses. He poured his in a coffee mug. There were only three jelly glasses.

"Everything's delicious, Mrs. Lychak," Anne said, which, in spite of David's suicidal mortification, was true. Stan, mouth somewhat full, proposed a toast to this effect. Betty blushed.

"Yeah," David said. "She's right. It is good."

This brought his aunt right back to her regular color.

"It's good," she said, "to have one's *own* opinions."

"That is my opinion," David said. "Jeez."

"I'm not much of a wine drinker," Stan said, "but this wine is really good wine."

⌘

AFTER DINNER DAVID didn't even ask for the keys; he just took them off the counter. His uncle didn't say a word about this. A few days ago this would have been unthinkable.

Anne thanked Betty and Stan for everything. They said it was nothing, really.

"What time are you going to be home?" Betty asked. She said it as David was in the motion of closing the door. They were already out. Anne was partway to the Willys.

David jerked the door open and gave his aunt an ugly look. "I'm *not* a child anymore," he said. "OK? And *you're* not my mother."

Stan, hunched over the table, did not move from his card-table chair. He stared darkly at the wine in his coffee mug.

Betty stood, came to the door, and lowered her voice to a whisper. "This girl," she said, "has no *idea* about Irene. Does she? Oh, David, how could—"

"I'll be home," David said. "When I'm home."

He slammed the door in her face.

⌘

THEY DROVE THE Jeepster to a park on the north shore of the island. They didn't say much, all the way there. David parked the car next to a picnic table. "Again," he said, "I'm so—"

"Don't say it," she said. "Don't say you're sorry."

"I am, though."

She threw open the door, got out, slammed it, strode to the rocky shore. The north coast of America.

David stayed in the car.

The bottle of wine David had considered sharing with Anne in the next century was still in the backseat. To open it, he used, for the first time ever, the corkscrew on his Swiss army knife (a graduation present from his father, that plus a new $50 bill, a union card, and a vague offer to take him to a whorehouse). He took a swig, right from the bottle, and got out, to go after her. When he stood up, he staggered.

This is the last day, ever, that I drink.

He leaned on the car. He took several deep breaths and went after her.

"How are your legs?" David asked.

Anne, her face lit by the burnt orange twilight, looked out across the lake, toward nothing David could see. "They're fine," she said. "They just look bad."

"That's good," he said. "Not that they look bad," he said. "That they're fine."

He handed her the bottle. She took it, took a long pull from it, and handed it back.

"I have to tell you something," she said.

"What," David said. "Is it bad?" She *has a confession for* me?

"Not really," she said. She took the bottle back from him. "It's just... well." She took a quick pull. "I'm not a sophomore at Vassar."

"You're not?"

She turned to face him.

"There's no other way to say this. I'll be blunt." She handed the bottle to David, then stood tall (five feet ten inches, as tall as she'd get), as if about to recite a poem. "I am sixteen years old."

He felt blood rush to his ears.

"I am, however, ahead in school," she said. "I start my senior year in the fall. Which is to say that I'm only a year behind you in school." She nodded. "So there. I've said it."

His heart raced.

"I'm engaged," he blurted. "I mean, I was. Engaged."

"Oh?" she said. She did not betray her surprise. "Actually, so am I."

She shrugged.

"Really, it's a secret," she said. "Which is fortunate. Because I haven't told him yet, but it's over." She shrugged again. "That was the other thing I had to tell you about."

Could've knocked him over with a single *barbicel* of a feather. "You haven't *told* him?"

"Surely he must know," she said. "By now he should have taken the hint. He's *such* a boy. Are you going to drink that or just breathe on it?"

"Take it," he said.

They sat on top of the picnic table and for a while didn't say much. They made fairly quick work of the bottle.

Darkness fell: cloudy, moonless, starless. At nearby, unseen campsites, fires crackled.

"Remember that gun?" Anne asked, after a very long silence and apropos of nothing.

"The one I shot?"

"Of course the one you shot, dummy," she said. She took hold of his hand, with both of hers, and put it in her lap. "That was *so* tremendous."

He laughed, softly. "It was," he said.

"'*They went thataway,*'" she said, cracking herself up, in a way that sounded phony.

"Yes," he said.

She stopped herself.

"I'm not a virgin, either," she said. "In case you were laboring under that delusion."

He didn't know what to say about that.

"I don't know what to say about that," he said.

"Yeah," she said. "No big surprise. Your not knowing what to say," she said. "Not the other. My . . . whatchamacallit. My experience."

He considered and came very close to telling her that he, in fact, *was* a virgin.

"Tell me about her," she said. "Your fiancée."

"I'd rather not."

She threw his hand back at him.

"I thought you said she was your *ex*-fiancée."

He couldn't remember what he'd said. This had been a hell of a bad day.

"This has been a hell of a day," he said.

"Maybe you should take me home," she said.

"Just like that?"

"Just like that!" she said. "After what you lied to me about—"

"You lied, too."

"—and after seeing the way you treat those sweet people—"

"Who?"

"*Who?* My god. My *god.* Your aunt and your uncle, that's who. The way you were talking to your aunt just about made me—"

"I don't treat them any way," he said.

"Exactly. You don't. Exactly right."

"As opposed to the way *you* treat *your* mother."

"You don't know my mother."

"You don't know my aunt and my uncle."

"So," she said. "OK." She jabbed her finger in his breastbone. "What happened with your mother? Why do you live with them?"

"I don't want to talk about it," he said. "If you don't mind."

"I think I do mind," she said. "I think I mind a lot."

"Then mind," he said. "See if I care." He got up. "Let's go," he said.

"Where?" she asked.

"Home," he said. "Like you said. I'm taking you home."

"Let me drive," she said.

"Oh, sure," he said.

She jumped down off the table, seized his face with her hands, and kissed him. He didn't pull away. He put his arms around her. Then he pulled her tight. It was an awfully long kiss.

"Let me drive," she said.

"I can't," he said.

She put his hand on her breast. Obediently, he squeezed.

They kissed.

"Let me drive," she said.

"I can't."

She took his other hand and put it through the neck of her summer dress and underneath her white all-silk brassiere. He squeezed.

They kissed.

"Let me drive," she said.

"I can't," he said.

"You're a greedy creep," she said.

"You're right," he said. "But, I mean, what I can do . . . ," he said. "It has nothing to do with . . . ," he said. "I just can't let you drive, no matter, y'know," he said, "what."

She considered him. She made a fast qualitative inventory of other places she might take one of his hands and put it. He was looking at her in what seemed like fear.

"I couldn't possibly care less," she said, "about your stupid car."

"It's not a stupid car," he said. Though he truly thought it was.

"It's a profoundly stupid car," she said. Though she truly thought it wasn't.

They persisted in this childish exchange. He was a champion debater, and she a born communicator a year ahead in school, and none of that, now, made a whit of difference. All this time he had his hands ludicrously criss-crossed, grasping one breast through two layers of clothes, the other by its clammy bare skin. He was only grasping now, not squeezing.

"Let go of my tits," she finally said.

"Nice mouth," he said.

"Let go of my tits," she said.

"Fine," he said, and he did. He looked grateful. He stuck his hand in his pocket. "Here," he said. He gave her the keys. "What the fuck. Drive."

"Nice mouth," she said.

"Drive," he said.

ᠺᠥ

FIRST CURVE, SHE took too fast. First turn, at the entrance to the state park, she again took too fast. "Easy," David said.

"I *know* how to drive."

Anne had no driver's license (she and her father had had an H-bomb of an argument over why the boys all got their licenses at sixteen but, for who knows what patriarchal bullshit reason, she had to wait until she was eighteen). But she did know how to drive (her brother Patrick had taught her last summer, before he moved to New York to become a television technician).

She glanced at her watch. "Ten o'clock!" she said.

David snapped on the radio. It was right where he'd left it from last night.

"*... This is your old pal Alan Freed. Welcome to ... the MOONDOG Show!*"

"All *right!*" said David and Anne, both, in unison.

The car radio was full of static, like there was a thunderstorm between here and there. Freed threw on the honking, hiccup-scream onslaught of Big Jay McNeely's "Insect Ball." Big Jay got it *going!* There was nothing for Alan Freed and Anne and David to *do,* but this:

"*Hey, ho, hey, play, go, ho, hey!*"

And this:

Pounding on the phone book! Pounding on the dashboard! Pounding, pounding, pounding, pounding, pounding on the steering wheel!

For most of the rest of the way back, which was to say Big Jay plus a real *rockin'* thing from Miss *Varetta Dillard!* (whom they had both gone to see sing and not seen, who'd been playing on the jukebox in the nostalgic, halcyon days of earlier this week), things were OK.

"I want to *dance,*" said Anne.

"Slow down."

"*Mercy, Mister Percy,*" sang Anne and Varetta.

"Easy," David said.

Anne stood on the brake. The car fishtailed, perpendicular to the road, the main one through the middle of the island.

"Stop it!" Anne said.

"Let me drive," he said.

"Men," Anne said. "Menmenmenmenmenmenmenmen. Men!"

The spin had killed the engine. The headlights shone across a parched grape arbor. The farmers could sure use it, some rain.

David laughed.

"I'm glad you think that's funny."

"Aw, c'mon," he said. "I'm sorry. Let's just go. Start it up and let's go."

Alan Freed was doing a commercial for Erin Brew. He opened a bottle, poured it, and drank. This made Anne and David feel queasy, but neither made a move to change the station.

The turn she was about to make, as she got close to the lake-gravel drive of Ashcroft, felt different from the rest of them. No wider, but faster.

David yelled.

Anne hit the brake and the Jeepster responded (naturally, Stan kept the brakes well maintained). Smooth gravel flew. It was a hell of a nice save.

If only that dead elm had been cut down, who knows what might have happened?

What if Kenneth hadn't been having a good writing day, if he'd broken form and helped John cut it down? What if things had gone differently with those boys from good families and Jane and one or two of *them* were around to help out? (A web of tangential *what-if*s stem from this one.) What if Alan Freed hadn't sent out into the Moondog kingdom winningly frenetic music that would make any semidrunk youth wish to drive too fast?

Then again, what if the elm wasn't already dead? Just a bigass healthy tree that Anne almost missed but didn't, grazing the trunk of it with the entire passenger side of the heretofore pampered Jeepster? Anne and David wouldn't have had to stew in the *what-if*s. They would have lost the chance to blame things on a dead tree.

On a better-tended estate, that big dead ex-tree would have been cleared out of there a year ago. It was slated to be cut down but still standing; near its base, its bark was strafed off and the wood underneath was streaked with yellow paint.

Even figuring out that maybe, even if the tree hadn't been there, even if the car hadn't hit it, every consequential thing the wreck seemed to have triggered still might have happened—even *that* makes a person's head hurt.

So who knows? A wreck is what it is. Things just are. A kiss is still a kiss.

All that can be said for certain is that if the tree had been cut down, Stan Lychak's mint-condition 1949 yellow Willys Jeepster, driven by Anne O'Connor (driven by David Zielinsky in the "official" version of the story), would have stayed that way. Mint. It wouldn't have collided with a tree that wasn't there.

In Anne's defense, it *barely* hit the tree that was there.

A scant few inches the other way, and nothing would have happened.

Upon such a principle are all of us conceived.

∾

DAVID SCREAMED AT her and called her a horrible, horrible name.

Anne tried to say she was sorry, but he would have none of it.

Her mother and her brother and her brother's friend and the cook and even a few neighbors heard the sickening crunch and ran out to see what had made it.

Anne fell to her knees and began vomiting on an oleander bush.

David stood next to the scored, crumpled side of the Willys, hyperventilating.

Everyone was OK. That was the most important thing.

"It was a deer," David blurted.

Anne was crying. Sobbing. He was nowhere near her. She was as crumpled as the car, and much more wrecked-looking, and David did not run to her side. He was screwed to the ground by everything that falling for this girl might have been about instead of love.

"It was a deer," David said, "and I barely swerved in time to miss it."

Anne's guts heaved and wrenched, and she wanted to look back at David and see the look on his face as he was making this stupid, chivalric gesture, but she just kept thinking about that other girl, that other *woman,* the fiancée. Abruptly, Anne was drenched with cold sweat. She retched, and out came another hot stream clotted with pinkish chunks of fish and corn.

Sarah O'Connor started doing the screaming now, about does he know who her daughter *is,* and about the wine smell that anyone would have noticed, roiling from that ruined oleander, and about all the things a woman like her would say to a boy like David.

Including that he was never to see her daughter again.

David still couldn't think of anything to say.

Anne heard him not saying anything. She realized he wasn't going to come to her side.

Sarah draped her arm around her sobbing daughter, helped her to her feet, and led her inside. Anne didn't look back. John told the neighbors to go away. John said that maybe the same should go for David. "You kind of blew it, buddy boy," he said. "Too bad we didn't cut down that tree today."

Kenneth, who claimed to know a lot about cars, deemed the damage superficial. "There's a lot of it," he said, "but nothing structural. Two hundred bucks, is my estimate."

This, in 1952, was nearly 5 percent of the average American household income.

David got behind the wheel, shaking.

He stopped at the fish shack, drank black coffee, and chewed peppermint candies (Life Savers, invented in Cleveland by Hart Crane's father) that he'd bought from the case near the cash register. The waitress kept asking if he was OK. He said he was. He put his hand up to his mouth and tried to smell his breath. He ordered pie. Apple. Finally he got up.

"You sure you're OK?" the waitress asked.

"Yes," he said. "I need the check."

"On the house." She was heavy. She patted his head. She let her hand linger in his hair.

"Thank you," he said. "You're very pretty."

"Excuse me?"

"I said you're very kind," he said.

She was the sort of young woman who'd always been told that she had a pretty face, and behind her back people said *if only*. "Are you sure you're OK? Because you don't look OK."

"Really," he said. "I am. Thanks."

When she walked away, he threw two bucks on the table and left.

Outside, on the street, two old men stood next to the Jeepster.

"Looks recent," one of them said to David.

"How can you tell?"

"You just can," said the other.

"Are you OK?" said the first.

"I am," David said. "It was a deer," he said. "I barely missed it."

"Damn deer," said the first. "Somebody ought to shoot 'em."

The second old man laughed very hard. "We try," he said to David.

David got in the car and drove off. The Jeepster drove just fine, no different from before.

Every light in the trailer glowed, like a huge tin lantern in the woods.

David had hoped against hope that he could start fresh in the morning, that everything would come clear in the morning. He pulled up to the trailer, making sure the wrecked side faced the other way. The split second he cut the lights, the trailer door opened.

Uncle Stan stood there, framed in the light.

"In or out," said Aunt Betty, from behind him. "The bugs."

Stan closed the door.

"Come here," he said. "Kid."

David obeyed.

"Hold still," said Stan.

David obeyed. The punch landed so fast and so hard on David's chin it might as well have been invisible. It made a sound like dropping a raw turkey. It was not a night you could see the stars, unless you were David Zielinsky.

"She's not your mother," Stan said. He lowered his voice to a whisper. "For which you should be grateful. You ungrateful prick."

He kicked David in the ribs.

"You skinny little cheat."

He spit on him.

Betty opened the door and called out to them in the dark. Stan was already picking David up off the ground. "He just tripped," Stan said.

"Are you OK?" she said.

David said he was.

"If I thought of you as a kid," Stan whispered, "I wouldn't have done anything."

"Thank you," David said. And in truth he was grateful. Few men have ever felt more justly coldcocked, kicked, and spat upon.

Crazy lake effect. The rain never did quite come. The farmers could have used it.

∽

THE NEXT DAY David and Anne did not see each other. In this, it had much in common with the several hundred days thereafter.

You couldn't say Stan Lychak was happy about his wrecked car. *Disbelieving* would be the word. He and David got up early the next morning to go fishing, hangovers be damned, and David told him about the accident, about the deer he'd swerved to miss and barely missed—that, along with the red pickup truck that was going the other way and did in fact hit the deer. David, thinking quickly, used Stan's pistol to put the deer out of its misery, but he missed and the startled deer got up and ran off and David and the guy in the truck, whose name David didn't get in all the craziness, looked for it awhile but couldn't find it. David should have filed a police report for insurance purposes, he knows, but is there even a police station here on this island? Wouldn't they probably just have to report it to a precinct station on the mainland?

During this whole story, Stan, dressed for fishing and slathered in mosquito repellant, stood stock-still, looking at his beloved Willys Jeepster and, occasionally, whistling.

"Damn" was all he said. "Damn."

They went fishing. They did not talk about yesterday. Out on the lake, the quiet settled on them. David caught the first thing, a barely keepable smallmouth.

"At least," said Stan, "no one was hurt."

"Except that poor deer," David said.

"Right," his uncle said. "Damn."

◌◌

ANNE DID NOT cry, the next day. A girl would cry. A little *girl*. The *hell* with that.

What she did was, she shook everything off and did not talk about what had happened, and she and her brother cut down the tree.

The whole time they were out there working, Anne kept glancing down the lakefront road, expecting to see David in the wrecked car, defying what the adults had said, defying good sense and the consequences, coming to see her despite everything, and to see what was possible. The sawdust flew, and the blows of the ax and whine of the saws felt drilled right into her hungover skull, and she suffered the pain with the masochism of a true penitent. As the day wore hotly on, Anne knew that he was not coming back. She realized she'd known this all along.

"This wood," John said as they finished stacking it behind the house, "should burn great."

Happily, it got cold that night. Anne built a fire in the main hearth. She burned the pieces with yellow paint on them first. He was a boy who did what he was told. She was a girl who pretended to be a rebel but did what she was told, too. She could go see *him*, right? She could ride her bike to the trailer, stand tall, knock on the door, take the blame for the wrecked car, suffer all the consequences, and do everything in her power to make David love her. She would not always be sixteen. He did not, Anne was certain, want to be engaged to that fiancée. The fiancée, Anne imagined, was someone David had settled for. Anne was *someone*.

But, of course, that's not what she was going to do. She told herself it was a summer romance, if that. A good learning experience. Then she threw her *Log* on the fire. She was in on the joke.

Cleave: "to sever." Cleave: "to join together." *Cleave* is its own antonym, the linguistic equivalent of one of those hermaphroditic worms that mates with itself.

Cleveland was originally called *Cleaveland,* after a guy named Moses (Yale, class of 1777). Not *the* Moses, but a good name nonetheless for someone who rises from a marshy river to found a promised land.

Cleveland's "a" was dropped for reasons upon which historians cannot achieve accord.

It's the Cuyahoga River that puts the cleave in Cleveland, separating East from Midwest, integration from segregation, a place that sees itself as America's westernmost eastern city from a place that sees itself as the easternmost midwestern city. The rest of the country sees it as neither, though it must be said that the rest of the country is perversely wont to misunderstand Cleveland.

As a dividing line, the river is a mess, kinked with arbitrary bends, navigable only by those born to it. But there you have it. On top of that, the river doesn't just divide. It also joins. All those bridges cleaving east to west. All those festivals and taverns, down by the river, places where people from east and west come together and play. All those steel mills and shipping yards, places where people from east and west come together and work.

In the early nineteenth century, the West Side was a thriving port town for the real Cleveland Indians: Seneca, Ottawa, Delaware, Chippewa, and Iroquois—the same Iroquois whose word for *crooked* gave the river its grand, unlovely name. The East Side was home to a few cowering white settlers. A generation later, the white folks were moving into the West Side, and the Indians were gone. In 1837 a dispute over which side of town should be named county seat resulted in a war between East Siders and West Siders, fought on a bridge high over the Cuyahoga. No deaths, though several musketeers were injured, and the bridge itself was attacked with axes and crowbars. Ale flowed. A cannon remained unfired. An attempt to burn the bridge down got nowhere.

Cleave.

WHEN IRENE'S FERRY pulled into the station, David was there, in his uncle's wrecked car, in a driving rainstorm, to greet it. He looked for her, standing tragic-looking and wronged against the ferry railing. But of course she had borrowed her grandparents' gray DeSoto. It was the first car off the ferry. Stupid; why would she get out of the car? The hard rain against the ragtop made it tough for David to hear himself think.

He honked.

She drove past, and he had to honk again.

She kept going.

David cranked the engine and followed her. How could she know where to go?

He caught up and honked again. Irene pulled the DeSoto to the sandy shoulder of the road and ran back to the Willys. She did not have an umbrella. David had to help her with the ruined passenger door, by which time she was soaked.

"My god," she said. "What happened to your uncle's car?"

"Deer," he said.

"Oh my god!" Irene would have been devastated at the thought of a deer killed for a reason other than sportsmanlike hunting, which all her male relatives had always done. "No one was hurt, were they? Who was driving? How did it happen?"

"Kiss me," David said. He meant it. He took her in his arms, wet and buxom and confused-looking, and his heart hurt. This was the right thing to do, Irene. He felt it. This was who he was supposed to be holding. This was someone who came from where he came from. This was a woman he was lucky to know. This was nobody to take for granted.

They kissed for a long time.

"Where did you think you were you going?" David said.

"I've been here," she said. "The trailer's my cousin's neighbor's. I stayed in it once."

David couldn't help but smile. *This* was a West Sider, his Irene: webbed into cousins, coworkers, friends, and acquaintances, everyone saving a buck on something because they knew somebody, nobody talking to anybody they didn't already know.

"So who *was* driving?" she said.

"Me," he said. "I was in it, alone, all by myself. I was running an errand. I missed the deer but I kind of ran into a tree. Just barely."

"Did he kill you?"

Grammatically, that might have meant the deer, but they both knew it meant Stan. "No," he said, though there was a welt on his jawbone from where Stan decked him. "He took it really great. It was just one of those things, is all."

"Wow," she said. "He's a kind one."

He is, David agreed. "The kindest," he said.

They kissed some more, and then she got back in her car and followed him to the trailer. Stan and Betty didn't mention Anne, and David wasn't about to. Anyone can err. David was human. It had been a brief mistake, quickly rectified. With Irene, he kept telling himself, it all came clear. A girl from the neighborhood. A girl who loved him and was nice, who understood him and was from his world. It was good. She was pretty, too, Irene. She was getting A's in all her nursing school classes and on top of being book-smart had common sense, too, which David had to admit was not always his own long suit. Plus, he was having a rough time keeping his eyes off Irene's full breasts. And also that ring of his mother's, on Irene's finger.

Things went great.

Irene slept on the foldout, David on the floor. The first night they didn't try anything, but their last night, in the middle of the night, on the floor of that rented house trailer, under a blanket Betty had knitted, Irene whispered that it was a good time, and David and Irene made quiet love.

᠆᠊᠊᠊

THE NEXT DAY he reported to the induction center and was measured at six feet three inches, an inch and a half more than when he first volunteered, an inch too tall for submarine training.

Over the summer, at an age where most men have stopped, David had grown.

The navy got wind of his loading-dock experience, and after boot camp David spent the rest of the Korean War and a short time thereafter in Long Beach, California, assigned to logistics. Departing goods. The piers: which by any other name were still docks. The navy's black market was a dullsville amateur hour compared to the intricate deals he'd seen presided over in Cleveland by men like his father. Long Beach was a sleazy nowhere. His shifts—twelve hours a day, twenty-fours every third day plus every other weekend—were a hell of inventory, paperwork, and monotony. The most interesting thing that happened to him in the navy was playing on the shipyard basketball team (he was again the reserve center), grabbing an inconsequential late-game rebound, and wrecking his knee. It would be thirty years before there was a widely available surgical procedure that would have done him any good.

～

THAT DECEMBER, AT the Union Club, on the meaty, influential arm of her father, Anne Elizabeth "Babe" O'Connor made her debut. She was the only Catholic in her deb class (though it was her mother's blood people saw, and her father's power—not his religion, which since the long-ago death of his Irish-born parents and, especially, the faith-rattling death of Steven, the O'Connors did not observe). Her parents did nothing to embarrass her. She danced with boys from good families. Everyone told her she was beautiful (which she knew, but did not like to hear). She had put her summer fling in socialist dreamland nicely behind her and returned to a life she could proficiently scorn. The boy she danced with the most that night was named Alton Herrick. Alton—born in Cleveland, but having been abroad often enough to have affected some inscrutable accent—was a smooth dancer, quite well-read, with (he whispered in her quivering ear) his own brand-new Indian motorcycle, a 3050. He was related to Myron T. Herrick, governor of Ohio and, later, in the years leading to World War I, ambassador to France (hence: *Myron T. Herrick, Friend of France,* by Col. T. Bentley Mott).

Her mother had come home from the island that fall, but rarely spoke to her father. As far as Anne could tell, they were never in the same room together except at formal obligatory social occasions. Her father traveled to Columbus and Washington more and more, and even when he was in town, he worked longer and longer hours. The few times Anne and her father were together at home, they eyed each other like friendly but wary coworkers.

Her brother Patrick was working in New York, but he had an offer on the table to come home and be the program director of the radio station his father partially owned. Patrick, twenty-four, was engaged to be married to the daughter of a former assistant attorney general of the United States. Anne's other brother, John, got the renovations to Ashcroft to a certain point and went back to California. Something happened with him and Kenneth. Kenneth moved to Paris.

Anne's senior year was a glory. She was the first student in her school's history to be editor of the school newspaper, its yearbook, and its literary magazine. She went out for field hockey, for the first time, and led the team in scoring. She kept (fruitlessly) asking why her school still had no Negro students. Other girls, even other seniors, openly told her they admired her and wished they could be like her. She remained steadfast in her dream of being a war correspondent. She wrote an essay about this on her entrance exam to Smith College and earned from them a scholarship she did not need a penny of.

Once, late at night, she wrote David Zielinsky a letter. It was a patriotic thing to do: every day the papers said so. *Write a soldier-boy.* This letter filled twenty-two pages of stationery and made no mention of any romantic anything. It had only the most glancing mentions of Kelley's Island. Instead, the letter told the breezy story of Anne's senior year and also all the news-worthy things that had happened in Cleveland that he might not have heard about, there in Korea. She had no way of knowing that he was not in Korea. She finished the letter and the next day called the number in the phone book for Stanley Lychak, to get David's mailing address. There was no answer. After that, Anne reconsidered. The letter was never mailed.

გა

IN THE SPRING, the weekend following her seventeenth birthday, Alton Herrick came home from Andover and casually relieved Anne O'Connor of her virginity. They took a suite at the Statler. Anne rigged everything, paid for most of it. Alton's casualness was an obvious front; girls from the debu-tante set were supposed to be off-limits in this way. Anne appreciated the front and did not call him on it. For her, the experience was a mixed one, but it was a safe time of the month. Alton was really very sweet and vulnerable about everything. He had decided he wanted to become a novelist, which in-terested Anne, too (it seemed like the kind of thing a war correspondent would do during her dotage), and after the deed was done, they spent a long time talking about J. D. Salinger and also Kenneth, whose book she kept looking for in the stores but never saw. As for her virginity, she was happy to see it go. It seemed time.

A few weeks later, she was elected her school's May Queen.

She came home with the news of that, but her father was away on busi-ness and her mother was—a servant said—upstairs with a migraine and not seeing anyone, even if sweet Jesus himself shows up. Which sounded a lot more like the servant than Sarah O'Connor. Anne went out back. The pool had just been cleaned and filled for the first time of the season. There was what looked like a huge black sweater submerged in the shallow end.

It was the dog. When no one was looking, the dumb wolfhound puppy had jumped in there and drowned. It never was much of a swimmer. It pined so terribly for John, Anne had a hard time not ascribing human emotions to the act, though she wasn't the sort of girl who thought like that. The dead dog did not float. She pulled it out of the pool herself (it seemed to weigh more than she did) and sat on the cement deck and stroked its wet, smelly fur. Anne thought she would cry, but what she felt was somehow too empty for that, and the tears did not come, and she was both proud of herself for this and ashamed.

Those girls at school, she thought, *don't have the first idea of what it is to be me.*

But then even *this* seemed like a silly, girlish thing to allow herself to think. She lay the dog gently down on the cement, got up, apprised one of the servants of the situation, and walked back to school, head high and untearful.

◌

EARLY ONE SEASONABLY cold morning, the first day of November, in the year of our lord 1952, a few hundred yards upriver from Collision Bend (where you can always make money from out-of-towners, betting them that this tanker or that barge will be able to make it around that sharp corner cleanly, without backing up and negotiating it twice, which the eyes of the uninitiated say is the only way and yet never happens), the Cuyahoga River caught fire.

The river burned.

It wasn't so much the river, but a huge oil slick *on* the river, though distinguishing one from the other was more a job for a chemist than a lay observer.

One theory says that the fire was touched off by sparks from a welder's torch. Could have come from a scrap yard or a shipyard or some minor bridge repair. It was a direct consequence of Cleveland's vitality that on that day, as on most, all of those places—scrap yards, shipyards, and bridges—had their share of fairly paid union welders working overtime.

Another theory says that the fire was caused by a flung cigarette butt. This could have come from some deckhand, or from the car window of someone driving over any of a half dozen bridges. Lots of people driving over those bridges that morning. High percentage of smokers. It was the golden age of smoking in the car.

Possible, even, that a spark might have been issued from the wheels of a streetcar or of a railroad car on the Norfolk & Western Railroad. If that kind of spark did, against all probability, endure its long windy fall from trestle to river, that's one badass spark, capable of historic, large-scale mayhem.

The Battalion Seven fire chief who investigated the fire entertained other theories as well. Spontaneous combustion. Bright early-winter sunlight refracted (à la a magnifying glass and immolated ants) through the windows of an office tower. Arson.

Official cause: unknown.

This was not, it should be said, the first time the river had burned and it would not be the last. But it was the worst—at least in terms of intensity, flame height, and dollar damage, and thus in fact. In truth, though, the worst was yet to come.

Because little patches of oily water routinely caught fire and smoldered for a while and burned themselves out (on the Cuyahoga and—let's be fair— on *several* of America's great industry-bearing rivers), for a couple hours no one thought to call the fire department.

By the time anyone did, the flames were sweeping through the Cuyahoga Valley, decimating the shipyards at the Great Lakes Towing Company, and leaping a full five stories into the air. When the first CFD pumpers arrived, the Jefferson Avenue Bridge was in flames. That's mostly where they trained their water cannons, on the logic that most of the water that hit the bridge would also fall on the river, thus diluting the oil and other flammables (sewage, solvents, lubricants, and an awful lot of paint). The next arriving trucks addressed the burning shipyards. The worst of it was out in an hour. The river itself, though, kept flickering on and off, like a novelty birthday candle.

This was news, but it was not big news. None of the three local TV stations sent a crew to get footage of the fire. Only two of three *mentioned* it. All three daily newspapers did, it's true, place the fire on the front page (only one used a picture). The stories, though, were midwestern-chipper: "If not the most disastrous fire [in the city's history]," wrote the *Plain Dealer,* "certainly the gaudiest."

The rest of the world hardly noticed. A small account of the fire appeared deep in the *New York Times.* No national magazine gave it a mention. None of the comedians who heard about the fire, there in the thriving industrial city of Cleveland, found it funny enough to use.

PART TWO

∾

BEST LOCATION
IN THE NATION
The Seventh City: 1954–1960

— 5 —

"AFTER SHE CAME out here," Aunt Betty said, "all we talked about were the shows she was in." By *shows* she meant movies; by *talked about* she meant in letters. In practical terms, for Betty Lychak long-distance phone calls had not yet been invented. News of her sister's death had come via telegram, not telephone. "Supposedly there were several. She was the most excited about a detective show with Jimmy Cagney and Mae West. Your mother was Cagney's secretary. She had nineteen lines, she said."

From the public parking area at Venice Beach, behind the windshield of a battered blue half-ton Ford pickup, David and his aunt stared out at the vast calm of the Pacific Ocean. Even on a weekday morning, the beach was filled with sunbathers, enjoying the benefits of the planet's still-intact ozone layer. The truck's radio did not go off with the ignition, and the jazz show David had it tuned to was still playing Chet Baker and Gerry Mulligan. "My Old Flame."

"You're kidding me," said David. "Cagney?"

"So she said."

"Oh. Right."

"If she was lying, she'd have said 'about twenty lines,'" Betty said. "But it was nineteen."

The truck belonged to one of the fellows David bunked with in a squalid apartment in Long Beach, who had it on permanent loan from a guy killed in Korea. Of necessity, Betty was behind the wheel. David had been discharged from the VA hospital an hour ago. His leg was still in the cast; he had to sit at an angle to fit in the cab. His crutches lay in the rusty bed. The truck's de facto owner had been nice enough to drive Betty from her hotel to the hospital and take a bus back to the shipyard. Betty hadn't driven a truck before. She wrestled with its steering. She was hell on the gearshift.

"You don't have to convince me," David lied. "I'm game. I'd like to."

Go see the house where she lived. Go to Santa Monica, see the beach where she'd drowned. Of course, he could have done it at any time these past two years. Any of the times he'd seen his father in Las Vegas, stayed with buddies at rooms Mikey Z got free from the Desert Inn, David could have asked for details—addresses, directions—and gone, as his aunt was putting it now, to pay his respects.

"Far as I know, none of those shows ever came to Cleveland," Betty said. Her head was tied in a scarf. She wore green-lensed cat-eyed prescription sunglasses. "Maybe they came somewhere. Out west here, or in Canada. Who knows."

"Hmm," David said. "Maybe."

He was not quite four years old when she'd left. The only firsthand memory of her that he trusted to be his was the wake. He was eight. He was kept outside the room with the coffin in it until the end, when his aunt and Grandma Luzinski ushered him in. He shut his eyes, except just a glimpse. Her brown hair was dyed blond. She looked waxy and like no one he knew. A month later the Japanese bombed Pearl Harbor.

"I suspect those shows never existed," said Betty. "A lie, to save face."

"Maybe," he said. *No kidding.*

"But somewhere out here," she said, "there *is* a screen test of her. I was visiting her the day they made it. What an interesting thing to watch. I was there. You should have seen her, David." She turned to him. "The way she came alive, under those bright lights."

"I'd love to have," he said.

Betty put the truck in gear, sort of, and pulled over the gate-entry spikes and out, lurching north on the beachside highway to Santa Monica, only a mile away.

She stopped at a red light.

David felt his stomach lurch. Sweat ran down his flanks.

"Let's not," he blurted. "Please, let's not." He was feeling dizzy, too.

His aunt looked at him. "Beg pardon?"

"The beach?" Where did it come from, this sudden panic? "Let's not. OK?"

"Can we drive by?" Betty said. "I'd like to be able to do that."

"Could we not?" He felt near tears. He punched himself in the thigh of his good leg.

The light turned green. Cars behind them honked.

"Fine," she said. "Fine."

She swung the truck across a lane of traffic and headed north, in second gear where fourth was called for. The truck lurched. David was too relieved to complain. David turned up the radio. Brubeck! Thank you, God, for Brubeck. Thank God for *you*, Brubeck.

◌◌

THE HOUSE IN the Hollywood Hills looked like every other stucco Moorish house in the Hollywood Hills: dull white walls, rust-colored tile roof, patio

[124]

out to one side. This one had a pool in back. A few families in Old Brooklyn had aboveground pools, but in California everyone seemed to have the money for in-ground.

"Well," said Betty, "it's not a bad little house, I suppose."

She parked the truck at the curb. Its abused motor hissed.

"Do you want to go in?" David said.

His aunt took off her sunglasses. Around her eyes, she was starting to look old. "No," she said. "Why would we want to do that? Who knows who lives here now. We shouldn't disturb them, I don't think."

"Charlie Parker," David said. His aunt took off her sunglasses and looked at him. David pointed at the radio. "Bird."

His aunt nodded. David turned it down. From inside that house came the sound of barking dogs. An army of them, sounded like. In the front window, through a gap in the drawn red velvet drapes, flashed glimpses of snarling, leaping poodle heads.

"I'm going in," David said. "I guess I should, right?"

Betty considered this. Finally, she asked if he wanted help with his crutches.

David opened the door. "No," he said. "I'm fine."

"Do you mind," she said, "if I don't?"

He did not.

"I just needed...," she said. "For my own, well, peace...," she said. "Oh, Joanie." She turned away from David and started softly to cry.

He planted his good leg and hopped toward the truck bed. David had never used crutches before, not even goofing around with a broken-legged friend's. That sloping driveway, up to the house, made a clumsy thing clumsier.

The doorbell didn't seem to work. He tried the knocker. The poodles sounded eager to deafen and then devour him. "Sweet!" shouted a woman's hoarse, slurry voice. "Sweet!" Then more adjectives: "Valiant! Happy! Precious! Misty! Gay!"

There was a great scuttling of dog claws against tile, the sound of a slamming door. The barking grew muffled.

A tall, slim, stunning woman opened the door, a redhead dressed in just a brassiere and a pair of men's pajama bottoms. The first thing David thought of was Anne O'Connor.

"You're young," the woman said. She pointed at his leg. "What'd you do to yourself?"

"I'm sorry to bother you, but—"

"Wait," she said. "You're not Sweet. Sweet's a Jew."

"Excuse me?"

"Who are you?" The woman had just the tiniest pudge at her waist, which was not like Anne O'Connor at all but was ungodly sexy. David was marrying Irene next month. He almost never thought about Anne O'Connor. "You're not from the studio?"

"My name's David Zielinsky. I just got out of the United States Navy and—"

"Oh, shit." She spun around and ran back into the house, but she kept the door open.

Every window had those red velvet drapes, all hung from iron spears. Unjacketed ten-inch records (which made David shudder) lay strewn on a cabinet-style hi-fi. On a glass-topped coffee table was a bottle of Pernod, something David had read about (in Hemingway) but never before seen (and would, if the occasion arose, have mispronounced), and two huge icy tumblers, each with a little silver spatula balanced on top, sporting a half-dissolved lump of sugar. It was still morning.

The woman returned. She'd put on a green silk blouse. "Look," she said. "I'm expecting someone important."

"Sorry to bother you." The blouse just made her hair prettier. A darker red than Anne's.

"Yeah, yeah," she said. "What you selling?"

"Nothing," he said. "My . . . well, a friend of mine. Used to live here." He kept looking at those records. He wanted to clean them, store them, to alphabetize and rescue them.

She laughed. "Lots of people used to live here. Now it's me and Brenda and her dogs. Who you looking for, huh, swabbie?"

"Nobody," he said.

"You came to the right place. Lemme guess." She pointed out at the blue truck. "That right there's your ma, and your pa is Tony Two-Jackets. Look, you wanna make a scene with Brenda, she's in Vegas with your pa."

David frowned. What in the hell? "Ma'am," he said, "my mother used to live here. A long time ago. Back around in the '30s. You wouldn't know her. I just wanted to see the place, I don't know why. I'm sorry."

The woman nodded, gravely. "I'm sorry, too, hon." She put her hand on his shoulder. "I'd give you the five-cent tour," she said, "but I'm meeting a certain someone."

Who knows why, she kissed him on the forehead. Then she closed the door.

When David got back to the truck, his aunt wasn't crying anymore. If things had worked out the way they were supposed to, Irene, Uncle Stan, and Grandma Luzinski would all be here. They'd all planned to come out for the surgery and then bring him home. But Irene couldn't get away from the hospital. Stan had just gotten hired to do some work on a murder case so big David had seen it written up in the L.A. papers. And Grammalu decided at the last minute she couldn't set foot in the city where her daughter had drowned. If any of the three of them had come, it might have put the kibosh on this lachrymose morning.

"How was it?" asked Betty. He was afraid she'd ask about the seminude redheaded woman. He felt guilty, like he'd done something with her. A kiss, or worse. All this time, he'd been faithful to Irene (*one hundred & ten percent true,* he once said in a letter, though this caused her to ask why he brought the subject up; why did she twist a nice thing he said and bring on the Spanish Inquisition? Women!)—which was more than he could say for *any* of his navy buddies.

"The place is probably about the same as then, I bet," he said. "It's nice."

"That's good," she said. "That's a comfort, I suppose."

"Yeah," he said. "Let's go."

In odd moments, of which this was one, he allowed himself to be honest. Losing out on a girl like Anne O'Connor was a mistake; given a once-in-a-lifetime chance, he'd had a failure of nerve. But that was just in odd moments. He'd known Irene for *years*. It's the *idea* of Anne he loved, and not the real girl. Wake up! No girl anywhere was more real than Irene Hrudka.

In this way, David tried not to think about his mother.

∽

EVERY OTHER TIME home, David had taken the train. But the travel allowance from the navy was enough to pay to fly, plus which his aunt, who'd rarely flown anywhere, was just nuts about airplanes. Like a little girl. It was fun to see, as their prop plane was buffeted high above the Rocky Mountains, and through and over any number of cloud banks. Among a planeful of sick passengers, Betty had the equilibrium and stomach of a test pilot. The joy of watching her got David through it. Still, he fouled several airsickness bags, each time handing it to the stewardess with the same feeling of shame he'd had when, in the second grade, he threw up inside his desk. Worse, even with double doses of the pain pills, his knee throbbed like mad.

Somewhere over what the pilot said was Nebraska, David sang/mumbled a medley of Louis Jordan hits, interspersed with a pallid Alan Freed imitation (*Freed, gone from Cleveland! Say it ain't so, Al!*). His aunt had no idea what he was doing but was amused—gleeful, too, over those cute little bottles of vodka, which, in moderation, she dribbled into her ice water and then kept when empty. During all those takeoffs and landings—Los Angeles, Denver, Kansas City, Chicago—while David popped pills and dug his nails into the arms of his seat, Aunt Betty, in the window seat, squirmed and pointed, beamed and giggled. If he just listened and didn't look at her gray eyes, he'd think she was someone his age, a girl.

Finally their airplane swooped in east of Cleveland, in a wide arc over sunlit Lake Erie, then banked south and came in, low, over the city. David could see Terminal Tower, and the Cuyahoga River, and all those handsome bridges.

They came in lower still, and there it was: Cleveland Municipal Stadium, still draped in bunting from last week's All-Star Game, its brown-gray husk and its green center gleaming in the summer sun.

His heart knocked against his ribs. His spirit soared. And he thought: *Home. I am home.*

☙❧

EXCEPT FOR DAVID'S father—in Chicago on business; he promised to be back in time to swing by the party—everyone was there to greet them, there at tiny Hopkins Airport: Irene, Uncle Stan, and even Grandma Luzinski, whom David used to call Grammalu and who stood at the gate, trembling in anticipation and from Parkinson's, holding a loaf of homemade zucchini bread. Irene ran to him, her face wet with tears, and she reached him and threw her arms around him and knocked his crutches away. Bystanders gasped. Irene and David fell in a heap on the hot tarmac, laughing, kissing each other with the manic speed of love-addled cartoon characters.

Don't worry about them. A fall like that is nothing when you are twenty years old.

Airline employees stood by to offer assistance. It was a long wait. Someone said something about hosing the couple down.

Irene had gained weight. David didn't care. She, too, looked like home to him. "You look like home to me," he said.

"Wait till you see the bridesmaid dresses I have picked out," she said. "The hall is great, too. Mom and Aunt Betty and I still have to go listen to bands. I love you, I love you!"

She smelled like Clairol hair spray and vanilla.

Aunt Betty handed David his crutches. His hugs of Grammalu and Uncle Stan were more subdued, but they, too, looked like home, even though Grammalu had moved from Cleveland to a house trailer in Tarpon Springs,

Florida, when David was six. She was confused about his knee. Her own (late) husband, Walter Luzinski (Grampalu), had been wounded in the thigh, fighting in France in World War I. She kept calling David's operation his wound and muttering things about dirty jerries.

Gone for almost two years and all David had in the way of luggage was his duffel bag and a trunk full of dozens of tiny pasteboard suitcases, themselves full of singles and long players on which he'd squandered several paydays. Grammalu had sliced the zucchini bread. Near where they were waiting was a newsstand. Stan bought the afternoon papers, the *News* and the *Press*. A banner headline in the *Press* read "SOMEBODY IS GETTING AWAY WITH MURDER!" "Even in California, that Sheppard case is news," David said. "How'd you get involved with that?"

Stan shrugged. "I came recommended to the family."

"Even in Europe it's news," said Betty. "Friends told us."

David took a second piece of zucchini bread. Grammalu beamed. He said, "So . . . ?"

His uncle frowned. "So what?"

"So did he do it? Dr. Sam."

"'Dr. Sam'?" he said, mocking. "As if you know him."

"Fine," David said. "Don't tell me."

Stan didn't say anything. He'd never liked talking about a case he was working on. Even at the office, David never heard him say much more about things than the bare exchange of information. Stan Lychak was the sort of man who did not wonder aloud.

David kissed Irene some more. He took a third piece of zucchini bread. Finally the trunk appeared. He tried to warn his uncle.

"Yow!" Stan stood back from it and rubbed his lower back. "What's in there, a body?"

"Records," David said. His uncle shot him a look.

"What kind of records?" Stan loved classical music but was a radio listener. David felt as silly as if he'd said *toy trucks*.

"Hi-fi records. Albums, long players, singles. Some Cleveland Orchestra recordings." One: Tchaikovsky's Sixth. Everything else was blues, R&B, or jazz. "The redcaps will help you."

Stan rolled his eyes. Outside of restaurants, he avoided the services of anyone who worked for tips. He disdained taxicabs, delivery services, and bellboys. He shined his own shoes, ignored street musicians, and would walk a crooked mile to avoid valet parking. In one smooth swoop, he brought the trunk up and onto his broad left shoulder, and grunted.

"Wow," said Irene.

"All in the legs," said Stan. His voice showed some strain. But he walked like a grown man who carried heavy things for a living, even though he did not.

All in the legs. David, hobbling crutch-aided toward the parking lot, found it hard not to take that as a gibe. Everyone knows the legs are the first to go.

∽

NATURALLY, THERE WAS a welcome-home party. Most of the men were in the garage, standing around a metal folding table. The table was covered by a clean new tarp and wooden bowls of pretzels, chips, and red-skin peanuts. Inside, where the Jeepster would normally go, was an iced-up fifty-five-gallon drum filled with Carling Black Label beer. The old icebox was out here (it had come with the house and was replaced years ago by a Frigidaire), filled with pop and the canned beer neighbors brought. The old living-room radio was out here, too, and the Indians were on. It's Early Wynn pitching for us, Virgil Trucks for Chicago. No score, top of the fourth.

On the lawn, as prescribed by what must have been an Old Brooklyn law: horseshoes.

The women were inside. Even with both leaves inserted, the Lychaks' dining-room table was so laden with food a card table was butted up to the end of it and covered with a Christmas-quality tablecloth. What food! Lugged here by friends and neighbors and overseen by Grammalu and ladies from the neighborhood she'd known all her life. It was all there, all the food David had been heartsick for. Chafing dishes full of pierogis: cheese, potato, and cheese-*and*-potato. Other chafing dishes brimming with kielbasas and sauerkraut. A ham the size of a watermelon, festooned with toothpick-attached machine-cut pineapple rings. Pyrex bowls full of potato salad: mustard and German both. The huge steel pot that came from Mrs. Mytczynskyj across the street—so big that when her son Lee was in kindergarten he could still use it to win games of hide-and-seek—now full of fifty pounds of mashed potatoes. Casseroles, casseroles, casseroles: topped with melted American cheese, corn-flakes, Bisquick/oleo crumbs, Durkee dried onions, or a combination thereof. Mayonnaised salads. Breadbaskets full of Parker House rolls from Hough Bakery. Four different Jell-O molds (three red and one racy green). Apple and rhubarb pies. All this, plus a five-gallon tub of rigatoni that Stan stopped off to pick up at Mama Isabelle's on Pearl Road.

Aunt Betty flew into motion, shooing guests from the davenport by the living-room window, clearing a place for David, who'd dispensed with the crutches and was hopping on one leg, his arm around Irene for support. Even when they sat down, he kept his arm there.

The radio blared "Hernando's Hideaway." The councilman for their ward and David's junior high English teacher, among the few men indoors, sang drunkenly along. The councilman had a fine voice, the teacher less so. On the wall above them family photographs—everyone's wedding pictures (except his parents'), a shot of a dog that had died before David was born, one of Grampalu and Grammalu moving into the trailer in Tarpon Springs—all at least ten years old. For the first time in his life, David actually *saw* them. Example: in that wedding photo his aunt was his and Irene's exact age. She looked even younger.

"Oh, My Papa" came on next. The councilman soldiered on solo. When he finished he got a hand from all the ladies. Two of the older ones were crying. Aunt Betty—who'd surveyed the spread and deemed it good—swooped back into the living room and turned down the radio.

The Lychaks still did not own a television set.

"That was interesting," Betty said, something she'd say only when she did not mean it. She turned the dial to the Indians game. "That's what you want," she said to David, "isn't it?"

Jimmy Dudley's voice boomed out of the console. For years Dudley's partner was Jack Graney, but now he had a new guy. That was how everything felt, both familiar and not.

"All I want," David said, "is already here." He kissed Irene, a peck on the lips, and made a big show of blowing a kiss first to his aunt and then his grandmother. The old ladies sighed.

The party swirled around him. He received guests, accepted hugs, and shook hands, all the time feeling like he was watching this through the window, from across the street, through a pair of official Boy Scout binoculars. He accepted business cards from people whose home phone numbers he knew by heart. He made a fuss over seeing people he'd known all his life and never once thought about the whole time he was in California. He smiled while people asked Irene about the wedding plans and at excruciating length she told them. Worst of all, David had to keep talking about his leg. He wished he'd used the ditto machine in his uncle's office to run off a hundred sheets reading *I was playing basketball for the base team, went up for a rebound, landed funny, heard a sickening pop, and the next thing I knew I was home.*

What really got to him during that party, though, was how absurdly *behind* he was. It had seemed the right thing to do, the navy; America was at war. But now he felt punished for it, with a ruined knee and the anxious feeling that he'd spent two years goofing off while everyone else buckled down. He and Irene had been engaged so long, party guests cracked old-maid jokes to her face. Guys David grew up with had joined the National Guard, gotten on with life, and found set-for-life jobs at steel mills and auto plants. Several others had received student deferments and gone to college; two guys he knew would be seniors this fall at Ohio State; one was going to be a dentist. One friend of David's, Gorman "Skeezix" Soltesz, had been drafted, served in battle, won a Purple Heart, returned home, and graduated from the police academy. The only one of David's close pals who'd enlisted—Carl, his old paper-route sub—was at Annapolis. That runt Lee Mytczynskyj, a year younger than David, was making good money at U.S. Steel, had a wife and a baby girl, *and was building a house in Parma!* Complete, Lee boasted, with a garage. David didn't even have a car. He didn't own a business suit. He had two neckties, one of them a clip-on. His most valuable possession was a trunk full of hi-fi records. He lived with his aunt and uncle, in a room with model airplanes dangling from tacked-to-the-ceiling lengths of fish line, dresser drawers stuffed with comic books and baseball cards, curtains that featured a cowboy-and-Indian print. He had a fiancée, but if he wanted to fool around with her, they'd have to sneak off in a dark basement or a borrowed car, and worry about getting caught.

David kept rubbing Irene's shoulder. He started whispering corny things in her ear, like *I'm the luckiest fella here* and *Hello, my life,* and, once, *Let's make a baby.* On this, she punched his shoulder, but she smiled when she did it. The wedding had been postponed until the end of the summer, so David would be able to walk and not hobble down the aisle. He didn't know if he could stand it, the wait.

◈

ALL ANYONE AT the party talked about were the Indians, playing better baseball than any team ever, and Sam Sheppard, the handsome young Bay Village osteopath who maybe killed his pretty wife. Local news, small in the scheme of things, writ large.

It was the year of the hubris-soaked flameout of Senator Joseph Mc-Carthy, yet—even though the most famous TV person in town, Dorothy Fuldheim, had, in denouncing McCarthy's demagoguery, beaten Edward R. Murrow to the punch by two months—if in Cleveland someone said *Red menace,* they were probably talking baseball, and about to start saying things like *Tribe on warpath, winnum skirmish over paleface Yankees, heap big smile!* Though it was the year of *Brown v. the Board of Education,* in David's neighborhood nothing about that could spark decent patio conversation. But, two weeks after Marilyn Sheppard's bloody late-night Fourth of July murder, everyone in the county could cite intricate details of the case.

On all this, too, David felt out of it. In Long Beach guys used to rib him about what a big Indians fan he was, called him Chief. Any summer day he could turn to the sports page and see Cleveland in first was a good day. And the Sheppard case: as soon as he heard Uncle Stan was working for the family, David devoured every scrap of news he could find. But now—hearing everyone go on and *on,* without the first idea of a life that stretched beyond the suburbs of Cleveland—David wanted to change the subject, to talk about world diplomacy, jazz music, or the Negro question. Anything that wasn't just about *here.*

He did nothing of the sort, of course.

Eventually, he finished thirds and then fourths of the food (Irene brought him his plates) and had a piece each of rhubarb (Mrs. Pfrenger's) and apple (Betty's) pie, and made his way out to the garage, where the ballgame was over (the first words anyone said to him, when he hopped there and sat down on a scratchy webbed-nylon lawn chair, were, "We won"). Cigar smoking (Dutch Masters, though Cubans were still available) and beer drinking (out of aluminum tumblers, still ubiquitous) had moved from harmony to melody.

Every woman still at the party was inside.

Every man was outside.

His father still hadn't shown and, without sending his regrets, never would. David spent the night expecting him. On those trips to Las Vegas, flush with complimentary cocktails and free rooms, things had gotten better between them. In fact, David had hoped that day to ask Mike to be the best man at his wedding, a southern tradition he'd heard about in the navy and thought would be noble. Also, he felt so distanced from his high school friends. Same with the navy friends. David was the sort of person who was friendly with everyone (he was good with names) but had a hard time making deep friendships. When he was a kid, Aunt Betty had said he was too picky. Last Christmas Betty got a few toddies into her and said that the absence of his mother had kept him from letting anyone get close (Betty, still chipping away at her college degree, was considering a major in psychology). This made her seize up with inadequacy and cry. David assured her that in all matters mother-related she'd been grand.

Now, at his homecoming, David accepted a beer and sat back, happy to melt into the crowd; the talk even veered briefly away from Dr. Sam and the

Indians. He laughed along with Mr. Biederman's old joke about the copulation between cat and skunk and Mr. Wisniewski's about the tiger and the horny monkey. Skeezix Soltesz told one he'd lifted from this week's *Milton Berle Show* and got called on it. Then, to David's astonishment, Uncle Stan reeled off three filthy gems. On the third he laughed so hard his face shone like red glass.

"So, David," blurted Fat Henry Biederman, "I hear you're going to work on the Sheppard case, too?"

Fat Henry was Mr. Biederman's kid, not yet thirty and already a professor at Fenn College. General business and accounting. He'd grown up here, but after he got the job moved to the East Side. He was the only person David knew who'd done that. David hardly knew him. Why he came to the party, who knows? Just in the neighborhood.

"I don't know," David said. "It's a possibility." His uncle's face was still a little red. "To tell you the truth, I'm still weighing some different options." Which was a pile of crap.

Stan got up and went to watch the horseshoes game.

"Right," said Fat Henry Biederman. "So how *is* your dad?"

"What?" David said.

"Your options," Henry said. "I presumed that's what you meant. Options, you know, in...let's call it the labor-management branch of the family."

The other men snickered.

"What?" David said. "What's so funny?" But of course he knew.

"Well, so," said Henry, rising. "David." Then pacing. He must be one hell of a prick in the classroom. "What *is* it you're going to do with the rest of your life? Your dreams."

More snickers, though David got the sense—wishful thinking?—that maybe the men were really laughing at Henry.

"Whatever I do for now," David said, feeling a wave of coppery impulse breaking over the back of his skull and shoulders, "someday I'm going to be mayor of the city of Cleveland."

No one but David seemed startled. No one laughed. No one thought he was being ironic (if people had, they'd have called him *smart*). After all, David had held class office all four years at Rhodes High. What else had he been working up to, if not this? Fat Henry gave David a patronizing little tap on the shoulder, but the other men shouted out things like "You betcha!" and "Why not?" The councilman allowed as how David might be an improvement on the current mayor, though this was just a figure of speech. Mayor Celebrezze was new and ethnic, a man of the people, who last year beat the candidate the machine put forth. People *loved* him.

What made David say that he wanted to be mayor, he could not imagine. Later, he will say that he never wanted to be anything else. But the first time the thought came into his head was the moment he heard himself say it.

— 6 —

DR. SAM'S STORY was that he was asleep on the downstairs sofa of his lake-front house when he heard a disturbance. He confronted a bushy-haired man, apparently ransacking the house for pharmaceuticals, and got conked on the head. He passed out briefly, came to, chased the man down to the lake, got conked again, and woke up hours later, revived by the waves.

The story the papers were more than hinting at was that Dr. Sam killed her.

Anne O'Connor, *Cleveland News* copygirl, would have done anything to get closer to the case. It was what made Cleveland bearable, that story. Instead she was assisting the women's page editor, at the smallest and most conservative of Cleveland's three dailies, the one making the least amount of hay out of the Sheppard case. This past year at Smith, she had, as a freshman, covered the Amherst police beat for the school paper. Now she was writing about weddings. Weddings! Also engagements, parties, trips to Europe, cotillions, teas, benefits, and meetings of the Daughters of the Western Reserve.

What questions to wrestle with! Every day Anne got curiouser and curiouser. Why wasn't the murder weapon found? Why wasn't the T-shirt Dr. Sam was wearing found? Why did Dr. Sam, supposedly in a semicoma from his injuries, stay for three days in Bay View Hospital, which his family owned, before he let the police examine him? Why didn't the bushy-haired man leave any footprints or fingerprints? Why would the bushy-haired man think Dr. Sam kept drugs of recreational interest in his home? Why no bloodstains outside Marilyn's bedroom, except on Dr. Sam's shoes? Why didn't the Sheppards' seven-year-old son, asleep in the next room, wake up while his mother was being bludgeoned? Why didn't the family dog bark? (If only the dog could talk!) What was Dr. Sam's *motive?* The whole city—the whole *country* even, the way the case had caught on—treated the murder like a delightful new craze of a board game. Anne was as guilty as the next person.

Unless the next person was Dr. Sam Sheppard. Anne was convinced: they don't come any more guilty than that sly boots.

෴

"BABE, SHE'LL KILL me," Patrick whispered. They were in his kitchen. Anne had cooked Patrick and his wife a bad roast beef dinner. Now she and her brother were doing the dishes. New dishes. Patrick and Ibby had been married a year, but had only weeks ago returned to Cleveland from New York. Everything in the apartment was new; the place looked like a sample room in the housewares floor at Halle Brothers. "Not that we have space. The nursery isn't—"

"You wouldn't be blaming it on Ibby," Anne said, too loud, "if you wanted to let me yourself, and so, OK, you don't. But why don't you? It's the perfect plan."

"Forget it."

Anne dropped a saucer.

"Babe!" he said.

"Accident," she said.

"Is there a problem?" Ibby called from the living room.

In unison, Anne and Patrick said no.

The apartment had an immaculate faded-deco glory, nine floors above Shaker Square. Ibby—short for Elizabeth—sat in the next room in their new BarcaLounger, watching some witless program on TV. She had a condition that, from the third month of her pregnancy on, required bed rest—a condition made more serious by this summer's record-setting heat. There were fans everywhere. Ibby was three years older than Anne and not a real blond. Her father was a former assistant attorney general of the United States.

"You're nuts," Patrick said, whispering again.

"Just until the end of the summer. You don't know what it's like. Why can't she move back to Ashcroft?"

"She goes up there all the time."

"She comes back. She's not living there. Look, Patrick, don't move a thing. I'll sleep on the floor if I have to. Really, you don't know what it's like."

She wasn't asking Patrick to give up his study. The baby was due in October. The nursery would be gathering dust until then. "Don't be selfish," Anne said.

"Selfish?" Patrick said. "Thus spake the pot. Wait'll you're expecting. Then you'll understand. And I do know what it's like."

Patrick had lived at home in the summers, too. What with all those years of boarding schools, summer camps, and summer homes, the O'Connor children went from the ages of twelve to eighteen without ever spending more than a few weeks at a time at home. Then came the college years. Family mythology had it that only Steven—poor, sweet, perfect, and doomed—spent a happy postprep summer at home. A year later he was dead.

"It's different now," Anne said. "Why don't you guys get a bigger place? A house?"

"It's not different," said Patrick. "It's exactly the same. Take it like a man."

This was Patrick's idea of a compliment. Anne smiled.

"Somebody!" called Ibby. "I need the television station changed in here."

"Go ahead." Now Anne was whispering. "Thumbkin."

"Here I am," sang Patrick. "Here I am." With his partially thumbless left hand, he gave Anne the lightest imaginable slap on the cheek.

"How are you today, sir," she sang.

"Very well I thank you," he sang, on his way to assist his wife.

Run and hide. Anne did not sing this or even say it.

They had been drinking. Even Anne a little. Now, watching Patrick come when called, she felt a little bit sick. She was almost sure it wasn't the wine.

Patrick had always been someone who came when called. This epiphany didn't make Anne feel any better. Her opinion was that married life and being the boss—he'd been doing well in TV, when, under pressure from both his and Ibby's parents, he'd returned to Cleveland to become the general manager at the radio station his father partly owned—did not suit Patrick. He was drinking too much, Anne believed, and those were the reasons why.

☙❧

ANOTHER THING THAT made her sick was the smell of ink. Not flu-sick, but light-headed. When she said something about it, Mrs. Apple, the horse-faced woman of indeterminate age who ran the women's page, threw back her equine head and sniffed (if Anne were telling the story, the word she'd use is *whinnied*) and laughed like a lunatic. "Ahh! The nectar of gossip!" She sniffed again, even more theatrically. "The blood of emerging fact!"

Anne tried to explain. She liked writing. She liked reporting. She liked action. She still hoped someday to be a war correspondent. Let her get out of the office and go cover something.

"One day," said Mrs. Apple, "you will be where I am and someone will be where you are, saying something as girlish as that. You will find no way of talking to that person, but your heart will go out to her." Mrs. Apple put a hand on Anne's shoulder. They shared that tiny office with a boxing writer who was never there. Anne used the man's little steel desk. Mrs. Apple, by her own choice, used a sewing machine trestle with a board on top.

"The ink really does make me sick."

[138]

"You're a girl," said Mrs. Apple. "With little experience. Patience, patience. May I borrow a cigarette?"

"I'll do all the work you need me to," Anne said, "and stay late to write something else. Or help someone report something. Anything that's, you know, out in the world."

Mrs. Apple looked at her.

"I don't smoke," Anne said. Which Mrs. Apple knew full well.

"'Out in the world.'" Mrs. Apple shook her head. She might have been thirty. She might have been fifty-five. "This," she said, "is the world."

What is the world? Her dumb desk? The editorial offices of the *Cleveland News,* which got beat every afternoon, in every possible way, by the *Press*? Anne gave up. She glanced at the filmy window. She couldn't see through it. "When do they clean these windows?" Anne asked.

Mrs. Apple handed her a stack of calligraphy-adorned envelopes. All she said was, "Ha." It was not said unkindly.

୭୦

ALL SUMMER LONG there was a record by the Midnighters, on rhythm-and-blues radio but also on pop radio and certainly every jukebox—everywhere a person went—called "Work with Me, Annie." It was not about working.

Anne loathed being called *Annie.* That summer it was worse than ever. At the *News* a cute (married) copy editor called her that once.

Once.

Anne still liked dance records, and she certainly loved music that frightened the oldsters. Radio and newspaper editorials (including one in the *News*) spoke out against dirty lyrics and what should be done about them. Were Reds involved? What did this say about morality these days? The naïveté these writers had! A person has to be pretty old to be so naive. They were *surprised* that their outrage just made the record more popular. They helped invent the teenager.

If only the song had been called "Work with Me, Carolyn." "Work with Me, Cathy." Anything else. Anne took enough ribbing from the kids in her crowd that, in weak moments, she found herself thinking maybe the bluenoses had a point.

୭୦

JOHN WAS IN California. Patrick lived on the other side of Shaker Heights. Steven was dead. There was no one left to buffer her from her parents.

One night Anne had been awakened by the sound of them arguing. This happened more and more. Even screaming and the sound of shoving, of falling people and broken glass. But this night it was worse. Anne came in off her sleeping porch and went downstairs. In the dark she could hear them running toward her: the sound of frightened people, clumsy from drink, running without a destination.

Suddenly, emerging before her like a horse bounding onto a highway, lit by moonlight, came her mother, wearing only a small cotton brassiere and holding a shrimp fork, followed by her father, stark naked, bleeding from a cut to his shoulder and carrying a service revolver, which, though Anne could not have known this, had been given to him by Eliot Ness himself.

They froze. Her mother was a vision—lithe, pale, and mean-looking. Her father's face was streaked with tears. Both of them gasped for breath. Both had been athletes, but that was a long time ago. Both looked disoriented, as if they'd been awoken from sleepwalking.

"There," her mother said. "You see? Are you happy?"

"Babe," said Tom O'Connor. But then he realized he was naked. He covered himself with the gun.

"Now that," Sarah O'Connor slurred, "is what I call a fig leaf."

Anne ran back upstairs. "No!" she shouted. "I am *not* happy!"

She didn't know there was a gun in the house. This was not a house that needed a gun.

∽

"WHY NO INQUEST? DO IT NOW, DR. GERBER!"

The editor of the *Press* was writing unsigned front-page editorials now, though everyone knew who wrote them. Louie Seltzer, the self-appointed voice of the common man. Legendary Louie, who'd worked at the *Press* since he was a teenaged office boy and been its editor since he was thirty-one. To Anne, eighteen years old and with the dream of becoming a war correspondent, Louis B. Seltzer was a local hero. She didn't yet understand that Seltzer, a little bald despot, was the chief rival to Anne's father's machine. Even if she had, the *Press*'s coverage of the Sheppard case was irresistible. Anne wasn't quite sure what an inquest was and why one was needed; it seemed merely a chance for public officials to show off, to do in public what they'd otherwise do in private, thus giving reporters access to everything. Access to everything was what America was supposed to be about. No daughter of a man as powerful as Tom O'Connor would really think America was about this, but that didn't have to deny Anne her ideals.

At the *News* offices the Sheppard case was all the rage. Anne would go out in the evenings with silly old prep friends and various boys from good families, home from the four corners of the earth, and they talked about the Sheppard case, too. Go for a walk, just to get out of the house on a hot night or weekend afternoon, and it wasn't just the strains of radio broadcasts of Indians games she heard. That first, yes. But she'd stop, ask the score, shake her head in wonderment over what a team this was, what pitching (what a fool her father had been to sell his share of the club!), but in no time she'd find herself talking about the newest news on the Sheppard case. Typically, this would be the stories that were in the *Press* that day. Not just the news, but what Louie Seltzer did with the news.

It was humiliating to work for any other paper. The *Press* owned Cleveland. The *Plain Dealer,* the competent morning paper, was number two (both second to the *Press,* Anne thought, and crap). The *PD* owned the *News.* The *News* was third-string; everyone knew it. Even then, working for the *News* wouldn't have been so bad, but they saw her as such a *girl.* Her father had gotten her the job, which made it worse. Someday she'd be a grandmother, with two Pulitzer prizes, a flat in Paris, and a ranch in Kentucky where her taciturn husband raised Thoroughbreds and wrote poetry about the land, and still her father would see her as some dumb girl.

"'Dumb' girl?" said Tom O'Connor. "Where'd you get that idea, 'dumb'?"

"Don't reframe the argument," she said. "It's the job."

"Reframing the argument." He smiled. "In this line of work, it comes with the territory."

"I'm talking about *my* job," she said. "'Comes with the territory'? Please. When did you become a traveling salesman? Don't be disingenuous."

He smiled more broadly.

"Don't condescend to me," she said.

He shook his head. "Good to know," he said, "this East Coast education of yours I'm paying for is worth the money." Her father was a midwesterner through and through. Despite his power and the money he'd married into, he was prone to the local parochialism, in both principal senses of that (he'd wanted her to attend a Catholic school, as the boys had).

"So," he asked, "what would you rather do?"

"Find my own job."

"Fine," he said.

This was the last thing she had expected him to say.

"Fine," she said. "Stop smiling."

"Fine," he said.

"I mean it, Daddy," she said.

"Fine," he said, and finally did.

"I didn't want you to feel I was ungrateful," she said, "if I looked for something else, something that more suited me." She did not say *a job at the Press*. She was afraid he could read her mind, though. "I don't have enough experience to get anything perfect, but I—"

"I applaud the initiative," he said. This was the kind of thing her father would say only if he was being insincere.

"I'm not quitting, though. Not until—"

"There's the O'Connor spirit." He looked at his watch.

This happened in his law office downtown, where he had not for years practiced any law. Anne was on her lunch break. In his lobby were two Negro members of the city council, and, across from them but clearly not with them, Bert Porter, the city engineer, the first wrong pony in years that Tom O'Connor had backed for mayor (Celebrezze was Seltzer's man). Though Anne had been shown in ahead of them, her father had given her just five minutes. The office smelled like peppermints and pipe tobacco. Her father didn't smoke. The walls were tastelessly thick with pictures of him shaking hands with any Clevelander worth shaking hands with. Over his shoulder Anne could see Terminal Tower. The Indians flag flew. She pointed. "Who's pitching?"

"What's it matter?" said Boss Tom, and now they smiled in sync.

Cleveland can't be beat! This, 1954, is our year!

⌀

THAT BOY ALTON Herrick had cozied up to Sarah O'Connor and came by often, but Anne had lost interest in him as any kind of boyfriend. Other friends, boys and girls, dropped in and out without warning, which is what happens when you own a pool during the hottest summer anyone can remember. These were people Anne had known forever, but they seemed like strangers, of no more interest than her mother's friends or her father's. Simply people to be entertained, as ubiquitous and little-considered as the help. All summer Anne was surrounded by people and felt entirely alone.

In the mansion next door, where once had lived the sisters Van Sweringen, was now a huge Catholic family, sired by the owner of a string of car dealerships. For no reason Anne could figure, he had every tree on the property cut down. His startled-looking wife was constantly pregnant. The children sometimes came over to swim, but Anne couldn't keep them all straight. Eight of them, nine of them, who knows? All the girls seemed to be named Debbie or Christina; all the boys were named Mickey. The way those people bred was just disgusting.

In the life of every woman, there are times when it seems like everywhere you look, every woman you see is pregnant. This was the first time Anne thought that.

৪৩

OF COURSE DR. Sam did it. Of course he did. Anne had seen enough.

There were affairs. His bad behavior. His complicated alibi, which flew in the face of Occam's razor (the favorite thing Anne had learned her freshman year). There was also what everyone knows but nobody says: the all-things-being-equal enormity of what husbands do to wives. Plus you have the wild sex-hungers of the nouveau riche. You can't underestimate that.

Dr. Sam is the husband; he did it. Of *course* he did it.

Banner headline in the *Press:* QUIT STALLING—BRING HIM IN!

৪৩

ANNE O'CONNOR DID not think about her father naked. She did not think about the slack pillow of flesh above her mother's pubic hair. She did not think about this, she did not, she did not, she did not.

Naked, in the moonlit center hall. Sweating. Hairy.

She did not.

৪৩

SOMEWHERE IN PENNSYLVANIA, Eliot Ness, donor of that .38, hooked up with a ghostwriter. (The gun was given to Boss Tom on the occasion of his having pulled a string or five and seen to it that Ness was able to stay as Cleveland's safety director, the only man in the twentieth century to do so under both Republican and Democratic mayors, despite the fact that Cleveland city elections are, in theory, nonpartisan.) "The book," said the ghostwriter, "will be called *The Untouchables*." Ness wanted to know how much money he could make. "Up front," said the ghostwriter, "not so much." He quoted a number. Ness took another slug of Wild Turkey and laughed and considered showing the writer to the door. The writer could tell. "But, Eliot," the writer said, "keep your eye on the ball. You have a good story. Believe me. And a true story, too," he said. "With a good, true story, who knows what can happen?"

The writer wouldn't have made a distinction between a true story and a merely factual one, but with Eliot Ness it will turn out that this distinction makes itself. The drinking belongs to no one's truth. Likewise the wartime crusade against VD. The long years of aging-boy, name-selling wheedling—forget that. The true story of Eliot Ness will, horrifyingly enough, stop short of Cleveland. He'll never get his ass kicked in a Cleveland mayoral race. He will never be a laughingstock. He'll be in Chicago forever. In any version of the story, true, he will wear a vested suit and bring down Al Capone. But, eventually, Eliot Ness will become "Eliot Ness," fighting villains invented by pseudonymous blacklisted scriptwriters. Thirty-three years from now, he will be the star of a major motion picture. His sidekick will be a bald Bond. James Bond.

Ness stayed in his chair and looked at the enormous picture of his young self that he'd hung above the mantelpiece. (A wedding picture, actually, though if this interferes with any reader's sense of truth, feel free to substitute a picture of Ness arresting Capone, with Stan Lychak slapping on the cuffs.)

The writer said, "No thanks," holding up his whiskey tumbler to indicate its still-full nature.

Finally, Ness agreed. "Damn straight it's a good story."

"Hell yes," said the writer. "And a true one."

"All true," Ness said. Then he laughed. Whatever else Ness was, any man who ever drank with him will tell you: he was a man who could tell stories. "All true," Ness said again. "Whatever the fuck that means."

From the next room, Ness's wife cried his name.

"Sorry," he said. "Whatever the *heck* that means."

The writer whispered that his wife was the same way. Eliot Ness closed his eyes and drank. The end.

⊙⊚

ANNE LIED ABOUT her age (twenty-four instead of eighteen; exceptionally beautiful girls adopt a wariness that makes them seem older than they are—especially those who've traveled widely and received actual poise lessons), about her education (a graduate of Smith instead of a sophomore there), about her broadcasting experience (some, instead of none whatsoever), and about being related to her brother Patrick ("Who?"). Hoot Thagard did not ask her about being related to her mother (cousin to Rockefellers) or her father (boss of everything). As references, Anne listed the young copy editor at the *News* with the appalling crush on her (he'd promised to lie according to a script they'd concocted together) and two radio stations in Massachusetts, both invented, call letters and all. Further, she left the station manager with the impression that she could work there indefinitely. She was due back in Northampton in twenty-two days.

Mr. Thagard, WCRB's station manager, was a genial, stammering, childless lummox with a gray crew cut. He'd studied agriculture at Ohio State and somehow parlayed that into twenty-three years (and counting) at a low-wattage station southwest of Cleveland, at the wrong end of the dial, housed in an unpainted cinder-block building surrounded by cow pastures. He admitted all of this, right in the interview! With clear and cartoonish pride, he pointed out that, unlike most radio and television stations, WCRB's call letters actually stood for something: West Cuyahoga Radio Broadcasting. To Anne's astonishment, he did not ask why a pretty young thing like her wasn't married. He asked nothing that a prospective employer could ask then but would not be allowed to ask now. Hoot Thagard did, it's true, run a radio station that featured his cabbage-faced wife's two-hour-long morning recipe recitation show; an afternoon show he hosted himself *(Swap Meet)* that amounted to live classified ads; instrumental music of a sort Anne found square (her grandchildren will embrace it as "ultralounge"); and such special events as daylong coverage of the Cuyahoga County and Lorain County Fairs, remote broadcasts from house-trailer sales lots, and live radio broadcasts of swimming meets (Hoot's nieces and nephews swam). Hoot Thagard had no talent for radio. But he was a good man. His professionalism stands up to the standards of another era.

With Anne still in his office—sitting on a much-shellacked oak chair of the sort typically seen behind the desks of grade school teachers—Mr. Thagard called the first reference. The copy editor. Mr. Thagard was the kind of large man who seemed never to know where to put all the inefficient parts of himself. He drummed his fingers on his green metal desk. He thrust his hands in his pockets and took his hands right back out. He twirled the phone cord, stood up, sat down, stood up, was leashed back nearer the phone, and sat down. Any pose he struck failed.

Anne was on her lunch break from the *News*. She'd told her boss, Mrs. Apple, that she'd be late. Just how late, Mrs. Apple couldn't have imagined.

The last thing Hoot Thagard said to the copy editor was, "That's a . . . a . . . a rare . . . a rare quality in these . . . ah . . . these. Right. Times. Thanks for listening."

He hung up and offered Anne the job.

"When, ah, ah, can you, ah," Mr. Thagard said, "start?"

"How's now?" Anne said.

"Now is *fa-a-a-a-n*tastic!" Mr. Thagard slapped his thighs, broke into a hayseed's grin, and leaped to his feet. Anne flinched. Thagard extended his hand. "Welcome back to radio!" His breath smelled of Black Jack gum, which he chewed incessantly.

"Glad to be here," Anne said. "To be back. So what exactly will I be doing?"

"General...ah...general reporting," he said. "Like I said."

"I report to what," she guessed, "the news director? To whom, I mean."

Hoot Thagard laughed. Obviously that laugh was where the nickname came from. "No, no, no," he said. "You report to me. '*News director*.' Oh, that's, that's...that's rich."

Turned out, for a salary of ninety-five cents an hour, Anne O'Connor (who *was* rich) had been hired to be the news *department*. Other than what she dug up herself, the operation was strictly rip 'n' read.

∽

SHE MEANT TO tell her parents that night, but when she got home they were both out. The dining room was decked out for a dinner that had, one of the maids said, been canceled for reasons Mr. O'Connor had chosen not to get into. Anne ate alone. Beef Wellington, of all things.

The next day she drove (eighteenth birthday present: a '54 Chevy Bel Air hardtop, turquoise and white two-tone) to the radio station and spent the morning trying to figure things out. There wasn't a machine in the place that she quite knew how to work: not a microphone, not the portable reel-to-reel tape recording machine, not the multiline telephone with a hold button. All she'd ever done at her brother's station was complain to him about her parents and pilfer extra copies of rhythm-and-blues records. Everyone at WCRB was nice to her, but Flossie and Hoot Thagard were busy with their own shows and no one would teach her anything. Even the receptionist had the twitchy look native only to much-beaten prisoners in psych wards and to grown men and women working at the lowest rung of their chosen profession. Anne had been given no direct responsibilities. She made neat, arbitrary piles of lightly edited press releases, including obituaries, and of pulpy pages of ripped wire copy. That took no time at all, though. She found herself going into and out of unoccupied studios and rooms, closing doors behind her and guessing what different buttons and knobs would do. One made Walter Winchell's reedy recorded voice boom out of a monitor and blow a fuse. Anne ran and hid in the ladies' room.

By noon the effort of trying to look busy had exhausted her. She skipped lunch. She locked herself in the smallest production studio (about the same size as the smaller of the two armoires in her bedroom) and called her brother.

Patrick's first reaction was to laugh.

"It's not funny," she said.

"What possessed you to want to work there? If you wanted to be in radio, Babe—"

"It's not funny. You know why I want to work here."

"I do?"

"Don't be stupid." Patrick—at least in moments he wasn't being hectored by Ibby to ask his father for a raise or his mother for a loan against his trust fund so they could buy a big house before the baby arrived—was capable of feeling just as queasy as she did about being beholden to their parents for everything. "Also, please please *please* don't tell Mother and Dad."

"When do you go back to school?"

"That's my point. No reason they need to know, with so little time left in the summer."

Patrick sighed. He talked her through the care and feeding of a portable tape machine. He gave her a tip on the Sheppard case, a bail hearing that afternoon. He gave her the names of people to talk to, though none of the unlisted phone numbers she'd need to get anything good.

That afternoon Anne O'Connor became a pack journalist.

At the county courthouse, dark-suited men with microphones and four-inch-wide reporter's notebooks smoked and swarmed and shouted and joked and complained and knocked into her without saying so much as *Move, toots*. Sullen cops walked unhurriedly among them. There were more women reporters than Anne would have guessed, but only because she would have guessed that there'd be none.

She didn't know where to go, and at first was afraid to ask, for fear of looking unprofessional. But how professional *is* all this? *It's like dancing*, she thought. *The way you think people are watching you but really they couldn't care less. One-two-three, one-two-three, one-two-three.* Just like that, she was in the thick of things, making it up as she went gracefully along. It was too late by far to get a seat in the courtroom, but within minutes Anne had wormed her way into a jammed hallway and was shoulder to shoulder with a score of sweaty reporters, getting the same story everyone else was getting.

Exactly what went on in a bail hearing, Anne couldn't have said. She knew the gist of it, though: Dr. Sam was guilty and this was a doomed piece of procedural wrangling his lawyer did for the sake of thoroughness.

She overheard conversations among the other reporters, who were already nostalgic for the highly entertaining coroner's inquest that, a couple weeks ago, was staged at an elementary school in Bay Village. A crowd-pleaser of a minitrial. During it the prosecutor had turned up evidence that a former medical technician at Dr. Sam's hospital was out in Los Angeles, as his kept woman. The jet-setting doc had been inventing medical conferences that covered his trips out there. Rumor had it there were other women. What exactly this had to do with a coroner's inquest, Anne hadn't the foggiest. Standing in the hall, she heard her new peers speculate about orgies and wife swapping. She heard them say the Sheppards were drinking pals and who knows what else with Otto Graham and his wife. Graham, quarterback of the Cleveland Browns! Someone said Graham might be called as a witness at the trial.

(Anne thought *orgy* was a synonym for *bacchanal* and had little idea what wife swapping was. She presumed it was not literal. By the standards of 1954, she was not an unworldly eighteen. She'd traveled through Europe. She'd smoked marijuana. She was not a virgin.)

Finally, the courtroom doors opened. A foursome of cops pushed through the reporters like football blockers. Behind them—with a pang of recognition so sharp it hurt!—came that big blond crew-cutted osteopath, his eyes narrowed in brutish self-righteous strickenness. (OK, sure: he was also squinting because of the flashbulbs and TV lights.) Around her, other reporters shouted questions.

Somehow, she did, too.

"Sam! Did you kill your wife?" The words just came! "Sam! *Sam!*"

Dumb luck: right by Anne O'Connor's microphone, Sam Sheppard turned to the swarm, his jaw clenched, and flatly said, "I believe justice will be done."

Never has any human sentence been more insincerely uttered.

But Anne was too excited to notice.

She ran for a phone booth. Fat chance. Taken, taken, taken, taken. She headed north, toward the lake, for blocks and blocks. Taken, taken, taken. Finally, near the stadium, she found one free. She placed the call. She was drenched with sweat. Next to the stadium—true story!—was the big-top tent of the circus. There was a big banner with Emmett Kelly's picture on it. Also mentioned were the Flying Wallendas.

Anne dialed and asked to be put through to the studio. The disc jockey, a tremendously fat man with a high voice, said she could just drive it there. It was too late to do a live broadcast.

She let loose an impressively profane tirade, goddamning him to hell and telling him to get ready to cue her or to put her through to Hoot, who (she lied) had personally told her to phone something in.

Three. Two. One.

"The Ringling Brothers aren't the only circus in Cleveland" was how she led. She set the scene. It was all ad-libbed. Only after she was into it did she think she maybe should have written something out, but by then she was *into it.* Inside it. Nothing she could write, she was sure, would be as good at this. "Finally, after the long day of testimony," she said, realizing only then that she hadn't the first idea about what the testimony had contained, or even how it had come out, "Dr. Sam Sheppard emerged haggard from the court-room. As WCRB listeners will hear in tomorrow's live interview with the accused osteopath, he continued to deny committing the alleged crime and to assert his faith that, and here I quote, 'justice will prevail.'" She was on dead-line. She did not mean to distort. "The question still remains: Is Sheppard this circus's ringleader? Its high-wire act? Its sad Emmett Kelly–like clown? Or its dangerous beast? Only time will tell. That, and a jury of his peers. This is Anne O'Connor, WCRB news, *live* from the steps of the Cuyahoga County Courthouse."

OK, a street corner several blocks away from there. Poetic license.

Dance! *One-two-three, one-two-three, one-two-three.*

Imagine: Mr. Thagard was *paying* her to do this.

When she got back to her Bel Air, its windshield sported a parking ticket, fluttering whitely in the lake wind. A ticket her father could but would certainly not be asked to fix.

෨෩

At the end of the week, Hoot Thagard gave Anne a raise. Up to a dollar five an hour. Mr. Thagard said that five was his lucky number. Everyone at WCRB made an hourly rate ending in five.

Flossie Thagard had her as a guest on the recipe show, raving about Anne's courthouse-steps reporting (which actually couldn't have been more pedestrian) and her résumé (which was fraudulent). Anne read a recipe Flossie handed her. It was for a casserole involving canned soup. It was hard to imagine anyone eating anything so vulgar. But, to be a good sport, Anne lied and said she'd made it for her (nonexistent) fiancé. *Wally McGuire.* "Wally just loves it," she said.

"The way to a man's heart," said Flossie.

"You betcha," said Anne. "That's my Wally."

"Hoot's the same way. As our listeners know."

"Thank you," Anne said. "I only hope Wally and I are as happy as you two."

Flossie rolled her eyes—faux exasperation. Flossie and Hoot Thagard were crazy about each other. "I'm sure you will be, dear."

Anne's whole time at WCRB, Flossie Thagard would be the closest thing to an obliging friend Anne would be able to find. Mr. Thagard was of course a dear, consistently so. But as for everyone else at the station, whenever Anne walked into a room, they stared at her and put their hands over what was in front of them, like schoolkids thwarting a cheater.

—— 7 ——

A WEEK AFTER David came home lame from the navy, his father swung by, early on a Sunday morning, driving a black Lincoln Continental that he left idling at the curb. Aunt Betty and Uncle Stan were at mass. The Lincoln was full of other unshaven men in dark suits and open collars. They'd driven all night from Kansas City, said Mike Zielinsky. Not Kansas City exactly. Let's just say Kansas City, for simplicity's sake. Long story.

"You're too late," David said. He stood on the front porch in a thread-bare brown Egyptian-cotton bathrobe that, in fact, had once belonged to his father. "I already have a job."

His father groaned. "With Stan," he said. "Am I right?"

"Gee. Lucky guess," David said. "He's training me. He's got this big—"

"Right," said Mike. "That thing. That fucking Sheppard thing."

"That's right," David said.

His father's breath smelled as coffee-fouled as a ditch at the bottom of an erosion-wracked Colombian hillside. He tugged the collar of David's robe. David had taken the robe from the house next door as his father was in the process of selling it and had no idea that it had been a wedding present from his mother to his father. "Figures Stan would get a piece of that."

David didn't want to ask how. It was a piece of his father's logic he could do without.

The job his father had come to offer him was a desk position at the union local that oversaw the stocking and servicing of every jukebox in greater Cleveland. The pay was twice what Stan was paying and came with a membership to a country club plus three weeks' vacation, one of which could be spent at a cabana hotel in Miami Beach. Plus pilferage privileges. "Crazy as you are about all that boogaloo-zigaboo music, I figured you'd be glad to get some free—"

"You figured wrong," David said. That wasn't true; it was just that he'd made a commitment to Stan. "Don't be sore at me, OK?"

"Looks like you're the sore one. You're the one turning *me* down."

"I'm not sore. I'm just tired."

He'd been out late with some guys from the neighborhood. They'd gone to a club on East 55th to see Wynonie Harris. David's idea. He was the only one who dug the music going in. Despite a spirited performance by the suave and randy Mr. Blues, there were no converts. The drunker they got, the louder they said *nigger*; at a crucial moment it had been necessary for Skeezix Soltesz (the worst offender) to pull his badge. A long night.

"Stan can't be paying you that much. Are you even making two thou?"

"He's paying me fine," David said.

"I bet. Stan hasn't paid anybody a fair wage since the twelfth of never."

Mike asked David how things were going with the wedding, asked if anyone needed any help with anything. The hall, liquor, whatever. He knew people, he reminded his son.

"We have all that covered," said David, though he knew nothing of the sort.

A chunky baby-faced guy David had never seen before (it was Jackie Presser) got out of the Lincoln and crossed the street to smoke a cigar. He sat on the opposite curb, nodding his head as if to a song only he could hear.

"Married," said Mike. "You, married." He shook his head.

"Yes," David said. "Me, married." He pulled back his shoulders, a defiant gesture that, on the crutches, made him wobble. His father reached out to steady him, then looked away, squinting in the morning light, his eyes determinedly not on the Lincoln or the baby-faced man.

"Fine institution, marriage, no matter what people say. Your aunt and uncle: living proof."

"Yes," David said. "Can I ask you something?"

"Shit. I knew this was coming." His father frowned. "I heard you went there," he said. "A little bird told me. Actually, she's a big fucking loony bird."

It took David a moment to figure out that his father was talking about that little house in Santa Monica, the last place his mother had lived.

"Not that," David said, and then just blurted it out: "I was going to ask if you'd be my best man."

Especially after last night, his neighborhood buddies hardly seemed an option.

At the request, David's father cocked his head, his face a combination of befuddlement and a big corn-fed grin. David explained how having your father be your best man was a southern tradition he'd heard about in the service.

"Even so," said Mike, "you'd think that, of all the fathers anywhere, I'd be the last one you'd think of as his kid's best friend."

"Best man," David corrected. He shrugged. "There's a difference."

"Smart guy," said his father. He gave David the slow, tender slap on the cheek that is a gesture of inchoate feelings on the part of people who know people.

They joked back and forth for a few minutes. Things *had* gotten better between them on those trips to the Desert Inn. No reason to fall back into how things used to be, back when David lived here and was only a boy.

Only in the midst of this did it click, for David. He'd had an opening to ask about his mother, and in his headlong lurch to ask about another difficult thing, albeit one much less difficult, he'd let the moment pass.

He was about to bring it up, it was right on the tip of his tongue, when someone in the Lincoln laid on the horn and his father gave whoever it was the finger.

"I'm glad to do it, the best man situation and whatnot," he said. "Just tell me what I need to do—I got a tux, by the way—"

"I'm not wearing a tuxedo," David said.

"Whatever you do, it's jake with me. I'll be all you ever wanted in a best man, but the point of my visit here wasn't just to hear you blow it by turning down that sweet job I got you—"

"You have a *tux?*" David said. "Why would—"

"—which by the way I knew you would do, but to—"

The horn sounded again.

"Fuck you!" Mikey Z shouted. He shook his fist at them. "You fucks! It's fucking *Sunday morning* here!" Across the street, Mrs. Mytczynskyj opened the upstairs drapes and stared out, her face framed by curlers. Unlike Betty and Stan, the Mytczynskyjs were late-mass people. Jackie Presser got back into the Lincoln.

Mike shook his head. "Long story, those guys," he said to David. "Hey, real quick. I need you to do me a favor."

Somehow, David had known his whole life a moment like this would come. But he was going into politics and could not risk compromising his honesty with even the appearance of impropriety. "Sure," he said.

"It's a small favor," his father said. "There's this thing coming up. Some, you know, what-you-call-it." He waved one hand, the gesture a one-armed ref would make for traveling. "Jesus, kiddo. I don't want to get into all of what I'm getting into here. If you're not gonna be working for me . . . well, you're not then. OK? You're not. OK?"

David shrugged.

"Answer me."

"OK."

"OK then. And so there are things you don't need to know and things it's better if you don't know. Things, you know, about the unions, and maybe one or two things about me. OK?" He paused.

"OK," David said.

"OK. *Hearings!* That was the word I was looking for. There's maybe going to be hearings. This hard-on Bender wants hearings." Congressman George Bender was running for the Senate against the Democratic incumbent Thomas Burke, a former mayor of Cleveland. "But my point, and maybe I can leave it at that, the point is that there are people, political crumbums and those newspaper fucks, who'll be saying things about unions in general and maybe yours truly, too. None of those things are going to be true. OK?"

"Right."

"Right. Some of the things that get said might possibly have in some small way to do with your mother, and *those* things, those things *especially*, will in no *way* be true. OK? No way shape or form. What I want you to do for me is remember that *none* of it is true."

"None of what is true?"

"Exactly," he said. He patted David on the cheek. "That's my boy!"

Anything anyone might theoretically say about his father, his mother, and his father's employers—all of it's false? David looked at his father. Right before David joined the navy, he'd been charmed by his father, and the last couple years what he felt toward his father was, in every sense of the word, entertained. But now all he felt was pity.

Grow up, David thought. *Never be this man.*

"Is that your favor?" he said.

"That's my favor," said Mike. "Exac-a-tackly."

"Anything," David said, "for my dear old dad."

His father either did not catch or else let pass the sarcasm. "Also, you might tell people to vote for Burke. For Senate."

"I can vote myself, you know. Do you even know how old I am?"

For the third time that hot morning, the horn of the Lincoln blared. His back to the car, Mike gave them a get-outta-here wave. "You're twenty years old, smart guy, and you turn twenty-one in October, and the day you were born was the happiest day of my life. I had on a new blue shirt with an egg stain on it, and your mother, when she went into labor that night, had the dog curled up at her feet and was playing ragtime music on the upright Steinway piano I'd gotten her for Christmas the year before. She'd gotten the sheet music at a rummage sale in Parma. It was snowing, can you believe that? October. That's Cleveland for you." He pursed his lips and looked to be trying to dislodge a piece of food from some molar. "Fucking Cleveland."

"We had a *dog?*" David said. Though he didn't remember ever having a piano, either.

"We had a dog," his father confirmed. "Actually it was more like she had a dog. Douglas Fairbanks the Third. A registered bulldog, papers and everything. That dog worshiped her. Jesus, you don't remember Fairbanks?"

"I don't remember having any pets. I don't remember ever seeing pictures of any pets."

"Well, we had Fairbanks. That was it. There was a turtle before that, named I don't remember what, but it lasted, say, maybe a week."

"That's two pets."

"Right," his father said. "If you count the turtle."

"I'm counting the turtle."

"So count the turtle, see if I care." His father shook David's hand goodbye, started down the porch steps, then turned around. "What I hear about the Sheppard thing, by the way," he said, "is that he didn't do it, the chiropractor."

"Osteopath."

"Whatever. The husband. Mrs. Sheppard was havin' an affair, and Dr. Sam was havin' an affair, and of course now all that looks hinky, but it don't mean nothin'. If all the people who were . . ." He let out an exasperated sigh. "Well, a lot more people would be dead than are dead."

David knew who it was that he and his father were thinking about. Not Marilyn Sheppard.

"Stan says there are a lot of leads that point elsewhere," David said.

"I got good sources," said his father. "Believe that."

"I do," said David, but he didn't.

"Course, whether a guy did a thing or didn't do a thing," his father said, "ain't exactly what matters in a court of law. Gotta go," he said, and went— without ever managing to ask his hobbled son the most obvious thing, which was, *How's that ruined knee?*

When the Lincoln turned the corner, David saw that the driver's side was strafed with blue paint. Robin's-egg blue: a color David would have chosen for his Thunderbird, if he could afford a Thunderbird, if he could even drive one, which, with the knee, he couldn't.

◠◡

AND SO IT was that, within a week of coming home lame from the navy, David found himself at his uncle's office, opening mail and answering the phone, dressed in one of three brand-new sport coats (a black, a blue, a gray) he'd bought forlornly off the rack at Higbee's tall department, and one of four thin dark ties that the clerk said would go with anything. The office was a gray-walled two-room job high in the Rockefeller Building, near the mouth of the Detroit Avenue Bridge, though the reception area lacked a view. The only things on the wall were three glass cases filled with state and municipal police department uniform arm patches from as far away as Coral Gables (Florida), Tijuana (Baja California), Provo (Utah; it had a beehive on it), and Alaska (the Territory Patrol; a good one), plus a dusty replica of *Blue Boy* that had been retired from Stan and Betty's living-room wall. Every day David wore the same pair of black slacks, which Betty had sliced at the seam to accommodate his cast. For the most part, David sat alone at his gunmetal-gray steel desk, coat on, tie tied. Stan's secretary had quit to have a baby. With the Sheppard case raging, Stan had no time to interview a successor but couldn't risk, under the circumstances, letting the switchboard take all the messages.

Not for the tips that came in, he explained. Just to keep the reporters at bay.

That's who the calls were mostly from, the newspapers. They wanted to know things David hadn't the first idea about. That, Stan said, is how you deal with reporters. If you don't know anything, you can't lie. David's first week home from the service, he was being quoted daily in Cleveland newspapers he'd heretofore only delivered. Not by name, but he could look at stories where they said "a source close to the Sheppard family would neither confirm nor deny..." and feel the pride of authorship.

The mail came mostly from crackpots, confessing the murder in spidery handwriting (the letters were surprisingly often carbon copies, occasionally from the already-incarcerated). Others claimed to know something that would break the case wide open. Nine times out of ten, these had something to do with Communists. The next most-common denominator was "niggers." Several suggested "Commie/nigger" conspiracies. One nutjob—confusing calcium, good for bones, with fluoride, good for teeth—wrote a letter a day, insisting that the key to everything could be found in investigating how this bone-doctor fellow got the city to fluoridate the water supply. The trail, he said, would lead past Sheppard, through the Vatican, and, eventually (the writer supplied diagrams), to Nikita Khrushchev himself. David kept telling his uncle he ought to write a book.

"You can't know what a bunch of sick morons make up the general public until you see it firsthand," Stan explained. "This kind of thing's pure you-had-to-be-there. Or here, as the case may be. Anyway, I'm no book writer."

Still, David thought. *If a person wrote it right.* And he would indulge a twenty-year-old's cherished fantasy: writing his memoirs. He'd include his many as-yet-unaccomplished accomplishments. His knee injury ought to be good for something. Adversity. You need that. He would devote a chapter to patriotism. The matter of being a motherless child with an absentee, semi-criminal father would need to be glossed over. The book would have a drawing of Terminal Tower on the cover. It would be called *The Times of My American Life*. He'd give copies away to hospitals, schools, and prisons. He'd become a popular member of the lecture circuit.

(David didn't know where this circuit went or how a guy got on it; even the word *circuit* intimidated him. He'd been lousy in shop class, especially the unit on electricity, during which David made drawings that his haggard, prissy teacher said would cause "mayhem, fire, or worse." But David had read about the lecture circuit. Most of the people on it had written books and/or were on the radio. He had no interest in being on the radio. He wanted to help his city. If he were a mayor of a city as grand as Cleveland, people would know his name.)

The leads David spent his days fielding weren't, for the most part, the ones Stan worked on. Stan mostly worked leads he drummed up himself: in-quiries any good cop would have pursued but that the Bay Village and Cleveland departments, pressured by the newspapers to arrest Dr. Sam, were ignoring. For instance, who didn't like Dr. Sam? Who didn't like the family? (Lots of people. For one thing, that newish hospital the Sheppard family ran encroached on other doctors' turfs. On top of that, traditional doctors hated losing patients to *osteopaths,* those bone-fetishist grads of Brand-X colleges.) Was someone sleeping with Marilyn? (The answer to all such questions—Stan told David—is *probably.* Nothing to do with Mrs. Sheppard per se. Just your law of averages.) Was Sam sleeping with someone (yes) who might want revenge? (Stranger things have happened.) What about any psychos in the area? (Every neighborhood has 'em.) What about friends, family, employees: anyone with access to and familiarity with the house? (Just because there was no sign of forced entry and no lights turned on doesn't mean, ipso facto, that Dr. Sam killed his wife.) Are any of these people bushy-haired? Would/could any of these people have hired a bushy-haired someone to kill Marilyn? (Not a day goes by in America without many similar pieces of work contracted.)

လလ

WORKING WITH UNCLE Stan was more a discipline than a job. Each morning David would get up at the stroke of five, in the dark, hobble to the bathroom, shave and sponge himself clean, hobble downstairs to the egg-and-kielbasa breakfasts his aunt made but never herself ate. He would read the dull, responsible morning paper, the *Plain Dealer* (sports first, but he now made a habit of reading the whole front page and everything about local politics, too), and bolt down two cups of coffee in perfect sync with his uncle. At six sharp, they pulled out of the drive and rode into the city in the (fully repaired, exquisitely kept) Jeepster, listening to classical music, talking about baseball, facing the rising sun before it rose high enough to be punishing, crossing the Detroit Avenue Bridge as, all over greater Cleveland, the owners of the cars that would constitute rush-hour traffic were only just beginning to heed their alarm clocks.

In the parking garage, David never asked his uncle for help with the crutches. Stan stood and waited.

They entered the Rockefeller Building together. His uncle stopped at the newsstand and bought the *New York Times* and the *Wall Street Journal*. They took the elevator together, nodding cop-hellos to Dino the elevator man and making their purposeful way to their respective desks. It was six-eighteen. You could set your watch by it.

Stan read his newspapers and David typed thank-you letters to crackpots. At seven Stan called the switchboard for messages. Then he went to have a cup of coffee at a diner where the first-shift detectives went, senior men on the CPD. David could have goofed off then, but instead he took out the typing textbook he'd borrowed from the library, took out his uncle's stopwatch, and gave himself tests.

Eight-thirty sharp, his uncle came back. He'd recite a blow-by-blow of his schedule that day and a list of clerical tasks for David to do. David wrote it all down. For most of the rest of the day, David was in the office alone. At nine the phones started. Not just from the *Press*, the *News*, and the *PD*, either. Ones from Akron, Erie, Columbus, Pittsburgh, Detroit, Cincinnati, even Los Angeles, New York, and of course the wire services. David took their names and questions and told them they should really contact the office of Mr. William J. Corrigan, the defense attorney and famous labor lawyer who was Dr. Sam Sheppard's attorney. When asked, as he repeatedly was, why Dr. Sheppard needed an attorney of the wattage of Bill Corrigan if he was not guilty, David said that all questions about this matter should be addressed either by rereading the United States Constitution or by speaking directly to Mr. William J. Corrigan.

The Constitution part was David's own little improvisation.

When asked anything about the case itself, David neither confirmed nor denied.

After talking to the reporters, it was a relief to hear from the rare tip-bearing goofus. Also diverting were the voices of young women who wanted to send Dr. Sam flowers.

$\backsim$

THE TINY TATTOO on David's shoulder appalled Irene, even though it was of her name. "It's barbaric, sweetie," she said. It was the first time since his return they'd gotten the chance to make love. This was at a house in the neighborhood, where for two weeks Irene was dog-sitting. The dog was ancient and no trouble. Irene insisted that the lights stay off, but eyes adjust. "I know you meant it to be, y'know, nice," Irene said. "But a *tattoo*."

"You have to understand," he said. "In the navy, a lot of—"

She put her hand over it.

"You know, I used to have a dog," David said, pointing to the collie. "A long time ago. A bulldog. Fairbanks was its name."

"How permanent is permanent?" she asked.

"Permanent as our love," he said.

"Oh, hell," she said.

They laughed about how full of it he was, then started tickling each other and got to laughing so hard that the old dog, outside the door to the locked guest bedroom, joined in with barking energetic enough to provoke a large gift-puddle of orange urine.

$\backsim$

TYPICALLY, IRENE MET David for lunch. She was another prompt one, Irene. David wasn't, but the combination of navy life, working for his uncle, and getting ready to marry Irene had brought out an uncharacteristic side of him. He was glad. How can a person dream of being mayor of a city like Cleveland unless he can adhere to a schedule?

Irene worked second shift at City Hospital, starting at three. At the stroke of noon, David would tell the switchboard to please take messages. He had forty-five minutes. When he got to the lobby, there Irene would be, sweaty and dabbing at her neck with a handkerchief.

David would look at her and feel heartbreaking tenderness and know he was doing the right thing, marrying Irene. She was a freely perspiring woman. This mortified her, but David found it arousing, the sweating. How could a man have made love to a woman on a day hot enough to render their bodies one slippery, cooperative whole and not think of sex every time thereafter he saw a reasonably attractive sweaty woman? It was a look Irene made sexier yet, accessorized by a white patent-leather purse and a small white leatherette book called *The Wedding Embassy Yearbook*, which she'd gotten free from Halle Brothers department store for registering there and which spelled out everything that was expected of one in planning a wedding. This had chiefly to do with etiquette. Middle-class weddings had not yet become vulgar, bankruptcy-inducing bacchanals. David loved seeing her carry that book, but he rarely looked inside it. (Once. The people depicted in there looked older than he and Irene were, and richer. More than one picture showed a square-jawed man with a cigarette holder. David admired FDR as much as the next person, more really, but a cigarette holder? It made him want to call the whole thing off. He'd snapped the book shut. He wouldn't look inside it anymore.) This was Irene's mother's show, with mandated assists from Aunt Betty (rehearsal dinner, bar bill, band, ad hoc consultation, which Betty did cheerfully even though she thought Mrs. Hrudka was a nitwit) and footwork courtesy of Irene herself. Once lunch was over, Irene would have a list of downtown tasks to accomplish, before hopping a 2:40 bus across the river and to work. The streetcars had stopped running in January. Now it was buses. Hundreds of hot, smelly buses.

The heat! Heat like David couldn't believe. It was hot enough that summer to get people in barber and beauty shops talking about if anyone had seen it get hotter. David hadn't. Not even in California, not even close. He was lucky to work in a building that had, right after the war, been retrofitted for air-conditioning. Every day since David had been home, the temp hit ninety. The air tasted like tar. Brother man, was it hot! Because of the heat and David's leg and the fact they didn't have a car to use, he and Irene ate lunch near his office. The Woolworth's lunch counter on Euclid Avenue or the dining room at Higbee's, where Irene would order a snowball of cottage cheese on an alarmingly green leaf of lettuce. She was certainly not fat. Her just-below-the-top-band-of-the-underpants belly seemed, in its milky plumpness, almost lewd—particularly in the unforgiving light of summer.

One day the tailor for her dress-fitting called in sick. Irene had some time on her hands and David splurged for a taxicab to take them to Short Vincent and to the Theatrical. Irene had been to the Hollenden Hotel but never to the Theatrical. After a wait that, David knew, would make him late getting back, they were seated at a tiny table near the ladies' room.

"This is the place you always talk about?"

"Shh," David said. "People will hear you."

When David came here with his uncle, he felt like someone who could aspire to belong. With Irene, he felt watched.

"It's just a delicatessen restaurant on a dark street," she said.

"There's Celebrezze," he whispered.

"Celebrezze!"

"Shh," David said.

"You're right," she whispered. Her round face glowed like a wet dish.

The mayor was across the room in a booth with Louie Seltzer, editor of the *Press,* who'd gotten Celebrezze elected, who was prosecuting Sheppard on the front page of the paper, and who was a threat to Thomas O'Connor as the political boss of Cleveland. All this intelligence came courtesy of Stan Lychak. David, in explaining things to Irene, neglected to cite his source.

"Don't look now," David said, "but behind you is—"

Irene spun around. "Dorothy Fuldheim!"

Fuldheim—the gnomish redhead who was a TV anchorwoman years before the term existed—was on her way to the ladies' room. She heard Irene, smiled her lopsided grin, waved, and said, "Hello, dear." It was a wave that involved wiggly fingers.

Once Fuldheim was out of earshot, David told Irene that famous people have also been known to urinate.

Irene looked at him and frowned. "This is a side of you I don't care for."

"It's just—"

She shook her head. She looked down at the menu and wouldn't talk. When the waiter came, she said that iced tea would be fine, just that. David couldn't persuade her otherwise.

"Don't ruin this," he said after the waiter left.

Irene met his eyes. "I'm not . . . ," she said. "Some . . ."

"I know you're not."

"Some hillbilly. Some rube. Just because you work where—"

"I know you're not."

"That's right," she said. "I'm not."

"I know," he said.

"I don't think you do."

He looked at her. What he thought was, *How will this woman handle being the wife of the mayor of Cleveland?* She was bright, good with math and money, a good judge of people. But she'd hardly even been to the other side of Cleveland. David had served his country in time of police action, had been to Hawaii on liberty, Las Vegas countless times on two-day passes, and come this close to going all the way to Korea. And, well . . . so what? Irene could go places, too. David could take her. They could grow together. Isn't that what marriage is supposed to be?

This was what he was thinking.

It didn't occur to him that there were all kinds of big shots there that day whom *he* did not recognize. For example, upstairs was a table of locally famous people who knew people.

David's mouth was spectacularly full of corned beef, which he chewed longer than necessary, buying time. What he finally said was this: "I'm sorry." He reached out to hold her chin, and she let him. "I'm not being fair. The first time I was here," he said, "when I sat where you sat? Figuratively, I mean. Not the same seat, but you know. Anyway, I was in awe."

He told her a short, rushed version of the Eliot Ness story.

She looked at him like she might cry. It's true, Ness's fall from heroism was a sad story, and at first David gave himself credit for a moving telling of the tale. But it seemed more than that. He asked her what was wrong. She wouldn't say. Or rather, what she said was, "Nothing."

On the way back, in the taxicab, as she was helping him with his crutches, she said, "Don't make me feel small. But who was Eliot Ness?"

"Is," David said. "He's not just a friend of Uncle Stan's; he was a real hero," he said. "But that was a long time ago. Almost twenty years."

"Before we were born," Irene said.

"Right as," said David.

Telling the story made David realize that all this time he'd been half-expecting his father to walk into the Theatrical.

"I'm sorry," David said. "It's just a story." This was a girl who knew where he came from, who waited for him when he was in the service, who'd known him forever: a girl who could keep him true to himself. "Really," he said, "I'm sorry. You're right. Look at me, please."

With obvious effort, she did. Irene was good at not crying when she didn't want to. She tapped him on the wrist, right on the watch. "I'll go get a taxi," she said. "You're late."

David told her no, they could go together. He left a sharp's-sized tip and lame-frogged his way through the trying-not-to-stare crowd. It was a nice gesture, Irene's, but how would it look, a girl hailing the cab?

When he got back to the office, his uncle was waiting for him.

"Even people with banker's hours," Stan said, "get back on time from lunch."

"Irene needed me," he unswervingly lied. "There was a crisis with the wedding bands. The rings. A situation with, you know, the sizes. It's all straight now."

Stan blocked David's shortest path behind the desk, his posture as straight as a man in a shirt ad. David didn't risk a pardon-me. He took the long way, the other way around. Stan watched him. David sat down. He adjusted his tie. Stan kept watching him.

"It won't happen again," David said.

"Forty-five minutes," said Stan, tapping his watch, gesture of a martinet.

"This never happens," David said.

"Happened today."

"True," David said. "What I—"

Stan waved it off. "Women," he said.

David nodded. Grown men said this a lot. Maybe one time in ten David knew what they meant. This was not one of those times. He was sure this was a thing a man grew into.

Stan handed him a pink message slip. "I thought you were supposed to be doing this for me," he said, but he said it kindly. "Here."

On the FROM line Stan, in his schoolmarmish cursive, had written out the whole name, even circled the MR.: *Michael Zielinsky*. Not, *Mike* or *Mikey Z* and not *your dad*. The CALL BACK box was checked. The number was local. The comment: *(Claims he knows you)*. Parentheses Stan's.

"Crazy," David said. "I was just thinking about him." He did not say *my dad*.

"I bet you were," Stan said. "Your thoughts to God's ears."

This was another thing that people said that David didn't really understand. (Usually they said *your lips,* but David was clear on that part, Stan's terse witticism.) God, if David had the story straight, heard quite a few things He didn't act on.

"Mind if I call him back now?" David said.

His uncle shrugged.

David hadn't told his aunt and uncle that his father had come by that Sunday morning. Now, David realized, his uncle was cheesed off both that David had taken a long lunch and that Mikey Z hadn't welcomed his temporarily crippled son home. David might have set the record straight, but it was likely his uncle's compassion over the latter was keeping him from giving David hell about the former. So David said nothing. He waited until his uncle went back out for the afternoon, then dialed the number on the message slip. It was a nightclub. "Are you his kid?" the bartender asked. "OK, then. As long as you are, I can tell you. Mr. Zielinsky just left."

⁓

MOST AFTERNOONS THE calls slacked off. About the only work Stan left was the answering of nutjob mail and clipping relevant articles from newspapers Stan was done with. This might have taken even less time than it did, except that David got caught up in reading the out-of-town papers. It was like taking a free trip someplace. You got to see where in different cities you could go hear Louis Jordan, Miles Davis, Nat Cole, or B.B. King—clubs with names like the Regal, the Top Hat, and the Metropolitan, dates sequential enough that you could have said what kind of summer your heroes were having. Plus you got to see how a given news story—made up of what you'd think are the exact same events—was worth more or less attention in cities other than Cleveland. He couldn't remember having ever read the *New York Times* before that summer, and he was astounded how much space they gave over to world events, how little time he'd ever before spent reading about things like that. He hadn't been a newspaper reader in the service; nobody he knew was. Even news about Korea he'd gotten through the grapevine. What sort of citizen did *that* make him? (Bad.) This fall he'd be voting for the first time. By this time next year, he could easily be a husband, a father, and a home owner, but right now his head hurt, thinking of all the catching up he had to do. Really, he looked back on the sad, failed twenty years of his life up until then—filled with pickup sports, snickering boon pals, rushed-through homework, and daydreams—and couldn't get over all the lost time.

With his uncle's approval, David spent much of his afternoons writing and rewriting his entrance-exam essay to Fenn College, where he planned to take night classes and at which he planned to double-major in political science and history, with a minor in American lit. That was the plan, though when he told it to people it sounded overly complicated and unlikely. *In today's troubled society,* he wrote, *when vigilance from the nefarious forces of Communism is as necessary at the school board meeting as it is among the brain trust of NATO . . .*

He ripped the sheet out of the typewriter. What dishonest crap. He bounced the wadded-up page off *Blue Boy.* He retrieved it and attempted six hook shots at the trash can until one fell. He took the paper out and kept at it until he made three straight. He was learning to compose at the typewriter, which made the going rockier. People said that things written on typewriters could never be as good as things written longhand, but David thought this was kind of backward.

He started again, a new tack this time. *The good young men and women of the present young generation face many challenges in redressing the many problems they will inherit and addressing the many problems as yet unforeseen.* The *redressing/addressing* thing was slick, but already this was getting away from him. David took out a thesaurus and changed the first *many* to *myriad* and the second to *manifold*. He took out the first *young*. He changed the second *problems* to *quandaries*. What a great word, *quandaries*.

He flipped open the platen, balled up the paper, and fired it so hard off *Blue Boy* that it banked clean and true into the trash can.

God, did he miss basketball.

In exasperation and self-loathing, David started typing newspaper editorials, verbatim, both for typing practice and, more, to feel the pleasure of classy writing flow through his childish mind, his clumsy fingers, and onto the page. Two steady weeks of this and he learned more about writing than he might have gleaned from ten semesters of freshman composition. One day he tried again, and his essay just happened. It was about the triumph of *Brown v. the Board of Education:* archly sanctimonious, derivative but no plagiary. Days later his GI Bill–expedited application was accepted. The letter contained a complimentary parking permit (for the car he didn't have) and a coupon good for his first semester's books ("$15.00 VALUE") in the campus bookstore, an award for writing an entrance essay of "exceptional originality and merit."

∽

LATE EVERY AFTERNOON Stan returned, a copy of the just-off-the-presses *News* and *Press* tucked under his arm, and, without fail, returned every call from every reporter. Without fail, Stan would say that all questions about this matter should be addressed directly to Mr. William J. Corrigan. With some of the local guys, men he knew, he chuckled as he said it and might go briefly off the record. Even then all he'd say is that it was a heck of a mess and that he'd never seen such a bungling coroner as this joker Gerber, and, hell no, you can't quote me.

(Meanwhile, David paged through the news and sports sections of the papers; once, in an idle scan of the women's page of the *News*, he saw Anne O'Connor's byline. *A rich girl with a job? Yeah, right.* It's a common name. Still, it made him think of her. That said, David wouldn't want you to misunderstand. He did not think about her, other than idly.)

Somewhere among the calls, Stan would also call Betty, to confirm that he wouldn't be late for dinner, and to ask what if anything he could bring home and also if she needed him to cook. Stan rarely worked late. He'd achieved midcareer mastery over a profession perceived as chiefly nocturnal (if you grab a guy from work he'll be less defensive than if you pop up at his house; likewise, housewives in the afternoon talk more freely than if their husbands were around). Typically, at five sharp David hobbled out of the office, and Stan locked the door and summoned the elevator. Betty rarely needed anything. And—though she was taking both Romantic literature and a demanding statistics class this summer at Baldwin-Wallace—she never took him up on his offer to cook, except on Wednesdays. Wednesday was hibachi night. Other people in the neighborhood had, for the most part, built barbecue pits alongside their bomb shelters (the ubiquitous former outnumbered the much-to-be-desired latter, 2 to 1), but the Lychaks made do with the driest basement in Old Brooklyn (Stan had a hundred Harry Homeowner tricks for this) and a puny hibachi. It had been purchased while David was away. Stan, clearly, had not instigated this purchase. Every Wednesday night he stared at the unresponsive coals as if they had something personal against his entire way of life. Then he'd take out the lighter fluid and booster-douse the coals, unflinching in the face of this explosion, and the coals would finally take. Stan didn't grill side dishes: no tinfoil-wrapped corn on the cob, no toasting the French bread from Hough Bakery. He grilled steaks—beef and, months after a winter in which Stan had gotten his deer, venison. Steaks, period. He stayed out there watching them, with his suit still on and his tie slightly loosened and without so much as a drink in his hand, until all three pieces of meat were painstakingly well-done.

David liked rare meat but said nothing.

On Irene's days off, David had dinner at her house. Irene was a fine cook, but it was Mrs. Hrudka's idea that while she still had the chance to look over her daughter's shoulder, Irene should work her way through not only Mrs. Hrudka's own card-file recipe box but also the entire *Betty Crocker Cookbook.* Irene poured undiluted cans of Campbell's soup over various gray meats. She layered the ingredients of creamy casseroles that would be topped with Kellogg's corn flakes, Durkee dried onions, or crumbs made out of Bisquick and butter. She came to see as kitchen staples the springform pan, the gravy boat, and the wall-mounted copper-colored Jell-O molds. She fricasseed, blanched, sautéed, braised, and parboiled things David couldn't imagine requesting or, right now, affording. Lamb. Salmon. Chinese spareribs. Milk-fed veal. Cornish game hens. Through no fault of Irene's, those were the worst of all possible foods, Cornish game hens: miniature whole chickens that, defying common sense, were to be eaten solely with one's knife and fork. When Mr. Hrudka tried picking his game hen up, his wife slapped him squarely on his bald head and called him a slob. Mr. Hrudka put the bird down and looked at his daughter. Irene shrugged. He looked at David, who smiled insipidly, then caught his reflection in the mirror over the porcelain-elephant–covered mantel and covered his mouth, pretending to cough. Mr. Hrudka rubbed the reddening crown of his head. He was a lean man who'd won a Bronze Star in the First World War and was a foreman at Fisher Body, supervisor of more than one hundred men, but at home he acted like someone accustomed to following orders.

Irene had three much-older brothers (Irene, as Mrs. Hrudka was mortifyingly quick to admit, was "an unbidden gift from God"). The brothers used to share a bedroom in the Hrudkas' modest frame house that Mrs. Hrudka had long since filled with a collection of porcelain-head dolls. Mrs. Hrudka called it a "sitting room," though, with the dolls covering the room's two chairs and daybed (not to mention its dresser, highboy, and old-fashioned console radio), there was nowhere to sit. After Irene and her mother finished the dishes, David left Mr. Hrudka alone in the den, to continue gape-mouthedly watching TV, and hopped his way to the rug-covered floor of the sitting room. They'd listen to Bill Randle on the radio. Randle was no Alan Freed, but Freed was gone, and Randle played the same swell music. Irene was a convert to R&B, although she had a maddening inability to remember who did what song.

"You really don't have to do all that on my account," David said one night.

Irene looked at him blankly.

"The cooking," he said.

"What makes you think it's on your account?" she said. "Aren't *we* full of ourselves?"

It took him a second to calculate how she meant this. "Oh," he said. "Sorry."

"Anyway, I think it's cute," Irene said. "It's Ma's way of saying she loves me. She's lonely." Irene waved, indicating the thicket of dolls. The sitting room was the only room he and Irene were allowed to be alone in, as if Mrs. Hrudka knew the creepy glass eyes of seven dozen dolls could irradiate any boy's libido.

"What is it about your mom and porcelain? Dolls, elephants."

Irene laughed. "Don't forget the collection of porcelain thimbles. She used to collect little porcelain bells, too, but she traded them to her sister—you've met Aunt Klara?"

He had. He'd been dating her long enough to know every relative, even the ones who did not live in America.

"She's a nutty one," Irene said. "Ma traded her half-baked collection of porcelain bells to Aunt Klara for Aunt Klara's half-baked collection of porcelain elephants."

"Why *elephants?*" A panic-pang hit David. "Your parents aren't Republicans, are they?"

"What if they are?"

"Are they?" When she didn't answer, a worse thought occurred to him. "Are *you?*"

"What if I am?"

"You'd cancel out my votes," David said. "I can't marry someone who's going to cancel out my votes every November. You're not kidding, are you?"

"People don't always vote for people from the same party."

"Who doesn't?" David said.

"People."

"People," he scoffed. "You don't know what you're talking about."

She frowned. "This is awfully narrow of you," she said.

"You really aren't kidding."

"Is this your way of telling me you can't marry me?" she asked. "Don't say that, David, don't bring the subject up, if you don't mean it."

"I don't mean it."

"Then don't say it."

"That's not what I'm saying," he said. "I'm talking hypothetically."

"Whether I marry you or not," she said, "I'd continue to vote. Maybe you should just marry me because it keeps you close, gives you a chance to convert me. Is that how you think?"

"You know how I think," he said.

"I'm starting to wonder," she said.

"That makes two of us," he said.

How could this have only come out now? He'd known her forever, and something this fundamental was only coming out now? David couldn't have named ten people in Cleveland he knew personally and knew to be Republicans. He'd have been less shocked, he was sure, if she'd told him she was somehow part Negro.

On the radio, Rosemary Clooney sang "Hey, There." He hated Rosemary Clooney, though years later he'll feel nostalgic for this music and, on a vacation to a beach house on the outer banks of North Carolina, whim-purchase a compact disc filled with her greatest hits, and, sitting in a hot tub, sipping a nonalcoholic beer, decide he'd judged her harshly.

"All right," Irene finally said. "I am kidding. Ma's not a Republican, and neither is Dad, and neither am I," she said. "But this is awfully narrow of you."

"OK, then," David said. "So what is it with your mom and porcelain?"

"You think too much," she said.

"Why would you collect a thing for no reason?"

"Why do you collect records?"

"I love music," he said.

"She loves porcelain," she said.

"What for? What's it good for?"

"What good is all that music?" she said. "It's not like the radio's going out of business."

David took a deep breath and held it. *One, two, three, four, five, six, seven, eight, nine, ten.* "You can't compare this," he said, holding up a porce-lain doll dressed to look like the boy in *Blue Boy,* "with a Charlie Parker record!" He drew himself up on his one good knee. "You can't compare bric-a-brac with things that capture the American experience. You can't compare dust-gathering souvenirs with a music *library.*" He felt like the very jazz mu-sicians he was riffing about, playing a solo from his soul to a sweet, sincere, large-breasted audience of one. As he talked, he felt long God-fingers of in-spiration curve warmly around his shoulders. "You can't compare commerce with art! You can't compare knickknacks and gewgaws with culture and heart! You can't compare thimbles with symbols!"

Irene burst out laughing. "Cymbals?" she said, pantomiming banging a set together.

"*Symbols,*" he said. "As in, *symbolism.*"

She laughed harder, shrieking now. It was contagious; he laughed at himself.

"Hey," he said. Irene was composing herself now. "I thought that was good."

"Work on it, tiger." She rose to kiss him. "I love you," she said.

"You're the one for me," he said. He couldn't possibly have meant it more.

❧

FROM THE BACKSEAT of a limousine, David and his father watched Irene walk into City Hospital. He'd been in limos several times before, in Las

Vegas as a guest of his father's, but it was Irene's first time. There had been unpleasantness at dinner. The limo ride, though, had unduly impressed her. She'd gotten out in what seemed like buoyant spirits. David wished she'd wear her uniform more often. She changed when she got there. Even today, when she'd gotten approval for a long dinner break, she'd changed out of it and into a dress and would change back. David would rather see her in that uniform than see her naked. True. Now, watching her from behind, he narrowed his eyes and pretended that was what she wore: white and clinging, wholesome, all-cotton, and true.

"Nice girl," said Mike, jerking his thumb unnecessarily, "your fiancée. Eileen."

"Irene," David said. "You've met her at least five times before. She and I have been going steady since the beginning of—"

"I know," he said. "Down, boy. What I'm saying is, she's a nice girl."

"Right," David said. "That's absolutely right."

"Hey!" He tugged at the strap of the rucksack David had brought. "She forgot her stuff."

"I didn't bring it for her," David said. His father had just assumed, for which David had been grateful.

David had been home more than a month. This was the second time he'd seen his father.

"Listen, sport, she didn't mean nothing by what she said," said Mike. "She thought it was good news, the Independence thing."

"I know what she thought," David said. He did not like the sound of it, his father defending Irene. "You don't need to defend her, OK? The last thing you need to do is that."

The limo was one of a small fleet his father had a piece of. Driving was Shoes Hoffman, the enormously fat man Mikey Z had punched years ago in the barbershop. He hadn't even been asked into the restaurant, right on the shore in Lakewood. Mike paid, of course. Also, in deference to Irene's tight schedule, he'd seen to it the food hit their table the split second they sat down: side salads and bread in place, then, *pow!* three steaming medium-well filets (the princess cut for Irene, king cuts for Mike and David). David liked rare meat but had said nothing.

"I'm pulling your chain, kid," his father said, "about not remembering her name. Irene. Of course I know it's Irene. Jeez-oh-man, here I am, father of a kid who don't know a joke when he hears one. How'd that come to be, I wonder."

"Funny," David said. "Har de har har."

"The problem with you," said Shoes, "is that the only time you're funny is when you're not trying to be."

"Problem with you is you won't shut the fuck up," said Mike. "Everybody's a critic."

"Everybody's a comedian," said David.

"Christ," said his father. He made a cross with his index fingers, as if warding off a vampire. "Truce, already."

At dinner Irene had talked mostly about wedding plans, and David and his father gamely feigned interest. Then she'd dropped the bomb.

"I have the greatest news," she'd said.

Whenever anyone says this, it's sixty-forty your life is going to change for the worse. David had braced himself.

(News of the pregnancy was to come later. Irene didn't know, yet.)

"My parents bought two lots in Independence," she'd said. "They're building a new home on one. We can have whatever time we need to scrape together the money to build on the other."

"Independence?" David said. "What were you thinking, sweetie?" *Independence*. It's only a few miles away, in the Cuyahoga Valley, but David wasn't sure he'd ever been there.

His father asked what the heck's wrong with Independence? Sounded like a great idea. Maybe he could help? There were builders who owed him favors.

"Honey," David said. He took Irene's hand in his. "It's sweet of your parents, really it is, but . . ." He raised his eyebrows cartoonishly. *How could she not get it?*

"But what?" she said.

Oh, for god's sake. Where to begin?

"It's not me, is it?" his father had said.

"You?"

"Me and your mother, living next door to her sister and Stan? It's not that?"

"What? Why would it be that? It's Independence." He turned to Irene. "It's a suburb."

"What are you doing with your eyebrows?"

David couldn't believe this. "It's the *suburbs*."

Irene frowned and started in on the obvious—what-all was great about the suburbs, beginning with the schools, continuing through disquisitions on public safety and appreciating real estate values, all of it latent with a fear of Negroes. Out of an indulgence that he would have called love, he curbed his instinct for swift, ruthless rebuttal. He let her say her piece.

"The suburbs are fine," he said, once she seemed finished, "for some people. It's..." He didn't want to tip his hand with his father. But what choice did he have? "We need to live in the city of Cleveland," he blurted. "For political reasons."

Aloud, it sounded ridiculous, but there it was. Only when David had swallowed hard and said yes, he was serious, only then did his father stop laughing. "Y'know," Mikey Z said, "I ran for office myself once. State senate. True story."

"I remember," David said. But Irene didn't know. David's father told a version of the story. He left out the part where his position on the Taft-Hartley Bill was that he'd paid it. Irene asked David why he'd never told her his father had run for office. His father, to his credit, allowed David to save face by reasserting that he'd run just for show. For the union.

Now, outside the hospital, Mike rapped his stooge on the back of the skull. "Home, Shoes," he said.

"Whose?" Shoes said.

"His, dumbfuck." Then, to David: "Cigar?"

"Let me out over on Archwood," David said. "I have some people I need to meet."

"Some people? What people? Your mayoral campaign staff?" He snickered. "Sorry, kid. That's not fair. You want a cigar or not?"

"I'm meeting some friends there," David lied. "Yeah, sure."

"So what *is* in the bag," his father asked, "if it's not hers?"

David had brought a rucksack full of campaign literature for Senator Burke. This was not going well. Really, though, after what came out at dinner, why bother lying?

"Campaign literature for Senator Burke," he said. "Also lapel buttons." He patted his cane, new this week. "I'm going to canvass my way home."

"No shit?"

"No kidding," David said.

"You sure the leg's up to that?" It was the first time his father had shown concern for David's knee.

"I'm sure," he said, though he wasn't. Probably it was. He wasn't at all ready for the cane stage, but anything to ditch those heavy crutches.

"We could drive you house to house."

"Oh, right. Now there's a great idea."

His father shrugged, handed David a cigar, and lit them both with the limo's built-in lighter. "Burke, huh?" he said. "I had no idea I had such influence on you."

"You don't," David said. He grinned, though. He saw the humor in this.

"Seems like," he said, "last time we talked I told you—"

"It's nothing like that," David said. "That's just a coincidence."

What David might have told his father was this, the truth: when David went to Fenn College to register for his fall classes and buy his books, he had, while he was at it, bought as pleasure reading a book required for a senior-level political science class. It was called *Careers in Politics*. Chapter 1: anyone contemplating such a career "should volunteer immediately for a candidate in whom he believes." David felt branded as mediocre to be starting out voting in a midterm election. Blessed are those who cast their first ballot in a presidential election. They must feel chosen. Important. Absent the chance to support the bright, cultured likes of Adlai Stevenson, David supposed he should volunteer for a local campaign, though it was a bad time for that, too. The mayor/council elections were next year, and David had no interest in judgeships and county officers. Where the action stood to be this election was the Senate race. It was already in full swing, and it sported, for David, the perfect candidate: Thomas Burke. How perfect? He was a Democrat. He was a former mayor of Cleveland. He was an incumbent, which meant he was likely to win. Volunteering on a winning campaign, said *Careers in Politics,* is "by far the most common path to a man's first paying political job."

True, Burke was the man opposing "that hard-on Bender"—who had in fact subpoenaed Mike Zielinsky for congressional racketeering hearings to be held (with naked election-year opportunism) not in Washington but Cleveland. (David both deplored the corruption of the rackets and admired their initiative. In his few weeks as a dockworker, he'd seen a hundred little scams, worked so that people who knew people would get work and/or money. This is the way of the world. To deny it, David thought, kept one's ideals intact—and safely on the bench of a little game called real life.) But Burke was also the man who, as mayor, had cleaned up the Mob-throttled corruption in the Cleveland Police Department by hiring Eliot Ness—and, as a consequence, Stan Lychak.

It was only this last part that David mentioned to his father.

"There can't be that many candidates I could volunteer for," David said, "who'd have both your support and Uncle Stan's."

"There can't be?" his father said.

"I'm serious."

"I'm serious, too. Is that what you really think—that there can't be?"

"You know what I mean."

"I doubt Stan's ever voted Republican, for anything."

"You know what I mean."

"Me, I vote the man, not the party. I've voted for some Republicans in my day."

"C'mon..." David was about to say *Dad* but caught himself. With his father he deployed the same tack he took with Mr. Hrudka, who'd told David to call him *Bud.* He couldn't bring himself to call Mr. Hrudka *Bud,* so he called him nothing. If he was in the kitchen and it occurred to him that Mr. Hrudka, too, might like another Carling, David would walk all the way back into the TV room, make eye contact, and ask. "You *know* what I mean."

They were on Archwood now.

All the way down, David told Shoes. The east end of the neighborhood.

"Christ, what a walk," his father said. "Sure we can't drive you where you need to go?"

"I'm going door-to-door," David said. "Exactly how would that work?"

His father shrugged. He started back on the politics. David had talked about this with his father as much as he could stand. Ticked off, his head swimming from the martinis at dinner and the cigar now, David summoned the nerve to ask what he'd been wanting to ask for years.

"Let me ask you something," he interrupted. "About Mom."

His father jutted his jaw. He nodded. Then he rose, spun, as agile as any large man you'll ever see in the back of a limo, grabbed the handle of the partition behind Shoes's head, and slammed it closed. David hadn't known there was a partition.

"How will he know where to stop?" David said.

"He'll know not to," said Mike. "He'll go in circles until I say the word. Look," he said. "There's no mystery to all that, and there's not that much to say. I don't know what that slut in Santa Monica told you, but—"

"I just want to know why Mom left."

"You know already," his father said. "She wanted to be in the movies."

"We could have moved," David said. "All of us. There are unions in Los Angeles."

"Not like here. Though that didn't have the first thing to do with it."

"What did?"

"She's in a bunch of plays at different playhouses here, right? Shakespeare things, *The Petrified Forest*, funny ones, you name it. She was in, what-you-call-it, the nose one. *Cyrano.* Anyway, some good ones, some not, but she's good in 'em all, see, gets great notices, and people put ideas in her head and say they can do things for her, make things happen, bald-faced lies every pretty girl in America gets told, only Joan buys it. Next thing you know she wants to be in the movies, which, as you may have noticed, is not a business you can get real far in," he slammed his fist into the leather seat, "*in Cleveland fucking Ohio.*"

He smoothed his thinning hair.

The punch had made a sound like a fastball exploding in a catcher's mitt.

"Your cigar's out, son." Mikey Z pressed the lighter down. "Draw on it, like this. Try it like this. See?"

David could feel his heart thumping. His hands shook. "I don't care about the cigar," he said. "Tell me about Mom. How it happened, what happened, all that."

On the porches and sidewalks of Archwood, Denison, and the numbered north-south streets, the weary lumpenproletariat of the near West Side stopped what they were doing (weeding and watering, dog walking and gossiping, debating the Sheppard case and listening to Mike Garcia pitch a shutout against the Tigers) to try to see inside the limo's long windows for the VIP inside. Years went by on these streets without a limo driving down them.

"Joan," his father said. "You want to know, what is it about Joan?"

"How about this," David said. "How about telling me why she killed herself?" *What is it about Joan?* His father talked about her in the present tense.

"What's your aunt Betty have to say about all this? She blames me, right?"

"She says it's a mystery," David said.

"Really?" Genuine surprise, by David's stars.

"Really."

"Your aunt's a wise woman."

"That's true."

"'Cause that's the part that *is* a mystery. The *why.*"

"You must have some idea, Dad."

Dad! It just slipped.

"Must I, Son?" His father raised his eyebrows.

The limo kept moving. The lighter popped up. David took it and relit the cigar. He and his father smoked and kept eye contact.

"I'm sorry, David," said his father. "This isn't easy for me."

David nodded.

"Best man, huh?" he said.

"Apparently, every wedding needs one." David was no aficionado, but this seemed like a good cigar. "I'd be real grateful if you didn't change the subject, though."

A few more blocks passed.

"You know what you need to know about that?" his father said. "About your mother's, you know. How it ended."

"Everything is what I need to know about that."

"Everything," his father scoffed. "That's what you think."

"That's what I know."

"I wish I was a kid again," he said, "so I could know everything."

"I don't know anything," David said. "Tell me the things nobody's telling me."

His father shook his head. "It's McCarthy's fault."

"Excuse me?"

"McCarthy. That fucking beady-eyed, cheese-sucking mick. 'Tail-Gunner Joe,' my ass. One look at him, you can see he's a coward. He's got everyone thinking there's conspiracies behind this, schemes behind that. Like an investigation of a thing that you put on *television* is going to smoke out anything resembling the truth."

"C'mon. McCarthy? Gimme a break."

"You asked. Your cigar's out." He pressed the lighter down again.

David affected an impassive stare.

"Here's the central fact about all that, OK?" his father said. "When a person kills herself, you can't know why. Period. The person who can answer can't answer. Not just on account of she's dead, on account of she was of a state of mind where she couldn't say why even when she was about to do it. A person who kills herself isn't acting like herself. By *definition.* If that was how a person was, she'd kill herself every fucking day, which is a *scientific impossibility.* OK?"

"OK."

"So listen: you can't know. Period. Once you know *that*—"

The lighter popped up.

"Once you realize that's all you'll *ever* know, *then,* by god you finally know something."

He extended the lighter toward David.

David threw his cigar out the window.

"Some bum's gonna have himself a great smoke."

"Bums? Here?"

"Bums, crumbums, same dif," he said. "Maybe a hobo."

"A hobo?"

"Why not a hobo? Every place has the occasional hobo. Or gypsy."

"Tell your driver I need to get to work," David said. "If I'm going to be home before midnight." He glanced out, recognized the corner. "Here is good."

His father yelled that Shoes should stop, Shoes asked where, and Mikey Z said, "Here, you stupid fat fuck, what's *stop* mean to you?" All of this shouted through the closed partition.

Shoes stopped the car.

"Need any help with that?" Mike held up the rucksack.

David got out, got situated, then reached for the bag.

"Cracks me up." Mike handed it to him. "You think Stan and me are so different."

David laughed. "What are you suggesting?"

They stood next to each other, on a square of crumbling sidewalk. In the distance, David could see the crest of Terminal Tower.

"You want to go into this politics thing, for whatever reason I don't know or care to," Mike said, patting the bag full of Burke buttons and leaflets, "then at least go into it knowing the thing you need to know not to be a schmuck."

David couldn't think of any way to keep from hearing it. But his father waited and waited for the cue. Despite himself, David smiled. "All right, Dad," he said. This time he meant to say it. "OK. What is it?"

Mike Zielinsky pointed at his son, then touched him, gently, on the breastbone. "You're seeing differences that don't exist, categories that are made up so that suckers'll think everything's a . . ." He used his head to indicate a nearby porch, from which a radio broadcast of the Indians game played. "They think everything's a fucking ballgame. Team one, team two, one you root for, one you root against, one in one kind of uniform, the other in another. Dig it: in life there's no uniforms, and every player worth a shit plays on both teams."

Mikey Z pressed his hand flat against his son's chest. David leaned on his cane. He was having a rough time keeping his balance.

"Everything is what it is," said his father, "and also something else."

David felt completely like a man, able to see this for what it was.

And then his father kissed him on the cheek.

And David could see that, too, for what it was.

The two men observed a brief, respectful moment of manly silence.

"'Dig it'?" David said.

"Whattaya?" said his father. "Isn't that what you kids say?"

"Some kids," David admitted. "Mostly it only works if you're a Negro, a bongo-playing poet, or Frank Sinatra."

"Ah, but you forget," said his father. "I've met Sinatra."

"That doesn't make you Sinatra."

"You should hear me sing."

"You can sing?"

"I'm kidding," his father said. "Tell everybody to, like they say, vote early and often. Oh, yeah. And one other thing?"

"Yes?"

"Your hero Burke? He wasn't the one who hired your other hero, Ness. You're thinking of *Burton*. Not Burke. Bur-*ton*. Harold Burton. Judge Harold Burton? Member of the U.S. Supreme Court? Ring a bell? You want to be in politics, kid, keep your fuckin' facts straight."

"Really?" was all David could say. "Wasn't Burke—"

"Really," said his father. "It's not your fault, though. Cleveland! If you have the right name, people will vote for you, see. Only reason Burton was ever a senator was because there was a Democrat, also name of Burton, which caused people to get confused and vote for a Republican, which is what Burton was, see. And then Burton, he's a senator for a while and then what happens? Truman, a fuckin' Democrat, appoints the honorable Mr. Burton to the Supreme Court. See what I'm trying to tell you?"

David wasn't sure. But by then his father was gone.

⌒⌒

THE CANVASSING WENT OK until it didn't. David was nowhere near ready for that cane. After about an hour, he asked an old lady in a tiny pink house full of decrepit Pomeranians, all seemingly as old as the woman, if he could use her phone. At first she said no. Mayor Burke had fired her late husband from the fire department. Also, the world being what it was, she didn't think it wise to trust people anymore. But she sized David up, drenched in sweat and in obvious pain, reconsidered, and showed him into her kitchen. The house smelled of limburger cheese.

His aunt answered, got the address (she didn't need directions), and said she'd be right there. When she arrived, in her car, Stan was there, too. When they went somewhere together in her car, she drove. You did not often see a man like that, at that time and in that place, who rode shotgun. More rare still was that Stan had ridden along not out of overzealous concern for his nephew but, David realized, just because he liked being with his wife.

When they got home, Betty asked how dinner was.

"Fine," David said. "Uneventful."

∾

LATE THAT NIGHT, when he couldn't sleep, he went downstairs and took out his aunt's scrapbook, looking for pictures of his mother. Easy to see how the Hollywood thing happened: any picture she was in, even snapshots at picnics or taken at cast parties, all seemed a little like pinups or, at their grainiest, like shots you'd see in some rag like *Tinseltown Tattle*—all because his mother, Joan Zielinsky, was tall, thin, straight-standing, and high-cheekboned, all because in every photo, even the blurriest one, she looked like a woman you'd never meet.

There were several playbills in there, too. Many didn't seem to feature anyone David knew, until he realized (from the photos in the newspaper clippings inserted into some of them) that she played around with different stage names. "Joanie Ames." "Janet Sheraton." The one she seemed to have settled on was "Gigi Madison." He'd not come across this before. But it suited her. She looked just the way someone named Gigi Madison would look.

When she'd left, David was almost four years old. Looking over the pictures, his ruined knee propped up on an ottoman, he realized how many of the things he remembered about her really came from these photos. As far as true memories went, David wasn't sure he had one.

He took out Betty and Stan's wedding album. In it, Joan Zielinsky looked painfully pregnant. She was in the wedding party (a pregnant woman as a bridesmaid is "customarily inappropriate," David had gleaned from *The Wedding Embassy Yearbook*), which seemed to have included no one but Stan, Betty, their parents, Joan Luzinski, and Stan's older brother (also a cop; he was killed at Normandy; Stan's younger brother was a pediatrician in Milwaukee). Everyone looked so serious. Even when they were clowning around, it looked forced, as if, off camera, a much-loved dying great-aunt had, as her last request, asked everyone to please be zany. One thing you think about, looking at old pictures, is that year by year the human race has gotten less serious. David ran his finger over an image of his mother, in

[179]

alarming profile. *I'm the same age now,* he thought, nonplussed in the hammerhead way of insomniac epiphanies, *as she is there.*

∽

SUMMER NIGHTS! WHAT is there to say about summer nights in Cleveland? This: *Rock it, daddy-o!* In Cleveland there is no spring. In Cleveland there is winter, then a wetter, meaner sort of winter (to be a Clevelander is to have a story about a ten-inch snowfall in April that you endured with good grace, a story you tell, whenever the chance arises, to horrified Sun Belt pantywaists). Then one day winter/wet-winter ends and, *bingo-bango,* it's summertime. After enduring what a person made of less-stern stuff than a Clevelander would confront in five winters, ten winters, maybe even a lifetime of winters, you've by god *earned* your nine and one-half paradisiacal weeks of nighttime glory. You're Goldilocks, baby, and you've spent twenty-some weeks in the too-hard bed and twenty-some in the too-soft, and you hit the sheets on Baby Bear's bed and you can't *believe* how heavenly it feels to feel just right. Just right!

But this ain't no fairy tale, jack. Get your fairy tales the pantywaist hell out of Cleveland.

Better switch metaphors.

After the brutal Cleveland winter, you attack and savor summer nights with (switching metaphors but retaining the heavenly) the fervor a righteous man might bring to the happy news that, here in heaven, stogies, single-malts, and rewarding multiorgasmic sexual intercourse as the preamble to social intercourse, rather than its holy, marriage-bound culmination, are devoid of unpleasant consequences and are in fact encouraged. To cite God's memorable phrase: "On earth, *bad;* in heaven, *good.*" Enjoy!

This was never more true than it was in the summer of '54. Hot, in every possible sense of the word. Oh, to be twenty years old, with your baseball team in first place all summer long, and your wedding coming up that fall, to the childhood sweetheart who's become your fiancée and is about to become your wife (and who's already pregnant; neither one of you know, though she has an idea). Oh, to be twenty, and, on the nights you don't spend with that fiancée, to ride around in the dark, frittering away nights with old boon pals you've outgrown but pretend not to have. Oh, to be driven around in souped-up cars like Skeezix Soltesz's '38 Mercury or Little Al Vronski's '48 Plymouth, and to turn up those tinny AM radios and to hear coming out of them *Bill Randle!* the rockin' and rollin' sound of *Bill Randle!* on *WHK rock-and-roll radio!* You were digging that music before anyone you knew and now your friends are on the bandwagon, a wagon driven not by Alan Freed but by Randle, Freed's pallid, annoyingly sane successor. Freed is gone and so is your childhood. You feel older at twenty than any of your children will, than any future American generation ever will, and so what? It's all *so* right, *so* perfect and true, to have summer night after hot summer night stretching out for you, and hot wind in your face and a college education on your horizon and a candidate you believe in and a career that you can feel passionate in the pursuit of! It's *so* right, *so* perfect and true, to have the love of a good woman in your present and future, and children coming, sooner than you think (and that will be great news! great news!) and to be able to ride through the hot Cleveland night and push those hard analog dashboard buttons! *Ksh-thum,* "...to present to you, the new hot wax from the Beale Street Blues Boy himself, the one and only Mister B.B. King!" *Ksh-thum,* "...and at the end of six, your Cleveland Indians 9, the New York Yankees 1!" *Ksh-thum,* "...who knows what evil lurks in the hearts of men?" *Ksh-thum,* "...good-rockin' hillbilly cat from Tennessee! Listen to that boy wail!" *Ksh-thum,* "...mambo, mambo Italiano." *Ksh-thum, ksh-thum, ksh-thum,* "...whether the Sheppard family will have any response to this latest bombshell remains to be seen," says a sexy voice at the end of the dial. "Reporting from Bay Village, this is Anne O'Connor, WCRB news."

LOCAL HEROES

୧୨

Second in a Series: The Longest Out
September 29, 1954

VIC WERTZ SWINGS. Swings that long, lethal, left-handed swing and connects! A smash, a screamer, a shot, a bomb: hissing and rising, to dead center. Man'll play seventeen years in the big leagues, and this—with the eyes of the world upon him, when it counts the most—is as hard as he will ever hit a baseball. There are Hall of Famers, immortals, who've never hit a ball so hard.

Watch it go.

(As it does, Cleveland is the best place in America. Iron-rich, irony-poor. Hot, exciting, burly, booming, industrious, earnest, capitalist, strong, civil, just, and free.[1] Winners. Everything Cleveland touches turns to high-grade steel. Example: the one thing wrong with the '54 Indians is that their first baseman can't hit. So, midseason, they get better by getting Wertz, a three-time All-Star Baltimore traded to Cleveland for next to nothing. Wertz, an outfielder, had never played first, but play first he does, and well, and the Indians win more games than any team in league history, and on the day they clinch the pennant, the day New York has to choke on its smirk and call Cleveland "champions," someone takes a tube of lipstick and, on the wide bald head of the twenty-nine-year-old Wertz, writes, WE'RE IN. A great shot;

---

[1] By the standards of 1954 America.

the photographers snap it, the wire services send it out, and the picture runs in every American newspaper worth its ink. Whose lipstick? What was lipstick doing in a Major League Baseball locker room? Ever get the feeling that the things you most want to know about history are the questions no one ever asks? That the essence of history is the details lost to it?)

Willie Mays. Polo Grounds. Game One. World Series. Day game. Wednesday. Cleveland 2, New York 2. Two on. Doby. Rosen. Top of the eighth.

(Bad enough that this has to happen; why does it have to happen in New York? Huh? Why, why, why, fucking why? Because. God is the most shameless of classical dramatists. Let us thank Him for our food. The ostensibly inconsequential moment that will presage Cleveland's descent into loserdom and laff-riot Rust Belt bathos necessarily must come at the hands of its nemesis: NYC. Apotheosized in the gloved left hand of young, racing, dashing Willie Mays. Christ. It figures. If a thing like this is going to happen, it figures it's going to happen to Cleveland. Cleveland gets past its nemesis, the Yankees, who won every damned pennant since Cleveland's last one. And what happens? Catch a train to New York to face the underdog Giants. Underdogs from New York? Right. New Yorkers may be surprised to learn that the rest of America has been scorned, abandoned, and upstaged by New York so often as to render "New York underdog" oxymoronic. Burn in hell, Yankees, Giants, Dodgers, Mets, Jets, Nets, Knicks, Rangers, Islanders, and most fitting of all Devils.[2] Burn in hell, ye fans of any of these. Also, your families. Your dentists, attorneys, insurance agents, greengrocers, neighbors, lovers, old flames, and the rest of your circle of immediate acquaintance. Burn in hell, anybody anywhere who has ever made a Cleveland joke. Present company excepted.)

As the ball rockets out of the infield, Doby and Rosen run. The ball's uncatchable.

Willie Mays plays the shallowest but also the best center field of his or any time, and he takes off running, running. His hat falls off.[3] Back, back, back, back, back. A dead run.

Forty feet from where the ball will eventually land, it passes a point that, in every other ballpark in the big leagues, would have been the outfield fence.

---

[2] Yes, yes: strictly speaking, the Nets, Islanders, and Devils never were NYC teams, and the Jets, Dodgers, and (football and baseball) Giants no longer are. You want to speak strictly, fine: the Cuyahoga River's worst polluters were upriver, outside the city of Cleveland.

[3] Look, nothing against Willie Mays, but he wore a too-small hat just for show.

In a cloud of dust, Doby, who'd come to this moment from the places Mays had (only more so), digs in his spikes. He runs back to second to tag up. Rosen couldn't have dreamed it, and keeps going.

Mays is all elbows and knees and wind and grace, and with his back to the plate, *460 feet from home*, still on the pure dead run, he sticks up his glove and as the ball shoots over his left shoulder he spears it—*spears it*—and in the same impossibly fluid motion, spins and fires the ball back to the infield.

A gape-mouthed world slaps itself in the forehead, so hard it hurts. Dis-fucking-belief. Learn it to the younguns.

(Watch it again: spears it, spins, fires the ball back to the infield. A spectator slaps himself in the head. Mays spears it, spins, and fires it back to the infield. A spectator slaps himself in the head. It is the highlight film to end all highlight films, destined to be threaded and rethreaded, played and replayed. It is television's first universally indelible sports highlight. If you are from Cleveland, it is a moment you cannot stand to see and cannot stop watching. Spears it, spins, fires the ball back to the infield. A spectator slaps himself in the head. Play it again. I can't go on; I'll go on. Watch it. This clip is to Cleveland as, nine years from now, the Zapruder film will be to JFK. As for Cleveland's demise: Mays did not act alone.)

Doby tags. He makes it to third. Rosen is nearly thrown out, trying to get back to first.

Had the game been played in Cleveland, the score would be 5–2. In New York, it remains tied. Goes to extra innings, which is to say that without the catch, Cleveland wins. One out, bottom of tenth, with Mays on second, Hank Thompson on first, and with Cleveland ace Bob Lemon still on the mound, Giants manager Leo Durocher[4] inserts as a pinch hitter a bench-warmer by the too-cute name of Dusty Rhodes. Pinch-hitting for Monte Irvin, the Giants' star left fielder and a future Hall of Famer? Crazy.

As Wertz (removed for a defensive replacement) watches from the bench, Rhodes lofts Lemon's first pitch over the spot where Wertz would have been standing and down the right-field line. Rhodes runs like hell. Routine fly ball.

In any park but this one.

Had the game been played in Cleveland, Indians right fielder Dave Pope

---

[4] Ironically managing the team about which, as manager of the Dodgers, he once gave the following pennant-chances appraisal: "Nice guys." He shrugged. "Finish last." Note that this was not said about Cleveland. Also that Durocher did *not* make the blanket statement "Nice guys finish last." That's a misquote. It may be the truth, of course, but it's not a fact.

would have hauled down the easy out. But this is the Polo Grounds, a former... well, polo grounds. Its ridiculously oblong perimeter results in the game's deepest center field and its shallowest right and left.

Rhodes's ball—hit 260 feet, barely half as far as Wertz's drive—sails over the fence. Guess who scores the winning run? Willie Mays. Final score: New York 5, Cleveland 2.

Wertz stands, watches, winces. He cannot believe it. For a moment, he cusses inventively.

Still, this is baseball. A long season. Can't get too high or too low. As he heads to the showers, Wertz takes a series of deep breaths and does not allow himself to think about injustice. Vic Wertz thinks about tomorrow. Today was just one game of a possible seven. Things even out. We'll get 'em tomorrow. That's what he thinks.

∾

GOD, IT GETS *so much* worse.

Game Two, the Indians go ahead early, 1–0. "Early": a good omen, right, with Early Wynn pitching?[5] Wynn is in command. Until: in the fifth inning, Durocher again pinch-hits that scrub Dusty Rhodes for Irvin, and Rhodes bloops a single to center, scoring (yep) Mays. Worse yet: Rhodes stays in the game and in the seventh hits (yep) another cheap-ass homer to right. Two homers in the Series that, together, traveled about as far as Vic Wertz's long out. New York wins, 3–1.

The Series takes the train back to Cleveland. No off day. In Game Three Durocher, ridiculously, pinch-hits Rhodes for Irvin in the *second inning*. Two-run single. By the end of the inning, it's 4–0 New York. Final score: New York 6, Cleveland 2.

Rhodes's three pinch hits are a World Series record.

"I ain't thinkin' about no records," says Rhodes. "All I care about is seein' us win."

Wertz is batting .500 for the Series. No other Indian is hitting his weight. "So nobody's won the Series after losing the first three," Wertz says. "So what? Nobody in our league ever won 111 games either. Maybe we're due for another first."

(For most of the rest of the American century, Cleveland will be tormented by the gulf between what it is due for and what it's going to get.)

---

[5] His real name. A future Hall of Famer, Wynn will win three hundred games in the big leagues. But not this one.

The less said about Game Four, the better. Rhodes doesn't play, Wertz goes 2 for 4 and Cleveland loses 7–4. It's over, and how. The heavily favored Indians were swept. For the record, it happened both in Cleveland and to Cleveland.[6]

(To be precise, the idea that if some strange and humiliating thing is going to happen, it figures it'll happen to Cleveland—that idea doesn't exist yet. You are present at the creation. Worse things will happen. Things of more consequence. But in retrospect, a forty-year diet of shit sandwiches starts here. "In case you need me," says the waiter, "my name is Gotham.")

New York is the Champion of the World. To think anyone would celebrate *that!*

New York an underdog? Please. Goliath kills David. That's what we're looking at. Dewey defeats Truman. Casey at the Bat swats a three-run homer. Things like that. The Giant eats Jack. New York punks Cleveland. Who the fuck wants to read *that* kind of story?

☙

WORSE YET.

The next season Cleveland, still a terrific team, is locked in a tight pennant race with (surprise) the Yankees, when in August Vic Wertz goes on the disabled list with polio.

(Yes, polio. Polio! Polo to polio. What's going to get him next, a politico?)

Without Wertz, Cleveland struggles. New York wins the pennant by three games.

Doctors say Wertz's career is over.

In truth, it was. But in fact, Wertz comes back. He hits a career-high thirty-two homers in 1956 and is an All-Star again in 1957. In 1958 he blows out his knee.[7] In the off season he is traded to Boston for a talented lunatic.[8] The year after that, Cleveland trades its best player, Rocky Colavito, for a washed-up former star named Harvey Kuenn. After fifteen years of being

---

[6] Only two other times that century were heavily favored teams swept: Philadelphia (Cleveland's East Coast soulmate) in 1914 and Oakland (the Cleveland of northern California) in 1990. Fellow long-suffering butts of jokes, brothers and sisters, we embrace you!

[7] Today, every sports fan knows what an anterior cruciate ligament is. Every team has a star who's torn it, had it replaced, and come magnificently back. Then, doctors had no idea how to fix it, to the lingering dismay of Vic Wertz, David Zielinsky, and legions of the semi-lame.

[8] Jimmy Piersall. Portrayed in the 1957 movie version of his life by *Psycho* star Tony

one of baseball's proudest teams (if perennial bridesmaids to the Yankees), the Indians embark on a string of thirty-five consecutive seasons in which they will not seriously contend.

Cleveland embarks on a string of thirty-five years in which it will not seriously contend.

As for Wertz, he manages to display what heartland sportswriters call *grit*—code for *this fellow is a mediocre, hardworking Caucasian*—and ekes out five post-Cleveland years in the majors, bouncing from Boston to Detroit to Minnesota, released and rereleased, until no one wants him anymore. When he is finished, he is an old thirty-eight. What little hair he has is gray. He is slower afoot than an arthritic dog.

Seventeen years in Major League Baseball. Four All-Star teams. And what is he remembered for? A long out.

In 1983, shortly before his death, with the Indians mired in last place and still twelve years shy of their first play-off appearance since that '54 Series, Vic Wertz tells a reporter he's proud of hitting that ball, happy to be forever an enabler of the greatness of Willie Mays. If it *had* been a home run, or even a double or a triple, Wertz says, would anyone remember me?

Now, his face is lost to history. His career is lost to history. But as long as there is baseball, as long as there are television sets on which to watch it, Vic Wertz's long out lives.

It happened in a World Series in which he hit an even .500, a Series his team lost through no fault whatsoever of his. Yet he is the personification of that loss. The man you never see, the man who hit the ball that became the catch you see all the time, the one you can't believe.

Spears it, spins, fires the ball back to the infield. A spectator slaps himself in the head.

By the time Cleveland makes it back to a World Series, Vic Wertz will have been dead for a dozen years.

He lived.

He died.

For the record, it is possible—examples include beheaded chickens, soldiers the split second after being bisected by a machine gun, or the city of Cleveland, circa 1954–1969—to be dead without knowing it.

Perkins, who threw like a girl, back when that simile offended virtually no one. Today, of course, things are entirely different. Today Piersall's condition could be treated with psychoactive drugs.

8

IN RETROSPECT, SHE was bound to run into David Zielinsky somewhere. In real life, Anne O'Connor didn't see it coming.

Where it happened was west of Cleveland, at the far edge of Cuyahoga County, under a big white tent, the hot dusk air tangy with the smells of fried dough, manure, and roasted corn. It was a Thursday, three days before she was supposed to go back to Smith College.

What brought Anne to the Cuyahoga County Fair was her job. What is there for a radio news reporter to do at a county fair? Anyone's guess— which was how Hoot Thagard had presented it. "Be extemporaneous," he'd said. "Follow, you know, your...ah, nose." Mr. Thagard said *extemporaneous* like a man stunned to have thought of the word. He'd be broadcasting a daylong version of *Swap Meet* (100 percent extemporaneously) from a panel truck at the edge of a parking lot, near the poultry barn. People brought what they wanted to sell to the panel truck and Mr. Thagard helped them describe it. Often this involved the livestock on exhibit or the vehicle the seller in question had driven to the fair. Back at the studio, fat paranoid DJs fielded bids. Anne's job was to come by every hour on the halfhour with the latest county fair news. Such as it was. It was good to have an assignment, however vague, but did it have to be something so square? (Questions she heard herself ask: "Could you characterize the difference between a house trailer and a mobile home?" "A *sulky* is what, now?" "What about the fourth *H* in 4H?" "Are aboveground pools here to stay?" "Did you always want to be a clown?") Plus, she hated taking time away from the Sheppard case. She had her bearings and was *this close* to digging up actual news. She could feel it. Instead, she was stuck at the fair.

At home, to allay suspicion, she'd packed her bags—for school, she knew her parents would think, though she had other ideas—and made a production of setting them in the middle of the upstairs hall. A steamer trunk and two hard green Samsonite suitcases that her brother John had given her when she graduated from prep school. She still hadn't told her parents, either of them, that she no longer worked for the *News*. Finished with her radio duties for the day, Anne had come to that big white tent to tell her father just that.

Anne recognized David immediately. This, even though his hair was longer and he was wearing what can only be described as Clark Kent glasses. His shoulders were startlingly more broad. He sat behind a table, dressed in a (sweated-through) starched white shirt and thin tie, handing out candidate-touting leaflets, key rings, pens, pencils, pins, and yardsticks.

The pang that shot through her! Never in her wildest. The shock, she told herself. The unexpectedness of this. What it was, was surprise. Period.

The tent was filled with volunteers and politicians. In the far back corner stood Anne's father, involved in what seemed like an unhappy exchange with three well-dressed Negro men. She caught his eye; he nodded and raised one finger.

Finally, David did notice her. But not really. As she stood there, frozen in the face of a confrontation other than the one she'd come there to have, he handed her a leaflet.

"Vote Burke," he said.

She took it with her left hand. She extended her right. "I don't know if you remember me," she said. "My name is Anne O'Connor. We played table tennis up at—"

"Oh my god." He looked up. Behind the glasses, and perhaps magnified by them, his eyes grew panic-wide. "It's . . ."

"I don't need this," she said.

She handed the leaflet back to him. She flipped her hair. She stood straight.

"What . . . ," he said. That was all he said. She let a few moments pass, to let him suffer.

"As you may remember," she finally said, "or perhaps not, since, if I re-call, I misled you about my age," she said, "I'm not old enough to vote."

"I remember," he said. It was hard to tell how he said it. "Of course I remember."

What was he doing here? Did he know her father? Had they talked about her, behind her back? Anne had a dream like this once. In it, she happened upon her Western civ prof (who'd made a clumsy pass at her) and her brother Steven (dead now for ten years), drinking Pepsi, playing driveway basketball, and acting like boon pals. Happily, Mamie Eisenhower and a bear dressed like a priest challenged Steven and Dr. Mangan to a game of two-on-two, and Anne woke up.

(Noninstitutionalized midwestern Catholics hadn't yet discovered psychotherapy.)

Anne and David looked each other in the eye, nodding like simpletons.

"Well," she said.

"Well," he said.

Nearby, drunken auto-plant workers swung sledgehammers and rang bells. A midway barker barked. A caterwauling toddler was asked if he'd like something to cry about. The tractor-sounding motor of a Tilt-A-Whirl geared up. Under the tent, other members of the party faithful laughed phony laughs. Over all this came the booming voice of Anne's father, summoning someone.

"So," Anne finally said to David. "We meet again." It was all she could think to say, this line of bad moviespeak. She hoped it sounded ironic.

"My god," said David. "Wow. Whattaya know? It's you."

"It is I." Archly grammatical; quasi-irony. All it got from David was more nodding. "Bang!" she said, holding her hand like a pistol. " 'They went thataway.' " She blew on the end of her index finger. "Remember?"

"I got into all kinds of dutch about that car," he said.

"If I'd have ever *heard* from you again, I would have paid—"

"Forget it," David said. "It was as much my fault as yours. Water over the bridge."

"Over the dam."

"Right." He laughed. "Right, right. Hey!" he said. "I heard you on the radio. Boy, that's impressive."

"That wasn't me," she said. Her father was probably out of earshot, but why risk it?

"Anne O'Connor," he said, oblivious. "Jeez, you look like a million bucks. I can't believe it. How've you been?"

"OK, *don't* believe it. I lied." She lowered her voice. "It was me. On the radio." Was that *million bucks* thing a crack? Did it have to do with her belated offer to pay for the wrecked car? "I've been swell. I can't believe it either, seeing you here. So you're a Burke man, huh?"

"Absolutely." He broke into an overprepared debater's litany of all that was wrong with George Bender—including his poor record on labor issues and how the racketeering hearings he's staging are a union-busting sham, a cynical attempt to get his name in the papers—and succinctly to extol the manifold virtues of that great American, Senator Thomas Burke.

She nearly told him that Burke was a friend of her family and that his appointment to the U.S. Senate (to fulfill the term of Robert A. Taft, a man known as Mr. Republican) had been brokered by her father. She stopped herself. Nothing more powerful than a loaded, unfired gun.

David just kept talking and talking about Burke.

"You're looking good yourself," she said, to put him out of his misery. "Older. I don't know: distinguished." That long, bean-shaped midwestern face, such a contrast to smirky prep-school smartalecks she'd been bred to fall in love with. Her girlish mistake at Kelley's Island had been to think that she could fall in love with a boy from such a different background. The thing to do was become friends with him, this vantage point to a world she found so much more real than hers. Friends. This was what she was thinking. It was then she noticed his leg, stiff and encased in a brace so elaborate his trouser leg was cut to fit over it. She pointed. "The war?"

"Excuse me?"

"Did you, you know . . . ?" For a moment, she flashed on an image of her brother. Smiling. Playing the cornet. Playing a note-by-note copy of a Beiderbecke record. No one talked about Steven. Steven, dead, shot down. Blown away. She swallowed. "In Korea?"

"Oh!" he said. "Yeah. I mean no. Kind of."

Despite herself, she laughed. This was funny enough that she stopped thinking about her brother. "Kind of?" she said.

"It's a long story," he said.

She would have thought she'd be mad at him. But what had gone on between them had happened two years ago—a lifetime. No reason at all not to be continental about it and laugh it off. She repeated it: *"Kind of?"*

He relented. The injury occurred during a basketball game, he said, at a naval base outside Los Angeles. He told her the story.

"That counts!" she said. "You wouldn't have *been* there to play basketball if you weren't, you know. Serving your country. Right?"

He shrugged. He blushed. "Yeah," he said. "I guess."

Men! Compliment something they've done and gain the upper hand. Simple, simple, simple. Tell everyone.

⚭

ANNE O'CONNOR AND David Zielinsky couldn't have avoided meeting again. They were bound, by accident (history's fulcrum), to intersect. No coincidence needed. Unthinkable that a Cleveland pol wouldn't come in time to know every reporter in town, and vice versa.

Everything is the same thing.

Plus, it can be scientifically proven that Cleveland is the smallest big city in America (also the biggest small one). It is a city where, metaphorically and often literally, everyone lives ten minutes from his mother. Even if he doesn't have one. Anne's running into David at the big white tent in the summer of 1954 was merely a matter of sooner triumphing over later.

Call it chaos theory. Call it Murphy's law. Call it history. Any chaos theoretician, Murphy's lawyer, or historian could sit you down in the parlor, pull out the slide projector, and show you. Grab a beer, friend. Watch sooner kick later's saggy-cheeked ass.

༖

"LISTEN," DAVID SAID, "about that summer—"

Anne shook her head. "Don't."

This flummoxed him.

"Really," she said. "Not necessary."

Under the corner of the tent, her father and a couple of his cronies were finishing with the Negroes. The man her father had called over had turned out to be Thomas Burke himself, which Anne, out of kindness, did not point out to David. Everyone was shaking hands. Her father smiled. It did not look to Anne like a real smile.

David was looking at her expectantly. On the fringe of her attention, he may have said the word *ketchup*.

"I'm sorry," she said. "Did you say something?"

"A pop," he said. "A milk shake, coffee, whatever you want. Lemonade."

To catch up. That's what he'd said.

"I can't," she said. "I'd love to, but I can't. I have to—"

Explanation failed her. She shook her head and, in frustration, wagged both hands the same way one would in a ladies' room that had run out of hand towels. She left him there, with his embossed combs and church keys, and went around the other end of the table.

Extemporaneous.

"Babe!" her father said.

She did not like to be called this anymore. As he hugged her, she flinched. She felt David watching this.

Thomas O'Connor asked her where her friends were. Anne drew a blank. "Oh!" she said. "My friends. They're over by the poultry barn."

This had been a lie she'd told him, that she was going to the fair with some old prep friends—a cover for why she'd be at the fair, why she'd be able to swing by and meet him here. (Though, in a broader sense, she will look back on her life and wonder where her friends were. A popular girl, surrounded by people, friendly with everyone in sight and yet friendless.)

"We need to talk. We need to go somewhere," she said. "And talk."

"This isn't a good time, Babe," he said.

"Right," she said. "Of course it's not."

He looked at his watch. Fine, he told her, OK; for her he could spare ten minutes. He lifted the back flap of the tent and showed Anne through. Anne glanced back at David. He wasn't watching.

Her father took her to someone's office underneath the grandstand. He had a key. The office was filled with bags of lime, dozens of folded folding chairs, a tiny desk, and two stools. The warped paneling was festooned with faded pictures of cars and pinup girls. Anne and her father sat on the stools.

"Do you know that boy?" she said.

"Which boy?"

"The one I was talking to," she said. "At the front table? David something. Zielinsky."

Tom shrugged. "Should I? Is that what you needed to talk about?"

She shook her head.

"Because if you want to talk about boys," he said, "go ahead. I used to be one."

She rolled her eyes. "That's as old as grandma's toe and twice as corny," she said, "and so is that."

"Smart girl."

"On the button."

"Cute as one, too," he said.

"Da-a-ad!" It was a reflex; she hated the way she sounded when she said that.

"So what is it? Shoot, sheriff."

She took a deep breath. She began. Her father listened, poker-faced, to her long explanation of her job and how she'd gotten it, how much she liked it, how at first it was just a lark but now she just *couldn't* leave for school, not with the chance to cover a national news story like the Sheppard case. Chance of a lifetime. She'd go back to Smith in the spring, or, if the trial dragged on, next summer. At the latest.

When she finished, her father let out a long breath. Over his shoulder were Betty Grable and a Studebaker President. Over the other one was a faded 1939 calendar (February; Gigi Madison; John Deere tractor), a long, bland Chrysler, and Lana Turner. "I'd been wondering," he said, "when you'd finally tell me."

Of *course* he knew. How could she not have known he'd know? "How'd you find out?"

"Last I checked," he said, "no one's found a way to make the public air-waves private."

She doubted he'd found out about this himself. WCRB's signal wasn't strong enough to reach the East Side; you'd lose it right about the time you crossed the river. But too many people knew her father; too many people were eager to cash in on the political favor they could get from telling him a thing he didn't already know. Why hadn't she used a made-up name? Ego? "Does Mother know?"

"If she does," he said, "it didn't come from me. Mum's the word. Ha."

"So?" she said. On with it.

Her father ran his hands over his thighs. "I should probably be angry," he said. "I should try to talk you out of it, but..." He stared out the office's one tiny window. "You're such a mixture, you know? Of... how can I say this? Of the most strong and stubborn parts of both your mother and me? *She* won't like this plan of yours, I can tell you, but..."

A grin betrayed him. He'd go along with Anne's plan because, at bottom, it was a matter of him and his daughter versus his wife. Anne was too young to grasp the downside of this.

"The Sheppard case, huh?"

Anne nodded.

"I can't, personally, think of anything more trivial," he said. "Not to diminish that poor woman who was murdered, but people get murdered every day. Why this case?"

When Anne started to answer, her father waved her off. "Rhetorical question. That's just me talking. It takes all kinds. I see what's happening with this... matter. I'm not stupid about how reporters pick the things they're going to play up. If you want to think this Sheppard thing is a story, think it's a story. No skin off my nose."

Years later Anne will appreciate what-all her father succeeded in not saying. She wanted to be a career woman, something no one on either his or his wife's side of the family had ever been, and he went right along with it. Plus, no politician could be thrilled at the implicit rebellion involved in one of his children becoming a reporter, yet never did he breathe a discouraging word. Worse, the Sheppard case was the pet cause of his nemesis, that demagogue Seltzer. The Sheppard case was just a symptom. The cause: in the '53 mayoral race, Seltzer had backed Celebrezze, and the machine backed Bert Porter, the city engineer and, not coincidentally, brother of the editor of the *PD*. Tom O'Connor disliked Bert Porter and feared he'd alienate the Negroes. This wasn't a fear shared by many others running the machine. Bert had paid his dues; it was his turn. When Celebrezze won, the machine was hobbled, and the *Press* had won a huge victory over the *Plain Dealer*. Months later, fat and sassy with victory, Seltzer used the Sheppard case to trumpet his new power, to extend its limits. The subtext to the Sheppard affair—readable, by those in the know, between every line of Seltzer's unsigned front-page editorials—was Louie the Office Boy's daily fuck-you to the *PD*, Tom O'Connor, and the machine. Anne was not in the know; her father could have (but did not) set her straight. But even back *then*, laboring under the crippling self-involvement of youth, she might have understood what a kick in the teeth it was for her to be gaga over the pet cause of her father's nemesis. To be forsaking college, as Seltzer had, to go to work as a reporter. This must all have occurred to Tom O'Connor. But he said nothing.

"So tell me," he said, "what is it that you need from me?"

Anne had it all figured out. "Tell mother," she said.

"Done," he said. Anne did not pick up on the sadism in his tone.

"And," she said, "let me move out. Let me get my own apartment."

He turned to her. He looked at her for a long time.

A long time.

He got up from his stool. He went to the things on the wall, the women and the cars, and began straightening them. With his back to her, he took out a tortoiseshell comb and ran it through his slicked and unmussed hair.

She did not think about her father naked. Naked, and holding that gun. She did not.

He sat down on the edge of the desk. Still he was facing away from her.

"I'm sorry, Babe," he whispered, "about how it's been. At home. Your mother and I aren't . . ." He tilted his head, as if out that window was a sight too curious to process. He straightened his tie. "It's complicated. I'm sorry for what—if any—part I've played in," he said, "any unpleasantness."

He was the sort of man who apologized without looking at you. This could have been part of why he'd only served one term as mayor.

He got up. He turned to his daughter, his arms extended to hug her, or at least touch her.

She pulled back.

"My own apartment," Anne insisted. The blunt, streamlined demands of the young! Anne's hands were balled into fists. She couldn't believe she was doing this. What it felt like to her was that her life was beginning.

Thomas O'Connor nodded. "I'll make you a deal. Keep your job, go back to school later. But no apartment," he said. "You want an apartment? Take the carriage house."

Outside, a keening tractor and the crowd it was entertaining had nearly drowned her father out, but Anne heard. The carriage house was a combination guest house and painting studio for her mother. Hard to believe, Anne thought, that her father liked the idea of guests in the main house, in one of the four empty bedrooms there, close to whatever domestic obstreperousness might erupt. Also, Anne really did want her own place. But (a) she couldn't afford it, and (b) she didn't want to push her luck. She'd come too far not to take what was being offered.

"You'll tell Mother?" she said.

There was a flicker of a grin, and he nodded.

⊙

THE NEXT MORNING Anne was up early and out of the house before her father could have had a chance to tell her mother anything. For years they'd slept in separate (locked) bedrooms, and her mother drank too much to be a morning person.

Before she met up with Mr. Thagard at the fair (he and Flossie were there already, interviewing concessionaires, reading recipes for sloppy joes and elephant ears, explaining how—with supplies they suspected their listeners already had in their homes—one could make a snow cone, sans special equipment, up to and including syrup of de rigueur, postnuclear colors), Anne swung by the studio to follow up on a tip she'd gotten on the Sheppard case.

It had come from the (married) copy desk editor from the *News,* who still called Anne once in a while, a connection she worked to her advantage when she got him to introduce her to one of the *News* reporters (a woman!) assigned to the Sheppard case. That was how Anne had gotten the name of the private eye the Sheppard family hired (the Sheppards hired more than one; it was a flawed tip).

"Lychak Investigations," said the voice on the phone.

Anne identified herself and asked to talk to Mr. Stanley Lychak. The split second she did, the name, which had rung a bell, rang a louder one.

"So," said David Zielinsky, "we meet again."

⊙

SUNDAY MORNING ANNE awoke to the sound of her mother and the cook dragging Anne's steamer trunk down the center stairs. The day had barely dawned. It was a ferociously unlikely hour for Sarah O'Connor to be awake, much less awake and wrestling someone else's luggage. Her own valise was already in the Cadillac.

"Where do you think you're taking that?"

"Hurry up, young lady," called Sarah. These were the first words she'd spoken to her daughter in two weeks. "We need to be on the road."

It was ten after six. Anne had been out late the night before, among the three carfuls of the fellow trust-funded who'd gone to a club on East 55th to see Big Joe Turner.

"I forbid it." Sarah and the cook stopped on the landing. "An apartment? Please. We've already sent your tuition in, and you're going. How are you going to afford an apartment?"

He didn't tell her yet?

"Affording it's not the issue," Sarah said. The cook averted her eyes. She was new. Anne didn't know her name. "Though god knows if you want money, you won't get it from us."

"I don't—"

"I shouldn't say that. Certainly your father will find a way to slip you money. I have no illusions to the contrary. *Would* find a way. I am speaking in the hypothetical, since none of this is going to happen. School days, school days, good ol' golden rule days. Shower up, Cinderella."

Anne came down to the landing and blocked her mother's way. "Actually," Anne said, "I'm moving into the carriage house. It was his idea, but I'm in favor of it, too."

Sarah slapped her. It was not a particularly hard slap. In silence, close enough to feel the other's breathing, Anne and her mother stared at one another.

The cook squeezed past them without even saying *pardon me,* without saying anything at all, descended the stairs alone, and walked right out the front door. Anne and Sarah didn't know it yet, but she wasn't coming back.

At the sound of the front door closing, Anne turned, ran back up the stairs, slammed her bedroom door, and locked it.

The sturdy doors in that grand house! Their fine locks! Just tremendous, tremendous quality. You can't buy materials like that anymore. And the workmanship that put it all together, forget about it. Those days are gone, my friend.

For an hour, and then an hour more, and an hour after that, Anne sat on her bed, her knees to her chest, rocking slowly back and forth, weathering wave after wave of the screaming and pounding and pure white-hot fury of Sarah O'Connor. Sobbing. Shouting. Name-calling. More fitful sobbing. At one point Sarah's pounding took on a metallic cast. Andirons, Anne guessed. The door began to splinter but did not come close to giving way.

Anne's father was in the house somewhere, presumably in his bedroom, but in this battle he had fired all the salvos he was going to. Never in all this did Anne hear her mother yelling at him. All of it was directed at Anne.

Anne withstood, and said nothing. Not a word. She held herself, rocked, did not cry, and waited. She held herself.

Late morning a lull came. It stretched for a half hour, then more. Anne wondered when this would be over. Now? She got out of bed. Unshowered, she got dressed—an ancient pair of chinos and an undershirt she'd worn home one time when she'd stayed overnight at Patrick and Ibby's: clothes she'd planned to abandon along with the room. She tied her hair in a kerchief. She had not often jumped out of her window, but it was possible. All there was to miss was a yew tree and a small hedge of rhododendrons. Jump out and over, hit with bended knees and roll.

There came a knock at the door. Softly, her mother said her name.

"It's not a matter of the carriage house," said Sarah. "You understand that, don't you?"

Anne cleared her throat. "I'm not sure I understand anything," she said.

"I can paint anywhere," Sarah said. "Outside. On the sleeping porch. In one of the spare rooms. I'm afraid you think I'm just angry about that. Is that what you think, Babe?"

"I'm not sure I think anything," Anne said. "Except that I want to keep doing my job and I want an apartment. If you're not mad about the carriage house," she said, "then what are you mad about?"

"I'm not mad, Babe."

She's not mad? "What do you call all that? The pounding? You're mad, all right."

"No, I'm not," she said. "I'm frustrated."

"Tomato/tomahto," Anne said. "Stop calling me *Babe,* OK?"

"Your father doesn't understand," said Sarah, pausing to take a drag from her cigarette, "the value of a college education for a girl."

Oh, sure: look how far it's gotten *her.* Look at her! In a different context, Anne would have said this. Now, though, Anne felt as if she'd absorbed every blow her door had. She looked like it, too. She'd gripped her upper arms so hard they were covered with mauve bruises. On her cheek was a pink outline of her mother's hand.

"I'm going back," Anne called. "No one ever said I wasn't going back. I'll get my degree. It's only a matter of when."

Her mother slapped the door, once. Then there was a long silence.

"It's fine," her mother said. "I'll help you move into the carriage house. We can fix it up for you, together." She said this the way she might have suggested a trip to go get ice cream.

Anne let another long silence stretch out.

"You mean it?" she said.

"Absolutely," said her mother.

"This isn't a trick?"

"Babe." Said in a *how-could-you* tone. "Sorry," she said. "Force of habit. I'm sorry."

Anne opened the door.

Her mother grabbed her. Anne's heart jolted and she prepared to be tackled, but what her mother was trying to do was hug her. Anne hugged her back. They held each other and cried, and it was a long time before either of them let go or said anything. Finally, when it happened, it was Anne who let go and Sarah who talked.

"Look on the bright side," she said, as if she'd been the one asking Anne to stay home from Smith. "You'll be here when the baby is born." Patrick and Ibby's. "When you become an auntie and I become a granny."

Through her ludicrous tears, Anne laughed. Her mother's face and hair were as much a wreck as an act 4 Lady Macbeth, but, even through this, she was a beautiful woman, no one's idea of a grandmother.

"Granny," Anne said.

"Auntie Anne, Auntie Anne," said Sarah.

"And Toto, too," Anne said, in note-perfect Billie Burke falsetto. *Auntie Anne* was fine. Better than *Babe* and light-years better than *Annie*. God, did she hate being called *Annie*.

⊚∕∞

THE THEATRICAL WAS about what Anne expected, right down to the brassy hipster music on the jukebox (as she entered: something new by Bobby Darin), the jar of slimy pickled eggs on each table, the cloud of cigarette smoke, and the film on the glass of the framed glossies of celebrities. She'd never been there. All those years, hearing her father and his friends allude to it, she had an idea. But her father had never taken her. It wasn't the sort of place you took a kid.

David was late. It gave her time—too much—to think. Only now did it occur to her that she'd worn capri pants the last time, up at Kelley's. She'd put altogether too much time into setting out clothes, changing, and rechanging.

(All David's shirts were white, all his ties were dark and thin, and still: that morning, he, too, endured the torment of sartorial indecision.) All to get reacquainted with a boy? A boy who no longer interested her, except as a friend? They were too different to be a couple. But friends, that could be interesting.

Ten minutes late, that was all. When he arrived, the cane, the leg, the terrible limp, gave him a good excuse. He was sweating and apologetic. Anne accepted. She said she'd only just gotten there herself. He asked Anne what she was drinking, and he followed suit: Cotton Club "Less Sweet" Ginger Ale.

"I thought you were a Pepsi-Cola man. At Kelley's that's what you drank, mostly."

"I remember drinking," David said, "but not Pepsi-Cola."

They both laughed. That wine!

He dabbed girlishly at his face with his napkin. "You *remember* that, me drinking Pepsi-Cola?"

"Maybe it was just what we had on hand," she said. "I do remember you drinking a lot of it, though."

"It was hotter than billy hell in that attic," he said. "Though not as hot as this summer."

"Don't flatter yourself, OK?" she said. "I remember a lot of dumb things." She shrugged. "So tell me about your wedding plans. It's the same fiancée, right? The one you got back together with?"

It was. Her name was Irene Hrudka (*These public school West Siders,* Anne thought, *and their industrious-sounding names!*).

David had been straight with Anne on the phone; almost the first thing he'd said, tripping over himself to blurt it out, was that he was getting married next month. It was that honesty, coupled with Anne's decision to be adult about all this, that made her agree to have lunch with him (also, she felt bad about being rude to him at the fair). It had been two weeks, though, before they'd been able to make their schedules jibe. David had to work all day, and most lunches he had to study (night school; he was the first person she'd ever known who went to Fenn College). In the meantime, they'd spoken on the phone nearly every day, as David fed her little scraps of information on the Sheppard case, explanations of other people who might have had motives. Someone Marilyn was "involved with," perhaps. Psychos in the area. Also friends, electricians, plumbers, handymen, dog- and baby-sitters: anyone with a key to the house. Anne didn't believe a word of it, but David's uncle was working for the family, so David *would* think like this.

David went on and on about wedding planning. This was not, to put it mildly, a thing that interested Anne. She'd started it, though. When he got onto the subject of the band he'd had to hire and how much it was going to cost and how he hated paying all that money for a band that, beyond a little Sinatra, was going to play square music David despised, Anne leaped on the chance to change the subject.

"Speaking of music," she said, "do you still like the same kind of things you used to?"

"I guess," he said. "The same only more so, if that makes sense. In California the R&B scene wasn't as good as it is here in the East, but I got to see a lot of jazz, and I bought so many records, I... Well, let's just say I bought a lot of records."

Here in the East? The only people who say that are Clevelanders who've never been east of East Cleveland. Her father talked that way, too, a vestige of his own narrow youth.

"What do you think of Bill Randle?" Anne said.

"He's no Alan Freed," he said.

"Amen, brother," she said. "He's on top of the world in New York, Freed is. He's making a movie. This past spring some girlfriends of mine and I went to one of his Rock 'n' Roll Dance Parties down there."

"In New York?" David was clearly impressed. Too impressed, though for some reason his being impressed by her—her job; going to NYC to see a Freed show—struck Anne as cute.

"Yeah. It was great. The Flamingos, the Clovers, Fats Domino, the Moonglows. The coolest. Unlike the one here, where they never even got through all the acts before—"

"The Moondog Coronation Ball?"

"Exactly."

"I was there."

"You're kidding."

David puffed up. "I got a ticket from my—"

"I was there, too."

"—dad. *You're* kidding."

"We snuck out of the dorm to go."

"Don't you live in Shaker?"

"So?"

"You live in Shaker, and when you went to school there you lived in a dorm?"

"You don't understand," she said. "A lot of people do it." Which wasn't especially true. "Where were you when the cops came?"

"What?"

"At the ball."

"Oh. Way, way in the back."

"We were off to the side. We were trying to bug my brother. He was the engineer for the radio broadcast."

"Wow, that's great!" he said. "Is that how you got into radio, your brother?"

"No," she snapped. "Nothing like that."

Anne couldn't believe that neither of them had said anything about this, up at Kelley's. But—as they told what they remembered, with the kind of nostalgia for the recent past that is the province of young adults—what was more incredible was how at odds their memories of that night were.

Anne remembered the crowd as almost entirely Negro, the most she'd ever seen in one place. David claimed it was about 10 percent white. Anne said the riot broke out right as Varetta Dillard went onstage. David said no way, it was during Tiny Grimes. Varetta Dillard never got anywhere near the stage.

"What was that first group?" Anne asked.

"Paul Williams and the Hucklebuckers."

"I don't think so," Anne said.

"It was!" David said. "Bet you."

"Bet me what?"

"Lunch?"

"Fine," she said. Just then the waiter came up. "I'll have the lobster," Anne said.

David looked stricken.

"Joke," she said. "You're so easy." She ordered a BLT, fries, and another Cotton Club, no ice. David ordered a steak sandwich.

"Anyway, if you're so sure you're right, what's to worry?"

"How can you forget Paul Williams and the Hucklebuckers?" he said. "They played that song, I don't know, four times."

"What song?"

"'Do the Hucklebuck.'"

"I don't think so. There were scads of those hucklebuck songs. They were all sort of the same, but they were different."

"I thought you said the first group wasn't Paul Williams and the Hucklebuckers."

"They weren't," she said. "They played later. After the Dominoes."

"The Dominoes!" he said, loud enough that people at other tables stared. "You've *got* to be kidding! The Dominoes never went on."

She shushed him. He apologized.

"That's not how I remember it," Anne said. "I remember the Dominoes going on first."

"Name one song they played," David said.

He pulled out one of those revolting pickled eggs. Who knew what hands had been in that jar? He ate it.

"I can't," she said. "I like the music, but to dance to. I don't have the need to collect all the records, like you."

"What are you saying?"

"Just that I can't remember any of the songs the Dominoes played. That's all."

"Because they didn't play any."

"Truce," she said. "OK? One of us should just go look this up. The library or someplace. The morgue at one of the newspapers. You know what a newspaper morgue is, don't you? It's like an archive."

He pulled out a dime. "Call your brother."

"Your funeral," she said, and took it.

Patrick had heard about David, "the boy who wrecked that Jeepster at Ashcroft." His mother had told him about it, John had told him, and Anne had told him, too. It was Patrick who eventually helped John grind the stump of that dead elm, the one into which Anne had run Stan Lychak's Jeepster (of course, everyone but Anne and David believed that David had wrecked the car). "The Dominoes never went on," Patrick said. "Varetta Dillard opened, then came Paul Williams, and the fire department broke everything up during Tiny Grimes."

"I thought it was the cops," Anne said. She was certain Varetta Dillard didn't open.

"Fire department," he said. "How's the new digs?" he said, meaning the carriage house.

"Great," she said, because it was. "I'm mostly squared away. Come by for dinner."

"I would," he said, "if we didn't have the well-being of an unborn baby to think of."

Anne loved being a bad cook. Dorothy Fuldheim, the news commentator at Channel 5, bragged about her lousy cooking on the air. Fuldheim wouldn't be caught dead reading a recipe. She did the *news*. Anyone famous who passed though Cleveland, Fuldheim did the interview. She was Cleveland's Murrow. Nothing against Flossie Thagard. But Anne did not want to wake up one day and find herself in Flossie Thagard's shoes. It would be *so* much better to be Fuldheim: smart, famous, respected, short, homely, prideful of her humble beginnings, and sure of herself. She had the store-bought classiness of someone new to her money, but that was just packaging. To Anne, Dorothy Fuldheim was a woman who laughed at what the world said a woman had to be.

When Anne got back to the table, their food was there. David had already dug in.

"I was right," she said. "About everything."

⌒⌒

IT CAME BACK to her, how easy it was to talk to this boy. He didn't show off; he talked to her as if she was a person. It was rarely like that, with boys. This one was a talker *and* a listener, and she was a talker. Once they got going, they got *going*.

That "Work with Me, Annie" song came on the jukebox, and Anne said how much she hated it whenever anyone called her *Annie*. David said he could understand. It made his skin crawl whenever anyone called him *Dave*—or, worse, *Davey*.

They talked about their jobs. Anne had not met many boys who would talk to her about this. Theirs, yes; hers, no. In fact, she had not met any. Take Alton Herrick (please). To the extent he took her job seriously at all, he used it to talk about what hacks reporters were. But she could tell he really didn't take it seriously. As far as Alton was concerned, Anne's job was a summer job and no more serious than his own (he coached swimming two hours a day for a summer-league country club team).

David was different. As she told him what it was she loved about being in the middle of a breaking news story, how it felt to know things that most people didn't, the feeling that you might get to be the person who tells thousands of people something they'll want to know, David nodded, ate his sandwich, wiped the juice from his chin, and kept his eyes fixed on hers. He said *hmm* at the right times. He asked questions that let her go into it more deeply: *When you're in a pack like that, how do you get anything that everyone else doesn't already have?* Little ones, too, like *How so?* and *For example?* Best of all, he didn't turn the conversation into one of those parallel monologues boys are famous for, where you say a thing and they say something vaguely related from their own experience, and you go back to you and they go back to them, until you both get tired of talking about yourselves, which for most boys takes forever.

When the conversation did turn to David and his job, it was Anne who asked about it. Not the job he had working for his uncle (Anne didn't want

[204]

him to think she was using him), but what he wanted to do once he was done with school.

That was when things really took off.

One thing led to another. In one of their phone conversations, he'd let slip that he was a political science major, that he might want someday to run for office, and that, yes, he knew who her father was but, no, he didn't *know him* know him. And so it was just darling, watching him choose his words, trying not to sound too gung ho about public service while at the same time being gung ho as all get out.

Anne asked him where this passion had come from, the navy?

"No," he said, "god no." He did not answer the question, except insofar as it led to him talking about how little sense of serving the public the navy had given him, how boring and gallingly wasteful the navy was. Looking back, though, he could appreciate what a stroke of luck it was, that boredom, how blessed he was not to have had to risk his life.

Lunch led to dessert. Anne had the Theatrical's "Famous Apple Pie"; David, the "Legendary Hot Fudge Sundae."

David's account of naval life led to Anne bringing up her brother who'd died. She almost never brought this up. Now, as she did, she didn't go into detail. David kept saying *wow*. This was all news to him. He stopped eating. "Steven was the good son," she said. "He's a standard we can't live up to." Her dinner plate had still not been bused; with one of her remaining french fries, she drew her initials in a pool of ketchup. "It's worse for the boys. Probably impossible for my parents. You'd be surprised how little I think about it. Isn't that awful?"

David said, no, he understood.

"It is funny," she said, "how we never talk about it, any of us. Not funny ha-ha."

"Funny peculiar," said David. "I know. Only it's not so peculiar."

It hit her. His mother. "I'm sorry!"

He started eating again. His sundae was a melted wreck. "Don't be," he said.

Dessert led to coffee.

"How'd you know I was thinking about my mother?" asked David.

"C'mon," Anne said. "I'm not a stupid person. I'm a year ahead in school."

"That's not a book-smart sort of thing you did there."

"No kidding," she said. "I was joking. It wasn't so hard, seeing what you were thinking. I'm sorry if you—"

He waved her off. As he said he'd do two years ago, he told Anne about his mother's death, what he knew about it.

"Hollywood!" Anne said. "John's in Hollywood! My brother John."

"The painter guy."

"He's acting some now," she said. "Trying to write."

"I meant—"

"I know what you meant." Painting the third floor at Ashcroft.

"How's that dog? The wolfhound?"

"Dead." Out of respect for David's mother, Anne did not say *drowned*. "Long story."

"Oh," David said. In fairness, what else was there to say? "And how's Kenneth?"

"John and Kenneth split," she said, "and then got back together. And then they split. And then they got back together. He's still writing that novel. Kenneth."

David nodded. He looked excessively thoughtful, as if it hadn't occurred to him that her brother and Kenneth were homosexuals, or perhaps as if he didn't know that there were such people. "I'd like to write a book," David finally confessed.

"Really," Anne said, as flatly as she could. She was starting to realize that every ambitious American means to write a book someday.

"A long time from now," David said. "If, you know, my career goes the way I'm hoping. I guess it would be an autobiography."

He blushed. A boy who, when he brags on himself, blushes!

"A novel's a lot different from that," Anne said.

"I know," he said. "I'm a year ahead in school."

He never told her this. "You are?" she said.

"Joke," he said.

Give led to take.

Coffee led to more coffee.

A late lunch led to a later one. Finally, the waiter asked them to settle up. David grabbed the check, but Anne insisted they go dutch. "Otherwise it's a date," she said. "I'm certainly not going to go on a date with a man who's engaged."

"I've been meaning to ask you," David said.

"On a date?"

"No," he said. He screwed up his face.

"You don't have to look so disgusted."

"Let me finish, OK? What I was trying to say, what I've been meaning to ask is," he said, "how's that fiancé of *yours?*"

She looked at him. He said he'd heard her on the air. What *did* he hear? The recipe show? "Do you mean Wally McGuire?"

"I don't remember," David said. "Jeez, has there been more than one?"

"There haven't been *any,*" she said. "That was just..." She waved her hands, frustrated to describe just what it is that was. "Show business."

David frowned. "What are you talking about?"

She explained. The fiancé she invented and mentioned on Flossie Thagard's recipe show.

Now it was David's turn to laugh. "That wasn't it," he said. "Up at Kelley's, you said there was a fiancé. I was just calling your bluff."

"So the wedding is when, now?"

He told her.

"Want to come?" he said. "You should come. I can get you an invitation." He winked at her. "I know some people who know some people."

Thrust and parry, parry and thrust.

"I can bring a date, I presume?"

"Sure," he said. "Naturally."

"Then I'd be delighted to accept," she said, calling *his* bluff. "Truly, I'd love to." On a paper bevnap (DRINK PRIDE OF CLEVELAND BEER!), she wrote out her address. Beside the street address, she wrote *Apt. #1A.* "Mail the invitation here," she said.

She offered him a ride back to his office, but he said, no, he'd take a cab. He insisted. He acted nonchalant about how late he was, but he was a pretty bad actor.

How different we are, she thought, *and yet too much alike.*
How alike we are, yet too different.

❧

ANNE O'CONNOR WAS a year ahead in school. Here's what it is to be a year ahead in school:

When you are in kindergarten, in fifth grade, or a freshman, you are the youngest person in the building. You are a year younger than the people you are competing against in sports, for the lead in the school play, for dates—at a time in human life when a year has the gravity of ten adult-years. Even if you are socially poised at a level far beyond your years (possible only for year-ahead girls), your teachers will note in your permanent record that will follow you for the rest of your life that you have a tendency to seek attention, to show off, to be a loud voice. There is no sense arguing with people who say this. This is how they see you. What being ahead mostly means is that you have been singled out as being special. This is bad. Parents of very smart children forget this, blinded by pridefulness over what zygotal alchemy their genetic material has wrought. Ha! Anyone who has attended school should be unsentimental enough to remember that to be singled out as special for reasons other than male athletic prowess or, to a lesser and infinitely more complicated extent, female physical beauty is bad, bad, bad, bad, bad, bad, bad, bad, bad, bad, bad, bad, bad, bad.

Though it has its good parts.

You are never unaware of a feeling that you are better than everyone else (it's true! be honest!), which, no matter what anyone tells you about the wrongness of thinking this, is a terrific feeling. (Also a nightmare, a burden.) It is a feeling that you are smart enough to know is utterly, utterly false. (And also true.) But mostly false. (No, it's not.)

But most of all what being a year ahead in school means is that you walk around feeling like you have a whole year of your life to blow. You could dynamite one whole year of your life, and what's the worst thing that could happen? People your age would catch up to you. Big deal.

You never feel like you are the age you are. You long to, but you never have. To be a year ahead in school is to feel both younger and older than everyone your age. Or, rather, to feel as if there *is* no one your age.

Ս

"GROOM'S SIDE," SAID Anne O'Connor.

She was late, but nothing was under way. The congregation (maybe two hundred people, distributed equally on either side of the aisle) was visibly fidgety. The organist, bizarrely, played "Greensleeves." The usher (Skeezix Soltesz) crooked his arm and held it out. Alton Herrick followed, swiveling his head to take in the stained-glass, flower-bedecked splendor of St. John Cantius Church. He smirked. Smirked! At what? The garishness of the flowers? The dresses? At the footwear of the other guests? At the Polish-language hymnals in the pew backs (Alton was unshy about ethnic jokes)? Truly, it was a lovely church, as fine as any downtown cathedral. Alton was a snob. Anne considered specific ways she might kill him.

Their usher, like the others, wore not a tuxedo but rather a blue suit he must have already owned (the suits did not match; some were noticeably worn), along with matching skinny navy blue ties (sporting a lone sternum-level triple stripe: aqua, white, aqua) and matching tie tacks (silver-plated). "Any score yet?" he whispered—to Alton, who did not care about baseball, which was part of why he'd been available as Anne's last-minute date.

"Not until tonight," said Alton, too loud. Then, in a bad Cockney accent: "'F you catch m'drift, guv." More smirking. Maybe he was just smirking at the very idea of a wedding.

The usher frowned. "They're not playing—"

"Zero–zero," Anne said. "Bottom of the first. Smith, Avila, and Doby went down one-two-three." She'd connived press credentials for Games Three, Four, and Five (this got her into the game and a seat in the auxiliary press area, a section of the right-field stands; because she was a woman, she was barred from the locker room, something that did not then strike Anne as at all strange; in fact, it would have seemed obscene). When David had invited her to the wedding, she didn't make the connection. She got to go to the game yesterday, but now here she was, with her Indians, inconceivably, down three games to none to the underdog Giants, spending Game Four at St. John Cantius instead of at Cleveland Stadium—all to call David's bluff.

"They should've pitched Feller," said the usher, still to Alton.

"He's a jolly good one," Alton said. "Feller is." He'd been drinking scotch from a flask with his fraternity letters engraved on it. Between that and too much Skin Bracer, Alton reeked.

"Lemon gives us our best chance to stay alive," Anne said. This was what the Indians manager had said after yesterday's game (in the locker room; it was a quote she read in the papers; the story she did for WCRB was filed from a press-box telephone and included nothing someone who'd listened to the game on the radio didn't already know). As soon as she quoted Al Lopez, though, she heard a voice in her head. An old lady in 1948. *Bob Lemon, the pitcher. The young man who used to be an outfielder. He's starting for us.* "Lemon was the winner," Anne said, "when we won it all in '48."

"True," said the usher. "Then Feller can go tomorrow and we're only a game down."

"They won't lose today," Anne said, taking her seat now. "Not at home."

"Everyone's a winner here," Alton stage-whispered. He spread out his arms, a whole-wide-world gesture, and sat. "I hope I don't cry!"

She elbowed him. He mouthed *sorry* and gave her what he must have thought was the sheepish grin of the charming rogue. It was strange, knowing he would do whatever she said. Knowing that most men would. It was something she knew and tried not to think about.

Time passed.

Murmuring in the pews ahead of her was a mix of ethnic-looking off-duty cops in ill-fitting suits (their women looked hopeful) and garishly dressed Jewish- and Italian-looking men with quite a bit of jewelry (their women looked tired). The bride's side was a sea of thick-torsoed ethnics. Throughout the congregation were more blue-haired women and white-belted men than Anne had seen in her life up to now.

The volume of the murmuring rose (in both the decibel and quantitative senses of *volume*). Something was wrong.

"Your boyfriend's got cold feet," Alton said. "Betcha five smackers."

The ushers had disappeared from the back of the church, Anne pointed out. Things were going forward.

Sure enough, a young priest came out and knelt in the aisle, whispering things to David's aunt and uncle. They stood and followed him, back to the sacristy presumably. It was the first time Anne had seen Betty and Stan since that wonderful, awful day in the Erie islands. Betty's cocktail-length dress looked terrific on her (never an overweight woman, Betty had toned up nicely, exercising along each morning with *The Paige Palmer Show*). Stan had shaved his mustache. His suit would have flattered the most discerning New Yorker; the crease in his trousers could have sliced carrots.

Anne had spent the first half of her summer writing about weddings, but this was the first one she'd attended since Patrick and Ibby's two years ago.

Moments later Betty Lychak reemerged unescorted, nodded to the organist and to the stocky woman about to be David's mother-in-law (according to the program: MRS. TEODOR "BUD" [AGNES] HRUDKA) and took her seat. The organist struck up the processional. At the back of the church, the bridesmaids gathered and, one by one, walked down the aisle. (Alton started to make a crack about the bridesmaid dresses; Anne shot him. A look.) On the opposite side of the altar from the organ came Stan Lychak. Then, badly limping and in a suit identical to his uncle's, came David.

By Anne's reckoning, he made a handsome, earnest, angry-looking groom.

Pow: "Lohengrin." Wagner's kick in the head to love. Anne was stunned to feel tears. Mr. Teodor "Bud" Hrudka, his mouth a quivering wreck, stutter-stepped up the aisle with his pretty, veiled, round-faced daughter. Anne saw into Irene's eyes; this was a happy woman.

Honest to god, Anne couldn't have been happier for these people.

As Irene and David took their place at the altar, flanked by Irene's sister-in-law Janice and David's uncle Stan, Anne glanced at the bulletin. It read, BEST MAN: MICHAEL J. ZIELINSKY.

Anne felt a rock in her throat. Where did she get off, pitying herself about having her parents as her parents? Poor David. His mother was *dead*. And now, apparently, his father was a no-show at his son's wedding.

There are people in this world, Anne thought, *with* problems.

The ceremony included a beautiful and interminable Latin mass, made infinitely more excruciating for the average attendee because of lingering anxiety about how the Indians might be faring. Also, the priest was impeded by a lingering case of the hiccups.

It was a record-speed recessional.

Anne (with Alton in tow) was aghast at how many people felt justified in ditching the receiving line.

In the St. John Cantius parking lot, car radios crackled to life. With two down in the bottom of the fifth, the score was New York 7, Cleveland 0.

Anne, as manners decreed, shook hands with the wedding party. Strangers—though from them Anne overheard talk that David's father had called and that he'd been summoned away suddenly on business. Elsewhere in the nave, a group of some of the more garishly dressed people were also talking about it; Anne could make out stray words. *Bender,* which made her think David's father had gone on one. Then she heard *subpoena. Florida. Bender* again. Bender the congressman. The hearings.

Finally the line progressed and she came to the familiar faces of Betty and Stan. Anne bent toward Betty to hug her, but Betty stiffened and pulled back. Anne froze, then stammered out an introduction of Alton. Alton shook Betty's hand. Stan looked straight at Anne and said nothing. Were they mad because so many people had left to hear the rest of the Series game? That made no sense. Anne extended her hand to Stan. He let it hang there. Surely they couldn't be mad David had invited her, an old girlfriend, and only briefly that?

She glanced over at David, just finishing with the people in line ahead of Alton and Anne. David was completely ashen. He nudged his uncle. Stan narrowed his lips. He had weaselly lips; he should never have shaved the mustache. He took Anne's hand and shook it. When he shook Alton's, Alton cried out in pain.

Suddenly, Anne got it. The timing of everything, two years ago. David had never broken up and gotten back together with Irene. He'd never broken up with her at all.

David took a deep breath.

Anne, however, had been subjected to a lifetime of social education, formal and otherwise, to prepare her for just such a moment. No observable behavior betrayed either surprise or epiphany. On cue, she introduced Alton Herrick, demurely curtsied to David, and, once he introduced her as "an old friend" to Mrs. David (Irene) Zielinsky, gave the bride the lightest-possible embrace, kissing the narthex air. "Best wishes," she said to Irene. Anne pivoted, as smoothly as a motorized statue in one of those big Bavarian clocks, to face David. "Congratulations," she said.

"Thanks," he said. "I'm glad you could come."

Alton was in hale-fellow-well-met mode, expressing his happiness for everyone with such slick, over-the-top fervor that no one, Anne feared, could possibly have thought it sincere.

She wasn't angry. It was a lifetime ago, she told herself, that week she spent with David at Kelley's. That Irene had been in the wings all along might have shocked another kind of girl, Anne thought, but to her the whole thing just made David human, a man, and more interesting. A more interesting *friend*. Period. But still friends. With all they have in common, why not?

Still, she did not go to the reception at the VFW hall (David had gotten a deal, being an actual VFW himself). She told herself it was because (a) she did not want to give Alton a chance to embarrass her, and (b) she wanted to see the end of the ballgame and hope against hope Cleveland could pull it out.

But the drive back to Shaker Heights took longer than the rest of the game did. Anne suffered through it all on the radio. Final score: New York 7, Cleveland 4.

She snapped it off.

Alton tried to make light of it. Happily, they were at a red light. She hauled off and busted him in the mouth.

In reflex, he spun toward her.

"Try it," she said. "I dare you."

He did not take her up on it. "I probably had that coming," he said. "Weddings bring out the worst in me. Weddings and scotch," he said. He rolled down the window, pulled the flask from his breast pocket, and flung it. It landed in somebody's yard. "There."

"Take me home," she said. "Take me straight home, and if you say another word, I'll . . ."

The light changed. She did not have to finish. He shook his head, put his roadster in gear, and—Alton Herrick, of the *Myron T. Herrick, Friend of France* Herricks—did precisely as he was told.

___ 9 ___

WHERE WAS MIKEY Z? Let's just say Florida. Various hotels. Let's just say he's got your fucking subpoena right here, pal.

Anne had never met him. She couldn't have guessed where he was and couldn't have known that looking into why he missed her friend's wedding, his only son's wedding, could have produced actual news. Even the city's best-connected, most-experienced reporters either did not know or chose not to know. So while David and Irene Zielinsky honeymooned (a four-hour drive to Niagara Falls, where they spent four days; David couldn't miss too much school), Anne joined most of the rest of Cleveland's reporters in returning to the Sheppard case, which was embroiled in petitions for a change of venue, with the arcana of jury selection soon to come.

Speaking of David's father, speaking of good stories, and even speaking of being young, precocious, and ahead in school: let us now praise Congressman George Bender.

On a late-summer day near the dawn of the American century, on the West Side of a great American city, near a wide river of legendary tortuousness, was born to pious Czech immigrants a boy wonder they named Georg Benda. While he was still in his teens, enchanted by another boy wonder, albeit an aging one, George (as he began to spell it) became a popular and effective speechmaker for Theodore Roosevelt's Bull Moose Party. More than once, the wavy-haired young Master Benda shook his fist at a large crowd and shouted, *"Down with the establishment!"* The Bull Moose Party was neither Republican nor Democrat, yet it was also both. It was a party that stood for many things, progressive things, though mostly it stood for one thing: Theodore Roosevelt. It was a lesson the boy wonder learned well.

The boy grew up, worked in advertising, for a newspaper, and as the manager of a department store. He did not smoke or drink and was active in his church. His forehead grew large; his features seemed crammed into the bottom half of his face. His hair remained attractively wavy. He married a woman to whom he would remain married. With the Bull Moose Party now extinct, he pragmatically joined his hero's old party. He changed his name from *Benda* to the less-ethnic *Bender*. At age twenty-four, on a pro-Prohibition platform, he was elected to the state senate.

Quick with a joke, eager to mock the legislature's slower wits, and consistently willing to go off the record, Bender was a favorite of his former peers, the newspapermen. In the state that was home to the Anti-Saloon League, Bender benefited from being a teetotaler and staunch backer of Prohibition. Yet he attacked a state law that allowed justices of the peace to hire private security officers to conduct liquor raids. These raiders, usually with ties to mobsters, would enter private homes (often of recent immigrants), seize a jug of homemade wine, bring the guilty to the JP, and watch as a $1,000 fine was levied (enough money, in those years, to purchase a house). The raiders were charged with collecting the money, at which they were skilled. Their commission was 50 percent. This did not count interest and collection fees. Bender thought this was wrong!

He raised signatures for a referendum to overturn the law. One day he hired a marching oompah band and showed up at the statehouse carrying a tremendous roll of paper. The band led the way into the senate chamber. Behind them came Bender and, for forty feet behind him, like the train of a bride's dress, slithered the petition. The newspapermen loved it! George Bender was now both for *and* against Prohibition. The voters loved it! Three years later, in a statewide election necessitated by Ohio's new-census legislative bounty, the still-young George Bender (though—filled with his wife's buttery cooking and a dollop too much of himself—he was getting jowly) was elected to the United States Congress.

George Bender had learned things, raising signatures for that statewide referendum and, more to the point, money to see that it passed. One thing was that Prohibition was becoming unpopular, both for its own sake and because of the organized crime it facilitated. Bowing to public opinion, and publicly patting himself on the back for doing so, he reversed himself. When the time came, he voted for repeal. Before too awful long, with all those Washington parties (it is a city that does the world's business during cocktail hour), Bender himself began to drink. Who should have a problem with this? It was the law of the land, the will of the people.

Another thing he learned was how good he was at raising money. He learned things about how money given to a committee doesn't get reported in the newspaper the way money given to a candidate is. Good to know. He became a resourceful pioneer in that most American of political gambits, the perpetual campaign. For a time, he directed the city commission that oversaw the construction and administration of Cleveland Municipal Stadium. What jobs he had to give! Thousands of them, during the Depression. This gave Bender a good feeling. If those newly employed people wanted to donate a token amount to the sort of organization that, it might be argued, helped create such jobs, that was surely their prerogative. Bender's indictments for embezzlement and perjury resulted in acquittal. He moved to the East Side, to a huge house out in Pepper Pike. At Christmas he gave his reporters such tokens as diamond cuff links, Swiss watches, boxes of Cuban cigars, cases of single-malt scotch. Pals look out for their pals. He was indicted for using campaign funds for personal use. Democrats were in charge of this, Bender cried. He was acquitted. He became a deacon in his church. His hair grew thin and straight.

And of *course* he learned, way back during the failed experiment of Prohibition, that organized crime was bad. George Bender was on the record about that! (Building the stadium had also opened his eyes. The people who got hired for that, though, weren't mobsters, just people who knew people who knew George Bender. Again, don't misunderstand: he was acquitted.) When the labor unions were reputedly infiltrated by mobsters, Congressman Bender was concerned. (Also there was the matter of Reds; Reds were also bad.) The racketeering hearings he held had *nothing* to do with the fact that the unions had never supported him. He was always against mobsters. Long before he found himself running for the United States Senate.

So he held some hearings. So what? Why *not* in Cleveland? A lot of what needed to be investigated was in Cleveland. Why *not* hold them three weeks before election? The business of the country shouldn't stop, he soberly opined, just because there's an election next month. George Bender had boxes and boxes of information just on the rackets that a Mr. William Presser was alleged to be conducting vis-à-vis jukeboxes. Bender was just getting started on dump trucks, but things there looked fishy, too! Very fishy. Also there were some allegations featuring a Mr. James R. Hoffa that needed to be considered.

The hearings started. People with names like *Moose* testified. (If Moose Maxwell, a Negro whose real name was Richard Finley, was to be believed, the going rate for bombing a non-Teamster truck was $225; torching a tavern that housed a nonunion jukebox fetched $400 for a private contractor such as himself.) About what happened next, accounts conflict.

Yes, Bender did go to Florida. The allegation that he was met at an airport there by John Scalish, don of the Cleveland Mafia, came from an American Federation of Labor guy. Bender said he wouldn't accept an endorsement from that union even if they offered it. (They never offered it.) Bender denied meeting with Scalish. Scalish hadn't even answered his subpoena! Bender said he and his wife went to Florida to take a three-day vacation in the sun. Health reasons. The allegation that he continued from Florida to Cuba and came back a millionaire wasn't made publicly until after Bender could no longer defend himself. Fair? Hardly.

Yes, the Teamsters switched their Senate endorsement from Burke to Bender. Yes, right about then, the hearings abruptly ended. Coincidence. Find the smoking gun, win a million dollars. Anyway, Bender said he'd resume the hearings in Washington in December.

Yes, less than a week before the election, there was a botched attempt to bomb George Bender's sensibly used 1946 Cadillac. Who knows what that was about? The cops' investigation turned up a big bag full of bupkis. Some say that Bender knew it was coming, that it was staged to get his name in the papers and give him a chance to speculate that the Mob was out to get him. Others say that the Teamsters had a perfect plan: endorse Bender, then right before the election, too late for anyone to do anything about it, have him killed, thus allowing Burke to win anyway.

Bender won the election by less than 10,000 votes. Make that less than 6,000 votes (there was a recount). Make that less than 4,000 votes (another recount). Make that less than 3,000 votes (yet another). Why did the numbers keep not adding up? It's complicated, an election. Lots of ballots and ballot boxes and machines and whatnot. A lot can happen. Let's just say, sometimes you can count and count and still not get a total that looks right. So there you go: "Senator George H. Bender."

Getting ready to get right to work as a senator is *very* time-consuming. Also, he was a lame-duck member of Congress. For let's just say logistical reasons, Bender was unable to continue the hearings.

In the Senate a much-mellowed version of the teetotaling boy wonder became a popular host. He had a fine house on the north edge of Georgetown, much-enjoyed by members of the Washington elite—Republicans and Democrats, reporters and ambassadors, lobbyists and millionaires alike. (Key word: *alike*.) The refreshments were ample. It is said that President Eisenhower enjoyed George Bender's company.

In the next election, Frank Lausche (yet another former mayor of Cleveland, the first big-time politician that Louis Seltzer ever helped create) left the governor's house to crush George Bender. Landslide for Lausche. Bender did not come home. Bender stayed in the District. He was hired by a Mr. James R. Hoffa to conduct an in-house investigation of Teamster rackets. Bender was pleased as rum punch to find nothing. Nothing at all! But his old friends in the Senate—many of whom had eaten well at Bender's table—denounced Bender's efforts as a whitewash and conducted an investigation of their own. Bender resigned. Months later, on a visit to the empty house in Pepper Pike, he was found dead in his garage, the door closed and that '46 Cadillac still unbombed, still running. The end.

THE BABY FLOATS *in a jar of yellowing formaldehyde in the coroner's office. Pregnant women have dreams like this. Pure grotesquery. A sick parody of amniotic fluid.*

The mother was buried, but some sources say the baby went into a jar. The jar went onto a shelf. Evidence.

Go ahead: look at it. Pick up the jar. It's the size of a family-sized jar of Miracle Whip. It is a larger jar than is necessary. Inside, the tiny body spins and gyres. Its gills are gone. Its eyes are closed. It looks human. It died four months ago, five months before it was born. Look at it. "It" is a baby. How gruesome, that we have to call him or her "it." Its brother, Chip, was asleep in the next room as someone bludgeoned their mother to death. It has no name. Daily, the fluid yellows.

Evidence.

∽

THE PARKING LOT outside the Criminal Court Building was a Hooverville of tents and panel trucks. Reporters were everywhere, too many to count. Lurching among them were competing Slavic-looking men bearing wooden trays laden with sandwiches, kielbasas, and warm pop, charging what the market would bear. One of the men wore a sleeveless undershirt. It was the first week of November.

Television cameras weren't allowed in the courtroom, though for some reason newsreel cameras were. Some stations had reporters there, to stand in front of the building and say what, at the end of the day, needed to be said. Most simply sought the most germane silent, exterior footage they could get. TV was nothing. The most-watched news broadcast in Cleveland featured the talking head of Dorothy Fuldheim and on some nights nothing else. No footage. The show was fifteen minutes long.

As for radio: tape machines were barred from the courtroom. Anne had hers in her purse. She doubted anyone would search a lady's purse. To be safe, she'd piled a stack of feminine napkins of top of the tape machine. No bailiff, no *man*, was going to rifle through feminine napkins.

In the crowded hallway, a reporter from Chicago struck up a conversation with her. He worked for one of the newspaper chains, smoked Chesterfield Kings, and claimed he had a degree in history from Princeton. He told her some of the rumors he'd heard. The Sheppards were members of a "key club." Sam was a bisexual dope fiend. Also a secret abortionist.

He was flirting with her. "Rumors," Anne said. "That's all those are." She'd heard them. David told him his uncle had looked into those things, and most if not all of them were wildly false. (She avoided talking about personal things with David. To her, he was merely a source.)

"I also hear Dr. Sam was sterile. He found out Marilyn was pregnant, lost his head, and killed her."

Cripes. These days, who *wasn't* pregnant?

"That's ridiculous," Anne said. "He has a son. Sam Junior. Chip. That poor kid."

"Who knows," said the man, "where *that* kid came from?"

"He looks just like his dad," she said. "Really, this thing is bad enough without—"

"It's just what I hear, is all." He smiled. "Mind you," he said, "I don't think he did it."

The doors came open. Six cops flanked the bailiff and head jailer.

Sam Sheppard, who was in a jail cell on the fourth floor of the building, had come down a back stairway. He was already in the courtroom. Anne and the reporters around her missed him.

"Passes only!" the jailer shouted.

Anne did not have a press pass, per se, but she did have a letter from Hoot Thagard on WCRB stationery asking whomever it may concern to extend to her all privileges accorded any member of the working press. The judge in the case, Blythin, had briefly been the mayor of Cleveland, and even though he was a Republican, a word from Anne's father would have gone a long way. That was not how Anne wanted to play it.

Ahead of her, the cops were turning people away. Members of the public, Anne presumed, come there to gawk.

"What's *that?*" the bailiff said. He shoved the letter back at Anne. When she objected, he interrupted her. "Space is limited," he said. "Talk to the jailer."

"I'm a member of the working—"

"Space is limited, talk to the jailer," said the bailiff. "How old *are* you?"

A cop herded her gently, forcefully aside.

"Twenty-four," she said.

"Baloney," the bailiff said. "Next!"

The reporter from Chicago had the right kind of pass. "Twenty-four?" he scoffed. "Twenty-four, my ass."

"Now I've seen everything," said the bailiff, louder than might have been necessary. "A high school newspaper sending a little girl to cover a murder trial!"

No one had looked in her purse. All around her, peers chuckled.

Inside the courtroom, the newspapermen with the best connections found themselves seated at a table before the bar, even closer to the action than the jury.

∞

"SHE LOOKS LIKE me," Anne said. The babies were arrayed in the glass toasters. While Ibby was in labor, Patrick had gone out and bought two whole cases of Dutch Masters cigars. He was giving them out by the boxful. The baby had been almost a month overdue and was huge. The biggest baby there. She could already hold her head up, Patrick said. Her name was Lucy.

"She looks nothing like you," Patrick said. "She's a blond."

"Like a cross between me," she said, "and Winston Churchill." *Something* that *size could come out of me? Never.*

"That's sickening," Patrick said. "You and Winston Churchill."

Ibby's parents and Sarah O'Connor had all been there for hours now, and, with Ibby herself drugged into the forested west edge of oblivion, Patrick was clearly overjoyed to have someone else to talk to.

"That's a horrible thing to say about my beautiful baby," Patrick said. "Lucy looks nothing at all like Winston Churchill."

"She's beautiful," Anne said. "Don't get me wrong."

"Everybody says that," said Patrick, "about Winston Churchill."

"Because it's true," Anne said.

"It's not true of Lucy."

"Only because she also looks like me."

"You're impossible," her brother said. "Have a cigar."

To his astonishment, she opened her box and did just that.

"Lucy's a good name," Anne said. She spit the end of it off. She had matches in her purse (also cigarettes, which, since the move to the carriage house, she'd taken up). "I must admit, though, I'm hurt you didn't name her after me." She puffed her cigar like no tomorrow.

Of *course* just then her father arrived.

"Those things'll stunt your growth."

But then he broke into that great booming laugh of his and hugged Patrick. "Nice job, buster," he said. "Congratulations for extending our bloodlines."

Our bloodlines? His tongue did not seem to be at all in-cheek. Neither did he seem overcome by emotion. All he was, was stiff. He accepted the box of cigars his son gave him.

Down the hall Ibby's father hefted and wrangled a stuffed pink panda bear as big as he was. Her mother stood behind him, telling him shrilly where to put it and what to watch out for.

Anne kept right on smoking. She couldn't blame this baby, four weeks late joining this family. Bright girl, Lucy.

∞

ALL THIS TIME on the Sheppard story, and all Anne had managed to dig up were trifles. She'd interviewed family members of the empaneled jurors (every paper in town repeatedly published the jurors' pictures and addresses). She did a phone interview with the lisping, shouting editor of the scandal sheet that offered $5,000 to Susan Hayes, the pretty nurse with whom Sheppard had an affair, for the exclusive rights to her story (*Playboy*, new that year, didn't yet have its act together enough to ask Miss Hayes to pose nude). On that last one, Mr. Thagard told Anne he appreciated her initiative but that she shouldn't give free publicity to "such, such, ah, distaste . . . ah, distastefulness. Such scoundrels." She saw his point. The story never aired.

Other, more wholesome ones did. Anne had (on tips David fed her) interviewed friends and former schoolteachers of Marilyn Sheppard's. WCRB's listeners learned that Marilyn, at the age of six, scored an intelligence quotient of 136. They learned she was a native East Sider, who despite the nice place on the lake in Bay Village complained to her friends (Heights girls all) about knuckling under to Sam's desire to live "way out west," near his family's hospital. She complained that Sam used his job as an excuse for not wearing his wedding ring (which he called a "nuisance"). One Thanksgiving Marilyn and baby Chip had dinner on the East Side with her family, while Sam had dinner on the West Side with his. Her favorite magazine was *Time*. She'd taught Sunday school. She was kind to animals. Two pals named daughters after her.

∞

ON ANNE'S DAYS off, for what she told herself was no reason at all, she'd take that turquoise-and-white Chevy Bel Air down to Amish country, roll

[221]

down the windows, and *drive*. A hundred miles an hour! The cold wind buffeted and knifed her; her long, whipping hair felt like a weapon she'd turned on herself.

The day her father had bought Anne the car—her eighteenth birthday—he asked her if she knew how fast this car would go.

She did not.

Fast enough to kill you, he'd said.

Anne loved that! It was the sort of question a person would ask a boy. At times, her father seemed to understand her.

Not that this changed anything.

She had to watch out for horses, out here. She had to watch out for the black Amish buggies. Cows. But there were roads she'd discovered south of Cleveland, straight and gently rolling, that made it easy to see what was coming. No matter how cold it was, she'd roll down the windows. Her car was so nice, she could get up to eighty and not feel much, but with the windows down, she'd be slapped about in the driver's seat (forget seat belts; that kind of precaution comes later) and the sound of the radio would be swallowed up (forget car stereo; that kind of power comes later), and Anne would blast past white porches and haystacks and red barns and pumpkins. Cows.

Sometimes she took friends along. They'd love it at first, the way she drove, but then she'd keep the speed up and they'd say OK, enough, and Anne would laugh at them in a way she hoped sounded evil and keep her foot stomped down until they would beg and break into tears. And then for a little while beyond that. Sometimes these drives would take her somewhere: Oberlin, Kenyon, Denison—day trips to schools where she had a casual friend (they were all casual friends). Typically, though, she went alone. Typically, she went nowhere in particular. She took this car out in the country and *stood* on the damn gas! She stood on the gas and rolled down the windows.

It was then she would realize that, really, she'd hardly ever had a day when she did not think about her brother. For ten years she would think about him and then not think about thinking about him. It was a skill she was out here driving fast and working to lose.

Steven. He had a name. Steven was the one who had taught her to read. He had been a star swimmer and a diver, and he was the one who had taught her to dive, who'd coached her through a child's natural terror toward doing an inward. He was the one who'd sing corny songs with her, family harmonies on "Big Rock Candy Mountain." He was the one who took her in his arms when Grandmother O'Connor died and held her and told her it would be all right. He was the one who could have been the star at Notre Dame. Once, his name had appeared in *Sport* magazine. He might have played professional football. He could have had a career in jazz orchestras. He could have become a professor of music. When he left for the war, though, he'd told his father that when he came back, he planned to pursue the law and become a junior partner in the firm. Steven wasn't perfect. That was a lie. Steven bought into the world the way people told him it was. He did not go his own way. He volunteered for things and was sickeningly nice, the kind of boy that nuns, priests, and parents say a boy should be. He could imitate Beiderbecke, but he couldn't play anything that didn't sound like someone else. When, freshman year, Anne read *Portrait of the Artist as a Young Man,* every stupid thing wrong with Stephen and even Cranly reminded her of Steven. Sure, he smiled. But it was a crooked smile, and one tooth was chipped (he fell from a tree; how sickeningly wholesome). He had a crooked smile. One earlobe was much bigger than the other. He could fart at will. OK, *that* was a good thing. That, let's face it, was just the *funniest.* At will. Everyone should have a brother like that. Steven needed to do more things like that.

Steven volunteered. Steven became an officer. He learned to fly an airplane. Would it feel like this, in a plane buffeted by a high cold wind over the Sea of Japan?

What she thought of all the time—almost every day, for years and years and years, though only now was she allowing herself to realize this—was Steven's crooked smile. There were a lot of things about him that she'd lost, but she could still see that crooked smile, with its chipped upper-right incisor, and what it must have looked like the moment he knew he was a goner. How much time did he have? Who else was in the plane? Anne had no idea. There was no one she could think to ask. But she could just *see* Steven, clasping his big, dry right hand on the shoulder of his weeping navigator, a plumber's kid (let's say) from Tallahassee, Florida. Steven says, *It'll be all right, buddy.* Out here, in the cold and punishing wind, she could see that. She can see his crooked smile freeze. It's more than he can bear, his death, falling in a metal firecracker toward the sea. The smile loses the force of Steven's conviction, but it's still stuck there. Steven keeps his hand on the navigator's shoulder. In a loud voice, Steven recites the Twenty-third Psalm.

Seconds from now he will die, far from anyone who loves him. Far from *her.* His plane and body will never be found. What's left of him, a star swimmer, will float in warm salt water, then settle lower and lower in the warm salt water. Anne can picture, crazily, one of his football cleats. She can see it spin and gyre toward the ocean floor. In a week or so, in Cleveland, his mother will come to the door in her bathing suit, get the news, and thank the officer who delivers it. She will go back to the pool and say nothing to Anne, who is diving, practicing one-and-a-halfs. Sarah O'Connor will say, "Oh, that was nobody." She will dive into the pool and—hugging the wall so Anne can keep practicing—swim nonstop laps for over an hour. Two weeks after that, his mother will pack up his things, give his furniture to Catholic Charities, and begin repainting his room. His letterman's jacket will be awarded posthumously. Their father will make a special trip to South Bend for it. There will be a moment of silence at halftime, a prayer directed at Touchdown Jesus. But for now, Steven is still moving. Dead, but still moving. Parts of him. Down through the water.

Steven called her *Annie*. Steven alone was allowed to call her *Annie*. It just sounded different, coming from him.

A hundred miles an hour! Fast enough to kill you.

੬੭

THE FIRST WITNESSES were the investigating cops, the coroner, and the crime-lab ghouls. Anne, on a waiting list to get a pass, listened in the hallway, scribbling frantic notes on half a steno pad (she chopped them herself on a paper cutter; WCRB had no reporter's notebooks). During recesses, the reporters were invited into a hot, marble-tiled, BO-smelling back room and, supervised by the bailiff, allowed to look at (but not touch) any and all exhibits entered into evidence. No cameras! But people cheated, and the bailiff looked the other way. Cameramen! Inside the courtroom they sat in front of the bar and stood on empty chairs to get the shots they wanted, and Judge Blythin acted like they were nothing more than flies.

The men, Anne could tell, had a hard time with all the blood. The older ones had no doubt been to war, yet they would glance at pictures of Marilyn's puffy, much-hacked face of death, then turn pale, then turn away. It wrecked them, these black-and-white photographs of a *woman's* blood. After a few days the exhibits contained more than just pictures. *Actual* woman's blood. Step right up.

Blood, blood, blood, and more blood. Pools of blood, drops of blood, splatters of blood. Clotted blood. Bloodstains, bloody clothing, bloody sheets. A fogged and bloody ladies' Longines wristwatch. A blood-encrusted tooth fragment in what looked like a half-sized pill bottle. Blood-soaked squares of wall-to-wall carpeting, hacked out of the middle of rooms. A brick-sized piece of wood, sawed from a stair riser, sporting one dull droplet of blood. A dungaree jacket with blood spots on it. Exhibit 27: a pair of bloody gloves.

Evidence.

Anne's pulse raced (more blood). She did not turn pale and she did not turn away. One day a well-respected (male) reporter from the *Plain Dealer* looked at something bloody, then wept, then vomited.

This trial, Anne thought, this *world,* was run by queasy, blood-fearing men.

The prosecutor held the state record for sending men to the electric chair. Bloodless death. Men.

Only men could make a trial like this bog down over the question of whether, as Dr. Sam's initial statement had indicated, Marilyn's mutilated upper torso had been left exposed by the killer or killers, her *breasts* naked, bruised, and visible (the men bent themselves into pretzels not saying the word *breasts*), or whether, as the first cop on the scene said, Marilyn's blood-smeared, much-punctured upper torso (including her *breasts*) had been covered by a sheet, thus—the prosecutor said—suggesting that the crime scene had been "manipulated." (The way he said that word: *manipulated.* Anyone listening thought of a man's hand on a woman's *breasts.*)

The coroner, Dr. Gerber (a man), mentioned Marilyn's spread legs and moved on. There was no cross-examination on this. No one had tested Marilyn Sheppard's body to see if she'd been raped. No one asked Gerber why not. Only men could have thought that too indecent to mention. Only men could gloss over the obvious and move on.

The defense lawyers tried to make all this blood seem innocent. They claimed it did not necessarily all come from the murder. There was a story about a houseguest who got a fishhook stuck in the meat of his thumb, racing bloodily through the house in search of kindly Dr. Sam. The family dog, an Irish setter named Koko, had just been in heat; some of the bloodstains on the carpet supposedly were hers. Then there was Dr. Sam's job. He was a surgeon. He could be called to the family hospital on short notice. Many articles of his clothing were drizzled with strangers' blood. The day of his wife's murder, Dr. Sam had spent the afternoon slathered in the blood of a beautiful three-year-old boy whose head and upper torso had been run over by a truck.

On the phone, David told her that his uncle had questioned a handyman of the Sheppards who said that if anyone found any blood of his type anywhere in the house, it was because he'd cut his hands on broken glass, changing the storm windows. (This did not come up at the trial.) As hot as it was that summer, Anne asked, why were the Sheppards having the screens put in as late as *June?* Makes no sense. David said a lot of things about this case made no sense. Are you saying, Anne said, that Dr. Sam didn't do it? I'm not saying anything, David said. Do you want the handyman's phone number? She didn't. Your uncle, she said, is grasping at straws.

"By the way," he said, "Irene's having a baby."

By the way? In this context, *by the way?* "That's wonderful!" she said.

"She's due in April," David said.

"That's wonderful," Anne said. October plus nine: July. Oh. "Just fabulous."

Was she the only woman in America of childbearing age who *wasn't* pregnant?

∽

ANNE WENT THROUGH channels to get a pass. Snake eyes.

Occasionally mere members of the public got in; these were *always* women, dressed as if for a lunch at the Union Club. Wives, it turned out, of judges, sheriffs, and high-level newspaper editors. Photographers (not allowed in the courtroom itself) snapped their pretty pictures. These would run atop chipper cutlines in the news section of the next day's editions.

Three weeks into the trial (at about the same time Dr. Sam's mother took an overdose of Tuinal, was rushed to the family hospital, and was saved), Anne's resolve shattered. She had connections of her own. A good reporter should use the connections she has.

The trial broke for Thanksgiving. The day after, Anne was in the courtroom.

The first witness she saw testify was a specialist in the matter of blood-stains. Her name was Mary Cowan. *Her* name. A woman. Both the prosecutor, who had called her, and Dr. Sam's attorneys apologized for the ghastly things they wanted to know. The bespectacled and impassive Mary Cowan, specialist in spilled blood, never flinched.

∽

NEXT CAME THE friends and family. Dr. Sam had a temper, it was said. Marilyn supposedly told their neighbor that Sam was a real "Dr. Jekyll and Mr. Hyde." Cleveland Heights friends of Marilyn's said that she'd buy a new pair of golf shoes or a new icebox and then cower in fear of Sam's reaction—this, even though the playboy osteopath squandered money on sports cars and even once risked his life driving in a sports car race at Put-in-Bay. A cousin of Marilyn's swore that once, when Dr. Sam was telling a story at the dinner table, little Chip had tapped him on the shoulder. Dr. Sam went "red with rage" and beat the boy.

During recesses all that the other reporters could talk about was Susan Hayes this and Susan Hayes that. Outside the court building, the cameras were ready for her.

Men. The way they think, it's just too much.

The men running things pretended to be interested in all this science and all these rules of law and evidence, but Anne wasn't fooled. She knew what they were thinking.

In this corner (Anne wrote in her notebook, bored during yet another defense-team attempt to ask the judge for a mistrial), *the contendah, the pretty, blond, and much-freckled other woman, now living with her parents in Rocky River, where she enjoys doing the dishes, listening to recordings of classical music, reading the Holy Bible, and shooing reporters off her parents' front porch, weighing in at a trim 108 pounds . . . Miss Susaa-a-a-a-a-an Hayes!*

In the other corner, the champe-e-e-en of the world, the martyred Sunday school teacher, the loving mother, pretty herself (only not as), young herself (only not as), slaughtered while carrying her second child and now currently decomposing in her grave, ladies and gentlemen, you know her! you love her! here she is, the wronged wife . . . Mrs. Marily-y-y-y-yn Sheppard!

It wasn't so much that Anne had changed her mind about Dr. Sam. If he didn't do it, who did? If his story's the truth, why doesn't the evidence better support it? But it gave her pause that almost everyone covering the trial from out of town had come to think Dr. Sam was getting railroaded. Anne wasn't so sure, but the more she saw, the less she could explain what this trial had to do with anybody's idea of justice.

⌘

"I KNOW THAT'S what I said," said Hoot Thagard. He'd slammed the office door so hard that his framed diploma—indicating that Tobias T. Thagard was worthy of a degree in agriculture and animal husbandry from the Ohio State University—had crashed to the floor. Broken glass. He did not pick it up. (Was he afraid of getting cut?) He had Anne sit down, across the desk from him. She'd never seen him even remotely angry before. "I still mean it. I'm not particular on what you report about, so long as you don't report on that."

When Mr. Thagard was angry, his stammer went away.

There had been complaints, he said, from listeners. "I warned you," he said.

"Not to not cover it at all," she said.

"You're the only reporter we have. There are more stories out there than that filth."

"Name one," she said.

"You're fired," he said. "Get out."

When Mr. Thagard was angry, he seemed to know what to do with his hands. They were folded on his desk before him. He sat perfectly still, made eye contact perfectly well.

"I'm sorry," she said.

He kept looking at her.

"I got carried away," she said.

He nodded. "Correct."

"I didn't mean to be arrogant, when I said for you to name one. I just meant that I was caught up in that story and I..." She smiled at him. She gave him that smile. She sat up straight. "I really was asking for you to suggest other stories for me to cover."

He reached into a wire in-basket, took out a file folder full of press releases, and dropped them on the desk in front of her. "Here," he said. "But listen. That's, that's...ah. Two strikes."

The morning Dr. Sam Sheppard took the stand, Anne O'Connor was on bended knee in the middle of the Christmas display at Halle Brothers department store, before a little house, her microphone thrust in the face of Mr. Jing-a-Ling.

Several WCRB listeners called in to say they liked the story. One, though, complained about the lack of a story on the Sheppard case. The listener asked to talk to Mr. Thagard specifically. "He thanked me for listening," said the friend Anne had put up to make the call. It was her old friend Jane, home for the holidays. "He said to call back anytime."

∞

THE TRIAL ENDED. Though Susan Hayes had been called as a witness in the coroner's inquest (under oath: thus, as the *Press* kept reminding the world, opening up the possibility that, irrespective of the murder verdict, she and/or Dr. Sam might still be charged with perjury for their disinclination to kiss and tell), she was never called to testify at the trial. The Sheppards' dead baby stayed where it was. It was not entered into evidence.

Four days before Christmas, about the time the baby had been due, the verdict came in. Guilty. Second-degree murder. The judge sentenced Dr. Sam to life. He avoided the chair. Seventeen days later, his mother locked herself in a bathroom at Dr. Sam's brother's house and shot herself in the head (imagine the blood). A week after she was buried, his father's stomach ulcer hemorrhaged. (*Hemorrhage;* from the Greek; "a copious discharge of blood.") He died, too.

∽

FOR MONTHS ANNE O'Connor did as she was told. She kept her distance from her parents, from her brother and Ibby (Ibby was *so* protective about that baby, a person couldn't get within a mile of them anyway), from David Zielinsky, from most of her old friends, from anything approximating hard news.

She found out that Bill Randle, the new rock-and-roll king of Cleveland, used to be in the CIA. She let it go.

In March Randle was filming a rock-and-roll movie—aping Alan Freed, yet again—in a high school gymnasium in the ticky-tack suburb of Brooklyn, the kind of place a person could live in Cleveland her whole life and need directions to find. Patrick had arranged for her to interview the director. That afternoon, though, on a whim, she stopped by her old prep school to watch a diving meet. The team was good that year. Anne sat in a corner and tried not to be seen. She was wearing flats, velvet pants, a silk shirt, a loosened Italian scarf, and a loose tweed Brooks Brothers jacket that had been Steven's; it was among a box of his things that Anne had found in the huge, leaky basement of the main house, things (she wrongly assumed) that her mother had overlooked. There, in her old school, Anne felt as if she were in costume, as if she had won the lead in a play and needed to make the audience believe she was thirty years old.

The star of the team had once been a gawky sophomore who hero-worshiped Anne. Now, look at her! She could do things Anne could never dream of. She had a grace and precision Anne was too aggressive to master.

Anne went out to the car and got her tape machine.

She came back in, watched the entire meet, missing the filming of the concert so she could do a story on her prep school swimming team and the hopes of its star diver to capture a state championship. After the interview, the girl drove with Anne to the station. They laughed and laughed like schoolgirls. Anne had the time of her life. She put the story together, read the news, and went out dancing with her old friend. They spent a lot of time at a Dog 'n' Suds drive-in. They flirted with boys (not men). At the end of the night, Anne went home to her dumb apartment in her dumb carriage house and, privately, broke down and sobbed.

Later, Anne would not believe she'd missed the chance to see Elvis Presley's first performance outside the South.

"Who knew?" Anne would say. She would labor to make not seeing him into just as good a story as seeing him.

⌇

"Is Mary Cowan here?"

The new Cuyahoga County Coroner's offices had been built on the campus of Western Reserve University. A modern facility, in the worst sense of that.

The receptionist was about Anne's age. "The job has been filled," she said. She was wearing cat-eyed glasses and a loud red sweater that had no doubt been knitted by her arthritic and myopic *busi*. "I started today."

Anne took out her letter from Mr. Thagard, now much-rumpled. "I'm not here about a job; I'm here to do one," she said. "I'm a reporter. I want to ask her a few questions."

The receptionist told Anne she could take a seat. The lobby was filled with Danish furniture. Teak. On the walls were framed aerial photographs of Cleveland. Everywhere a person looked there were shiny new things of the sort a bourgeois person would think of as "classy." Ficus, ficus, ficus.

Anne waited for a good solid ten minutes.

Finally, out came a young man with a very bad case of acne. He said he was Mary Cowan's assistant. Anne bluffed her way in. She had her homely reporter's notebook, but she had not brought a tape machine.

The young man spelled his name out to her. She wrote it down. He was a medical student. Before they even got to the evidence-storage room, he had asked her out.

She took out her notebook and scribbled a fake number. "Call me," she said. "I get off work at seven-thirty. How's eight?"

"Great!" He laughed. "Eight, great. I'm a poet, and I don't know it, but my feet show it, Longfellow." The man's name was Dennis. He stopped to show her his feet. "Actually, I have very small feet. Runs in the family."

"You know what they say," she said.

"No." He looked baffled.

"Small feet," she said, "warm heart."

The room was in the basement, filled with industry-grade metal shelves and rows of what looked like overgrown filing cabinets.

The young man knew right where to go. "We never put all this stuff

[230]

completely away," he says. "You'd be surprised how many requests like yours there are, and Dr. Gerber thinks there still might be an appeal."

The baby was gone.

"Crap," said Dennis the med student. "I'd've sworn it was still here."

"You lost it?"

"No," he said. "That would be impossible. We don't lose anything around here."

He looked and looked.

"What I bet happened," he finally said, "is that the family buried it." He seemed psychotically cheered up by this. "I'm sure that's probably what happened."

Manic now, Dennis told her to wait right where she was. A moment later he came back, toting an empty glass jar about the size of the ones on the bottom shelf of the grocery aisle. "It was in one just like this," he said. He was very pleased with himself. "It was a girl."

Anne held the jar.

For some reason she opened it. She smelled it, but it didn't smell like anything.

"I brought you a jar," he said, "so you could picture it."

He described to her what it looked like. Dennis was the sort of young man who thought that if he could shock a girl a little bit, she would think he was brave.

"You are a very literal-minded man," she said. "I like that."

She ran her hands over the surface of the jar. She put the lid back on, held it up to the light. "You sure keep things clean around here," she said.

"You have to," he said, "with evidence."

She went back to WCRB, did a story on the missing fetus, apologized to Mr. Thagard for having acquired what was no doubt her third strike, quit before she could be fired, and admitted to him that she was only nineteen years old.

Anne was back at Smith in time for the summer session.

She took her car. She still drove it too fast, but, let's face it, if it's your time, any speed is fast enough to kill you.

LOCAL HEROES

∾

Third in a Series: The Anchorwoman's Tale

1957–1960

IT'S SEVEN MINUTES after nine when a big white Lincoln Continental, empty except for its driver, pulls up in front of the blunt, new, cement-box building at the corner of Euclid and East 30th. The driver wears white gloves and is alone. But wait. In the passenger side, barely visible over the dashboard, is a shock of flame-red hair. The door opens, and out rolls a near-visible cloud of tuberose perfume. Dorothy Fuldheim has arrived.

Wearing a blue-and-white taffeta ball gown.

A little after nine on a train-wreck of a Monday morning so far, and Dorothy Fuldheim is decked out in pearls and heavy bracelets and wearing the gown already, and a pox on anyone who might think it's too early. Can it be too early to be elegant? For ten years she's read the news and commented on the news, the first woman in America with her own TV news show, and all those years she wore smart, stylish suits—suits of a cut and cachet that she could barely afford and could not afford to be without. But today calls for the gown. She has a closet full of gowns, of course, but today warrants a brand-new one, the heck with what it cost. A dress like this, Aunt Molly would have said, is not an expense. It's an investment.

Dorothy Fuldheim is sixty-four years old.

She crosses the sidewalk, lugging a leather book bag, thinking of the advice Aunt Molly gave her a half century ago. *Walk like a woman whose business it is to be a woman.* She does. She sways, she swishes. That dashing young man, one of the station announcers and the singer for her new show, opens the door for her. "Hiya, Red," he says.

She gives him a queenly nod and does not break stride. The way this morning has gone,[1] Dorothy does not want to talk. The young man offers to carry her bag. She ignores him.

The young man breaks into song. *"You're a symphony,"* he sings, *"a very beautiful sonata, my Inamorata."* His Dean Martin is spot-on. *"Say that you're my sweetheart, my love."*

In the lobby the receptionist, one of the salesmen, and two members of the public, waiting on a sofa, all stop to applaud.

"Bah," she says. "You should have seen me when I was your age," she says—to the young man, but playing to the crowd. She can't help herself. "I was quite something, you know. You'd have sung the whole song, on bended knee."

"Back then, you wouldn't have given me a second look," says the young man. At the radio station where they'd both worked before television existed and they came to work here (both Scripps-Howard operations, same as the *Press*), he was singing in one studio when she arrived in another, and she waved coquettishly at him and tripped and fell; she went on anyway, read the news and allowed him to take her to the hospital; her arm was broken. "You'd have never stood still to listen to all of it."

"And I shan't do so now," she says, and keeps going.

That could be her motto: *She says, and keeps going.*

Her office is crammed with flowers. Most she sent herself. She looks through the cards. Roses from Scripps-Howard, a carnation arrangement from her producer, bouquets from viewers. None of the flowers are from P—. She drops her bag on the floor, sits heavily down, breaks out the gingersnaps, and starts on the coffee.

---

[1] You're entitled, Dorothy. Your mother smeared herself with feces. In the back room, your fourteen-year-old invalid granddaughter undertook a bout of otherworldly bleating that began before the nurse arrived and was still going on when the driver honked. The poor Lhasa apso cowered in the breezeway. Throughout this, your agreeable sad-sack husband—#2 in a series—sat at the kitchen table, talking endlessly about hydrangeas. That a morning like this was not unprecedented is no reason for you to accept with docility what happened. And you don't. Thank God, in whom you would like to believe, for Junior. Junior tended to the crises on all fronts. Imagine how much worse things would be without Junior! You cannot imagine.

In Studio C stagehands spread white tablecloths across two dozen tables. Coffee brews. One by one, members of the Joe Howard Orchestra arrive, sprightly Caucasians decked out in swallow-tailed morning formal wear. The lights come up on a smartly arrayed parlor, the new set: a convincing fireplace; a sofa, armchair, and coffee table all with Queen Anne legs; walls painted robin's-egg blue (Dorothy's favorite color), decorated with Stiffel sconces and oil paintings by accomplished local artists. The pastry chef at the Hollenden Hotel delivers twenty cheesecakes himself. He will oversee their service. It's New York-style, an irony that occurred to Dorothy Fuldheim only after she placed the order herself.

All morning people flit in and wish her well on the new show. She finds herself being snappish. She loves the attention, she does. But can't they see she has work to do? Without closing her door, and without being rude to anyone, Dorothy Fuldheim has no choice but to assume the position; she has the remarkable ability to hunch her gnomish body over her big desk with such Talmudic zeal that any passerby would, and does, find it intimidating.

The books are new, ones she might review on the show. She will return to book reviews on this show, the producers have promised. Pitiful ten-minute segments, not the hour she'd been given during her years on the lecture circuit, but she'll take it. Book reviews are what saved her and sustained her, what paid the bills and fed her soul and made her famous. She takes out the first one. *Atlas Shrugged*. She sets it in the middle of her desk. She opens it from the back cover; 1,168 pages. She looks at the book some more. She puts one cheek on the desk and considers the book from this angle. It sits on her desk, like a big fat threat. She takes out another one. *On the Road*. She diagonal-page skim-reads it. She never reads every word of a book. It's a gift, she tells people. Kerouac takes her half an hour. Ugh. These unkempt beatniks, what do they think their rudeness might change in this world? Where are the Thackerays of today? The Gissings? The George Eliots? Not that she does not love many of today's writers. Give her Noël Coward. Give her Dawn Powell. Give her a biography of Marie Curie, Booker T. Washington, or Catherine the Great. Give her *Profiles in Courage*. Give her *Raintree County*.

She holds out her hands. They're shaking. All these years, and she's nervous?

She shudders, shakes it off, takes out the *New York Times,* which she's already read at breakfast (it was that or talk about hydrangeas). She drinks too much coffee. That could be part of the nervousness (but then into what, pray tell, would she dunk her gingersnaps?). In and out of the ladies' room she goes, in that grand, rustling dress, her jewelry jangling. She is perspiring somewhat freely. She dabs herself into a low glow. She reapplies the tuberose.

The public is arriving, about a hundred strong. They had to write for tickets, and write they did. The doors to Studio C open. The people are shown to their seats. On trips to the bathroom, Dorothy Fuldheim takes the long way back to her office, to spy on them, her public. She tiptoes into the wings and cranes her head to see.

"They love you, Red." It's the young man. He's changed clothes. He's in a swallow-tailed coat now, too.

"Have you seen my fountain pen?" she says. It is the first excuse to pop into her head.

"I'll keep an eye out for it," he says. "Don't worry," he says. "You'll be great."

"It's rude," she says, "to sneak up on people."

She rustles down the back corridor, back to the offices. She and that disc jockey, the cohost with whom she's been saddled, have a brief meeting with the station manager, the producer, and the floor director. They run through the show for the day, what comes after what. Dorothy Fuldheim listens and offers the stray opinion. Once she's out there under the stage lights, she will do what she wants, without a script and without notes, as always. That's what she does. Sometimes she makes notes, to put straight her thoughts, but she leaves them purposely in her office. Scripts are not what she does. If they don't like it, they can just look for someone else.

She doesn't mean that. Neither does she say it.

When the meeting is finished, she hurries back to her office. Finally, thank God (in whom she would like to believe), the phone rings, and it's Dorothy Fuldheim Jr. They live in the same house, and have for all of Junior's life, but every morning they call each other. Junior, a thirty-eight-year-old college student with a congenitally weak heart, has a break between classes now. They giggle and chat and kvetch, like sisters. They are both widows. One dead husband apiece, both of weak hearts. Dorothy's was a weak-hearted attorney, father to Junior's condition. As for Junior's husband, he came home from the war and saw his baby for the first time, and soon thereafter swallowed calcium cyanide on his parents' front lawn. Gerber, the coroner, ruled it a suicide—a weak heart of a different sort. Aunt Molly had, before the age of twenty-five, buried three husbands. At twenty-five! At the same age, Dorothy was an old-maid schoolteacher in Milwaukee who'd scarcely had three *dates*.

Junior tells her mother to break a leg.

Dorothy Fuldheim tells Junior she's her shining light. She hangs up. At last, her hands are still. She goes to touch up her makeup.

She never told Junior about New York. Spilt milk now anyway. Good heavens. How, realistically, could she have *ever* disentangled her life enough to go to New York? Bah. Plus, as proof of how things even out, now here's this show: a show that lets Dorothy Fuldheim do all the things she does. She will comment on the news. She will interview the news makers of our time. She will work without a script. She will speechify, edify, testify. She will act.

Having a cohost was not her idea. Especially the cohost they picked, a glib disc jockey answering on occasion to the nickname of Smoochie. Smoochie! A name for a poodle, if you ask Dorothy Fuldheim. Poodles, however, she liked. Any kind of dog. That poor old dog of hers, this morning, skulking into the breezeway to lie down and quiver.

My word, look at the time!

Eight minutes to air. Dorothy Fuldheim takes a deep breath. This is forever, if you're a pro, if this is your life.

She hurries to the wings. She is sixty-four years old, ready to make her debut. Her hands again begin to shake. Must be the coffee. Must be.

She catches the eye of the young man, the singer. He winks at her.

She rolls her eyes, then closes them, holds her breath, and makes her entrance.

She sweeps forward, sashaying across the studio. When the audience sees her, there emits from its members a guttural *ooooh*. They *love* her gown, her jewels, her walk, her presence: they love *her*! They break into applause! She has done nothing, but they applaud. She is a *star*. They applaud. She is a force of nature. They applaud. A room changes because she, the public Dorothy, has entered it. There are few men in the room (six or seven in the audience, plus the orchestra members and the men behind the cameras, running the sound and managing the station), but the looks on their faces make it plain: even at her age, this has everything to do with *sex*. Women love her because she is not beautiful and therefore not threatening, and men love her for no reason they will allow themselves to consider. Also, she is smart. She knows who she is. She is perfect.

They applaud.

Dorothy Fuldheim takes her place in the Queen Anne chair. There is a little box at its feet on which she can rest hers. The disc jockey sits on the sofa. The floor director begins the countdown to air.

Welcome to television! Whatever the heck that is. Ten years into the game and still no one really knows. But, hey: Welcome to it!

The cameras roll.

The orchestra holds aloft its instruments.

In the control room, a sound-effects man bongs a chime once. Into his microphone, the young man tells northeast Ohio what time it is.

And now, ladies and gentlemen, live from downtown Cleveland, Ohio, the Best Location in the Nation, welcome to *The One O'Clock Club*!

⮞⮜

ONCE UPON A time, in a great midwestern city renowned for its engines and beer, there was born under the sooty skies of poverty the youngest child of three: a girl. Her name was Dorothy.[2] Her brother and sister were good-looking, but Dorothy was not. Her brother and sister grew tall, but Dorothy did not. Her brother was a gifted musician, her sister was a gifted dancer, but Dorothy had no talents anyone could see. She read twelve books a week. On her every trip to the library, she hid at the top of the grand marble stairs and waited until no one was watching; then, pretending that the books cradled in one arm were the imaginary train of an imaginary ball gown, she held her head high and descended the stairs, waving like royalty to imaginary well-wishers, blowing kisses to imaginary suitors, smiling benevolently at her imaginary subjects, basking in a roar of imaginary applause.

The girl had a beautiful godmother named Molly. Aunt Molly was the loveliest woman in Milwaukee, yet despite or because of this she was cursed. Her lips were made to be kissed, it's true, and her body was made to be held by men, of this the young Dorothy had no doubt. Yet men would fall in love with sweet Molly and die. She must have been a sad and miserable god-mother indeed, but she loved Dorothy very much and did not let the girl see anything but grit, pluck, and womanly wiles. Molly taught the girl how to walk. She taught her how to be brave and strong in a man's world. She taught her the three R's of womanhood: repartee, remuneration, resilience.

The girl's father was also able to see Dorothy's inner beauty. He, too, undertook to equip her with magic powers. He took her with him to the Milwaukee County Courthouse, where they sat together in the gallery, listening to silver-tongued, gold-motivated oratory as if it were music. For in fact it was! Dorothy learned to hear it. Before long, Dorothy was learning to make it.

---

[2] From the Greek. Meaning "a gift from God." Your family was not Greek; they were Jewish, though nonpracticing. This is in contrast to another girl growing up in the same Milwaukee neighborhood, Goldie Mabovitch. The Mabovitches practiced, man, practiced. Years later, after both Goldie and you had traveled the world and done things no woman in your by-then-respective countries had ever done, you interviewed her. By then her name was Golda Meir. It happened in Cleveland, on your turf. The word *myth* is also Greek.

One night while she was still a girl, her father took her and his other children to his lodge: a great hall of elders. Her brother had a talent: he played the piano for them, and they applauded. Her sister had a talent: she danced, and they applauded. When it was Dorothy's turn, she did the only thing she could think of: she talked. She gave a lecture about isolationism. Lecturing was still a song she was learning to sing, and the elders were, Dorothy could tell, bored. But this was the Midwest, home of politeness, and when she finished, the elders applauded. For the first time, she did not have to use her imagination!

∽

"THEY CALL YOU *the Toe?*" Dorothy Fuldheim asks.

"Some of the guys call me that," says Lou Groza. "I think the reporters started it."

"And why do they call you that?"

"I'm a kicker," he says. Groza is not wearing formal wear; just a coat and tie. "A tackle, too, but the nickname, it has to do with my kicking."

"What I don't understand," she says, "is why you only kick with one toe."

Groza chuckles. "Are you serious?"

"Don't I look serious to you?"

"Yes, ma'am," admits the Toe. "You do. Very."

"Believe it or not," says the disc jockey, "you're right. She's serious."

Dorothy Fuldheim gives the disc jockey a look. In Cleveland her interviews of sports figures are legendary. She asks boxers about their home runs, shortstops about their touchdowns. No one is clear about the degree to which this is or is not pure shtick, which is how Dorothy Fuldheim would like it to stay.[3]

She soldiers on. "Tell me, Mr. . . . How do you pronounce that name of yours again?"

"Groza."

"Mr. Groza. You are a football kicker. Exactly how high do you kick the football?"

The audience laughs and the disc jockey positively guffaws. Dorothy Fuldheim's face isn't one you would call straight: its mouth is lopsided, and she contorts it with her every nimble thought. But right now it is as straight as it will go.

"How high?" says the now-troubled tackle.

---

[3] You were a trained stage actress. Also a television pioneer. Tomato/tomahto. Which is not to say you knew thing one about sports.

"Yes."

Groza frowns. He can't tell if his chain is being yanked. "It goes I would say thirty feet in the air. But the point really is how far it goes."

"How far does it go?"

"That depends," he says, "on where the team is on the field."

"I see." Or so she says. "And where *is* your team on the field? When you kick, I mean."

"It varies," he says.

"I see," she says.

Groza looks around the studio, as if for a substitution from the bench. Off camera the floor director wolfs down cheesecake and shrugs.

"I led all kickers in points scored last year," Groza says. "This year I'm leading again."

Blankly, Fuldheim considers him. "Let's talk about your coach. His name, they tell me, is Mister Paul Brown." She squirms in her chair. Her hands dance; full-force-five gesticulation.

"Coach Brown," Groza says. "He's a genius, Coach Brown."

"Are all the teams named after their coaches?"

"They wanted to call us the Panthers, but some fella owned that name, so there was a contest. The fans picked Browns. I don't know the whole story."

"You don't? Then why are you here?"

Groza shifts in his chair. "I don't know the whole story on that story."

"I see." Fuldheim puts a finger to her cheekbone. "What, then, is a 'Brown'?"

"It's just a name, is all."

"It doesn't mean *anything?*"

"Sometimes you see a picture of an elf," he volunteers. Lou Groza has hope in his eyes.

"An elf?"

Helpless, Groza looks at the disc jockey.

"A brownie," the disc jockey says.

"I believe that's right," says Groza.

"Not the Girl Scout kind," offers the disc jockey.

"Definitely not," Groza says. "For a while there we had a midget for a mascot. Maybe that's how the elf came about. I'm not sure what was first, that midget or the elf cartoon."

"I see," says Dorothy Fuldheim. "Have you ever been to Scotland?"

"Ma'am?"

"*Ma'am.* You know, Mister Toe," she says, "you have lovely manners."

"Thank you."

"You're welcome," she says. "Scotland is *marvelous*. You really must visit it. Brownies are a kind of elf that comes from Scotland. They come into your home at night and help with the housework. Isn't that just grand! I have a brownie myself, only her name is Mildred and she comes during the day and I have to pay her."

The audience loves it!

"Huh," says Groza. Now it's his turn to soldier on. "Um, some teams, y'know, in the sports world, some are just named for colors. There's, what, the Grays. The Blues. The Reds."

"The Reds! Yes!" says Dorothy Fuldheim. The vehemence of her epiphany makes both the disc jockey and Groza jump. She wriggles in her seat as if its cushion were imbued with biting ants. "I read that they changed their name. To the Redlegs, and do you know why?"

"Go ahead, Lou," says the disc jockey. "Tell her."

"So people wouldn't think they were Commies?" Groza says.

"Exactly!" She can still get a little thrill from leading a horse to water and watching it drink, a joy born way back when she was still Miss Snell, old-maid schoolteacher. "What *are* your feelings about Senator McCarthy?"

"Senator McCarthy?" McCarthy died recently. Call it natural causes. "Jeez, I don't know. It's kind of sad?"

By now Groza is looking to her for approval.

"It is sad," she affirms. "Personally, you know, he was a charming man, impeccably polite. It goes without saying that his professional conduct was another matter."

She does not gloat. She interviewed McCarthy and, later, denounced him in a commentary—*weeks* before Edward R. Murrow's famous version of the same thing. She feels no need to remind her audience of this. In truth, few among them need reminding.

"Hmm," Groza says. He has his hands clamped tightly to his knees.

"Is it hard for Mr. Brown," she asks, "coaching his son?"

"His son?"

She gets up and reaches behind the couch for a copy of today's *Press*, a prop from the last segment, an interview with Louie Seltzer. She pulls out the sports section. "This young man, the rookie the people are so excited about? He's not Coach Brown's son?"

Groza cracks up. "Am I on *Candid Camera*?"

"The name of the show," the disc jockey says, directly into the camera, "is *The One O'Clock Club*."

The audience is nearly in tears. No one is drinking coffee, for fear of committing a ferocious spit-take.

"Well?" says Dorothy Fuldheim.

"Miss Fuldheim," Lou Groza says, softly, "Jim Brown is a Negro."

Dorothy Fuldheim sits back down and examines the paper more closely. "Well," she says. "So he is."

The audience is *so* with her! What a show!

"You know, my late husband used to drag me to baseball games," she says. "The coach in baseball wears a uniform. But now look here." She holds the paper up. She keeps it still. She knows what the cameraman needs. She is a natural. "Your Coach Brown wears street clothes."

"All the coaches wear street clothes."

"Not baseball coaches."

"Baseball is different," says the disc jockey.

"Why is it different, Mr. Groza?"

Groza looks at her. He is, by the standards of the day, a behemoth. His eyes are wide with fear. "It's just different," he says. "You should ask a baseball person that question."

"Why would I want to do that," she asks. "I don't know *anything* about sports, I *never* cook, I eat gingersnaps for breakfast!" she says. "And if I *knew* the answers to my questions, I wouldn't ask them."

The audience explodes in applause.

Cut to commercial.

One segment still to go, but, to use a term germane to football, baseball, boxing, theater, the movies, popular music, organized crime, and television: It's a hit!

⌒

ALWAYS, IN A true myth, there must be the intervention of supernatural aid.

So: Dorothy grew older and wiser. She went out into the world to seek her fortune.[4] By day, she trained the young minds of Milwaukee. By night,

---

4 The young men of Milwaukee, like young men everywhere, were endowed with the most literal sorts of imaginations. They could not imagine themselves with you. You could imagine yourself with them. Eventually you met a sweet, weak-hearted young man with a law degree, working for an insurance concern. By then you were twenty-five, scarcely of marriageable age. You married. He had to have known, even then, that he was destined to wind up in a footnote. Not even that, if it weren't for you. He can't complain. You made that clear to him.

she was a member of a theater troupe. On a stage she could disappear, and reappear. She could become someone else: herself.

One fateful night Dorothy found herself in the City of Broad Shoulders, starring in a play. In it, she played a woman furious that the state treats women as mere breeding animals. The character is a mother of two sons. One suffers from hideous birth defects. The other is able and handsome. The character rages at the injustice of a state that forbade her to have the "THING"[5] killed and yet summons the able, handsome son to war. In the audience was an angel.[6] It was a midwestern angel, one who showered blessings upon common sense and the downtrodden. The angel felt in Dorothy's fiery performance a force for good.

There came a knock at the stage door. Dorothy opened it. Before her stood the angel! To Dorothy's wondering ears, the angel offered to send her to a faraway land, a City of Brotherly Love, to give a speech that would promote world peace and social justice. There would be other speakers, older and more famous, but the angel deemed Dorothy worthy of being in their number. Humbled, Dorothy could do little but accept.

The speech was a success, but rather than continuing on that path, Dorothy found herself married, and she moved with her husband back to his hometown, another great midwestern city, perhaps the greatest of them all.[7] Dorothy had a baby and named her Junior. Dorothy and her little family continued their journey through life in an apartment on the East Side of that great city and were very poor. One day Dorothy was walking the baby in a stroller when a rich woman, a stranger, stopped her. Aren't you the woman I heard in the City of Brotherly Love? said the rich woman. You are the answer to my prayers![8]

The rich woman said she needed a speaker, someone to do a book review at a meeting of the Women's City Club. The book was about supermen who ruled the world.

Dorothy had no idea what this entailed, but it had to do with a book, and public speaking, and it paid ten dollars. She accepted, spent three dollars

---

[5] All caps in the script.

[6] Jane Addams, director of Hull House and an official inspector of the streets and alleys of the city of Chicago. Winner of the 1931 Nobel Peace prize.

[7] The slogan "Best Location in the Nation" was coined by a Cleveland utility company that placed ads in national magazines, seeking to draw business to the city. It came to be semiofficially adopted by the city. You called it "witless Babbittry."

[8] You wanted to believe in prayers. You were a person full of the spirit. You envied those able to believe. You didn't say this to the rich woman.

on the material for a fancy gown, and made it while she read the book. A week later she climbed to the podium and atop a little box behind the podium, and even then had to stand on tiptoe. She talked about the book for an hour, acting out the good parts and scaring the bejabbers out of rich women of the city. Supermen might really someday rule the world! Stranger things have happened. It got Dorothy not only a free meal and ten dollars but also a standing ovation! Everyone loved her.

The next thing she knew, she was on the lecture circuit, giving hour-long book reviews from one end of the earth to the other (in myths, the earth has ends). But the presence of the angel endured, and though Dorothy remained short, her stature as a speaker grew. She spoke about the world and what it was coming to. She was a prophet of her times. She took to the very airwaves, speaking about the issues of the day and performing improvised miniature biographies of the famous. Whenever she returned home to speak, she was so beloved, they decorated the meeting hall to match the gown she wore.

k

WHEN THE SHOW comes back from commercial, there she is, Dorothy Fuldheim, seated on the stairs to the set, her dress arrayed around her like a pool of shiny elegance, her eyes fixed squarely on the lens of the camera. For this, the final segment, the book review, Dorothy Fuldheim has left her chair. She's descended the steps of the set, in plain view of flesh-and-blood well-wishers. It was all she could do not to blow a kiss.

Instead, she brings fire.

James Gould Cozzens. *By Love Possessed,* which everyone this year is calling the Great American Novel. No notes. She isn't even holding the book for a prop. No spotlight. The stage remains lit. It's just her. She does voices. She acts out stories from the novel. She burns. Yet, amid all this passion, she manages to reassure the viewers that this important book is for more than just the eggheads.

She looks out into the darkness, across a plane of coffee-stained tablecloths, and her audience, her public, stares back at her, utterly still, mouths agape. They're *hers.*

"Again and again," she concludes, "poor Arthur Winner is amazed to learn a lesson we all, sadly, must learn again and again in our own lives. It is a lesson as hard to learn for the somewhat-well-to-do as it is for the humblest stevedore, or the most straitlaced schoolmarm. The human heart is unruly. It will not do what it is told."

The next few weeks are a cascade of congratulations and well-wishers.

Telegrams galore: Mayor Celebrezze; several council members and county commissioners; strangers of every sort (rich ones, poor ones, beggarmen, thieves; East Siders *and* West Siders); the management at Kornman's, Halle Brothers, Higbee's, the Theatrical, and someone with a sense of humor in the offices of the Browns. Friends and neighbors.[9] Junior takes time from her studies to come watch a show. Daily, bouquets arrive. Quite a bit of chocolate. The station is besieged by requests for tickets to the show. Somewhere in there comes a massive horseshoe of chrysanthemums from P—.

Dorothy Fuldheim can do it all: hard news and entertainment, politics and showbiz. She expresses firm opinions. She approaches the world with genuine and unflagging curiosity. She is on television, in the historic present tense.

Dorothy Fuldheim owns Cleveland.

At first, she doesn't think so. *Owns?* She's been a tenant all her life.

But the more time she spends on television, the more she gets the best tables in restaurants. The more any celebrity passing through Cleveland feels the obligation to come see her, often bearing gifts, as if she were a monarch to whom tribute must be paid. When a blizzard makes her late for a performance of the Cleveland Orchestra (yes, a blizzard; no evidence exists that it had anything to do with P—), they delay the concert until she arrives and is seated. It is a sublime concert, a tribute to the recently deceased Jean Sibelius, pride of the Finns, and thus—if anything—enhanced by the snow outside.

She doesn't trust it, any of it.[10] Clevelanders can *tell* she doesn't trust it; a lack of trust can't be faked. Naturally, this makes everyone love her more.

People who've never met Dorothy Fuldheim feel like she's a member of the family. She can't believe it. Before television, there was nothing like this. For a stranger to feel like one of the family, people need to *see* you. They need to feel like you are real.

Dorothy Fuldheim, they see. Even in black and white, it's plain how colorful she is. Dorothy Fuldheim is present. She's real.

ༀ

YOU WERE THE sort of person around whom myths arose.

You said so yourself.

---

[9] Your husband sent a card. He was, by the standards of his times, very supportive. You would want us to be clear on that. He was a graduate of Cleveland Law School. He had a one-man practice in a walk-up office a few blocks from home. He did his best.

[10] Except Junior. You couldn't have trusted anyone more than you trusted Junior.

(A concession? A confession? An advertisement?)

Of *course* you were—in any good dictionary's first-string sense of the word: a traditional story dealing with a hero who embodies a culture's ideals and truths. But you were a journalist.[11] Journalists tend to use that word, *myth*, in the sense any good dictionary relegates to fifth- or sixth-string status: half-truths, scurrilous and/or resonant rumors, things to be dispelled, debunked, and quashed.

For example: you did not have a photographic memory. You wrote things out merely to get your thoughts straight. Then you'd go on and, even after the advent of the TelePrompTer, be extemporaneous. You weren't there to read, you said, but to communicate. This had nothing to do with any quote-unquote photographic memory.

Inevitably there were rumors you would go to New York. *If you're so good, why are you still here?* Were you good? Most thought so. Were you still here? You were. You had your reasons. These were reasons you did not want to talk about. So you talked about New York, all the offers, in *spades* you had offers! You talked all the time about how you should have gone to New York, how in New York the station would have provided you with a driver. How true was all this? Gospel. How factual? Let's put it this way: no one can say there was not at least one substantial offer. A myth? Yes (in the classical sense) and no (in the journalistic).

That Cleveland Orchestra story? Delaying the performance for you? Never happened, you said.

You were a flirt. No argument there. You bragged about how far you'd come, from a girl yearning for her luck with boys to change, to a woman who believed any man in her company was lucky. As a consequence, there were rumors of suitors. But when coworkers noticed the lavish gifts that came to your office signed only "P—," you said you had no idea what that was about. A secret admirer. It was a matter about which you were aflame with unsatisfied curiosity!

---

[11] Some said you weren't a journalist, although you played one on TV. Also because. You were accused of being less a journalist than a personality. Your accusers? Journalists (some of whom would give anything to become a personality). To co-opt their odd language for a moment, though: look at the facts. You were doing a journalist's job, better than almost anyone in town; ipso facto, no? Eventually, in a career long enough to see *TV journalism* go from an oxymoron to an overenrolled course of study in American universities, you began to call *yourself* a journalist. Why not? What else?

And for heaven's sake: Edward VIII, the self-deposed king of England and a guest of yours (his second-ever TV interview), was not your one true love. That was a journalistic myth, one you would gladly go anywhere to disabuse. Again and again. No substance to it at all. Really. You mean that. Really. Is that microphone on?

∽

IN THE YEARS that follow, she continues to do her commentaries. She never stops. (*She says, and keeps going.*) *The One O'Clock Club* is a nice red cherry on top of that big hot fudge sundae she likes to call *success,* but its novelty is sure to wane. It's the commentaries that matter. *The One O'Clock Club* could exist without her, she supposes—they could find a younger woman who'd be less acid in her exchanges with the disc jockey—but the commentaries: who would they get for that? Her commentaries on the news and on the hard, prosaic truths of life (these made frequent reference to Aunt Molly) are as much a part of the station as its call letters or its network affiliation. She does one during the six o'clock news, a different one during the eleven (filmed at 6:35; her days are long but not *that* long). Hundreds of them a year! She'll use a good one over and over, like a speech on the lecture circuit, like a play performed anew each night of its run.[12] Powerful people call her to ask what she's going to say on a particular issue.[13] Throughout the Cuyahoga River watershed, when her image appears on a turned-on, half-watched television set, people stop what they're doing. For three to five minutes, dishes soak in the sink, stews go unstirred, children are told to hush up, vacuums lie silent and abhorred, cocktail shakers are set down, and arguments cease. How does she know this? They tell her. They telegram, they write, they call, they stop her on the street and they tell her.

She doesn't even trust that.

She is sixty-four years old, then sixty-five years old, and then sixty-six. She signs one-year contract after one-year contract, privately certain each will be the last.[14] Most television stations have no women reporters or news-

---

[12] You helped invent the rerun. At Junior's urging, you reconstructed some of the popular perennials and sent them off to *Reader's Digest*. Reruns of reruns of reruns; you were the patron saint of midwestern industriousness. Our hero. No irony intended.

[13] You never told. Tune in, you'd say. You coquette, you!

[14] To station management, you complained how little you were paid, threatened to quit, suffered no fools gladly.

[246]

casters. As they start to, the women they hire are young and pretty (blonds and pert brunettes, though eventually, inevitably, one hires a young and pretty redhead). Dorothy Fuldheim is interesting-looking. She can command a man's attention. But old: who can do anything about old?

"You take me for granted," she tells the news director, "because I'm old. You think I have nowhere else to go but here."

"Don't be ridiculous," he says. Like everyone else in the station's news operation (except Dorothy Fuldheim), the news director came to his job from newspapers. "This is journalism, Dorothy," he says, "not the Miss America Pageant. We *like* it that you're older.[15] Our *viewers* like it that you're older."

At home Dorothy Fuldheim stays the course. She endures. She sees after her mother's needs.[16] Her mother was never in a moment's danger of being sent to a home. If Dorothy is hosting, say, a dinner party, and Mother is having a good day, Dorothy has people carry her downstairs. When she dies, it happens in Dorothy's house.[17]

As for the granddaughter: it's possible to know Dorothy Fuldheim for years, to be a close associate or friend, and never lay eyes on her. Dorothy protects her. She will not allow her to be photographed. She displays several photos of Junior in her office; none of the granddaughter. Dorothy Fuldheim claims that what afflicts the poor girl is infantile paralysis. She foots the bills. She pays neighborhood kids to play with her, nurses to attend to her, therapists to come to the house and strap her into elaborate braces and confront the hopeless task of helping her.

---

[15] He said *older,* not *old.* He was scared of you. He loved you. He was the younger Irish cousin you never had. He ran the operation without benefit of a single person holding an MBA degree. He would have had to look up the phone number of the station's attorney. He would manage to retire without ever saying the word *demographic.*

[16] You were your father's daughter. He was a smooth talker who got curiously good deals from the lady at the butcher shop. A handsome charmer who one day moved on. This isn't to say you did not love your stolid mother. Still. Your mother might have lived out her days with her oldest, your talented brother, who'd gone to Hollywood and was making a nice living playing piano on Esquivel records and directing orchestras that recorded film scores and Muzak. Or her middle child, your talented sister, who'd had a life that, let's just say, was a good means of comparison for how far women would come, later in this century. The burden fell perversely, as it almost always does, on the child the parent loved least. In this case: you. You shouldered the burden. You were rarely heard to complain.

[17] Only fair, you said, since I was born in hers. Despite and perhaps because of everything, you were the good daughter.

Dorothy Fuldheim, owner of Cleveland, says this is why she keeps working. Not out of passion for her job or a lack of imagination about what she might do to fill her time. Not out of an urge to prove to the world what a woman or a golden-ager can do. It's for that granddaughter nobody sees. Dorothy is afraid of leaving her indigent, terrified she'll wind up in an institution.

On top of her withering duties at the station, Dorothy Fuldheim will also go anywhere and speak to any organization that will pay her.

That said, anyone who sees Dorothy Fuldheim work—even as she's standing on tiptoe on a box behind a podium at one of those supposedly mercenary speaking engagements, her alarmingly red hair blowing in the cold and lake-effect wind that calls Cleveland home—witnesses something in its day miraculous: a woman doing a thing for its own sake.

She says, and keeps going.

∾

IN ANY MYTH worth the powder to blow it to hell, the hero must confront evil.

Dorothy underwent the trials and travels of the lecture circuit, all over the country of her birth and then, as her fame and ability grew, in hostile and faraway lands. While traveling through the unfamiliar landscape of the country of her ancestors' birth, Dorothy heard a speech by the land's small and evil leader. What a speaker he was! The crowd loved him. Dorothy knew how much skill went into being a small person who could make a crowd respond like that. But horror washed over her, hearing the hatred on which he chose to expend his gifts.

As a prophet of her times, Dorothy sought an audience with the evil man. She went to his office, happened to run into him in the lobby, and he granted her an interview. She let him talk. And talk. She could not believe what she was hearing. He seemed not to know she was of the same ethnicity as the bankers he said were ruining the world. Dorothy returned home. On the lecture circuit, she tried to warn people about the madman running the country of her ancestors' birth. She was seen as too theatrical. She faced a disbelieving public. Her warnings went disastrously unheeded. She was without honor in her native land.

War broke out.

One world ended.

For the good of mankind, Junior's sweetheart was called to face death;

they married; he went. While he was gone, his baby was born. Doctors said the baby would never be right.[18] The burden of this fell on Dorothy and her husband. The soldier faced death and survived. As it does for us all, facing life proved more difficult.[19] He came home, saw his lot, returned to the soil of his parents, and took poison.

Several nights later Dorothy sunk to her knees in the cold, wet grass of the front yard of her own house, a house filled with grief, and looked to the skies and cursed a god in whom she did not believe. That was that.

⟳

THE ONE O'CLOCK *Club* can't exist without her.

That's what Dorothy Fuldheim is thinking, concealed in the wings of Studio C and watching the audience stream in, watching the lighting, sound, and makeup people minister to the younger woman on the sofa. (The Queen Anne chair is gone. Let's say it broke.) Dorothy, at age sixty-seven, said she wouldn't do the show any more unless (a) the station paid for her car and driver and (b) gave her a raise. She took her removal from the show with grace. She'll be given interview segments during the news. On large issues affecting the city, she'll get to do the odd half-hour special.

Over the years the formality of *The One O'Clock Club* has been toned down. The swallow-tailed coats have been replaced by suits. Dorothy only wore her most elaborate gowns on special occasions.

The dashing young man is still the show's announcer. He is older now. These days he rarely sings. "It'll never be the same without you, Red."

"Bah," she says. "I'm right here, aren't I?"

"You know what I mean."

"I'll outlive you all," she says. "Watch me."

"Who'll do the book reviews?"

"They're doing book reviews? I was told the book reviews were being discontinued."

"My point exactly."

---

[18] You weren't a bad person. It was a different time. The words *differently abled* had not yet crossed any human lips. It was a time, however, when no one found infantile paralysis shameful. So, OK. Infantile paralysis. Polio. Whatever. We're with you, Dorothy.

[19] He was a soldier, but you could have taught him lessons about soldiering on.

"Don't get fresh with me," she says. "You know, it's rude, sneaking up on people."

"Yours?" He pulls out a fountain pen. "I found this on the set."

"Under the chair, I suppose," she says. She smiles. She turns to leave.

"Exactly," he says. "Gosh, I wonder what did happen to that chair?"

"Shh," she says. No one is nearby to hear. "It's not my pen," she says, and keeps going.

The show goes on, without Dorothy Fuldheim. She watches the opening segment on the monitor in her office. The younger woman and the disc jockey hurl no barbed exchanges.

Dorothy always suspected the novelty of the show would wane. So be it. She turns off the set. She's busy. She has commentaries to write. Plus, she's got all sorts of news interviews coming up in the next few weeks. Billy Graham. Jimmy Hoffa. William O. Walker and John O. Holly. Margaret Chase Smith. Herbert Gold. Bob Hope. Alfred Kinsey. She needs to prepare. She couldn't *be* more busy.

She hunches over her desk.

When the new cohostess and the disc jockey get back to their respective offices, each finds flowers and a congratulatory telegram from Dorothy Fuldheim.

"There's just something about a telegram," she says when, independently, the disc jockey and the new cohostess traipse down the hall to thank her for the thank-you. "You trust it," says Dorothy, "more than you do a card or a smiling face. Now scat."

⁊

ANOTHER WORLD BEGAN.

It was a world that included a magic picture box. The box eventually became a world that included the world.

As that miracle came to pass, Dorothy was inside the box.[20]

Some said the box was evil. Others said it was good. Dorothy said the box itself was neither good nor evil. The box, spake Dorothy, was what the people inside of the box made of the people outside of the box. From inside

---

[20] You were hired for licensing reasons. The station needed local talent and you were both. You were famous in the neighborhood. The sponsors of your news broadcast, Duquesne beer, asked why you read the news without . . . well, reading it. No notes. It's not what I do, you told them. They figured in a year or so they could fire you.

the box one night, she told the people of her native land that they could look at the box from a certain angle and what did they see? Themselves. A mirror. Then they could look at the box from another angle, and what did they see? Light, pouring into their homes. A lamp.

Guided by the benevolent ghosts of her father and Aunt Molly and the eloquent lawyers of turn-of-the-century Milwaukee, Dorothy strove to tell the world about the world.

৩৩

DOROTHY FULDHEIM AND Jimmy Hoffa are talking about childhood. They have this in common, their bleak beginnings.

"Everyone," says Dorothy Fuldheim, "should have been born poor. Don't you agree?"

"Yes, ma'am," says Hoffa. "I do. I really do."

These are two people charmed silly by one another. Dorothy Fuldheim loves nothing more than to get a guest talking about the upbringing he or she has overcome. Viewers love it; Dorothy loves it. It's a conversation that can lead anywhere.

"Having to do without," he says, "having to be embarrassed about what the other kids in the neighborhood thought of my house, my folks' house, it makes a person humble."

"That's the least of what it makes a person," she says.

His eyes narrow to slits. What is Dorothy Fuldheim saying?

She looks back at him. She knows how to use silence in an interview.

"You appreciate what you have," he says. "You remember what it was like, when you were the little guy."

"Is that the problem with big labor?" she says. "That they've forgotten the little guy?"

"No," he says. No hesitation. "You have to understand, the press is anti-labor, always has been. Look at all the newspaper strikes these days. The press prints all sorts of negative stories on us, but in the Brotherhood of Teamsters, the fellas out there driving and hauling? They know what I stand for. They know I'm behind every one of 'em, a hundred percent."

She asks him hard questions. She asks about the violence. About the rackets. About accusations of fraud in the Teamster elections. Hoffa tells her these things have been blown out of proportion. The men involved aren't true Teamsters. Some were even revealed to be Reds. That's a fact! The few who were real Teamsters, he says, have been weeded out. He is helping the good men in the Justice Department with their investigation. He has nothing to hide.

"Yes," she grimaces, "but what about locally?" There go the hands! Waving, waving. "What about the troubles of Bill Presser?" she says. She explains to the viewers that he is the local Teamster leader and a close friend of Hoffa's.

"Mr. Presser was a victim," says Hoffa, "of the men around him. I can assure your viewers, Mr. Presser has disposed of those bad apples. I expect him to be exonerated yet again."

"What sort of people are we talking about here?" she says. One finger to her temple. "Mobsters?"

"Mobsters?" He says it like he's never heard the word. "No. Some of it is a matter of good men who got carried away. People who, let's say, knew the wrong people. But, look, I admit, there were—and I say *were*, because we've cleaned this up—but in the local here, there were some whatchacall, some opportunists. Petty crooks. Things of that ilk."

"That ilk?" she says.

"Correct," he says. Hoffa cites the huge number of members the Teamsters have—in Cuyahoga County, in Ohio, and nationwide. "You take that many, let's say, churchgoers. And I'll guarantee you with that many people, you're going to have a rotten few that shouldn't be touching the collection plate."

She pounces. She asks about the Central States Pension Fund.

The camera catches a split second of savage rage on Hoffa's face. It was an opening he gave her himself. The probe has been in the news, but few particulars have come out. Dorothy Fuldheim, it would appear, knows some people herself.

Hoffa recovers. "I'm sure you can understand, Miss Fuldheim," he says, "that due to the Justice Department investigation, I can't comment on that at this time. I would like to, believe me."

"Many of your union members would like to believe you." She puts her hands together, fingertips to fingertips. Her face is as straight as it gets.

He lets another long-for-TV silence pass between them. "You're very good," he says.

"So are you," she says.

The interview ends. She throws it back to the anchorman.

Cut to anchor.

He thanks Dorothy for that interesting exchange. In other news relating to Miss Fuldheim, he says (here, a still photo of mailbags appears over his shoulder), the viewers have spoken. The cards and letters have been overwhelming. Beginning Monday, Dorothy Fuldheim will resume her presidency of *The One O'Clock Club*.

Viewers can hear people in the studio clapping. Viewers themselves clapped, tens of thousands of hands clapping, in living rooms throughout the Cuyahoga River watershed.

Dorothy Fuldheim is having none of it. She's already gone—out in the lobby, thanking Mr. Hoffa for being so kind and candid. He is thanking her for having him on, for giving him a chance to explain himself.

"Anytime," she says.

"Anytime?" he says. He asks her to forgive the personal question, but just how long does she have until retirement?

She thanks him again.

⌘

YOU NEVER RETIRED. You did not outlive them all, but, sister, you gave it one hell of a try.

You kept doing *The One O'Clock Club* until another station in town stole the idea, pumped money into it, attracted bigger celebrities, paid their guests, and knocked you off the air. The only twists *(quelle surprise!)* were that they made the man the star and the woman a second banana who did no book reviews. The role of the disc jockey was played by Mike Douglas. Playing Dorothy Fuldheim: Zsa Zsa Gabor. That role proved too much, though. Someone new played it every week. When tapes of *The Mike Douglas Show* hit New York, it begat *The Merv Griffin Show*. This list of begats after that would fill a book twice this length.

You kept going. Interviews, commentaries, specials. Every speaking engagement that came with a check. Husband #2 died; that series was canceled, too. P—'s identity, or (to toe the party line) if you even knew P—'s identity, remained a secret. Junior finished college, finished grad school, and became a college professor. She never remarried. She never left town. She never lived as far as ten minutes from you. Ten seconds was more like it. Her heart got weaker. You threatened to throw yourself out the window if she died. In the middle of an attack, she pointed out that you were on the first floor. She got a pacemaker. She died.

You kept going.

You watched as Cleveland caught fire, went broke, and went to hell, yet you almost managed to live through it, to a reversal of fortune few imagined possible but that you, in your commentaries, predicted.

You kept going. When you were seventy-eight, you got a twenty-five-year mortgage. When you were eighty-nine, you signed a three-year contract. When you were ninety-one, you interviewed that dopey kid President Ronald Reagan. Minutes later you had a stroke and never recovered and wound up in a home, not your own. *Still* you kept going, five more years.

You died.

(The granddaughter was taken care of. After seventy-five years of working full-time if not more so, you'd made enough money for that.)

What a run you had! You were the first TV anchorwoman, a job you performed before it had a name. You introduced Marilyn Monroe to Joe DiMaggio (it happened in the Theatrical, on Short Vincent Street). You interviewed queens and kings and Martin Luther King. You interviewed FDR, Hannibal Harry, Ike, JFK, LBJ, Tricky Dick, Gerry, Jimmy, and Dutch—all while in office. You interviewed mobsters and crimebusters, writers and people who work for a living, evangelists and strippers, hippies, yippies, hipsters, and squares. Has-beens, wanna-bes, never-weres, and stars. You interviewed every local hero worth mentioning. You published two memoirs,[21] a book of reportage,[22] and a novel.[23] You were a guest on the *Tonight Show.* On *Nightline.* You owned Cleveland.

You laughed. You cried. You loved.

Shouldn't you be more famous than you are?

You should.

Why aren't you?

Is it because you turned down the offer in New York? Because you never left Cleveland? In a perfect world, this would have made you *more* famous, but you, of all sad people, knew what a perfect world this isn't.

Cleveland: if you can make it there, you'll make it anywhere.

But who'll know? Not even you.

For the record, Dorothy Fuldheim, outside the city of Cleveland and the

---

[21] *I Laughed, I Cried, I Loved* and *A Thousand Friends.*

[22] You insisted the station send you to cover the Arab-Israeli war. "Are you crazy?" said the station manager. "You're seventy-three!" You told him he was the crazy one. If he'd been running a station when Octavian's galleys attacked Cleopatra's fleet at Actium would he have refused to allow his chief news analyst to cover the event? What could he say to that? He'd sent you, if you'd agree to take a bodyguard. Fine, you said, but only if he's strong, good-looking, bright, and has a good name. You and former Indian third baseman Al Rosen went to Israel. The book was called *Where Are the Arabs?*

[23] *Three and a Half Husbands.* Aunt Molly, in the novel, becomes "Molly."

sorority of the first wave of women who tried to be journalists on television, has been lost to history. For reasons impossible to defend, she did not make the cut. Inside the city of Cleveland—until everyone who saw her on TV dies, too—she lives. Her ghost can descend any public staircase it wants. Her perfume lingers. Her blown kisses will find targets.

∾

PART THREE

HOME OF THE BROWNS
The Eighth City: 1960–1964

— II —

IRENE ZIELINSKY PULLED up in front of Stan and Betty's old house in her green '53 Buick, a hand-me-down from her parents, and honked the horn. She didn't even pull in the driveway, which David was sure was supposed to mean something. She could be that way. She'd never tell you anything straight. When you cracked the code, she'd deny there even *was* a code. Teddy and Lizard were in the back. They'd already been to early mass.

David came out onto the porch in just his pants. He waved at them to come in.

"Daddy's naked!" shrieked Lizard. "*Na*-ked, *na*-ked, *na*-ked!" She was four, but nearly the same size as her brother. She still had on the bubblegum-pink dress Betty had made her for Easter and that Lizard insisted on wearing to mass every Sunday. She'd wear it every day if Irene didn't hide it in the liquor cabinet. She was just as stubborn about her nickname (an endearment David initiated); she wouldn't even answer to *Liz*, *Beth*, or *Elizabeth*.

"We're already late," called Irene. "There's no time."

"Shut up!" Teddy said to his sister. He pushed her away from him.

"Mo-o-om! Teddy said *shut up*."

"Come on," David said. "Come see how it's coming."

Irene stuck her wrist out the window and tapped on her watch.

David had been painting and wallpapering his old room. It was going to be Teddy's.

"Relax," David said. "We have plenty of time. We'll make it."

He went back inside, certain she would follow.

Moments later, when she did, he was disgusted—appalled she hadn't stuck to her guns.

"Lizard's stupid," Teddy said. "Daddy, Lizard doesn't even know what *naked* means."

"*Stupid* is a bad word," said Irene. "We don't call people *stupid*."

"Ha-ha," Lizard taunted. "You're in trouble."

"Are they going to change?" David said.

Irene had worn a simple navy blue dress that could go anywhere, but the kids were going to look ridiculous in their Sunday clothes at an amusement park. Teddy wore a blue suit and a clip-on tie. White shoes, black belt. His black dress shoes didn't fit; Irene was waiting until she got paid next week to get him new ones.

"You drive, and I can change them in the car," Irene said. "I promised my mom and dad we'd get pictures of Tammy playing."

Tammy Hrudka, Irene's oldest brother's kid, played sax in the Independence High School band. Tammy's parents and Irene's parents would be at the airport, too, cameras in hand, and would also be at Euclid Beach Park when the band again played for Senator Kennedy. Irene was the third line of photographic defense. Bud Hrudka had passed his belt-and-suspenders ways on to all four of his children.

"I can change myself," said Lizard.

"You cannot," said Teddy.

"Can too!"

"You're crazy," Teddy said. He looked at David. "She thinks she can do everything."

"I *can* do everything!" said Lizard.

"Your mommy will just help," David said.

"OK, Daddy," Lizard said.

"So, all right," said Irene. She was wiping her shoes, which were clean, on a piece of cardboard, which was not. "What's new?"

Behind Irene, and without being told, the kids wiped their feet, too.

"Upstairs," David said.

All day yesterday David had been there with friends—two of the other law clerks from the firm, one of the associates, and, off and on, guys who were still in the neighborhood: Jimbo Schmidtke, Skeezix Soltesz, guys like that. Lee Mytczynskyj had been visiting his mother, across the street, and had escaped to come over and help install a new toilet. David bought them all beer, and he didn't get home until after midnight. He was back here before six.

"Everything up here is finished, I think," David said. "Except the carpeting, of course."

Irene was still shopping for that. She couldn't make up her mind.

"You guys did a great job," Irene said. "Wow."

She didn't say it with any enthusiasm. She was hurrying from room to room.

"Even the curtain rods are up," David pointed out.

"That's great," she said. "Are you about ready?"

"I am," he said. "Is that all you're going to say about this?"

Lizard had gone into Aunt Betty's old sewing room and was spinning around and around, chanting, "*Mine, mine, mine, mine, mine.*" Her room at the house in Independence was bigger. But she was in love with this room: its tiny window seat and its long windows.

Teddy was in his new room, too, sitting Indian-style in the middle of it. He was only five, but he had a look on his face like an adult who is too sad to cry. Teddy didn't like sports, but he was sore about missing the ballgame. That might not be the reason for these particular blues, though. Teddy was a sad kid. He didn't need reasons.

"What do you want me to say?" Irene said. "It's great, all of it."

"What do I *want* you to say? I don't *want* you to say anything."

"Mine, mine, mine. Lizard is great, Lizard is great, Lizard is great."

"I'm sorry." Irene softened. She ran her hands over the chair rail in the master bedroom. "This is impressive, honestly." The room was now yellow. Irene had bought the paint. The hardwood floor was paint-splattered; knowing wall-to-wall carpeting was coming, he and the guys hadn't bothered with drop cloths. "Sorry." She looked at her watch. She kissed him on the cheek. "You guys did a great job. Terrific. I'm a little under the weather."

David nodded. "OK," he said. "Two minutes. Under the weather from what?"

"I've seen your two minuteses," Irene said. "Hurry up. We'll be in the car."

"Which?" he said. His car was a hand-me-down, too. The Jeepster.

"Mine, definitely. It's nothing."

"What's nothing?"

"A stomachache, is all."

"Oh. Good. Not good about your stomach, but . . ." Why did everything have to be so hard? "You know what I mean." David didn't want to drive the Buick, especially on a nice day, one of his last chances to drive with the top down, but it wasn't worth arguing about. "Maybe even a minute and a half," he called. He went to the bedroom to grab his things.

Stan and Betty had moved to Lakewood five years ago, and five years of renters had taken its toll on their old house. Holes in the plaster, coats of cheap paint over coats of cheap paint, weird stains on the linoleum, scrapes and gouges in the floorboards. Outside, the rosebushes had gone wild and the lawn hadn't been fertilized since who knows when. The neighborhood wasn't what it used to be either, but it was still solid. Unlike Independence, Old Brooklyn had a history. David was known here, and so was Irene. It was a neighborhood he had a stake in, a place he thought he could help improve. A place that would elect him.

The house was sixty years old, but *built*. The house in Independence, beside Irene's parents' house, had nothing of the style or workmanship this old frame house had. That's the problem with our world, David thought. People don't rebuild things. They don't adapt. They tear things down and start over. They move away and start over. It's the American way, he supposed: screw things up and light out for the territories. But this was *1960*. With the pie-in-the-sky exception of the moon, what territories were there for a person to light out for?

⁓

THE YEAR-OLD INNERBELT bridge, Ohio's widest, was so monstrously nondescript it lacked a proper name. Cleveland's other bridges were named after the streets they connected. This one connected nothing; to drive it was to drive a few thousand feet of blank federal government freeway. The grandest bridges—the carved-stone Lorain-Carnegie and the graceful steel double-decker Detroit-Superior—had such *perfect* names. The streets on the Midwest-looking West Side were named after working-class cities west of here. The streets on the East-looking East Side were named after a rich guy and a prevailing attitude. The bridges were the hyphens that joined them.

The Zielinskys, in a hurry, had taken the innerbelt bridge, theoretically the fastest route from the West Side to Burke Lakefront Airport. Now they found themselves stuck in traffic, inching across the damn thing.

"Indians flag!" said Lizard, pointing at Terminal Tower, which, aside from other cars, was about all the view this bridge afforded. "Wahoo! Wahoo! Wahoo!"

"Shut up," said Teddy.

"Teddy!" said Irene. "That's a bad word."

Two words, David thought, but did not say.

"Lizard's an idiot," Teddy said. Three weeks of kindergarten were showing results. David can't remember the boy ever using the word *idiot* before.

"I'm not an idiot," said Lizard. "You're an idiot. Daddy says that when there's an Indians flag—"

"I *know*," Teddy said. "I knew that when I was two."

"I knew it when I was one."

"I knew it when I was zero," Teddy said. "I hate baseball."

"I love it," she said.

"Just . . . be quiet," Teddy said. "Please."

It broke David's heart, how softly Teddy said *please,* how much mercy the boy seemed to need.

So maybe it was the game David was sore about: the last home game of the year, meaningless except that it would have been Teddy's first Indians game. Also, David had a thing about the last home game of the season. He had a five-year streak going. He'd bought the tickets in March, long before he knew when the Democratic Steer Roast would be. Kennedy had spoken at the last two, and David had been at both of them, but this time Kennedy was running for something, the big something: president. All over the city, the ward leaders had made it clear that attendance was mandatory. Not that David wouldn't have gone anyway, not that he failed to recognize the value of being seen at an event like this. But he felt bad about it, for the boy's sake. David had the tickets, in fact, and had slipped them into a pocket of his plaid sport coat. He'd asked around at work and at the law school, but he couldn't sell them and he felt too broke to give them away. Maybe he'd run into someone who could use them.

Lizard started up again, chanting that she loved baseball.

"Your brother said *please*," Irene said. "So do be quiet."

"But—"

"Lizard." That was all it took, David saying her name.

Irene let out her breath. She did it again. It was a stunning day, bright, warm for September but not too warm. Despite this Irene was sweating.

"What?" David said. "Are you all right?"

She nodded.

"Because you don't look all right." Even by Irene's standards, she was sweating a lot.

"I'll be fine. It's nothing." She reached over and turned on the radio. Wretched, syrupy piano music: Ferrante and Teicher, playing some ghastly showtune. She left it there.

Now it was David's turn to take a deep breath. Ferrante and fucking Teicher? But he pulled an Irene. He didn't object. He didn't change it. He let her have her way, with a sickened-looking expression on his face that ought to keep her from enjoying her little victory.

It was a clear day, but in the Cuyahoga Valley, the air was too hazy to see the Huletts or the steel mills. From the lane they were stuck in, David couldn't even see the water.

⟡

THE MOMENT THE charter plane, a Convair, touched down at Burke Lakefront Airport, the band came to attention.

The plane was fifteen minutes late. David had just arrived himself. He struggled to hold his position, blasted by a sulfurous wind off the lake and jostled by band boosters, family members of the band, and fervid Democrats.

Three thousand people, David would say (he'd been to enough political rallies to get good at such estimates). It wasn't the best circumstance to try to figure out how to use Irene's Brownie camera, which he'd given her for her birthday last year but which she'd never used. Irene, looking pale, had gone to find some shady place to sit. Her mother was watching the kids. Tammy's father, Sonny Hrudka (like Bud, a lifer at Fisher Body), wielded a clumsy movie camera and had no better vantage point than David did, but Bud Hrudka was right in front, with his Polaroid Land camera mounted to a tripod. He had a look on his face like he'd been standing there for hours. Although, David thought, his father-in-law always looked a little like that.

As the plane taxied across the tarmac, young women began to scream. A few at first, then hundreds. As if it were Elvis! Between that and all the other elbowing, camera-toting relatives, it was hard for David to keep a bead on Tammy Hrudka, Irene's niece, a plump kid not much taller than her saxophone. Why would a kid that short play baritone sax?

The door of the airplane opened, and the Independence High School band broke into "Anchors Aweigh." Like David, Senator Kennedy was a veteran of the navy. The band pumped it out, the drums and brass drowning everything out in the way of high school bands, making themselves heard over the cheers and screams, the wind and the locustry of whirring cameras.

On the other side of the restraining rope, David, without a scorecard, recognized the players: Governor DiSalle, Senator Young, three congressmen (including the one who didn't appoint David to Annapolis), Jack Russell (the council president, unmistakable in his cowboy boots and white Stetson), and Tom O'Connor (ergo, no Seltzer; ergo, the otherwise-curious absence of Senator Lausche and Mayor Celebrezze).

The way Senator Kennedy walked seemed, in its famously injured vigor, oddly brave, especially in the hard lakefront wind. Unbent. Balanced between an officer's gait and a regular-guy shamble. His hair blew wildly. His smile was supremely white. He had a hangdog look to his eyes and a suntan, neither of which the newspaper photos of him captured.

Flanked by Secret Servicemen and followed by the Ohio Democratic elite, the senator moved straight into the crowd, more gripping people's hands than actually shaking them (the way David imagined that one might milk a cow). Senator Kennedy was a man who looked good in his clothes (the thirty pounds David had gained since his wedding day had taken him from too skinny to slightly paunchy, with maybe four days' transition when he felt the way Kennedy looked). He was a man whose every gesture said *money* and yet at the same time looked like someone who'd be good to tilt a

glass with. For years David had admired the senator, but there was something different about him now, as if he'd been sharpened by the process of
becoming who the country needed him to be. He looked like a guy who was
a member of a club you weren't, but also like the one most likely to nominate
you to join. Moving through the crowd he gave the appearance of having
stopped to greet you without ever stopping. His lips kept forming the words
thank you and *good to see you,* but David was far too far away to hear.

There would have been a moment where Tammy Hrudka was in the
same frame as Senator Kennedy, but David missed it (so did Sonny, whose
ancient movie camera jammed, and Bud, who was *too* close: any view of
Tammy and her horn was blocked by the beaming Kennedy retinue). All his
shots of the senator were either facing him but far away, or of his back, some
time after he passed. As he passed, David froze. He shot nothing.

There goes the epitome of everything in this life that I will never have.

No sooner did the thought cross David's mind then, at the far edge of the
senator's meet-and-greet party, he saw a robustly tanned man. His father.
Michael "Mikey Z" Zielinsky, acting vice president of two different locals in
the International Brotherhood of Teamsters.

Of course. Of *course.*

Although David had managed to score a pass to get him and his family
into the tent at Euclid Beach Park near where the actual steer would be
roasted and served (where he could shake hands with people whose hands it
was good to shake), he'd pulled every string he could think of with the ward
leaders, trying to get into one or more of the meetings the senator was about
to hold in the Hollenden Hotel (the motorcade's first stop), but nothing
doing. Every string he could think of. Right. Jesus. And there his father
went, toward the line of open and guarded convertibles, trailing in the senator's wake like a shark sucking down the chum.

For years Irene had been telling David, make things straight with your
dad; you never know what can happen. What's past is past, she'd say. Maybe
this was a sign, David thought. Maybe his wife was right. Maybe it was time.

༄

IRENE HAD SLIPPED away and decorously vomited behind a parked airplane. She insisted she'd be all right, though, that she was feeling a little
better. She didn't look one bit better, but that was Irene: appease, appease,
appease. St. Irene the Good. Why couldn't she just say it, that she feels like
hell and could they just take her home? But no. The kids had never been to
the park before, and, to forestall the boredom that was sure to lay them low

once the speeches started, David and Irene had played up—overplayed—the joy and rapture of the rides, attractions, and exotic food available only at Euclid Beach Park.

And so, eschewing public transportation, as any good midwesterner would (also because the Kennedy-belittling *Press,* in one of Louie Seltzer's many thousand veiled swipes at the Irish Catholic Tom O'Connor, the city's biggest Kennedy-backer, had advised that "persons bent on attending the rally go by public transportation") and avoiding St. Clair—the route Senator Kennedy's blue convertible would take in two hours, a route already filling with a crowd that the (Democratic) city traffic commissioner would later estimate at a quarter million people—they went to the park, anyway. The whole fam-damily, as Bud Hrudka would say.

"I saw Mike," David told Irene. They were getting close to the park. "My father," he added. "He was part of Kennedy's whatchamajig. His entourage."

"That's great," she said. "Isn't it?"

"Sure," David said. It wasn't as if he didn't talk to his father. They'd cross paths downtown. Once in a great while, he'd take David, Irene, and the kids out for a swanky dinner at which the drink flowed and the conversation did not. Mike Zielinsky's way of atoning for not showing up for the wedding had been to send David and Irene a ludicrous amount of cash as a gift. They'd went back and forth, arguing about whether to give it back; they kept it. "It's getting about time for another dinner," David said.

"Under better circumstances than the last one," Irene said.

"He was actually charming at that," David said, meaning the family dinner after Grandma Luzinski's funeral, a couple months ago, "especially considering she didn't really like him."

"Maybe once we move," Irene said, "we can have him to the house." Mike had never once come to the house in Independence. David couldn't have told you his own father's mailing address, though Irene probably had it somewhere.

"What do you mean?" David said. *Was that a crack?*

"Just that he knows where it is, is all."

"Is that a parade?" Lizard asked. They were stopped at a light, ten or so blocks from the park.

"Is what a parade, honey?" Irene said.

"That."

There were twenty-some Negroes with placards. Euclid "BLEACH" PARK, said one. PROFILES IN DIS-COURAGE, read another. Another, EUCLID

BEACH PARK POLICE BEAT NEGROES, sounded to David more like a sports score.

"A strike," Irene said. "I would guess."

David caught Irene's eye and shook his head. He pointed. Parked at the curb was a police car. City of Cleveland, even though by then they were outside Cleveland and inside the Euclid city limits. Inside were two cops, both white.

"A strike like in baseball?" said Lizard.

Teddy laughed, too hard. "Lizard thinks those people are playing baseball."

"It's complicated, sweetie," David said. "It's a grown-up situation."

Lizard accepted this and went back to singing the first line from "Old MacDonald" over and over and over.

"What's it about?" Irene said. She was all but drenched with sweat.

David wasn't sure, but he'd heard through the grapevine that the Negro leaders were boycotting the Steer Roast, even though it had been held here for years, to protest a long string of incidents involving the park's thuggish police force. This was a place, after all, that had closed down its dance pavilion rather than integrate it. That was awhile ago, though.

"Way over here?" said Irene. "What do they think they'll accomplish way out here?"

"I doubt it's their choice," he said. "I don't think things like that accomplish anything anyway," he said. "I'm certainly sympathetic, but for other people"—meaning *white people*—"picketing just scares them."

"Maybe." Like a lot of girls, Irene said *maybe* in lieu of real disagreement on an issue. "But why not just let them have their say?"

David wasn't sure about that either. "There are security issues, I'm sure. You just can't do a thing like this anywhere you want," he said. "Also, it makes the city look bad on TV."

"That's ridiculous," she said.

"It is," he said, "but what's Kennedy supposed to do, not come here? To win the election, he needs Ohio. To win Ohio, he needs a landslide in Cleveland. To get that, he needs to come to the Steer Roast. It may not be right," David said, "but it's a practical matter. In the end, what are the Negroes going to do, vote for Nixon?"

"That's awful," Irene said. "*Practical* is hardly the word."

"I agree," he said. "I agree completely. But, I'll tell you one thing. Things are changing. Things won't always be this way."

She looked at him. "Oh, really?"

"Really."

"If you think you can do something about that," she said, "more power to you."

"Screw you." But the second he said it, he regretted it.

Irene closed her eyes. "Why do you always take what I say the worst way possible?"

"I'm sorry," he said. "I just thought—"

"You thought wrong."

Irene may not be crazy about him getting into politics, but David had to admit, she was a progressive girl. Most of the people from the neighborhood had the sort of attitudes about civil rights that her family did (with whom it was not safe to watch so much as a football game, for fear one of them would see Jim Brown hit a hole and scream, "Run, you lazy nigger, run!" at the TV). Irene was different. Maybe David took that too much for granted.

⟲

ROCK AND ROLL *has gone to hell. Bunch of drippy Bobbys and Frankies.*

Even as David minted the thought, though, passing through the castle-like archway to Euclid Beach Park, heading in the other direction of a sign pointing the way to "The Bill Randle Rock 'N' Roll Party," he knew he was rationalizing. He wanted to go. The show was free and featured four pop acts David didn't know. The whole pop music business was a swamp of sappiness and bribery. Little Richard quit, Elvis got drafted, Chuck Berry's going to jail, Buddy Holly died, and the great Larry Williams couldn't *buy* a hit. Alan Freed was going to jail, too, looked like, all of which goes to show you: fly too close to the sun, you're *gone,* daddy-o. The few records David could afford to buy of late had been jazz, and why not? What rock-and-roll bands today are doing anything that, say, Roy Milton and His Solid Senders weren't doing (better) ten years ago? Still, David liked to try to keep up.

"You have to be impressed with Senator Kennedy," he said to Irene, underneath the echoey cement Colonnade, at the edge of Kiddie Land. "You can bet your last samolian Dick Nixon doesn't have rock-and-roll acts warm up the crowd for a campaign appearance."

"Oh, my god, the smell," Irene said. "All this!" She waved her hand, gave David a knowing tap, and ran to the nearest ladies' room.

The kids were already in line for the Kiddie Rocket Ships. They were holding hands. It melted his heart when they were like this.

It was a long line.

David wasn't sure he'd ever seen the park this crowded. Stan and Betty avoided crowds. Stan would take a day off work to avoid coming here on a weekend.

The ticket line was even longer than the ride line, and by the time David got to the kids, they were at the front, waiting. An ancient man in green denim coveralls had pulled them aside. "These yours?" He was eating a big yellow onion as if it were an apple.

"I told you he'd come," said Teddy. "Stupid."

"No, *I* told *you*," Lizard said. "Stupid*head*."

"Yep," David said. "They're mine."

The Kiddie Rocket Ships were a small-scale replica of the Rocket Ships, one of the park's trademark rides. The glistening stainless steel rockets were modeled on ones from the Buck Rogers comic strips and were welded into being right on the premises. Teddy and Lizard were too small for the real Rocket Ships, of course. They were too small for anything except for the carousels, that miniature train, and the rides in Kiddie Land. David had never been here when he was that small. He'd never done anything in Kiddie Land but walk past it.

The kids finished, and he gave them tickets to the Kiddie Swans, and, holding hands, they got in line. Look at them! He loved them. He was a lucky man.

He bought himself a cigar. The kids came running back to him; he sent them off with tickets to the Kiddie Land Hook & Ladder, and he sat down to smoke his cigar.

Strange: here he was, at Euclid Beach Park, and he wasn't going to ride the Thriller, the Racing Coaster, or best of all the Flying Turns (that barrels-on-a-wooden-bobsled-run coaster). Ten years ago he and Irene came to the park on a double date with Jimbo Schmidtke and Doris Blatchly. Summer of '50. Doris had never been on the Flying Turns before. She peed her pants. Attendants on the ride saw the wet spot on the seat and, like a racing-car pit crew, stripped off the cushion, replaced it, and had the car moving in David would say eight seconds flat. Doris sat under a tree crying while Jimbo went to the car to get her a beach towel and Irene and David rode the ride five more times straight, laughing and French-kissing and laughing.

He wouldn't be doing any of this. He was older now. A father. A *dad*. A husband.

The kids came running back to him; he sent them off with tickets to the Kiddie Autos.

David looked around him. There were others of his kind, smoking, watching the kids, footing the bill, worried and stunned silent. Responsible young men of the New Frontier. He'd been going to night school year-round, nonstop, full-time, six years without a vacation. Straight A's. He'd been a faithful husband and, even though Irene kept working, a good provider. He'd worked on campaigns, he'd been president of the Fenn College Young Democrats, and at Cleveland-Marshall he'd been captain of the moot-court team. Almost every Monday he went as a spectator to watch parts of the city council meetings. When he got a chance, he watched the city's hot trial lawyers in action: Mike Climaco, Norm Minor, Lou Stokes, and most of all John Patrick Butler (not because he was Mikey Z's attorney, in spite of that; when trials ended, jurors lined up to ask for Butler's autograph). All through this, David worked—the last two years as a full-time law clerk (Stan had closed up shop to become head of investigations at the same firm; David came with him). At times like this, watching his kids and breathing hard, he wasn't sure how he did it. He did it. One foot in front of the other. Summary makes heroes out of ordinary joes. David would finish school this term, pass the bar, set up a campaign organization, raise money, get elected to council, change the world. Anyone with a plan could do the same. A man with a plan can work backward from it and accomplish a lot.

"I'm fine," Irene said.

"Jesus. Don't do that. You scared the crap out of me."

She sat down beside him on the bench. She looked a world better. The color was back in her face. "In case you were wondering."

"Sorry. You scared me. Sorry about in the car, too. Was it something you ate?"

"Do you mind?"

He held the cigar so the smoke blew away from her.

"Where are they?" she said.

He pointed.

"Where's the camera?" she said. She waved to the kids, but they were locked in some kind of centrifugal torpor and didn't see.

"Damn," he said. He'd left it in the car. "I'll go get it."

He did. As he slammed the trunk of the Buick, across three long rows of parked American cars, he saw her.

Or someone who looked like her. Walking hand in hand with a man. The man was laughing and handsome, and the woman, who may or may not have been Anne O'Connor, had a wry, postcoital look on her face, the way joke tellers do. Her red hair was bobbed. She had on a hat of the sort the senator's wife famously wore. Whoever it was, she was a knockout.

David couldn't be sure. He used to see her sometimes at rallies and fundrasiers, but it had been two or three years. Last he heard, she'd finished school and was working for a TV station in New York, as a reporter.

He stood there behind the respectable back end of his wife's parents' well-maintained green Buick, his wife's Christmas-gift camera dangling from one hand, a cheap cigar from the other. He watched the handsome man with hair like the senator's and the stunning, posture-perfect woman who looked like Anne O'Connor walk away, toward the rock-and-roll show, toward the tent where the roasted steer was being served. Only when they were out of sight did David realize how tightly he was gripping the strap of the camera.

Crazy. He felt as guilty as if he'd kissed her, the woman. Also as betrayed as if she, the woman, were cheating on him.

Old flames. An innocent, bittersweet, inevitable, whiskey-cured pleasure of manly life. Sinatra taught it to us all. It wasn't even her, probably.

David ditched the smelly cigar and jogged back to Kiddie Land. He loved his life. He was a lucky man, and true.

∽

WHEN HE GOT back, Irene and the kids were already in line for the Surprise House. "Do you think this one will be OK for them?"

"It's just a funhouse," Irene said.

"Is it scary?" Teddy said, eyes wide. The boy could detect the slightest adult anxiety.

"Teddy's a scaredy-cat!" said Lizard.

Teddy punched her in the arm. David picked Teddy up, gave him a quick swat on the bottom, and set him down. He didn't cry. He said nothing at all.

"It's more funny than scary," Irene said. "A funhouse."

"Surprise House," Teddy said. He said it as if a surprise were a punishment. Teddy held out his hand, his sister took it, and, as a family of four, they moved forward.

They drew nearer to the glassed-in portico that housed Laughing Sal, the motorized fat-lady mannequin, whose throaty, incessant laugh was famously rumored to be a recording of a woman having an orgasm.

Lizard clamped her hands over her ears and started to cry.

"It's OK, Lizard," Teddy said, resigned. He reached over and stroked her hair, softly. "It's not real."

David and Irene exchanged a look.

"I know," Lizard said. "But it's awful."

"It is," Teddy admitted. "It's very, very awful."

"You don't have to do this," Irene said, squatting down to be eye-level with Lizard. "Sweetie, if you're scared—"

"I'm not!"

"She's not," Teddy said. "We're fine. Both of us."

The line kept moving. Mercifully, Laughing Sal's laugh receded, and as they were about to enter, Lizard began to cheer up.

"I *was* wondering, by the way," David said. "You didn't give me a chance."

"Wondering what?" said Irene.

"How you were. Jesus. How are you? You look better, a little."

"Oh, that," she said. "I feel better." They were on the threshold of the Surprise House. She pointed to the sign above the entranceway. "This is as good a time as any, I guess. Surprise," she said. "How I am," she pulled him to her and whispered in his ear, "is pregnant."

He could still hear Laughing Sal, just not so loud. He looked at her. She nodded. He pulled her aside and hugged her. "I love you," he said.

He waved for others in line to pass.

"I love you, too," Irene said. David always said it first; she was the chimer-inner.

"I really do," he said. "This is great."

"Great?" Irene said. It was hard to tell if she was being sarcastic, or if she was really interested in how he felt about this.

"It is great," he said. "A blessing, all those things. I know what you're thinking," he said, meaning the vast range of financial speculation that this news made more tenuous, the house that they'd now outgrown before they even moved into it. "But it's great."

"C'mon!" Lizard said, tugging at David's sleeve. "It's our turn!"

"This isn't the time," Irene whispered to David.

"C'*mon!*"

"Stop it," said Teddy. "They're busy."

David looped his arm around Irene. They walked into the Surprise House. He hadn't walked with her like that since when? The last time they were here? Since they were kids.

If this wasn't love, David would like to know what was.

⌒

TOM O'CONNOR WAS the master of ceremonies. He introduced Mayor Celebrezze, who did show up for this. Celebrezze announced his endorsement of Senator Kennedy, sending up a cheer from the crowd so vigorous the ground hummed.

The Zielinskys were behind the podium, in the big-top tent.

The tent was filled with long tables, decimated plates of food, and briskly moving busboys. David could have used a beer. But there was none; the park was famously dry. Funny how not being able to have a drink makes it sound like the thing you just have to have. Man, could he use a drink! In one corner of the tent, a group of men huddled around a television, watching the Browns play Philadelphia. David was surprised, coming late and with the program already under way (they could take Tammy Hrudka's picture at the end of the festivities, Irene had said, indulging the kids in yet another ride), how many people there still were in the tent: milling around, pressing the flesh, and not yet seeing fit to leave the realm of the pass-bearing chosen for the unredeemed world of mere audience.

David did not see the woman who probably wasn't Anne O'Connor.

Instead he saw his father.

Mike Zielinsky caught sight of his two grandkids and let out a whoop. "My angels!"

Teddy and Lizard sprinted into his arms, screaming, "Fat Grampa! Fat Grampa!"—which is what they called him, and what he claimed to like being called, despite the fact that he was more beefy than out-and-out fat. He was in his late fifties, but you'd still like the idea of him blocking for you in a backyard football game.

As David kept his distance, his father shamelessly performed his shtick: cartoon-character voices, quarters pulled out of the kids' ears and given to them, grabbing them by their legs and dangling them upside down while they laughed in a way David could rarely provoke. David supposed he should be happy, that his kids had two grandfathers and a great-uncle they called Grandpa Stan, and loved them all.

Mike hugged Irene, too, and set about his usual course of flattery. She looked like hell. What shit, hearing his father say she didn't. David walked away. He opened the flap of the tent.

Christ!

His *heart* skipped a beat, the crowd was so vast. David knew it was big, but this was beyond reckoning. A pinkish sea of close-cropped heads, roiling and shiny in the most perfect autumn day a Clevelander would dare imagine.

It would be the biggest crowd of the whole campaign: at least a hundred thousand, maybe half again that much. Bigger and whiter than the crowd at that Satchel Paige game, bigger and whiter by far than the Moondog

Coronation Ball. The biggest crowd David would ever see. The biggest crowd John F. Kennedy would live to see.

Some people elbowed past.

Again, David saw the red-haired woman. Maybe forty yards back from the stage, on the edge of a platform that held a television camera and a handful of other spectators, including a handsome man who put an arm around her. It was pretty far away. It probably wasn't her.

He let the tent flap fall.

He took the long way back to his family, so he could get a Browns score, he told himself. Halftime. Browns 24, Eagles 10. Cleveland's going to be great this year; everyone can feel it.

On the podium now was the governor. He welcomed the amazing turnout of all you fine people of Cuyahoga County (*CuyaHOEga,* he said, not *CuyaHOGA,* thus branding himself an outsider). Yes, he acknowledged, he and the party leaders in this part of the state have had their differences, and to be honest, he and Mr. O'Connor, or, rather, the leaders in this part of the state, still do have differences. But! This should *not* stand in the way of them uniting, along with the rest of you wonderful people, this great crowd, in support of Senator Kennedy. It shouldn't!

Another baby, David thought.

He loved his wife and kids. This was the greatest news a grown man can receive. Something to get used to, is all. They could add to the house. The backyard was small, but David knew the people a person would need to know to get the right permits.

Suddenly, the smell of all that charred meat got to him. Sympathy nausea. David sat down on a wooden folding chair.

They were walking toward him. Mike had Lizard on one shoulder, Teddy on the other. David wasn't sure he could have done this himself. Actually, he was sure he couldn't have, though in his defense, he had a wrecked knee. Both kids had looks on their faces like this was the best ride in the park. Irene was trying to take a picture.

"You look like you seen a ghost," Mike said.

"Boo," said David.

His father handed him a flask, engraved with the Teamsters logo and Mike's initials.

"Saw you at the airport," David said, taking it. Maybe a drink would be just the thing. "Irene? I don't think there's enough light, hon."

She kept shooting. He drank.

"Ouzo," his father said.

David shuddered. "I should know better," he said, "than to drink what you're drinking." He wiped his tongue with his hand. "So, how were the meetings?"

Mike set the kids down smoothly and took back the flask.

"More!" Lizard said, jumping up and down. "Again!"

"Politics," Mike said. "Jeez, it's terrific to see you."

"Presser out yet?" Of jail.

"Last week. Just wait, sweetpea," he said to Lizard. "I'm jawin' with your pa."

"Yeah," Teddy said. "He's jawin' with our pa!"

"'Pa'!" said Lizard.

They collapsed in a fit of the giggles.

"Why wasn't Presser the guy? In the meetings."

Mike gave David the soft pat on the cheek. "You're cute," he said.

OK, dumb question.

Irene asked the kids if they needed to use the bathroom before the next president of the United States spoke and took them before they could answer.

"When're you done with school?" Mike asked. "You're gonna have more degrees than a fuckin' thermometer."

"December. It's just two."

"Two?"

"A bachelor's and a law degree."

"Plus high school."

"That's not a *degree*."

"What is it then? Huh?"

"It's nothing."

"Tell it to a dropout," Mike said. He took a long pull of the ouzo. Ouzo! Yeesh. "*This* December? Man alive. What are you going to do with yourself now?"

"This and that, I guess."

His father of course knew what David was going to do. "I was telling your wife—"

"She has a name."

"Touchy, touchy. I was telling the lovely Irene"—*was that a cut?*—"that she ought to pack up her two angel children and her pale, overworked wretch of a husband and come down to Miami Beach for a week sometime. Tina and I'd just love to have you."

Tina? This was an old gambit, except for the Tina part. He had a place down there. David and his family had never been.

"Did you meet Tina?"

"Who's Tina?"

"My new lady friend?"

"Lady friend?"

"Fresh guy."

"No," he said. "Sorry. I'd like to, though. Where is she?"

Mike looked around the tent. "I told you about Tina. I'm sure I told you about Tina."

"Now that you mention it," David said, "maybe you did." There was a parade of these I'm-sure-I-told-you-about-her women, new names every time.

"Well, Tina's here somewhere. Women, huh?"

On the podium a congressman called the sight before him the largest assemblage of Democrats in American history. The crowd loved that!

Irene and the kids came back. "Want to find a place to watch?" she asked.

Mike crouched down. "Guess which hand," he said to Teddy.

"Why does he get to go first?" Lizard asked.

"You go first, then," Mike said. "If that's OK with you, sport."

"Yeah," Teddy sighed. "It's OK."

She picked left. It was a fiver. She grabbed it and ran around in tight circles of joy.

"Tough luck, sport," he said to Teddy.

"It's OK," Teddy said. His body went a little slack. "I don't care."

You cruel fucker, thought David.

But Teddy, being Teddy, followed through. He touched Mike's right hand. It had five bucks in it, too.

"Thank you," Teddy said. He didn't lose his cool though. "I sincerely appreciate it."

David caught Irene's eye. She was beaming, proud. *I sincerely appreciate it?* Teddy was five. He was a scary kid.

⌒

"AND NOW, LADIES and gentlemen," says Anne O'Connor's father, "the next . . . president . . . of the United . . . States . . . *of America!*"

Not in Elvis's wildest! Screams *and* applause *and* the hard *basso profundo* of male approval, a hundred fifty thousand *strong,* and we do mean *strong,* Jack!

"Republicans argue," the senator says, "that the vice president is a man of long experience."

Boos! He's not! He's a beady-eyed, slouchy-shouldered bad man! A *child* can see that!

"I don't know what kind of experience he had"—though of course the senator does, having been elected to Congress for the first time the same year Nixon was—"unless it was helping conduct the worst witch-hunt this country has seen since the darkest days of Salem."

Yes, that!

"Unless it was hiding for eight years in the president's cloakroom, or wherever he's been."

Yes! Where *has* Dick been?

"But whatever that experience is, I don't think you want it for the next four years!"

No way, Jack! We don't! We're with you!

"The fact is, in 1958 the president gave the vice president his first executive function. He was named chairman of a committee for price stability and economic growth. The committee met and talked and studied. They didn't bring prices down. They didn't send our growth rate up. But you know what they *did* do? They filed a report!"

Reports! We laugh! Washington and their wacky reports! This way demons lie.

"The *Washington Post* called it one of the most redundant, uninspired, and generally useless documents to come off the government's mimeograph machines."

That's bad! Think of the competition!

"The *New York Herald Tribune,* a Republican paper, said it was like something you wrote in high school."

That's worse! High school! Oh, Jesus, what crap we wrote in high school!

"The cost of living now is at an all-time high. I think we can do better than that."

Of *course* we can. We're with you, Jack!

The senator turns to the matter of ending discrimination.

"We want to finish it, north, south, east, or west. We stand for the American Constitution and the Declaration of Independence. We want fair treatment for all people, no matter where they live, no matter what their creed or color."

Well, now who can argue with that! The man looks presidential!

The senator thanks Ohio for its crucial support, both in winning the nomination and in turning out the greatest crowd he has ever seen.

We're great! We're great! It's true!

"Ohio is the key," says the senator. "The next president of the United States will carry Ohio."

Of *course* he will.

"Look at the world!" says the senator. "If you're satisfied to have things as they are for the next four or eight years, vote for Mr. Nixon!"

Boo! Boo! No! Not that! Anything but that!

"If you think we can do better..."

Yes!

"...if you think we can hold the banner of freedom high..."

How high the *moon*, Jack!

"...we want your help. I ask for your help, not because of my candidacy but because we have a great opportunity to serve mankind. I want you to join me in this campaign to demonstrate to the American people, to a watching world, that we will be second to none."

We are Cleveland! We *know* what it is to be second to some! We used to be the fifth biggest city in America, then we were the sixth, then we were the seventh, and just this year we fell again, and now we're the eighth. Eight is not great. We want your help, Jack! Help us be second to none. We want to join you!

⌒⌒

"I THINK WE can do bettah than tha-a-a-t!" Teddy said. The Zielinskys were driving home, heading west in heavy traffic on Lakeshore Drive. The boy was a remarkable mimic.

"Yay!" Lizard said. "Yay! Kennedy's great, Kennedy's great!"

"I think we can do bettah than tha-a-a-at!"

The sun was low in the sky. David had the Indians' postgame show on the radio. Cleveland had lost to the White Sox, 4–0. The same day, the Pirates and the Yankees had each clinched the pennant. The Yankees, led by Roger Maris, who'd started with the Indians and been traded for what, a load of freshly laundered towels?

"I think we can do bettah than tha-a-a-at!"

To David's astonishment, Teddy had watched the senator's speech as if it were a sporting event. If Teddy liked sports, which he didn't. David felt responsible. His own choices had warped the boy. "He's amazing," David said. "Have you ever heard him do that before?"

"All the time," Irene said. "Where have you been?"

[278]

He rolled his eyes. "Don't start," he said.

"It's usually cartoon characters," Irene said. "You're amazing, Ted."

"The next president of America," Teddy said, exactly like the senator only much higher, "will be from Cleveland!"

"Ken-ne-dy! Ken-ne-dy!" shouted Lizard. "Ken-ne-dy! Kiss my knee!"

"That's stupid," said Teddy, in his own voice. "Nobody would kiss your ugly knee."

"You're stupid," Lizard said. "Go back to being Kennedy. I love him!"

"Why don't you marry him?" Teddy said.

"He's already married," she said.

"How do you know that?" Irene said.

"You have to be married to be president," Teddy said. "Everybody knows that."

David smiled. Cleveland was 74–74 for the year. Fourth place. The season was dead before it started, killed in the spring by the soul-sapping trade of Rocky Colavito to Detroit. Colavito was gone, and Maris was gone, too. Cleveland was doing well to be mediocre.

"That's not why I know he's married," Lizard said.

"How do you know, then, sweetpea?" David said.

"I just know," she said. "He's got a wife named Mrs. Kennedy."

"You don't know anything."

"I know everything," Lizard said. "Go back to being the president."

Teddy didn't correct her. "Old MacDonald had a fa-a-ahm," Teddy said, in the manner of John F. Kennedy. He went through the whole song. Lizard was laughing as if he *were* a cartoon.

At one point David had sunk to the lowest of the low, taking Irene's Brownie and slithering through the crowd to where the Independence High School band was, and looking up through the cheap telephoto lens at the woman on the platform who may or may not have been Anne O'Connor. (This is not to say that David did not get what he imagined were several fine photographs of the Independence High School marching band in general and fourth-chair saxophonist Tammy Hrudka in particular. A roll's worth.) The bobbed-hair woman on the platform was sharing a bucket of popcorn with the boy, the man, who looked a little like the senator, if you looked at him the right way. David did not look at him the right way.

Crazy. David was pretty sure now it wasn't her.

What he thought of, when he thought about her, wasn't really her, either. He recognized that. The woman he thought of when he thought of her was some weird ideal. Not a woman, and not a woman he had known or ever been in love with.

He knew this. He was in control of it.

"We can add onto the house," David said. "I think I can get it done cheap."

Irene put her hand on his knee and squeezed it.

"I know," David said, "what you're giving up. Moving. It'll be best, though, for all of us. Even, you know. Well. All of us."

She kept her hand there, resting on his leg.

"I'm lucky," he said. "Behind every great man, right? I know how lucky I am."

"No, you don't," she said, "but I love you anyway."

This struck David just right. "And that," he said, "is what I love most about you." That edge, he meant.

"We ca-a-an get it done cheap," mimicked Teddy. "Tha-a-at is what I love."

"Yay!" said Lizard. "Ken-ne-dy, Ken-ne-dy!"

"You ought to be on TV, Ted," Irene said. "You ought to be on *Ed Sullivan*."

They would be home in time for *Ed Sullivan*.

They were on the Shoreway now. They drew near the stadium. If David had gone to the game, he realized, he'd still be there now. When the last game of the season ended, David would stay in his seat, sipping a beer and making notes on a legal pad about the season as a whole. The grounds crew would start pulling down the outfield fence and attacking the job of girding the stadium for the long, cold months when the Browns were the sole tenant. One year the ushers tried to herd David out. He slipped them a buck to let him stay until the grounds crew dug up home plate. David kept the notes inside the scorecard. He kept his last-day scorecards in a file folder separate from the others.

Opening Day was to baseball what Christmas and Easter were to Christianity. What marked you as devout was the last home game of the season. Each of the years David had been there, the game had meant nothing but pride. No one there to be seen. No pollyannas. No fair-weather fans. The stands were more empty than full, peopled by hardscrabble realists who came to see a game for the sake of a game. David had been at Cleveland's last home game in both 1950 and 1951, then missed 1952 and 1953 when he was in the service. He missed 1954—the World Series, no less—to get married. If that wasn't love, David didn't know what was. Joke. But for five years straight, he'd been there.

"Here." On impulse, David pulled the pair of unused tickets from the breast pocket of his sport coat and handed them to the boy. "A souvenir."

As soon as he did it, the illogic of the gesture kicked in.

But Teddy took the tickets, unquestioningly. "Thank you," he said. "I sincerely appreciate it."

"Can I have some?" Lizard said.

"We can share," Teddy said, and gave her one.

"Yay!" she said. "Lizard is great! Teddy is great, too!"

David loved, loved, loved his wife and kids. Loved them!

That's what he was thinking.

What his family saw was a big, silent man with no particular look on his face, squinting into the sun, piloting the family sedan over a bridge to the West Side, turning up the radio to hear highlights from a football game. Browns 41, Eagles 20.

෨

MEANWHILE, AS THE Zielinskys headed south, toward one of their last remaining nights in Independence, the senator caught a charter plane to Chicago. The next day Khrushchev took off his shoe and banged it on a table at the United Nations. The next night the senator and the vice president went on television for what technically was not a presidential debate (anyone who'd been on a high school debate team could and would tell you that) but in truth was exactly that.

Who won? Famously, that depended on whether a person watched the pageantry in person or on TV. How many watched it in person? Hands? On TV? Hands?

Exactly.

The New Frontier.

The following weekend, David Zielinsky moved his family from his old new house to his new old house. He started working up the nerve to ask his father for money, to build an addition.

The next president of the United States lost Ohio—by more votes than he lost any other state. Would've been worse, without Cleveland. Cleveland was great guns for Jack.

The New Frontier! Blast off, baby! Duck and cover! Vig-ah! Dig it.

── 12 ──

IN MANHATTAN, THE day before her father died—the newspaper accounts would say Thomas O'Connor had a heart attack on his boat, while fishing in Lake Erie, which was untrue (the boat belonged to Sarah; also, he detested fishing)—Anne O'Connor reached across the table at the Century Club, took the hand of her beau, a vigorous older man who had that afternoon lost two out of three sets of tennis to her, and declined his offer of marriage. He nodded. He ran his unheld hand over his gray crew cut, as if he were trying to spark enough static electricity for balloons to stick to his head. The other hand held on for dear life. "That quickly?" he said. He was a senior editor of a publishing house. He and Anne had been dating for six months. "You don't even want to spare me, tell me you need to think about it? No, just like that, no?"

What could she say? When it's no, it's no. She'd never told the man she loved him. She'd been careful. They had been inventive, bohemian lovers, had made a handsome couple, but *marriage?* "I'm sorry," she said.

The man let go of her hand, called the waiter over, and ordered a bottle of Dom Pérignon.

"If you think that's going to change my mind—," Anne said.

He waved her off.

"One glass," he said to the waiter. "The lady, unfortunately, can't stay."

He looked her right in the eyes. The waiter left.

"That's just lovely," Anne said.

"Yes," he said. "Isn't it?" He had been married twice before.

The next day at work, Anne finished the weather segment for the noon news and the station manager asked her to join him for lunch, not in the executive dining room, but in a bar across the street. She knew exactly what was coming. He was married. How he knew she'd dumped the editor, she hadn't a clue. Men smell it.

Or maybe he didn't know. What men smell is less opportunity than opportunism.

"Have a drink," the station manager said. The bar was preposterously dark. It was a red-velvet, Delmonico-steak sort of place. Anne had dodged other passes there.

"Water's fine," she said. "Eight glasses a day."

He looked at her in horror.

"For good health," she explained. She could still wear the clothes she'd worn in college.

"You must live in the loo."

He was new at the station and British, but he'd been in the States so long his accent sounded like an American stage actor affecting one. He was dimple-chinned, easy on the eyes, and well aware of it. He got away with wearing a cravat, he was that good-looking. He'd been an anchorman in Boston before getting this job. Good-looking men got rewarded for it. Good-looking women knew they'd been hired for it: it only, another way of saying they were punished for it. Anne had thought the weather-reader job would lead to a reporter's job. Three years later she was still affecting enthusiasm for needed rain and doing on-air commercials for cleaning products that, in real life, she hired someone to deploy. She'd wanted to be a war correspondent! Good god. Like a little boy who wanted to grow up and play shortstop for the Indians.

All through lunch the station manager talked about nothing. She wanted to get this over with, and giving him any part of herself would make things worse. She listened and he talked. He was a talker. Kennedy this, Kennedy that. The strengths and mostly weaknesses of the new fall schedule. He was also a drinker. What was weird, he started talking about his wife and kids— a lot about his kids and their school situations. Odd gambit.

The split second their plates were taken away, he sat up straight, adjusted his necktie, and cleared his throat. "Anne, there's something I have to tell you."

"Don't," she said. "Please."

"I have to," he said. What a tortured look this one was capable of! "I have no choice."

"You do," she said. "Really, you do."

He frowned. "There's no easy way to say this."

"Then don't," she said. "It's not a thing you have to say. I'm flattered, but . . . well, let's just put it behind us, OK?" She shrugged, in a way calculated to be diplomatically coquettish.

"Flattered?"

He'd had four drinks. A fifth was en route. She'd become a drink-counter. Genetics.

"You're an interesting man, of course," she said. "Perhaps under other circumstances . . ."

"Excuse me?" He frowned. "What are you suggesting? Are you suggesting something?"

"No, sir," she said. *Sir:* always a good touch.

"OK, then," he said. "Look, I'm sorry, Anne, and if it was up to me, I wouldn't be doing this, but the ownership, they have, well, ideas."

"It's about time," she said. They were the lowest-rated station in New York.

"Not ideas exactly," he said. "Plans."

"Oh." Oh god. *Now* she got it.

"So." He swirled the ice in his glass, drained it, then stuck his finger in the glass, pulled out the cocktail onion, and ate it. "So. Well. You're, um. Um. Fired."

He looked away, toward the mirror over the padded patent-leather bar, and began to chew his ice.

Anne tried to decide if he was really bad or really good at this, firing people. She looked toward the same mirror. It was too far away for her to see herself. She would have liked to have a picture of this, her life exploding in a dark Manhattan bar. Old, spent, unmarried, foolish, smarter and prettier and richer than everyone and punished for it. At twenty-five you are not prepared to be replaced with someone younger.

Things can always get worse, she thought. She thought she believed that. She didn't. It's a thought you mint only if you don't believe it.

Really good at it, she decided.

She pointed at his empty glass.

"What do you call that drink?" she asked.

"A Gibson," he said, still not looking at her.

These things come in threes. At about the same time Anne was getting fired, give or take a few hours, her father took the Chris-Craft (a new one) out from the dock at Kelley's Island and had the heart attack that killed him. He was missing for three days (threes on top of threes!). Ibby, of all people, called to tell Anne. Ibby was bawling, as if she had the right. When the boat washed up on the Canadian shore, the call came from Patrick. He was crying, too. Their father was still in the boat, dead for two days and wearing only his underpants (briefs, which, on Anne's father, were inaptly named). No other clothes on the boat, not even a life jacket, but the boat was gassed up and his wallet was in the glove box, thick with twenties. There was a ladies' wig, blond, which Patrick said their mother claimed as hers, and an ice chest full of beer and sandwiches, enough for three or four people. One of Tom O'Connor's eyes had been plucked out by a gull. A copy of Kenneth's new novel was also on board. Patrick stopped crying to tell this part. He paused for Anne's reaction.

"What are you suggesting?" she said.

"You know exactly what I'm suggesting," Patrick said. "Have you read it?"

"Of course."

"All right then."

"You're a cretin. You're saying the book killed him." *The wig killed him, stupid.*

"I'm not saying anything. You said it, not me."

"You should get out of the Midwest," she said, "for the occasional visit at least."

In fact, the book was most likely left on the boat by Sarah (to whom that particular copy was inscribed). Ridiculous, to think a book could kill a man.

The odd details of Thomas O'Connor's death appeared only in the *Press*. The *Plain Dealer* showed more restraint. The *News* had been out of business for a year now. Radio stations increasingly relied on plagiary of newspapers for their news, and on this matter they chose to plagiarize the *PD* and not the *Press*. As for TV, who relied on TV for news? Further, television still, touchingly, believed it had a responsibility to children who might be watching. And of course there was the matter of not having footage of the derelict boat. What they did have footage of was last fall's Democratic Steer Roast, of Thomas O'Connor shaking hands with the handsome young man who was now our president, and of course that was what people saw.

☙

"The king died," Kenneth said, "and then the queen died of grief."

"*Ha!*" John O'Connor said. "She's fine. Look at her." From where John, Kenneth, and Anne stood, across the crowded room from her, in the largest funeral parlor in greater Cleveland, they couldn't actually see Sarah O'Connor. They all turned, though, in the direction of where they knew she was: dutifully near the coffin, Patrick (the child who had not abandoned her) at her side, swimming in thousands of dollars' worth of standing flower arrangements, receiving the city's rich and powerful. "It's like she's in the winner's circle at the Kentucky Derby, all those flowers," John said. "She's in her glory. She's free. She's a winner, baby."

Kenneth slapped John on the back of the head. "She," he stage-whispered, "isn't the queen I was talking about."

"Not funny," John said.

John and Kenneth were no longer a couple. Kenneth was there as a friend. They both lived in Key West, but not together and not as a couple. Kenneth was writing; John was not. John had abandoned Hollywood, gone to grad school (UCLA, American lit), and, with only his dissertation to go, abandoned that too, moved to Key West, and became a bartender.

"I thought Steven's was bad," John said. "But this is ridiculous."

"I don't remember Steven's," Anne said.

"Of course you do. How can you not? You were, what, eight? Who doesn't remember important things that happened to them when they were eight?"

"I don't."

"You don't because you don't want to," he said.

"I don't because I don't," she said. "Period."

"Your brother John," Kenneth said to Anne, "loved your father to pieces. Loves. No matter what happened, and no matter what he says. If he tells you anything different, stick your fingers in your ears and hum."

"You don't know anything," John said. "If it'd been Mom who died first, you wouldn't even have been allowed to be here."

Kenneth shook his head, exhausted.

A (white) state senator and his wife came up to Kenneth and warmly introduced themselves. The wife claimed to have loved his new book. Kenneth said that made one of her.

Kenneth was among a great many Negroes in attendance. Every important Negro attorney and politician (wives in tow) made an appearance: testament, Anne imagined, to her father's pragmatic attempts to integrate the machine. The people who came up to tell Kenneth they admired his work, though, were white. His first novel, the second he'd written, was the sort of misfit preacher's-son story of which the subject-matter police approved. On the strength of that, he'd revised and published the one he started at Kelley's, a book loosely based on his and John's friendship, which began when they were football teammates. The John character was the protagonist. Not to give away the ending, but: the Kenneth character (unlike the exquisitely dark-skinned Kenneth) is passing as white. Negro and liberal white reviewers (everyone assigned to it, in other words) savaged the book. Anne would have thought James Baldwin's success would have paved a way, but that got used against Kenneth, as if library shelves could hold but one homosexual Negro.

When Kenneth was through with these latest well-wishers, John put his hand on Anne's shoulder. "I'm warning you, Babe," he said. "When Dad's good and buried, and when all the people clear out, I plan to take a good long piss on his grave. You're welcome to join me."

"I can't believe you," Anne said.

"Believe me," he said. His eyes were cowboy-squint remorseless.

She was not going to cry. Bad enough her father was gone, worse she had to try to cope with it in front of anyone who was anyone in Cleveland. So be it. But if she had to perform, if that was the given, she was going to turn in the sort of performance *she* chose. She took a deep breath. Then another. "I love you, John," she said, "but if you mean that, you're a monster."

"Believe me," John said.

"You're fooling no one," Kenneth said. "You're too old for a stunt like that. Cry, already. What's wrong with you people?"

ৎ৹

ANNE HAD BOUGHT three new dresses. The one she had on was a Chanel, the darkest possible purple, a color beyond black. Gloves to match. But tomorrow, she'd buck nothing: a black A-line number so by the book she could imagine Mamie Eisenhower choosing it for a state funeral, which of course this was. White gloves.

What possessed Anne to buy the third dress, also black but slit high and so low-cut only a slut would wear it in church? She liked the way it looked. She liked the way it made her look. She liked the idea that she could live long enough to have a day when it would be the just-right thing to wear. A place to go where that dress would be just the ticket. She closed her eyes and wondered what it would take to get there, to that fine day. She came up empty.

ৎ৹

THE VIEWING PART of the wake went for six punishing hours, three to nine. Except for Sarah, the family took turns stepping out. The undertaker had set up a buffet in a side room. Family only, supposedly—though a few guests, accustomed to VIP suites and free food wherever they went, wandered in, sat down, and snacked. Cold cuts and crudités, waxy-looking fruit, weak coffee, and a small mildewy refrigerator stocked with bottles of pop.

It's hard, hearing hundreds of mopey people tell you they're sorry, without telling them to shut up and stop apologizing. Anne managed. She performed her role as well as could any Broadway actress sent to play it (at least if that actress were directed not to cry). She accepted embraces, and closed her eyes and nodded somberly. She got that move *down,* jack. Sometimes she even swallowed, as if she were choked up, and sometimes she wasn't even

[287]

acting. She agreed with every nice thing anyone said about her father. Because why not? Some of it was true. Yes, he will be missed. No, there will never be another one like him. He was the last of a breed and one of a kind. (She did not point out the contradiction there.) She was at what seemed like the worst time in her life to field questions about her job and social life and all things New York, but she took the questions and answered them vaguely and politely, and turned the conversation back at the questioners. *People don't want to talk about you; they want to talk about themselves and, at best, you insofar as it affects them.* Say what you want about deb class, more of it came in handy than Anne ever could have imagined.

Who *didn't* come to the wake? Every relative, shoestring and otherwise, managed to show up looking distraught. Schoolmates of Patrick's, of John's, of Anne's, even of Steven's. Officers in the Notre Dame Alumni Association, a retired assistant football coach, even one of the legendary Four Horsemen. Everybody from Tom and Sarah's old crowd—back when they were a legitimate couple and took vacations to Europe and Cuba with other couples and their families—came blubbering up to the casket. Neighbors, too. At one point, late in the day in the break room, Patrick handed Anne a soda and asked her to name someone who owned a house in Shaker Heights of five thousand square feet or more who didn't come. Anne couldn't. "Who are you thinking of?"

Patrick shook his head. "All here, is what I'm thinking."

Speaking of all here: the politicians! Any Democrat who'd ever run for anything beyond middle school student council, plus the county's four or five electable Republicans. Friends. Enemies. Cronies. Up-and-comers, gone-and-wenters. In power, out of power, seeking power. A complete set. Collect 'em! Trade 'em with your friends!

It was a collection that included David Zielinsky. Of course. She'd heard he was running for council, news that made her feel both like she'd done nothing with her life and like anyone who stayed in this city could become famous in the neighborhood.

Happily, she saw him before he saw her. He was going gray at the temples and had lost the little paunch he used to have. He had a tan. His limp was all but gone. Left hand; wedding ring; check. He looked like he'd been to politician school, sliding through the crowd in an unpretentious off-the-rack suit, shaking hands and clasping shoulders and looking genuinely (and not too) sad. Clasping shoulders. His wedding ring was silver.

Not a conversation she felt like having. She ducked into the break room. Louie Seltzer was in there, weeping.

"This is just for family," she said, though a few other strangers were in there. "Get out."

He cocked his head, like a gallingly stupid dog.

"Get the . . ." She was still no good at swearing. "Get out, you despicable martinet."

Some of Sarah O'Connor's cousins applauded. They were from New York themselves and probably had no idea who Louie Seltzer was.

He rose. "Wait," he said. "You're the daughter."

"Are you deaf?" she said.

"I'm sorry for your loss," Seltzer said. "I truly admired your father."

"I'm happy to beat you senseless," she said. "If that's what it takes."

Seltzer smiled. "You've got his spirit."

She swung at him. He ducked.

Off balance, she fell against a table, knocking a plate of crackers to the floor.

"I didn't know this was for family," he said. "I didn't mean to offend." He scuttled out.

Anne sat down. She was hyperventilating. Someone went for help. Patrick and Ibby were the first to respond, but by then Anne's hyperventilating had turned to sobs.

She couldn't stop herself. She hated herself.

"That's OK, sweetie," Ibby said. "Oh, honey. I know."

Ibby held her. Her sister-in-law, who came from the same sort of family and had been in this family long enough to know what's what. Who until that moment had never seemed like an ally, or like anything at all. The woman who took Patrick away from home. Totally unfair.

Anne sobbed. It cleared the room, except for Ibby and Patrick, and Ibby told Patrick to go. "Oh, honey," Ibby said to Anne. "I know."

Anyone would have imagined this had everything to do with her father, with grief. Grief was part of it. Grief was all of it, but grief for so many things, too many things. Her shoulders heaved and she could not breathe, battling for air and control, sucker-punched by grief for the person she had set out into the world to be and was not. Grief for the life she might have had with a man who was not born and bred to be a suitable mate. Not a man, *that* man. She *hated* herself, crying over a man, crying over someone she'd barely more than kissed, crying over someone she was in love with the idea of loving. *God,* how she was poisoned! By fairy tales and other women and love and sex and grief. And guilt! How *dare* she be crying about anything other than her father! Ambition, shame, failure: how can any of it matter now? Too much, all too much, all of it bound together and dropped on her and exploding in a mushroom cloud of self-loathing that anyone watching or listening would have called grief, and was grief.

No one could have imagined what Anne's life felt like, these past few days, and what-all she was crying about. Even Anne could not imagine this. Ibby did not try to get her to stop crying, the way a man would have, or to tell her everything would be all right, the way a young man would have. She let Anne cry. Ibby gently rocked her and said nothing. Ibby smelled like baby powder, French perfume, and applesauce. Her dress was made of rayon. She rocked her.

After what could have been five minutes and could have been an hour, Anne regained control. Even that took awhile, deep breath after deep breath. There were hitches in those deep breaths, hiccuppy aftershocks of sorrow.

"I love you, Ibby," Anne finally said.

"And I love you, Annie," Ibby said. "You *have* had a long day."

"Don't call me that," Anne said.

✂∽

WAS THE OTHER woman there, at the wake? The one with the wig, who'd panicked when her father had the heart attack and thrown his clothes into Lake Erie and swam for it? What had possessed her father, taking that woman up to Kelley's Island, his wife's sanctuary?

Anne had gone to all-girls schools all her life, but she'd always under-stood men better than women. Except, she now realized, the man who was her father. All she did was love him. She knew the facts of his life well enough to write his obituary, but as for the truth needed to get at biography, she knew only enough to be dangerous. Glimpses. Man in a role. "Father." "Boss." That she understood this is all that kept the danger sheathed.

Mostly, it suited Anne that no one in her family talked about anything. But after years of that, people die and you can't talk to them about any of the things you thought might someday emerge. All the questions she'd like to know the answers to, but never enough to ask. What, Dad, were the worst means you acceded to in the name of the ends? What did you know about how the world really works, things you would not in life have told us, your own children? Tell! What's it really like to lose a child? To disown one? Tell! And the truth: When, Dad, did you stop loving Mother? Sadder: What if you never really stopped? Was that possible? Tell!

If her father came back from the dead, expressly to satisfy his favorite child's curiosity, even *then,* Anne knew, she couldn't ask a single one of these questions.

Who was she, the wig-woman?

Imagine her, making it to shore. Say she's a wife of a friend. A bored woman whose own husband was a cheat, who went out into a world of proscribed choices and made revenge-love to Thomas O'Connor. She could do much, much worse. Picture that woman, emerging from the foul, dying lake. She is no athlete. Her chest heaves. This is the farthest she's ever swum, the most exercise she's gotten since she was a girl at summer camp, twenty-some years ago, and she can't believe her luck. She's made it. Then she reassesses how lucky she really is. What petty vengeance the Lord stoops to exact. Imagine her on the rocky shore, sitting on a stump, full of self-loathing, wondering how long it will take her clothes to dry, and trying to decide what to do, how to make her way home. How *did* she make her way home? Wouldn't it have been like one of those dreams where you're naked in public and need to find your way home before anyone notices? Anne had this dream a lot. For that woman, it would have been no dream. How would she do it? How *did* she do it?

That's assuming she made it to shore at all.

Anne knew nothing, which made anything possible.

The wig, the underpants, the sandwiches: logic decreed that these things were getting discussed, right in the funeral parlor. But it was kept from any corner Anne inhabited. She wanted to know but wasn't seriously tempted to bring it up. They were not that kind of family. They did not bring things up. Anne was proud of this. She was. Knowing things you don't want to know but already know: whom does that make free?

Maybe there *was* no woman.

Anne knew nothing, which made anything possible.

A blond wig, though. How that must have hurt her mother, claiming to own a blond wig. Her mother had lustrous dark brown hair. Not a strand of gray. Jackie Kennedy hair.

৩৩

BACK AT THE house, the impromptu family part of the wake ended up going for *another* six hours. What doesn't get said, enough, about funerals is, despite everyone's efforts to be somber and respectful, how much fun they turn out to be. (Weddings: vice versa.)

John and Kenneth certainly hadn't lost their knack for turning stragglers, long-lost relatives, and acquaintances into very special new friends, and within an hour of the time everyone got back to the house, and John and Kenneth had executed a superfluous liquor run, Sinatra's *Songs for Swingin' Lovers* was pumping out of the Swedish hi-fi that John, Patrick, and Anne had bought their parents last Christmas. It was a warm night for September, and Sarah was sitting in the yard, catching up with cousins she hadn't seen since who knows when. Patrick and Ibby had stowed the kids with her parents and were among the couples dancing. Kenneth found a legal pad and went around asking people to tell stories about Tom O'Connor. He presided over the music, too, slapping swing disks on, and warding off rock and roll, which he called "evil juvenilia." Anne grabbed a bottle of Bushmill's and sat at the groaning board with her father's two older brothers and their kids and kids' spouses, and the next thing she knew she was lost in talk about the president and going to the moon and Jim Brown and the time her father misplaced his Lincoln. They raised a toast to Roger Maris. They raised a toast to the memory of Bill Corrigan, who died last month and was succeeded at the helm of the equally dead Sam Sheppard case by some arrogant Boston kid a year out of law school named F. Lee Bailey. They argued about Anne's father's lone touchdown at Notre Dame (a fumble recovery? an interception return? the return of a blocked punt?). They talked about movies with Anthony Quinn in them; Uncle Stephen—a retired trial lawyer ten years older than Tom but a dead ringer for him, and, despite the spelling, Steven's namesake—loved that Anthony Quinn. Uncle Seamus took ice in his Bushmill's, to the horror of everyone at the table. This just shows what people know, he said. "Good Irish priests like me," he said, "drink nothing neat."

Everyone laughed, especially Uncle Seamus. He was never a priest; he dropped out of the seminary to marry Aunt Gwen and had spent his adult life as a math teacher in Baltimore.

Inevitably, the reunited O'Connor wing of the family pulled out pictures of babies and children and passed them around the table. Cries of *so big, so big!* Inevitably, this led to talk about Anne and when she was going to have snapshots of her own to pass around.

"Would *never,*" Anne said, "be such a tragedy?"

"Wash out your mouth, missy," said Uncle Seamus.

"Coming from where we came from," said Uncle Stephen, looking showily around the grand dining room, "it's amazing we all got where we are. We lucky boys. We lucky, lucky, lucky boys. God *bless* America."

"More Bushmill's, Uncle Stephen?" said Anne.

"To your father," Stephen said, taking the bottle and raising it. "To Tommy."

⟋⟍

A TOUCH FOOTBALL game sprang up on the flood-lit front lawn. The bigger part of the group went out to play or watch. Sarah came in and switched the hi-fi to a classical music radio station. Britten's Third.

Anne, who'd gone upstairs to change (a cotton sweater that had been her father's; drawstring Bermuda shorts of her mother's; barefoot) and was on her way out, put a hand on her mother's shoulder. "How you holding up?"

Her mother nodded. She smiled sadly. "Oh, you know."

"Dad would have loved this," Anne said.

"I know," Sarah said. "He would have been the ringleader." She laughed. She made her hands into a megaphone. "Step right up," she said.

Anne gave her mother's shoulder a squeeze. The world's slightest hug.

"We need to talk," Sarah said. "At some point."

"Of course we do," Anne said. "Mom, you don't need to tell me. Things don't last forever, etcetera. I'm not a kid. You and Dad loved each other. A marriage is complicated—"

"It's about the house," Sarah said.

Anne shook her head. "Your business," she said, heading for the door. "Keep me out of it. Whatever you do, you do."

The football game went on and on, into the night, through a complaint from the vulgarian car-dealer neighbors and two trips from apologetic Shaker Heights cops. Anne was Kenneth's main deep threat. She was faster than most of the people in this crowd, even though they were almost all of them men and some had played college football and she was barefoot. She was younger and could always see well in the dark. Also, she'd had little to drink and did not have the disadvantage, as most of them did, of playing in a tight, increasingly ruined suit.

The game ended, as these games always do, when someone got hurt.

By the time Anne and Kenneth ferried John back from the hospital, it was after two. The postwake had broken up. The house was postparty wreckage. There wouldn't be anyone there to clean it until morning. The soundtrack to *The Magnificent Seven* was playing. Sarah and Patrick sat under that big Italian chandelier, smoking pipes.

"Who do we have here?" John said, managing surprisingly well with his crutches. "Sherlock Holmes and his lovely mother?"

"Sprained?" Sarah said, pointing at his ankle.

"Broken," Kenneth said.

"Thank you, Charlie McCarthy," John said. "It's broken," he said. "Not badly."

"That's foul," Kenneth said, fanning the smoke with his hand.

"You're kidding," Patrick said. "Broken? Jeez, I'm sorry."

"I slipped," John said. "Don't give it a second thought, Thumbkin. Dad's pipes?"

"Excellent deduction, Watson!"

"That tobacco must be a hundred years old," Anne said.

"It was in the humidor," Patrick said.

"It's not bad," Sarah said. "I could learn to like this."

"Mother!" Anne said.

"The problem with you, kiddo," Sarah said, "is that you're a prude. Listen, now that I have the three of you here—"

"Right, right," John said. "Patrick and Ibby are moving into the house and you're moving to Ashcroft again. Big secret."

Sarah turned to Patrick and slapped him on the bicep. "You told them?" Sarah said.

"Gotcha!" John said. "Am I good or what?"

"Don't let him fool you, Mrs. O," Kenneth said. "He's not that good."

Sarah convulsed in laughter, too hard, and then started hacking on the pipe smoke.

"How'd you even know to guess?"

John shrugged. "Ibby told me."

"There are financial implications of this," Sarah said, "that I think we should discuss."

"Where is Ibby?" Anne said. The record had to be her father's. He loved that movie.

"Home with the babies," Patrick said. They had four kids, ages six to six months; Patrick was wont to call them *the babies*.

"Of *course*," Anne said. "Naturally."

"What do you mean by that?" Patrick said.

"It's too late and I'm too tired," Anne said, "to mean anything by anything."

"I'm going to be sick, I think," Sarah said.

Anne followed her mother to the bathroom and held her thick, sweaty, and undyed hair while she vomited. This was something for which Anne had a talent. Even in college, holding the hair of sporadically retching sorority sisters, she'd never once succumbed to sympathy barfing. A moment like this made her think she might, after all, make a terrific mother.

When the vomiting slowed, Anne brought her mother a glass of water and a saltine and sat down cross-legged beside her. "I have some things to tell you, too, Mom."

As she began, out in the living room, Patrick and Kenneth were singing "Happy Birthday." Excellent, excellent harmony. John was telling them to shut up. It really was his birthday. Anne had totally forgotten. Her big brother's forty-first birthday.

"My god," she said. "I have a brother who's forty-one. How did that happen?"

"I have a son who's forty-one," her mother said. She put down her empty water glass. Anne handed her a fresh towel.

"We're old as the hills," Anne said.

"Speak for yourself."

Anne went ahead. She told her mother everything.

☙

ANNE SLEPT SURPRISINGLY well but was up not long after dawn. She was staying in her old room, the one she'd grown up in, the one with the andiron scars on the door. She was showered and out of the house before six. The cooks and maids were already at work.

Her mother's new car was the cutest thing, a Studebaker Avanti, which looked like what a Corvette would look like if you drained its designers of 20 percent of their testosterone. It was butternut-gold.

She went out to inspect the city.

That had been one of Uncle Stephen's stories last night. Anne hadn't heard it before. During her father's mayoral term, he was stopped late one night, coming home. "Sir," the cop said, "you're weaving like the devil." Her father smiled. "I'm not drunk," he said. "I'm the mayor! I'm out inspecting the city!" The cop let him go. No one would have been the wiser—except that the cop's brother worked for the *Press*. Brothers! What are you gonna do, eh!

She took Fairmount to Cedar Hill, where the Heights met the city, where, suddenly, Terminal Tower loomed on the horizon. Euclid Avenue was a pitted, potholed mess. Stores and restaurants were boarded up. The faces on the street were resolutely black. Traffic was still thick, though, and the faces in the cars were a model of integration Dr. Martin Luther King could have pointed to with hope. Downtown Cleveland was in a down cycle, but it was still a place where people worked. It made her feel like she was a part of something, this workaday, weekday drive into the city. A funeral pulls a person out of life, out of what day of the week it is. That was not like her father. He was a man who worked hard, played hard, rose early, and set a good example for the junior partners. He was a man who knew what day it was.

This was his route to work.

Once, Euclid Avenue was the richest street in America. Millionaires' Row, it was called. Now, what, maybe five of those mansions left? Subdivided into dark apartments. Crummy men's clubs. Underfinanced nursing homes.

The stoplights were hopelessly out of sync. The traffic was awful, by Cleveland standards. But she'd lived in New York long enough, even though she did not of course have a car there, to appreciate how awful this wasn't.

Downtown drew closer. The river drew closer.

Cleveland had become the sort of city where newspapers and department stores were going bankrupt. People lived in the suburbs and never came down here. Companies were starting to leave, not just for the burbs but for the South, in nowheresvilles too small for a full complement of network TV stations, too vulgar to field a decent symphony orchestra.

Anne kept thinking these things. The hell with thinking.

What she felt was her heart quicken. What held her attention were those last great, doomed mansions and the brave little skyline, and what she felt most of all was that she was in a place that interested her. A place she knew but hadn't *seen*, not the way her father had. She'd been raised in Cleveland but outside of it, too: in the Heights, in prep schools, among the wealthy, able to travel abroad on either parent's whim. As a kid, she couldn't wait to leave. Staying in Cleveland for the long haul was an option she never considered.

After she moved to New York, when she'd come back here to visit, it was like the time she gave a talk about being a successful TV reporter to her old third-grade teacher's class and stopped into the girls' room in the elementary school wing and felt like the star of *Attack of the 50-Foot Woman*. In New York, when she'd say she was from Cleveland, people would increasingly say, well, what a good place to be *from*, and Anne would tell them they had *that* right. Both of those things felt false now.

She pulled into a taxi space in front of the Gothic building that, stories above her, housed her father's law firm.

When she'd dumped the last would-be fiancé, about this time last year, during their trip here for him to meet her parents, her dad had talked Anne into staying an extra day. He'd taken her to the movies, shopping, to the art museum: a dopey, good-hearted effort to do things she liked. He said nothing about the previous day's unpleasantness. The next day, on the way to the airport, he stopped here and with a straight arm reached across the seat and gripped her shoulder. "What you don't understand about love," he said, "is that you don't fall in love with someone in spite of his flaws, but because of them. Don't think I'm criticizing you, Babe. I'm so proud of you, I could split wide open. What I'm trying to say is, when the things that are wrong with a person are things that interest you—not things you think you want to fix, God spare the world from that. Things that *interest* you. Then you know you really have something."

He was so alive as he said it. So sure of himself. He was a man in love with control, losing his grip on the city he loved. A man in love with a city that had stopped loving him back. After he imparted his advice, Boss Tom gave her a hug and a hundred-dollar bill, got out of the car, and one of the law clerks, a woman, drove Anne the rest of the way to Hopkins Airport.

That was the last time she saw her father alive. She hadn't even come home last Christmas. In the past year David Zielinsky talked to him more often than she did. To him, her father was a giant.

A doorman rapped on her window. "Excuse me, miss," he said, "but you have to move."

Excuse me, miss, but you have to move.

In New York, this is not what a doorman would have said.

She used to joke that the state line of Ohio was like a parking garage exit with those spikes and a sign that says DO NOT BACK UP, YOU WILL PUNCTURE YOUR TIRES. A kid's ruthless joke, made at the expense of people she loved, for the benefit of New Yorkers.

Excuse me, miss, but you have to move.

She moved. She drove down to the empty stadium. She parked on the north side of it, outside Tower B, where the Browns' offices were, in a space marked GUEST. She got out and walked across a parking lot and past a union building, to the lake, just east of the mouth of the river. The railroad bridge was cranked down, and a freight train without beginning or end rumbled westward, across the Cuyahoga, across Whiskey Island, disappearing into the earnest edge of the Midwest. On the west horizon rose mountains of gray salt, mined from caves extending for miles under the bottom of the lake, stacked high in preparation for the coming winter. A silt of dead fish covered the breakwater. The wind blew so hard Anne could hardly breathe.

— 13 —

THE FUNERAL PROCESSION was so long that few midday motorists on the East Side were spared. Stuck at green lights, they banged fleshy, unsentimental fists on their steering wheels as motorcycle cops barred their way and a black river of flag-bearing American cars passed and passed and passed and passed and passed. The oblivious mourners entered Lake View Cemetery on the Euclid Avenue side: at the crest of Murray Hill, six miles from City Hall, on the edge of Cleveland proper. Lake Erie was miles away, too, visible from nowhere in Lake View Cemetery except for the top of the Garfield Monument, the first principal structure that the procession confronted.

Carved from native Ohio sandstone, the monument's circular tower rose almost two hundred feet in the air. In front of the tower, with two smaller towers on its corners, was the monument's memorial hall, the size of a chapel in a suburban parish and filled with mosaics, stained-glass windows, and white marble statues celebrating the life of James A. Garfield, twentieth president of the United States of America, born and buried in Cuyahoga County. His was the requisite American story. Born not only poor but in an actual log cabin. A knack for oratory. Quick with a toast. Storyteller. He was a college professor, an attorney, an antislavery state senator, a Union general, a progressive Republican congressman, and a semireluctant compromise candidate for president. As a condition of his nomination, Garfield agreed to an open-secret backroom deal: if elected, he would share political appointments with Roscoe Conkling, his chief rival. Garfield won. He reneged. Four months later Charles Guiteau—who walks hell wearing a sandwich sign that, on both sides, reads DISGRUNTLED OFFICE SEEKER—shot him. Two months after that, almost exactly eighty years before the procession that bore and followed Thomas O'Connor passed by, Garfield died.

Disgruntled office seekers do not get buried in a cemetery like this.

It was almost a century old, spreading out over two hundred wooded and hilly acres. Ohio-cut stone (with some Barre granite and Italian marble spirited in) fashioned into Romanesque obelisks, Byzantine spires, and craggy Gothic gingerbread. Sunny clearings. Paved roads black as a new hearse. Fastidious horticulture. Ponds made from a system of dams on Dugway Creek. This was a cemetery for millionaires, martyrs, and heroes.

Near the north entrance, a low-lying populist part of the cemetery, was a monument to the 172 children and teachers who died in 1908, in a fire at an elementary school just east of here, deaths that spurred the implementation of fire-safety measures worldwide. Nearby was the final resting place of Charles W. Chesnutt, the best writer to live most of his life in Cleveland (born there, worked as a reporter in New York, came home). When his best books failed to adhere to uplift-the-race dogma and thus failed to find readers, Chesnutt quit writing and lived out his days as an attorney and civil rights pioneer; he died out-of-print and bitter. Not far away was the grave site of Cleveland Indians shortstop Ray Chapman, only big-league player to die in a game, killed during a pennant race by a pitch from the hand of a New York Yankee. Chapman's tombstone was paid for with the dimes of distraught baseball-loving children; his epitaph was not but should have been *If a thing like this had to happen, it figures it would happen to Cleveland.*

The procession came in the other way and did not pass those graves. Instead, on its left, the hearse, limousines, and mere cars behind them drew past the tomb and the tall, spare monument of John D. Rockefeller, distant relative of the new widow. It drew past monuments to the ruthless, bearded men who built Cleveland, men with first names like Josias, Newton, Jeptha, and Cyrus. The hearse went around a bend; passengers in the procession could look across a meadow and see, built into a hillside, the tombs holding what was left of the Van Sweringens, O.P. and M.J., Carrie and Edith: gone to Lake View Cemetery, food for the worms.

A tastefully undersized white tent covered the O'Connor family plot.

The day was cold for September. This was Cleveland, and no one was unprepared or even surprised. The funeral-goers emerged from their cars in overcoats and warm leather gloves. Rain was not expected and in fact would not come, but the sky was the gray that was the exclusive province of a city like Cleveland.

A true local, of which this funeral boasted hundreds, would notice the gradation of gray that was Cleveland's alone. A true local would not believe there to be a city *like* Cleveland.

Already interred in the plot: STEVEN FRANCES O'CONNOR, 1922–1944. AMERICAN WAR HERO. The headstone had a fighter plane carved into it. The tent had been set up so one of its sides blocked mourners from stepping on Steven's grave. Someone, out early this morning, had already laid a red rose there.

Thomas O'Connor, son of a truck driver and a laundress, raised in Ohio City, wound up buried in the epicenter of the prettiest two hundred acres in

Cleveland. His tombstone, modest by the standards of Lake View Cemetery, was still more than what a boy who grew up where and when Tommy O'Connor grew up might ever have imagined. Feldspar! He survived the Great War and did not brag about it. He did not even talk about it. His adult life was devoted to the impossible task of running a great city. He married a beautiful woman, a rich girl, who did not ever lose her looks, who survived him, and whose name was already carved on the stone beside his. He fathered three surviving children (only two of whom had borne or would bear him grandchildren), each attractive in his or her way, each mourning in his or her way. Hundreds of rich and powerful people watched as the oak casket bearing his big, dead body was winched into the ground. Few there did not owe him something. Important people wept. The debts they owed Boss Tom O'Connor were in theory retired. A trumpeter played "Taps," then a shameless cornetist played "Danny Boy." Thomas O'Connor's wife and children sobbed. The end.

14

DAVID ZIELINSKY'S UNCLE worked with Tom O'Connor (though Mr. O'Connor, who didn't practice law per se, had an office suite on the floor above) and David had once been enamored of Mr. O'Connor's daughter, but, until the funeral dinner, David had never been to the house. He tried not to stare.

He'd garrotte nuns to have a house like this: high ceilings and dark wood, servants, a swimming pool, a gazebo *and* a guest cottage, oil paintings (not dead relatives, but art! abstract art!), thick rugs, and the largest chandelier he'd ever seen in a private home. He went to the bathroom and was startled to see in it two toilets, side by side. Then he realized one was a bidet, something he'd read about but never seen. He double-checked the lock on the door, then played with the bidet, operating its little fountain. It was hard to see that water squirting and not wonder whether this was an apparatus Anne O'Connor customarily used.

A bidet—something David only vaguely understood—in an American house! David opposed the rich in aggregate. Severally, he couldn't have loved them more if they were family.

He finished in the bathroom. He should get going. David intended only to pay his respects. He'd been careful not to be creepy about pressing the flesh. He was there out of a sense of honest loss. Tom O'Connor had coached him and seemed, when he died, on the cusp of endorsing him. But David had a spaghetti dinner to go to, then two separate coffees, on opposite sides of his ward. The primary was a week from today.

But he couldn't leave without saying a word of condolence to Anne. Mourners swarmed her, of course, and David did not want to intrude. He kept waiting for the right opening. He would certainly not want her to get the wrong idea.

He never got the perfect moment, but when he saw that she was nowhere near her mother (Sarah frightened him), David, strapped for time, had no choice but to take a deep breath and walk across the marble floor of the living room, right up to her.

"Your father," David blurted, "was a giant."

"That's incredibly sweet of you." Anne did not look at all surprised. "It was good of her to come. Of you to come, I mean." She slapped herself in the head. "It's been a long few days."

Her face was scrubbed of makeup. Her eyes were bloodshot, her arms were lightly bruised, and her hair looked like she'd been caught in a tornado. She was a wreck. He had never seen her so beautiful.

"He was a great man," David said. He hugged her. She flinched, just a little. He couldn't help himself: politicians are huggers, especially West Siders. Worse than Italians. As bad as southerners. He would not have wanted that hug to be misunderstood. It had been nine years since their last embrace. She smelled like Ivory soap. A rich girl, but Ivory soap.

And then she hugged him back.

She held it a few beats too long, and he did not try to pull away until she let him go.

David could hardly breathe. He breathed.

"Your father stood for all the right things," he finally said. "You still in New York?"

"I am. I heard you were running for council."

"Your father," David said. His voice cracked. He could feel himself blushing, badly blushing. He wondered what an asthma attack felt like, and if maybe he was having one. He breathed. "Well, he was a big help, is all."

"Do you think you'll win?" she asked.

"Hard to tell," he said. "You never know. It's just heating up now."

She nodded. She narrowed her eyes. "We should catch up," she said. She lowered her voice to a whisper. "I could use a break," she said, "from all of this."

"I'd like that," he said. "When do you go back?" His ears went hot.

"I'm not sure," she said. "Actually, I may have a job here. Listen, are you in the book?"

He was. But he gave her his card, which had only his office number on it. Not the campaign office (he did not have a separate line in his basement, just an extension he'd rigged for himself and was not paying for). The law office, where he never was, where, by the grace of his uncle, he was allowed to share a desk with another associate, one attached to the firm in more than name only. The receptionist would give him the message.

That he did not give her his home number told himself something right there, and filled him with guilt all the way back to Old Brooklyn.

The smell of the spaghetti sauce at the Moose Lodge snapped him out of it. Show time.

DAVID FIRST WENT to see Tom O'Connor six months ago. For over an hour David sat in a hot reception area, sweating in a leather club chair. Finally, a secretary came out, apologized, and said it would be necessary to reschedule. They'd call him, she said.

Two weeks later the secretary called to invite him to the Country Club for a round of golf. *Golf?* He wasn't sure he'd heard her right. For one thing it was April. April, in Cleveland.

"Unless you'd rather not golf," the secretary said.

"Golf is fine," David said, flummoxed. "Which country club?"

"*The* Country Club," the secretary sneered.

"Oh," David said. "Right. That's fine then. I'll be there."

The Country Club was out in Pepper Pike, on land that once belonged to the Van Sweringens. David didn't want to look a gift horse in the mouth, but why on earth was Mr. O'Connor willing to let David have three or so hours of his time on the golf course? Was it because David had used his friendship with Anne as a foot in the door to get that first meeting? Or had people who knew people whispered in Mr. O'Connor's ear that this was a kid he maybe could do a favor for? Even more than that, he was unnerved by the idea of going to meet a man this powerful over *golf*. David couldn't possibly turn down the invitation, but what he was thinking as he accepted it was, *Please, God, don't let me embarrass myself.*

David could golf, but he was no golfer. Over the years he'd played a few times, for laughs and with borrowed clubs. He wasn't half bad, and he'd been meaning to get serious about the game (men of consequence golf). So, OK. This was his chance. He charged a set of clubs at Sears, and for two weeks took daily lessons from a pro at a driving range in Westlake. The pro said that for someone so tall, David had a decent aptitude for the game. The day before his game with Mr. O'Connor, David went out in two heavy sweaters to play a brown, public, par-three course. David was grouped with three strangers, two Slavic barbers and an old man who sold insurance. On his first drive, he topped the ball so badly it only went fifty yards. On his second, he hit the daylights out of the ball, but it sliced so badly that the ball cleared a nearby road and was lost. The younger Slavic barber started making fun of him. A hole later, the younger barber drove two straight balls into a water hazard, while David drove the ball over it, straight, just short of the green. He chipped the ball badly—too hard—but it bit at the edge of the green and David made a long, lucky putt for par. The older barber started to razz his brother, and the younger barber said he hated playing with bad players because their lousy skills rubbed off. The next thing David knew the man

[303]

was swearing and throwing his clubs. The insurance man was a big cheater, insisting on gimmes and mulligans, kicking his ball all the time and citing winter rules. The older barber called the younger a menace, and the younger threw a club at him. At the turn the brothers told David and the insurance man to find new partners. David was cold anyway. He went home. The next day the East Side got a foot of snow (the West Side, nothing). David called to reschedule. The secretary said she had a cancellation for late that afternoon.

Fifteen minutes early for the meeting, David opened the door to the suite and ran into Mr. O'Connor. Literally. "There you are," he said, reaching down to help David up. No apologies, just a hand. "C'mon," he said. "Let's go for a walk."

Mr. O'Connor moved fast, light on his feet for a fat man, and, as they crossed Public Square and headed up Superior, David struggled to keep up. His knee was killing him. It was about to rain.

"Big fella like you," said Mr. O'Connor, "you ever play any sports?"

What was he saying? Did this have to do with golf? With David's slight limp? "Basketball," he said. "That's how I got the bum knee."

Mr. O'Connor nodded. They were in front of the Richardsonian arched entrance to the Arcade. He held the door open for David.

"Think of a ward race," he said, "as a pickup basketball game. You choose someone for your team, then you and that guy whisper about who you're gonna pick next, and so on. One good player per precinct," he said. "All you need to win a council race."

"That's what I'm hoping you can help me with," he said. It wasn't like that at all, David thought. A person you picked had more choices than to play with you or go home. "I was hoping you'd help me pick my first player, maybe help me get him to want to play on my team."

Five stories above them, heavy gray spring gloom pressed down on the Arcade's vast vaulted iron-and-glass roof. It was three o'clock on a Friday. The scrolled balconies that ringed the Arcade were nearly empty.

Mr. O'Connor grabbed David's arm and pulled him into an alcove. It housed a two-chair shoe shine stand. Both chairs were empty. David had done his shoes the night before, but he sat obediently down.

"All right, so why should I back you?" said Mr. O'Connor. "Aside from your being a friend of my daughter's." He shook his head. "A lot of people are friends of my daughter's."

David started to answer, but Mr. O'Connor cut him off.

"Just tell me this, son," Mr. O'Connor said. "Would *you* vote for you?"

"Excuse me, sir?"

"People will ask you that. *Why* would you vote for you?"

David gave a windily diplomatic answer, about being young and progressive, about the declining public schools his children were attending, but mostly about Erieview—what a boondoggle it was to prop up downtown businesses that don't need propping up, with money that could be used to build schools and fund urban renewal in neighborhoods like Glenville, Hough, Central, and Fairfax. The two shoe shine men were Negroes and thus, David was aware, probably lived in one of those neighborhoods. The men never made eye contact with either David or Mr. O'Connor. David never once said the word *Negro*.

Mr. O'Connor shook his head. "Which ward did you say you're in?"

David told him, though he must surely have known.

"Your father's Mike Zielinsky, right? Mikey Z?"

David's heart sank. "Right."

"That's good. It's a labor ward. That has to help you then, right?"

David wasn't so sure, beyond the money part. "Right."

"If memory serves, he ran for state senate once. That's the same Mike Zielinsky, right?"

David closed his eyes and nodded.

"That's good," said Mr. O'Connor. "It doesn't matter how it turned out, you see? In Cleveland, just that the name *Zielinsky* has been on a ballot before, that's a plus for you."

David pursed his lips and made a face to indicate that Mr. O'Connor had a good point.

"And of course Stan Lychak's your uncle," he said. "You have an in with labor, plus you have the Eliot Ness law-and-order angle, and your defining issue is your objection to *Erieview*? Erieview's not even in your ward. And you're against it, why? Because it takes money away from *other* neighborhoods that aren't in your ward?" In other circumstances, and in a less-echoey place than the Arcade, Tom O'Connor's great booming laugh would have sounded warm.

"Erieview takes money away from my ward, too," David said. "I want to be my own man, Mr. O'Connor. I don't want to ride on anyone's coattails."

"Right," he said. "Of course. So what are you doing milking your friendship with my daughter so you can talk to me?"

David went red. He'd worked his ass off, volunteering for Burke, for Celebrezze, for JFK, even for the congressman who had not appointed him to Annapolis. He'd accrued more than enough sweat equity for this—certainly more than any of his opponents had. The man to beat was the son of that congressman, who didn't live in the ward and hadn't even worked on his father's races. He couldn't think of a way to say any of this without pissing off Mr. O'Connor.

"Don't be a chump, kid," said Mr. O'Connor. "Ride any coattail that'll support your weight. That doesn't mean you can't still have integrity."

Mr. O'Connor insisted on paying for both shoe shines. David had to admit, his shoes looked 100 percent better. They climbed a wide marble staircase up to the third-floor balcony, to a steak joint there, and a maître d' ushered them to a private dining room in the back. A waiter asked what they'd like to drink. David ordered pop. Mr. O'Connor shook his head sadly and ordered Bushmill's. When the drinks came, David's was in a Collins glass, so full of ice there was hardly any pop in there. Mr. O'Connor was given a shot glass and the whole bottle.

Prompted by a signed glossy of Paul Brown, they talked about the Browns for a long time. The Indians' season had started, but it was the Browns.

(Meanwhile, Irene was at home, in the early stages of labor, dialing her mother for a ride to the hospital, disgusted that she had called around and been unable to find David.)

Mr. O'Connor was only sipping at his drink. "Ward elections," he said, "are the purest, cleanest form of democracy. Especially our ward elections."

Our ward elections, as if he owned them. Which, as far as David was concerned, he did.

"Council elections are nonpartisan," Mr. O'Connor went on, "and are held only in odd years, and do you know why? I'll tell you why. Low voter turnout. Low voter turnout is good. You hold these things the same year as a presidential, and know-nothings who couldn't tell their councilman from the man in the moon would pull the lever anyway. This way, we keep power in the wards, grassroots, in the hands of the people who choose to care."

Mr. O'Connor took out a fountain pen and a bar napkin. "How many people in your ward, about twenty thou?"

"About that," David said. He wasn't sure.

Mr. O'Connor threw back the rest of his drink. He looked at Paul Brown's photo, squinting. "Eight hundred votes in the primary gets you on the ballot in November," he said, seconds later. "Probably 2,101 wins it outright, which you want to do, obviously, if possible."

David cocked his head, like a dog. "Just like that?"

Mr. O'Connor ignored him. Twenty thou, he said, means about twelve thousand registered voters. In the primary, figure a turnout in that ward of 40 percent, of which about a fifth will only vote for mayor. Round it up: about four thousand people will cast a vote in the council race. One in ten people and you win. If there's at least three serious candidates in that ward, which there will be, that means eight hundred should be good for second place, which gets you to the general. Two thousand and one is a majority, and it's over. "Break the ward down by precinct and figure out where to get two thousand votes," he said, "then get your wife to promise to vote for you and—huzzah!—you win."

(Meanwhile, Irene was telling Teddy and Lizard to go over to Mrs. Mytczynskyj's and stay put until Aunt Betty got there. As can happen three kids into the game, Irene's labor was going to be absurdly brief. She was a nurse and an experienced mother; she recognized the implications. She didn't have time to make it to Parma Hospital, where she worked, and instead had to go to Deaconess, where she used to work. It was only blocks away. She drove herself. She gave birth in the emergency room. It was a boy. Bradley. David got there an hour later. Irene was furious, which struck David as unreasonable. It was the early 1960s, ten years shy of when people started pretending fathers had something to do with childbirth. "I'm sorry, honey," he said, "but you can't believe how important that meeting was to my future. To our future." Irene said he had it right the first time: *his* future.)

Mr. O'Connor handed David his business card. Already written on the back were three names: precinct captains. "Here's some people you might want to pick for your team," he said.

The waiter came back and asked if they were going to order any food. Mr. O'Connor said, yes, when the party he was meeting here arrived.

He gave David a look. He had not said the party *we* are meeting.

David thanked him and got up to leave.

"You might be a good candidate, son," said Mr. O'Connor. "The ingredients are there. But everything I told you was just strategy." He poured himself another. "Mere strategy." He did not tell David to sit back down. "Strategy is cute, but all it tells you is how to win." Theatrically, he took a sip. "What you might think more about," he said, "is why you want to."

☙❧

Two days after Tom O'Connor's funeral, as a rainstorm raged outside, the Optimist Club sponsored "Meet the Candidates Night" in the cafeteria of the same middle school where David Zielinsky had been a B+ student. The place still smelled like wet wool and mop water. Only four of the six candidates attended. Willis Young, the Negro candidate, had apparently seen this as a waste of time. The other no-show was a doddering Socialist crank who probably forgot. For the most part, the audience was made up of people working for or related to one of the candidates. The exceptions: a surly, gold-bricking janitor who'd been at the school forever and did not even live in the ward, militantly bored reporters from both the *Press* and the *Plain Dealer*, nine Optimists (all with name tags), one table full of extra-credit-grubbing seventh graders from Miss Schrag's Ohio history class, and about a dozen golden-agers, mostly women, relishing the attention they got from professing to be undecided. David had been in Miss Schrag's class himself. She smiled at him and discreetly waved. Her seventh graders asked most of the questions, reading them from their composition books while tiny Miss Schrag made notes. The reporters, one very old and one very young, ignored the proceedings and talked loudly to each other. David kept expecting them to leave. They did not: patience rewarded them when Fat Henry Biederman's cousin accused David's father of murdering David's mother.

"This ward is a ward made up of families," said Bruce Biederman. "I don't think we need to be represented in city hall by someone from a broken home, or at least it would have been a broken home," he said, smiling incongruously as he delivered the blow, "had not the criminal element in that family played a part in there never being any need for"—and here he took a deep breath and practically shouted—"a *divorce!*"

The reporters, neither of whom were from the neighborhood, snapped to attention, brows furrowed. The seventh graders also looked confused, though they were twelve years old and thus stuck with that look for a few years. Several of the blue-hairs clucked.

David looked at a water stain on the wall, over the head of a randomly chosen blue-hair.

Bruce Biederman was a certified public accountant and just as big a prick as Fat Henry. Better-looking, though. Bruce had the wavy blond hair, white teeth, and high cheekbones of the callow, too-pretty guy in the movies who loses the girl to John Wayne.

"It's a concern I share, as a matter of fact," chirped Mrs. Richard Kastleman, a real estate agent. "We've all heard the stories." She lit into an "as a wife and mother" tangent that was all she had to say, publicly. Privately, she'd talk openly about ways of keeping more Negroes from moving in. At present, most were on the East Side, though about two hundred lived in this ward now, most on the edge of it, in houses behind Deaconess Hospital.

David glanced at the son of the outgoing councilman. He was also an attorney and like David had moved back into the ward to be elected from there. This had become a huge issue, too. The councilman's son had a big wart on his eyebrow. He was pretending to be concentrating on his little stack of index cards. He'd been well-coached, too, and wasn't biting.

Outside, it thundered, unusual for a September storm.

"Mr. Zielinsky?" said the moderator, the Optimists' treasurer; a Ford salesman. "Any reaction to these allegations?"

David almost said *allegations of what?* That would have been what he'd have said a year ago, and that would have sunk him. But that was before he met with Mr. O'Connor a few more times, before David picked up a few good players for his team. "I'm sorry my opponent has seen fit to bring up for political gain a painful and personal matter," David said. He made eye contact with Bruce Biederman. *Thanks for teeing it up for me, fuckhead!* "And if what you mean, Mr. Biederman, about 'the criminal element' is my father's passionate and lifelong involvement in labor unions, all I can say in response to that is that I, myself, have been a member of a dockworkers local, and I'm as proud of that, and of my father's long fight for the rights of the working man, as I am of being a veteran of the United States Navy in time of war."

David's constituency—about twenty people: Teamsters, Longshoremen, bowling alley owners, drivers for Yellow Cab, and cop friends of Skeezix Soltesz, who'd quit the force and wanted to be called Gorman—broke into applause. The blue-hairs went for it, too, as did Miss Schrag and most of the seventh graders. Miss Schrag had always liked him.

Whack it!

"I'm especially sorry my opponent thought it necessary to bring this up," David said, "when the real issue in this election is Erieview. The real issue in this election is whether you want to keep pumping your hard-earned money into the pockets of fat-cat businessmen when neighborhood schools like this one"—and here he pointed to the janitor, who was positioning a metal trash can in the corner, to catch a slow drip—"can't get their roofs fixed properly. The supporters of Erieview don't care about the roof of your school or how often the snowplows come down your streets, but I do. They're building office towers downtown while neighborhoods on the East Side turn into slums. They don't care, but I do. Is this neighborhood next? The supporters of Erieview don't care. Who cares? I do."

The Optimists were with him now.

"I may be the youngest person in this race, but I care. They're using *your tax dollars* to subsidize hotels," David said, "to make things cushy for out-of-towners, but who's looking out for the people who *live* here? Who's going to stand up for you, you and all the rest of us who haven't taken the cowards' way out and abandoned Cleveland for the suburbs?"

It slipped out. He was on a roll, and it slipped out. Damn Irene. If it wasn't for the Hrudkas, David never would have left.

Bruce Biederman, though, missed the opening. "I have proof!" he said instead, waving a file folder. He had the look on his face that the actors he resembled use right before they get shot down in the dusty streets of Old Tucson. "The coroner's report *and* the police report!"

Thanks to Stan Lychak, David had copies of these already. Had, since June.

"It saddens me," David said, "to see this private matter dragged into a place where it doesn't belong. I have nothing to hide, but I'm here to talk about issues that affect this city. If Mr. Biederman wants to wallow in the mud," he said, shrugging, "that's beyond my control."

The Optimists' treasurer looked for guidance from his clubmates. David saw one tap at his wristwatch.

Both reporters had their hands raised. (This was before reporters thought they were the most important people in every room they deigned to enter, before naive cynicism reigned unchallenged among them.)

"Thank you for coming!" said the treasurer. "Let's give our candidates a big round of applause, and don't forget to vote next Tuesday!" Even as the applause came, the man's eyes darted about. He didn't look like he believed he'd get away with this. "Except you kids, of course. You'll, heh heh, have to wait, oh, ten years. But, uh, please vote then. Good night!"

"They will," said Miss Schrag. "I make them all sign a pledge."

David remembered. He still thought of it, every election day.

The reporters came up afterward, but by the time they got the copies of the coroner's report from Bruce Biederman, David was heading for the door. "Busy campaign, fellas," he said as they caught up to him.

"Your father was investigated in the death of your mother," said the older reporter. "Any comment on that?"

"I know you have a job to do," David said. "You have to ask me that question, I know." More of Mr. O'Connor's coaching, that. "All I can say in answer to it is this: we live in a country," he said, "where people investigated for a crime aren't assumed to have done it. I'm saddened that this resolved, painful, and private family matter was dragged into the public arena for nothing more substantial than venal political gain."

David turned and walked away, and Gorman Soltesz, Stan Lychak's assistant and David's campaign chairman, blocked the path of the reporters. Gorman was prepared for this. He went over the report in detail. He'd been a football star; being in front of reporters again brought him to life. Yes, Mrs. Joan Zielinsky's death had been investigated as a murder. Several people were questioned in this tragic matter, but the coroner, as you can see, ultimately ruled her death an accident. Not a murder, not even a suicide. Leads pointing elsewhere were at best inconclusive. As a former police officer and currently licensed private investigator in the state of Ohio, he had personally reviewed the police work in this matter and deemed it outstanding. He spelled his last name out to them three times, and still they both got it wrong.

Six opponents running in the same ward David was, it was inevitable someone was going to say unsavory things about David's father and/or David's mother. David knew it was getting said behind his back. The wonder was, it took this long to go public.

The next day everywhere David went—a pancake breakfast with the Kiwanis, a coffee in the house of a retired librarian, lunch at Mama Isabelle's, door-to-door in the little Negro neighborhood, and on his home turf (west of Pearl and south of the zoo)—people told him they couldn't believe it, what Bruce Biederman had done, what the papers had chosen to print. The papers, actually, both omitted Biederman's quasi-allegation of murder. (This happened millions of years ago, when newspapers rarely reported a rumor someone had said on the logic that someone had said it.) What they did report was Mike Zielinsky's various indictments on racketeering charges and his lone conviction, on tax evasion, for which he'd paid a $2,350 fine. The older reporter also managed to connect the name Zielinsky with the guy who got clobbered running for state senate after he said his position on the Taft-Hartley Bill was that he'd paid it.

Still, the possibility that David's father had killed his mother or had her killed was something people were talking about. They'd been talking about it before. But more of them were talking about it now than at any time in the twenty years since she died.

༄

THAT JANUARY, BEFORE he even declared for the race, David and his family had taken his father up on his offer and gone to visit him in Miami. The more pregnant Irene got, the more she'd started complaining about money, what it was costing them to add on to a house where she didn't want to live, to send her kids to a school she didn't want them to attend, to live in a neigh-borhood that would never be what it used to be, and for what? The chance David would get elected? If it happened, great, but what if it didn't? Plus, win *or* lose, where was the money for the campaign going to come from? She wouldn't have taken a vacation if it had cost them anything, but it didn't. Mike Zielinsky had sent them four plane tickets, along with a note saying their money would be no good in Florida. Cherry on top: Cleveland was in the Runner-Up Bowl, there in Miami, against the Lions, and Mike had scored a pair of seats on the forty-yard line. Still Irene didn't want to go. She thought they owed his father too much already. "Think," David said, "what a slap in the face it would be to say no to him now."

When David, Irene, and the kids landed in Miami, cranky from a flight during which none of the four of them had exactly behaved well, Mikey Z and his girlfriend Tina were waiting for them, dispensing Browns jerseys the way people supposedly hand out leis in Hawaii.

Tina and Mike already had theirs on. Mike's was pulled on over a guyabera shirt. All were number thirty-two, Jim Brown's number. Lizard put hers on right away and ran down the hall screaming for someone to throw her a bomb. Teddy thanked his grandfather and held the jersey out in front of him, as if he'd never seen such a thing. Irene and David said, gee, you really shouldn't have. "You've done so much already," Irene said.

Too much, that's what she meant. David gave her a look. She folded her arms and turned away from him.

"I'm happy to do it," Mike said. "That's what family's for, am I right?"

The loan for the addition to the house lay between them, as unspoken and badly underfoot as a mute pig that thinks it's a kitten.

"You're right," David said. "Lizard! Get back here."

Mike handed Irene a gift box, wrapped in silver foil. Inside was a baby-sized Browns sweatshirt.

"I made the number myself," Tina said, "and sewed it on the back. See?" Even in a football jersey and matching brown slacks, she looked like an aging starlet, complete with blond hair, pulled-back shoulders, and a tobacco-hoarse voice. Her breasts were so large David was embarrassed for her. He couldn't not look, though. Like a burning building, those breasts. "They don't make jerseys for babies," Tina said.

"It's terrific," Irene said. "Very, very thoughtful."

"We couldn't find a place to get this crap down here," Mike said. "Had to have some people pick it out and mail it to me. I got the sizes right, huh?"

"You did," David said, though the kids' jerseys were much too big.

"Very, very thoughtful," said Irene.

Teddy and Lizard were throwing a wadded-up newspaper back and forth, haplessly. Lizard was chanting, "How now, brown cow?" Teddy, who had an earache and had cried almost all the way from Cleveland, was so relieved to be off the plane he just let her yammer.

"You look great," said Tina, who had never seen Irene before.

"I'm fat."

"No!" Tina said. "Take that back! You look . . . well, *glowing* isn't the half of it."

"See?" David said. "I tell her the same thing, but she won't listen."

"For once, the boy's right," said Mikey Z. "Look at you! More grandbabies for me!"

Now Irene gave David a look. She was six months pregnant. The first time she was pregnant, David had found it erotic as hell. Irene rebuffed him. Kick a dog long enough, it'll turn on you. Now, the third time around, he was as disgusted to look at her naked as she was loath to let him. What he told her, though, when he told her anything at all, was that she looked great. The party line, and he toed it.

Mike was driving an Eldorado these days. Gold body, black vinyl top. This year's model, but the new smell was gone.

David hadn't been to Miami since he was a kid, but, as always, it gave him a walloping headache. All that sun, bouncing off all that blue water, all those bright white buildings. Also pink and turquoise. Miami was a city decked out like somebody's remodeled bathroom.

Mike Zielinsky's place was in Miami Beach, right on the water, the top-floor, four-bedroom suite of a six-floor hotel the union seemed to own. David didn't want to know about who paid for what.

The TV was on when they came in. *The Untouchables*. Mike pointed at the set. "Ever see this?" he said. Who hadn't? "Remember that guy? What a load of—" He looked at Teddy and Lizard. "Bullcrap, eh? Weedy little do-gooding hypocrite. Turn it off, would you, hon?" But Tina didn't obey. The TV remained on, and Mike said nothing more about it. Tina had an easel set up in the corner, by the French doors to the balcony. She smoked cigarettes and painted scenes of the surf and of small boats in the moonlit ocean while she maintained whatever end of the conversation was hers to uphold.

"Those are so good," Irene said, and seemed to mean it.

"I'll give this one to you," Tina said. "When I'm done with it."

Even though it was dark, David and Mike took the kids down to see the beach. By the time they got back, Irene and Tina were girlfriends. There was no telling, David thought, who Irene was going to take a shine to. He was done predicting.

A five-day trip: more time under the same roof with his father than David could ever remember spending. That said, Mike was gone often as not. Business to attend to, things that kept popping up. Every lunch and dinner was takeout, delivery, or, if Mike was there, restaurants. David and the kids spent their time in the hotel pool and on the beach (Lizard wouldn't take off her Browns jersey; Teddy was afraid of the water but enjoyed making sand castles), and the women watched whatever idiotic drivel was on TV and drank coffee all day. Outside of David's suitcase, there were no books in the apartment. Irene hadn't brought one. David couldn't believe it: he was watching the kids, not complaining about it one bit, the way most men would, and all Irene could find to do was watch TV. When he wasn't watching the kids, the women kept them inside, watching TV and playing the very occasional game of cards. It wasn't so different than at home, really, where Irene relied on her mother or Aunt Betty to watch the kids—even now that she was on leave from the hospital (their policy was that no one could work after her fifth month). David would have supported anything she wanted to do. School, reading, a hobby. But all she did was watch TV and talk on the phone to people she'd known all her life.

Mike did manage to be on hand for the Runner-Up Bowl. Tina had freshly laundered his and David's Browns jerseys, though neither had been dirty.

The Runner-Up Bowl pitted the second-place team in the Western Conference (Detroit) against the second-place team in the Eastern (the Browns). It was played (unlike the championship) at a warm, neutral site, far from either team's fans and, absurdly, the week after the championship game. It should have been called the Second-Runner-Up Bowl. The true runners-up were the Green Bay Packers, who'd lost the championship to Philadelphia last Saturday. But say this much for the Runner-Up Bowl: it settled all those off-season arguments about whose team was the third-best in football.

The Orange Bowl was half empty. The game was sloppy, but close. David and his father drained a flask full of whiskey and who knows how many one-dollar beers.

Playing in the Runner-Up Bowl was indignity enough. On top of *that*, Cleveland lost it, 17–16. David bought a pennant for the kids.

Mike, so drunk he could barely walk, said he'd rather finish last than lose a horseshit game like this. They were outside the Orange Bowl, looking for his car.

"It wasn't so bad," David said. "There are all kinds of cities who wish they were where Cleveland is."

"Name one."

David rattled off a list. Pittsburgh, Washington, Baltimore, St. Louis, on and on. "Plus cities like Miami. Miami doesn't even have big-league sports."

His father laughed at him. "Miami, believe me, doesn't wish it was Cleveland."

David couldn't accept this. "I can't accept that."

He sat down. He'd had less to drink than his father, but he needed to sit down.

They stopped at a Big Boy's for coffee. Lots and lots of bad, bottomless-cup coffee. When they got back to the hotel, the kids were in bed and Irene and Tina stopped talking the split second Mike put the key in the door.

"Speak of the devil, huh?" he said. "Fat Grampa's here! Where're my grandbabies?"

"We weren't talking about you," Tina said. "You're not waking those kids up."

"You *weren't* talking about me?" he said. "Looks like I need to get more interesting." He lifted her up off the couch and swirled her around. David started toward Irene, to follow suit, until he saw the look in her eyes. Which was good. She'd gained a lot of weight this time. David's knee probably wasn't up to any wife-swirling.

That night in bed, in the kind of whispered conversation about people in adjoining rooms that constitutes one of marriage's most salient features, Irene asked David what, really, he knew about his mother's death.

∽

"WILLIS! DAVID ZIELINSKY here."

Here being his campaign office, in his basement. The Ping-Pong table was covered with stacks of campaign brochures. His desk was a door on two sawhorses. There were three typing tables—two bearing huge black typewriters, one a postage machine. Behind him was a six-foot-wide map of the ward drawn by a volunteer, a draftsman by profession, husband of the lady who cut Aunt Betty's hair. Upstairs the baby was crying; Irene was yelling at Teddy about eating breakfast. Lizard was quiet. Too quiet. Outside a crew of roofers was shingling the addition.

"What's this about?" said Willis Young, cutting off a string of David's pleasantries. "I have class in four minutes." Young taught at a high school in Hough. In the past ten years Hough had gone from 10 to 90 percent Negro. He taught drama and driver's ed.

"Missed you at the Optimists' event last night," David said.

"I bet you did."

"I'll cut right through it, Willis."

"I wish you would," he said. "I also wish you'd call me Mr. Young."

Fuck him. "Are you still in the race?"

"I don't have time for this."

"I'd like to sit down with you," David said. "Are you by any chance free for lunch?"

"I can't leave the grounds of the school."

"Coffee, then, this afternoon. A beer. I think we could—"

"I understand what you're doing," Young said. "What you're saying. White people are always looking for one nigger to speak for all the others."

"That's not—"

"Why don't you wait until after the primary? I imagine we both have plenty to do until then, hmm?"

Now the baby had stopped crying and Teddy had started. He was six! Was he ever going to stop crying? The roofers were hammering like madmen.

"It's possible, you know, that someone will win the primary outright," David said, putting a hand over his other ear, "and then what clout will you have?"

"Anything is possible," Young said. No one was going to get a majority, not with six names on the ballot.

"It's also possible the top two," David said, "will be people who, unlike me, see your endorsement as the kiss of death."

"It's possible I'll be one of those top two, sir."

The way he said that! *Sir.* David took a deep breath. "Sure. Anything is possible."

"I don't even know you," Young said.

"Born and raised in the ward," David said. *Unlike you.* "That's why I'm calling, really. To give you a chance to get to know me."

"Lucky me."

David counted to five. "You know I'm against Erieview, Mr. Young," he said. "You and I are the only ones."

"Carrigan's against Erieview."

"Carrigan's a *Socialist.*"

"They've already started building it," Young said. "I'm not sure there's anything to be done about that now."

"They want to expand it. I don't have to tell you, Mr. Young, what this is really about."

"Yes," Young said. "Well." He didn't seem to know *anything*.

Upstairs Irene gave Teddy a spanking. Lizard broke into a shrieking rendition of "Blue Moon." The baby, Brad, started crying again. Teddy did not. "You'll be sorry someday!" he yelled. Doors slammed.

After a long pause Willis Young said he was sorry if he sounded rude. "I hear you've been campaigning in my neighborhood," he said, "which is more than I can say for some people. Let's just see what happens Tuesday, and we'll go from there."

Shit. "All right then."

"I read about what Biederman said," said Willis Young.

"I'm only sorry he didn't want to stick to the issues," David said.

"I'm sorry for your loss." Which proved he'd done more than read about it.

"Thank you," David said. "It was a long time ago."

"I have to go," Young said. "Thank you for your interest, and good-bye."

Upstairs Aunt Betty had arrived to watch the baby and finish sending the kids off to school. The phone rang again.

"Is David Zielinsky there?"

"Anne?"

She'd never before called him at home. "Is this a bad time?"

Upstairs Betty immediately imposed peace. Even the roofers seemed to be making less noise. She should have had ten kids of her own, Betty. She'd found her calling.

"Not at all," David said.

Anne apologized for phoning him at home. She'd lost the card he'd given her. She was sorry about that, too. It's been a long few days. For him, too, judging from what she read in the paper. "Are you free for lunch?" she said. "Or, I don't know, golf? Do you golf?"

Irene opened the door at the top of the basement stairs. He could see her white nurse shoes. "Good-bye," she hollered, and did not wait for him to say anything.

☙

Two in the morning, the night before the primary. The house was dark when David got home. He went down in the lit basement and told Gorman

[317]

and three Teamsters to go home and get some rest. They'd done what they could. Today was exhausting (he could hardly remember all the petty little groups he met with), and tomorrow would be a longer day yet.

He watched his friends drive away, took off his necktie and his shoes, and flicked off the porch light. He went in the kitchen for a glass of water. Instead, he opened the pantry. He poured some bourbon in a jelly glass. The top of the bottle was crusty. David wiped it off. He wished he had some Bushmill's. He'd never had Bushmill's. He was more of a beer guy.

I'm a beer guy. Something he'd actually said aloud in the campaign. (Context: the councilman's son had a wine cellar in his house in Westlake, which he still owned; his apartment in the ward was a semifurnished sham. David would have made more of this, except that he still owned the house in Independence. It hadn't sold and now they were renting it. The plan was to put it back on the market in the spring. During a bad recent argument— about money, naturally, money that his father had scared up for them and that had no certain repayment terms attached—Irene had threatened to take the kids and move back there as soon as the tenants' lease ran out. As far as David was concerned, that was just argument talk. It was like suicide, he thought; people who talk about it never do it.)

David walked around his dark house in his stocking feet. Irene was asleep, diagonal across their double bed. Snoring. The baby was in a cradle, near her side of the bed. The bedroom TV (Bud and Flossie's old one) was still on, gone to static. David turned it off.

Lizard lay in the middle of her bed, on her back, straight, the covers utterly undisturbed. A bomb wouldn't wake this one up.

Teddy was curled up in a ball on the floor, covered by his pillow and the pennant from the Runner-Up Bowl. He woke the split second David stepped into the room. "What're you doing, bucko?" Teddy was groggy and said something incoherent about Cub Scouts. David lifted him up, tucked him in, and went and sat down in the living room.

When David was a kid, they didn't use this room. Now it was filthy with Irene's tchotchkes and the kids' toys, full of hand-me-down prewar furniture. Once David took over the basement for an office, the notion of a formal living room became absurd. They couldn't do without the space.

This was the house David had grown up in, but it was so changed from then, he could hardly see it that way anymore. Except in the dark. The walls were still where the walls had been. The light from the streetlights still came through the windows the way it always had.

Anything could happen tomorrow, of which he was altogether too aware.

David was a lawyer with an undergraduate minor in English. That more than canceled out his time as a dockworker and a navy supply clerk, which is to say this: David had too much training in seeing things from different perspectives. Seeing things from many different perspectives is good, Mr. O'Connor had said, when you are governing, though not all the time, but it's bad when you're running for office—always.

David couldn't help himself. Better to think too much, he figured, than not enough.

On the one hand, Bruce Biederman was probably cooked for playing such a dirty trick. On the other, he could be seen as a tough guy, and benefit.

On the one hand, Willis Young was tilting at the ward's white windmills. On the other, David—young, progressive, an opponent of Erieview, the only other candidate to campaign in the Negro neighborhood—would have been the one to get the Negro votes otherwise.

On the one hand, Mrs. Richard Kastleman was a Republican; there were a clutch of Republicans on Schaaf Road, in homes that came with their own greenhouses, but that was it. On the other, council elections were nonpartisan. People wouldn't necessarily know she was a Republican, which could multiply her white-flight message by the lowest common denominator.

On the one hand, the Socialist was a crank. On the other, his name was Carrigan; Cleveland had a history of voting for certain names, and Carrigan was awfully close to Corrigan.

On the one hand, the councilman's son was a no-personality, no-issue wartbrow who didn't really live in the ward. On the other, he'd run a clean, well-financed campaign and had the same name as the outgoing councilman (he'd filed suit to keep the "Jr." off the ballot).

On the one hand, David didn't have to beat him now to get to the general election. On the other, if David ends up losing anyway, why run for another month, racking up expenses and tilting at his own dumb windmills?

He was never going to be able to sleep. He went in the kitchen and got more bourbon.

What could he do? He'd done what he could.

Except for the outgoing councilman and his current competitors, David had talked to every single person who'd run in that ward, win or lose, for the past ten years.

He'd gotten two candidates bounced off the ballot for irregularities on their petitions. Two down, five to go.

He secured endorsements from three different union locals, including the Longshoreman, whose new local president (Danny Greene, David's age, who painted the union headquarters emerald green) sent out a letter (on green paper, with darker green ink) reminding his members that David once worked the docks himself (each recipient was docked $5 for the enclosed two raffle tickets, which he was free to resell; first prize was a color TV, which, later, no one could prove was *not* awarded). David kept scrupulous records of all donations the union members saw fit to supply.

David was initiated into Lodge 658 (a veterans-only lodge) of the Free and Accepted Masons. He was told that every single American president had been a member of the Free and Accepted Masons.

Eliot Ness's name appeared three times in David's brochure. In his stump speech, David talked about how Ness was an American hero long before TV made him one, and he used Ness as an example of how it's possible to fix things in Cleveland that people say are beyond repair.

David had learned that there were people, a surprisingly large number of people, who'd drive to the polls a certain way just to pass certain houses and see whose yard signs were in the yard. David learned the people whose yards mattered most and did what he could to get his name planted there. There were blue-hairs who'd vote for whoever took them to the polls; David had Teamsters on his side and rides galore lined up for the old folks. There were certain poll workers who, if they were handing out your literature on election day, meant more votes than others. David was paying poll workers more than any of the other candidates.

He got up again and went to look at his wife. She had not lost the pregnancy weight and was starting to get so moonfaced David hardly recognized her. She'd refused, because of her weight, to be photographed for the campaign brochure. But in the dark, outlined by the glow of the new security light mounted to the unfinished addition, what David could see of her looked the same as ever.

— 15 —

THE STORY TINA TOLD IRENE

TINA HAD KNOWN David's mother, known her as Gigi Madison. Not well, but they traveled in the same circles. Tina had no idea back then that Gigi was married, which was odd, because she talked about herself more than anyone Tina ever met. Knowing Mike as Tina did now, she realized a lot of what Gigi said was hooey. Gigi Madison, liar. "So take some of this," Tina said, "with a whole box of Morton's."

There were all kinds of gals out there, the prizes of rich men who'd promised them they'd throw some money and weight around, to get their young girlfriends a part in a movie, even a studio contract. You knew these men had ties to things you wished they didn't have ties to, but you were young, see, and didn't think about it. These guys were fun. They picked up the tab and set you up in nice digs and with nice clothes. Looking back, it was like the casting couch you climbed up on before you ever got a chance to climb onto the real casting couch. That wasn't how it seemed at the time, but that's how it was. Men like this, they had houses they bought and furnished just so they could set you up there. Other girls had cried themselves to sleep on pillows you'd think of as yours. You knew about those other girls, but you didn't think about them. Tina wasn't one bit proud of any of it. She'd gone out there, age sixteen, high school dropout from Kingman, Arizona, population who cares. Running away from the usual things, let's leave it at that. She'd gotten a fake ID so she could lie about her age, but no one cared. Everyone in Hollywood, Tina said, was a liar, too. No one called you on it. If you don't believe a word a person says, you can take everything at face value—that's the lesson she took away from Hollywood. Tina answered phones by day and tried to go to the right dark velvet nightclubs. Before long she got involved with some crooked characters and then with a famous song-writer looking for someone to be his public girlfriend, never mind his name or why. Tina was older and wiser now, and didn't want to talk about that.

What she did want to talk about was Gigi. Gigi Madison was in the same circles, but different. First of all, she was a tall drink of water with talent. She could act rings around people, could cry on demand and also dance. Her face was a little lopsided, but there were girls less pretty who were getting movies. Gigi dyed her hair too often, and it was going to straw from that. Plus, her height was a problem. "Most actors are practically dwarfs," Tina said.

"No!" Irene said.

"Yes!" said Tina. "Dwarfs with gigantic heads!"

None of which was to say Gigi wasn't pretty. She was. ("She actually had a large head, too," Tina said. "Who knows why the camera loves people with big heads?") And as far as the singing went, she was taking lessons, but she was no slouch. She even got jobs in little jazz joints, nothing special, but a chance to practice. The guy she was involved with was a handsome sugar daddy, just the classiest guy going. He built hotels. Later on he built a lot of the ones out in Las Vegas. One of those old guys with lots of silver perfect hair. It had been Tina's impression that those two, Gigi and the man, had met in Cleveland and been together for years. He wasn't married, apparently, and whatever kind of life they had together, it looked like love to Tina Rae Bettis. Tina hadn't brought this up to Mike, of course, for fear of what the story might exactly be. Knowing what *not* to talk about, Tina said, that's the secret to love. But put it this way (and no knock on Mike, who's a great guy in his own right): Tina would've traded places with Gigi Madison in a heartbeat. Tina expected that Gigi Madison would become a big star.

Where it all went wrong, if you asked Tina, was this guy everybody called Sweet. Why Gigi would want to leave the man she was with to be with Sweet was a mystery. Another mystery was why he was called Sweet. Sweet was a crude, heavyset lout, a bad-sheep in-law, or something along those lines, of that guy Scalish in Cleveland.

Irene had no idea who John Scalish was. She and Tina were drinking wine and watching the last light of the day shimmer on the green-black ocean and wondering when their men would be back from the Runner-Up Bowl. Lizard and Teddy were watching a Western on TV and arguing whether it was possible for there to be girl sheriffs. (Teddy's logic, prefiguring chaos theory, was that if it was possible, there would *be* a girl sheriff, but neither he nor Lizard could name one. Lizard said that was just dumb.)

"Scalish," Tina said. "You know. He's in charge of, you know, things."

Irene had to have Tina explain the word *don;* immediately Irene told her bickering children to turn off the TV and go to bed; she'd be right there to tuck them in. She said it with enough edge that even Lizard obeyed. Irene was having a hard time breathing. She poured herself more wine.

(When she told the story to David later that night in bed, she was furious that his father had done business and, for all she knew, still did business with the Cosa Nostra, and that here she was, *married* and *trapped* and *endangered* in this situation. She couldn't believe it! David was drunk enough to laugh at her. "Cosa Nostra!" he said. "Oh, god, that's a good one!" That really set Irene off. "Think of the children," she hissed. She went on and on about the children. "Here we are, in a gangster's apartment," she said. "Shut up," David said. "Whatever else my father is," David said, "he's not that." She said she wasn't sure she could stay with him, under the circumstances, and David said she had to be kidding. That was the last thing either of them said that night, even though they were both awake for a long time thereafter.)

Sweet was a big talker, but they all were. According to Tina, Gigi met Sweet in one of the clubs where she sang and that he owned part of. The next *day* she woke up and dumped the hotel builder, *over the phone,* and moved into some place Sweet had, up in the Hollywood Hills.

(David said he didn't want to hear any more. Irene said he really needed to hear this.)

Right about then, Gigi started landing parts. Bit parts, sure, and to be honest Tina couldn't remember the names of any of them, she was so jealous. Gigi was on her way. Whether this had to do with the balls the hotel builder had rolling for her already or whether Sweet really made things happen, who knows? There's also the possibility that Gigi landed the parts herself.

"For what it's worth," Tina said, "Gigi was a drinker." But then, most people in that crowd were drinkers. Quite a few popped pills and smoked marijuana, too, but Tina stayed away from all that, honest. Gigi started looking old for her age. So it could have been that Gigi got so close to success she could taste it, only to realize her ingenue days were already gone, and she drowned herself. It's possible she was drunk. It's possible she wasn't much of a swimmer.

But the word was, she was killed. Open secret.

"A lot of people said it was the jealous husband, but take it from me," Tina said, "Mike is just the nicest guy and could never do a thing like that." Some people said Gigi told Sweet she was going back to the hotel builder, and he had her killed. Some people said it was the hotel builder. The cops ruled it an accident, but, believe Tina, the cops in L.A. did what they were paid to do—by the person who'd paid them the most to do it.

Irene finished telling David the story.

David listened to the ocean, on the other side of the continent from the one where his mother had died. Who would he be, now, if she hadn't died? He didn't want to think about that.

"Don't you have anything to say?" Irene said. "Are you going to talk to your dad?"

"No," he said.

"Which?"

"Both." They lay there for a long time. "I'd love to see those movies," he said.

"Oh, grow up," she said. "There weren't any movies."

"There were movies," he said.

"Have you ever seen them?"

"I've never seen Paris," he said, "but I know it's there."

"Are you sure it's not your father?" she said. "This is a horrible thing to say, but..."

"I've never been to another country except Canada, right there at the falls," he said. "But I'll bet all of them are there. All the countries in the world."

Another long silence lay between them.

"You're drinking a lot," she said. "Maybe that's where it comes from, your mother."

"There's nothing in that ridiculous story that I hadn't already heard about."

She sat up. Even in the dark, he could see she was furious. "How could you not tell me?"

Because he didn't know it. Because he was lying.

"I just thought you knew," he said. "Past is past. Good night."

She kept at it. It exhausted her, though, and finally she went to sleep, which was more than David could say about that night. He was no artist, but years later he could have painted a picture of that ceiling from memory.

THE STORY ANNE TOLD THE STATION MANAGER

PHIL WEINTRAUB HAD seen Anne O'Connor's audition reel. He had her résumé. He'd deemed both *solid*.

Solid is not fluid. Solid is not brilliant. Nothing precocious about solid.

Anne thanked him. She wanted to tell him the truth about the résumé, the story behind the reel.

(Phil Weintraub was new. Born and raised in Cleveland, he'd spent twenty-one years as a sportswriter in St. Louis, then eight years as a news director of a UHF station there. Now he was here, the lowest-rated VHF station in Cleveland. His office was being redone. He was having it carpeted: the floors, the walls, and the ceilings. He showed it to her, then had her tag along with him on a story he was doing about Cleveland's new basketball team, the Pipers, whose season started next month. He said he wanted to keep his hand in, as a reporter, though he came there with no camera crew, carrying no notebook, nothing but her résumé. This was how Anne came to be interviewed for a job in the stands at the Cleveland Arena.)

That first job, Anne volunteered, the job at the now-defunct *News*? Family connections led to that job. That second job, in radio, she'd lied to get. That's why there's no references from those jobs. Still, she was just a kid when she did all that, and so consider the experience. Most people that age, if they're working at all, are caddies, soda jerks, or lifeguards. How many people is he interviewing for this job, she said, who actually covered the Sheppard case?

"True?" Phil said. He arched a bushy eyebrow at her.

"True," she said.

"That poor schmuck got railroaded," he said.

Anne said she thought not.

He said he liked a reporter who stuck to her guns.

The seats in the Cleveland Arena were splintered, bowed, chipped, and hard. The place smelled like coffee-drinker's urine and sawdust. The Cleveland Pipers came out to practice: gawky white men, frankly sexual as they broke into sweat, running about the floor in their underwear. Phil Weintraub had his eyes on them, not Anne, but he said he was all ears, and to continue. He actually had the smallest ears Anne had ever seen on a grown man. She continued.

She'd finished her education, she said, graduating Phi Beta Kappa and magna cum laude. All those summers, she'd had that impressive string of internships in New York, which she got legitimately and on her own. She had several opportunities after graduation, but she wanted to work for a station in New York, to prove something to herself. In six months she worked her way up from assistant floor director to on-air talent. Mission accomplished.

She thought that would cinch it. On-air talent in New York, New York. A fish grows to the size of its tank. She'd swum in the *ocean!*

Phil Weintraub was not impressed. He'd been to New York a million times and other than Ebbets Field, which is gone anyway, you could have it. He said this without looking at her. Anne couldn't tell what he was getting at, how he meant that.

For a while they watched basketball.

It was still supposed to be a job interview. Anne didn't know how to get it back there.

Finally, she said the team looked good to her. Their coach, John McLendon, was the first Negro to coach professional basketball, which, Anne said, was fitting, don't you think?

Phil Weintraub didn't react.

Because of the way the Browns and the Indians had pioneered integration in their respective sports, Anne said. Her father had actually been a part-owner of the Indians during the period they became the first integrated team in the league, did Phil Weintraub know that?

Still, he didn't react. Instead, he spotted the owner of the team and waved him over. The owner was a fast-talking shipbuilding executive not much older than Anne. He said he had some phone calls to make, that he'd be right back.

"So," Anne said.

"Get with it," Weintraub said, "because when that Steinbrenner kid comes back, I need to talk to him." Phil Weintraub was actually there to discuss broadcast rights, not to do a story.

The truth, Anne said, was that she'd been fired from the station in New York. Their loss, she said. She was supposed to get the chance to report, but they had her pigeonholed as the glamour-puss weather girl, and to hell with that. She wanted to be a war correspondent. Maybe that was a childish fantasy, maybe not. Maybe it was an impossible thing for a woman, but the only things worth doing in life, she said, are impossible things.

That got Weintraub to look at her. Blankly. "You're very young," he said.

"You're very bald," she blurted. At least she didn't mention his ears.

He looked startled, but only for a moment. "I think maybe I like you," he said.

Happily, he sounded avuncular when he said that. He'd worked for other men who did not sound avuncular when they said things like that. She soldiered on.

To be frank, she said, becoming a war correspondent was still the plan, someday. But as he so astutely pointed out, she was young. She had time. For right now, some family matters had transpired that made her want to come back home. That was what this was, *home*. It seemed like the right time to take a few years and make some sense of that through adult eyes.

Example: this place. The Cleveland Arena. The last time she had been in this building was the Moondog Coronation Ball, the first rock-and-roll concert in the history of the world.

He said he was not a fan of rock and roll, but she told him the story anyway. Pointing to where the stage was. Pointing to where the bar was. Doing a nice little impression of Alan Freed. Phil Weintraub knew who Alan Freed was. Now Phil Weintraub was looking at *her*.

Halfway through the story, Anne knew she had him.

"A riot?" he said, incredulous. Looking at her.

"A riot," she said. "All because the authorities overreacted. There's a lesson in there for everyone."

"I suppose there is," said Phil Weintraub.

"This town is my town," Anne O'Connor said. "No outsider could know Cleveland the way I know it. Express an opinion on anything in this city," she said, "and what's the first thing a Clevelander says to you? He sizes you up and says, *How long have you lived here?* Right?"

Phil Weintraub laughed. He hadn't told her he was from Cleveland, too. Only the St. Louis part. Later Anne and Phil would look back on this and laugh. "What the heck," he said. "I'll bite. Tell me the kind of a story you could find that someone else wouldn't. An example."

"OK," she said.

"Anytime now."

"I'm thinking," she said. "How about this. How about that man who won that West Side city council ward by six votes?"

(A majority of six, in the primary. The only nonincumbent to win in the primary. The councilman's son demanded a recount; released yesterday, the recount resulted in the same exact total. The councilman's son cried foul, claiming that *proved* the election was rigged.)

"So?" said Phil Weintraub.

"David Zielinsky. It so happens I know him. It looks like it was a surprise, him winning, but I know how it happened."

"How?"

"Hire me," she said, "and I'll report it for you."

"Report it for me," he said, "and I'll hire you."

George Steinbrenner was heading their way.

Weintraub told her, yes, he was serious. If the story was good, she had the job. "Oh, and one more thing," he said. "Even if I do hire you," he said, "you have to dye your hair."

"Dye my hair what?"

"Anything but red," he said.

"Red's my real color."

"Red is Dorothy Fuldheim's color. If you want to compete with her in her town—"

"She wasn't born here."

"—you'll have to dye your hair."

"You can't tell what color my hair is," Anne objected, "in black and white."

"People can tell," said Phil Weintraub. "You'll have to dye it."

Anne had already interviewed at the station that employed Dorothy Fuldheim and been given the kiss-off before the interview was even over. The third station had belonged partly to her father. She was either getting this job on her own or not coming home. That left this station.

She accepted the challenge. It didn't strike her as much of one.

THE STORY STAN LYCHAK TOLD DAVID

AUNT BETTY WOULD not in many tandems be the less attractive person, and to be honest Stan never saw her that way, but she saw *herself* as Joan's younger and less-attractive sister, in the shadow of the homecoming queen. Funny thing is, it was for the best. Betty grew up with her head on straight and Joan, forgive him, was a me-first loony bird. Joan got it in her head that she was this great beauty and that that was the only thing in the world. Stan shrugged.

Betty could have escaped it, thinking of herself that way. She and Stan could have stayed in Chicago. It didn't work out like that, and that's life for you. Betty and Stan got married and bought a house next to Joan, who by then had married David's father.

Joan was the big actress in high school, and she kept at it. She was good, Stan said. She landed roles in community theater right off. Some of the plays she was in were flaky, but Betty never missed any of them. Stan went to some, too. Even in a bad one, Joan'd be good.

Your father, said Stan, was more enthusiastic than anyone. Don't look so surprised. He has half a college degree. He almost never missed a performance. He encouraged her.

(David and Stan were in Stan's oak-paneled office at the law firm. June 1961. It was bigger than most of the partners' offices. Stan had worked there for three years and hadn't hung anything on the walls. His police-force patch collection now hung over the fireplace in the new house. On his desk was a single framed snapshot: Betty on the lip of a fjord, blowing him a kiss. Last year on vacation they'd gone to Norway, Sweden, and Denmark. From the things he did in the war, Stan had connections all over Europe, and lately he and Betty had been going for a couple weeks every year. Stan's filing cabinets were the only ones in the firm with locks. Big combination locks Stan special-ordered from a place in Maryland.)

Joan started getting good notices in the newspapers. Your aunt still has them someplace, Stan said, you should ask her to see it all. A few years of that, though, Joan got to be a big fish in a small pond, and the newspaper jackals turned on her.

David nodded. He understood: *If you're so good, why are you still here?*

Late one night Joan rang the doorbell. Ten o'clock. Stan and Betty were already in bed. There was an inch of ice covering everything, followed by a foot of wet snow. David was bundled up in a snowsuit, just to come next door, and was holding her hand. Remember that?

He did not.

Well, Stan would never forget it.

Stan excused himself, went to the window, took a deep breath, and sat back down.

Never.

Joan asked her sister if she'd watch David. She warned her that it might be awhile. Betty never hesitated. All this time the snow kept falling. Joan left during a blizzard. Don't ask Stan how she got out of town. She got out.

In L.A., well, things happened. Her dreams didn't come true. Four years later she died.

Betty got the news by telegram. David was at school. She called Stan at work and told him to come home right away, she wouldn't say why. When he got there, she was rolling on the living-room floor, crying so hard she looked like a feral beast. Neighbors stood in their yards.

Stan told the neighbors to mind their goddamn business. That was the only way to say it.

"The thought of Betty, that broken up," Stan said. "It almost kills *me*," he said, "even now, just to think of it."

David shook his head.

"Do you know," Stan said, "what she kept saying, what broke her up the most? Do you?"

He did not.

"She was crying your name. Her sister, who she loved so much it scared me, had just died, and what's Betty concerned with? *You*. How you'd survive.

How you'd be able to get through it. She cried your name for hours. Hours. Can you imagine what that was like?"

He had no memory of that day. He sat there and shook his head some more.

Stan started crying, too. Stan was the sort of man who cried at just the right times, in a way never less than manly. David would have done anything to join in, but he didn't have it in him. Whatever it takes to cry, it was broken. This happened ten years before that struck people as bad. It struck David as a bad thing now. In this way he was ahead of the curve.

Stan wiped his face with his hand. He opened a drawer, took out a file, and slid it across the desk to David. But Stan's hand still rested on it.

"What sort of man do you think I am?" Stan said.

Stan hadn't aged since David was a boy. It was spooky. "What do you mean?"

"Do you think," Stan said, "that my sister-in-law could die without me looking into it?"

This had never occurred to David before.

"You never asked," Stan said. "I always figured you'd ask, but you never did. Not," he said, "until you decided to run for office."

David did not like the way Stan said *office*. But there wasn't anything to say about that.

"Please," Stan said, "don't tell me if you came here planning to ask me to go look into it. Now that you're running for office. To ask me to do you a favor and go out there."

"I just wanted to know what you knew, Uncle Stan."

Stan nodded. "Everything there is to know about it," he said, "is in that file. And has been for years. Do you think," he said, "your father did it? Is that what you're worried about?"

"I don't think anything."

"Roger that," said Stan. He shrugged. "Well, he didn't. The police report is what it is. The men who worked on it were good men."

He lifted his hand. David took the file.

"Accident," Stan said.

David nodded.

"Hey, hey! Mister Councilma-a-an!" Stan said.

"Don't jinx me."

"Mister—what?—twenty-eight-year-old councilman? Right? Twenty-eight?"

"I'll be twenty-eight by the time I got sworn in."

"You're *going on* twenty-eight," said Stan. "Perfect."

"When you and Eliot Ness were together in Chicago, you were younger than that."

Stan pursed his lips. His face went blank.

"I'm curious about something," Stan said.

David waited a long time for Stan to ask. Out Stan's window, David could see the cranes working on Erieview's first office tower.

"If your mother's death had to do with your father," Stan finally said, "do you think your aunt and I would have just sat still and done nothing?"

"I don't think anything."

"Do you really think he'd still be alive?"

"Who'd have killed him?" David said. "What do you mean? People from . . . the union?"

"Please," Stan said.

"You don't mean you. Do you?"

Only poker champions and spooks could make their face look as blank as Stan's. That, for David, was when a lot of things started to click about Uncle Stan.

"You do mean you," David said.

"Please." Stan pointed at the door with both hands, double-barreled. "Go."

THE STORY DAVID TOLD IRENE

IT WAS A week after the primary. It was still dark outside. David put his golf clubs in his trunk and when he got back inside, Irene and the baby were in the kitchen. The baby, Brad, crawled at startling speed across the linoleum. The boy had a sense of *mission*. David hadn't the foggiest when the other kids started to crawl, but this one seemed to do it sooner. He was, what? Six months old? He doubted even Lizard had crawled that young.

"You have an interview *this* early?" Irene said.

David shrugged. "Reporters," he said.

Irene, wearing an appallingly huge white bra and a ratty pair of pajama bottoms, scooped up the baby and deftly plopped him in his high chair. Brad started bawling.

"What's that supposed to mean, 'reporters'?"

"It's not supposed to mean anything is what it's supposed to mean,"

David said. "Christ. If you're not in good with the reporters, nothing you do is going to amount to anything."

"Fine," Irene said.

"Yes, fine," he said. Had she seen him load up his clubs? David didn't think so.

Irene fed Brad baby food from a jar. For the other babies, she'd made everything herself.

"You should really wear a robe," David said. "The kids are getting old enough, you should really wear a robe."

She draped her free arm across her stomach. "No one's up," she said. "I am not on display in my own house."

"Maybe you should be."

"Supposedly my own house," she said. "How could this ever be my own house? Who moves *back* to Cleveland?"

Of course it was her house. If it was his house, he certainly would not have hung Tina's tacky painting of the moon over Miami on the wall over the breakfast nook. Except, maybe, if and when Tina visited. Tina had given the painting to Irene. Irene seemed genuinely to like it.

"Don't start," David said.

"Start? *Start?* This is *not* something *I* started."

The baby howled, in that red-faced way you have to be a baby or someone with a freshly severed limb to achieve.

Teddy came into the kitchen in Superman pj's, his Halloween costume last year. (Superman, famously, was created in Cleveland. It was pride of place that had prompted David to persuade Teddy to be Superman. Teddy had wanted to be JFK, and Irene was at a loss about how to make a JFK costume. Irene had said why not take an old sheet, poke two holes in it, and go as a ghost. This, from a woman who prided herself on being a good mother.) "You guys," Teddy said, rubbing his eyes. "Do you mind? Some people are trying to sleep around here."

"What six-year-old talks like that?" David said. "Irene, what's wrong with him?"

"He's doing an impression of you," Irene said.

"Do you mind?" Teddy said. Staccato, angry, deliberate, accent on each syllable. The look on his face was impassive. He was a mimic, not an actor. "Do you mind?"

"I get it," David said. "Good one." He grabbed an old James Dean red windbreaker from a hook beside the breakfast nook and kissed the screaming baby on top of his head. He tried to kiss Irene; she cheeked him. He and Teddy shook hands manfully.

"You really should wear a robe," Teddy said.

THE STORY OF THE JOURNEY, NOT THE DESTINATION

DAVID DROVE ACROSS the city at dawn, into the sun, against the grain of traffic from the time he crossed the river and kept heading east. He wanted to call Anne O'Connor at the Country Club to cancel. He really did! He didn't have the right kind of windbreaker, couldn't golf worth a damn, and was treating this situation too much like it was a date. He had that feeling in his stomach like he'd just driven too fast over a dip. (He hadn't. The land was far too flat for that.) How long had it been since he'd had that life-giving fear tingling through the marrow of his pelvis? The last time he'd been with Anne? David had been a faithful husband. Despite the copper-tasting thrill of the way this anticipation felt, he intended to stay so. It was not now, nor would it ever be, a date. Just a quick round of golf with an old friend.

He pulled into a service station to use the pay phone. But he didn't even get out of the Jeepster. He sat in it, motor running. Suddenly, he banged on the steering wheel, cussed himself out, stomped on the gas, and, without looking, shot out into traffic. A horn blared. A red-and-white milk truck, tires squealing, swerved and missed him, barely. David waved *sorry*.

His rib cage muscles hurt, the way they will after a close call on the highway. He kept going. He took several deep breaths. Before long he'd put the close call out of his mind.

It was still sinking in: David Zielinsky was a councilman-elect. What this feeling reminded him of was the time he got the news that he hadn't been appointed to Annapolis. For days he walked around in a stupor, wondering what was going to happen with the rest of his life. Big plans, botched or fulfilled—either way, the aftermath felt the same.

It was supposed to get up to seventy today, hot for October. It was probably twenty degrees short of that now.

On impulse David pulled over again, whipping into the parking lot of a bowling alley, to put the top down. He hadn't had the top down all year. It had been a rainy summer. Plus, the car was thirteen years old, and the top was original equipment. Imagine a wind-warped, much-used canvas umbrella, thirteen years into its life, only heavier and more cumbersome. David wrestled it, swore at it and at himself, too, for the stupidity of this task and also the broader one.

He looked at his watch. He'd made himself late.

"Hey, friend!" A tiny man had come out of the bowling alley. He was yelling across the parking lot in a deep voice that did not match his body: he was about five feet tall, with long hair and a beard, dressed in a gray baseball uniform and carrying a broom. "Whattaya call that car?"

"Willys Jeepster, 1949."

"They still make 'em like that?" He and David remained about fifty feet from one another, shouting.

"No," David said. "They stopped."

"This country," said the man, shaking his head. "It's going straight to fucking hell."

"Right after we go to the moon." David liked where he imagined this country was going.

"I'll believe that when I fucking see it," the man shouted. This was at a time when yelling the word *fucking* was a bold and devil-may-care thing to do; David, product of his times, hoped no women or kids were within earshot. "The moon won't change anything down here," the man said. "Believe you me."

"Gotta go," David said.

"You interested in selling that?" the man said. "I don't care for the yellow. Fuck yellow. Yellow! But I like the car."

"No." Actually, he did need a new car, something better than an increasingly rusty hand-me-down ragtop. What could he afford, though? "Well," he said, "what'll you give me?"

"What'll you take?" The man stood his ground. He came no closer.

"I have to go," David said.

"Keep me in mind!" said the tiny man.

David got back in the car and kept going.

A baseball uniform? A baseball uniform. Wonder what *that* guy's story was?

As David left Cleveland, the land started getting hilly. It was an unfamiliar landscape. Horse farms and big houses, old and new, set far back from the road. The car, too, felt strange. It had been a long time since he'd driven it with the top down.

Finally, David pulled up to the gate of the Country Club. "Open sesame," he murmured.

A guard asked him if he could help him.

Putting the top down had made David late, but it felt worth it. True, a part of him still thought he should turn around and go home, but a bigger part of him felt as if he belonged. Top down, sunglasses and James Dean windbreaker on, heater roaring, newish golf clubs in the trunk.

"The name is David Zielinsky. I'm here," he said, "as a guest of a Miss Anne O'Connor."

The guard—a pimply kid, though not much younger than David— checked a clipboard, then nodded and hurried to open the gate.

There's something about the last time of the year you put your top down. Something about using that indefinite article as he imparted the password. Something about arriving in a club that would not (yet) have him as a member. David was proud of himself, that he'd shown enough restraint not to introduce himself as *Councilman-elect David Zielinsky*.

None of this could have happened if he hadn't gotten a majority in the primary. So blame the voters. Blame the people who knew people who, let's just say, would vote a certain way if it was shown to be worth their while. Otherwise, David would have been too busy campaigning.

Accidents will happen.

THE STORY BEHIND THE STORY

TO BEGIN WITH, he said nothing about her hair, which, yesterday, she'd dyed Jackie Kennedy brunette. He hit his first tee shot long and straight and birdied the hole. When Anne complimented him, David muttered a nonchalant thank-you. Even their caddy seemed to buy it. The other two members of their foursome—two mossback old club snobs the starter had placed with them—told David he had honors. He begged their pardon. "Low score tees off first," said one of them, rolling his eyes. David said he knew that; he just hadn't heard them.

On the second hole, standing in a sand trap and chipping for bogey, David felt the need to tell Anne he was still really just learning the game.

"True of everybody," Anne said.

The caddy—a hulking, pimply kid named Gary, who looked like a high school defensive end but claimed to be only twelve—said that the sand trap on this hole was trickier than it looked, that it gave fits to the very best golfers. The two old guys hadn't come anywhere near it. They stood by the green, talking with their caddy, an older boy they'd requested, and watching.

"I'm better," David said, "at sports with bigger balls."

"Oh, *really?*" Anne smirked.

David blushed. The caddy giggled (OK, maybe he *was* twelve).

David addressed the ball and then pounded it. The cloud of sand went farther than the ball, but the ball did make it out of the trap.

Anne thought it was charming, the way doing poorly at golf was eating him up and how hard it was for him to hide that. "Not Ping-Pong, is it?" she said. "Speaking of small balls."

"I'd played Ping-Pong before," he said. "I'd played lots and lots of Ping-Pong."

David chipped it onto the green, then three-putted and took a nine.

"Golf's a hard game," Anne said, by way of reassurance. "Takes years of practice. More than Ping-Pong, even."

David laughed. *A man who laughs at a cut like that,* Anne thought, *is a man.*

"In reality," David said, "I'm better than this hole and not as good as that birdie."

"Aw, just play. That's why there's eighteen holes. Your average will assert itself."

"I should be able to hit it better, though," David said. "Longer. The ball just *sits* there. There's no excuse for not hitting it solidly."

"You can't think like that," one of the old guys said. "Don't think too much."

"Better than not thinking enough," David said.

"It's not an either/or, bucko," said Anne.

"A happy medium," David said. "I know."

"Someone who gets paid before the séance," she said.

He cocked his head like a dumb puppy. "What?"

"A happy medium is someone who gets paid before the séance."

"I get it," David said. "Good one."

Anne had no short game and could not hit it as far as the old guys. What she could do was hit the ball string-straight, every time. Anne kept waiting for them to ask if she was related to her father (who'd have been about their age), but they never did.

Six holes into it, as David lost two straight balls into a water hazard that anything airborne would have cleared, the men said that they had work to do today and went ahead.

"I'm really not this bad," David said. "I'm just having a bad day of it."

Gary the caddy pointed out that David could take a drop. David ignored him. He was, as Anne would have guessed, the sort of guy who just kept slamming them. Another one went in the drink. Then another. It seemed like David was starting to affect a limp. An alibi. Men.

The caddy told David to try the four-iron rather than the three. Just to get more loft.

David took it, teed up another ball, and blasted it. The caddy let out a low whistle.

"There!" David said. "That's more like it. *That's* what I'm capable of."

The caddy tried to take the blame for giving David the three in the first place, and David let him. But the three-iron, for a man David's size, had been the right club.

David parred seven. Anne disregarded Gary's advice on the break of the green—shouldering their bags, he looked so much like some lummoxy dock-worker, it was hard to take him seriously, plus which this was her home course—and double-bogeyed it.

David stepped to the eighth tee. He stood there for a long time, his lips moving as he muttered something, his weight shifting like a man who had to pee. He pulled the club back once, then started over, twice, then started over.

"Keep your head down this time," she said to David. "Keep your left arm straight."

"I know," he said. "I took some lessons."

"Ask for your money back," she said. "You're a lawyer. Sue him."

David looked up at her. "Do you mind?"

She held up her hands, the "OK, OK" gesture. Gary the caddy gave David a thumbs-up.

David hunched over the ball, his body a repertoire of twitches. Finally, he brought his driver back, swung, and topped the ball so badly it didn't even roll as far as the ladies' tee.

"All right, then," Anne said. "Dick out."

David frowned. He looked at Gary.

"It's a tradition," she said. "A man who doesn't clear the ladies' tee on his tee shot has to play the rest of that hole with his, you know. Dick out."

David kept looking at the caddy. "It's not a rule," the caddy said. "It's more like what she said. A tradition. Actually, technically, it's against the rules. Club rules."

Behind them came another foursome.

"Gotcha," Anne said.

"That was a joke?"

"No," Anne said. "But I wasn't going to make you do it."

"Have you ever seen anyone do it?"

"No," she admitted. "My brother John claims he made my brother Patrick do it once." Patrick had been eleven at the time. Anne wasn't going to humiliate David with that. The male ego is like thin ice. It'll support just so much before it spider-cracks, breaks, and returns from solid to liquid.

"What about you?" he asked Gary.

"Yes, sir," Gary said. "I've seen it. But, you know. Not in mixed company."

Anne granted David a mulligan, and, as he went to retrieve his shamefully stroked ball, she told the next foursome to play through.

"Just learning the game, eh?" said a man, probably about forty, pinching her shoulder.

"It's a hard game," she said.

"Nothing to it, darlin'," he said. "Just keep your head down." He looked at Gary and David, grinned, and mouthed the word *women*.

Anne did not correct him. There was only frustration to be had in doing it. There was power in not needing to.

"She's actually whipping me," David said. "I'm the one who's learning."

The man said that's golf for you: everyone's always learning.

The foursome disappeared over a hill. Before long Gary told David it'd be OK to tee off. He hit it hard but sliced it. Anne hit the same drive she did every time: a hundred and fifty yards and down the fairway. She wound up with a bogey, David a double bogey.

On their way to the ninth tee, he asked her how she managed to always hit it so straight. She said she didn't know, she just did. Gary the caddy tried to explain what-all Anne was doing right, in what seemed like a naked attempt for a big tip, but David just shook his head. "Show me," he told Anne.

Gary pulled her driver out of her bag and handed it to her. She took a few practice swings. David studied her. Gary kept his mouth shut. David really studied her. Anne O'Connor was a woman who was used to being watched, a woman who was watched for a living, but this felt different somehow.

"This is nutty," Anne said. "I'm not good enough to be anyone's ideal."

David just let out a long breath.

Anne teed it up. She could feel her heart beating in her ears. She hit her longest drive all day, two hundred yards, easy. "Golf shot," she said, tooting her own horn.

"Yes, ma'am," the caddy said. "You bet it was."

David approached the tee and said he still wasn't sure he understood what she was doing that he wasn't. *Avoiding all those twitches, for one thing*, Anne thought. "Don't think so much," she said. "Here," she said. She came up behind him. "Like this." She wrapped her arms around him, guiding his left arm through a few practice swings, her fingers digging into his left forearm in a game attempt to get him to keep the arm straight.

Amazing, how much a game like golf—where all people do is walk slowly around and swing a steel rod a hundred-odd times, half the time just these little taps—makes a person sweat.

David teed off. Again, he hit it short of the women's tee. She could see that it was killing him—and killing him, too, not to be able to let it show.

"Let it show," Anne said.

"FUUUUUUUUUCK!" He danced around in a foot-stomping spectacle worthy of Rumpelstiltskin. Then he looked at her, eyes wide.

"Most people," she said, "yell *fore*."

He laughed. "Most people hit it past the women's tee."

"Dick out," she said. She liked it, somehow, that he said *fuck* in front of her.

David touched his zipper. He unbuckled his belt.

"Go ahead."

Gary the caddy looked away, toward the top of a line of trees.

Neither Anne nor David moved. She kept her eyes on his eyes. She wanted the kid to take a hike.

David did not call her bluff. Instead he asked her what she'd done with her hair.

"I dyed it," she said. "I was tired of the other."

"The red was natural," he said, "wasn't it?"

"We live in the space age," she said. "Who wants natural?"

"It looks great," he said.

"You wait this long to say anything about it," she said, "and you expect me to think you think it 'looks great.' "

"I don't expect you to think anything."

"Lucky for you," she said. "C'mon," she said, pointing toward his ball. "You used your mulligan already."

Gary told David the yardage to the hole and recommended an iron, even though a wood would have been the obvious (if more difficult) club. David hit the three-iron fairly well. His limp was getting worse, whether from all the walking or from the temper tantrum or whether he was faking it, who knew? Anne asked him if it was his knee that was bothering him, and he said that he was used to it. The limp diminished slightly. On his next shot he hit a lovely seven-iron, curving it around a tree and landing it right in front of the green. It rolled to about fifteen feet of the hole. It was his best shot all day.

"Take that one," Anne said. "Pick it up. It's a gimme."

She was serious. It would have been the perfect note to end on. But David just laughed. He three-putted, then spread his arms and looked heavenward, affecting the eyes-closed beatific countenance of a martyr. "Go ahead," he said. "Shoot me."

Anne suggested they call it a game and go into the club for coffee. For the first time all day, Gary the caddy looked like a kid, like someone whose father reconsidered and did not spank him. Anne whispered to David that only members were allowed to tip (a lie) and slipped the kid a twenty. He did not look as grateful as Anne might have expected.

"So," Anne said on their way into the clubhouse, "whatever happened to that car?"

"I'm still driving it," David said. "Didn't you see me pull up? Didn't I ever tell you the story about the car?"

"I wasn't that eager," she said, "and you weren't that late. And, no, you never told me." In reestablishing their friendship, in matters regarding the murder of Marilyn Sheppard, she and David had kept things on a certain plane. Beyond the broad outlines, they'd avoided talking about the circumstances of their first acquaintance. "How old is that car now?"

"Not as old as you'd think," he said.

They sat down and ordered coffee and a basket of muffins, too. He started talking to her. Really *talking,* confessing and gossiping, the way men won't.

He told her about the lies he told his uncle: the deer, the shot he didn't fire at the deer that didn't exist, how the reason his aunt and uncle were weird to Anne that day in Put-in-Bay had to do with Irene, and about the murderous right cross he absorbed for insulting his aunt (He hadn't meant to! He loved his aunt! Like a mother, then and always!).

Anne would have guessed at everything David said, except the particulars of the deer and the reason his uncle punched David out.

"What about Chet?" David said. "Whatever happened to that creep Chet? Or your friend Jane? You ever see them?"

"Jane, once in a blue moon," Anne said. "Chet, never."

The mention of Chet led to a lengthy debate about the scoutmaster who'd lent David a tire pump to reinflate the tires of the Jeepster.

"That's ridiculous," Anne said. "Why would someone on a Saturday night in Kelley's Island be walking around with a scoutmaster's uniform on?"

"Why does anyone do anything?" He was on his third muffin, each slathered in butter. "Why would I make up a detail like that? The scoutmaster."

Anne insisted it was impossible for the man to have had a scoutmaster's uniform on and for her not to remember it.

Anyone observing them would have mistaken them for a married couple in the throes of a petty contretemps, but Anne was having a ball. Which is to say that the inner workings of any human relationship are unknowable except to those involved (they, typically, don't know much). Anne believed (incorrectly) that she was smiling.

She remembered that she'd fallen for this boy as a means of rebellion. What a crock. He was a boy just like the boy who married dear old mom. Not that that was a good thing or a bad thing. It was just a thing. He *got* her, though, in the same way a person gets a joke. They were fighting in a way that wasn't fighting. There are people Anne hadn't seen in a week with whom she'd have a harder time reestablishing a context for conversation. Example: anyone and everyone she'd known in New York.

Who knows why there are times when time stops and the talk just flows? David and Anne sat in the Country Club's empty lounge, catching each other up on their respective lives, drinking cup after cup of coffee, pausing for bathroom breaks delayed to near-medical extremes, for Anne to call into the station and confirm that the camera crew would meet her at the zoo at two-thirty, and for David to call into work and say that his TV interview was running much later than he'd thought (not a lie; as for the law firm, he was only of-counsel; he had little to do there).

They told each other all the stories in this chapter.

They talked at length and from the heart about their parents.

Anne told David stories of New York, and—taking a risk that did not feel like one, crossing a line that as she crossed it was no more tangible than the line that divides wards, cities, counties, states, or countries—the men there she'd grown sick of.

David listened, attentive as a girlfriend.

David talked about Irene.

Anne listened, attentive as a drinking buddy.

Just before they went out for Anne to see the ungleaming present state of the Jeepster and to leave in separate cars for the zoo (after some persuasion on Anne's part, she drove the Jeepster; David, the Avanti), David told Anne this story.

THE STORY OF A BETRAYAL

IT WOULD HAVE been premature, and expensive, to have a big election party for the primary. Just a small thing, to reward the key volunteers in case they lost and to energize them in case David won and went on to the general.

Betty volunteered to come to her old kitchen and cook sloppy joes and bake a half-dozen apple pies, and the owner of a carryout store, the captain of the precinct where David lived, sold them chips and beverages at cost. Irene worked that day. The hospital asked her to work an extra half-shift and she did. Her mother was watching the kids and Irene called to tell David they'd just spend the night in Independence.

"That's ridiculous," he said. "They should be here." If he won, a photographer might come by. It was good to have the family at hand. He put his hand over the mouthpiece. He was on the kitchen phone. The house was filling up with people. Too many were coming uninvited into the kitchen. "Why," he whispered, "would you take an extra half-shift, today of all days?"

"We need the money," she said. She had to go.

The first returns they got had David ahead by a landslide. The councilman's son was a distant second. Carrigan third. The rest didn't have enough votes to say so.

Stan Lychak sat in a corner, reading *Time* and not talking to anyone.

Longshoremen in green windbreakers and Teamsters in blue cloth jackets came, got food, and went to respective corners. David wasn't sure they'd been invited, but of course he was glad for their support and told them so, one by one. He said he knew nothing about who won the TV raffle.

The sloppy joes, everyone agreed, were the best sloppy joes Betty had ever made.

The next totals they heard, David was even further ahead. People with early-morning jobs said their congratulations and headed out.

At about nine-thirty Irene called to say it was an impossible night. Full moon. She was going to have to complete the double shift. She was sorry. "You don't sound sorry," David said.

She was, she said. She had to go, she said.

When David hung up the phone, it rang again. He let Gorman Soltesz answer it. When Gorman was done, he stood up on a dining-room chair.

"Ladies and gentlemen," he said. There were twenty-odd people there, all Caucasians. Gorman was dressed in a gray suit, and he looked like the prom king he once was. He poured a can of Carling's into a wineglass. "Here's to our ward's next city councilman!"

David told him to get down.

Gorman shook his head. "You got a majority, sport!"

The room filled with shouts and laughter. Betty, doing the dishes, screamed and came running and was the first to hug him. She called his name over and over and she was in tears. "Somewhere," she whispered in his ear, "your mother is smiling. You know that, don't you?"

"A majority of what?" David said to Gorman.

"Get this, everybody," Gorman said. "Here's the best part. A majority by *six votes!*"

A moment like this, a victory, a man should have his wife and kids with him. Was David wrong?

That wasn't the worst part. The worst part was when Irene finally got home that night. She never took time to vote. She forgot. She claimed. Close as it was, and his own wife didn't vote for him.

THE STORY

THE ANCHOR SETS it up as, heh-heh, a true-blue David and Goliath story—with a twist!

We see Anne O'Connor, brunette, in a tan raincoat of European cut, standing at the gates of the zoo. She catches the viewers up on the basic facts. She asks David to account for his slim win in the primary. She reaches up to him. The camera tilts up; the camera work could be better. He extols the hard work the members of his campaign put in, the old-fashioned shoe-leather politics this win redeemed. He adjusts his glasses. He looks vaguely professorial, like an earnest young lab technician explaining a new advance in physics to people who'll never understand it.

Cut to three man-on-the-street talking heads. They like what David stands for! They like what he is fighting!

Footage of Erieview. Stock footage of a bleak tenement, not even in David's ward.

Anne O'Connor, now in front of David's house. Cut to: still of David's induction picture into the navy. A picture of Eliot Ness. A picture of the biggest union local in the ward. Stock footage of City Hall.

Exterior shot: Deaconess Hospital.

Interior shot: a hospital lobby. Standing up against a wall, a hard-looking nurse who won't look into the camera says she's sure glad it was by six votes instead of one. She says people would be surprised how busy a hospital can get. But it all turned out well.

The camera pulls back to a three-shot. David leans into the microphone and says he's proud of his wife and her career. He looks right at the camera. Throughout the Cuyahoga River watershed, viewers are thinking that *here* is a man who is (despite his eyeglasses) Kennedyesque. David smiles, in a way no viewer would call insincere, and says he can only hope to serve the city as effectively and faithfully as his wife has, does, and will continue to do.

The camera stays on the three-shot. The nurse folds her arms and looks like a person waiting for a late bus. David looks into the camera. Anne O'Connor, professionally grim, stands straight and says her name, the call letters of the TV station, and the word *news*.

Cut to: the fatherly looking anchorman.

He looks like a man who's just been paid. He gives Anne his thanks. He smiles in the reassuring way that people outside the confines of TV do not smile. He welcomes her to the team.

THAT'S THE STORY OF, THAT'S THE GLORY OF LOVE

A PERSON CAN be in love with the idea of love. A person can fall in love with the idea of another person. Less commonly, a person can fall in love with another person.

In fact, a person *always* falls in love with the idea of another person, not the person. Falling in love with the actual person takes time and too much honesty. In the time it takes for it to be enough time, and to summon the strength it takes to mount enough honesty, it's too late. A person is calling something love that isn't love.

Unless it is. Some people luck out. The thing they've been calling love turns out to be just that. Such people exist. Film at eleven.

Factor in: how in love a person is with any unfulfilled idea of what his or her life should be. Young people, whose lives are still principally about what they set out in life to be, instead of who they are, are impossible on this count. Loving a young person is like trying to lasso water.

Leave aside: the hairsplitting of loving a person versus being *in* love with a person.

Don't forget: the vastly underrated role of setting. A person can fall in love with the place where a person falls in love. Better to bypass the intermediary and fall in love with the place. Love of place tends to be more honest. People know when what they feel for a place is lust or idle fantasy—which is to say: the idea of the place. The sort of dumb-bunny promiscuity that gets lavished on beaches, mountains, or Florence, Italy. To love, let's say, Cleveland, Ohio, U.S.A.? Brothers and sisters, if a person calls that love, it's love.

All that said: yes. A person *can* be in love with another person. A person can love another person. But this is territory occupied more often than it is possessed. A title claimed more often than it is won.

— 16 —

IN 1961 THE *new owner of the Browns—a New Yorker, a man with no football experience but who knew people who could set a guy up to buy an NFL team with no more of his own money invested than it'd take to buy a nice brick home—guaranteed that Cleveland would win the championship. He had a distressingly nasal voice. His name was Art Modell.*

Paul Brown, longtime coach and general manager and the team's namesake, pulled Modell aside and explained how dumb that was. It gets people's hopes up. Makes the fans harder on the players. Messes with team morale. Modell shrugged and said, "Hey, I'm a fan myself." Paul Brown told him to cut it out. Modell shook his head and said, "Hey, I'm your boss." Days later Modell moved Paul Brown from a large stadium-front office to a small one in back.

Brown's fine secretary quit, citing "Mr. Modell's Machiavellian mind."
The 1961 champions of the world were the Green Bay Packers.

After the season Brown traded a future Hall of Famer to Washington (sending Bobby Mitchell from the NFL's first integrated team to, with Mitchell's arrival, its last) for the draft pick that became Ernie Davis, Heisman Trophy winner, a halfback who broke Jim Brown's records at Syracuse. Again Modell guaranteed a championship and his coach winced. Modell paid Davis more money than he was paying Jim Brown, the greatest player in football history. Again the coach winced. Jim Brown said nothing to the newspapers but was royally pissed off. He was a man able to put royalty into royally pissed off. He liked Ernie Davis personally.

To mend fences with (and line the pockets of) his pissed-off badass star, Modell got Jim Brown a local TV show. This was a violation of Paul Brown's team rules. The TV station's management encouraged Jim Brown to be as candid as possible.

Believe me, you don't want that, Brown said. Where do you see a black man being candid? Kitchen tables, front porches, barrooms, and jail cells. Not TV. How long have you lived in America?

You're the greatest player in football, said Phil Weintraub. That's what people see when they see you. That first. Not a black man. A football hero.

America, shit. Jim Brown asked what planet Weintraub came from.

Earth.

Where on Earth?

Here, actually. Though I spent a long time in St. Louis.

Things are no different here than in St. Louis, sir.

It's your show, Jim, Weintraub said. I really do want you to be yourself.

Brown laughed and said he'd be as much of himself as he could without starting a riot.

Start the riot, Weintraub said, shrugging. It'd make good TV.

When training camp started, Ernie Davis showed up with a toothache. The tooth was pulled but the gums bled and would not heal. The team doctor gave Davis a new physical. Acute leukemia. Ernie Davis had yet to play a game in Cleveland and was already a goner.

He went back to training camp. Every day he'd show up in a gray hooded sweatsuit and help warm up the quarterbacks, then jog slowly and alone around the perimeter of the fields. He'd go by, and his teammates stood still. Even the coaches stopped yelling. Runs like a deer, a player would mumble. Still looks good, another would say. He'll pull through, a kid like that.

The players were used to being around men with bum knees, sore shoulders, elbows full of chips and fluid, broken bones, pulled hamstrings. But this? They stared *at Ernie Davis.*

Like September fog on the Cuyahoga, up rose Cleveland's lament: If a thing like this is going to happen, it just figures it'd happen here.

୧୨

THE GREAT CLEVELAND newspaper strike began the day before Thanksgiving 1962. The Newspaper Guild wanted a $10-a-week raise and a union shop. If you asked management at the *Plain Dealer,* this was a pissing-for-distance contest between the Guild and Louie Seltzer. If you asked management at the *Press*—Seltzer, aka Mr. Cleveland—this was the fault of the union-busting brass at the *PD,* the leadership at the Guild (with whom he'd until now been cozy), the meddlesome leadership of the local Teamsters, the appalling lack of leadership in city hall (people who, for the most part, served at LBS's behest), the erosion of the American work ethic, and who knows what-all. Perhaps even that dastardly Dr. Sam. Anyone but Seltzer.

Who was right? Accounts conflict. But whatever brought this thing to a head, no one can say the management of either of the city's dailies welcomed the idea of a true union shop.

As the strike began—as, on behalf of the Guild, warmly dressed Teamsters, their steamy breath rising in the clear night, climbed out of their cars, accepted signs from men in vans, and formed a well-muscled picket line around the loading docks at both the *Press* and the *PD*—Anne O'Connor sat at the anchor desk to do the eleven o'clock news, shuffling wire copy, fiddling with a strand of pearls, smoking a cigarette, and mumbling. It would be her debut as anchor. She was twenty-six years old, alone at the blunt, functional formica desk, a gigantic aerial photo of the city behind her, the cameramen most in need of double-time holiday pay before her (their union defined all holidays as commencing at 5 P.M., the night before the day). For weeks the Guild at the *Press* had been grousing about a possible holiday-season strike, a knockout punch right smack in the ad dollars. Neither newspaper had written much about the possibility of a strike, and what was written gave readers the impression that nothing would happen. None of the stories Anne was about to read mentioned any possibility of a newspaper strike.

Anchoring the news on a holiday night was no lucky break for Anne. She had no desire to be a news reader. She saw herself as a *reporter*. Just this month she'd done a great story on Carl Stokes, who'd just become the first Negro Democrat elected to the Ohio legislature, a story in which she'd used her personal connections (Carl's mother had once been the O'Connors' housekeeper) to win Stokes's candor (though his candor was as easy to tap as a spigot, and as refreshing). The story had provoked complaints from people claiming to be affiliated with the Klan. Get calls like that—including a bomb scare—and you know you're doing *something* right.

Phil Weintraub hadn't even told her she had to read the news until that very afternoon. She'd been in an editing room, finishing a home-for-the-holidays story about the former mayor, Anthony Celebrezze, JFK's newly confirmed secretary of health, education, and welfare. She'd known better than to complain. "Sounds like fun," she'd said. Trace element of sarcasm.

Phil Weintraub only shrugged. He got it. He was good.

Anne was under contract, and not union, and thus received no extra money for doing this, a thing she didn't want to do. She also had to read the weather, something she'd sworn never to do again. Sports was supposed to be done by a part-timer, a raspy-voiced tavern owner who did color commentary on Cleveland Pipers games. But an hour ago he'd begged off, too. A skeleton staff of technicians was still here (the widowed, the divorced, the haggard ones most deeply in debt), but as far as any viewer would be able to see, everything fell to Anne O'Connor, alone.

She'd taken the time to call David's house, on the off chance he'd gone home early, and let it ring for a long time. She'd called her apartment; not there, either. The operator at City Hall would be long gone, and Anne was certainly not going to call him at his wife's house. Anne would have liked him to see this, just for laughs, but she didn't care *that* much.

The floor director cued her. The lights seemed to grow brighter, hotter.

Anne straightened the papers, sat up straight. The brassy theme music was a Mancini knockoff, lifted from the score of a jazzy detective movie.

The floor director lowered his arm.

Anne suppressed the impulse to laugh. She welcomed Cleveland. She mentioned the name of the people for whom she was substituting. "Here," she said, "is tonight's news."

A house fire. (She'd rewritten the copy to remove the word *blaze*.)

A car wreck. (She'd rewritten the copy to remove *pileup* and *tragic*.)

Footage of slow-moving traffic on the Innerbelt, so people can see themselves and know they're real. A sanctimonious reminder (which, as she heard herself saying it, Anne wished she'd have cut) to be careful this holiday weekend.

Next, a story about a local boy made good: Celebrezze, America's first Italian American cabinet member, once the longest-serving mayor in Cleveland history, dressed in a sweater that looks home-knitted, playing with his children, parading a camera crew through his kitchen as his wife cooks, walking down the street in front of his house shaking hands, and sitting still for a few questions—speculation about America's future (bright); his profound thankfulness about the resolution to the Cuban Missile Crisis, for which he'd had a ringside seat (the ex-mayor deemed the president's leadership "brave and inspirational"); his thoughts on Cleveland (he misses it).

(The camera off her, Anne watches this, her own story, and does not do what the people in the booth and studio—all of them men—would expect of a woman, to check her hair and makeup. She feels them watching her.)

Commercial break. Scattered applause on the studio floor.

"Don't patronize me, fellas," Anne said.

One cameraman said he knew she was nervous and admired the way she hid it. She told him he was full of crap.

There was a phone call. "I'm not nervous," she said. "Which line?" The only thing that made her nervous was that people kept asking her if she was nervous.

Phil Weintraub, line two. He was someplace loud; a party. "You're amazing," he yelled. "The camera loves you."

"How can you see it," she said, "as loud as it is there?"

"Precisely," he said. "I can see it, just not hear it. As well as you're doing, I don't have to hear it. TV is about pictures, dummy." He was one of those men who could call you *dummy* and make it sound better than *sweetheart*. "You nervous?"

"No," she said. "Should I be?"

"I don't believe you," he said, "but no. Here's your cue, right?"

She looked up, hung up, welcomed Cleveland back.

Next up: a still photo of a flatbed truck, hauling a fifty-foot Douglas fir destined to be the Christmas tree at the Sterling-Lindner department store.

Then several mentions, sans footage, of volunteers at the Old Stone Church, feasts for those less fortunate, places donations might be left.

Then another still photo, of the Nike missile base in Parma, its payload poised to strike incoming Soviet ordnance (the missile evokes a stylized but exemplary human erection): how thankful we should be tonight for peace, etcetera.

Quick international roundup, all without pictures: two-sentence stories of border squabbles among the world's hot-tempered swarthy people. The thankful-for-peace story, which she did not write, was of course at loggerheads with the international news wrap-up, which she'd assembled. As she read things like *Pakistani frontier* and *Ho Chi Minh*, she could hardly wait to get to her kicker, the student riots in Ankara.

"Speaking of Turkey," she said, "another group that wishes it had the sort of peace the United States at present enjoys," she said, "is the world's doomed and panic-stricken population of..." She smiled wickedly. "Turkeys."

Then the obligatory network-feed story about turkeys: how dumb they are, et cetera.

(Anne was unduly proud of herself; years later she realized that the wire services always send out both Turkey and turkey stories the week of Thanksgiving.)

"We'll be back," Anne said, shivering to foreshadow what would come after the commercial, "with a look at the North Coast's most accurate weather forecast."

ᖫ

SHE SLEPT AS late as she could stand to.

When she woke up it was still dark. David was still not there. She considered calling his house, even picked the phone up off the nightstand to do it. She dialed the first number, a nine, and had the handset back on the cradle before the wheel of the dial stopped spinning.

She got up, went to the living-room window of her apartment, and looked out at the falling snow. Wet early-winter flakes dropping straight and heavy through the windless dark. Two hundred feet below her, barely visible, were the plain white lights of Shaker Square. The Christmas lights didn't go up for another week.

Snow had not been predicted. Bitter cold, but not snow. Nice forecast.

She opened her apartment door. The paper wasn't there yet.

She went into the kitchen to make coffee. When she flipped on the light, she saw the clock. It was only four. She took out a church key and a can of beer David had left. Anne was a vodka drinker, but she was hardly going to pour herself a drink at four in the morning.

Say this much for Anne O'Connor: at least she didn't have cats.

She put on a Thelonius Monk record (one of the solo piano albums), pulled her copy of *Ship of Fools* from a polished-steel bookcase, and sat down at the kitchen table. She drank half the beer. It wasn't going to help, not with the erratic hours she worked. But she wasn't going to go for pills. David took a pill now and then and kept a bottle of them there. For Anne, taking a sleeping pill would feel like slipping into a pair of her mother's un-laundered underpants.

She couldn't concentrate on the book. Outside her window, fat snowflakes fell. Better than counting sheep. Anne put her head down on the opened novel. At seven she woke up again and went to the door. The paper was always here by seven. Not today. She called the *PD*'s general number, which she knew from memory. Busy. Again. Busy. Again. Busy.

The phone rang while she was in the shower. She'd be damned if she'd give David the satisfaction. She didn't care what he did, as long as he did what he said he was going to do. He'd said he was swinging by after a meeting of the planning committee. So swing, baby.

In just a towel, she started calling the *PD* again. Busy. Obviously things were running late because of the snow.

∽

"I'M HOME!"

David yelled it in a way calculated to sound sarcastic to Irene and enthusiastic to the kids. Wasted effort: all that greeted him in Independence was a yapping poodle (Irene had named it Precious), the sound of an unwatched television, the smell of pumpkin pie, and some kind of metallic bleat he couldn't place. Irene and the kids were already next door.

It was about 11 A.M. David was hungover and wearing the suit he'd worn yesterday. His father hadn't even called him about the strike until Anne

[350]

would have already been at the station. What was he going to do, call and ask for free PR? David had left City Hall, met his father at the *Press* docks, watched the strike begin, waited for TV cameras to come by so he could stand in front of them and demand that Locher, the do-nothing appointed to fill out Celebrezze's term, show some leadership and mediate this crisis. But the cameras didn't come. His father and a man from the Guild each thought the other was going to have someone tip off the TV people. By the time the snafu was parsed, it was nearly midnight. Mikey Z gave thumbs-up to his best team of linemen, then asked David to go for a drink at the Hollenden. When they got there, Mike was a fury of pounding fists and spilled peanuts. "What did the fucking guy think," said Mike, "that the strike was gonna get reported in fucking newspapers that don't exist? That we'd start up his strike for him and take care of the publicity too?" It took a long time for his father to settle down. David sat there irrationally afraid his father would blame him; David hadn't even told his own father he was more or less living with a TV reporter—that's how discreet things were. As Mike simmered down, David knew he should go, but by then he was in a just-one-more mode. Next thing he knew it was last call and he was more drunk than he wanted to be and so took his father up on his offer of a room. Then it was now.

The floor was an obstacle course of strewn Legos, Matchbox cars, baby rattles, half-naked Barbies, and—still on, vibrating—that electric football game, featuring inch-high plastic men painted as the Browns and inch-high plastic men painted as the Packers, which David had bought Teddy for his birthday but which Lizard had taken over (Barbie coached the Browns; Skipper, the Packers; Teddy's G.I. Joe had been commandeered to be Barbie's assistant).

David turned off the TV and the bleating football game. He got down on his knees and gave the dog the attention it wouldn't rest until it received. (Precious! David rests his case.) Then he took off his clothes and got in the shower.

Any second Teddy or Lizard would come by, happy to see him.

He got out, got dressed, still alone in the house, except for Precious. Precious was curled up asleep on the bed, on the side where David would sleep if he slept there.

Irene had baked that morning. Apple pie and something involving bread crumbs and mayonnaise. Dishes were stacked high in the kitchen sink.

As David did them, he kept looking next door. Bud and Flossie's house was essentially identical to the one where David nominally lived. A porch-free ranch-style, half-brick (sandpaper-colored), half-(brown-)aluminum-sided house. Arborvitae in front, poured cement patio in back. Detached peak-roofed garage. Birdbath. Welcome to paradise.

David was tall enough to look out over the top of the curtain that covered the bottom three-fourths of the window above the sink and see into the kitchen and dining room next door, where the Hrudka women smoked cigarettes and assembled Thanksgiving dinner. In Bud and Flossie's backyard, a flock of grandchildren in wool coats and severe haircuts toddled, squabbled, ran in circles, and cried, while drawn and paunchy men stood shivering in the mouth of Bud's garage, eyeing the old refrigerator inside, checking their watches, longing for noon.

David wanted to bound down the back steps, slap the men on the back, in-laws and out-laws alike, and accept from them a cigarette he didn't smoke and at noon a beer he'd be happy to drink, and talk football. He wanted the women to fuss over him, the way they used to, years ago.

He watched them and felt like he belonged in their world. At the same time he wondered what the fuck he was doing among these vulgarian freaks.

His in-laws didn't approve of Irene and him living separately. No one would talk about it to his face, but, especially from the women, there'd be arched eyebrows, affected shoulder angles, legs pointed away from him, with no interest in what and how much he ate.

He saw Teddy and he saw Lizard, and they both looked like they were having fun. Even Teddy! Narrow as these lots were, they had to have seen him drive up. But the kids kept playing. David put the last dried dish away, then picked up the toys. He didn't know where anything went but did his best. He found G.I. Joe's pants. That was good. He put them back on G.I. Joe.

⌒⌒

ANNE PLAYED MUSIC on the car radio on the way to her old house, though in fact the only stations that had the story were the ones that had managed to get through the busy lines at the *PD* and learn from the management person answering the phone that both city papers were on strike. What raised Anne's suspicions was that the snow was melting and all the newspaper boxes she passed still held yesterday's edition.

Ibby's family was all over the house. They were, by and large, large: a race of bearish men and tall, translucent-skinned women. They looked enough like Anne's family to be Anne's family, which of course by marriage they now were. When Anne came through the front door without knocking, everyone shouted hello to her and made her run a gauntlet of hugs, kisses, compliments, and proffered drinks. Several of them said they had seen her on TV last night and that she was brilliant. Patrick interrupted some board game he was playing with his and several other people's children to tell her he was proud beyond words.

"I hated doing it," Anne said. "But thanks, Thumbkin."

"You don't like things you're good at," he said. "I know. Just don't sell yourself short."

Children were calling his name.

"You're needed," she said. "Thanks for the advice, chum."

He rolled his eyes. "Glad you could make it," he said.

Ibby and her three handsome sisters were in the kitchen. Ibby was the oldest. This was the first Thanksgiving that Anne could remember that wasn't served by a hired cook.

Ibby dropped the potato she was peeling to run across the kitchen and hug Anne. Ibby was pregnant again. Her sisters were smoking marijuana.

"Hey, sweetie," Anne said. "Smells good."

The sisters laughed. One of them had served a stint in San Francisco as a far-out beatnik jodhpur angel, and now they all smoked. Anne declined their offer. She had to work.

"It *all* smells good," Anne said. "Anything I can do?"

"We have it under control, I think," Ibby said. "You can see how Patrick's doing with the kids." Ibby grinned. "Or you can watch for the Grand Dame. I always like a little warning."

For the first time ever, Sarah was wintering at Ashcroft.

"As cold as it got last night," Anne said, "I wonder if the ferry ..."

Ibby shook her head. "Nope. The Grand Dame flies. She told me she thought that if she slipped the pilot a little something extra, he'd fly her all the way in to Burke."

"A little something extra," Anne repeated. "For Christ's sake. She just thinks—"

"I don't think so, doll," Ibby said. "I think the pilot's sweet on her." There was something appealingly dirty, moll-like, in the way she said that. Ibby was the only person Anne had told about David. "Oh, don't look so horrified. Want a belt?"

Not the accessory. Booze. Took Anne a second. "Where's your newspaper?" she said. Anne opened the pantry door a crack. Patrick had two kids on his back and was singing to them in French. "I can't drink. I have to work." Someone's opened pack of Salems was on the counter. She took one and lit up.

"We saw you!" said one of the handsome sisters. "You were stellar."

"I hated doing it," Anne said. "Thanks, though."

That was when she heard about the strike. Ibby's youngest sister was engaged to a boy whose father ran Halle Brothers department store. The strike, according to the prospective father-in-law, could last awhile, which, according to Ibby's sister, had him about ready to crawl out on a ledge, worrying about not being able to advertise for Christmas.

Anne's first newscast, and she'd missed the biggest story of the day (all three Cleveland TV stations missed it). It wound up being the biggest story of the year. In the case of the stature of Cleveland TV news, the biggest story ever. But superlatives are a function of historical perspective. Anne was in television, a medium that inculcates its practitioners to think of time as a thing to fill, historical perspective as something a tweedy geezer might be asked to provide during unwatched Sunday morning public affairs programming. What Anne was thinking—nibbling on gherkins and the leavings of sweet potatoes in a dirtied bowl—was how embarrassed she was, how hard it will be to anchor the news again today, with only a skeleton crew of reporters and no local papers to filch from.

She looked longingly at the sisters' marijuana cigarette.

"I can't stay," Anne said. "I'd like to. At least," she said, elbowing Ibby, "to go on scout duty for the Grand Dame." She was supposed to go in at three, but, under the circumstances, she needed to take off.

In another sort of family, a person who comes for a big holiday dinner and leaves within ten minutes would elicit a chorus of arch-browed lament. This wasn't that sort of family.

࿇

MODELL CONTINUED TO *guarantee a championship. Paul Brown kept telling him to cut it out. Green Bay was the talk of football. Vince Lombardi—who got hired (he'd been an assistant with New York) on Brown's recommendation—was called a genius on the cover of* Time. *As for Brown, football's erstwhile genius, talk was that the game had passed him by. Modell would buy his players steaks and drinks, and shake his rueful, bulbous head as they complained about the coach's stifling game plans. Then Jim Brown hurt his wrist. It can be scientifically proven that a coach with a healthy, in-his-prime Jim Brown is more of a genius than one without.*

[354]

Modell called his coach into his office, offered him a seat (Brown stood), and told him to get the gray-skinned, still-fleet Davis into a game. Have him return a kick. It'd be an inspiration to sick kids, et cetera. The doctors say they've got the thing arrested. So what's the holdup?

The coach bit his lip. You mean a publicity stunt, he said.

Look, said Modell, you think this is the football business? It's the pub-licity business. That's how the modern world works. Every business, when you get down to it, is the publicity business. Do I make myself clear? I got eighty grand wrapped up in that kid. A publicity stunt's the least I can expect.

Paul Brown didn't say anything. He didn't do anything, either. He was a bald, deliberate man who did not swear or drink. He'd complained about the TV shows some of the players had gotten, and Modell overruled him. After a career where Brown won championships as often as not, he was mired in a season of injury and loss. Modell shrugged. What the fuck, I'm just a fan.

How many fans, Brown said, get to watch games in the press box?

When you going to put Davis in a game? I thought I told you to put Davis in a game.

He's dying, Brown said.

Watching the team you put out there, Modell said, I know the feeling. What I hear is, Ernie Davis is getting better. Unlike this team.

I won't do it, Brown said. I don't want to hear any more about it.

During the weekdays between games, Ernie Davis kept coming to camp.

⌒⌒

TWO WEEKS INTO the strike, the Teamsters' national office ordered their men back to work. The strike did not, they publicly said, involve issues that concerned the Brotherhood. (Less publicly, the newspaper brass and Jimmy Hoffa—theoretical opposites, though we don't live in a theoretical world—met and managed to reach, let's just say, a meeting of the minds.)

That same day David closed his office door and motioned for the shovel-faced Negro developer, a man about fifty, to take a seat.

David was the only council member without a window in his office. (If he'd had one, it would have revealed a curtain of thick gray snowflakes.) Behind David were his Fenn College and Cleveland-Marshall diplomas and a selection of family photos. In the largest of these—taken this summer, a sitting conducted for the church directory—Lizard is so tanned she looks Italian, Brad is in a baby sport coat sound asleep, Teddy is pale as oatmeal and biting his lower lip, and Irene (who lost twenty pounds in anticipation of this picture and has since gained it back) sits tall and affects a Mona Lisa smile. As for David, he couldn't look *more* the part of young pol on the rise.

On cue, the phone rang. It was Gorman, in the outer office, placing the standard-issue call just to make someone wait. David held up one finger. The developer held up one not-to-worry hand, his laughably unsubtle briefcase already across his lap.

"That's a concern we all share," David said to Gorman. "The young turks, that is."

"Hear anything from your pop?" Gorman asked. The Teamsters were going back at three, the end of the first shift.

"You know I'm always there for the workingman," David said.

"Think there'll be problems?"

"I plan to look into that further," David said. "But as you know, my stand on that issue is a matter of public record."

The desk was new and steel. A donation to the city from the Brotherhood of Teamsters. Across from its thicket of haphazardly stacked paper were two wooden chairs. David had sawed a couple inches off the legs, a tactic of Uncle Stan's. The developer was about David's height, and now David was looking down at him. On the wall behind the developer's head was a ward map of Cleveland, filthy with pushpins.

"You bettin' the Browns this week?" Gorman said. "I heard you aced yourself tickets in the mayor's box."

"Correct, on both counts." David declined the developer's proffered cigarette but pushed an ashtray his way. The developer chose not to light up. "I'm not the sort of person," David said, "who sits back and calls for studies. I'd rather do something than nothing."

"Whattaya," said Gorman. "Green Bay's giving seven and a half."

"Point well taken. Let me put it to you this way. I'd rather do something and take the chance of being wrong," said David, "than do nothing and never know."

"I'll call Shoes," Gorman said. "One A-Jax or two?" Twenty or forty bucks.

"The latter," David said.

"I can never remember which one that is."

"Neither, then. How about five?" A hundred bucks. What the hell. "I'm not in office for the sake of being in office," he said. "I'm here to serve the people. That, ma'am, means you."

"Roger that, sweetums," said Gorman, and hung up.

David smiled and apologized to the developer, who waved the apology off.

"I don't want to take up too much of your time," the developer said, snapping open the latches of his briefcase. "I know you're a busy man," he said. He'd grown up in Cleveland but had a southern accent. He was in the business of rezoning property for multifamily use—not a slumlord per se, but one who paves the way for them. "But you're also a young man." He motioned toward the picture on the wall. "With a beautiful, lovely, beautiful family."

David dug his fingernails into his thighs to keep from laughing. The man wasn't even going to try for subtlety.

"What it costs to set a family up these days," said the man, opening the briefcase up so he could see its contents and David couldn't, "I hate to even think about. It was bad in my day but now"—he made an explosion noise—"I can't hardly imagine."

"Double negative," David blurted.

The developer frowned.

"Forget it," David said. He reached across the desk and down, pressing the briefcase lid closed. "Don't show it to me," David said. "I don't want to know."

David wasn't shocked. This was a Friday. Every Friday a lunch-sized brown paper bag showed up in each council member's mailbox. As far as David knew, everyone accepted this money, no questions asked, and had for years. David didn't know who, in fact, put it there. Everyone got the same amount, so it'd be hard to say what exactly it was buying. As the developer ran though a litany of what-all his rezoning project would do for Cleveland, David's packet was tucked in the breast pocket of his sport coat. It would go where that money always went, in the bank. Campaign war chest. David had not yet spent a dollar of it. True story.

"My vote," David said, "simply isn't for sale."

"I wasn't suggesting—"

"Eh-eh-eh-eh." David was doing the waving-off now. "Don't make it worse."

David didn't care about this project. He would, in fact, vote for it. Jack Russell, the blowhard cowboy poseur who'd been council president since Christ was a cricket, was against it. David, thus, was for it. Take the money, lose the high road.

"You might work on your style, sir." David rose, opened his door, and began to usher the developer down the hall. "You watch too many movies. You're a clown."

"Actually," the man said, managing both to brighten and to frown more deeply, "my father was a clown. Professionally."

"You don't say." David couldn't remember ever having seen a Negro clown.

"I just did say."

"So you did. You're an awfully literal-minded extortionist." They were in the lobby now. "I know I'm the new man," David said, raising his voice. "So, for the record, I do *not* take *bribes*. You're lucky I don't call the *cops*." David was shouting. The receptionists stood to watch. Up and down the corridor, colleagues stuck their furtive balding heads out their office doors. A group of Negroes came through the door to the lobby: every Negro member of council plus several others, too. The senior member of this group looked at David and rolled his eyes.

"Call the cops?" The developer feigned outrage. "Sir, you may have lost your marbles."

Rolled his eyes! David was a friend to the Negroes' cause. Other members of council—you could see it in their faces, even now—were troubled by the mere sight of a group of political Negroes. Paranoid fears. David was different. David was on the record as being different, and he didn't appreciate being treated as if he were one of the bad guys, just for turning down a bribe. Were they offended? If any of them turned down a bribe to a white developer, do they think he'd be offended?

The flustered developer put his hand on the shoulder of one of the Negroes in the group, a woman. "I can't imagine," he said, "what your young friend here is talking about."

She shrugged, and kept going. The group disappeared around a corner. As they did, David caught sight of the only other councilman his own age. "Get out of my sight," David said, nudging the developer toward the door. "Don't make me say the word *bribe*."

"You're a fake," the developer whispered. "You're worse than your uncle."

David turned his back on the man. "Dumb son of a clown."

The other young councilman was still watching. The other young man winked.

David made his right hand into a revolver, closed one eye, and, grinning, mime-shot his young white peer. *We're the New Frontier. The space age. Look upon our future, ye mortals, and despair.*

It's good to be seen for what you are. David liked this guy more all the time.

David kept walking. He was back in his office before what the developer had said really registered. Not *your father*. It was his father David was used to hearing about, being compared with or against. But the man had said *your uncle*. Maybe not so odd, David reasoned. He knew little about the developer, but it was no leap to imagine him involved with things ideally kept from the scrutiny of a good investigator. Still: Stan, a fake?

On David's filing cabinet was a framed picture of his aunt and his uncle, cutting a white cake at their anniversary party last year. An Italian cassata cake. They were cutting it with a saber Stan had impulsively pulled from the wall at the VFW hall. Just look at those laughing, windburned faces. What a life they'd shared.

Then he called Anne. She was out.

૭૦

THE STATION DID not develop its own film. They used a little lab on Carnegie and 66th, calling ahead on a two-way radio so that someone was ready for them. Anne stayed in Hugo the cameraman's car, her heart still beating hard and, with a manual typewriter on her lap, banging out a draft of the story. Inside, in the lobby of the lab, Hugo flipped through a magazine while technicians went about their brisk, unfrantic business. Anne looked up and saw them blasting the film with air, to dry it so it wouldn't stick to the reels. Only a few moments now.

Hugo came to life, ran the cans to the car, tossed them into the backseat, and drove like mad to the station. Anne rocked in her seat and rewrote the story in her head.

Behind the station Hugo pulled into the lot, hit a patch of ice, skidded into a parking space, and ever so slightly clipped a fence post. The car was his (by the time he retires, he'll be at the helm of a station-owned remote van, complete with a motorized satellite dish), but he didn't even cuss. He and Anne grabbed the camera and film cans and, without even closing the car doors behind them, ran though the back door to the station, past the startled boozer of a security guard, jostling past interns, talent, guests, and techs, though slippery cement-floor catacombs to the editing room.

"Stop it!" said Hugo the cameraman.

"Stop what?"

"Stop chanting."

"Chanting what?"

"'Jesus, Jesus, Jesus, Jesus.'"

She hadn't known she was chanting.

"I'm Catholic," he said.

"So am I," Anne said. "Jesus, Hugo! You've got frozen blood all over your coat."

Splattered and smeared. A failed kids' art project.

Eight minutes to air.

They pulled off their coats and their gloves and balled them up and threw them in the corner. Hugo's cold hands fumbled with the take-up reel on the editing machine. Anne stood in the hall and screamed out the name of the newscast's senior film editor.

Phil Weintraub came running.

"Phil! You can't believe—"

"Right," he said. "I can. We're going to—"

"If it bleeds, it leads, Phil!"

"Fine, fine, fine, fine, fine."

The editor was right behind him, a serene, pear-shaped man who looked like a professor of library science. He slid into his chair. His hands moved as fast as a grocery store's champion bagger's. His expression could have been no more untroubled if he were dead.

Hugo the cameraman and Phil and various onlookers darted in and looked on and hovered and came in and out and asked questions about when it would be ready, and the editor cut film, and Anne sat behind a typewriter and pounded out the anchor's intro for the story.

The newspaper strike, the Newspaper Guild, the Teamsters, Jackie Presser, Louis Seltzer, no comment, bloodshed on the loading docks, this exclusive footage, Anne O'Connor.

She would sit at the anchor desk, beside the anchor, and narrate.

On the huge sleigh of that editing console came flickering images of shadows and blood, men in parkas beating on other men in parkas. Anne looked up from her typewriter. The footage wasn't as good as she'd hoped. Hugo had been badly jostled. Though that was good in a way: it *showed* chaos and violence. It gave the viewer the blurry what-next sense of being *there*.

The makeup person came in to fuss with Anne, right there in the editing room, because there wouldn't otherwise be time, and Anne at first shooed her away. "You can't go on like that," the makeup woman said. "For god's sake, you've got blood on your face."

"Jesus, Jesus, Jesus," Anne said.

"Anne!" Hugo said. "Stop it."

"*Nothing can* stop *me now*," Anne sang. "*'Cause I'm the Duke of Ear-r-r-rl.*"

"You can't go on," the woman said.

Anne smiled. "I'll go on."

"Duchess," said the schoolmarmish editor.

"*Duke-Duke-Duke,*" she sang, syncopated by her typing. "*Duke of Earl, Duke-Duke, Duke of Earl, Duke-Duke, Duke of Earl, Duke-Duke, Duke of Earl, Duke-Duke . . .*"

૭૭

RADIO THRIVED. TELEVISION news ratings doubled and then tripled. Ad rates for TV and radio tripled. If you had a piece of that, great. Everyone else suffered.

Guild workers couldn't get strike pay unless they stood in subzero temperatures for two hours a day. They stood.

Christmas drew near. Without full-page newspaper ads enticing them downtown, Clevelanders increasingly shopped in the places they increasingly lived, which is to say not Cleveland per se. Greater Cleveland. East. West. Away from the center.

George Steinbrenner's Cleveland Pipers folded, and so did the American Basketball League. The team's few hearty fans showed up for games clutching tickets in mittened hands, looking through the locked glass doors of the Cleveland Arena and cussing with a fury distinct to the spurned sports fans of a great northern city.

Forget trying to sell a house. Forget trying to hire someone, or to be hired.

Movie theaters handed out listings of show times at nearby grocery stores. Grocers handed out sale flyers at the movies. Men destined to trigger two of the worst riots in American history took over, respectively, as Cleveland's chief of police and Ohio's governor. In Cleveland their deeds went essentially unreported. The chief of police began to spend his unscrutinized spare time cruising the snowy streets of Hough, carrying an automatic rifle, looking for snipers.

White people desperate for news began to buy the *Call & Post*, the Negro-owned paper. Many of these readers had heretofore considered the term *northern migration* germane only to butterflies. The newspaper, aware of its new audience, broadened its news coverage and narrowed its editorial-page focus to near-incessant hammering on the city's spending millions of dollars on Erieview's unneeded office towers (one of which would house the *Press*) while families in Hough were served by crowded, filthy schools, predatory landlords, and an adversarial police force.

People died. Obituaries were haphazardly read on radio, on TV, in the *Call & Post* and the suburban weeklies, but people often heard about dead

[361]

friends after all official mourning had been completed. Lapsed churchgoers returned just to read the bulletins. As for the dead, even after their sparsely attended funerals, they remained unburied by the hundreds, their caskets stacked in cemetery barns until the snow and bitter cold subsided enough so that—in this, Cleveland's snowiest and coldest winter ever—their graves could be more easily dug.

∾

ON CHRISTMAS EVE, on a wide salted sidewalk in front of Guild head-quarters, filmed for broadcast later that night, Anne's Jewish boss hands out canned hams. His station is the only one in town unaffiliated with either newspaper. Parka-swaddled striking workers make their grim, slouchy way to the front of the line. Off to Phil Weintraub's left, Anne O'Connor leads several members of the Old Stone Church choir in a rendition of "Good King Wenceslas." The film stock is brittle, old, and silent. Anne opens her mouth so wide the world's weakest lip-reader could tag the carol in question as "Good King Wenceslas." (The snow nearby is deep, but neither crisp nor even. More like heaped and grimy.) Anne's shoulders are pulled back. Her chest is stuck brazenly out, god knows why. She must have used a can of hair-spray, but the wind is too much: it lifts hanks of her hair, like plasticine flaps. Tears stream down her cheeks, probably from the cold. She is both smiling and frowning, but one thing she seems not to be doing is crying.

It'd be great to hear her voice, but the story was done with one of the turret-lensed windup cameras, not the station's lone SA-16. Her singing was never recorded. It happened but is lost to history. Run this film through the projector once more and it'll be gone, too.

∾

ERNIE DAVIS DID *not, of course, dress for games or travel with the team.*

The last game of the season, in San Francisco, fog closed the airport, and the Browns' plane landed in Sacramento. During the layover Modell pulled a few players aside, bought them drinks, and asked about Paul Brown's waning creativity. Had the game passed him by?

(Paul Brown, who had rules against drinking, sat with some of his coaches in a waiting area. There is no historical record of what was discussed.)

The man, said Jim Brown, controls everything. We can't audible. They make me run tackle to tackle. What happened to sweeps? What happened to a deep threat that'll open things up for me? Don't get me started on those fucking IQ tests. We all know what that's code for.

What's it code for? said Modell.

Those tests are bullshit, Art. We'll just leave it at that.

What I hear from Paul, Modell said, is that you have a problem with authority.

You ought to consider the things he has problems with.

What are you suggesting? said Modell.

He's what he is. Don't get me wrong. For a man of his generation, he's a saint.

The fog lifted. The team reboarded the plane. The next day Cleveland won the game, 13–10. Despite the time he'd missed due to his injury, Jim Brown, for the season, managed, briefly and just barely, to achieve the milestone of a thousand yards. But with the game winding down, he got the quarterback to call an audible, to let him try something. An end-around. Brown was thrown for a loss. He finished 1962 with 996 yards. The Browns finished with a record of 7–6–1.

∞

"PENNSYLVANIA, THERE'S NOTHING worse than the Pennsylvania fucking Turnpike." The day after Christmas, and Anne was driving a rented Chevrolet across Pennsylvania. Traffic was not what you'd call heavy. Snowfall was. Anne could feel herself coming down with something. She felt her forehead. Hotter than she'd feared. She lit a cigarette.

"There's Nebraska." John O'Connor looked up. "Iowa. You can't believe what it's like to drive across Iowa." He'd been reading the Holy Bible. That was how he always spoke of it: *the Holy Bible.* It wasn't all he read—he'd just finished a dissertation on Whitman and Hart Crane—but since their father died, the Bible was what John read for fun. John was forty-two and looked younger. "What possessed you to take up that filthy habit?" He pointed at her cigarette.

"I've smoked for years." Why? Who knows? The problem with people, Anne thought, is the compulsion to explain. Assignation of motive. She's more guilty than most. Occupational hazard. More addictive than smoking. "Especially in the car. Just not around the family."

"Hmm," John said. "Well. There's that eastern half of Colorado. Criminetly: only half the state's flat and soul-sapping to drive, and when you're doing the east-to-west of that you can see the mountains and even Denver, so you'd think that'd make it easier, if only for the view, which it both does," he said, "and mostly doesn't. Slow *down*."

"Shut *up*," Anne said. "Who says *criminetly?*"

John had sworn off swearing. Anne couldn't bring herself to swear off ragging him for swearing off swearing.

"Of course, Florida, north-south," John said, "is unrelenting." He'd rented that Chevy in Key West, driven it the 1,400 miles to Cleveland. "But *Kansas*," he said, "is the worst, baaaaaar none." He dragged the word out to fill the feet in the line where a younger John would have said *bar-fucking-none*. A younger John also wouldn't have lectured her. "Please slow down."

She sneezed. John blessed her. Anne made a point of not thanking him.

"If I go any slower, I'll have to throw it in reverse." She was barely over the speed limit.

"Too fast for the conditions is what the law says. If you're driving through a blizzard—"

"It's hardly more than flurries." But she let the car drift below the speed limit. Only tailing state troopers and her oldest brother could have made her do this.

John was a driver. He denied being afraid to fly. Anne had made this trip east dozens of times, when she was going to school at Smith and when she was living in New York, but she'd never driven farther west than Detroit. Flown, yes; driven, no. John was going to New York to participate in a convention of English professors, at which he had job interviews. Anne's official story was that she was going to New York to see some old friends, which, except for the plural, was not untrue.

"Thank you," he said, pointing at the speedometer, then patting her knee.

He was so self-satisfied, she was tempted to speed up. She didn't. She took a long drag on her cigarette, then sneezed.

"Bless you," he said. "Are you OK?"

She shrugged. She took a long drag off her cigarette.

"It's not as if you have a spotless driving record."

She did not at first have any idea what he was talking about.

"That deer," he said. "That deer you almost hit and hit that dead tree instead."

She did not say anything.

"At Kelley's," he said.

Here she was, on this long trip, and here was her chance. Her opening. She'd been meaning to do this. Dying to. A thing wasn't real unless you told someone. The only person Anne had told was Ibby. Ibby had made it real, but she was also married and bored and too eager to live vicariously through Anne. For this to be real, someone needed to be at least a little bit shocked. But not too much. That made John the perfect person to tell.

"I wonder," John said, "whatever happened to—"

"I swear to *God*," Anne said. "Can't anybody in this family live down anything?"

"What's that supposed to mean?"

"Just what I said," she said. "I have one accident in ten years and you want to make a federal case out of it. As if somehow—"

"Ha!" John bounced up and down in his seat. "I knew it! *Iknewit-IknewitIknewit!*"

A chill ran through her. How could he know? She'd been the world's most discreet lover. She felt her forehead. Burning. She sneezed again. A sequence of three. She swerved the car. John reached out to grab the wheel. She shot him a look.

"You think you're so clever," he said.

"Hello, pot. Kettle here."

John smiled. "At the time," he said, "you said *he* was driving."

"Who?" she said. Her fever, were she to guess, was probably 101.

"The tall boy. Whatever his name was. Gatsby. I *knew* you were the one driving that yellow car. *Dai-sy, Dai-sy*," he sang. "*How does your garden grow?*"

"That's not how that song goes," she said.

"You'd know," he said.

They drove for several miles in silence.

"That *boy* was at Dad's funeral, you know," Anne finally said. "He's on city council."

John cocked his head and gave her a *do-tell* look.

She kept driving.

"That's all," she said.

"I don't remember seeing him at the funeral," John said. "I'd have remembered him."

"He was there," she said. "The whole city was there."

"The whole city was not there. It's a pretty big city, dear, and most of the people there don't give two hoots—"

"You know what I mean."

"How could Gatsby be on the city council? How could a kid—"

"A kid?"

"A kid."

"Dad was younger than he was, that kid, when he first got elected to council."

"Dad was Dad."

"Hard to argue with logic like that. Christ."

She glanced at John to see if that made him wince. But no.

When she again triple-sneezed, John insisted that she pull over. He'd drive. They'd stop at the next plaza and see what medicine could be had. If need be, they'd even get off the turnpike, find a real drugstore in a town somewhere.

She did as she was told.

"So," John said, back on the road, "you ever see our Boy Councilman?"

"He's on the council. That's not exactly my beat, but of course I—"

"You know what I mean."

"He's married," she heard herself say. Her head was so congested, her own words sounded echoey.

John let out a theatrical sigh. "These days," he said, "all the good ones are married."

◦◦

"THERE'S SOMETHING DIFFERENT about this snow," David said. "It doesn't look like snow in Ohio. Somehow."

He had the curtains pulled back. They were in a suite on the twelfth floor of the Plaza. He still had on his boots and his overcoat and a scarf his aunt had knitted and given him for Christmas. The faux suede gloves were a present from his kids. He'd also gotten a bottle of Brut and the usual school-project crap. He and Irene had not exchanged gifts in years.

"Don't be ridiculous." Anne sat on the back of the sofa, smoking. "Snow is snow."

The day was new-dime bright, yet despite this snow fell—a roiling cloud of mote-sized flakes, dense enough to obscure the view of Central Park. They'd paid extra for this view. *Anne* had paid extra. Anne had made the arrangements. But she'd let slip that rooms with this view were more. How much more, David did not want to think about. This was his first time in New York. Everything he said and did felt to him like the words and deeds of a rube.

If anyone had accused him of this, he'd have been furious.

The plan was to do what lovers would do who meet in New York two days after Christmas and stay until New Year's Day. And so despite Anne's fever and whatever it was that was making David sullen, they went out walking the streets of Manhattan. They went to Macy's, Gimbel's, and Tiffany's. They saw the Christmas tree at 30 Rock. They made their way to the Village, where they saw Sonny Clark and Dexter Gordon at the Blue Note. There, in the dark and sipping martinis, they started holding hands and things began to feel better.

That night Anne was too sick to sleep.

She told David not to mind her, and she stayed in the outer room, watching TV. In the morning she ordered room service, to feed her fever. It was the first time David had seen a bagel. David told her it was A-OK with him if they just stayed in the room all day. Anne smiled and said, right, she bet it was. Instead, she sent him to a drugstore to get a bagful of over-the-counter whatnot, washed it down with coffee, gamely got showered and dressed, and insisted they go as planned to Radio City (the Rockettes, a matinee of *Lawrence of Arabia*). Afterward they ordered cured-meat sandwiches from abusive waiters in a delicatessen.

She kept getting sicker. David asked her what she was trying to prove and she said nothing. Again that night they slept apart. In the morning Anne said that she'd gotten a surprising amount of sleep, slumped in that chair. She felt slightly better. They had lunch and dinner reservations at the kind of restaurants you read about in books (Anne had been to all of these before), plus tickets to *A Thousand Clowns*.

She spent the night coughing and sneezing. She wouldn't allow for the possibility that maybe she had pneumonia. Just a bug. David stayed up with her and rubbed her shoulders and went out in the middle of the night for chicken soup and hot tea with honey and lemon, which, miraculously, he had no trouble finding. In the middle of the night. New York, New York.

She spent a day in bed, moaning and refusing to see a doctor and chugging Vicks products and telling David that she'd be fine and to stay away, she was no doubt contagious. Go see a movie or a play or a museum or the sights. He stayed in the room with her, watching television and, when she was not sleeping, talking mostly about work. David managed to come up with a few lame suggestions for how Anne could expand her role at the station, how possibly she could get her own issue-oriented show. She had all kinds of ideas about how David could position himself to run for mayor. David went out and bought an armful of out-of-town newspapers (the New

York papers were, coincidentally, on strike, too, but, unlike Cleveland, papers from other cities were plentiful). They'd never spent so much time watching television.

When Anne woke up the next day, she said she felt fine. She came out of the shower and did indeed look fine. Unspeakably fine. Fine in a way most men never get to see a woman look. Water droplets were magnificently involved. David was fully dressed for the day, and Anne was wet from the shower and stark naked and, standing on the towel in a room at the Plaza on the morning of New Year's Eve, they embraced, and held it, and held it, and did not say anything. As far as David was concerned, there was nothing that needed to be said.

Anne said that what she wanted to do was go to Central Park and go ice-skating. Yes, she was sure. Yes, fine, she was crazy. He ought at least to know *that* by now.

After, David tried to start a lover-playful snowball fight. The snow, he remained convinced, was different.

They saw *Who's Afraid of Virginia Woolf?* and went for an after-theater supper at the Algonquin. Reservations courtesy of Anne. David kept looking across the room, at the people seated at the famous round table. When he told Anne that he was surprised how small the table was, she kissed him and whispered that the table over there wasn't *the* round table; it was merely *a* round table. *The* round table was long gone. He had to laugh at himself.

When their champagne arrived, David asked Anne about, you know, the holidays. By which he meant of course Christmas. She said she didn't know what he meant.

"This situation," he said. "Christmas makes it . . . well, strange. Maybe awkward."

He and Anne had also agreed not to exchange gifts. Anne gave him a first edition of Sandburg's *Lincoln*. David gave Anne an expensive fountain pen and, although she did not know it yet, a Labrador retriever puppy. The dog would be delivered the day they got home. Her building does not allow dogs, and she will have to return it.

"I don't know what you mean," she said.

"Even this," David said, "away from it all, and it's been like we're brother and sister."

Anne flinched.

"What?" he said. This had been a fine vacation, at least given Anne's cold (it was actually asthmatic bronchitis). What's not to love about New York, New York, capital of the world, decked out in lights, snow, and money for Christmastime? But they'd made love a grand total of not once. They both seemed to love the other. But neither had said *I love you,* not even during sex. They were also people whose ability to cry was broken. "I'm not accusing you or us of anything. I'm just thinking out loud."

"More like being thoughtless out loud," she said.

"You were the one," he said, "who said this was something like ideal."

"Are you trying to, what? Feel sorry for poor me?" She laughed. It looked like real laughter. "Spinster other woman on Christmas day, pining for her married lover?"

"Keep it down," David said. "Please," he said. "Honey."

Anne rolled her eyes.

David tried to laugh himself. It wouldn't have convinced a deaf person. She wasn't the other woman anyway. He did not live with Irene. Irene seemed fine with this. It was only for the kids and for political reasons that the situation with him and Anne developed the way it did.

"You look like a million bucks," he finally said, because he had to say something. When a person is at a loss for words, he should say something true. She had on a black dress, slit high and low-cut. Pearls. Her hair was freshly dyed black and in a Cleopatra cut. "I mean, I apologize for the cliché." And the reference to money. "But you look just amazing."

"I never said this was ideal."

"You did," he said. "You said you didn't want to get married. You said that under the circumstances, your career and everything, that this, you know, arrangement, that it was what fit into the space you had in your life for, you know."

"No," she said. "I *don't* know."

"Romance," he said. "Men."

She lit a cigarette. It triggered a coughing fit. Finally, she got her wind back. "Don't put words in my mouth," she said. "I said most of what you said I said, but I never called this ideal." She pressed her index finger hard against his shoulder, right where the tattoo of Irene's name was. She kept pressing until he could not possibly mistake what the gesture meant. "This," she said, "is *not* ideal."

David took a long swig of champagne. Then he took a deep breath and told Anne she was right and he was sorry.

"Aren't you going to ask me," she said, "what *would* be ideal?"

"No."

"Good," she said. "You're learning."

"Happy New Year," he said, though it was only eleven.

"You're educable," she said. "Nice quality, in a man."

He raised his glass, to toast whatever. They made short work of that bottle and ordered another, and before you could say *Guy Lombardo* it was 1963.

∞

SIT DOWN, SAID *Art Modell, I've made a decision. You're fired.*

Paul Brown sat.

As both coach and as general manager, said Modell.

I have eight more years on my contract, Brown said.

Modell shrugged. We'll pay you. This team can never be mine as long as you're here. People think of the Cleveland Browns, they think of you. I come to the stadium, I feel like it's your house I'm coming to. From now on, there's only going to be one dominant image. Me.

Brown sat there silently for a long time, then said he would like to talk to his wife and then perhaps to his lawyer. That was all he said. He got up, left the room, said nothing to anyone, took the back stairs down Tower B, got in his car, sat there silently for about an hour, staring out at the frozen lake, then turned the key and drove straight home.

Modell held a press conference. It seemed less like the firing of a coach than the launching of a magazine. He'd hired strike-idled Cleveland sportswriters to prepare a magazine on the firing, to be given away at newsstands throughout the Cuyahoga River basin. Modell referred to it as if it were a reference book, as if it had not been written to his specifications.

The magazine spoke of Paul Brown's uncreative offense. It savaged the team's recent decisions: draft choices and trades and other roster moves. It accused Brown of inattention to financial mismanagement within the team's ticket office. It cited thirteen players (none of them named) who said they would not return to Cleveland in 1963 if Paul Brown remained as coach.

The magazine also contained a statement from and several photographs of that dominant image, Art Modell. The statement complained that Brown had not consulted him in making important player decisions. It thanked Brown for his years of service in making the Cleveland Browns the New York Yankees of football.

Modell, at the press conference, elaborated on his statement. There were no Cleveland newspapers to carry these comments. The TV and radio stations hit the high points. For those who didn't know to go to the newsstand—by now, people were out of the habit—the rest of the story was lost to history.

As for Ernie Davis: he got better. His condition was arrested. Almost no one knew about it. There were no newspapers to report a good-news off-season story like this. There was radio and there was TV, but no Cleveland station kept a reporter constantly on the Browns beat. Plus, this was only a playing out of the story the way it had been reported, when last it was reported. The official story was that Davis would be ready to start next season.

The Browns had a basketball team that, beginning in January, played games for charity and to give the players a way to stay in shape. Davis was that team's best player. (Jim Brown did not play on that team. As it began its season, Jim Brown was having dinner with civil rights leaders and politely expressing qualms about the integrationist approach.) These games were not covered on radio or TV. None were played, as they would be now, against teams of TV personalities. No record exists of anyone reporting these games. No stats were kept. There remains throughout Cleveland and among Cleveland expats exiled in Florida a living few who saw these games in person—as player, ref, ticket taker, or fan. The story that gets told is how unstoppable Davis was. He wasn't flashy. He kept his head down most of the time, a model of humility and, in the eyes of many, a credit to his race. But make no mistake, the man could play.

಄

ANNE NOSED HER Avanti through the falling snow and snowbank-canyon streets of Independence, a neighborhood of essentially identical houses—distinguished under all that snow by fake shutters or the lack thereof and by who had or hadn't removed all their Christmas decorations—until she found the right street and saw David's ancient Jeepster, whopper-jawed in an unshoveled drive, and a big sign on the mailbox that read THE ZIELINSKY'S.

She kept going. The Zielinskys still had a wreath on the door, and the snow-covered hummock on the roof was probably some vulgar plastic Santa. Its cord was frozen into a huge icicle under the eaves. The first week of March, in the middle of David's kids' spring vacation, and Santa was still on the roof. Why? Because the man of the house wasn't in that house, that's why. Anne went around the block and pulled her car to the curb, far enough up the newly plowed street that she doubted she'd be seen. She lit a cigarette and turned up the radio. Bartók.

She caught a glimpse of herself in the rearview. Look at me: an other woman, with too much makeup and expensively dyed hair, hair a *man* told me to dye, driving around in the middle of a snowstorm on a day that, if there were a God, might have been one of the best days of my life, and yet here I am, arrived at a pointless destination, motivated by I don't know what, listening to longhair music the younger me would have mocked, hiding in my childishly sporty car, smoking cheap lipstick-smudged cigarettes in the Land of the Misused Apostrophe.

All to spy on my lover, for no reason, while he's in there doing what? Celebrating his daughter's seventh birthday.

Perfect. This, she thought, is why I hate women.

Her birthday wish for Elizabeth: a world in which things for women were different.

Anne could not have been any more specific than that.

A black Cadillac pulled up in front of David's house. His father got out, opened the trunk, and took out a stack of presents bigger and wider than his torso. This, in addition to a magnificent red bicycle. He'd pulled the car too close to the snowbank; Tina climbed across the seat and climbed out the driver's side.

Anne put the Avanti in reverse. David would be coming out to help.

Sure enough, the door opened.

Anne kept going backward.

When she looked up, though, it was not David who'd come outside, but *her*. The plump childbearing wife. Irene. She had a name, the wife. Irene.

And, worse, the girl. Elizabeth. Lizard. Shuffling down the snowy drive-way in a party dress and her father's galoshes, hatless and laughing, her long blond hair whipping in the snowy wind. When she saw the bicycle, she shrieked so loud Anne—up the block and in her car and playing Bartók to the point of distortion—could hear it as well as if the girl were sitting next to her. Elizabeth hugged her grandfather and as Anne backed the car up, the adults around Elizabeth watched and shouted (noiselessly, from Anne's vantage point) and the girl put the bicycle down in the snowy driveway and tried to ride it, and managed to make it out into the street. Her hair kept whipping in the wind, and nothing bad happened. She was a happy, strong, and daring girl, undaunted by the cruelty of a wintertime birthday.

Anne kept going backward, but she was sure Irene had seen her.

Especially when Anne rammed the Avanti into a snowbank.

Anne tried to extricate her car, but panic just made things worse. Her tires spun and dug ruts. Down the street, the girl got off her bicycle and took a bow, and her father put his arm around her, and the Zielinsky family bus-ied itself carrying big festive boxes into the house.

Anne swore and pounded the steering wheel and blamed herself for everything. She couldn't tell if David had seen her.

A city snowplow stopped to help. The driver recognized Anne from TV and asked for her autograph. She'd been asked for her autograph often enough that this did not seem absurd. It was a function of sitting at the anchor desk. She got ten times the mail she'd ever received before, some from the professional letters-to-the-editor crowd, cast adrift by the strike, but most of it fan mail. Women praising her hair and makeup. Women writing in with hair and makeup tips. Mash notes. Old women writing in to fix her up with their lonely schoolteacher son. As rattled as she was, she did not hesitate when the driver handed her a piece of brown paper towel. She signed it. Under her name she wrote the call letters of the station.

She kept sneaking glances down the block to David's house. Everyone was inside.

Another plow came by, this one carrying a driver and the city's director of public works. The driver who'd gotten Anne unstuck had called them on the radio. They, too, wanted autographs. Again Anne complied, this time with pages torn from her reporter's notebook.

As she and all the city workers prepared to go their separate ways, the director of public works, a cute little old man with a round face, shouted out for Anne to wait. He jogged up to her window and motioned for Anne to crank it down.

"I almost forgot to ask," he said, grinning like a schoolboy. "What's Dorothy Fuldheim really like?"

Just then, a white Pontiac with David's aunt and uncle passed by. Anne resisted the urge to duck. "Just like what you'd think," Anne told the old man. "With Dorothy, what you see is what you get."

"I knew it!" he said, beaming, strutting back to the snowplow as if he'd just won a bet.

Betty and Stan parked on the street and got out. They did not seem to be looking this way. They, too, seemed not to have noticed her. More than ten years ago she had spent a day with them. More than ten years ago she had been a threat to David's marriage to Irene. More than ten years, and where had Anne come in all that time? A long, long ways, and—just look around!—no place at all.

◯◯

ANNE HAD NO place to go until the City Club debate, two hours later, but she headed downtown anyway.

What had she expected, coming down there? Punishment? Some kind of a sign? This thing with David had worked out because of what it was *not:* a marriage, a public relationship, an arrangement in which he would expect her to cook or decorate his arm or his living room or even be at any given place at any given time. It fit her life and who she was trying to be and what she deemed important. That he was married, she'd told herself, limited things in ways she appreciated having them limited. If he *weren't* married, she'd told herself, it would be even worse: a rising-star politician involved with a rising-star reporter—the equivalent, in a small town like Cleveland, to young royalty. Too complicated, too ill-advised, too *silly*.

If only a person's heart, that spurting capricious thing, could be ordered around to do the things its head devised.

That wasn't it.

There were other people involved, whole lives and choices. There was, fusty though it was to consider, the simple matter of right and wrong. Though, in Anne's experience, this is never a simple matter. She wondered, as she drove, if she were only thinking about this because of John and his newfound religion. John had accepted a professorship at of all places John Carroll and, come this fall, would be around all the time. If there was one person whose disapproval she could not endure it was John. She hadn't even been able to *tell* John.

That wasn't it, either.

Anne had thought that what she was working herself up to do, to end, was finally a matter of escaping clichés that were otherwise inevitable. Things were workable now. But how could this whole thing *not* end in disaster? The ruinous item in the gossip column. The impossible legacy of a failed diaphragm. Or, most tiresome of all, the confrontation with the wronged wife, or with anyone who comes up to her unbidden and says, *We need to talk.*

Yet that wasn't it, either.

Anne feared she was not in love with David. She liked him and found him muscular, genuine, attentive, and smart. But she couldn't shake the anxiety that she loved David for what he represented. Wasn't the same true for him? Could he ever, really, get past the idea that she was a pretty girl who came from money and power? He told her how things really worked in Cleveland: how routine $100 bribes reduced charges, even murder, a degree or two; how golf dates and horse races accounted for how and when some trials ended; how conversations council members hold in private made actual meetings into mere theater; how, *forget* politics, it was this fellow Scalish who ran everything in Cleveland, except that he didn't sweat the details and even had the vision to let the Negroes keep most of the profits from numbers-running, which, fair's fair, they'd brought up here from the South. She'd played her role by telling him what Rio de Janeiro was like; how a trust fund works; how to order wine; what President Kennedy was like (she'd met him as Senator Kennedy and didn't know him well, but still—what a charmer!); how her father, in an attempt to keep the machine together, had backed as mayor a party loyalist (a raving bigot who happened also to be the brother of an editor at the *PD*) while Seltzer threw his support behind that populist lummox Lausche, and how that was what put Seltzer into power and in a roundabout way kept the Negroes out of the machine, which her father had been working to change and which Seltzer, shortsighted as he was short, didn't care about.

All of this was hopelessly entwined with the burlesque echo she and David were (and were too aware of being) of Tom O'Connor, working-class semi-ethnic Catholic Super Pol, and his wife, Sarah, acerbic and neurasthenic nicely dowried shoestring cousin to the Rockefellers.

Anne parked her car in a garage next to the City Club.

She banged her fists on the steering wheel. That wasn't it, either.

It was that girl, running down the driveway, seven years old and laughing, jumping onto a bicycle in the deep snow, and riding it, no matter what anyone said, and not falling down.

Life will make her fall down, of course. Happens to everybody. What makes a person into a person who matters is to have ideals, then to realize everything's tainted, then to grow up and reimpose your ideals upon the unjust and indifferent world. Thesis; antithesis; synthesis. Idealism; cynicism; hard-eyed optimism. Or, as Anne thought of it: The world is my oyster; the world is a big fat lie; the hell with you, I'll go on.

Seven years old is too young for any of this.

No seven-year-old should have to consider anything real. When Anne was seven, Steven was still alive (but already gone), and her family was still a family (but already gone). The war had started and too many real things were already in the chute. Anne can see that now. Seven was the end of her childhood.

Anne was not going to participate in giving that girl the slightest dose of premature reality.

That laughing hatless girl, whose father loved her, whose whole family was gathered in her honor, running down the driveway in a suburb south of a doomed city, her blond hair stringy and damp in the wind, happy on her birthday, jumping onto her new bicycle and riding it improbably well through the unshoveled snow.

ᕲᕰ

As SARAH O'CONNOR and her pilot sweetheart headed down the freshly plowed and salted runway at Kelley's Island, the first time the plane had left the island in two weeks, the first time since Christmas Sarah had left Ashcroft, Anne O'Connor found her seat at the City Club. Fifteen minutes to show time and already the place was full.

Louie Seltzer sat in his chair on the dais, legs crossed, as comfortable-looking as a man at his kitchen table waiting indulgently for his wife to finish getting ready for church. He wore a plain blue too-wide necktie, a worn but tailored suit, and a sanctimonious grin.

At the opposite side of the dais, the leader of the Newspaper Guild wore an off-the-rack, nice-enough suit, so obviously new that Anne kept looking it over for tags.

The cameras in back were not from Anne's station. This debate had originally been open to any station that wished to cover it. Things changed—as anyone familiar with news too good to be true, with a gift too fervently wanted, could have predicted.

Dorothy Fuldheim strode onstage. Onstage with the elfin Seltzer and gnomish Fuldheim, the Guild spokesman looked like a member of a doomed, inefficiently made species.

Anne rechecked: no, the cameras in back were, happily, not from Fuldheim's station, either. What she was doing onstage was anyone's guess. She was Dorothy Fuldheim, is what.

There had been a time—a whole week, in fact—when the word was, Anne O'Connor was the one tabbed to moderate this debate. She'd gotten Weintraub to back her, and she'd contacted old associates of her father's, people who, under lesser circumstances, she'd have been loath to milk. One day she'd gotten a phone call and it was a tentative yes. Anne had made the mistake of celebrating. She had taken David away for the weekend, to Detroit, to celebrate.

Speaking of Detroit, that's where Sarah O'Connor and her pilot were heading. She had cabin fever and knew a wonderful little Italian place downtown, near a small art gallery, where, later that year, she was supposed to have a small show. Her pilot sweetheart had the ways and means of getting her there. Who wouldn't want a beau who was a pilot?

Less than a week after that celebration, though, the job of moderating this debate had in fact gone to Dorothy Fuldheim. Anne called to see what had happened, but her call did not get returned, and then, for reasons never explained, Fuldheim, too, was dropped. The rumor was that it was because she was a woman, but Anne had also heard that this was a rumor Fuldheim initiated. All the more galling, since Anne suspected it was true. And Anne could not promulgate it, out of fear of being perceived as whiny.

They have us, Anne thought. *The system is so rigged it's ridiculous.*

Fuldheim came to the edge of the stage. Out of nowhere, two excessively handsome men appeared to help her down the steep stairs, assistance that Fuldheim both rebuffed and clearly relished having the coquettish chance to rebuff. You had to hand it to her: this was a woman who, homely and Jewish as she was, would have been the star of any deb class.

The moderator was a former newspaperman, newly hired as the anchorman of the third station in town (of which Anne's father had been part-owner). He was an accomplished, courtly man. Anne found him even-handed, smart, and worthy. She wished him dead.

As the moderator reached the stage, Anne saw that David, too, had finally arrived, breathless, his tie crooked, hair still wet with snow. Despite herself, she smiled. This was what Cleveland wanted in a politician: a flummoxed man with a crooked tie and wetly mussed hair, lurching into a room late because of his daughter's seventh birthday party. He took his place, a seat reserved for him in a thicket of Teamsters functionaries and councilmen. When his eyes met Anne's, she turned away.

The plane's wings iced immediately. The pilot was good and familiar with this, and so did not panic, did not even tell Sarah O'Connor exactly what was happening, just that they would need to turn around. By this time the Sandusky airport was the closest place to land.

The moderator welcomed everyone, then, cued by his floor director that they were having snowstorm-triggered signal problems, apologized, stalled, and welcomed everyone all over again.

Seltzer began by saying how surprised and sad he was that no one from the *Plain Dealer* had chosen to participate. He was of course neither. The *PD* people wouldn't talk to anyone with a microphone in his hand. Or her hand. The *PD* people wouldn't even let you inside the office outside the office where they worked. Louie Seltzer practically stood on the street and flagged down passing news vans.

Every time Anne glanced over at David, he was staring at her. She considered leaving. She considered frowning at him. She considered going over to him and slapping him. What she did was, she took out a reporter's notebook and a chewed pen and did her job. The room was filled with newspapermen with nothing to do and nowhere to go, there out of anxious curiosity and who, out of habit, filled their notebooks with quotes. Though it must be said that some of the more debt-ridden among them executed profane doodles and libelous running commentary. The closer your livelihood was to this, the more you were likely to see this as a confrontation in which, like most stalemates, everyone is wrong. Anne felt these men and few (very few) women scribbling along with her. These people looked down on TV reporters, but she, at least, had a place to file her stories. She, at least, had an audience that would listen to her.

Seltzer looked right into the camera. He looked like a kid in the school play who'd been told by his drama-teacher director to look sincere. "How ironical," he said, "that the other paper in town, run by the Ivy League sons of wealthy men, a place openly hostile in its business practices and on its pages to organized labor in all its many forms, is not only not here but also claims that they have been dragged into this matter, this tragic and expensive strike. They wouldn't let a union in there except over their dead bodies. And yet me, a friend to the workingman all his life, who went to work full-time at the age of twelve and came up himself from the humblest ranks of the humblest workingmen, *me,* who helped sign up fellas at my own paper for the union in order to help you fellas out, how ironical that *me* of all people finds himself here, in this situation, both run afoul of what the fat cats in Washington call the Taft-Hartley Bill and at the same time the target of what the men on the picket lines, and there are women on the picket lines, what you good people want. How strange that is."

His face came to life, as if his drama teacher had said, *Smile!*

"Once this is all settled, we'll see who really has the interests of the workingman at heart," Seltzer said. "Me, or my distinguished employee here, who, from what I hear, in conversations I have had, not with the union bigwigs, but with the people, *my* people, is out of touch with what the workingman—or woman!—wants." He turned away from the camera and toward the chapter president of the Guild, a master pressman in Seltzer's employ. "I can't promise," he said, "that when all this is over, that's not something you'll have to answer for."

At the time Anne hardly understood what he meant. No one in the audience booed or even said *ooh.* No one watching on TV could have guessed that here was a turning point in the history of the city. Macbeth was a goner long before Burnham Wood actually stormed his castle.

The chapter president of the Guild did not rise to the bait. He took out some index cards. He explained that all the union wanted was a $10 a week raise and a union shop.

Anne wrote the men's arguments down but was too distracted to analyze thing one. Plus, she was good enough at her job to know that the arguments were unlikely to matter much. As things progressed, it became increasingly clear that Louie Seltzer was playing the role of pal. One thing she'd learned from David, who'd learned it from his father, was that no one who proclaims himself a friend to the workingman really is. He kept conducting himself as if the sheer power of personality sparking off lightbulb-headed Mr. Cleveland would be enough to set things right. He kept making jokes about how the Guild president would be in the doghouse with both his constituents as well as LBS himself for ignoring the truth—that LBS is a little guy fighting for the interests of little guys. The enemy here consists of outside agitators who don't understand that this is Cleveland. What works in other places isn't necessarily what works here.

The pilot could not get clearance to land at the Sandusky airport. He appealed to the tower for them to reconsider; as he did, his voice did not betray him. Sarah O'Connor had no idea this was anything more serious than an automobile making an annoying pinging noise. When the iced-winged airplane made its emergency landing, the rear wheels hit a patch of ice and spun out, and the plane flipped over. Its top smashed into the tarmac and the pilot was crushed, killed instantly. When the plane finally skidded to a stop, it burst into flame. But it was a polite and decorous flame, one which began not with an explosion but rather with a sound like a large huff of breath. As the rescue trucks bore down on the wreckage, they saw alongside it the figure of a tall thin woman in a man's leather jacket, shaking her head and looking pissed off. They asked her if she was OK, but all she would say, over and over, is that this just figures.

⌒

THE FACTS SAY 1962–63 was the snowiest and coldest winter ever to hit Cleveland.

Who knows if that's true?

Yes, the ground was covered with snow nonstop from November to March. Yes, one day in January it was a record nineteen below zero. Not a record just for that day: the coldest day on record in the history of the city of Cleveland.

Be that as it may, there have been and will be other brutal winters. In Cleveland this is to say: most of them. They all have their selling points. Things like forty-eight inches of snow in twenty-four hours (to cite 1996's grim claim to fame). Also, just as there was no way to know what the newspaper strike meant while it was going on, there's no way to assess a winter when you're in the middle of it. Function of time and perspective.

The superlative invites schoolmarmish kvetching from our friends the fact fetishists. The superlative invites not just argument but pain.

Look at it like this: when the ads calling Cleveland "The Best Location in the Nation" were first submitted to *Time* (a magazine once published in Cleveland), the powers-that-be asked for proof about that "best" claim. Facts were supplied; officials at *Time* verified same; the ad ran.

True story.

So: peace.

Let's just call it a hell of a winter, in a place that knows one when it sees one.

The strike ended when the *PD* let it be known they'd give everyone the $10 a week raise if they dropped the demand for a union shop. This, coupled with Mr. Cleveland's performance on TV, was the end of the matter, though of course in other ways it was the beginning of the end.

∽

ON A WARM day in April, the presses again rolled. Both papers were thick and practically all ads. The next day both contained a big section full of obituaries (among many others this included Bela Teodor "Bud" Hrudka, 66, retired auto plant foreman, felled by a sudden and manly heart attack while shoveling snow from his daughter's driveway next door; and Thomas Reese, father of Marilyn Reese Sheppard, a broken man living in a motel room, who wrote on the free motel stationery "I am sick of everything, goodbye" and took his own life with a shotgun). News stories that might have made the front page the day after they transpired—Sam Sheppard's in-prison engagement to a rich German woman who happened to be the sister-in-law of Joseph Goebbels—were buried in a news digest.

In other cities—even New York, despite the less severe but more widely publicized newspaper strike there—the people's reliance on television as their primary source of news was still a generation away. In the matter, Cleveland was a trendsetter. As with rock and roll, urban riots, and economic and psychological dependence on its professional sports franchises, Cleveland was ahead of the American curve.

IN THOSE DAYS *most of the Browns stayed in Cleveland year-round. Few made enough money from football to support a family, and their association with the team got them off-season jobs as salesmen for car dealerships, appliance stores, monument engravers, and liquor concerns. The thinking was that your average joe from Parma would get a kick buying, say, a Westinghouse washing machine from a member of the Cleveland Browns who'd squeezed himself into an uncomfortable suit and, for only the price of, say, a Westinghouse washing machine would sit down with average joes from Parma and talk football.*

In this endeavor as well, Ernie Davis was one of the team. One of the fellas. As he continued to work out and to come back from the condition he and his doctors had with all due diligence arrested, Davis held down a nine-to-five as a salesman for a beverage distributorship. Among his duties was to go to grocers in Negro neighborhoods and get them to devote more shelf space to Cotton Club pop, to stock varieties other than the famous Cotton Club "Less Sweet" Ginger Ale. Throughout greater Cleveland and also exiled to Florida, there exist living people on whom Davis made sales calls. What they'll tell you, again and again, is this: Ernie Davis was a nice young man who could flat-out sell.

What they will also tell you is that he was the picture of health.

One Thursday in May—with the strike less than a month settled and the sun shining and the Indians playing (and en route to losing) a day game at the stadium—Ernie Davis, head down, quietly checked himself into a Cleveland hospital. Didn't even tell his mother. Saturday, he died. It was in all the newspapers.

—— 17 ——

THE SIX NEW identical houses, beige brick on the bottom floor, brown siding on the top, alarmingly cubic, sat on a bluff that did not quite overlook the river. Once, maybe it did. Now, any river view that might naturally exist was blocked by the valley of steel mills, their black towers topped by pillars of blue flame, housed in buildings that could contain whole hockey arenas, buildings clad with a gnarled, functional lattice of beams. Beams that beget more beams. American steel. These mills still ran day and night. Their future owners were still young Japanese men, into whose wildest dreams the Cuyahoga River was yet to flow.

On the last Friday of the summer of 1963, nine weeks before election day, David and Irene Zielinsky and their three handsome children moved into one of those houses, the fourth of the six to be occupied. They led the moving van there in the Buick Roadmaster they'd inherited when Irene's father died. David drove. He wore green sunglasses, chinos, and a white dress shirt with rolled-up sleeves. Beside him on the front seat were Irene, who had lately starved herself into something close to slenderness, and the baby, Brad, who was two and not really a baby anymore, riding unrestrained on his mother's lap, eating Sugar Smacks from a plastic cup and singing endless repetitions of "Take Me Out to the Ballgame." In back, scrubbed clean, combed, and wearing the first of their new school clothes, were Lizard—seven and blond, bigger than her older brother and singing along with the baby—and Teddy, eight and mousy-haired and reading a comic book (Aquaman, his favorite, even though Teddy refused again this summer to get in the water during Red Cross swimming lessons). Underneath the children's feet was the family dog, Precious, a white poodle/yorkie mix, a porkie, heavily drugged so it would not barf in the car and ruin everything. What a picture they made!

Which was fortunate, since when they pulled into their new driveway, two TV crews were already there. Irene looked at David. He shook his head. The reporters were both men. Neither was even from the same station as Anne O'Connor.

David got out of the car. The movers, a crew of four warned to expect a scene just like this, backed the van into the driveway. Lizard carried the poor sedated dog and stood grinning and adorable by her father's side. Brad needed a diaper change. Teddy would not get out of the car until he had finished his Aquaman.

At the microphone David smiled and draped his arm around his wife and dog and said that this was his proudest moment *so far* as a member of the Cleveland City Council. He said that it was residential initiatives such as this that could save the city. He said he hoped it might spur the city's leaders to move their focus away from the subsidizing of unnecessary downtown office towers and onto the *neighborhoods*. The *people*. "We do not, after all, live to work," he said, blessed with the political gifts to sound sincere, which he was. "We work to live." That he could say this and not sound unctuous, any viewer could see, explains a lot about why David Zielinsky was a rising star at City Hall. He thanked the other members of council (not by name) who helped him spearhead this initiative. He hugged his daughter and catatonic dog.

The van and the Zielinskys had come straight here from the house where David mostly grew up, the house that had been Uncle Stan and Aunt Betty's. The house in Independence had been discreetly sold (along with Irene's parents'; Irene's mother had moved to Florida to be with her sister). The Zielinskys had all been living together in Old Brooklyn for weeks, and now were moving everything from there to here. Who was the wiser? Not the TV crews.

They thanked David and asked if they could stay and film for a while. David said of course. He pitched in and worked with the movers. The movers were union and expensive, though of course this was not costing David a dime.

Throughout all of this, the boy stayed in the car. When the camera crews left, he asked if it would be OK if he slept at Grammie and Stan's tonight. It was not OK, and so Teddy asked if he could sleep out in the yard in a pup tent, but Irene said, no, the yard has too much straw in it still. Lizard called Teddy a big fat dumbhead, and he took a swing at her. One thing led to another, and as the boy's sister arranged her room and his parents changed clothes and got busy setting up the kitchen and TV room, Teddy was allowed to find his tent and pitch it in the bare scalped hard-clay dirt of what would someday be a flower bed.

But at eleven they all convened to watch their house and themselves on television. Even the baby. They sat in an otherwise dark room, and when the glowingly favorable story was finished, the best thing imaginable happened.

The camera swung to Dorothy Fuldheim.

She did a commentary on what a marvelous thing this was, a politician living not just with his decisions but inside them. "If this is what we can expect from this new generation of leaders, inspired to public service by our young and inspirational president," she said, "the New Frontier is destined to be quite the desirable neighborhood." She flashed that wry, lopsided grin. "Perhaps even as desirable as the one created and now occupied by Councilman Zielinsky."

The phone started ringing immediately. Precinct workers. People he'd gone to school with. A guy he'd worked with at the docks, what—eleven years ago? Other council members, more than one of whom mentioned that it might be time for a new council chair, one from the West Side (two and two were not explicitly tallied). David would put the phone on its cradle, and before he could let go, it would ring. Brad and Lizard went to bed. Teddy returned to his tent. As Irene tucked them in, David talked on the kitchen phone and rifled through boxes, looking for candles. When Aunt Betty got through, she was so proud she was crying. "Dorothy Fuldheim!" she said. "Imagine! And all for leaving that run-down old house of ours!"

A box marked, in Irene's perfect handwriting, *Miscellaneous* contained cookbooks and scorecards from Indians games, including the one from this summer he'd framed because Held, Ramos, Francona, and Brown hit four consecutive homers—a record. And in a box filled mostly with half-empty liquor bottles was a sight that made David's heart slam against his rib cage. A dusty bottle of wine.

"It was a *great* house," David said.

It was, he was sure, the same kind he'd drunk at Middle Bass Island, eleven years ago, that day with Anne O'Connor.

"It *was* a great house," said Aunt Betty. "But times change." She and Stan had moved again, this time to a penthouse suite in a high-rise on the Lakewood shore. "I wish your mother would have been here to see this, you know?"

"I know," David said.

"I'm just glad *I* lived to see it," said Aunt Betty. "Dorothy Fuldheim!"

He picked up the bottle. The vintage was 1951. Where did this come from? He'd *drunk* this bottle. David resisted the urge to throw the wine away. He closed the box. In the next one he found a cache of twenty-some candles.

Betty asked what Irene thought about the bracelet (paid for by money he'd borrowed from his father, but that Irene had gone with David to pick out). David hadn't, he said, had the chance to give it to her. He asked after his uncle, back from the hospital after hip surgery, and told his aunt, yes, they'd be there for Sunday dinner. After that he left the phone off the hook.

It was midnight. No need to make well-wishers think he's overeager. Besides, Irene should be done with the kids any sec.

He spread the candles around the kitchen and lit them all. When had they acquired so many candles?

David went outside and got the champagne from under the seat of the Buick. He went into the crawl space and got the diamond bracelet and the flowers from the Styrofoam cooler where he'd hidden them yesterday, and he waited in the kitchen, petting the still-docile dog and waiting for his wife. The bulge the jewelry box made in his sweat-damp chinos felt like a tumor.

He knew the move here would work, he just *knew* it, but, Christ, a coup like this can't be anything else but a sign. Can it? It can't. Fate, baby. Ride that wild pony!

This wait stretched on. He presumed it was because of one of the kids, but when he went to check, they were all asleep. His heart raced.

When he finally found Irene, she was sitting on a battered chest of drawers in a corner of the box-choked garage, crying so softly he at first mistook it for laughter.

Being a man, he asked and asked what was the problem and was she OK? His heart would not slow down. She did not say anything. When it entered his thick skull to hug her, she returned the embrace.

"I have a surprise for you," he said, "in the kitchen."

She looked at him and shook her head. He wiped a tear from her cheek. "What?" he said.

"From you," she said, "no surprises. Ever."

"I love you," he said.

"I mean it," she said.

"I know you do." His fingertips traced the perimeter of the concealed jewelry box, like an itch he couldn't not scratch. "We're going to be fine," he said.

She looked at him.

"You know me better than anyone," he said.

"This is not really about you," she said. "You know that, don't you?"

"Sure," he said. Lied. "Of course."

He pulled her close to him, and she was the one who leaned in for a kiss. It was a cold night for late August, and the kiss was as crisp and juicy as a winesap apple.

He smoothed her hair.

"Don't do that," she said.

"Why not?"

"OK," she said. "Do what you want."

"I want what you want."

She closed her eyes. "I love you, too," she said, and they kissed again. "My dad..."

She teared up. She shook her head and waved David off.

"No," she said. "It's not..." She took a deep breath. "My dad used to tell the boys, there's nothing like an unthrown punch. It was advice for boys. You know?"

David put a hand lightly on her thigh. He kept his eyes on her eyes. If life had taught him nothing else, it's that when a woman stops crying and starts talking, shut up and keep your eyes on hers. But she kept not saying anything. He wasn't good at the shutting-up part. "What," he finally said, "was that supposed to mean?"

"I think he picked it up in the service." What she took it to mean, she said, was that there was strength in having power that you displayed but did not use. Bud Hrudka had been a mustang CPO in the navy and was an intuitive Cold Warrior. "Advice for boys," she said. "Women know this in their bones."

"I have no idea what you're talking about," he said.

She nodded. "Exactly," she said. At last, she brightened. "You think our...whatever you want to call it. Moving here. Our reconciliation. You think it has to do with you."

"With *us*," he said. He thought that was the right answer.

"Right." She wiped her eyes. "*Us*. Which contains *you*. As long as it has to do with you."

"I don't understand," he said.

"No kidding." She was grinning now, so incongruously it made David a little afraid. "Part of it," she said, "but not all of it, is that I know how far back it went."

He was afraid to ask what she meant, certain he knew.

"Long before she did that story on you," she said.

"Can we not talk about this?" he said. *Betty told her.* Of course. He'd hate to see the *thrown* punch.

"Even if we did talk about it," she said, "you wouldn't..." Her voice trailed off. "You couldn't possibly..."

He knew as soon as he gave her the bracelet she'd start crying again, but maybe that was the way to go. And so he produced it. He popped the box open. "I want you to know I'd marry you all over again," he said. It was the line he'd rehearsed.

She did not cry. Her eyes got big, but she did not cry. She took the bracelet from the box and held it up to refract the light from the naked light-bulb in the garage rafters.

Suddenly, from out in the dark came the sound of footfalls slapping on the new driveway concrete, and a shrill voice screamed: *"Fire!"*

In tandem, Irene and David jumped off the dresser.

Teddy stood in the mouth of the garage. *"Fire!"* he shouted. *"Fire! Fire!"*

Irene ran to scoop Teddy up, who was shrieking and saying it was *everywhere!* David sprinted into the house, shouting for Lizard and Bradley to wake up, and into the kitchen, cursing all the way, thinking, Shit, *it just figures, on a day where everything was going so great, it just figures,* shit.

But the candles were all fine.

He ran through his new house, sniffing and hurdling boxes. Nothing. Lizard and the baby were both sound sleepers and did not wake up.

Teddy was, it turned out, half asleep. There was no fire.

As near as David and Irene could figure, he'd either seen the candles flickering in the kitchen window or was talking about the blue-orange flames in the valley, shooting up from the remote mills. The boy was shaking all over, and Irene told him of course he could sleep in their bed, poor thing, and that's how they spent the first night in that house, with Teddy thrashing between them. Irene wore the bracelet to bed. At some unholy hour shortly before dawn, Teddy woke them both up, again. Irene smoothed Teddy's sweat-damp hair. David touched her cheek.

"I've never been happier," David said, because after everything that day and night, it was, on balance, how he felt. "I mean that."

"I'm glad," Irene said.

She kissed her fingertips and applied them to David's dry lips.

Shortly, she was back asleep. He watched her newly thin torso rise and fall. He watched those ample breasts that she complained about as too large, as nuisances, but which most men would die to have access to. He watched as, despite the cold night, a thin and sexy line of sweat formed on her upper lip. He watched the bracelet on her strong wrist sparkle in the glow of the security light outside their window. He watched as her long, luscious right foot kicked out from under the covers. He couldn't remember not knowing her. Irene. Was there ever a time when, deep down, he had not known that this was the girl for him?

Teddy pulled into a fetal ball and muttered something in his sleep. Something that sounded like *Ghoulardi*. Or maybe *glad*. Glad. What's that supposed to mean, glad?

I'm thinking too much, David thought. *Glad is good.*

Dorothy Fuldheim, he thought.

No one else had, as of yet, declared for the council race in this, David's ward.

Might be time for a new council chair, he thought, *from the West Side.*

Remember this day, he thought. *Fire,* he thought, and smiled. He stroked his son's short curly hair. *A day,* he thought, *for the memoirs.*

He thought about the part of this day that he'd leave out of the memoirs. That kept him awake for a while. That kept him awake for what seemed like forever. He started to count not sheep but his ample blessings. Things were not perfect. But things were working out. Who, he thought, has more things going their way than I do?

Swiftly, David made it back to sleep, besotted with love for the world.

As he did, she strode into the intersection between awareness and dreams, and took her place under the grape arbor that his father set on fire the day after she left, dressed in dungarees and a red-checked shirt, picking grapes and rehearsing the national anthem. She was supposed to sing it before a boxing match someplace. She turned to him, her blond hair quivering in a light breeze, her broad face free of makeup, her cheekbones gleaming in the grape-leaf dappled summer sun, and in short pants he toddled toward her, a kind of running, his arms out, scared or injured by something long forgotten. Her face fell at his fear, and she held out her arms to him, eager to scoop him up and whisper something magical, something sane, something that would help. He was, he thought, bleeding. He was, he thought, not two but his age now. Whatever that was. He had no idea. In what may have been sleep, at what may have been memory (again, he had no idea), David Zielinsky murmured a single word. *Mother.*

— 18 —

WHEN ANNE ARRIVED at the faculty dining room at John Carroll, a startlingly young boy at the maître d's podium recognized her from TV, greeted her by name, took her coat, and handed her a piece of paper. For a split second Anne thought it was something she was supposed to autograph, but it was pink, a phone message. Ibby had called to cancel. One of her kids had a fever and had to stay home from school. Patrick wouldn't even admit there *was* a problem and so was certainly not going to come to lunch in her stead. Anne was shown to a table by the window. *When* did *college boys start to look this young?*

It was a sunny day. Still, outside, snow flurried. Not yet Thanksgiving, and snow.

Moments later John joined her.

"Ibby canceled."

John rolled his eyes. "Please." He liked Ibby. This was more about Patrick than Ibby.

"It was legitimate," Anne said. "One of the kids is sick."

She handed him the message. He read it, shaking his head, then balled it up and threw it at Anne.

"Hey!"

"Perfect," John said. "So here we are." He waved his hand. "The son 'who is not a marrying man,'" he said, making quotation marks with his fingers, "and 'Babe, the spinster daughter'"—more quotation marks—"at a luncheon to discuss what to do with our mother, when we both know we won't do a damned thing. Perfect. *Hel*lo, there. I'll have the club sandwich."

"If this keeps up, let's go skiing," Anne said. She lit a cigarette. She hadn't had a chance to size up the menu. The waiter asked if he should come back, but she said no. "Believe it or not, there's a place. Down in the valley. It opens this year, I'm not sure when. Maybe now."

"'Ski Cleveland!'" John said. More quotation marks. Somebody should slap him. "I heard." They had, as a family, gone skiing in both the Rockies and the Alps. Naturally, Steven had been the best skier. Patrick and their father were pathetic. John, Anne, and their mother were all good, but not in Steven's class. "Not interested."

"Then let's go sledding," Anne said.

The waiter tapped his order pad with a pencil.

"Sledding?" John said.

"I can't tell you how long it's been since I've gone sledding." She handed her menu to the waiter. "I'll have the same."

Anne had grown up about a mile from John Carroll, but until her brother was hired here, she'd never set foot on this campus. She'd always thought of it as a decent-enough college. An all-boys school. John, the sort of man who always detested his job, called it Catholic High to Grade 16. He was an English professor, but when the powers-that-be found out he'd played at Notre Dame, they reduced his teaching load so he'd have time to be an assistant coach. He accepted. That was his idea of a joke.

"It's not supposed to keep up," John said. "The snow."

"I know. I was just . . ." She took a cube from her ice water and tossed it at him. "I have to go to work anyway. When did college boys get so young?"

"Ba-a-a-be." John wagged a finger at her. "Look, but don't touch."

"I'm old," she said. She was twenty-seven.

"You're a baby."

"I *feel* old."

"You look great. Although that one," John said, "wouldn't be interested in you anyway." He arched an eyebrow. He could do it better than any cartoon character you ever saw.

"I thought you said—"

"I'm offended," John said. "And untenured." He pointed at her with a Hough Bakery Parker House roll. "Do you know how many kids who come here to play sports are afflicted by"—more quotation marks—"'the love that dares not speak its name'?"

"Stop that," Anne said.

"Most of them," John said. "Stop what?"

She demonstrated.

"Oh," he said.

"Most of them?" she said. "Come on."

He sat back in his chair and shrugged. "Lots of them. They're in love with Mother Mary and with the priest who first taught them to love Mary." He heaved a theatrical sigh. "And with the handsome and oblivious golden-haired tailback."

"That's not how it is at all," Anne said. "Look, I'm not the enemy here. You're terrible."

"I'm a very *good* man," he said. "I'm just a very bad wizard."

She didn't get it.

"*The Wizard of Oz*," he said.

Their food came. John bowed his head in prayer. This went on longer than Anne would have thought possible.

"Amen," she said, and together they crossed themselves.

They got all the way through lunch talking about this and that, nothing and everything, before Anne insisted they talk about their mother. "She's going to hurt herself. She can't, can't, *can't* spend another winter up there. She'll die, and I don't mean figuratively. *Die* die."

"Should we really have this conversation," John said, "without Patrick or Ibby? Who, after all, aced her out of her house and precipitated her descent from functioning madwoman to that which we see before us?" He again waved his hand. Another new pet gesture. The new toys were the quotes and this flourish thing. Anne imagined his students sitting there making tally marks in the margins of their notebooks. "Hmm?"

"Come on," Anne said. "That's crazy. Dad was the one who loved that house. That house had nothing to do with anything."

John had asked to live in the old studio where Anne had lived. Ibby said yes, but then Patrick said they needed it as a guest space. John was convinced it was because Patrick was afraid he'd turn their kids queer.

"Really," Anne said. "Don't you think we should do something?"

"I suppose," John said, "I could go up there, knock on the door, say, *Hello, mother!* and then pick her up and sling her over my shoulder and take her to a nuthouse."

"Not a nuthouse. But a hospital somewhere, don't you think?"

John softened. "I'm sorry," he said. He nodded.

Sarah O'Connor was drunk constantly and also taking who knows what concoction of pills. She'd run through so many maids and cooks, live-in help was out of the question. Right after the pilot died, she'd taken up with an out-of-work quarry worker John's age. Within the past year, she'd been brought in by the Kelley's Island police four times for sitting on the porch and firing pistols at god knows what, and would have been arrested if she hadn't been who she was and if, after the third time, she hadn't dumped the quarryman for the island's chief of police. She got on the phone late at night and tried to make threatening long-distance calls to J. Edgar Hoover. Just last week she went into Port Clinton and auditioned for a dinner theater production of *Oklahoma!* When the role went to a younger woman who did not sing as well, their mother wound up in the hospital for alcohol poisoning. *Dinner theater!* Sarah O'Connor wasn't the sort of woman who would even *attend* dinner theater.

"I talked to someone," Anne said, "at the Cleveland Clinic. If we . . ."

"Not Cleveland," John said. "Mayo. The last thing she'd—"

"Fine. Mayo. Doesn't matter. Point is, that to get her committed somewhere we need a court order. We go to probate court and say she's a danger to herself and others. That's the magic term. Then we get a judgment, and she goes someplace where she can get help."

John's expression was blank, his gaze level.

"Don't worry," Anne said. "When I talked to the man at the clinic, I made it sound like I was doing a story."

"How did you know what I was thinking?"

"Never play poker," Anne said.

"I'm good at poker."

"No one who says so is." This was, actually, something she'd heard Hoot Thagard say. Goofy as he was, Mr. Thagard could really play poker.

"You're the answer girl, aren't you?"

The snow stopped. It wasn't sticking. The sun still shone. Hatless book-toting boys in neckties and wool sport coats stayed obediently on the sidewalks. Across the quad a big black sculpture of someone's head glistened.

"I'm sorry," John said.

"For what?" Anne said.

"Thanks," he said. "OK. Problems: number one, how do you get a court order for a thing like this and keep it out of the newspapers?" He did the wave-dismissal thing. "Yes, yes, or off TV. I remember the days when *television news* was an oxymoron."

"You're *some* kind of moron," she said, "that's for sure."

He pursed his lips, as she knew he would.

"Number two," he said. "I already said. How to get Muhammad to the mountain?"

"Mother to Mayo?"

Again the wave motion. "Call it what you will. I'm not going to do it, and for damn sure loverboy's not going to do it."

The Kelley's Island police chief.

"Oh. Him. No," Anne said. "It wouldn't be him. The county sheriff would do it. As for number one," she said, "don't be naive."

"Naive?" He took his napkin and fanned himself, like a belle. "*Moi?*"

Anne frowned.

"Fine," he said. "Fine. So, Miss Lois Lane. Miss Edwina R. Murrow. Whichever." Again, the wave.

"Stop that, too."

"Stop what?"

"That." She mimicked him.

"Stop *that*," he said, pointing to her cigarette. "In all your reporting, did you ask about the going rate for bribing the constabulary? Hmm? Or was the fine art of the bribe something you picked up from Gatsby?"

She got up so fast her chair fell to the floor. John grabbed her by the wrist and apologized and asked her to stay, begged her to stay. He picked up the chair. She sat down. He apologized again. He said it was hard for him. He wasn't feeling himself. She made a bawdy crack about that. Then everything was jake.

That was John: serve and volley, thrust and parry, offend and apologize.

"A *very* bad wizard," John said. "So, fine. What's the next step?" He signaled for the waiter. "All this talk of her drinking makes me want a drink."

"We should talk to Patrick and Ibby first," she said, meaning Ibby, "but there's a man at Dad's firm who could handle it." Meaning Stan Lychak. "With discretion, I'm sure."

"Of course you're sure. It must be nice to be so sure."

"It is," she said. She took a deep breath and tried not to say anything.

The waiter came by. John did not order a drink. The boy gave him the check and John signed for it. "Your money's no good here, Babe," he said. "You have to have an account."

The waiter took the signed check but kept standing there.

John looked up at him. "May I help you?"

"I was kind of wondering . . . ," the boy said, with a crooked and mortified grin.

John was right! Good lord. No one says *I was wondering* who does not want a date.

"You want my sister's autograph," John said. "Don't you?"

"I do!" The boy's wide, pimply face was awash in relief. He whipped out an order pad. "We watch you every night, ma'am. You have lots of fans on campus, let me tell you."

She's not even *on* every night.

"The university only hired me," John said, "to get to you."

"I want to be on TV, too!" The boy was blushing so badly it looked medically dangerous.

"These days," John said, "who doesn't?"

[393]

Anne looked down at the boy's gravy-stained order pad. *It's not about being on TV; it's about THE STORY.* That's what she wanted to write. Instead, she asked the boy his name, wrote it, wrote *w/ all good hopes*, signed her name, and added the station's call letters.

"I hear you're a great teacher, Professor O'Connor," the boy said. "I hear you played for Notre Dame."

"Ah, the non sequitur," John said. "Take my class and—"

"I know what that means already," said the boy. When did they all get so young *and* so insolent? "Thanks, Miss O'Connor. Thanks for the encouragement."

That, too, seemed said with an edge.

On their way out, they walked through a hall lined on one side with photos of Jesuit martyrs and on the other with trophy cases and glossies of uniformed posing athletes.

"Get a load of this." John pointed at one of the athletes. "His father."

"Whose father?" Anne said.

"Don't play stupid," John said. "You're not equipped for it."

He took her by the arm. With his other hand he rapped a knuckle against the glass of a photo of a leather-helmeted Michael Zielinsky. He looked nothing at all like his tall, lean, long-fingered, and pretty son. "Gatsby's father. He went here. Something of a legend, it would seem."

During the breakup (or, to be precise, right after it), Ibby had told him about David. John steadfastly claimed to have known all along, which was impossible. He only wanted to save face. His, for not knowing, and Anne's, for not telling him. Everyone in the family showed flashes of the political gifts Boss Tom embodied. No one could manage more than flashes, though, with the mythologized exception of Steven.

"Gatsby is ancient history," Anne said. She'd never met David's father. She'd seen pictures, but none this old. "Can you believe they ever wore helmets like that?"

"That's not what I meant," John said.

"Don't play stupid," she said. "Even though you *are* equipped."

"Har de har har." He turned away from her and kept walking. He'd always wanted it both ways. He enjoyed it that people liked him for having played ball, but he hated it that anyone would think he was a dumb jock. Faggot jokes didn't faze him, but call him stupid and he saw red. "I saw where Gatsby won in a landslide."

"He was unopposed," Anne said.

"Still," John said.

John walked her to the visitors' parking, and they hugged good-bye and resolved that by the end of next week at the very, very, very latest, this situation will have been resolved. Anne said she would talk to Patrick, meaning Ibby, and John said he would pray about all this, not that he hadn't been, and said that Anne might try it, too, and she asked what made him think she hadn't been, and John made the wave motion and Anne got in and drove away. As she did, she caught sight in her rearview mirror of two students, a boy with a red crew cut and a boy with a blond crew cut, standing on the front steps of the library, hugging each other and, it would seem, weeping. Yes, definitely. Holding each other and weeping, on the steps of the university library. The boys held the embrace and held it, and when Anne turned the corner, the last glimpse she had of them they were still holding it.

She shook her head. Could it be that John wasn't kidding about his students?

She drove to her old house with the radio off. She pulled up not to the garage in back, where she'd always pulled up when she had lived here and, usually, even after, but rather in front, into the loop of the carriage drive. The snow flurries started up again, and now the sun fell behind a bank of clouds. This house theoretically looked exactly the same, especially in the front (in back, the gazebos had been leveled and the pool filled in, and Ibby had had a tennis court built). All that was different, Anne thought, was that most of the trees had been cut down. Dutch elm disease, and then a bug problem for which the pines close to the house were unfairly blamed. It was more than the trees, Anne thought. She pulled up directly in front of the front door. It was something more than what met the eye that had transformed that house, *this* house, *her* house, into the most familiar thing imaginable. Or, maybe not like that exactly. It was familiar, but grotesquely wrong and fake. Like a version of itself created on a motion picture soundstage. She turned off the engine and, impulsively, prayed the Lord's Prayer.

She finished. She got out of the car. Ibby stood framed in the doorway to the house, a baby on her hip, both of them sobbing.

Anne did not need to be told what was wrong. *Mother's dead*, Anne thought.

"What's wrong?" she asked.

"Oh, honey. Oh my god," Ibby said. "You haven't heard. They did it. They shot the president."

── 19 ──

THE DAY PRESIDENT Kennedy was shot, David woke up to see the sun shining a bright winter-pink against the corrugated steel roofs of the mills, and to hear the man on the radio say the snow flurries that had a slight chance of falling had a vastly better chance of falling on the East Side. Viva la lake effect! Irene woke up and purred and reached down and grasped him, and grinned and said, "Good morning, lover," and nature took its sweet, athletic course. Marriage: hang in, champ, and these things happen. When they do, David thought (making love to his beautiful wife from behind, electrified when at the most-perfect moment she swiveled her head and looked back at him with that sweat-damp familiar face), *everything* seemed worth it. Everything was worth whatever it cost.

Afterward, the water in the shower ran hotter than usual. The kids woke up on their own and got ready on their own. David put an Ornette Coleman record on the hi-fi, and no one complained. He put on a suit, fresh from the cleaners, that he'd just lost enough weight to wear. Irene made eggs. Teddy and Lizard slid him their homework; both had performed flawlessly. They ate without being cajoled. They headed off to school with minimal fighting or complaining. Aunt Betty came by to watch the baby right on time, which, in recent months, had become an unreasonable thing to hope for. When Irene went off to work, she French-kissed him good-bye. And the wispy-bearded kid who was coming to buy the rusty yellow Jeepster showed up, nine sharp, cash in hand. Exact change. The Jeepster belched white smoke. The kid seemed not to care. He drove off with the window down, waving.

When David got to City Hall, Gorman Soltesz was waiting for him in the reception area. Pacing. "Did you hear the news?" Gorman said.

David said he had not.

"Have I got news for you," Gorman said. It was news too good for Gorman to sit in his office and wait. Two more votes were in David's column for council chair. Plus one of the Negroes from an East Side Negro ward had confessed to Gorman that he was so fed up with Jack Russell that he was about to commit to David, too.

The thirty-three newly elected council members would meet tomorrow night at the Hollenden Hotel. No one had anything close to a majority. By

Gorman's count, David was going in there with eight and maybe nine votes. Enough to be kingmaker. Possibly enough to be king.

David frowned and pretended he was irked at Gorman for airing this out in the reception area, then they went back to David's office and exchanged a manly hug, and then David spent the rest of the morning meeting with people from his ward and calling around to various people in the water department and to builders who'd been awarded or who wished to be awarded various city contracts and to people who knew people at different Teamsters' locals, matchmaking demand with supply, feeling as good about himself as an unbeatified man can.

He was having lunch at the new Theatrical with Uncle Stan. He left early. He wanted to swing by the Hollenden Hotel on the way.

He walked. The sky had grown dark, but no snow fell, and the city throbbed with thundering trucks and a panoply of yellow taxicabs. The sidewalks teemed with sensibly dressed Clevelanders. It was a short walk through a big city, eighth largest in the United States of America. Still, David saw people he knew—stevedores, law school classmates, cops, guys he'd played basketball with, people from the neighborhood, and people he knew who knew people. He waved and he shook hands (*grasp, squeeze hard, lay the left hand on top of theirs, make eye contact, smile*). About forty years ago Cleveland had a mayor named Fred Kohler. Irked that other people in city government were taking credit for civic improvements, he used city money and city workers to erect orange billboards all over town that said *I, FRED KOHLER, ALONE, AM MAYOR*. Kohler ordered that every park bench, every piece of playground equipment, every signpost, every fireplug be painted orange. *Cleveland is a great American city*, thought David Zielinsky. *I am of it, in it, leading it, loving it*. As he waved and braced himself against the wind, he chanted the cadence of that, matched his walk to it: *of it, in it, leading it, loving it*.

The doorman at the Hollenden Hotel greeted David by name. Turned out, he'd played football for Cathedral Latin and had played against David's father, who'd played for Ignatius. David shook hands with him, asked about his family.

"I still can't believe they're tearing this place down," David said.

"Price of progress," said the doorman. "To be honest with you, I won't miss it." The new owners of the property had given him a job at one of their apartment towers on the Gold Coast in Lakewood. "Better tips there, better weather, better clientele, better neighborhood. Better what-have-you."

David congratulated the doorman on his good fortune, then headed off to the lobby bar and ordered himself a Rob Roy. He thought better of it and ordered a Pride of Cleveland. As the bartender pulled the tap, David could practically hear his father's reproach. He could practically feel his father's breath on his neck as he yelled at David in a way that was supposed to be hale but was really just loud. *A man oughta know what he wants to drink and not second-guess himself like a fucking schoolgirl.*

David took the glass out of the bar and marched up the back marble staircase to the Tom L. Johnson Room. Men in sofa-fabric sport coats milled around the doorway. A hand-lettered sign welcomed members of the Ohio Mobile Home Dealers Association. It hadn't occurred to David that the room would not be empty. The men stared at the cold beer in his hand. He smiled wanly. He considered setting it down but did not. That'd call even more attention to it. Besides: fuck 'em. There wasn't a house trailer or a house trailer dealership within fifteen miles of David's ward. He ignored the men and he ignored the woman who asked him his name so she could find him his name tag, and he stood on the threshold of the Johnson Room and admired its smoke-smudged red-and-gold velvet wallpaper and its silver chandeliers. He imagined how the room would be set up tomorrow night: several rectangular tables made into one big rectangle. Mums, coffee cups, and placards, with them all seated around it. Thirty-three chairs and no staff.

The oil painting of Tom Johnson, the progressive mayor who made Cleveland great, was a good ten feet tall. You couldn't help but notice that it was flaking badly at the bottom. You had to wonder what would become of that painting.

⟳

THE NEW THEATRICAL was not the old Theatrical, which had burned down and been rebuilt on the same site. It was an ugly-functional box of a building. The north side of Short Vincent Street had been demolished to make room for a bank building, a project that—for complicated reasons and despite the boarded-up storefronts the bank tower would replace—David had voted against. Inside the new Theatrical, a person who didn't know better might assume the glossies on the wall were from the old days. Those photos had been destroyed, of course; these had been bought at flea markets and estate sales. Some of the autographs were no doubt forged. Still, it was the Theatrical. There were pickled eggs and huge sandwiches, and David and his uncle spent the last hour they would spend together laughing and talking about the happy manly nonsense of sports and automobiles and music.

Stan told David he should have sold the Jeepster ages ago, and David said he couldn't believe Stan would feel that way, and Stan shook his big bald rueful head and told David to live in the present.

All through lunch, David kept trying to work up the nerve to wish Stan a happy birthday. He didn't manage it until they paid (David had called ahead and rigged it so the tab would be his) and left. David would have ignored Stan's adamant distaste for observing his own birthday this year, too, except that it was his sixty-fifth. He was being made to retire from the law firm, and, though it would not be Stan's actual birthday for two weeks, David didn't want his gift to get lost in the inevitable gold-watch horseshit.

It was a pair of season tickets to the Cleveland Orchestra. Fifth row center.

Stan opened the envelope. For a long time he turned the tickets over and over in his hands. His eyes welled with tears. "This must be . . . ," he said. "A mistake. We just sent in—"

"I talked to Aunt Betty," David said. Stan had for fifteen years been buying frugal six-concert packages. "She was in on this. She didn't mail your renewal check."

Stan looked toward the dark clouds gathering to the east, and for a long time did not say anything. "They're calling for snow, can you believe it?"

"Just east."

"Sure," Stan said, nodding, kicking the toe of his brogan against the cement of the gutter. "Lake effect."

David slapped him on the back.

Stan looked at him. It was hard to tell if he was surprised, frowning, or confused. He'd had a very slight stroke, and the muscles on the right side of his face sagged. "You shouldn't have," Stan said.

"Exactly," David said. It's true this had not cost David any money; it's not true it didn't cost David anything. Every schmuck has a little money. The capital David used to pay for the passes was that of a more precious coin.

Things unsaid lay between these men, as substantial and apparent to each as stacks of bagged sand. Stan held the tickets in front of him, his lips pursed, as if there were a decision to be made. He nodded, and put them in his pocket.

"Sometimes I think you don't know me at all," Stan said. "Then you go and do a thing like this."

"Sometimes I think you don't want me to know you," David said. "Then you go and do a thing like *this*."

"A thing," Stan said, "like what?"

David took a deep breath and forced himself not to brush the tear from his uncle's cheek. It could, after all, have been caused by the wind whipping off the lake and up Sixth Street.

"Like nothing," David said. He said the credit for the gift should go to Betty and Irene (not true; it was David's idea all the way), and Stan said he'd always liked that Irene, like a daughter, he said, and he asked after the kids, and the men shook hands and did not hug and went their separate ways.

Stan's heart attack hit him as he got into his car. It had been a late lunch. His body wouldn't be found until a little after five.

∽

DAVID HADN'T BEEN inside Record Rendezvous for years. He didn't exactly know what made him want to go there now except that he wanted to buy a new recording by Herbie Hancock that he'd read about in *Down Beat*. Also, he had time to kill and felt amazingly great about himself and the large, well-meaning city in which he lived. Among the times in his life he'd felt this way before were the years before he joined the navy, when he still expected to go to Annapolis and he thought of himself as someone with a secret identity: hepcat white boy who dug those rhythm and blues.

The neighborhood around the store wasn't a place you would want to go, if you didn't know where you were going. Worse than it used to be. Broken glass and scarred-earth vacant lots. The few remaining Victorian houses that, once, had made Prospect Avenue a half-assed version of Euclid's Millionaires' Row now were either boarded up, falling down, subdivided beyond reason, home to storefront bail bondsmen, or some combination of all of these. The few pedestrians were gray-faced round-shouldered Negroes dressed in menacing-looking army-surplus overcoats. The East Side had these more-progressive-than-thou airs, but ask anyone where the race problems are, and it's all east, east, east. Hey, ask Jack Russell! Buckeye Road gets blacker by the day, and that fake cowboy (he was born Paul Ruschak) watches while his bloated flank gets more and more exposed.

Inside the store it seemed at first like nothing had changed.

Two-thirds of the people in there were Negroes. The listening booths hadn't changed a bit. The walls were still covered with posters for dances Alan Freed and Leo Mintz had staged.

But the music. Christ. That drippy British shit. And in between those older posters were other ones, some of them for shows not even in Cleveland.

How was it that the music he'd liked so much as a kid, music by adults and for adults, music that painted a picture of adulthood that was cartoon-ish but true, how was it that this music got transformed into something else, music by kids and for kids, music that painted a picture of adolescence that was mythologized and false? These days just about all David bought was jazz, and he couldn't remember the last show he went to, but that would have been jazz, too, and probably some local nobody somewhere. Except for Sinatra, popular music was a wasteland.

David asked what it was that was playing.

The Beatles. Of course.

In the space of the past two weeks, David had gone from never having heard of the Beatles to hearing them wherever he went. David didn't under-stand why people didn't see the group for what it was: one young Brit who wants to be Little Richard, another who wants to be Carl Perkins, someone else in there who harmonizes flat, and a drummer who sounds like a tenth grader in a high school swing combo in a white neighborhood. What soul-less shit. But look around the store: even *Negroes* were falling for this crap.

From the back office came Leo Mintz. He looked like hell. He was in his fifties, but he needed to lose weight and give up on the comb-over, and he was muttering to himself like some old pigeon-feeding crazy. Mintz and David's father were drinking buddies back when Mullins Saloon was still there. The last time David saw him was at last year's Democratic Steer Roast, when he'd gotten stuck in a corner of a tent with Mintz and a group of teen-agers to whom he was adamantly asserting himself as the man who invented rock-and-roll music.

"Leo!" David said, hand extended. "David Zielinsky. You and my dad—"

"He's dead," Mintz said.

David flinched. There was an Irish wing of the Teamsters coming up. Deep down, David had known forever that a day like this would someday come.

"Shot dead," Mintz said. "Can you believe it?"

"I can," David said. His legs buckled. He fell against a bin of show-tune records.

Nothing would ever be the same.

It would be years later, of course, before his father was actually killed.

It would be a few hours yet before David would hear about his uncle's death.

It would be days after that before David started resenting how the presi-dent's death kept Stan Lychak from getting the attention he deserved (even, to some degree, from his own family, who watched the president's funeral during Stan's wake, on a portable TV set in a room adjacent to the coffin).

It would be months after that before his uncle's reputation was ruined and his uncle would seem to die again.

It would be years after that before Aunt Betty died, too, of the requisite syllogistic grief.

It was still three years before the whole city would seem to burst into flame.

Four before a great wave of high hopes hit the beach of Lake Erie and the banks of the Cuyahoga.

Five before the city ignited again and dashed those hopes.

Six before the city's most famous fire ever; six and a half before anyone gave a shit.

Seven before the Cleveland joke became a ham-fisted American birthright.

It would be fifteen days until the thirty-three members of the 1964–65 Cleveland City Council met in the ladies' dining room at the Union Club to elect their term's chairman. It was too late to meet in the Hollenden, though the Hollenden wouldn't have been right, anyway. Even aside from the wrecking ball. Too many of them had fresh memories of Jack Kennedy meeting with them there in 1960. It felt right to see the place fall. Those fifteen days left time for more maneuvering than usual. *Maneuvering* is the polite word for it. David went into that meeting toting what he believed were eight or maybe nine votes and expecting a fight: ballot after ballot, long into the night, slapping cold water on his face, loosening his tie, with nothing less at stake than the future of the great city of Cleveland, Ohio. Jack Russell, current council chairman, was the first nominated. The Negro councilman who was David's maybe-ninth vote raised his hand. Russell recognized him. The nomination was for the other young West Side councilman, the only other person David's age and, like David, a second-termer. David balled his napkin in his fist and tried to squeeze it to pulp. He looked at his fellow young turk; only last week he'd claimed he was going to vote for David. Now, the guy trained his lizard eyes on David as if nothing had happened. The senior Negro councilman was nominated next. Finally, a man representing the Near West neighborhood that included the docks nominated David. Nominations were closed. Speeches were made. David got to the podium and looked around and saw how it was buttered. The people he'd thought would support him wouldn't even look at him. Deals had been struck. The ballot would be a show of hands. The candidates were presented alphabetically. That meant the first name announced would be the other young councilman. He got seventeen hands, and like that it was over. As a formality, the vote proceeded. Russell finished second, the senior Negro third. By the time David's name was finally mentioned, everyone but David had already cast a vote for somebody. David kept his hand at his side.

It would be two weeks and a day before David would realize that the next mayor of Cleveland had to be a Negro. It would be a long time after that before he could convince all that many people. He would never convince his father. He would never convince his wife.

When David looks back at these years, he will say a lot of the same things Clevelanders say about Cleveland.

Nothing was ever the same after the Indians traded Rocky Colavito.

Nothing was ever the same after Jim Brown, at the peak of his powers, retired from football.

Nothing was the same after the Democratic machine failed to take into account the emerging political clout of the Negro population.

Nothing was the same after Cleveland succumbed to white people's unfortunate tendency to look for one black person to speak for all black people.

Nothing was the same after Euclid Beach Park closed for the season forever.

Nothing was the same after the riots. (We do not say which riots.)

Nothing was the same after the river caught on fire. (We do not say which time.)

Nothing was the same after the mayor's hair caught on fire. (We do not say which mayor. OK, we do. It was the same one who declined an invitation to a White House dinner because it was his wife's regular bowling night. This, it should be said, was not our worst mayor ever.)

Nothing was the same after Cleveland became a running gag on a TV show called *Laugh-In*. Nothing was the same after our thin midwestern skin triumphed over our thick midwestern blood and we asked for an apology and it was granted and thus, like an apology someone's mom exacts from the neighborhood bully, ruined everything.

Years and years later, a marriage counselor with a shirt open one button too far will tell David Zielinsky that a feeling is not right or wrong, a feeling just *is*. David's feeling, if he is honest (the counselor is big on honesty but seems not really to appreciate what a difficult standard that truly is), is that all his dreams in life were destroyed—or at least bashed into practical splinters—the day John F. Kennedy was killed.

Yes, David knows, for a man like him it would be better if this were a Cleveland thing. But that's how he feels, OK? OK.

Plus, for him, it *was* a Cleveland thing.

It was about that day at Euclid Beach Park when he saw the man speak, and saw a vision of what was possible in his own gawky, optimistic life.

It was also about a day in Cleveland when everything seemed to be going David's way, when the whole city and everyone in it seemed to love and accept him. Thereafter (and this is *so* Cleveland), whenever he felt remotely like that, he girded himself for apocalypse.

It was also about being in Record Rendezvous, a Cleveland landmark, when Leo Mintz, a mere acquaintance, a red-faced Jewish man who claimed to have invented rock and roll, gathered his shaken self and gave David a bear hug, and David learned that it was not his father who had been shot, it was the president.

David was strangely not relieved. He felt no less devastated. He stammered for a while, and people gathered around them, and David finally managed to speak. "Where?"

"In the head they shot him," Mintz said. "Can you believe it?"

"No," David said. "Where did it happen?"

When Mintz said Dallas, David was—finally, briefly—relieved.

If a thing like this had to happen, he thought, *thank god it didn't happen here.*

LOCAL HEROES

෨

Fourth in a Series: The Legend of Luee the Offis Boy

July 1964

LOUIE SELTZER'S PHONE has been ringing on this Sheppard business all day. Now there's even a girl with a TV camera in his outer office, cooling her stylish black heels and waiting for news. In the old days, no one thought interviewing another reporter was a story. She's the weekend anchor at her station and also the daughter of one of the old party bosses, a dragon Seltzer helped slay. She is wearing dark lipstick and a beige suit that probably cost more than a serviceable used car and has a look on her pretty face like someone who has not had to wait for things. An hour ago he asked her to leave and she didn't.

He looks up. She is, of course, staring at him. She mouths the words *any news?*

Louie Seltzer rolls his eyes. Of course *she* has to ask *him*. TV *news* is an oxymoron. The law is an ass. We have met the enemy, and he is us. *Madame Bovary, c'est moi.* The simplest explanation is best. We hold these truths to be self-evident. He shakes his hairless head.

The phone rings with more calls asking Seltzer for his comments on the matter, which he's not giving to anyone. Especially the pampered harpy. Look at her. This is the future, isn't it? Earlier this year she did a series of stories on the "Red Scare, Ten Years Later," as if Communists were no longer a

[405]

threat to anyone, and on the people who ruined people back then—thereby ruining people now, many of whom, like Eliot Ness's old acolyte Lychak, were dead. Louie Seltzer has been interviewed by *Edward R. Murrow*, understand? He's drafted and orchestrated the election of every Cleveland mayor for twenty-three years, every Ohio governor for seventeen. He's spent more than fifty years in this business. He expects, in the unforeseeable future, to die in this shiny downtown tower his personal influence built, in this lovely office his wife decorated for him, right after he puts the day's last edition to bed. A man like that is not going to sit still for an interview with some vindictive weekend anchor.

She still has her eyes on him. He looks away, pretending not to have glanced at her.

Some jobs just won't stay done, Louie Seltzer thinks. That's what he thinks about this Sheppard madness. As he editorialized somewhere around appeal number nine, a prizefighter who lost a unanimous decision can't very well hire a lawyer to undo what happened in the ring.

Yes, Louie Seltzer takes this latest tedious appeal seriously; he's got six reporters and two shooters on it: outside Columbus, where the convicted wife-slayer is in prison; Cleveland, for the local angle; Dayton, where the judge is. But Louie Seltzer has a newspaper to put out. When this crazy maneuver fails, the story will run below the fold. Meanwhile, there are a hundred decisions to be made that have nothing to do with the convicted wife-slayer and his headline-whore lawyer.

Were he to grant that girl out there a candid interview, he'd tell her this is a people's newspaper. People want *stories*. Murder. Boxing. Baseball. The rise and fall of the visionary Vans. The rise and fall of Eliot Ness. The fall of racketeers and bosses. People want flagpole sitters. They want the Heartache Baby. *Stories*, not in the journalist's sense of that, but the way his father used the word. Yarns. Tales. Legends.

An unsolved murder is a story. An unsolved murder that's unsolved only because the authorities are coddling the chief suspect in a way they'd never coddle a regular joe is a great story. A good trial with sex and blood and a college-educated pretty boy who thinks he's above the law and gets convicted of murder because of the influence Louie Seltzer could bring to bear—that, young lady, is a *whale* of a story.

People come in and out of his office, more staff than reporters. The phone keeps ringing. He cancels lunch with Mayor Locher. The girl in the outer office keeps sitting there. Whenever Louie Seltzer makes eye contact, her big green eyes widen in what he interprets as exasperation.

Yes, Louie Seltzer would concede, some of the things that happened after Sheppard got sent to prison are also stories. F. Lee Bailey is a pain in the neck, but he's a story. The live cancer cells Dr. Sam agreed to have injected into his body in some crackpot research study is a story. The best one is the rich blond divorcée, the German. She's—get this—the sister-in-law of that Nazi rat fink Goebbels. She read about Dr. Sam in some German magazine, wrote to him in prison, got engaged to him the first time she came to the States, kissed life on the Riviera good-bye, moved to the West Side, and bought a house on the fat-chance possibility Dr. Sam would one day join her there.

What's not a story, except maybe in the hands of a giant like Dickens,[1] is a decade's worth of legal wrangling. By the count of Louie Seltzer's own paper, twenty different judges have reviewed or ruled upon the case and thirteen separate appeals, and where has that gotten Sam Sheppard? Nowhere. He's still in jail where he belongs. He's lucky he didn't get the chair.

Louie Seltzer's ulcer flares. Back in the days when they called him Little Bromo, he got bottles of Bromo-Seltzer as gag gifts. Now he buys his own.

When the call finally comes, from Louie Seltzer's man in Dayton, Louie looks away from the weekend anchor and out across his gleaming newsroom, filled with metal desks and ringing phones, wire machines that sound like small churning trains and blue electric typewriters that sound like alien invaders in a B movie. Even their bells sound wrong, insubstantial and too sharp. That's how he thinks of it, *his* newsroom, the same way he thinks of *his* city: there for the good of everyone but—let's not kid ourselves—shaped by yours truly.

"They're letting him out," the reporter says. "They're letting him go."

Somehow, Louie Seltzer knew it. It makes no sense, but what these days does? The way things have been going, it figures. "In my gut," he says, "I saw this coming."

The reporter is too excited to tweak his boss for this slightly mixed metaphor and goes on to tell Louie Seltzer the worst part of the story.

The judge, in calling Sheppard's "carnival atmosphere" trial a "mockery of justice," condemned the coverage of the press in general and the *Press* in particular.

As the reporter reads the germane and savage passage, Louie Seltzer slumps down in his hard wooden populist desk chair. He shakes his head and both cannot believe what he is hearing and finds it all too predictable. He

---

[1] There are no giants like that anymore, believe you me.

wants to laugh, and he wants to cry, and instead he looks at the row of his father's books lined up on a custom-built oak shelf behind his desk. He looks at his new brown shoes. He looks at the pictures of his family and tries not to think.

You want to know what Louie Seltzer's thinking? America the beautiful is going to fiery hell, *that's* what Louie Seltzer thinks.

As soon as he thinks it, he remembers the people, *his* people, and the city, *his* city, and the *Press, his* newspaper, and he's disgusted with himself for succumbing to old-man pessimism. That's what they want him to think. That's how they want him to act. He's a year past corporate mandatory retirement age, and they want him out. He is a youthful sixty-six. He will not fan the flames of his own undoing. He will not think the thoughts of an old man. Kookie, lend me your comb. Ask not what your country can do for you. Beatles forever.

But it's true. America is going to fiery hell. Louie Seltzer stands and looks out his window at the nearly empty street below. Cleveland may already be there.

༺༻

THEY CALLED YOU Mr. Cleveland.

Who's *they?* Out-of-town journalists. Lickspittles. You called you that. *They call me Mr. Cleveland,* you'd say. You became fond of telling your own story. You became *they.*

Once, you were us, or so you'd have us believe. And we do! It's a classic: us versus them. *The* American classic.

Your destiny was born nineteen years before you were.

In 1878 Edward W. Scripps—a six-foot-tall red-bearded man who claimed he drank enough whiskey to keep four burly stevedores drunk—started the *Penny Press. They* all laughed. The *Press,* half the cost of other papers, reveled in stories about the common man and attacked the rich and powerful. When it revealed that Leonard Case Jr.—one of two visionary never-married brothers whose fortune helped lay the foundation for the modern Cleveland—died not of natural causes but by chloroforming himself in his bed, the *Press* became the number-one paper in town. Once, the father of one of the rich and powerful men the *Press* had smeared (it had, in the story, implicated the wrong person) retaliated by having thugs ambush the reporter and pour so much thick black paint on him he was in danger of suffocating. Scripps wrote an editorial demanding justice and ran it on the front page—the exact same story, day after day, until the men responsible were brought to justice. Scripps started what eventually became the Scripps-Howard newspaper chain. He started United Press International. His autobiography was called *Damned Old Crank*. At the age of thirty-six, he quit the paper to travel the world. Thirty-six years later he died off the coast of Africa in a mysterious yachting accident.

By that time, you—exactly like Scripps and also his opposite—were twenty-eight, more than half those years spent as a newspaperman. You were positioned to become his professional heir.

There are no stories like yours anymore. Couldn't happen now.

You were born on the northern coast of a vigorous young empire, on the Near West Side of a great northern city, in a one-story cottage behind a fire station. It was the end of the antepenultimate century of the last millennium. Your mother was a saint, had four more children, and managed weekly to transform a dime's groceries into a dollar's meals. Which was fortunate for you all, because your father was an unpublished novelist. After supper he commandeered the kitchen table, and your mother hushed the babies, and—as his family piled on the blankets to endure nights in the drafty, inadequate cottage—he ignored the sporadic clanging of fire wagons and worked by lamplight until dawn, conjuring up images of bloodthirsty indigenous people, strong Caucasian women in bonnets, exotic saloon girls with initially hidden sentimental streaks, and sharpshooting, square-jawed Caucasian men, all set against a backdrop of a frontier its author had read about but never seen. He slept all fitful morning, clamping pillows over his head to drown out the din of the firemen. He woke in time to greet the mailman and read, over lunch, each day's rejection letters. He spent his afternoons nursing migraines. After supper the table was cleared, the babies hushed, the lamp lit; back to work he went.

When finally one of your father's stories was published, the way you tell it, your mother did not cash but rather framed the check and hung it over the kitchen table.[2]

You started in the newspaper game at the age of seven, with the required paper route. Your money went to help the family. Your father started to sell more work, but there were only so many pennies to be squeezed from dime novels. Things at home remained grim. In the middle of your eighth-grade year, you ditched school and applied for a job as an office boy at the *Cleveland Leader*. The editor looked at your application and asked if you were related to

---

[2] In the America of that era, or at least its stories, such daft idealism is always rewarded.

Charlie Seltzer, the Western writer. You were the proudest boy in Cleveland and also hired. You begged your parents to let you drop out of school. Your father, who had less formal education than you and harbored quixotic dreams of sending you to college, relented only when you agreed to undergo a great-books curriculum he'd devise and administer. Starting with Mr. Dickens.

In an attempt to look older, you bought yourself a floppy black bow tie and wore it every day. One Monday, while you were still new on the job, you were delivering copy from City Hall to the Leader Building when you saw a streetcar plow into a horse-drawn pie wagon. No one was hurt, but the wagon was destroyed, the horses were spooked, and a hundred warm pies were smeared on the front of the derailed streetcar. The pies that weren't completely pulverized provided merry snacks for opportunistic passersby.[3] Who knows what got into you, but you paid a waif even more forlorn than you a nickel to deliver the city council story, then you whipped out a reporter's notebook you'd swiped and talked to those involved, and then ran back to the paper and asked if you could write the story. The editor laughed, and indulged you, and the story ran and was cute. Next thing you knew, they gave you your own column. Thirteen years old, and you had your own column in a big-city American daily.

Your byline was "Luee the Offis Boy." The shtick was that you, a hapless working-class kid, would go interview colorful people—politicians, mobsters, cops, judges, circus people, drawbridge operators, salty-tongued dockworkers, racetrack habitués, actors, et cetera—and do so in a flummoxed, wide-eyed way, then come back to the office and try to squeeze humor from the situation by misspelling as many words as possible, including your own name. Each column was accompanied by a caricature of you in your bow tie and engaged in some pratfall. You sort of were and sort of weren't in on the joke.

When the joke wore thin,[4] they fired you. They said you didn't have what it took to be a newspaperman. They said you wouldn't know a story if it bit you on your bony ass. Before you were old enough to drink, you were yesterday's news. But you endured. At eighteen you got married and landed a job at the *Cleveland Press,* determined to prove them wrong.

⌒⌒

In the next day's paper, the story runs above the fold.

The police chief says he's no lawyer but that it seems to him that when

---

[3] RIP, LBS, and all who wrote like you.
[4] Surprisingly, this took two years.

lawbreakers get all the breaks, it's decent people like you and me who get hurt.

The chief of detectives says this is the greatest miscarriage of justice he's ever heard of.

The coroner boasts about his meticulous filing system. He says he invites a new trial.

One of the jurors says everyone was unbiased toward Dr. Sam and unaffected by the publicity. He calls the federal judge's ruling hogwash. He calls the whole business a publicity stunt by the Sheppard family.

The county prosecutor vows to issue a warrant for Sheppard's arrest. The Ohio attorney general flies home from San Francisco, where he'd been a Goldwater delegate at the Republican National Convention, and vows to appeal this mess to the U.S. Supreme Court if necessary.

The judge who tried the case is dead. It has only now come out that, during the trial, he told syndicated columnist Dorothy Kilgallen she should go home because Sheppard was "guilty as hell." The *Press* calls into question Kilgallen's hearsay account of this as well as her curious failure to report this newsworthy tidbit at the time.

In print or aloud, Louie Seltzer does not comment.

He is hectored by television squirrels to do so. When he gets home from work, they are camped on his front yard, all three stations, and when he leaves for work the next morning, they're still there. He says nothing to them, and when he shows up at work, there are more television people blocking the sidewalk in front of the *Press* building.

"I will not," he snaps, "under any circumstances make any comment on any aspect of the Sheppard case—period. I'm going to be a stuck record and say nothing. I'm now the Sphinx."

He is proud of himself.

He imagines this crazy thing may take care of itself today. He's made calls. What he hears is that Sheppard is going to be let out of prison and be rearrested by a gang of waiting state troopers.

This doesn't happen.

Sheppard is released. He's free. He goes and hides in a motel. What Louie Seltzer hears is that if Goebbels's sister-in-law shows up, the state police will burst in on them and arrest him for fornication.

This doesn't happen, either.

The next morning Sheppard and Ariane get in a rented green Lincoln Continental with F. Lee Bailey and his wife and head west, five miles an hour under the speed limit and through a hard rain. Ariane drives. They're followed by a police helicopter and twenty-some journalist-bearing vehicles. When they cross the Indiana line, the helicopter turns back, and Ariane stomps the gas and starts driving like someone from the Hurricane Hell Drivers stunt show, running red lights and zigging and zagging and U-turning and going a hundred miles an hour in the rain. The *Press* has two cars in the procession. Two counties into Indiana, she's lost them both. The longer-lasting reporter compares his experiences to the wild chase in *It's a Mad, Mad, Mad, Mad World*. One by one, the other cars drop off the pace, too. By the time Ariane shoots through Gary and crosses the Illinois state line, only one car remains.[5] The Lincoln heads straight to the Chicago Tribune Building and its four passengers are rushed inside. The *Tribune* was where the reporter comes from who wrote the first book claiming Sheppard was innocent, of which there are now several, all written by out-of-towners (or by a Sheppard with an out-of-town ghostwriter). Turns out, that reporter rigged it for Sam and Ariane to be married right in the Trib Building with Bailey and Mrs. Bailey as witnesses, just to get a scoop.

When Louie Seltzer hears this, he pauses to give the misguided devil his due.

Then he picks up the phone to fire every reporter who's been assigned to the case. But there's someone on the line. The phone hadn't even rung.

"The phone didn't even ring," says Louie Seltzer.

"Tell us," the voice says, his boss, "what you know about this Bailey character. What you've said to him."

It's New York calling. Louie Seltzer is being summoned to New York.

He wouldn't have done it really, fire those men. He's just mad is all. Give 'em all raises. Tell 'em it's been your pleasure to have them as colleagues. An honor. Send flowers to their wives. Kiss their babies. God bless America.

⚬⚬

DR. RICHARD KIMBALL, *an innocent victim of blind justice. Falsely convicted for the murder of his wife. Reprieved by fate when a train wreck freed him en route to the death house.*

The creator of *The Fugitive* claims that in fact it has nothing to do with the Sheppard case, but, in truth, no one believes him.

In Cleveland the TV station that airs the show, Tuesdays at 10, is WEWS,

------

5 It is not from a Cleveland affiliate.

the same station that employs Dorothy Fuldheim. The EWS of WEWS stands for Edward W. Scripps.

The Tuesday after Sam Sheppard is released from prison, Louie Seltzer, who's had a long day, makes himself a Manhattan and heads straight for his BarcaLounger, and what he chooses to watch is *The Fugitive*. Anyone watching him would see wheels within wheels, ironies within ironies, and expect Seltzer to shoot or kick the TV screen, or at minimum suck down the Manhattan and make himself another. Truth is, Louie Seltzer sits in his well-lit living room and sips his drink in winning moderation, watches the show, finds it entertaining, nothing more or less, then watches the news on the same station, goes to bed, makes love to his wife, sleeps like a baby, and wakes up the next morning, glad to be alive.

∾

YOU STARTED AT the *Press* on the police beat, a beat many of the other reporters—dandified college men who scoffed at you, the self-taught outsider—found beneath them. You did not find it beneath you. Your reading had taught you that stories have chiefly to do with adultery and violence. So you'd have gladly drowned a warren's worth of cute little bunny rabbits to be on the police beat.

You wrote about murders, holdups, and domestic mayhem. You wrote stories of peccadilloes gone obstreperously wrong. You traveled with daily frantic zeal all over the city. What you learned was that, on one hand, there are stories; on the other, there's how things really work. Stories lie. The popular lust for the sex and blood of stories distracts the masses while *they* control the politics and money. *They* don't want you to know this, but you learned it. For a time, before you became they, you tried to write about it.

You wrangled a new beat for yourself. For almost ten years your exclusive job was to chart the rise and fall of the Vans, the two visionary never-married brothers whose fortune helped lay the foundation for the modern Cleveland. Next thing you knew, you turned thirty and were named editor in chief of the *Press*.

The weekend after your appointment, you sat alone in the *Press*'s morgue and read (page by crumbly yellowed page) the legacy Mr. Scripps left you. You emerged from the morgue and resolved anew to be an independent advocate for the little guy.

You piloted the *Press* through the Great Depression and a World War. You saw to it that every few weeks there was in your pages an appeal for money for a family left homeless by a fire. Or fatherless from a foreign war. Or—in the case of the Heartache Baby—destitute from giving birth to a child who was a panoply of limblessness and deformed organs. You wrote front-page editorials signed LBS. You made the paper number one again.

You pressured the city to hire the golden-boy Fed who brought down Al Capone, and you charted Ness's rise[6] as he brought down organized crime here. When a new mayor was elected, one from the other party, you pressured him to retain Ness. He obeyed. The party bosses despised you. You retaliated by handpicking Cleveland's mayors for the next quarter century. Again and again, you wrote that this candidate, *your* candidate, would smash those shadowy party bosses and be answerable to no one.[7] You broke the machine.[8]

So, OK. The Sheppard case.

It happened on a slow news day, the Fourth of July. The tall, handsome couple involved had been the king and the queen of the prom, were friends with the quarterback of the Cleveland Browns, and were a part of a family that owned a hospital. No one can say it wasn't news.

As for how you played it: (a) other papers made a big deal of it, too; it was a national story, for heaven's sake. And (b) people should see what you heard about and *didn't* print.

What was the family trying to hide that made them lock Dr. Sam in their hospital and not let police or doctors (other than his brothers) examine him? It was four days after the murder, *four days,* while evidence grew cold and nobody was doing anything except conspiring against a proper investigation, before you ran the first headline people later complained about. And what was so wrong with that one? TESTIFY NOW IN DEATH, BAY DOCTOR IS ORDERED. It was the authorities, not you, who were doing the ordering.

The next day: DOCTOR BALKS AT LIE TEST. Facts are facts.

A full week later: THE FINGER OF SUSPICION. The Bay Village police seemed to be protecting one of their clubby own.

Four days after that: SOMEONE IS GETTING AWAY WITH MURDER. Obviously.

Next day: WHY NO INQUEST? DO IT NOW, DR. GERBER! You want results? I got your fucking results right here. That very afternoon the coroner called for an inquest. If you know you have the power to make things happen and don't exercise it, could you sleep at night? No.

---

[6] When he fell, you charted that, too. Men were built up and torn down, and in the end, again and again, the last man standing was Mr. Cleveland.

[7] Rumors that candidates called you to ask if they might void their bowels may be false.

[8] And, after a fashion, became it.

Two days later the Cleveland police took over from the Bay Village bumblers. Soon thereafter, your headline was POLICE CAPTAIN URGES SHEPPARD'S ARREST, because he did.

After that, you became fond of questions.

WHY DON'T POLICE QUIZ TOP SUSPECT? you wrote two days later. A question everyone had. WHY ISN'T SAM SHEPPARD IN JAIL? Ditto. Later that day he was.

How about this question: If this wasn't what the people wanted—a populist, crusading paper that asked the questions they wanted answered, that had the courage and power to seek results, to get results—then why did your circulation skyrocket?

BUT WHO, you wrote, WILL SPEAK FOR MARILYN?

You. Asked and answered, Mr. Cleveland. You.

                                         ◌◌

THE CEO, HIS top two lieutenants, and a pride of lawyers meet not at lunch but in the boardroom, without so much as coffee or ice water. Louie Seltzer has never before been summoned to New York and has never needed to have a conversation with the brass in New York that was so serious it couldn't be held in a restaurant.

Like any newspaper editor, Louie Seltzer has been sued before. More all the time, but only, he says, because that's the kind of world we live in now. In better days people solved their problems without running frivolously to court.[9] He has not, however, ever been sued for $400 million. "It's a publicity stunt," he says. "A bluff. Believe me."

The CEO—who comes from the Howard side of the operation, not the Scripps—reminds Louie Seltzer that a federal judge cited the *Press* as directly responsible for denying Sam Sheppard a fair trial. A doctor falsely imprisoned for ten years? A tall, young, handsome doctor who was a model prisoner and whose son is a mess because of all this?

"In terms of damages," blurts one of the lawyers, "the sky may be the limit."

Another one of the lawyers, who taught at Harvard and had Lee Bailey as a student, says Louie Seltzer doesn't know what he's dealing with.

Louie Seltzer laughs. He cannot believe they are taking this so seriously. "If Bailey was serious," he says, "he'd ask for a realistic amount of money."

---

9 For example, some chose to seek vengeance by pouring enough thick black paint on a man to provoke fears of suffocation.

He rubs the bridge of his nose and laughs again. It's a small and brittle laugh. "The judge said nothing about false imprisonment. The judge only ruled that the trial was unfair."

Around the mahogany conference table, everyone is looking at Louie Seltzer. But nobody says anything.

"There will be another trial, believe me," says Louie Seltzer.

Crickets.

Finally, the lawyers start to tear into him with their opinions, and the meeting goes on like that for an awfully long time, so long that it comes as an actual surprise when the CEO changes the subject and pulls out a thin stack of charts and graphs, showing the alarming dropoff in circulation since the newspaper strike. Many of these charts display trends relative to the *Plain Dealer*. One of the lieutenants puffs up; clearly he is the charts-and-graphs man. The other one taps a long thin finger against his long thin lips, a gesture that looks as if it's been practiced in front of a mirror. Louie Seltzer cannot believe what he is hearing.[10] The CEO's presentation is so rehearsed, he presents it without discernible pauses; when Louie Seltzer tries to interject, the CEO frowns and, like a crossing guard, raises his hand. Stop. It was, Louie Seltzer thinks, what a person would do to silence a hapless old man.

The film of the City Club debate lies in a can, beside a projector, on a portable cart in the room's darkest corner.

ᕲᕲ

YOU WERE SINCERE. You worked hard. You were a faithful husband, a temperate drinker, true to your country, and faithful to your God. You never chucked everything to travel the world. You did not die in a mysterious yachting accident off the coast of Africa. You died surrounded by weeping members of your family, in the city where you lived your life, to which you'd given your life. You called your autobiography *The Years Were Good*.

For the record, you'd do nothing different. It's right there in *The Years Were Good*, the last sentence of your chapter on the Sheppard case: "I would do the same thing over again under the same circumstances." On the day F. Lee Bailey became a famous American trial lawyer, that was one of the lines he read aloud to the United States Supreme Court. More than one justice was seen to shake his gray and troubled head. You were a little guy from a poor family who

---

[10] That's not true. What you heard was what you were most afraid he'd say. When you hear a thing like that, you can never believe it. And you can also never believe it took so long.

grew up to become "Mr. Cleveland" and have parts of your life story read into the record in the highest court in the land. It was not well received.

You got fired.

It was called something more polite, but nobody was fooled, you especially. You were not in fact fired because of the Sheppard case, but nobody was fooled, you especially.

Fourteen years separated your professional and physical deaths. Fourteen fitful years of earthly hell. You looked on, silenced and aghast, as mayors you would not have chosen were chosen, as a famous murderer you helped send to prison was given a new trial and acquitted, as your city became a war zone and a laughingstock, as it caught fire and went broke and went to fiery hell.

A judge threw out Sheppard's lawsuit against you and your newspaper, blaming everything that went wrong in that first trial on Judge Blythin, who, lucky for him, was dead. Nothing that happened was your fault.

The *Press* was never the same without you. Under you it had been number one. You were convinced you could have made it number one again. Without you it became permanently number two. As in shit. In your unheeded opinion.

You lived. For fourteen years you watched as your legacy was dismantled and reviled, and every day of those fourteen years, you died. Finally, in 1980, your dying stopped. Two years later the *Cleveland Press* died, too.

They called you Mr. Cleveland. For the record, it was meant as a compliment. To your ears, it remained forever thus.

— 20 —

ANNE FINISHED ANCHORING the irksome, low-rated noon news—for today and forever; the new man had served his no-compete clause and started Monday—and was alone in the station's smallest editing room, going through her stories for the year, trying to pick four so she could submit an audition reel for the Press Club awards, when Phil Weintraub summoned her to his office, that cave of carpet. It was a Friday, two weeks before Christmas. The actual summoning had been done not by Phil but rather by the weasel-faced lickspittle the new station manager brought with him from Dallas. Not good. Phil was a meet-you-on-your-turf man.

The first thing Phil asked about was Anne's new fiancé, who was a second-string lineman for the Browns, and how he thought they'd do in New York tomorrow.

"Blah, blah, blah," Anne said. "Get to the point. I'm fired, right?"

"Fired!" Phil laughed. Through his unpaned window, snow fell in flakes so thick Anne couldn't see the parking lot. "What, may I ask, gave you that idea? Please, sit down."

"Nothing." For one thing, she was doing the Press Club reel herself. When she'd asked Phil if the station would nominate her and have an editor help her cut the reel, Phil had looked up, as if the answer were printed inside his forehead, and said she should ask the station manager. Who'd said no. She'd worked in *New York*. She'd willingly come back to Cleveland, and now, what? They were going to fire her? In her own hometown? "Nothing at all."

Phil nodded. "I wanted you to hear it from me," he said. "They want you to coanchor the news. The nightly news. During the week. Starting next month."

"They?" It was almost worse than being fired. "What do *you* want?"

"It doesn't concern me," he said. "I'm taking a job in Atlanta."

"Atlanta, *Georgia?*" Who'd move from Cleveland to a mountain-william town like that?

"My god!" he said, eyes cartoonishly wide. "I didn't ask! Is there another Atlanta?"

She sat speechless across his desk from him, hands on her skirted knees. The desk was bare except for his gold cigarette case. His carpeted walls, she suddenly realized, were mottled with clean unfaded rectangles where things once hung. Against one wall was a neat stack of boxes. She'd been too caught up in her own paranoia to notice any of this.

"I wasn't fired either," he said. The Atlanta gig was a station manager job, he said. The offer was, at his age, too good to pass up.

He was lying; Phil was a news guy all the way. And he never mentioned his age like that.

"Pretty hot there," Anne said. She used to do weather. She'd never been to Atlanta.

Phil jerked a thumb at the falling snow. "Hot I can live with," he said. He bent over the desk, toward her. "Look," he said. "You'll be great. Anchoring. You *are* great. I know you hate it, and I know the raise that comes with this you don't need."

She wanted to say she didn't *not* need it. She couldn't remember Phil ever making a crack about her coming from money.

"I also know you don't hate to anchor as much as you let on." He winked. He belonged to the last generation of American men who could wink without seeming creepy.

Whether he was right or wrong, point is, anchor jobs are dead ends, especially for a woman. It's reporters who go network. Not that Anne really wanted to go network. Not that she wanted to leave Cleveland. But still. Plus, it's certain that a woman anchoring the news in competition with Dorothy Fuldheim will be accused of being pretty. And of knowing the right people. And worse. These were just facts Anne was thinking then. She was sweating. She needed a cigarette.

"You're a natural at anchoring," he said. "The trouble with you, kid," he said, "is that you don't value things that come easily. Cigarette?"

Anne dug her nails into the flesh of her knees. Runs broke out on her nylons.

She accepted the cigarette. Phil lit it with the engraved gold lighter he'd gotten when he quit his newspaper job to take this one. He quit smoking years ago. He kept the matching gold cigarette case stocked just because it would have been a waste not to use it.

Reporters didn't get fired because they weren't twenty-eight anymore. Women reporters. Actually, they might. But, these days, anchors were sure to. Anne knew this. Phil knew this. Anne knew Phil knew this and vice versa. They stared at each other across the clean, empty desk. Nodding.

This would be the moment, Anne supposed, for one or the other of them to get up and move toward the other, and then hug. For a long time, other than the nodding and the fading smiles, neither moved.

Finally Phil stood. Anne stood, too. They almost missed out even on a handshake, but, as Anne turned to leave, Phil thrust his arm out. He had a nice grip. The hug never came.

AUDITION REEL, ANNE O'CONNOR
STORY #1—*"Crushed by a Bulldozer: The Rev. Bruce Klunder Story"*
AIR DATE: *April 7, 1964*

Going in, all Anne thought she was covering was a peaceful little protest in Hough, led by five well-meaning clergymen. If anyone could have guessed what was going to happen, the station would have sent someone else. The other stations would have sent people, too. Anne was the first TV reporter on the scene. Even then, she arrived at the construction site after the minister's crushed body had been removed but before his martyrdom commenced. She had footage of Negroes running up the streets of Hough, toward the accident. She had footage of a phalanx of white policemen trying to keep everyone back. She had footage, though not great footage, of the bulldozer driver, a big man in a white hard hat, being led away, sobbing. She had footage of the bulldozer's bloody roller. She used it all. Black and white makes blood look even worse than it looks. On camera Anne is seen to be shivering. It's a windy day. She's dressed for it, but there's that. The wind.

The Hough District. When she was a kid, this wasn't a bad place. It was on their way downtown. Her father drove through here every day. Once, this was the richest part of town. Later, it was a Jewish neighborhood and solid. Now it was black and hopeless. Once, the Indians played on the edge of this neighborhood and, even after they left, the Browns used the husk of the old ballpark for practice fields and classrooms. The Cleveland Clinic, one of the world's great hospitals, was on the other edge of it. Now, League Park was a crumbling ruin and the clinic hired its own police force. Poor Negroes from the South moved to Hough by the tens of thousands. Slumlords bought grand old buildings and subdivided them silly. Drugs. Prostitution. Gunplay. Next year a young numbers runner named Don King will preface his later career as boxing's evil genius by stomping a man to death on a sidewalk here. Earlier this year the chief of police testified to the state legislature that if the death penalty is abolished, black nationalists in places like Hough will murder cops and overthrow the government. Chester Avenue, a block south of Hough Avenue, was widened to four lanes, and people from the Heights now take it, not Hough, downtown. As they do they drive as fast as possible. The sympathetic cops issue no speeding tickets on Chester.

After years of spending almost nothing on Hough, the school board and city council approved construction of a new grade school there. Great, right? People in Hough fought it. Cleveland's full of half-empty grade schools, they said. This one was being built not to serve the children of Hough but to keep them from being bused to schools where the white kids go. Yes, finally some money was being spent on Hough, but for what? To sustain segregation. Several councilmen, all East Siders but two (David Zielinsky and the other young West Sider) went from supporting to opposing the school. But it was too late. End of story.

That was the conventional wisdom. Which is always wrong. It wasn't the end of the story; it was the foreshadowing of a bigger one.

Five ministers—three of them white, two Negroes—organized a protest in the style of peaceful resistance that Dr. Martin Luther King was using in the South. They showed up at the construction site before the workers. When the workers did arrive, they sat on cinder blocks and sipped coffee and watched the dozen or so people walk around with signs. No one sang. The foreman called the mayor's office. The call went unreturned.

Finally, the foreman ordered his men to work. Four of the clergymen lay down in front of the bulldozer. The bulldozer driver backed away from them. He hadn't the slightest idea there *was* a fifth, lying behind him. Bruce Klunder, a thin, bearded twenty-six-year-old Presbyterian minister three years out of Yale Divinity School, was crushed. Observers claimed he didn't even scream. The noise of the bulldozer's engine drowned out the cracking of Klunder's bones, the bursting of his organs and skull.

Anne did not get an interview with the bulldozer driver. The foreman was curt in a sentimental, manly way he must have learned from the movies. One of the other ministers talked about the cause for which Bruce Klunder had given his life.

She did not at the time realize what it meant that Klunder was a young white man, how two thousand Negroes could have been squashed by that bulldozer and it would not have preached so eloquently to those outside the choir as that one white martyr. Martyrdom is a function of time, or at least perspective. When Anne's story ran, Bruce Klunder had been dead less than six hours. The demonstrations that his death inspired—an angry march upon the Board of Education Building, a funeral with fifteen hundred mourners and two hundred cops for security—were several hours away. The reporter sent to cover them was someone more senior.

———

THE DAY AFTER Phil Weintraub quit, the Browns went to New York and on a muddy field thrashed the Giants, 55–20. The Browns would have won at least two more championships if it weren't for New York. Now the Giants were falling apart, Cleveland kicked them while they were down, and New Yorkers had to watch it. It was the last game of the season. Winning it earned the Browns the right to play Baltimore for the championship of football. The game would be in Cleveland. The salted, potholed streets of a great American city sang.

Right before she went on the air that night, Anne announced that if anyone made an on-air comment about her engagement to the second-string lineman she would have them ritually disemboweled. The sports guy did it anyway. He didn't even have footage of the lineman (though, with all that mud, who'd have known the difference?). Anne, as far as any of her viewers could see, found the remark charming.

Two days later Anne and the second-string lineman went skiing. Monday was date day. They both had Mondays off, the lineman because the Browns didn't practice then, Anne because she anchored the weekend news.

He asked if she could drive. He had a bone bruise on his right leg and the ski resort, Brandywine, was almost an hour south of Cleveland, built on a landfill-enhanced valley, all trails leading down toward the Cuyahoga. The resort only opened last year. The lineman, who loved to ski but had given it up, said he'd heard the resort was "world-class." He knew she'd skied in the Rockies and the Alps. Still, he'd suggested it for her sake—he would only watch, of course—and that was the sort of thing she loved about him. She'd been around too many football players in her life (her father, her brothers, a great many of their friends) to make generalizations about them. So: vis-à-vis *men in general*, this one was more gentle and eager to please than most. Much more. She'd be happy to drive, she said.

He lived on the West Side, in a rented, barely furnished house way out by the airport.

Halfway to Brandywine he started groaning. He insisted he was OK, then insisted he wasn't. "Honey?" he said. "Can you pull over so I can get in back, maybe elevate it?"

"We don't have to do this," she said.

"Don't be ridiculous," he said. "This is nothing. I'm fine. It's Monday."

She pulled to the side of the road. He heaved his bald and broken body out of the car, hobbled a step or two, hiked up a pant leg to reveal an archipelago of purple and yellow blotches, scooped up a huge bare handful of filthy roadside snow, rubbed it up and down the leg, and made low, satisfied noises like the noises he made on the rare occasions when they made love. During the season the lineman behaved like a superstitious prizefighter. The Browns, like any pro football team, sported a full complement of booze-hounds and womanizers, but the lineman was an old-school small-town boy from Florida. Also, before he was traded here, he'd played for Vince Lombardi. You did not want to get him started on the subject of Vince Lombardi.

"Are you OK?" Anne said.

"I'm great," he said. He pulled down his pant leg, got in the back, and wedged himself in there so his leg was raised. He took some green-and-yellow pills out of the pocket of his parka. Anne passed him her half-full paper cup of tepid coffee. More soft noises. "Much, much better."

Brandywine wasn't crowded, but they didn't even make it across the parking lot to buy lift tickets before people recognized them and wanted autographs. They both obliged everyone who asked. They had each, often, said to one another that when the day comes that signing an autograph is a chore, please shoot me.

He would stay in the lodge and watch Anne ski. This was how a lot of their dates went. Somewhere inside his aching body lived someone fun. But he was trying to milk another improbable year or so out of himself. He was, he told her, at the stage of his career where one twisted ankle might mean the end of the line, and the end of the line might mean a career in sales. (In the off-season, he sold cars at a dealership owned by a more famous teammate.) One Monday the lineman had stood on the ground and taken pictures of her jumping out of a perfectly good airplane. Another, their second date in fact, he'd sat in the stands at a county fair demolition derby on the periphery of the station's signal area, as Anne came in fourth in the celebrity division. The lineman looked on with something like devotion, but it was a devotion fragmented by autograph requests. In Cleveland even an ancient second-string lineman (he was thirty-two) is a god.

Today, skiing.

Anne went straight to the trail ranked most difficult. She crouched into a ball, her weight as far forward as she could coax it, and shot straight down the slope, a reckless, finesseless blur. It was a long steep trail with deep powder. She could have handled this one when she was eleven years old. She hit the first graduated incline, rocketed off it, and landed clean. S he hit the second one, rocketed off it, landed fairly clean, but lost her balance and, after teetering for about ten yards, fell head over heels. She was just rusty. She wasn't hurt. She was near the bottom; there were only two inclines.

At the top the lineman asked her if she was OK. "Looked," he said, "like an H-E-double-toothpick of a spill."

She kissed him. "Cuss," she whispered. "I like it."

He blushed.

She'd been meaning to tell him this for months. Now that she'd said it, she secretly hoped he wouldn't take her at her word.

He hugged her. "I just can't," he said. He laughed at himself.

It wasn't what you'd think. He was no prude. When called upon, he was an inventive lover. His mother had been the first woman high school principal in a four-county area, and his attitudes toward women were what you'd expect from the unrebellious son of that mother. His father was the football coach and taught Sunday school and English; he'd instilled in his son a love of the King James Bible and of American literature, each in its depraved unvarnished glory. Plus which all the lineman's years playing ball with Negroes had made him a zealot on the subject of civil rights. Being around him made Anne realize what a snob she was about religious people (especially, but not only, her own brother John). Like most Catholics, she'd never read a book of the Bible straight through.

She made four more runs, all straight down and fast and perfect. She was not a mogul girl. All that hopping. Forget it. What was in it for her as a skier was the speed of it.

She and the lineman took a hot chocolate break. That's when she told him about the anchor job.

"That's amazingly great!" he said.

He was the sort of man who'd say *amazingly great*.

"Isn't it?" he said, seeing her face. "Jeez. It isn't?"

She explained. It was an explanation broken up by four separate requests for autographs. Two for him, one for her, one asking for both. Kids were off for Christmas break and the place was getting crowded.

"I'm sorry," he finally said. "I thought it was a good thing. Sounded good. I'm just a—"

"Don't say it," she said. "You're not. You're really not."

"True," he said. He had a great smirk, but it was hard to provoke him into flashing it.

More interruptions. People really couldn't stop talking about that football game. Five touchdown passes for gray-haired Frank Ryan. What's he really like? What's Jim Brown really like? How you gonna stop Baltimore? They're favored, can you believe they're favored?

"It probably *is* a good thing," Anne finally got the chance to admit. "The job. I'm just crazy on the subject. Plus Phil. My god. What am I going to do without Phil?"

"Thrive, probably," said the lineman. "I've always thought he looked at you too much like a daughter or something. Even you complain about the stories you get sent on."

"I'm not the only reporter Phil has," she said. "Had. Or the most experienced."

"Still," he said. He went to get them more hot chocolate. When he got back, she pulled out an engraved sterling silver flask of schnapps. (A gift, for being in Patrick and Ibby's wedding.) The lineman, to her astonishment, grinned and nodded. She spiked both cups.

"To your good looks," she said, "and my good fortune."

Because he really was a good-looking man. Not boy. Man.

They drank.

"We win the championship," he stage-whispered, "I get like eight grand."

Again they drank, but as they did a group of about twenty kids came up to them and asked for autographs. All from both of them.

"OK," Anne said. "Shoot me."

Her very next time down the mountain (right, right: not *mountain;* the *hill*), she hurtled too far off the left edge of the first incline, which was the last thing she remembered. She broke her left arm in four places. She was knocked cold before the pain hit.

AUDITION REEL, ANNE O'CONNOR
STORY #2—*"The Sphinx"*
AIR DATE: *July 16, 1964*

Thing was, she was on his side, Seltzer. She, too, thought Sam Sheppard did it. She, too, thought he was getting out on a technicality. But Seltzer treated her like she was out to get him, made her wait outside his office, wouldn't talk to her until he was surrounded by a whole crowd of reporters and cameramen on the front steps of the *Press* building. For that, she had about the same footage as everyone.

What makes this story is the rest of it. The shots of the inflammatory front pages of the *Press* that, the day before, she'd had the forethought to dig out of the library and have the cameraman shoot. Shots of Louie in his office, playing phone jockey, wiping sweat from his face, frowning and turning away from the camera like a man with things to hide. Anne reads the judge's hot-off-the-wire damnation of Seltzer's excesses into the camera with no particular inflection but sporting an oddly delicate look of bad-clams revulsion.

The Sphinx thing, even though everyone else has the same footage, is in and of itself great—vainglorious, didactic, and dumb. Louie Seltzer, who was in newspapers all his life, may have known how a no-comment like that would read, but look at him! He has no idea how it looks.

୦୦

RIGHT ON TIME, the lineman pulled up in front of Anne's apartment building in yet another new Chevrolet. Silver this time. Dealer's plates. He got these essentially interchangeable demos even during the season. It gave the other salesmen a chance to talk football. Anne, waiting in the lobby, pushed open the front door with her hip. She'd had her hair done that afternoon, surrendering to the forces of the bouffant, which, she had to admit (catching a glimpse of herself in the mirrored walls of the lobby), looked *smashing*. She wore a sleeveless sheath dress, with vertical red jacquard stripes and an Audrey Hepburn bateau neck. She draped a bulky wool overcoat over her like a shawl. A thick cast kept her left arm at a ninety-degree angle. A small steel rod formed a hypotenuse between forearm and bicep. No one with any sense would wear a sleeveless dress in the dead of a Cleveland winter, but what choice did Anne have?

This time yesterday she was still in the hospital. Now, left to her own devices, she wasn't going to take her pain pills or even drink to kill the pain. A matter of will.

"I'm fine," she said. The lineman opened the door and helped her in anyway.

"You look like a mil—," he said. "You look great."

"You should try washing your hair with this thing. Bathing with this thing. Getting dressed with this thing. Putting on a goddamned *bra* with this thing. Despite it."

"I told you I'd help."

"I'm not *quite* up to that." She pinched his butt to clarify what she meant. "Yet."

He asked if she'd taken her pills. She said yes, the precise recommended dosage. He nodded, solemnly, and drove her to her mother's.

This past week Anne's mother had come to the hospital every day, like a real mother. Where that came from (pharmacology? psychotherapy? age?), who knows? Gift horse.

[426]

The carriage house could hardly have been more brightly lit. Sarah O'Connor—back from the clinic and sober for three months—had decided to compete (for the first time ever) in the Shaker Heights Christmas decorating competition, but she hadn't put up (or ordered someone else to put up) a single decoration. No Santas, no mangers, no giant plastic snowmen. Only lights. In an era ruled by colored lights, every light Sarah had deployed sported a clear bulb. Two strands of lights ran along the house's every roofline and corner, around the perimeter of the door and every window. The shrubs and trees were balls of white light.

Sarah had guests. The whole living area of the carriage house, in fact, was filled with seated, wrinkled women, more than a dozen of them, playing cards and sipping cordials. Sarah greeted Anne at the door, mink stole in one hand, bottle of Pepsi-Cola in the other.

"I never once saw you drink from a bottle," Anne blurted. Then, realizing how her mother might take that, clarified. "Drink pop, I mean." Another slip: it galled her mother when the children said *pop* instead of *soda*. "I mean—"

"Forget it." Her mother drank. "There," she said. "Satisfied?"

"I am." Anne accepted the stole. She stood in the stone foyer, and her mother did not invite her in. The carriage house had been gutted since Anne lived there, first by Ibby, who turned it into a playhouse for the children, then, radically, by Sarah, who'd stunned everyone in the family by accepting Patrick and Ibby's de rigueur invitation to move back into the guest house of the mansion in which she'd once suffered and reigned.

"I can't believe you're going to this thing," Sarah said. "Especially considering." She tapped Anne's cast. "Also: *high school?*" She shuddered. She only went to college reunions.

"I like your lights," Anne said.

"The hell you do," said Sarah. "I know you."

The hell you do, Anne thought. But did not say. Vis-à-vis the lights, her mother was correct. "Well, it's cheerful, anyway."

"Have it back by midnight, Cinderella," Sarah said. The stole. "And you, Prince Charming. Treat her nice."

"Yes, ma'am." This whole time the lineman had been standing, silently, behind Anne, crouching slightly, knees bent, as if ready to catch her if she toppled sideways.

"Midnight?" Anne said.

"Joke," Sarah said. "Keep it forever. I'll die before I have a chance to wear it."

"I'm sure you don't mean that, Mrs. O'Connor."

She ran a hand along the lineman's jawline. "He's cute," she said to Anne. "Say there," she asked the lineman, "what are our chances next week?"

He said they'd sure give it all they had.

"Mother doesn't care for football," Anne said. "She's full of it."

Sarah smiled at the lineman, narrowed her eyes, and whispered: "Go Browns."

"Thank you, ma'am." He was thrown off by the *full of it* crack. As soon as they got back in the car, he'd mention yet again how he disliked it when Anne talked to her mother like that.

Sarah turned to her guests. She raised her bottle of Pepsi. "I said, *Go Browns!*"

The women raised their cordials, like unsteadily opening blossoms, and shouted back: *"Go Browns!"*

෨෧

"TAKE CHESTER," ANNE said.

The lineman did as he was told and didn't even seem irked. He was God's perfect stoic, even about backseat drivers. A person had to love that.

"I love you," she said.

"Why?" he said.

"Why? What kind of a question is that—'why?'"

"Causal," he said. He reached over and squeezed her left thigh. "I love you, too," he said. "Did your class have a ten-year?"

Her tenth reunion had been in the summer and poorly attended. Anne had been on vacation in Florence. Tonight was a dance/fundraiser/general re-union for alums of the Classes of 1950–55. "From what I gather," Anne said, "the thinking is that Cleveland is the sort of city where prodigal daughters come home for Christmas. So we'll see. About attendance."

"I wish my class would have reunions some other time of year than August," he said. He'd missed his fifth, his tenth, and just this year his fifteenth. "They're always during training camp. Boy, I'd sure love to go."

"You were captain of the football team, right? Dated the head cheerleader. Royalty."

He shrugged. "I'd rather have been valedictorian."

"He'd have rather been you."

"She," he said. "That was who I was in love with, not June," he said. They'd had the former lovers talk. June, the head cheerleader, had been The First. His ex-wife, Barbara Jean, was a cheerleader, too, at a rival college.

They met when he knocked her down on the sidelines. "Pansy wanted no part of me. She hated me and everything she thought I stood for."

"*Pansy?*" she said. "I hit a nerve, eh?"

"Not really." He waved her off. "So were you popular in school?"

"I don't know," she said.

"Then you were," he said. "If you weren't, you'd know."

"I was salutatorian," she said. "No one remembers the salutatorian."

"No kidding!" he said. "Me, too!" He frowned. "Don't look so surprised."

"I'm not surprised." Though she was.

"It was a crummy redneck public school, I admit."

"That's not what I was thinking." Though it was. "Tell me more about . . . *Pansy*."

"Looking back, it maybe wasn't her so much," he said, "as the idea of her. She was pretty, but not all that pretty. We were rivals, you know, but not real big rivals. She said the only reason I got the grades I got were because teachers wanted me to like them." He shook his head. "Of course, she was right. I got given everything. She was a *hundred times* smarter than I was."

Anne reached across her body with her good arm and stroked his cheek. "Fishing for compliments, are we?"

He hooked an index finger in the crook of his mouth and pulled. Anne laughed. Snow fell. In front of them, a big green truck spread rock salt on Chester Avenue. In the swirling haze cast by the truck's yellow cherry-top light, the lineman looked a little like Steven. Her brother Steven. She'd never noticed this before. She felt a lump in her throat. This was ridiculous.

"You're smart," she said.

"Thank you," he said.

"Smart to be with me," she said.

"I know," he said.

The truck made a U-turn. As the yellow light died, he looked more like himself. It could have been the concussion that made Anne think that, she thought. Or the pain in her arm. He really looked nothing like Steven.

"So," he said. "Will I know any of these people?"

"I don't even know if *I* will," Anne said. "Half the people in my class live in Cleveland, and eleven years out of school I never see any of them except by accident."

"That's sad," said the lineman. He said he still was in touch with at least thirty of his high school classmates. "How'd that happen?"

"Gradually," Anne said, but other than that she couldn't say. In school she couldn't sigh without blowing the hair of a girl she'd have called a friend. She'd been voted "Most Popular." She'd been voted "Prettiest." She'd been captain of teams, editor of the school paper. Eleven years later she knew what seemed like nearly everyone in Cleveland, but only to a point. "My god," she said. "I have no friends. Turn here."

"You have friends." The lineman listed people he'd met from her job, people he'd met at fund-raising dinners for the March of Dimes, the NAACP, and the Junior League.

"That's not exactly what I mean," she said. "I sure as hell don't have girlfriends."

Even Anne didn't know what she *did* mean. Her concussion was more unnerving than her badly broken arm. Everything seemed one inch up and to the left of where it really was. Also, she felt like she'd died a little, like this was not really her life anymore but some grim, slushy dream. Her doctor had said this was common. She would at least have liked to be original.

The lineman was rattling off more names from the Junior League and also two newspaper reporters he'd met at a dinner party they'd gone to last month. He told Anne not to be so hard on herself. She had more friends than she thought. She affected more lives than she gave herself credit for. He asked her if she'd ever seen that old movie *It's a Wonderful Life*.

"I need a drink," Anne said. She despised that movie. Everything in George Bailey's life would be better if he had money, and, in the end, it's money that makes everything into sweetness and light. "Scotch. I want a double scotch rocks, no water."

He put the car in park, waiting for the valet. He looked at her.

"I'm not taking the pills," she said. "Not a single pill. And I don't plan to."

༄

THE UNION CLUB was full of women in pearls and small bouffants and men in thin ties who didn't want to be there. It smelled of damp wool, French perfume, and American cigarettes, and it looked almost exactly as it had for Anne's own debut, right down to the balloons (green; at her debut they were pink), the chrysanthemum-laden centerpieces (white at both), the tablecloths (bloodred at both), the giant ice sculpture of the state of Ohio, and the musicians (chamber music, featuring moonlighting members of the Cleveland Orchestra). Had the planning committee let her party be their guide? Or was all this a consequence of the concussion? Was any of this even here? Was there really an ice sculpture at her debut? Could the planning committee really be so square as to not find a rock-and-roll band? Was this all just a big wad of déjà vu?

"We watch you every night!" said a too-excited Dot Depester Haynes (a math genius who used to be fat but was now cancer-patient haggard; her weasel-faced husband was a thoracic surgeon at University Hospital). Then, "My god! What did you do to your arm?"

Anne rolled her eyes, adopted a chagrined look she'd actually practiced in the mirror, reached into her purse, and handed Dot a business card that read I BROKE IT SKIING.

"Anne! Your arm!" said an already-drunk Janet Hillman van der Boeck (Anne's understudy in three school plays; voted by her classmates both "Best Dancer" and "Sweetest"; her bearded bald husband was rising slowly through the ranks at Cleveland Trust). Anne handed Janet a card, which Janet, like Dot, thought was a hoot. Then, "We watch you every night."

Again and again, more or less the same drill.

Followed by an exchange of compliments about what each woman wore (Anne had kept the stole on, to deflect attention from the cast; it had the opposite effect), and an apologetically tardy introduction of the husband to her fiancé.

Followed by congratulations. (Everyone seemed already to know they were engaged. Everyone seemed to be lobbying for an invitation.)

Followed by gender-specific splinter conversations: Anne's schoolmate interrogating her about the as-yet-unplanned wedding while the husband engaged the lineman in a starstruck exchange about football. The women all had opinions. The men all played a little ball themselves, you know.

Next (inevitably, worst of all), Anne's schoolmate—an aging girl in outsize earrings, wearing organza and taffeta, either a princess-line dress or one of the many identical boatnecks—would reach into her gleaming clutch purse and whip out a stack of baby photos, brandishing it like an unholstered pistol.

Anne gamely marveled. No one but the babies' own mothers could look upon such fat, misshapen creatures and not wince. Happily, some of the kids were older. No matter how old their kids were, though, the mothers would somewhere in here affect beatific smiles and tell Anne that motherhood in general, and childbirth in particular, has been the greatest experience of their lives.

Only, Anne started to think, *because you've had* no *experience.*

Finally, the lineman would sign an autograph for the husband and Anne's old classmate would sign Anne's cast.

These were the girls with whom Anne had smoked, cheated in algebra, dissected fetal pigs and the enigma of boys, dove and ran track, gone to deb class, snuck out of the dorm to see Alan Freed shows, exploded beakers in chem, run naked one night across the snowy quad, endured the bad-breath lectures of stammering Mrs. Hetuck: the whole giggly megillah.

Anne had lost touch with them all.

Some of these girls must have grown up and not married, or grown up and gotten divorced. There were stories of such girls, among the nonattendees. All night Anne found only three other single women—all of them also engaged, or claiming to be.

These people did *not* watch her on TV every night, of course. Still, she spent the night thanking them and not correcting them.

Until she slipped. Sheila Moody Wade (who'd run the first leg on the 4 × 100-yard relay that Anne had anchored and led to the state meet; her dress-gray husband had just been promoted to colonel; they were stationed in West Berlin) said she was *so* very impressed that Anne had made a mark for herself here in town. "My mother and father watch you every night."

"I'm not even *on* every night," Anne said. "You fatuous phony."

Sheila Moody Wade folded her arms. "I *beg* your pardon?"

"She broke her arm skiing," said the lineman. "I blame myself. She actually is going to be on every night. Or was. The arm probably's going to delay that now, but maybe not. But—"

Anne frowned at him.

He raised his eyebrows, nodded toward Anne's drink.

"You're the one with the Browns, aren't you," said the colonel. "I played center at West Point, you know."

When the football thing ran its course (throughout which Sheila Moody Wade stood with her lips pursed and her purse closed), the lineman said he thought maybe they should go.

"Let's dance," Anne said. The quintet was playing—could this be? was this the scotch? the concussion?—"I Love to Laugh" from *Mary Poppins*. Boisterous waltzers filled the floor.

"With your arm like that?" he said. He was actually a terrific dancer, a member of the Jackie Gleason light-on-his-feet tribe of big men. "I think really we ought to go, darlin'."

Darlin'. Late at night, he'd get more southern. "OK," she said.

"Really?"

"I thought you'd never ask," she said.

On the way out, she slipped into the ladies' room and took one little pill. Her arm was killing her. Passing out sounded like heaven.

Anne's mother dated a man who used to be a quarryman. The Beatles used to be called the Quarrymen. That's what Anne thinks of when she does the Beatles story.

She has footage of them coming off the plane. John Lennon mouths *We love you, Cleveland.* In her voice-over, Anne says that he used to call himself Johnny Moondog.

After the concert she does a live stand-up, on the windy street in front of Music Hall. She has on a trenchcoat and smiles primly (editing this, she wants to slap the look off her face), while behind her girls ten years younger than she is stumble by in torn dresses, tear-blasted faces, and mad-scene hair, holding each other up.

"Fad?" she says, wrapping up the story. "Or phenomenon?"

These aren't, she'll realize later (cutting this story onto the reel), mutually exclusive.

"Time will tell," Anne says. "But tonight these young people sent a message from Cleveland to the Beatles, the group that has taken America by storm. *We* love *you.* Yeah, yeah, yeah." She smirks. "I'm Anne O'Connor," she says. *"Eyewitness News."*

❦

TWO DAYS AFTER Christmas, Anne finds herself in the wives section of sold-out Cleveland Stadium, swaddled in two blankets and four layers of ripped-to-fit-around-the-cast clothes, strafed by a knifing wind coming off Lake Erie, and, when the occasion arises, dispensing with a mittened hand her I BROKE IT SKIING cards. Anne says she's been here a million times and can't remember the wind ever being worse. Thrown footballs wobble like paper wads. Footballs punted into the wind seem to be sucked high, smack into an invisible wall, and drop straight down like wing-shot starlings.

The wives find Anne's cards funny. It was, she tells them, a get-well gift from her brother and sister-in-law. On Patrick's desk he has two silver business-card holders, one with normal ones, the other with a stack Ibby gave him, reading I BLEW OFF HALF MY THUMB WITH A CHERRY BOMB THE LAST TIME

CLEVELAND WON THE WORLD SERIES. As the years since that victory stack up like cordwood, the cards keep getting funnier. Patrick had to get another box.

Sixteen years! Sixteen years into the Hundred Years' War, the soldiers thought things couldn't go on like this much longer. They felt like they'd been fighting forever.

On the field, before a national television audience and seventy thousand screaming, miserable clothes-fattened Clevelanders, neither team can move the ball. The Browns are facing the wind and have an excuse. Everything favors the Colts, the highest-scoring team in football. They have the wind at their backs. They're facing a team that played semishoddy zone defense all year, yet came out today and—against Johnny Unitas, a quarterback to whom man-to-man defenses have been his own happy briar patches—played man-to-man. The wives of the defensive players jump and shout like the aging cheerleaders they mostly are, untroubled that their husbands are blitzing and hitting and tackling like other men altogether.

Anne's fiancé is, as usual, riding the bench.

At halftime there is no score. Nothing like a scoreless tie at halftime when you're slightly goofed on pain pills and fried from the caffeine you've ingested from the coffee you've chugged to keep yourself warm, in desperate need of a trip to the ladies' room and increasingly afraid your toes may be frostbitten.

The line for the ladies' room looks like a refugee camp in Siberia.

Anne can't wait. She climbs a series of ramps and stairs to the press box. The old gatekeeper had been there when her father owned part of the team. At first Anne pulls a press ID card from her purse. "Nothing doing," the man says. He points at two men walking past them, at the bright-red passes pinned to their coats. That's what you need. She hates to sink lower, but she's going to explode. She invokes her father's name. She says she used to sneak into the rest room here all the time. Doesn't he remember her? She begs.

The old man shakes his head. Beside him, a security cop tells her to move along.

She climbs back downstairs. Head down, she joins the uncredentialed in line. At a moment like this, it's hard not to dream that someday soon, when you're the second full-time female TV anchor in the history of the city of Cleveland, the wings of your own fame will show you to an available ladies' room, anywhere in the city. There are such places. She's been there. She'll be there again, she's sure. But now she is stuck in line and her vision is going blurry, whether from the concussion or from having to pee so badly she can't be sure.

The third quarter begins. The line inches grimly forward. Water drips from cracks in the cement. The din of the crowd rolls into the caverns of the stadium and makes it impossible to hear anything from the tinny PA speakers but defeated squawking.

Out on the field ancient Lou Groza, Lou the Toe, the oldest player in pro football, as much a fixture in this town as Terminal Tower, lines up near midfield to kick a field goal. Finally, the wind is at his back.

It's good! It is *so* good!

Anne hears trampling feet and a tide of crowd noise; she looks up, half expecting to see blocks of unmoored cement raining down on her. The women in line ask each other what happened. Like suppressed news of assassinated Communists, word spreads.

On the field, Baltimore fumbles. The news is still traveling Anne's way when her fiancé throws a block and Jim Brown jukes around him and one of the Colts and runs right over another Colt, as if the defender were just a hoop wrapped in paper, and keeps going, almost fifty yards before he's caught. At about the time news of the fumble reaches Anne, Frank Ryan zips the ball to Gary Collins in the end zone.

Anne hears about this and that the Browns are ahead 10–0 just as she gets a stall. Good news on top of good news.

A stranger asks her if she needs help. Anne loves Cleveland!

Inside the stall she wishes she hadn't declined the offer. Though she manages.

As she gets back to her seat, her toes are warmer and the edge is off all her pain. Frank Ryan rolls out, heaves the football—*how did we get the ball back?*—and Anne looks downfield and—*how can this be?*—there's Collins, alone. He makes the catch! *He makes the catch!* Groza kicks the point-after. Browns 17, Colts nothing.

Cleveland is not supposed to win. Everyone in the wives section knows this and has not been allowed to say or even believe this, and now, in just over five minutes, their husbands have scored seventeen unanswered points.

Anne grabs hold of the other women and gives hugs as mighty as anyone and plants chapped-lips kisses on anyone she can grab.

It's not over. It's still only the third quarter. But it's over.

In the fourth Groza will kick a field goal into the wind, Ryan will heave a rainbow pass that somehow Collins will grab for his record third touchdown, and the defense will against all logic hold, and the Browns will win, 27–0. The fans will storm the field. Jim Brown will be escorted off by white cops. The goalposts will be torn down. "The name, Cleveland, in the dateline of every American sports page," Louie Seltzer will write, "will be read by business and industrial executives, many of whom plan and attend conventions. This will impress them. It makes Cleveland a big town in their minds. And a big place is a good place to hold conventions."

The conventions will remain largely unheld. What Cleveland will become in the American mind is a big joke.

Before Cleveland wins another championship in any sport, the American century will end. The Browns themselves will leave town and go to play in, of all places, Baltimore.

When the game ends, Anne stays in the wives section and pops a pill to ease the pain in her jostled arm. She looks down at the field, straining to see in the swarm the man who will be her husband. She is happy. She remembers what Alan Freed used to say and how he said it.

Live it up!

AUDITION REEL, ANNE O'CONNOR
STORY #4—*"The Red Scare: Ten Years Later"*
AIR DATE: *January 8, 1964*

This one fell in her lap, and Phil Weintraub let her run with it. It would be years before, as a norm, stations ran sweeps-week investigative series.

Anne's series was poorly received. Councilman Zielinsky called a press conference to denounce the portrayal of his uncle. Both newspapers ran editorials excoriating her. The mail the station got was 6 to 1 against. The Cuban Missile Crisis was less than two years ago. JFK was shot by who knows whom only weeks before. Americans accused of being Communists—however slightly affiliated, or not affiliated at all, however railroaded or blacklisted—still looked to a lot of people like the Enemy.

None of which was why she almost omitted this story from the reel. The series was the best reporting she'd done all year, but it was crummy TV: talking heads, spliced with pans of photographs nailed to dingy wallpapered walls, shots of tombstones and the exteriors of brick apartment buildings, scratchy file footage of Senator McCarthy. She only included the best of the four stories. In it, handsome children in shabby overcoats placed wilted roses on their father's snow-covered grave and burst into tears.

In a perfect world, Stan Lychak would have lived and, instead of being the basis for these stories, been around to cash the check he'd gotten to keep Sarah O'Connor's trip to the Mayo Clinic out of the newspapers (where it had received prominent play). In this world, Stan died. His file cabinets at her father's old law firm were (after two locksmiths failed) opened by a reformed safecracker. The senior associate (who called *himself* that) called Anne with the news of their contents only because he was trawling for a date.

Stan Lychak had, probably, been CIA during the war and for a while afterward. There were mixed signals in the files about this; the greater surprise was that there were signals at all. From another angle, it made sense. This was the world's neatest filer. His system was complex but, as his codes became clear, easy to navigate. The papers inside each file were impeccably aligned. There were files kept both on cases and on individuals. There was no file on her father. There were no files on any of the attorneys there. Anne presumed these had been removed before she'd been called.

She told the associate she was seeing someone. She mentioned the second-string lineman. The associate's eyes got big. Sports-loving men, Anne's brother John contended, have homoerotic feelings. She had, at this point, only been on three dates with the lineman. On every one, other men approached them and talked to him in a way that did resemble flirting. She promised the associate she'd get him Jim Brown's autograph. After that he left her alone with the files.

Stan Lychak had worked both sides of all kinds of things. He'd investigated racketeers and the politicians looking to get reelected by challenging racketeers. He'd accepted money from politicians running against one another. He'd worked for competing corporations. He'd been consulted by people on both sides of protracted criminal and civil cases: tax evasion, money laundering, libel, murder, countless divorces—you name it.

One exception: Communists. This occupied two file drawers. Stan remained on one side of this issue. He worked on these cases, some in Cleveland (the basis for Anne's series) and most elsewhere, in the years before he joined the law firm, back when he had his own little practice. David Zielinsky would have worked for him during some of those years, but apparently Stan purged his files of every iota of his nephew's work.

Stan Lychak, or someone, must have purged other things from these files; there was, for example, in all those Communist-investigation files, not a single piece of paper with J. Edgar Hoover's signature. Another example: Stan's files on the Sheppard case included nothing a person couldn't find in a morning at the courthouse and an afternoon in the library.

But the only perfectly empty file in the whole meticulous mountain of paper was the one labeled GIGI MADISON, which rang no bells for Anne O'Connor. Until it did. A few days into working on this story, Anne remembered: David's mother's screen name. The folder label was the color Stan used for organized crime. The code he wrote in the right corner of the file tab was the one he used for murder one.

☙

PART FOUR

CLEVELAND: NOW!
The Twelfth City: 1965–1969

─── 21 ───

"Hey. Remember me?"

The knock on David Zielinsky's office door and the entrance Anne O'Connor presumed to make came in tandem. It was only two, but he'd finished his last meeting of the day and was packing his briefcase, about to call it a week. She was ash blond. Her hair was chopped bluntly short. He hadn't seen her in—what?—two years. Except on TV. Even on TV, last he saw, she'd been a long-haired brunette. Also, she was a little wrinkled around her eyes in a way that didn't show up on TV. Or maybe it did. She'd be— what?—twenty-nine? And holding. Anne's news broadcast wasn't one he often saw.

She stopped at the threshold of his office and leaned in. She cocked her head. "I'm Anne O'Connor?"

David snapped out of it and stood. "Do I *remember?*" He extended his hand. "Jesus. Come in. I'm sorry. It's just a surprise to see you is all." He didn't say anything about her hair, afraid it had been that way a long time. He was careful to leave the door open.

"How's your father?" she asked.

"It's nothing, just a broken arm," David said. Mike Zielinsky's car had been blown up. Last month. It had been parked next to the wrong car, the one that was wired. Freak thing. The story was that someone else had been the target. The story was not untrue.

"I wouldn't call a broken arm *nothing,*" Anne said.

"You know what I mean," he said. "Hey, I guess congratulations are in order."

She frowned. More wrinkles yet. "For what?"

That, right there, was what was wrong with her. She was the sort of woman for whom good fortune was such a given that congratulations could be for any of too many things. Awards, promotions, contests, stock splits, inheritances: who knows what-all. She was the sort of person who could ruin your uncle's reputation and barge into your office a year or so later, faking trepidation, sans appointment, and act like nothing happened. "Your wedding?" David said.

Anne squinted and shook her head in that cartoonish shake-out-the-cobwebs way. "You didn't hear?" she said.

"Hear what?" he said.

"You must be the only one in Cleveland."

The invitation had inspired Irene to break several pieces of newish Corning Ware. David took the invitation from her and tossed it in the garbage. He assured her he hadn't seen Anne, hadn't so much as *crossed paths* with her, had no idea why she invited them to her wedding with the lineman. He didn't point out that Anne had been invited to *their* wedding and had come. Happily, Irene seemed not to know or remember this. Late that night David fished the invitation out of the trash. He had no choice: he was a politician; he sent a gift. In his defense, one of the council secretaries picked it out. One in particular specialized at this. You'd give her *X* amount of money and she'd buy an appropriate thing and have it delivered. She lived in a very nice house. "You mean you got—"

"Left at the altar? No. Anyway, that's part of what I'm here for." From a massive awning-striped handbag she pulled out a long, still-wrapped box. She set the box on his desk when David failed to accept it from her. Candlesticks. He could give them to someone else.

"I'm sorry," he said. "I really didn't hear."

She considered this. "OK," she said. "I thought the congratulations were a dig. It's just, you know." She looked away from him. "Great office. You're coming up in the world."

The sky was thick with puke-yellow haze. A column of purple smoke rose from Whiskey Island. A thunderhead drew near. The lake, only blocks away, was a brown, indistinct rumor. Leaving the door open was as bad as closing it, David thought. What if someone walked by and saw her in his office and word somehow got back to Irene?

"Even second-termers get a window," David said. "Most of the offices have them."

"About to be a third-termer."

"Don't count my chickens," he said. Though he had no serious competition. He motioned for her to sit down. He'd turned his desk so the chairs were beside his and not across the desk from it. He'd read in a magazine this made people think you were approachable and kind. The chairs were still lower than his.

"So your wedding—"

"Long story," she said. "Ever *been* to Washington, D.C.?"

"Yes." The lineman, David now remembered, had been traded to the Redskins for (if memory served) two flashlight batteries and a half-used can of coffee. David hadn't put two and two together. "I wanted to go to school at Annapolis."

"I remember." She shrugged. "It's not a place I care for. Not Annapolis, Washington. But anyway. That's not why . . ." Again, she looked away. "Why I'm here."

She was looking right at the pictures of Irene and the kids on the wall, next to the window. This reassured David. Kept her visit innocent. Next week would be his eleventh anniversary. He and Irene were celebrating tonight and tomorrow, making a weekend of it.

"I never apologized about that story," she said. "About Stan. I'm sure you're sore about it. I can tell. Which is fine. I guess I don't blame you."

She guesses she doesn't blame *him!* "Forget it," he said. "Water under the dam."

"Under the bridge."

"You know what I mean."

"Sorry," she said. "This is very awkward." She screwed up her face. "*Ob*viously. Look. I don't know how to say this except straight out. What, really, do you know about . . . you know. About your mother's death?"

Not this again. "I know what there is to know." If he was going to talk about this, this was not the person he wanted to talk to. "This is pretty old news, Anne."

"Right," she said. "I know. Only . . ." She pulled one of Stan's old files from her handbag. "Only there's this."

It was empty.

"Big clue," David said. "You *stole* this?"

"Keep it," she said. She explained that this had been the only empty file in his files. She explained that the code on there was for murder.

"Stan looked into it to see if it *was* murder," David said. "It wasn't murder. That's why the file's empty. As far as all the papers, the police reports . . ." He swallowed. "The autopsy. I have those." He rapped his knuckles on his file cabinet. It was actually the drawer that had all his baseball scorecards in it. It was true, though; he did have those papers. "Probably, you should go. Before you start dragging my father into it."

That explained the chopped-off hair, he thought. The breakup. Women did that. Though Anne hadn't done that when she'd ended things with David, one bitter night, during a snowstorm, parked in front of her apartment in a car that had been her mother's and that Anne had just taken and called hers, the way another sort of person might do with a sweater. A Studebaker Avanti. The heater wheezed full blast and the radio played that insipid wimoweh song, the one where the lion sleeps tonight. Who sang that? *Right:* the Tokens.

"I'm not dragging anyone into this," she said.

That story with Stan had been over a year ago. David picked up the folder. "How long have you been carrying this around?" he said. "How long have you been working on this story? You *are* working on a story. I know you."

"Who said I'm not working on a story?" she said. "And you don't, really," she said. "Know me."

He took a deep breath. "I have an appointment," he said. "I need to go."

"All right." She mentioned two men and asked if David had heard of them. One was that man Sweet, though Anne didn't use his nickname. The other was the sugar daddy, the one in Las Vegas his mother had been with for a while.

"Don't you think," he said, "this is a conflict of interest for you? This story?" The only reason she'd gotten away with the story about Stan was that David had more to lose in revealing her conflict of interest than she did in having it revealed.

"They're both dead," she said. "Did you know that?"

"You should stop going to the movies," he said. "People die. There's not a story behind every person who dies."

"If there's not," she said, "there should be."

"Right," he said. "Sure. Just a matter of airtime. Spare me, OK?"

She mentioned that Sweet had been murdered a few years ago. The case was unsolved.

"What are you trying to prove?" he said. "Huh? My mother was a young woman with big dreams. Just like you but without all the goddamned money. OK? OK. She made some mistakes and wound up with some creeps, and she realized it. One night either she went swimming drunk," he said, "or she killed herself. No one's ever really going to know which. Or why. OK? OK. The mystery of that isn't a set of facts to be unraveled. The mystery *is* the fact. The facts. That's the problem with reporters. You want complicated things to have simple answers. You think mysteries exist to be solved. Don't you, Nancy Drew? Huh? Mysteries exist to be *endured*. Don't you understand *anything*? To be *accepted*, not unearthed. Do people ask you all the time about your dead brother, huh? *Steven?*"

She flinched.

"Big fucking war hero?" He mimed the use of castanets, a whoop-de-do gesture.

She got up to leave. He fought the urge to tell her to stay. He fought the urge to tell her he was sorry, that he was just angry. In his neck and temples he could feel his heartbeat. The opposite of love is not hate, it's indifference. She stopped in the doorway and turned around.

"I'm not," she said, "working on a story. By the way. I wouldn't do that."

Her eyes were lit. Her face looked ten years younger.

"My mother was...," he said, his voice softening. "For god's sake, Anne. For all intents and purposes, Betty was my mother."

"You don't believe that," Anne said. She shook her head, said no more, and left.

◌◌

GIFT NUMBER ONE was a scarf: silk; silver with black squares; Italian; he'd picked it out at Sterling-Linder himself. Gift number two, David said, was what he was going to do with the scarf. But the moment he reached across the gearshift and blindfolded his wife, he knew he'd screwed up. Irene set her lips in a way that suggested a willingness to be kissed but looked to David more like a person awaiting punishment. He could smell the Chanel perfume he'd given her last Christmas. He kissed her. Aunt Betty was inside the house, watching *The Mike Douglas Show* with the two younger kids and, as far as David knew, Teddy, too, but when David looked up from the kiss and from rechecking the knot behind his wife's round reluctant head, there was Teddy, standing in the rain in front of the car, frowning, holding an umbrella, his head cocked like an abandoned old terrier. David rolled down the window. A ten-year-old with an umbrella! What next? A pipe? A tweed jacket? "It's a surprise for your mom," David said.

"Teddy?" Irene called. "Go on and get out of the rain, OK?"

"They use blindfolds when they send people to firing squads," Teddy said. He had on alarmingly thick glasses and a Ghoulardi sweatshirt he bought with birthday money David's father had given him. No one on either side of the family needed glasses this thick, even the old people. Teddy adamantly maintained he had a disease he'd read about in a Ripley's cartoon, the one where kids die of old age before they turn thirteen.

"Who's 'they'?" David said.

"The government," Teddy said. "The Stalinists. The Nazis, too."

"Right," said David. *The Stalinists?* Other people's kids weren't so weird, David was sure. "That's where I'm taking your mom. To a Nazi firing squad."

"*David,*" Irene said. "Teddy, magicians use blindfolds." Gamely she kept the blindfold on.

"Not in the car," Teddy said. "Magicians don't use blindfolds in the car."

"He knew I was kidding," David whispered. "Teddy? I'm taking Mom somewhere fun." He turned on the ignition. "I just want her to be surprised when she gets there, that's all."

"Go on inside," Irene said. "I *like* surprises, sweetie."

Teddy hated surprises. So, now that David thought about it, did Irene. David hated it when Irene called the boy *sweetie.*

He put the car in reverse. "Take good care of everyone," he said. "You're the man of the house now."

"Aren't you coming back?"

At this, Irene removed the scarf. "We're always coming back, Teddy. C'mon, now." She blew him a kiss.

"C'mon, sport. We'll be back Sunday right after the game."

"I doubt it," Teddy said. He was just sore, David thought, because he didn't get to go to the game himself. It was the Browns' first home game of the season.

Betty opened the front door and called to the boy. Teddy folded his umbrella, hung his head theatrically, and trudged up the front sidewalk. From inside the house came the sound of "The Well-Tempered Clavier," à la Jerry Lee Lewis. Lizard had natural ability but hated to practice. Everything she played—Bach, Brahms, Chopin, Joplin, Gershwin—she pounded.

"He'll be fine," David said, backing out of the driveway.

"You want me to put this back on?" Irene said.

He shrugged.

"I'll do whatever you want," she said. "If it's what you want, I'll do it."

"I really don't care, I guess."

She sighed.

"I mean it," he said. "Anything *you* want."

She put the scarf back on herself. Her hair looked great, some kind of angular-helmet thing that all the movie stars were wearing this year. The scarf had messed it up. She didn't put it on that well, either. She could probably see whatever she wanted to.

"I like your hair," he said.

The car headed down a steep back road to the valley floor.

She smiled. "I thought you'd never—"

"Never?" he said. "You just got it done *today*."

"Joke," she said. "Sheesh."

This was the sulfur-smelling edge of David's ward. No one lived down here. The road made a hairpin. The car faced the skyline. From down in the valley, though, with due respect to Terminal Tower and to the valley's jagged ridge of priapic black smokestacks, what David saw of Cleveland's skyline was the heaps.

Piles. Mounds. Hillocks. Hills.

Small mountains of slag. Of gravel. Of coal. Of salt. Of splintered timbers and jagged rocks of plaster. Of smashed-flat automobiles. Of rusted white refrigerators. Of old tires. Of broken cinder blocks. And of whatever it was that lay heaped under those vast black tarps.

These heaps had become the true skyline of Cleveland. In the unwieldy, insoluble gray city David had chosen to love and try to run, this was where earth met sky. A skyline of heaps: raw material and refuse. It would take an expert to tell X from Y.

He handed the guard at the gate his business card and said they were there to see the plant manager (who lived on the bluff four houses down from the Zielinskys and who'd been one of the people who persuaded David that the best way to become mayor eventually would be to swallow it now and support the reelection of that do-nothing Locher for one more term).

David parked the car. Surely Irene must have peeked.

He took off the scarf. Her hair was wrecked. "Surprise!" he said, trying too hard as he said it, and thus sounding remarkably unlike a human being saying *surprise!*

Irene put her hand over her mouth. "What in the world?" she finally said.

David spoke the name of the steel mill.

"I know what it is," Irene said.

"You've never been in there, though, I bet." *I think too much. I hate myself.*

"We're going *in* there?"

"A private tour," David said. "A short private tour. I've never been in there."

"For our *anniversary?*"

Last year, for their tenth anniversary, David and Irene went to Hawaii. David spent a day attending seminars for the National Council of City Governments convention. A lesser man would have ditched the conference altogether. A lesser man would have socked the taxpayers of Cleveland with the cost of the convention (junket is *so* accusatory). David paid for everything but the hotel room, which had been donated by the Longshoremen's local.

"You don't get it, huh?" David considered just putting the car in gear and driving off. But he persevered. That was how he liked to think of himself. It would make a good epitaph.

After this, David said, they were going to dinner at the new Theatrical, in a private red velvet room, and then would catch a movie at the Palace Theater.

"Eleven years," he said. "The, uh, steel anniversary. I looked it up."

Irene laughed, not unpleasantly. "Only you," she said, "would think like this."

"Be a sport," he said. The rain was slowing down.

"The steel anniversary." She shook her head. Then laughed a little harder.

"I could have gotten you a car," he said. "But we can't afford a car."

"We don't need a new car." She was out of breath. Her car, a Buick Roadmaster, had been her father's. "I like this car."

She reached across the gearshift and hugged him so hard it hurt.

"What?" he asked.

"Nothing," she said. After a while she said, yes, she wanted to go in, and they did.

They were back in the car and driving downtown, against the grain of fleeing rush hour traffic, before they noticed they were each coated with a fine black sheen of factory smut.

∞

WHICH WAS A blessing.

It made them check into the hotel early, so they could shower.

Irene stepped into the shower with him.

Outside, it was still daylight. Their children were ten, nine, and four. How long had it been, Irene said—grinning, grabbing, soaping—since . . . you know. In broad daylight.

The rain had stopped. Still, it was less broad daylight than gold, fiery, crisp autumnal dusk. And there was enough humidity in the air that David's knee was hurting him, which thwarted one or two of their more athletic erotic options.

From their window the sun seemed to be setting in some faraway bend of the river.

They ordered room service.

"Let me dress you," David said.

"Dress me?"

He shrugged. Three kids into the game, and her body looked about the same as always: pudgy in a way that, when he stopped to consider it, he preferred.

"Did you see that in a movie or something? Did you read that in a book? Did you—"

"Fine," he said. "Dress yourself."

She smiled and kissed him. "No," she said. "I'm sorry," she said. "Dress me."

๑๑

THE PALACE THEATER was still the Palace Theater, a movie house like they just don't make anymore, big enough to seat the adult population of a small suburb, filled with red velvet seats and contained by a carved, gilt-scrolled ceiling that was once a better version of God's sky. Overlooking the wide floor were grand private boxes (now closed) and a huge, hormone-summoning balcony (now closed).

Irene and David were two of eleven people in the audience. They seemed to be the only white people.

They went to see *The Great Race,* starring prissy steam-powered cars, Jack Lemmon, and everyone else in Hollywood. It was packing movie houses all over the suburbs. Irene had been talking about wanting to see it ever since the radio started playing that sappy Johnny Mercer song from it, "The Sweetheart Tree." David no longer listened to anything on the radio but news, sports, and classical, but Irene had bought the sheet music and played the song on the piano Betty had given them. Betty gave lessons to Irene and the kids, and was such a good teacher everyone was encouraging her to take on some students, just to keep herself young (Betty would never do it; at Baldwin-Wallace she'd finished all her requirements for degrees in psychology, music, and English, yet she never applied for graduation). Irene loved to play, and Teddy, too. Lizard was as heedlessly talented at this as she was at everything. Betty claimed that the one to watch was Brad. Brad was four. He could play "The Sweetheart Tree" without looking at the sheet music. So that was the movie they saw.

It was very long.

The theater smelled like urinal cakes and dead animals. The darkened air danced with motes of plaster and asbestos. David could hear the rustling of pigeons, the scritching of mice, and, he imagined, the slow peeling of the long sheets of water-stained velvet WallTex. All this, plus the movie, yet David's mind kept running back to that afternoon. Today, of all days. His anniversary.

[449]

He wanted to think about his *wife,* not his mother and sure as hell not his . . . not Anne O'Connor. He reached over to Irene and squeezed her thigh. He leaned over to Irene and kissed her. How long had it been since he'd leaned over in a movie theater and kissed his wife? She kissed him back. They held hands.

Natalie Wood was the one who sang "The Sweetheart Tree." In the middle of a ruined movie palace, the wide silver screen—sliced in two places, mended in several others—was covered with a white woman so pretty it didn't matter how she sang, singing a song so slight it meant little to the plot of the movie. This wasn't one of the funny parts, but people laughed.

"Should we take a cab?" Irene asked after the movie. They were in the mouth of the dank tiled lobby. Behind them, white teenaged ushers rushed to sweep the floors and lock up.

"What'd you think," David said, "of the movie?"

"Should we take a cab?" Irene repeated. The hotel was only blocks away, right by Terminal Tower, which was visible from here. Terminal Tower was visible from everywhere.

David looked out at the yellowy wet darkness of Euclid Avenue. No cabs in sight. Hardly any traffic. Across the street a woman in thigh-high boots stood slouched in a doorway. Wads of newspaper blew by. "Hey, look," he said. "Tumbleweeds." He put his arm around his wife. "We can take a cab," he said, "if you want."

She kissed him. They walked. Marriage. Eleven years. Maybe you've been there.

∽

THE ICE IN the champagne bucket had melted entirely. It had arrived too late for this afternoon, too early for now. David opened the champagne anyway. Irene drank right from the bottle's spewing neck.

What's not to love?

The bed in the hotel room faced the television. David was against having a television set in the bedroom, yet, in a hotel, he kept the thing on, even during sex, even into the night. For the novelty, he supposed. The TV came to glowing life on the newscast Anne O'Connor coanchored. David jumped up and snapped the dial to another station.

Irene stayed in the bathroom for a long time. Like a bride.

On TV it was a night that explained why a person liked sports.

In Cleveland there were shots of housefires and slums and dead people under bloody sheets on cracked sidewalks, followed by comments on the up-coming mayoral debate between the two doomed losers: Carl Stokes, a state rep who'd bolted the party to run as an independent, and Ralph Perk, a wild-haired dim bulb sacrificial-lamb Republican. David liked Stokes, who was that most seductive, elusive, and electable of oxymorons: a brash pragmatist. (David believed himself to be a brash pragmatist.) But running as an inde-pendent was vainglory: bad for the party, the city, and the Negro cause. In Los Angeles the city smoldered from the aftermath of the riots in a place called Watts (David, who'd been stationed in Long Beach, had never heard of Watts). In Vietnam generals and newscasters weighed earnestly in on the sub-ject, broached this week by a froglike war correspondent with the smug, ironic name of Morley Safer, that America was losing. The subtext of every-thing said was America's unbeaten streak. America has never lost a war! We beat the British empire, our bad southern selves, and the Axis powers! Now we're losing to *Vietnam?* It felt to David like watching a pitcher lose his no-hitter and also the game when the other team's unlikable toothpick-hitting shortstop swatted a home run.

Well, it did.

Speaking of baseball: it was Friday night, but the sports segment led off not with high school football or with a preview of Sunday's Browns-Cardinals game or with a dismal story about another dismal loss in the Indians' dismal season but with two-day-old footage of Satchel Paige, on the mound, in a Kansas City Athletics uniform. In the bathroom, water ran. On the bed, David's heart clenched. He knew the story, but such were the TV broadcasts of presatellite sporting America that two-day-old highlights of games not broadcast on a network feed of some sort could be trotted out as news. And it was! To see it, it was! Satchel Paige, sixty years old, and now—after spend-ing the past few weeks sitting in a rocking chair in the K.C. bull pen, smiling crooked-toothedly, and waving at the meager crowds his bad baseball team drew while a uniformed nurse (*nothing* more sexy than a uniformed nurse) brought him cups of coffee—he'd become the oldest man ever to enter a game in a major American sport. A *stunt* they said *(who's they?)*. What did Paige do? He mowed down those Boston hitters, one right after another. He pitched three shutout innings, in front of only nine thousand people, which made David, who'd never been to Kansas City, vow never to go to that jerk-water noplace. For show, Paige came to the mound to start the fourth. As he walked off, the stadium lights were doused. The crowd held up matches and lighters, and joined together in the singing of "The Old Gray Mare."

"My god," David said. Paige had looked just the same as he had seventeen years ago, all elbows and knees, arm angles more appropriate to the rubberman from the circus. "My *god!*"

Irene flung open the bathroom door. "What?"

David shushed and pointed at the TV like a man witnessing a terrible accident. Which in a way he was. If a thing like this was going to happen, it by rights ought to have happened in Cleveland, in front of a sold-out crowd at Cleveland Stadium, the largest-capacity park in the game, for a team owned by Bill Veeck, the most famous man near whom David had ever been shaved, whose departure from Cleveland David now felt certain spelled the end of adventure, sport, and fun. The provocateur was a low-rent Veeck manqué named Charles O. Finley. And instead of Cleveland, it happened on the western fringe of the American League, in a city so pathetic only nine thousand people were willing to leave home to see a miracle.

"My god," David said. His head felt hot, fevered, on fire. He could feel the cold blade of the barber. He could see Eliot Ness's face. He could see that old black man, McNabb, and hear the sweet southern tang of his voice: *Yonder's Satchel.*

Irene sat on the edge of the bed. On TV the story ended, supplanted by journalism. She'd draped herself in the white terry cloth hotel robe. She had on who knows what underneath. "What?" she said.

David grabbed her by the shoulders. He looked her in the eyes and kissed her. *"Satchel Paige,"* he said, as if that explained everything, as if those two words unlocked divine secrets.

"You should see yourself," Irene marveled.

"You don't know it," he said. "Christ, I hardly knew it myself. I *didn't* know it myself. But it, that, was the greatest day," he said, "of my entire life."

"What was?"

David slapped himself on the head, pounded himself in the head, with joy and epiphany and frustration about feeling more than he could figure out how to say, even to this fellow traveler, his wife, about the day he became the man he was, or really the best part of the man he'd become and wished to be. The day he *felt.* A boy like David Zielinsky, from the West Side, who grew up to become a man who was not a bigot and who held before him like a chalice the enormous dreams of a great northern city.

The robe slipped from Irene's shoulders. What she had on was wispy, silky, and red.

"Wait," David said, replacing the robe. "First," he said, "I need to tell you a story."

— 22 —

LOOKING BACK, IRENE Zielinsky would mark September 1965—a weekend dedicated to the celebration of her steel anniversary—as the time her husband, David, lost his mind. Or at least his way. In those years, in the aftermath of a separation and mortifying affair, David made a production out of their anniversaries. He was then the third-youngest member of the Cleveland City Council. He lost his way on a Friday, at the end of a strange and wonderful day, while she was in the bathroom and he was watching the news. At the time it seemed to Irene more like a big fat wad of naive self-regard. He thought the best day of his life was some baseball game that didn't even count? Not the birth of his children. Not the day he proposed to her. Not his wedding day. A ballgame he saw when he was a boy. He talked to a Negro and bloomed into adulthood. He seemed serious. He had a look in his eyes like Burt Lancaster in *Elmer Gantry*.

The next day he seemed fine. He took her bowling at an alley his father had a silent interest in, and bowled a 485 series, just shy of his average when they'd been in a couples league together in high school. Irene found the pocket for long stretches in all three games, won them all and the series, too (552); David did not use his knee as an alibi, and he cheered her all the way. He took her to a clambake at the Country Club, at which the Zielinskys were newly fledged members. After dinner they danced to an orchestra composed of middle school music teachers from the east suburbs who wanted to be Woody Herman and the Thundering Herd, and after that they stayed downtown in the Sheraton Cleveland. Probably this was no longer safe, but they stayed very high in the air. On tap the next day, Sunday, was a trip to a target range and then to Cleveland Stadium, for a Browns game. She was an ER nurse in a hospital on the near west side. She saw what guns could and did do, more all the time. But she did love to shoot. It reminded her of her late father. He was a wiry cautious man named Bud Hrudka, foreman at an automobile plant, a man with cops as hunting buddies. This gave him, and his family, irregular but free access to police shooting ranges. From girlhood, Irene knew she had a gift, however useless.

The range was on the lakefront, in the basement of the International Longshoreman's Association building, a square, barracks-like building painted kelly green—as in Danny Greene, the president of the local, a big, sunlamp-tanned, balding Irishman. To get there, they'd had to go through a steel-paneled upstairs lobby that looked like a room you'd pass as you entered a prison. Once they'd been buzzed inside, the offices were as nice as any you'd see anywhere downtown, except for all the green. Green carpet, green patterned wallpaper. On the bulletin boards, most of the memos were green. Greene was in his office, icing down kegs of beer and singing a song she didn't know. He had a tenor voice good enough to be in a high school play but too effortful compared to the ones Irene heard on original Broadway cast recordings. On a low mahogany table in front of his desk was a block of cork the size of a bathroom vanity. Stuck in the middle of it was one of those knives. What do you call them? Like from *West Side Story*. Not a switchblade. The other. Greene held up one finger, finished with a bag of ice, went to his desk, pulled out two Smith & Wessons. A cigarette dangled artfully from the corner of his mouth. He handed the guns to David and Irene. "Plenty of ammo downstairs," he said. "So." He clapped a hand on Irene's shoulder. "You're a shooter, eh?"

She wanted to say she sure was but found herself blushing.

Greene cackled and poked David in the ribs. "Watch your step, Councilman. Married to Annie Oakley here."

Downstairs David turned on the lights and fumbled about in the ammo case before Irene told him to get out of her way, she'd do it. As she did, she asked about the knife.

"A stiletto," her husband said.

"*That's* it," she said. "How do you know that?"

He shrugged. "How does a person know anything?"

She was married to a man who was friendly with someone who did business behind an armored lobby and had a bunker in the basement of his office. David's father—a sometime local leader with the Teamsters and who knew people she'd rather her husband not know, *who got his arm broken in a car bombing!*—was a big part of this. But not all of it.

This all happened in the years before the invention of safety.

The firing range was made of cement and steel, but neither David nor Irene, who'd both done this before but never together, gave a second thought to ear protection. Protective eyewear? Please. David wore heavy, breakable-glass eyeglasses. Irene, nothing. She had 20/15 vision and secretly blamed her husband for her oldest child's dimming eyesight. Every time she stopped to look at Teddy's thick glasses, she wondered what marrying her high school sweetheart had cost her. But of course, that was silly. Without David, there'd be no Teddy, no Elizabeth, no Brad. There would be other people, maybe. The thought of the other people that other decisions would have created made her woozy. She sat down. Also she'd had too much red wine last night.

"I'm fine," she said. He was hovering over her. "You go first. Go."

She'd mentioned to him that she'd started her period this morning. He was easily intimidated by anything he thought might have to do with that, with anything female. The range could accommodate two shooters at once, but he obeyed.

The targets were cop targets, the kind with a grimacing man drawn on them. Unlike the cop ranges she'd gone to, there were no bull's-eyes to aim at. Just the grimacing man.

"Go for the head," Irene said.

David looked at her in a way you'd expect from a man with his politics.

"You have to decide," she said. "Otherwise you could hit the heart by accident and say that's what you were aiming for."

"Like our love." Then he smiled in a mincing way, like some British fop, perhaps a bad impression of someone in *The Great Race*. "Darling."

She stared at him. Then she got it. Who did he think was in the audience? He spent his days shaking hands and talking to people all around the city, and then he came home and sat in the dark and drank Wild Turkey, and what she got from him at night was too often something like this: a witticism. This was not the earnest boy with whom she'd set sail. "Shoot, OK?"

He stood there holding the thing at arm's length. Like a stinky diaper or a wounded rodent. Back in high school, when he played basketball, he did the same sort of thing when he shot free throws. Dribble, dribble, dribble. Hold the ball straight out from his chest. Breathe in, breathe out. Then back to the dribble, dribble, dribble. In the stands, other kids gave *Irene* the business, just for being sweet on a nerveless boy like that. Though in some ways he was brave. He pretended he could do anything. And so, OK, maybe someday he *would* be mayor. Stranger things have happened, though not to anyone she knew. The gun wobbled in his hand. David shifted his weight. So timid, so brave. Such a good husband and such a bad one.

He believed she'd always been faithful to him, she was sure. Unlike him, with that television harpy, Irene had never had anyone serious. Two interchangeable cutters at the hospital—tired, cynical men ideally suited for what she told herself was revenge.

"We're going to miss the game," she said, though it was hours away, and she didn't really care if they missed it. It was just hard to watch him.

He squeezed out a round. Then another. He let his arm down. He hadn't hit the head with either shot. The guns had been modified to be semiauto-matic and held twelve-round clips. Irene wasn't sure she'd live that long.

David abruptly jerked the gun up into position, bent his legs in some ap-proximation of someone he'd seen in a movie—probably a good guy, know-ing her husband—and emptied the clip.

One round in the head, one near it, one in the neck, the rest scattered. Four missed the paper altogether. The air had that sexy cordite smell.

"Your turn." His mouth was turned down in a poor-me way that both their boys inherited.

She took a breath and stepped to the line in the other bay. Her stance was open and more stooped than her father had taught her, but she was a better shot than he'd been, too. She fired one round evenly after another. The right song could have been sung to it, her rhythm. Her grouping was ordinary: three of the twelve missed the head, and the rest were scattered all over it. "I'm rusty," she said.

"You told me you were good," he said, "but I had no idea."

"I'm rusty," she said. "Your turn. This time, the heart."

He looked at her.

"What?" she said. "Really, that's how it's done."

"I'm used to bull's-eyes," he said. His uncle had been a cop. He'd taken David shooting a grand total of twice.

David found a middle ground between his tics and being a bad actor at the OK Corral. Mostly, he did manage to stay within the target's torso.

As he sat down, he started back in on his crazy baseball story. Earlier this week some Negro baseball player David had seen as a kid had done something amazing at an age, apparently, where that was both unlikely and unprecedented. This had, somehow, launched David onto a riot of self-congratulation about how, despite where he'd grown up, he wasn't a bigot—oblivious that she, of course, had grown up in the same place—and going on and on about how to put together a coalition of the progressive politicians and the Negroes. He'd talked her to sleep last night, started back up at breakfast, and now he was at it again.

"Shut up," she said. "Honey."

He apologized, which was hardly the same as shutting up. She turned to face him. He raised his hands, like a helpless twit in a stagecoach robbery. "Don't shoot," he said.

"I'm trying to," she said. "It's like golf, right?" She didn't play, but he was getting avid. "Etiquette, right?"

"Right."

"Put your hands down," she said, and readdressed the target.

A coalition to do *what* exactly? To fan the flames of the greater glory of David Zielinsky, that's what. Which she was essentially for. It scared her to death, though, that this had to do with the Negroes. Her father would have said that it was the Negroes that had brought about all these problems and that it was foolish to think that casting your lot with them would solve anything. That was how she was raised. She knew that wasn't the way to raise her own children in this modern world. Still: read the papers! Getting involved with a "Negro caucus" or a "Negro coalition" was a good way to get killed. Just when they were getting things right. Just when they were getting used to each other, in positive ways.

"Nice shot," he said.

She turned around, the gun prudently at her side. This was the worst imaginable idea for how to spend their eleventh wedding anniversary. That was what this city was ever more full of: the worst ideas for everything. Once this had been a great city. Now her father was dead. Her mother moved to Florida. All of a sudden the lake smelled like dead fish, the river looked like a backed-up toilet, and her husband was in love with himself because he figured out why he so loved the downtrodden Negroes. Nothing made sense.

"Sorry," he said.

"You ever fire a gun at anyone?" she blurted. Sometimes it's not amazing how many murders there are, but how few.

"No," he said, in a way that sounded like *yes*. She didn't want to know. "Why do you ask?" he asked. He stroked his face. "Have *you?*"

"Only in my dreams," she said.

"What's that supposed to mean?" He looked stricken: caught. She figured he knew exactly what it meant.

"Nothing," she said. "I love you."

It came back to her, the shooting, as she knew it would. This pattern was a beaut, no bigger around than the mouth of a paper cup.

"You're scaring me," David said, looking it over, whistling, tracing with his long index finger the big tattered hole all the little holes had made.

"I wish," she said.

"What's *that* supposed to mean?"

"Why does everything have to mean something?" she said. "I love you." What she meant was probably something else, but she couldn't have said what she meant.

They kept shooting. David improved. He was the sort of shot who would hit something if the thing he needed to hit came into his sights after ninety-nine rounds of practice.

Upstairs the footfalls of party guests multiplied. Several drink-wielding loudmouths trickled down and sat on benches and gave running commentary. They were strangers to Irene. David failed to introduce her, and they had to introduce themselves. She'd met a couple of them and apologized. David was also embarrassingly slow to realize these other people had come down there to shoot, too. Irene had to be the one to offer to step aside.

Half an hour until noon: what her father and brothers used to call beer-thirty. She and David went upstairs for a drink. Her ears rang. She asked David if he'd ask around for some aspirin.

"Not for *that*," she said. Everything menstrual made him go pale, as if he were the one losing blood. She tapped her ringing head. "Just from the shooting."

Danny Greene's windowless, mahogany-paneled office, bigger than any room in Irene's house, even the garage, had filled with judges, councilmen, state reps, county commissioners, the works. The other people were wives and labor leaders. Familiar faces, but Irene was bad with names. David rarely thought to help her out. He saw these people every day.

The first person she could identify was her father-in-law, and the first thing she heard him say was *oh yeah?* "Politicians are like football coaches," Mike Zielinsky said. His arm was in a cast, and the cast was swaddled in rabbit fur. "They gotta be smart enough to understand the game and dumb enough to think it matters."

The ones laughing the loudest were, Irene knew, the politicians. As the laughter waned, a gin-swilling churl in the corner yelled out to Mike that he'd heard that somewhere.

"That's the difference between politicians and regular people," Mike shouted back. "You mooks think you've heard everything."

Mooks. Irene could see how they loved it, these chuckling ex-lawyers, to stand around in sweaters and get called slangy names by a guy they called Mikey Z.

A console radio blared the Browns' countdown-to-kickoff show, too loud. But these were for the most part people who talked for a living. They overcame.

On the wall were framed flag-sized oil paintings of John F. Kennedy and the Pope. In a lit glass display case was a thick Bible that was probably worth a lot of money and a book called *The Last Hurrah,* opened to the title page, signed by the author.

Irene had never met an author, that she knew of. She was afraid she was the only one in the room who hadn't. She knew David worried that she was not the right sort of wife to accompany him to the places he needed and wanted to go. Minutes ago she'd been scaring her husband and blasting paper men into shreds, into nothingness. One on one with him, she had a happy marriage. Apart, or in a big group, it got complicated.

"Warehouses," said Mike Zielinsky, coming up to them and giving them hugs. David had started to hug people now that he was getting closer and closer to his little-boy's-dream of becoming mayor of the city of Cleveland, but with his family, even with his children, he could be counted on to flinch.

"Ah," said his son.

Mike kissed Irene on the cheek and flattered her a little. The cast thumped softly against her back, like a big rolling pin, and the fingers on that arm tapped her fleshy hip.

"No matter what happens in this world," Mike said to David, "it involves stuff of some kind. Goods. What those goods are, that changes, but as long as the world's still here and not bombed to a crisp, those goods are never all going to be where they're meant to be, which means that people need someplace to put that shit in the meantime." He held out his arms like a man expecting to be hugged yet again. He had a bloody mary in one hand. In the other, the arm with the cast, he held a cigar. He was wearing a black mohair sweater with gray-diamond panels, bunched up on the broken arm above the rabbit-fur sheath. "Am I right? And warehouses, the workers in warehouses, they're not union, not a single one of 'em. You should invest. You and, you know, the wife. I got people you can talk to." He winked at Irene.

The wife. They had no money to invest. They could barely afford their mortgage. Teddy and Elizabeth needed braces. Brad needed corrective shoes. To save money they used David's aunt to watch the kids when Irene worked and any other time they needed a sitter, and now Brad called Betty *Mama.* Every time Irene turned around, David bought a new suit, which (though he'd bought them in normal stores when they were younger) he said he needed to have custom-tailored, because of his height.

"That's great," David said. "Thanks for the tip. We've been talking about investments, actually." He sounded sincere, but his enthusiasm was confined to the lower half of his face.

She touched that lower half of his face. She stroked his soft cheek.

He blushed.

His father started to razz him, and Irene leaned toward her husband and kissed him full on his rough lips. He smelled like the spiced-rum cologne she'd bought for the kids to give him this past Father's Day.

Party guests hooted. She was thirty-two years old. Irene wrinkled her nose and girlishly buried her face in her husband's neck, and the party guests hooted some more, and Irene June Hrudka Zielinsky felt certain this was the last girlish moment she was ever going to have.

Eleven years is *nothing*. She knew that. Her parents had been married for fifty-two. What Irene understood so far about marriage was that it proposed an ideal and delivered a compromise, and that it meant sharing your life with a stranger you knew so well it thrilled and bored you. No one had told her this. Again, eleven years is nothing. But you can decide on things. You can decide that the weight you're never going to lose doesn't need losing. You can decide you don't need any more revenge. You can decide to stay married. You can decide to figure out the impossible. You can keep going on your rounds, helping the maimed, easing the pain of the doomed, watching people die, and accepting that no doctor anywhere will appreciate what you're able to do and forced to withstand. You can decide to hold tight to what scares you most. You can decide you know what marriage means. You can decide to take a different set of feelings from the ones you once called love and call the new ones love instead.

I shoot straight, she thought, releasing herself from her husband's embrace, feeling him wipe from her cheek a tear she hadn't known was there. In reflex she wiped the same spot on his face, which was dry. She patted his cheek and smiled. When he said, "What?" she said, "Nothing."

Danny Greene materialized at her shoulder. He dropped to one knee and with a bowed head and an extravagant wave of his arm, in imitation of a knight bestowing jewels upon the queen, extended his fist to her. People who knew people (Irene knew people, but for the most part not like that) would later call him the Unkillable Danny Greene. But that's a story for another book. For now, he turned his hand over and exposed his palm. It was full of aspirin.

David, she knew, felt upstaged. She thanked her host and then squeezed her husband's hand, for reassurance, and then took two aspirin, the recommended dosage, and went to the bar and washed the aspirin down with a wholesome glass of uniced, fluoridated tap water. She went to the ladies' room and prepared herself to go to a football game she'd go to instead of doing what she wanted to do, which was return home to spend a day with her kids. *I shoot straight,* she thought. *I have a gift.*

—— 23 ——

AT SUNSET, ON a hot Monday night in July 1966, with the promise of rain balanced on a mauve, unnatural horizon, a slim young black man in a white shirt and a dark tie walks into a corner bar—on the corner of East 79th and Hough: the 79er Cafe—and asks for a glass of water. Behind the bar the owner, a white-haired man born in a European country that ceased to exist, folds his arms before him, closes his eyes, and shakes his head no.

Clevelander v. Clevelander.

The black man stands tall, in an exaggerated way, and points out that what the owner is doing is illegal. The owner says he's been through this and through this; he reserves the right to refuse service to *anyone*. Behind the bar there's a sign to this effect. It's a common policy. Why pick on him? The other people in the 79er are for the most part other merchants in the area, unwinding at the end of their day in the dry cleaners, barbershop, or grocery store, among their own kind now. Other than in times like this, the owner has nothing against colored people. The man who fixes his Plymouth is colored. So's the weekend fry cook and the woman who comes into the 79er every morning and cleans. But *this:* it's not the first time, it's not about water, and he's sick of it. The least these people could do was order something that cost money. If he *does* start serving them, he's not going to start with a free glass of water.

The black man points out that state liquor laws require any business that serves liquor to serve everybody, regardless of etcetera.

The owner starts yelling. This is his business! He's free to run it how he pleases and to serve the people his customers are comfortable eating and drinking with. He left the country of his birth when the government started telling people how to run their businesses. He came here to take part in the free enterprise system. This is America!

The black man agrees. "Yes. This is America." He says it slowly and does not raise his voice. He maintains his posture, points out that this isn't the end of the matter, then does as he's told and leaves.

Stapled to the rough-hewn wall is a cardboard sign advertising beer and displaying the 1966 schedule for the Cleveland Indians, who are playing on a TV set above the bar and losing. Once they played just around the corner. People on their way to and from League Park stopped here for bratwurst and beer. Tonight the Indians are in New York, getting humiliated. The owner rips the sign from the wall. Staples fly. Staples ping onto the linoleum. He grabs a black Magic Marker, writes (the squeak of the marker louder than the TV) THIS PLACE WILL NOT SERVE COLOREDS, and holds it up to show his customers. A cheer goes up. They laugh and slap each other on their wide, hairy backs. The owner puts the sign in his window. He shakes his fist at the black people gathered on the sidewalk: *his* sidewalk. He turns, faces his clientele, and bows.

It is the hottest summer since 1954.

Clevelanders v. Nature.

Along Hough Avenue air-conditioning units are as rare as white people. The air-conditioning units here have run so constantly even many of the newer ones have conked out. Repairmen, even black ones, go to other neighborhoods first. All of which is to say that many more people are outside than would be usual, sipping more cold adult beverages than they would have on a cooler night, wetter with sweat than they'd have liked, in a worse mood than might have been ideal, looking to those rain clouds and wondering why they're stalled on the darkening horizon, above the west suburbs, torturing the good people of Hough with relief that will not come.

These are the people who see the sign go up in the barred window of the 79er Cafe, inside which they are not free to go.

These are the people who come down off their porches, stoops, and rusty fire escapes, to see what the people are looking at in the barred window of the 79er Cafe.

These are the people who switch off their televisions (the waning minutes of a rerun of *The Rat Patrol*) and look outside and see all those other people, and hear the sound of sirens and lock their doors and move their fitfully sleeping children away from the windows.

The deadbolt lock on the front door of the 79er Cafe clicks closed. Customers sneak out the back.

Seconds later there are five squad cars on the scene. Before the screaming policemen have the chance to separate the curious from the bellicose, a helicopter appears in the now-inky sky, training swiveling spotlights on the sweat-drenched people of central Hough.

Clevelanders v. Machine.

Now ten squad cars.

Someone yells at the cops that they'd take hours to come to your house if you had your car stolen or your apartment burglarized, but some scared white barkeep calls you and, fuck us, here comes the fucking cavalry!

Now fifteen.

The first shots come from no one knows where. Immediately, people run and push and cry and scream and scatter and call out the names of lovers, parents, children. Everywhere there is the sound of breaking glass. The bullets are coming from above, and people keep running. Rifle shots, from the roofs of buildings, and there's not a person there who knows if the shooters are on our side or theirs, and the sides are inscrutable anyway except along the most awful and obvious lines. Dripping-wet black people run into dark alleys and back to the homes that are in truth already gone. Cops dive behind parked cars and draw their weapons and look up at the helicopter pilot and wonder if he really wants them all to die, but instead of shooting at him they shoot out the lights: streetlights and even the swirling cherry tops and burning headlights of their own squad cars.

One of the snipers is firing what seems like a tommy gun from the roof of a nearby theater. Someone else is firing a deer rifle from on top of an apartment building. The apartment building is on fire. The cops who made it back to their squad cars have broken out the tear gas and are lobbing and shooting it indiscriminately onto the roofs of the Hough District. Through the haze of smoke and tear gas, how many snipers there are and where they are is anyone's guess.

More breaking glass and shrieks of running people. How and why the fires started who knows? The air shimmers with its thick smells: gasoline and burning tar, cordite and human sweat, the tangy ozone of coming rain. The head winds of the storm blow in from the lake, bringing with it the odor of fishy, sulfuric muck.

None of which a person too near the tear gas can smell.

On one corner a group of young black men assemble in a tight fearless circle and chant, *"Vietnam, Vietnam, Vietnam,"* and a terrified, sympathetic cop whose brother died there takes a nightstick out and tries to follow procedure and at the same time press these men gently away from the corner and to safety, and soon the black men are singing a hymn and the cop gives up and walks away and is ignored. He mutters a curse and a bullet catches him in the calf.

Clevelander v. God.

Four fire trucks roar into Hough, horns blazing, bearing eager young white men with axes and riot gear, but the trucks can't get past the panic-stricken people running through the hot dark fire-lit streets. Soon the fire trucks are pelted with pop bottles and bricks. Men run out of the darkness and get in fistfights with the all-white complement of firemen, and other men pull the hoses off the trucks and slice them with steak knives.

Inevitably, someone—an actual person, though by now even the people there don't feel like individuals; in the days that follow, incredulous authorities will tally up the ruined, the jailed, the homeless, the wounded, and the dead, and faces will reemerge, altered but once again real, and the living will see all this in terms of Man v. Society—uses a tire iron to pry the white metal bars off a drugstore window and the looting begins. Next door to it is a supermarket and that's next. Aggrieved and snarling people siphon gasoline out of bullet-riddled cars and into beer bottles, and stuff strips of their own torn clothing into the bottlenecks. Still the rains don't come. The supermarket—the only one that did not close when the last white person left the neighborhood, but instead forged bravely on by raising its prices across the board on the days the welfare checks arrive—explodes into flame. Looters run through the burning store, dodging popping aerosol cans and the pyre of the tissue/napkins aisle, ducking under the bleach fumes, until a natural gas line ruptures and the store explodes into flames four stories high.

Behind the store, utility poles go up like matchsticks. Power lines fall to the ground, sizzling and sparking, dancing like mythical snakes. The fire is hot enough to detonate gas tanks in cars parked across the street.

"Matters might have been worse," says the *PD*'s senior police reporter, dictating his story on deadline from a desk sergeant's phone at the Fifth District Police Headquarters, corner of Chester and 107th, close enough to smell the smoke, even with all the windows closed and the AC blasting, "if not for a good number of conscientious Negroes in the area."

An hour before sunrise, a hard rain begins to fall. On the wet pavement, blood mingles with ashes, spent cartridges with shards of glass, lost shoes with hair ribbons, all washed into the storm sewers, together sluicing its commingled, mucky way toward the dead river, toward the wide, twisted ditch that bisects this wounded city.

֍

WHY THAT PARTICULAR incident triggered things is anyone's guess. That's riots for you.

The Hough Riots went on for a week. Exactly what happened would be an imperfect composite account—more coherent years later, as memory fuzzed things, than it was to anyone stuck or stationed in the middle of it.

In the days and weeks that followed, the slim young black man would be called an instigator. A militant. The most powerful young black member of the Cleveland City Council noted that if the man had done what he did in 1776, he'd have been called a patriot. The man's identity will be lost to history. He was not the powder keg, not the fuse, maybe not even the match. Just a man. Do cities get the Rosa Parkses they deserve? Possibly he was nothing more than a thirsty guy on a hot night, blundering into history and finding his way right back out. But who is he? Who was he? It's a question no one pursued. The city burned. Shot-up sirens moaned and caterwauled. Bystanders died. White people acted surprised. Black people acted surprised that white people were surprised. Pundits embraced their sanctimony. Violence begat violence. The riot contained seeds of change for the better (as American riots tend to do). And the man (we don't know if and when he loosened his necktie) walked straight off the grid, into nonbeing, revealing the fault line of his city's true conflict.

It's pretty to think that this is Cleveland v. New York. Or Cleveland v. the World. Or Cleveland v. Rust. Or even the West Side of Cleveland v. the East Side.

It was Clevelanders v. Themselves. Not v. Other Clevelanders. Themselves.

Ourselves.

America v. Itself.

The end.

— 24 —

HER CHANCE TO be a war correspondent, and Anne O'Connor blew it.

Her eleven o'clock newscast mentioned the late-breaking news of a five-alarm fire in the Hough District. As the anchorman read (of *course* it had not been handed to her), Anne suspected this had been a cut-in (a) to add drama to the city's lowest-rated late newscast, (b) for the mellifluousness of the phrase *five-alarm fire in the Hough District*. Plus the station had sent a camera crew to the scene and would have footage tomorrow. This teased the viewers for that. Then came the weather. To Anne's surprise, the forecast did not call for rain. Her forearm, when she put weight on it, burned enough to make her jump. Her arm hadn't been wrong yet.

The newscast signed off. Anne left to go home. Had she stayed three minutes longer, she'd have been there when the news director—a thirty-seven-year-old West Sider named Len Petocek, recently sacked by let us say another network and hired here—heard some new details of the scene over the two-way radio and decided to send every available person to cover the story. A shooter did in fact run out the back door to see if he could catch her, but Anne was out of sight.

She drove toward the lake and took the Shoreway east. As the riots raged, she shot by the lakefront airport and the lakefront warehouses at seventy-five miles per hour, protected from getting pulled over yet again (they never ticketed her) by cop-depleting forces she couldn't have imagined. She was a mile north of apocalypse but oblivious to it, her radio blasting snarling new British rock music. She was thirty years old and had begun to dislike mirrors and hate herself for caring. She'd just this year been allowed to start spending money from her trust fund. The first big thing she bought was this car, a hardtop blue Corvette. The second was a Victorian house on a wooded lot in Bratenahl, on a cliff overlooking Lake Erie, so far east it wasn't Cleveland anymore. She lived alone. No cats! Her dog Babe was a sweet-tempered shepherd-mix bitch.

As she came around the bend of her long blacktop driveway, she saw her brother John's white pickup truck, parked in the grass on the far side of the driveway. He was shooting baskets at the hoop mounted to her garage. Patrick was with him. Her dog had been let out and was running around in jumping, overjoyed circles. Patrick was wearing an undershirt, Bermuda shorts, and canvas basketball shoes. John had on a tailored white dress shirt, chinos, and penny loafers. They were both drenched with sweat. Anne's Corvette was so new her dashboard clock still worked. Midnight.

She leaned out the window. John sized up a long set shot. "Keep your elbow in," she said.

He grabbed the ball, faced her, and dribbled it once, with two hands, like someone angry to have been assessed a personal foul.

"Hi, Babe!" Patrick waved and grinned like a simpleton.

He'd been sacked six months ago at the radio station he'd managed. Change of ownership. Since then he'd been managing family real estate and was talking about buying a real estate company and running that. A wet grocery sack cresting with beer cans sat on the flagstone sidewalk. The dog heard its name, ran over, knocked Patrick down, and licked his face.

"What's wrong with *your* court?" Anne said. "Either of you. I'm tired."

Patrick had a hoop, and so did John's apartment complex.

"Pat has family," John said, "I have neighbors. It's late. Where've you been?"

"Work," she said. "I don't suppose you watched." *Pat has family.* What kind of a dig was that? Coming from *John?* Anne pointed at the bright vapor light at the peak of the garage roof. "That wasn't the light I left on."

"We broke in," Patrick said. He wrestled Babe to submission. Ibby had taken up dog training (Anne was meaning to take Babe but had been busy, busy, busy), in hopes of learning enough to train seeing-eye dogs. Patrick had picked up a thing or two. The dog sat beside him, utterly still, its tongue inside its mouth.

John extended the ball her way. "This is your ball, too."

"How long have you guys been here?"

"Go get a beer," Patrick said. Babe ignored him. "Now *that* would be a trick."

"Listen," John said. "We walked down to the lake. You have a problem."

"I know, I know," she said. "The same guys I had out to fix the stairs are coming out next week to work on the dock. They did a good job on the stairs, don't you think?"

"It's not just the dock," John said.

"Hey, isn't this a school night?" Anne said. She could never figure out why, but he always taught summer school.

"If I had a dog who'd go get me beer," Patrick said. "Well, that'd be the dog to have, eh?"

John pointed at the house with his thumb. "Five years," he said, "and that whole thing's going to go sliding into the lake."

"Ten to twelve." Anne's arm ached from wrist to armpit. "I had a guy come out for that, too. He said ten years minimum. He gave me a price for moving the house back fifty feet."

John asked her how much, and she gave him a number that was half of the real number. He asked her how many years and she said more than any of us would ever live to see.

"I wouldn't have had to have kids," Patrick said, "if I'd've had dogs like that." He began making baby-talk noises and nuzzling the dog. Babe softly growled, a sign of utter happiness.

"Pat's drunk," John said. "Want to know why?"

In this family? A reason? "Could I please park my car first?"

John shrugged. He looked hurt that she hadn't said *why?*

"Want to open the garage door for me?" Anne asked.

"A dog that could open the garage!" Patrick said. "Maybe *that'd* be the dog to have."

John opened the garage door.

"Want a beer?" John said.

"They're warm," Patrick called. "Can we have some of yours? If they're cold?"

Anne parked the car, greeted her dog, and went to get herself a glass of wine. Her phone was ringing. Anne was certain it was Ibby. She and Patrick had had their problems before. Since Anne moved here this spring, each of them had come by furious with the other, spent the night at Anne's, and gone home by the chagrined light of the next morning. It was the house. Anne blamed that house. Someone should burn that house down. She let the phone ring. She was determined not to take sides. She was angry with John for taking sides.

(The phone call was not from Ibby.)

She put her hand on the receiver. If she was honest with herself, she was only certain it was from Ibby because she was afraid the call was not from her but from the other. The home.

(The phone call was not about her mother, either.)

Outside, her brothers had resumed a game of one-on-one.

"What'd you do to my dog?" she asked. Babe remained essentially still, watching.

They ignored her. They were playing to ten. Anne pulled down the tailgate of John's truck. The dog jumped up and put its head in her lap. She sipped her wine. She petted her needy dog. She'd named the dog Babe so everyone else would stop calling *her* that. It hadn't worked. John won the game 10–6.

"Not bad for an old man," John said. "Want to play me?"

Anne frowned. "What are you here for?"

"What bad habits you've fallen into," he said. "Didn't you notice what that sentence ended with?"

"Fuck you," she said. "Or should I suggest what someone should fuck you *with?*"

"A preposition!" Patrick said, like a game show contestant. At the edge of the grass, he counted down an imaginary clock—*five, four, three, two*—and at *one* heaved a hook shot. It banked hard and went in.

"The Giants win the pennant!" Patrick shouted. "The Giants win the pennant! The Giants win the pennant!" He flailed around the court. The dog finally snapped and joined him. "I can*not* believe it!"

"The younger you," John said to Anne, pointing at her, "would play me."

"The younger me," Anne said. "Feature that."

She glowered at him. Earlier this summer the station manager had hinted that Anne should consider plastic surgery. She'd told John about it, and *only* John, in strictest confidence and so he would reassure her (to be fair, he'd done precisely that). How could he, now, betray her? How could he be so mean?

Patrick rummaged through the empty cans in the grocery bag and found a full one. "I'm taking the rest of these in," he said, "and putting them in the freezer."

"I'm really sorry," John said. "That wasn't what I meant. At all."

Anne shook her head. It might have had something to do with the *fuck you with* line. The profanity always bugged him, which always made her want to do it more. Plus, he started it. Still and all: she was too tired to contend with her family. Had she been covering the riots, she no doubt would have been revived by adrenaline, fear, and ego, riding toward fire and gunfire in the backseat of a young West Side cop's squad car, while he muttered *nigger* this and *nigger* that. Instead she was home, oblivious and beat. "Forget it," Anne said.

"I'm getting married," John blurted.

"Married?" said Anne. She studied his heedless, craggy face. "To a *woman?*"

"That's how it's usually done, no?" said John.

Patrick stood behind him, nodding, his face still split by that insipid grin.

John sent the ball her way with a crisp chest pass. He had a look on his face that made it clear he wasn't kidding. "Want to go with me to tell her?"

The way he said it, it was clear he meant their mother. Two years ago Sarah O'Connor quit drinking for good. She lost weight, joined the church choir, started dating and attending benefits and parties. For the first time in decades, she was written up admiringly on the women's pages of the *Press* and the *PD*. This lasted six months. In the past year and a half, Sarah had come down with emphysema, had a stroke, a heart attack, another stroke, and been admitted to a nursing home.

"Who *is* she? The lucky girl, I mean? How'd you meet her? How did she . . ." Anne didn't have the right word for this. "Convert you?"

"I'm no passive agent for the feminine wiles," John said. "Doreen's are powerful, though, I'll give her that. Shoot."

Anne dribbled. *"Doreen?"* It sounded like the name of a woman who lived in a trailer.

John looked injured. Doreen, he said, worked in the admissions office at John Carroll, one of the women they'd hired to help the school go coed. Her father was an English prof, too, and she and John had been friends for ages. John claimed he hadn't been with a man in two years. Doreen had drafted John to travel with her on a recruiting trip—speeches to prep school assemblies, sitting behind folding tables in the offices of guidance counselors, that sort of thing—and eventually one thing had improbably led to another. She was twenty-five years old.

Anne picked up her dribble and shot the ball. She missed everything. Patrick and Babe chased it, out into the dark slope of her backyard.

John was forty-five.

"OK. I'm sorry," Anne said. "But, look, I've been engaged a hundred times and—"

"Five by my count."

"—it's not a good sign to be conceding things at this stage."

"Conceding things?"

"Trust me. 'I'll give her that,' you said. That's concession. I know concession when I hear it. I'm the great conceder."

This wasn't what she really wanted to tell him. What she really wanted to do was accuse him of doing this because it's what the Catholic Church said he was supposed to do.

The dog was trying to get the ball in its jaws. Patrick was laughing. The wind picked up, and so did the sound of the waves. The dog wailed at its own futility. Patrick broke out singing that old Buddy Holly song "That'll Be the Day." John yelled at him to shut up, and Patrick pretended not to hear.

"Doreen of course has no idea—"

John waved her off. "Don't presume to know what the lovely Doreen has ideas about, all right?" He smirked. "So," he said, "do you want to go with me to tell her?"

For a split second she thought John meant Doreen. Then she got it. "Don't be ridiculous. Visiting hours are—"

"We're going to break in."

"Right."

"Pat's idea. It's a good one. Join us."

Patrick got Babe to give up the ball and, on command, to roll over. Anne hadn't even seen him rehearsing that trick. It wasn't a trick the dog knew, but there it was. And Babe did it again.

"You'll be arrested," Anne said to John. He laughed. She wasn't sure whether he was laughing because he was kidding about breaking into the home or because of how unlikely it was that someone in their family would be arrested for anything. Then he reached out for a hug.

"Ugh." With her good arm, her right, she stiff-armed him. "You're sopping wet. OK, you won't be arrested," she said. "Have they been practicing that?" She pointed at Patrick and the dog. Again it rolled over.

"A little," John said. He called for the ball. Patrick reared back and fired a strike to his brother. Babe sprinted behind it, a keep-away natural.

"A woman," Anne said. "Oh, *John*."

"We might be," he said. "Arrested. You never know."

John had a terrible hitch in his shot, always had. Baskets went in for him. No one could explain it. John swished an ugly ten-footer. The dog hit the falling ball with its nose, sending it past Patrick back out into the yard. They raced toward it. Thunder rumbled from the west. A moment later Patrick said, "Oh shit," and called out that everything was fine, he'd buy her a new ball. It had fallen off the cliff.

"As long as it's not the dog!" Anne called.

"It's not!" Patrick said, and then ordered Babe to speak—another command the dog hadn't known earlier today. The dog barked.

Anne drained her wineglass and asked John for a cigarette. He made a face.

"Does Doreen know," Anne said, "that you're doing this as a gift to your dying mother? I suppose Doreen's pregnant, huh?" She touched the scar below her elbow, worrying it, feeling it burn, and not reacting at all.

"I'm *not* 'doing this as a gift for my dying mother.'" John made his fingers into little claws to denote the quotation marks. Occupational hazard. "Al*though*," he said, shrugging, "now that you *mention* it . . ."

ANNE AND PATRICK piled into John's truck and drove to the rest home to see their mother. They got no closer than the parking lot. John parked in the farthest space from the door, and they sat in the cab of his truck with the lights doused and the windshield wipers on high, watching the building's lit lobby glow through a hard, fat rain, watching steam foggily rise from the still-hot blacktop, choking down warm beer, and talking vaguely about love. Anne sat in the middle (happily, the gearshift was on the steering column), smoking just to irritate her brothers, which helped her fight the effects of the wine and the one pain pill she'd taken for her aching arm. To her right, Patrick passed out. To her left, John talked quite a bit about Catholicism and Doreen's sensible nature and ventured that if this baby was a girl perhaps he'd name her Anne. The beer ran out. At dawn a new shift of nurses arrived, a pride of laundresses and janitors left, and a security guard so young he had freckles came out and, with what looked like a high school class ring, rapped on their window—which woke Patrick up—and asked if he could help them. In unison, as a family, they all said no. They drove home. When they dropped Anne off, Patrick asked to hit the head. The *head?* Their father used to say that. He'd been in the navy. Patrick, because of his thumb, was 4F. Not that this was any reason to refuse her brother urinary privileges.

Inside, her phone was ringing. That, finally, was when Anne convinced Patrick to pick up the phone and talk to Ibby. Only it wasn't Ibby. "It's for you," Patrick said, handing the phone to Anne. That was when she found out her boss's boss—the station manager, not just the news director—had been trying all night to reach her.

LATER THAT MORNING, as the rains ended and the punishing sun re-emerged, Anne and Len Petocek, who was driving, pulled up in front of Al's Cutrate Store. The car had the station's logo on the door. Twenty desultory looters scattered. These were not all kids and not all black. From the passenger seat of the car (a four-door Rambler, two years old but rusted through along the bottoms of the doors and quarter panels), Anne saw a uniformed cop pocket a fistful of flashlight batteries and—without bothering even to conceal it—a wheel of cheese. He walked right past the old white man at the counter and disappeared out the back of the store.

Al's Cutrate Store lay in ruins of plaster chunks, broken glass, and bent metal shelves. The whole front wall was gone. A rusty tricycle was lodged in the wall. Below it, near where the door would have been, were the scars of a small, vanquished fire.

Anne had showered but not slept. She'd applied her makeup hastily and too thick. It was hot against her itchy skin.

Petocek was the sort of news director who bragged about having done every job there was to do at a TV station. He'd spend a whole day answering the phones when a receptionist was out with the flu, ignoring his own job and damn the consequences, then preen for days about how he had the common touch. The station had only four shooters, so, today, he'd pressed himself into service as the fifth, as this and every station in Cleveland practiced total-immersion coverage; even the sports guy was working the phones, interviewing professors of urban affairs and spokesmen for the Negro cause. Petocek panned across the ruins, squealing with porcine glee (later, he would concede that the other shooters had gotten better versions of the same thing). His voice was very high. Sometimes he went on the air and did commentaries. During these he'd get carried away and mug for the camera like a bombing vaudevillian. Everyone at the station and half the TV viewers in greater Cleveland did unkind imitations of him.

"Sir, are you Al?" Anne said. The old man looked to be about eighty-five.

"No Al," he said. He sat on a wooden stool behind his cash register. Its face had been smashed and its drawer gaped open. As for his face, it was shaped like a coffee mug. His skin was translucent and blue. "The store, I buy it from Al, fifty-eight years."

The footage here was fine, but the interview wouldn't work on TV. These were the days before TV people used subtitles when faced with anyone speaking accented English. The SA-16 camera had a magnetic strip on the edge of the film that recorded the sound and, for reasons Anne never fully understood, was slightly out of sync with the pictures. It had to be matched up in the editing room, time no one was going to take to impart the plight of poor, sad not-Al.

"You're just going to sit here," she said, "watching these people walk away with pieces of your store?"

These people. It didn't sound the way she meant it.

"What you want?" said not-Al. "Huh? I am sit here. You want I kill them? I'm not a gun man. Never no gun." Not-Al frowned. He pointed at the logo on the side of Len's camera. "Your TV station, we don't watch. OK? You go, huh?"

Only then did Anne notice an old woman there, too. A meat slicer had been thrown through the glass deli case. The man was so old this old woman might have been his wife or his daughter, there was no telling. She was picking shards of glass from what meat remained.

Anne waved Len over.

"No TV," said the woman. She put a hand over her face. "You go to hell."

Her accent was lighter than not-Al's.

Len Petocek pulled his head away from the eyepiece. "Don't you want to tell your story?" he asked. "C'mon. Tell Cleveland. Look right in here and let people know."

He made one of his faces. The woman raised her eyebrows and said, "Oh, you're him. That guy, the one who knows everything." *So they do watch us!* She looked straight into the camera and let loose. "I don't know everything like you there," she said, "but I do know that these people aren't human. Look around, yes? The human beings don't destroy their own homes. Do they? They don't."

All spoken right into the camera.

Always, when Petocek played shooter, he came back from stories with too many people looking right at the camera. It was footage that would never get aired if it had been shot by anyone else. You wanted the reporter in there. You wanted the person from the station to mediate. To control, listen, shape, interact. You wanted the family bending asynchronously over its flotilla of TV trays in the living room to observe everything and be accused of nothing.

Anne nudged Petocek and said didn't he think they should get out of there. As they walked, he lectured her about how people really wanted to tell their stories. About how you had to dig. They passed the tricycle, and Anne gave one of its protruding wheels a spin.

Beside the station's rusted Rambler stood two young black men, in coats and ties despite the heat. They looked like people who'd been queued up all morning and had finally been delivered to the head of the line. As Petocek and Anne approached, the men extended their hands. Anne shook them. Petocek did not.

"All night the police beat people for no reason," said one of the men. The other's lip was swollen. His white shirt had a few drops of blood on it. He stood in front of the turned-off camera and said he was living proof. "Someone has to tell our story."

"We have to go," Petocek said.

Anne did a quick stand-up with the two men, but mostly to appease them and only after giving Petocek a look. A small, curiously docile crowd of black people gathered around the Rambler. A few got in the background, smiling and waving at the camera.

This was not the story. This would never in a million years get used.

This all happened on the edge of Hough and was for Anne O'Connor as good as it was going to get.

The police had sealed off the worst part of it, and no one not already inside could get in. No one except cops, firefighters, newspapermen, and one TV crew per station. Behind the lines guns still fired, but sporadically. Somewhere the haggard, stubble-faced chief of police had his deer rifle drawn and was eyeing rooftops. Somewhere a newly married couple afraid to leave their tiny third-floor apartment made quiet love, fearing it would be their last chance. Somewhere TV crews leaned against bullet-ridden fire trucks, sipping coffee and waiting to capture on film the coming invasion of the Ohio National Guard.

∾

WHEN THE FILM he and Anne shot came back from the lab, Len Petocek looked at about half of it and decided it wasn't worth the time it would take to sync the sound. Each edit took about thirty seconds, as the editor literally cut film, glued it with rubber cement, and held it together by hand until it began to dry. Petocek said he liked some of the images and thought they could be used behind some of the stories people had written, just to give a sense of scene.

Three hours until the six o'clock news: too little time even to think about cutting together anything not sure to air. Anne was too unsurprised and too exhausted to argue, and also enough of a pro to realize this was hardly the time.

Anne looked over the shoulders of the two harried film editors and did some rewrite and drank a preposterous amount of coffee and took one and only one more pain pill and rushed around answering phones and yelling at people and completing not a blessed thing she started. Where you feel it first, the lack of sleep, is the thighs. Off and on all day, sneaking away to the ladies' room or her own tiny office, she'd whimper and almost cry from it all, blaming everything on her lack of sleep. Then she'd reemerge and hope no one had any idea.

Cans upon cans of film were returning from the lab, hundreds of feet of static footage of smoking rubble, angry black people, and clench-jawed police spokesmen. The mayor and the white councilmen hadn't wanted to go on camera. Even Carl Stokes—the state representative who, in narrowly losing the mayor's race last November, had become a semiofficial if semireluctant spokesman for the black people in Cleveland—said only that his thoughts and prayers were with the families of the four people who'd died. Anne had covered Stokes before. She was sure she would have gotten more from Stokes than that. But it had been her own choice to go to Hough, to be closer to the action. She should have known by now the best way to fail to get what she wanted was earnestly and directly to seek it.

The best story of the day came from behind the lines, an interview that the first reporter sent to the scene last night had gotten with the mother and children of the first casualty, a woman who'd heard the commotion and in a panic run home to protect her babies and been shot through the head. No one knew who'd fired the bullet. A stout old black woman said that her twin seven-year-old grandbabies, Lynnette and Jynnette, woke up this morning crying and asked if their mother was coming back. The woman—who stood up straight, spoke evenly, and didn't cry on camera—said no, she's gone. On camera the old woman said she'd been waiting for something like this to happen for a long time, only she'd prayed it wouldn't hit so close to home. God in his wisdom had seen fit to make it happen here anyway, for reasons it would be prideful to hope to understand. She hoped her daughter's death would mean something. She hoped people would wake up and see how it is for people down here. She waved a meaty hand in a way that made Anne think of a model on one of those game shows, pointing out a fabulous prize.

Anne watched the story get edited with tears running down her face.

"It's not *that* sad," said one of the editors.

She called him a string of awful names, and he said he was kidding, and she said, "Kidding? Right." In truth, until he'd pointed it out, she hadn't been aware she was crying.

She found the man who brought back that story and told him what good work he'd done.

At four Governor Rhodes sent in the National Guard. It wasn't until five that they rolled into Hough, in wave after wave of four-vehicle squadrons:

three Jeeps, each with three guardsmen and a machine gun, escorting a fire truck from across town or even the suburbs; in the passenger seat of each fire truck was a Cleveland cop with a shotgun across his lap. At five! Len Petocek screamed into the two-way radios that the timing of this was contrived to make it impossible for the six o'clock news to feature those Jeeps and machine guns and helmeted young men diverted from Vietnam training to invade Cleveland. He sent a runner to get a can of film. There was little chance of getting this on the air before 6:30, but nobody said anything.

With a story this big, the person doing the daily 5:28 cut-in during *Bowling for Dollars* would be the anchorman and not Anne.

Minutes to air Petocek knocked on Anne's office door to ask if she was all set. "Oh, jeez, I guess you're not." He pointed at her and made a rubbery face at the clock on the wall.

She had no idea what he meant. She pulled a final page of freshly tweaked copy out of her typewriter. "What do you mean?"

He stroked what would have been his beard, if he'd had one.

Her face, she understood.

She looked in her mirror. She did her own makeup, of course.

"No offense," he said, "but you look like crap."

"None taken." She heard herself say that and shook her head, fast, like a boxer trying to shake off a punch. "It's been a long day."

"Roger that," he said. "Listen, I've been in this business a long time, and—"

No longer than she had.

"—I hear, you know, rumblings." He made another bug-eyed face, this one apparently meant to indicate mock surprise over something shocking. "It might be time. You know?"

She thought he meant the newscast, but there was still almost ten minutes. "Your mother thought you were amusing, didn't she?"

"I know someone good," Petocek stage-whispered.

He was out her door and gone before she realized what he meant was plastic surgery, that the station manager had put Petocek up to this and Petocek had chosen now of all times to drop this bomb.

Eight minutes to air. A lifetime if you're a pro.

Anne looked in the mirror. Half an hour ago she'd scrubbed her face and reapplied her makeup, but the dark circles under her eyes had reasserted themselves. At her jawline the color of her foundation didn't quite match her pale throat. Her throat, truth be told, had the slightest beginnings of chicken neck. The slightest possible. The wrinkles in the corners of her eyes, men had told her, made her *prettier,* less like a doll and more like a woman. She heard that a lot. More all the time.

Was there anything at all a woman could do where her professional well-being wouldn't be threatened by things a man wouldn't even have to consider? *Other* than being a mother. Which didn't count. Mothers have no professional well-being. Just the booby prize of being uniquely suited to do a job men aren't able or willing to do.

Anne took out her compact of concealer and held it to the lights of her makeup mirror.

I can't go on like this, she thought.

She took a deep breath. *Right,* she thought. *That's what you think.*

⌾

THAT NIGHT, EVEN as Clevelanders tuned in to watch their city burn, four viewers (Anne harbored a vain hope it was the same crank four times) called to comment on Anne O'Connor's aging face. The newscast also included combat footage from Vietnam. Things ran together. Everything was what it was and also something else. Everything was the same thing.

Footage of the guardsmen and armed fire trucks riding into Hough didn't arrive in time to make the six o'clock news. The runner was a young beatnik-type from Cleveland Heights, home for the summer from some good college. Petocek fired him on the spot.

Guardsmen kept riding fully armed and frightened into Hough, until there were fourteen hundred troops stationed there. Still, for three more nights the riots reignited. Smoldering. Aftershocks. Fires kept burning. People kept getting hurt. A black family fleeing a burning building jumped into their old sedan and raced away, and the woman in the passenger seat, yet another mother, was shot in the face by a guardsman. She lived. Everyone who was killed was killed the first night.

The worst of it was over. Surely the worst was over. Everyone wanted to believe that, and no one did.

For those interested in lies, damned lies, and statistics: 4 dead, 30 injured, almost 300 arrests, at least 240 separate fires.

Four dead. On the air Len Petocek made a grim face and said he hoped these deaths would be a lesson for everyone—a force for change. Maybe the good that could come out of our city becoming a battlefield would be to do whatever was necessary to see that violence like this would not repeat itself.

Journalists filled hours of airtime and forests of newsprint giddily explaining the unexplainable. Politicians rushed toward microphones to testify about ideas they had for solving the insoluble. Fixing the broken. Reimagining a city that had seen the unimaginable. Opportunism and sincerity are in fact not mutually exclusive.

Right was wrong and wrong was right and up was down and down was up.

Black was sure as hell not white, though. East was still not west. The twain continued not to meet.

Otherwise, go figure.

Anne had lived her life thinking it was a curse she'd been born too pretty and now, what? She was going to undergo plastic surgery because her boss at a job she disliked more all the time told her to? Yes. It was crazy, but she was. Strike that: it was crazy, *and* she was.

Dr. Sam Sheppard and his young bulldog lawyer Bailey had gone before the Supreme Court of the United States, the highest court in the land, and secured a new trial for Dr. Sam. It started any week now. The highest court in the land! The new trial would be in Cleveland, which once seemed to Anne like the home of everything sensible. Anne had a bad feeling about the retrial. Privately, she no longer felt so certain about what *she* felt about the case. Maybe he *wasn't* guilty. Everything in the case didn't fit together as neatly as she'd thought when she covered the first trial. Where does it go, that certainty of youth? Why doesn't anyone tell you life is a slow, unswerving descent into doubt?

Louie Seltzer, Mr. Cleveland, editor-for-life of the *Press,* had finally been overthrown, deposed, and exiled. Nothing more unmoors a world than the loss of a clear enemy.

Jim Brown, on the set of the filming of *The Dirty Dozen,* asked to report to camp late. Art Modell (who'll own the team for another thirty cursed and title-barren years, then in a gesture of Learlike caprice, move it to Baltimore, Cleveland of the East; he'll place garbage-eating birds on the helmets and cloak the players in hideous purple jerseys) said OK. But there'd be a fine. "A fine?" Brown said. "Fuck it. I have nothing more to prove in the game of football." He retired.

The best player in the game, at the top of his game, and he *quits?* Bob Feller would never have done that. Satchel Paige, hell no. Tom O'Connor, never. The Vans, never. Sam Sheppard endured and kept fighting. Give the devil his due, even Louie Seltzer went down screaming. Brown did not get traded or go to New York. He quit the game and went to Los Angeles. *Quit! Los Angeles!* To participate in the creation of made-up stories, in the city where this whole business of riots got *started*. We are living in the final days, my friend.

Of *course* two days after Jim Brown retired the city erupted into flame. Naturally.

The Cleveland Anne knew was her father: big, broad, productive, lightly cultured, hard drinking, jovial, and respected.

The Cleveland she lived near and worked in was the subject of four-part articles in newspapers all over the world about America's Urban Quandary.

The Cleveland she lived near and worked in was a place where the Beatles (who since their last visit here had become bigger than Jesus) could return on a warm, breezy August day to play a concert in the biggest place in town—a rusting stadium scarcely older than Anne that had in her lifetime gone from eighth-wonder-of-the-world pretender to a drafty hulk that was a source of pride only to people who didn't get out much—and draw only twenty-four thousand people. In Cleveland this looked like a success: a month after the riots, twenty-four thousand kids, mostly white, were willing to go to downtown Cleveland at night. The Indians certainly did not fare that well. Outside Cleveland, though, the turnout was a joke.

The Cleveland Anne lived near and worked in had become shorthand for the worst place in America. Second prize: *two* all-expense-paid weeks in Cleveland. That sort of thing.

Right was wrong and wrong was right and up was down and down was up.

Steven was the martyr. Patrick was the amiable family man. John was the athletic homosexual bon vivant. Then John became Dr. Catholic Professor Man and now was going to get married to a woman named *Doreen* and vote Republican and present their drooling, dying mother with an issue she may or may not be coherent enough to know she has. What next? Patrick and Ibby getting divorced? Steven revealed to be a coward, a frequenter of prostitutes, and a Communist spy?

No one wants to be pigeonholed and no one enjoys seeing other people escape theirs.

Meanwhile Anne—what? What was she doing, she'd like to know, and what was it all about? Why did everything decay and die and burn and degenerate into filth and inconsequence? Why had she been punished by coming home? What did Cleveland ever do to hurt anyone?

Once Anne thought her life might go any which way. Now that it had, it was all wrong. It was not enough and just too much. She'd missed *everything* a person would want to have from having lived a life. She'd traveled everywhere and seen nothing, embraced the city her father had loved simply because he loved it (which, true, was not simple), and had been knifed in the heart for her troubles.

What's more exciting than to go where life is horrible and violent, to stand in front of rubble with a microphone in your hand and let the world know all there is to know? No life for a woman, her teachers had said.

Any day now the city, *her* city—the one her father had foreseen but not lived to see, or to remedy—any day now Cleveland would be overrun by plagues of toads and locusts.

Human beings don't destroy their own homes, do they? In Anne's experience, they do. We do. Everyone does. Animals don't destroy their own homes, but look out your window: how could anyone say the same for people? Rome burns. Has burned, is burning, always will *be* burning. Look harder. Smell it. It's not Rome we're talking about, sport. (Who knows but on the lower frequencies, Cleveland burns for you?) Yet you sit there. We sit there. Don't move.

੫

The Saturday of Labor Day weekend, Dr. and Mrs. Richard F. Hackberry requested the honor of Anne's presence as their daughter Doreen Marie joined in the sacrament of holy matrimony with Dr. John Xavier O'Connor. The ceremony was held in the building on the John Carroll campus that served as the Jesuits' dormitory, in a dark ground-floor chapel that smelled like stale beer and was about the size of a handball court. Doreen's sister Debbie was the matron of honor; Patrick served as best man and was the only man there with a tuxedo. John himself wore an Italian suit, but the scruffy professors on Doreen's side of the aisle all wore off-the-rack sport coats, if that. One had on what looked to be a homemade dashiki. The professors might have chosen to sit on the groom's side (there were no ushers) but did not. Doreen's father was a severe-looking hawk-faced man and her mother was Italian. Their side was packed.

In an elegantly simple blue A-line dress Anne had bought her for the occasion, Sarah O'Connor sat in a wheelchair in front of the front pew, stationed alongside the wedding party, and seemed to be following most of what was happening. Only her broad, unguarded smile gave her away. Before the strokes she never ever smiled like that, even for John, her secret favorite.

Other than John's immediate family (this being Patrick, Ibby, their well-behaved children, and Anne), the only people on the groom's side were the school's football coach and his humpbacked wife, several of John's students, all male, and John's old friend Kenneth, who'd flown in from Paris and was the only black person there. He didn't have a tie on, but his cream-colored linen suit looked like it had been pressed thirty seconds ago, and it stayed that way all day. Kenneth had stopped writing novels, he said, but his essays on matters of race were in demand by the best-paying magazines, and he was often invited to go on TV and talk about racial issues. The morning of the wedding, in fact, he'd taped an interview with Dorothy Fuldheim, which he didn't mention to Anne and which aired after he left town. Up until the point when it did air, Anne thought it was great to see him. The fringe of hair he had left was cottony white, and he'd gained enough weight to seem less severe. He made felicitous sport of the professorate and the earnest, shiny-skinned students and was able to coax a look of genuine recognition out of Anne's drooling mother. He whipped out his pocket square and dabbed her wet chin. She winked at him.

It was Kenneth's glance—more than Patrick's, even more than Ibby's—that Anne sought when the young hairy English professor in the dashiki got up and, in a voice so in love with its own sonorousness it needed to be accompanied by bongos, read some incoherent mystical poems he'd written for the occasion. When the poems went on and on, the priest (who was also a professor at the university) stood and edged toward the pulpit. Kenneth's head was purposefully bent down; his shoulders shook with stifled laughter. The chapel was hot. John and Doreen were arm in arm and weaving. Someone, soon, was going to faint. The priest placed a hand on the poet's shoulder. The poet stopped midpoem, stepped down, then paused to intone that if anyone was interested, copies of the poems had been dittoed and were available in the narthex, along with copies of his last book, which he'd be happy to sign in commemoration of this happy day.

Anne caught Kenneth's eye, and he lost it, covering his guffaw with a feigned coughing fit. The priest ran through the rest of the otherwise traditional service with great dispatch, and nobody fainted.

The reception was a sit-down dinner in the faculty dining room. Kenneth and Anne sat together and spent a couple of happy superficial drunken hours talking about books, old times, the Hough Riots, the Watts Riots (which Kenneth's sister had seen firsthand), and Paris. All night they studiously avoided the subject of homosexuality.

The closest they got to it was to talk about Doreen. Everyone who really knew John must have been talking about this. She was a short, swarthy woman with enormous breasts and hips. She looked even younger than she was, and her dress was cut low enough and cinched high enough to flatter her up to the cusp of stunning.

Doreen had no idea, Anne was sure.

Doreen's sister Debbie had six kids, and Doreen, in toasting her parents at the reception, made a crack about the catching up she had to do. *Child-bearing hips.*

"I don't see it," Anne whispered to Kenneth. "The appeal there."

Kenneth shrugged.

Just that? A shrug? "C'mon," she said. "I'm confessing something unforgivable here. But I can't see what she sees in him or he in her."

He shrugged again, but now he smirked. He sipped his vodka, which he'd begun drinking neat but was now pouring over ice.

"Money?" she said. "Child-bearing hips?"

He shook his head. "I put other people's marriages," he said, "right up there with the origin of life, the demise of the dinosaurs, the missing link, Amelia Earhart, and who shot JFK."

"Really," Anne said. "Why do you think he fell for . . . you know. Her. I certainly didn't see it coming. She's a nice kid, sure. But the world's full of nice kids."

"Why does a man," he said, "fall for any woman?"

He looked at her with eyes grown heavy-lidded from fame and French food, and what she wanted to say was that he had a good point there, presuming he meant that as a rhetorical question. "I'm presuming you mean that," she said, "as a rhetorical question."

"Look at it like this," he said. He had a bottle of vodka in front of him that he'd mostly drained himself. "I only write about things I don't understand, hoping to learn something. But only hoping. You see? If I wind up knowing, I'm a goner. I burn it. The thing to do is try to understand what you can't, and to fail interestingly." He swept his arm in the air. "Why isn't there any music at this thing? What's a wedding without a waltz?"

"You're drunk," she said. "And just changing the subject."

"Remind me," he said, refilling his glass. "The subject is what exactly?"

She wanted a cigarette but was trying to quit. Her doctor had told her it was not doing her skin any favors. "So do you still hate rock and roll?"

Kenneth claimed never really to have hated it. He listed as friends several rock musicians who frequented Paris, all of them white. He claimed to have smoked marijuana with John Lennon.

"You're a liar," she said.

"For a living," he said. At first she thought he meant smoking marijuana with the Beatles but then realized he meant lying.

At the end of the day Anne and Kenneth exchanged phone numbers and promised to cross paths again soon, and embraced. Kenneth climbed into a taxi. They never saw each other again.

∽

PATRICK AND IBBY came to New York for the procedure itself and again during her convalescence, hiding out at her old friend Jane's house in Westchester. Jane and her husband had loud arguments behind closed, inadequate doors. John and Doreen came to Westchester once. Everyone bore flowers and smiled too wide.

Anne let her hair grow out. She was afraid what would happen, but she did it. For the first time since she was a kid, it was red again. The shade was darker, but there was no gray.

As her healing progressed, her doctor, a stout and hale man with a booming laugh and gentle touch, said he was happy with the results, and only mildly concerned it was taking her so long to heal. He was chief of plastic surgery at a famous teaching hospital, and one of his worshipful interns asked if it was normal to bruise this much.

"People in my family bruise easily," Anne piped up. A nurse was rebandaging her face.

"Normal," the surgeon said, "is a dangerous word." Until that moment he'd reminded Anne, just a little, of her father.

LOCAL HEROES

ᕲᕳ

Fifth in a Series: How to Get Elected by White People
November 7, 1967–July 24, 1968

AFTER A TV crew records him shaking hands with the last few voters at a grade school in Mt. Olive and pretending not to hear the question about if he planned later tonight to meet with Dr. King, Carl Stokes thanks everyone, flashes a thumbs-up, and pulls aside the off-duty cop assigned to flank him and without breaking stride whispers that he'd just like to have some time alone. There's another car of Stokes workers who came there with them; they have room. The cop, a friend, says he doesn't think that's a good idea, but by then Stokes is jogging to his car.

Now, for the last time today, tonight, and possibly the next two years, Stokes is alone, quiet, and in no hurry. The song on the radio fades out, and Stokes turns that off, too. He doesn't want to hear the news. Good or bad. It's dark. The polls have closed. Downtown, hundreds of people wait for him—in the hotel suite at the Sheraton Cleveland, or in the balloon-filled ballroom there, or at his campaign headquarters in the Rockefeller Building. All waiting to stand next to him and celebrate a victory he hasn't yet won, but that they already see as theirs.

Which is fine with Carl Stokes. Accepting that, encouraging it, has brought him this far.

In silence he drives northwest down a hill on a road that will one day be named for his brother, a road his mother traveled on countless city buses, before countless dawns, on countless subzero mornings. Stokes is forty and looks younger, a big brown handsome man with a round head, closely trimmed Afro and mustache, and a dazzling, unfaked smile. Even though he's alone, even though his heart knows[1] that the great-grandson of a slave[2] is kidding himself if he thinks he'll be allowed to whip a man[3] who is the son of a heroic U.S. senator[4] and the grandson of an American president,[5] Stokes cannot stop flashing that smile.

Stokes starts, in fact, to laugh—a slow rumbling chuckle at first, but by the time he's at the bottom of the hill, heading down Chester and past the Cleveland Clinic, he's helpless with laughter. He drives along the south edge of Hough, laughing so hard he has to pull over, onto the concrete apron of an abandoned filling station. He is laughing that hard: hard enough that when he looks at himself in his rearview mirror his high cheekbones shine with tears.

✺

ONCE UPON A time, in the ghetto of a cold northern city, among a proud people who'd once been enslaved, there lived two brothers, Billy and Brother.

Before the older one was born, friends called his mother's swelling abdomen Little Billy. His mother delivered him and gave him another name, but all who knew him best called him Billy. Two years later the younger was born. Billy called him Brother. That stuck, too.

When Billy was four and Brother two, their father died of a pain in his gut. At the funeral neighbors clapped Billy on shoulders broad for one so young and told him he had to be the man of the house now. And so Billy steeled himself and became the oldest four-year-old alive. Brother had no memory of his father, and throughout his life no curiosity.

Their mother worked as a servant in mansions in the Heights, scrubbing floors, washing clothes, and changing the diapers of other women's babies. She barely earned enough to afford shelter. In their rickety house, her sons pounded tin cans flat and nailed them over rat holes. To keep warm they slept in one small lumpy bed, along with bricks heated in an old coal stove.

---

[1] Carl Stokes's head believes otherwise.
[2] Which is what Carl Stokes is. All four great-grandparents were slaves, in Alabama.
[3] Seth Taft.
[4] Robert Taft, known as Mr. Republican; JFK included him in *Profiles in Courage*.
[5] William Howard Taft.

Billy was a studious, responsible boy. Brother always sought new mischief. He played in the streets, learned games of chance from drunkards, and got in fistfights for fun.

One day, when the boys were thirteen and eleven, a miracle happened: those who ruled the land took small heed of the poor in their rat-holed houses and gave to them tall buildings full of warm rooms, running water, and machines that washed clothes and kept food cold.

For Billy, the tall buildings were grand: clean, safe, filled with other studious children, and near the neighborhood post office, where smart black men trained in the law, in the arts, in the classroom, were able at least to find work. On days when Billy had all his schoolwork done, he'd go to the post office, sit in a corner, and listen to those men talk.

Brother, too, loved their new home, especially the gaming room that was part of the tall buildings. Brother played pool, practicing his shots and his angles and winning other children's milk money. He played Ping-Pong and won a city championship. He stepped into a ring and fought boys of all colors, boys who were not his enemy, in hopes of winning gloves of gold.

One day the teachers at Billy and Brother's school announced that classes would be suspended so the boys and girls could go hear a man speak. They kept his identity secret, except to call him a "role model." Excited children filed into a great hall. Soon a velvet curtain drew back. There, center stage, was an old man known as Bojangles.

Billy was disgusted. The man was a *tap dancer!* Were the teachers saying that the only way to escape poverty, to escape trials hurled your way because of the color of your skin, was to be an *entertainer?* Billy *had* a role model: his mother, a woman who preached to her boys about the importance of learning, who ruined her back and knees so that her boys might eat.

Brother loved the stories Mr. Bojangles told. And *damned* if he couldn't still dance!

When after school Billy told him how sore he was, Brother saw his point. Still, Brother was glad he saw a legend like that—a man, he imagined, who'd been everywhere and seen it all.

❧

PURELY FOR THEATRICS, Carl Stokes knocks on the door of the hotel suite. His wife opens it. The room is crammed with people, roaring with joy and laughter. How all these people—not just family, clearly—found out about this suite, Stokes has no idea, but as far as anyone can see, he's thrilled. He shakes hands with everyone and works the room so gracefully, you can tell it wasn't taught. Without seeming to try, he works it so he's in a corner with the people he really does owe: his wife Shirley (#2 in a series), his brother, Louis, and—sitting strong and iron gray in a chair by the window—his mother.

"My baby!" She shakes her head in wonder. "Mayor of Cleveland. Mm-mm-mm."

"Have you heard?" Shirley says. "We're behind."

"The white precincts," he says, smoothing the hair of his beaming mother and turning to face his wife. "They report first. They have faster machines, more experienced poll workers."

"See this yet?" His brother, a lawyer for the NAACP, hands him that afternoon's *Press*. "They never let up, do they?"

Carl shakes his head. Two years ago Seltzer used a screaming headline to report the record black turnout and white voters ran out to the polls and Carl barely lost. Seltzer is gone now. But the *Press* is predicting that if the turnout is low, Stokes will win.

"As scare tactics go," Carl says, shrugging, handing the paper back.

"You're right," says Lou. *This one's mild.* Understood.

"From those jackals," Carl says, "this is like a nomination for sainthood."

"They're saying turnout is higher than last time," his brother says, meaning '65 and pointing at the TV set. "Possibly another record."

Lou Stokes looks strikingly like his brother. He's about the same height, though more angular. His posture is more stiff. Where Carl's a bit of a dandy (check out that double-breasted suit and red pocket square), Lou wears dark single-breasted G-man–style three-button suits. A blind man couldn't tell their voices apart.

"We're going to win this thing," Carl says. "Just watch."

The suite crashers cheer. They've been watching Carl and Lou talk as raptly as if this were the last episode of *The Fugitive*.

Carl excuses himself and goes into the bathroom to change. On the chrome towel rack is a box full of crisp white shirts. No one is more aware than Carl Stokes that the pictures from tonight might wind up in the history books.

When he emerges all eyes are on the TV, including the off-duty cop, who arrived in the meantime. Taft is up by ten thousand votes: four times Stokes's margin of defeat in '65. And *that* was to an incumbent Democrat.

"It's getting worse," Shirley says.

"When do our votes come in?" someone says.

Correct Carl Stokes if he's wrong, but isn't there a hint of relief in Shirley's voice?

"Still *very* early." Carl, all smiles, rubs his palms together. "I'm starving. How's that buffet downstairs?" In the ballroom, he means.

From the gallery all around him come happy testimonials.

"Well, good. Let's go. Some of you folks look like you could use seconds." He gently pinches a skinny bystander in the gut. Carl Stokes knows he can't set foot in the ballroom until much later—either to claim victory or accept defeat. He gives his brother a look and Shirley, too. They understand. He gives his mother a wink. The off-duty cop nods and follows.

Friends and campaign workers pack the brass-walled elevator. At the bottom Stokes excuses himself again, apparently to shake hands with a clutch of hotel employees, both black and white, and the next thing his gallery knows, he and the off-duty cop are gone.

The campaign is headquartered in a streetfront suite in the Rockefeller Building, a brownstone tower just up a small hill from the east bank of the Cuyahoga. The main room is full of about thirty campaign workers and draped with red-white-and-blue banners, posters featuring Stokes's photo (for black neighborhoods) and those with just his name (white). Banks of phones and electric typewriters sit on eight-foot folding tables. Three mismatched console TVs, donated independently to the campaign, are each tuned to a different station. There are no boxes of unused flyers, buttons, bumper stickers, posters, anything: what they have was dispersed.

The mood here is upbeat. The latest numbers show Carl Stokes closing the gap. Coffee is brewing. With any luck, it'll be a long night.

"Look on the bright side," Stokes calls. "If we *do* lose, the situation with Martin handles itself."

The room falls silent.

"Horse goes to the vet," Stokes says. "Vet says, 'Why the long face?'"

All that gets is a couple slight grins.

"Man, we are *not* going to lose!" Stokes says. "OK? Not this time."

In Stokes's lobby is a TV crew from CBS News in New York and reporters from the *New York Times,* the *Washington Post, Newsweek, Life,* and *Time.* Against the wishes of William O. Walker, editor of the *Call & Post* and one of Stokes's advisers, Stokes gives everyone in turn a few minutes inside. Even the men from the *PD* and the *Press.* He needs to give them what they want and get them out of here before Martin comes.

On the eleven o'clock newscasts, the local stations show Taft beating

Stokes, with the gap again widening. One station's pretty anchorwoman calls it "a stunning upset in the making." All three sign off with the race too close to call. Stokes's head pollster, who's been predicting victory all day, pulls out an adding machine and rechecks his numbers.

Stokes flits around the room and in his office, slapping people on the back and working the phones. He is relentlessly upbeat, both because he has to be and because he *is*.

One of the calls is from Martin's people. They are encamped in the new Hollenden Hotel. Win or lose, Martin plans to hold a press conference. Stokes says he'd be the last person on earth to presume to tell Martin what to do.

"We're going to win this thing," he keeps saying, either whispered into people's ears or when there are no reporters in the room. "Trust me."

At midnight he is down twenty-one thousand votes, with only thirty thousand left to count.

ೲ

LIKE ALL THE greats, you were misunderstood. *Great-grandson of a slave* didn't begin to tell your story. You lived in the present, dreamed of the future, and, until you were an old man, thought little of the past. And in a country with a fascist's love of victory, few understood that you rode into history on a rocket called defeat.

In 1958 you lost for sport. A year after you passed the bar exam, already restless with the law, you put your name on the ballot for state senate, then did nothing. You wanted to see how many voters would vote not for you but your name. In Cleveland people with names like Corrigan, Sweeney, Pokorny, and Russo got elected without being related to the Corrigans, Sweeneys, Pokornys, and Russos who'd held office before. When Anthony Celebrezze was mayor, Orlando Calabrese—a bouncer in a Short Vincent nudie joint—changed his name to Anthony Calabrese, ran for state senate, campaigned hardly at all, and won. You got five hundred votes.

In 1960 you ran for state rep. You campaigned all over the county. You put a hundred miles a night on your car. You stole your strategy from the ethnics: to your people you talked about your culture and the way others oppressed you; to every other kind of crowd it was three cheers for the melting pot. You went where no black man had gone before: spaghetti suppers in Little Italy, Kiwanis meetings in Parma, bingo nights at the Slovenian American Club, clambakes at the Old Brooklyn Legion Hall, Teamster Day at Euclid Beach Park. In these futile places, the ethnics looked at you like a

Martian. When you opened your mouth and English came out, they liked you, a little, just for that. You didn't push your luck by using their toilets or drinking fountains. Many of them came up to you afterward and said more Negroes should be like you.

You won.

But no: when the official tally came out, you lost by twenty-three votes. The Board of Elections charged ten bucks a precinct for a recount. You were tapped out, but outraged black folks sent you money. You got wadded-up dollar bills from welfare mothers and out-of-work machinists. Everyone in a high school civics class skipped lunch and sent you their lunch money. You paid for your recount. You won, by nineteen votes.

But no: your opponent, son of a congressman, had his lawyers point out the flaws in the Board of Elections' methodology. The Board paid for another recount. You lost by eight votes.

You conceded.[6] Suddenly everyone in Cleveland knew you. You were famous for being supported by the dimes of the downtrodden, famous for having an election stolen from you, famous for being gracious and dignified in defeat. In 1962 you won in a breeze.[7]

In 1965 you decided to run for mayor. For a generation the winner of the Democratic primary was a lock in the general. But what was left of the Democratic machine still had the juice to rig the primary for their befuddled ethnic incumbent. So you decided to make it a three-way race and run as an independent.[8]

You built a new machine. Your people were preachers, schoolteachers, bookmakers, pool-hall owners, outfielders, linebackers, R&B deejays, and the fabled little people, for whom you'd fought in the state legislature. You contacted everyone who gave money to any of your campaigns. Every ex-con assigned to you when you were a probation officer. Every Cleveland member of the NAACP. Everyone from your old housing project. Everyone from the high school class you didn't graduate with.

At your first press conference in May, you made your meager stack of petitions into a Michigan bankroll, which looked great on TV. No one thought to look at the blank ones in the middle. With the cameras rolling and reporters scribbling in their notebooks, you pledged that by your thirty-eighth birthday next month you'd have thirty-five thousand signatures—an

---

[6] Genius.

[7] In 1964 and 1966 you were reelected.

[8] Career-making genius move #2.

artificial deadline and more names than you needed, a pledge made purely to get attention. For a month, in cars, on buses, motorbikes, bicycles, and on foot, people who'd never worked on a campaign in their lives came to your indulgent brother's law office, asking for blank petitions and returning with full ones. On a Friday, four days before your media-event deadline, you had only eighteen thousand names. The R&B stations told people Brother Stokes was in trouble. All weekend the same people who once filled the stands for barely advertised Negro League ballgames came to the law office and wanted to know what they could do. On your birthday you had thirty-eight thousand names. You made photostats (you were no fool about what could happen at the Board of Elections) and called a press conference. When a TV reporter asked if all those names were from Negro neighborhoods, you said no, at least 10 percent were white people. As with the Michigan bankroll, no one called your bluff. A certain kind of white person wanted to believe you, which in fact gave you your 10 percent.

You rode in any parade you could find. Black children broke out of the crowd flanking the route and skipped along behind your car: laughing, proud of you, proud of themselves.

You went to the *PD* and the *Press* to seek their endorsements, and they didn't laugh until you left. The unions, the cops, and the firemen wouldn't even talk to you. Neither would the mayor. No one in council would back you, not even the Negroes. The closest thing the machine had to a boss— Bert Porter, nominally the county engineer—barred you from ward meetings and said you had no future in his party. His brother was executive editor of the *PD;* the *PD* called the Democratic incumbent the only safe candidate. Every Clevelander could translate *safe.*

The mayor refused to debate you. But when you told the Republican nominee—Ralph Perk, the county auditor, a dim bulb with the shock of shellacked hair all West Side ethnic pols seemed to sport—that, yes, the debate could focus on financial matters, he chuckled and agreed.

You holed up for a week in a small room in the new Hollenden Hotel and crammed.

Perk went first. He strode to the podium with a box of poker chips. He placed them in four teetering stacks. Each stack represented the people hired by each of the four previous mayors. "This is what needs to be done at City Hall." Perk swung his meaty arm and swept the chips off the podium. They rattled impressively to the floor. "Clean the place out."

He tried to look gruff after that, but the corners of his mouth kept twitching.

"I don't know if Mr. Perk is right," you began, "if those poker chips are employees the city doesn't need. But I do know this: they represent people. You don't smash people."

You smashed Ralph Perk. You spouted facts about the city's budget too arcane for anyone to question. People expected you to try to be a great Negro orator-hero, and instead you untheatrically carved up Perk's bromides and served him up with a candied apple in his mouth.

Election night you had two headquarters, one at a ballroom in the Sheraton Cleveland and one in the *Call & Post* offices in the ghetto. At each was assembled a band of rich and poor, young and old, men and women, blacks and whites, preachers and atheists, a handful of political pros with idealistic streaks peppering a roomful of slack-jawed naïfs.

You lost. With the unformidable exception of the black churches and the *Call & Post,* every institution in the city was against you, and still you buried Perk and came within twenty-three hundred votes—less than 1 percent of the vote—of the mayor.

Nothing would ever be more fun than that. Ever.

Eight months later the city broke into flame and armed soldiers occupied Hough. White people sought one man to speak for all the Negroes. Cleveland rethought the definition of *safe.*

∽

At about one Carl Stokes enters the ballroom. He is greeted by a booming chorus of *noooooooo.* Outside, idling at the curb, are six squad cars, summoned by the Stokes campaign itself, in case things get out of hand.

It's the hotel's biggest ballroom, twice the size of the one he'd been able to afford in '65. The crowd is much whiter and more expensively dressed than in '65. Dotted throughout are several big Afros, bigger than anything people had dreamed of two years ago. In the corner one of the R&B stations has a sound system set up and is broadcasting live, piping into the ballroom a feed of the latest Marvin Gaye duet. There are no TVs in here, but at least a dozen cameras. The election results have been announced all night from the podium.

The TV crews are asked politely and severally if they would leave, told that this is not going to be what it looks like, and they comply.

Stokes takes the stage, triggering an even louder *noooooo.*

The podium is a heavy oak thing, like the ones from school only unscarred and finished off with brass accents. The microphone won't work. Stokes tries to do without, but the yelling is too loud. Then he extends his arms wide, like a supplicant, and gestures downward with his hands, flipper-like. The shouting subsides, and the room grows rapidly, alarmingly quiet.

"I am not here," he says, loud enough he hopes to reach everyone, "to concede this race."

The room explodes in a cheer.

"But," he says, again deploying the flipper gesture, "at the risk of asking even more from people who have already given so much, I *am* here to beg for a favor—a favor from each and every one of you."

He pauses. There is a spooky, clammy silence. Faces look up at him with expressions stuck in some no-man's-land between anger and willingness.

"These historic campaigns for mayor," he says, "have not been about Carl Stokes; they've been about you." He asks how many worked on an election for the first time this year, how many for the first time in '65? He reminds them of the endorsements not he but *they* had won this time. "Win or lose," he says, and there is booing now, "either way we have made a difference. People all over the world have noticed what's happening here in Cleveland, have noticed *you*. This race," he says, "is not over, but as someone who's been involved in political fights maybe just a little bit longer than some of you, I'm asking you, imploring you, *begging* you, not to reject the system. What you people can do, what this city can be, it's bigger than Carl Stokes. It's bigger than any single election. It's bigger than any defeat, and it's bigger than any victory."

They're with him! Stokes knew he could do it.

His brother emerges from the wings, taps him on the elbow, hands him a piece of paper. They exchange a glance. Lou nods.

"We need," Carl says, "about 80 percent of the uncounted votes to go our way." He pauses. The crowd doesn't know how to take this and pauses with him. "My brother just handed me this. It shows that in the most recent precinct to report, we received..." He lowers his head. The microphone pops. It's on. Carl Stokes isn't startled. That's what the paper says: *Try the microphone*. He brings his mouth toward it and in his lowest baritone says: "Ninety."

This isn't complete bullshit. The last precinct he heard about, they'd gotten ninety-five.

He climbs down off the stage and works the reenergized crowd, making his way back out. The radio feed comes back up, and the deejay reads the results of other elections. Turnout is high. There will be at least one new black councilman. But the only West Side councilman to back Stokes got destroyed—the first Democrat to lose that ward since it was drawn.

When Stokes gets back to his office, both phone lines are ringing. He lets other people answer.

Martin is on line one, asking what chance Stokes thinks he has.

Seth Taft's press secretary is on line two, calling to say that Taft is about to claim victory and saying that as far as they're concerned, Stokes can concede either before or after. His choice.

Stokes drums two SETH TAFT FOR MAYOR pencils on his desk, then uses one to punch the button for line one.

"Every precinct left," Stokes says, "is ours. It's a matter of by how much." He invites Martin to come down to the office, have a drink, some coffee, and wait. He clenches his jaw. This is the best olive branch he can think to devise. "We still have an excellent chance, I believe." He really does. "I really do."

Despite everything, it's a thrill to hear that voice, to know a man your age could make such a difference in the world, and to realize he's in your city because of you.

By the time Stokes finishes with that call, Taft's press secretary has hung up.

൭൦

IT CAME TO pass that on distant shores a great war broke out. Billy and Brother's people were expected to fight and to die, and yet they could not share a tent or drinking fountain with their lighter-skinned countrymen. Still, young men volunteered to defend such a country. It was a war that needed fighting. Billy finished school and went to fight it.

Once he left, Brother quit that school and enrolled in the school of the streets. In the hall of pool, his teachers were A.C. and Big Al. A.C. was a great shooter who practiced hard but fell apart when riches were at stake. Big Al, king of the hustlers, shot no better than a bumpkin in a damp village basement, but with riches at stake he'd say and do things that made his opponent expect to lose. Just outside was another teacher, a woman named Ruth. Ruth and her husband were poor and desperate and started a business. Ruth provided a service at a nonnegotiable, reasonable price and did so on her terms, not in alleyways, doorways, or automobiles. She loved her husband. Work was work. One day a moving van appeared in front of her apartment. Ruth and her husband moved to the Heights. They opened a house-cleaning business; it thrived. They joined a church, started a family, and kept a well-tended yard.

Meanwhile, Billy found himself riding through the South in a train full of soldiers and enemy prisoners. The train stopped for lunch. The light-skinned soldiers went in and so did the prisoners, but the soldiers in Billy's train car had to go around back and eat in an alley. Goaded by these and other trials,

Billy was ready to riot. But he, too, was guided by the teachings of wise elders. Older, learned men in his battalion told Billy if he could corral his anger, he could be something. When he confessed to them that his dream was to use the laws of the land to make the world better for his people, they didn't tell him he couldn't. They told him he could.

Billy kept sending money home to his mother. He spent his liberty working in a mill, so he could send more. One day he was sent deep underground, to a hot, fetid room where a wizened man just shy of his allotted three score and ten was shoveling rotten sugar-beet husks. As Billy shoveled alongside him, sweating and barely able to breathe from the stench, he vowed to take whatever means necessary to keep from winding up like that old man.

When the war ended and Billy returned, Brother became a soldier and left. He was sent South and faced trials Billy had already endured. He was sent to the occupied country of the vanquished enemy, a distant land with many halls of pool. Brother, too, sent much money home.

Billy pursued his dream. By day he worked a menial job and every night he went to school. During his lunch breaks, he went to the courthouse and watched eloquent men argue.

Brother came home. He had not yet forged a dream and so followed Billy's example. He graduated from the school he'd quit and signed up for more schooling. To pay for this, he took a job as a driver for a small, greasy-haired wizard.[9] Brother drove the strange man throughout the land, watching as the wizard ensured that his people would support the ruler[10]—not because he truly believed in the ruler, he explained, but because doing so enhanced his wizardly powers. The wizard gave no public proclamations. In each village he sought out three or four villagers, spoke to them, and left. In every village, he explained to Brother, there are villagers who know villagers. This, said the wizard, is the way of this world.

⁖

AT FOUR IN the morning, after every TV station and most of the radio stations have long since signed off, it finally comes time to concede.

---

[9] John O. Holly, head of the Future Outlook League. A generation before King emerged, Holly organized peaceful boycotts and pickets of businesses that didn't hire Negroes. When the businesses relented, all Negroes hired became dues-paying members of the Future Outlook League. This wasn't a labor union. It was organized but no crime. It was politics, but what isn't? *"See?" said Leo Mintz. "It's all connected."*

[10] Frank Lausche, governor of Ohio for a zillion years, before that mayor of Cleveland.

The off-duty cop stands outside Carl Stokes's hotel suite; inside, everyone has cleared out but family. His son and daughter, six and four, are asleep on the beds in the darkened next room, dreaming. His mother—who, earlier, alone in the suite with the children, called housekeeping and bragged to the two young black women about her boys as they cleaned the rooms around her; when they finished, they had their picture taken with her, hugged her, and refused the tip she offered—keeps nodding off and pretending not to. Lou Stokes has gone downstairs. Carl and Shirley sit next to each other on the couch, holding hands. Carl is on the phone. "I'm not going to tell Martin what to do," he tells his press secretary. "If he wants to hold a press conference, that's his business. I'm not about to stop him. *We're* not about to stop him. Understood?"

Shirley shifts in her seat and pats her hair with her free hand and seems to be having a hard time getting comfortable. At a lull in the conversation, Carl leans over and kisses her.

There is a sharp knock. Carl finishes up on the phone. "Come in," he calls.

The cop opens the door.

In walks a slim, tanned, tennis-handsome white couple: Seth Taft and his wife, he bearing a bottle of wine, she an armful of roses. Carl and Shirley Stokes stand and accept the gifts. Handshakes are exchanged. The women kiss. Carl Stokes says he could not have asked for a more classy and gentlemanly opponent, and Seth Taft thanks him and finally lets go of his hand.

The Tafts leave. Carl persuades Shirley to let him wake the children and take them downstairs, too. He flicks on the light, shakes each of them by the flank, and they can tell by the look on his face that they've won. In sync they each stand and jump up on the beds, chanting *Mr. Mayor, Mr. Mayor, Mr. Mayor!*

Their parents and their grandmother stand back, watching and laughing. The laughter keeps pouring out of them, in gasps and shouts, like a thing too long suppressed.

The kids hurry to pull on some clothes and comb their hair, and the family leaves the suite as one. They're not even to the elevator before their little group gathers mass, like a rolling snowball. People fall in alongside them, running down the hall and, when the elevator proves too small, sprinting down the stairs. In the lobby more and more people fall in, *at four o'clock in the morning they fall in,* and they are for the most part strangers to Carl Stokes. Everyone wants to touch him! He's *pummeled,* but it's the kind of pummeling lavished on a ballplayer who's just slammed a home run. Suddenly comes the flash of a hot white light. They're beset by a plague of TV crews—both the bleary, bewildered locals and the barking self-satisfied men from the networks. Over this mess washes a wave of blue: fifty Cleveland cops careful to look strong and methodical on TV, parting a way through this mass of reporters and celebrants. What Carl Stokes notices are the jubilant faces and the churning arms and legs, and he would be afraid for his family but this crowd *itself* is his family, isn't it? He can feel it.

Before it's apparent exactly how he got there, he's backstage, just him and his family, concealed now for just a few moments from the crowd. There's his brother, who gives him a hug so hard it lifts him in the air. Lou and his wife embrace the rest of Carl's family, too. It's not until Carl makes a quick head count, to make sure everyone's made it through that happy gauntlet intact, that he sees his mother, looking curiously unsurprised, shaking hands with Martin.

Carl Stokes and Martin exchange a look. This is not, Stokes thinks, how they'd left it. Martin wasn't going to come here. They approach one another. Stiffly, they shake hands. The handshake dissolves into one of those hybrid midwestern half-hugs.

"Congratulations, Mr. Mayor," says Martin.

Stokes can't bring himself to ask if Martin plans to follow him up to the podium, and he can't bring himself to tell him not to. Stokes is a happy and exhausted man, too spent for any more politics now. "It's a great day," he says, "for us all."

Martin places his hands on Stokes's shoulders. He's dressed in the same kind of studiously plain suit as Carl's brother. For a long time nothing is said.

Stokes thanks Martin for everything, turns his back on him, regroups his wife, his kids, mother, his brother and sister-in-law, and heads toward the podium. He does not look back.

As he emerges onstage, someone flips on the houselights, and from the ballroom comes a thunderclap of applause, such as no one in the city of Cleveland[11] has ever faced before, an explosion of self-congratulatory, joy-throttled human noise that nearly knocked him down.

Hidden from view, surrounded by the police, Martin watches Carl Stokes raise his hands and his family's hands, too, listens to the new mayor's first triumphant words of acceptance, and with his entourage slips away, undetected, out of this hotel and toward another, wading out into the darkness just before dawn, down Euclid Avenue, his coat collar drawn against the re-

---

[11] Runners-up include Satchel Paige, Alan Freed, JFK, the Beatles, and Jim Brown. It's an honor just to be nominated.

lentless wind off the lake, undetected amid a fleet of honking cars, undetected as the people of Cleveland leave their warm homes and pour out into the streets.

They do not feel that hard wind. Without the need for music, they join arms, join hands, and dance.

☙

You knew you'd win. Or didn't think you'd lose, which matters more.[12] You won because you lost in 1965. White people didn't much vote for you. Because of how far you got without them, it made them *willing* to vote for you. That's how white people think. If they feel like they've given you something, they'll crush you. If you do it on your own, they'll scramble to give you anything.

After you lost Cleveland fell apart. Daily, it seemed, the federal government stripped money from the city for misappropriation, segregation, incompetence. When the riots broke out, white people feigned surprise and blamelessness. Into more and more white breasts was kindled the hope that they might be saved by one good Negro. They looked to the skies for Superman.[13]

You had your feet on the ground, but your eyes were on Washington. The Feds ordered Ohio to redraw its congressional districts. You thought you'd be a lock in the Twenty-first District. But when the new Twenty-first was announced, it was worse than before: the East Side black neighborhood had been parceled out to three different districts. The *Press* and *PD* looked upon this oddly shaped map and shouted *huzzah!* How grand that the Negro people will be represented in several districts rather than to have to settle for being the majority in only one! Perhaps limitations of space kept two such large news organs from pointing out that Ohio's chances of electing its first black congressman went from sure thing to fat chance.

You fought this in the legislature but finally handed off to your brother. He'd taken two other cases to the Supreme Court and won. If this one had to go the distance, he was the man.

Time passed. You decided you'd only run for mayor again if your brother lost, but the case dragged on and the deadline for the mayor's race

---

[12] Thus spake Big Al.

[13] He, too, came from Cleveland, debuting in a high school newspaper in Glenville precisely twenty years before you and your brother opened the law offices of Stokes & Stokes there.

was the one that came up first. The mayor was such a joke by now, it was clear you could run as a Democrat and beat him. So you filed.

You had your machine in place, and on top of it, you had the frightened white establishment lining up to anoint you Head Negro in Charge. You had a delicate coalition built. Your victory seemed like only a matter of time.

That's when you heard that Martin Luther King was coming to town to register voters.

This, in a nutshell, is what politics forces upon a person: you cozy up to your enemies and stiff-arm your heroes. King had lost every battle he'd waged outside the South, and he needed you more than you needed him. You needed him like you needed a suntan.

When King came to town, William O. Walker arranged a meeting at the *Call & Post* offices. It was the kind of meeting where the pleasantries went on forever. Quite a bit of this conversation involved sports and your common disdain for the Kennedys.

How were you supposed to tell King that you'd already registered black voters galore? How do you tell King his presence will scare white people, disrupt your coalition, and do more harm than good? Even if you do summon the wherewithal to say that, how do you explain your rejection of King to the ministers in the black churches, who'd been with you from the start?

You said it. King outlined what good he thought he could do in Cleveland, and when he was done you took a deep breath and said, "I'd rather you not stay."

King stayed.

Do you want to be told to place your money in a Negro bank? read a letter sent to people throughout Cuyahoga County. *Do you want to be told to sell your home and used car through a Negro newspaper? This is what the King-Stokes combine stands for.*

The letter was from the county engineer and Democratic Party chair Albert S. Porter. He denied writing it, but you, for one, did not believe him.

The King-Stokes combine. To say anything about this, one way or the other, was God's perfect lose-lose position.

Again that year it was a very hot summer.

You kept your head down and did what you needed to do. Business leaders, including an influential organization called Group '66,[14] supported you. White politicians, even a few West Siders, supported you. Black politi-

---

[14] A group whose own leaders included a brash young man named George Steinbrenner.

cians either supported you or got out of your way. In September the *PD* endorsed you.[15]

Game, set, match. Whitey loved you, man.

In the primary you cleaned the mayor's sprung clock.

The Republicans drafted Seth Taft to run against you in the general. You couldn't have been happier. He was a forty-four-year-old Pepper Pike lawyer and political tyro who leased an apartment in Cleveland days before the filing deadline. America, for one brief shining moment, wasn't the sort of place where it was an unalloyed advantage to be the grandson of a president and the son of a senator, particularly in Cleveland, where the labor vote now had to choose between a black man and the scion of a family with a century-long record of being noisily, powerfully pro-management.

No Republican in a generation had received more than a third of the vote. You knew Taft would get more than that. What was different about him, you joked, was his inexperience and the way people love a carpetbagger.

You debated him four times—the last time at the City Club preceded, like a title fight, with an undercard debate between a supporter of yours and one of his, yours earnest and white and his savvy and black; your debate, the main event, was broadcast live on all three local TV stations and excerpted at length by the networks, here and all over the world. *The world!* Seth Taft was professional, good-looking, a little shy, and a gentleman. You couldn't have asked for a pigeon with a more poetic lineage.

Three weeks after you won—only *three weeks;* you had to wonder about the timing—your brother called you.

"Listen, Brother, we just won your case."

"Hell, man," you said. "I don't want to go to Congress. I'm the mayor of Cleveland." A painting of you had appeared on the cover of that one-time Cleveland magazine, *Time.* Suddenly, becoming Ohio's first black congressman paled.

But when three black city councilmen lined up to run for the seat, you flipped. Where were these clowns when you ran in '65? Where were they when you fought your own party to create a district where a black could win? You'd be damned if you let them reap the benefit.

---

[15] The *Press* endorsed no one. There was a time when the *Press* owned Cleveland, and that time had been served. During one of your debates with Seth Taft—and not even the televised one—Louie Seltzer was the moderator. The format of the debate was such that all he really did was serve as timekeeper. Sic transit gloria fucking mundi.

At a Sunday morning meeting of the local leaders of the NAACP, at Pier East on Shaker Square, you asked your brother to run. He hadn't seen this coming. He was a lawyer, not a politician. He tried to defer. But you paid the tab. You drove him to your house. You told him about your machine. You talked him into it. Everyone, even Lou, thought he'd just be keeping the seat warm for you.

◦∿

THREE WEEKS AFTER Martin was killed, on a cold day for April, with storm clouds bearing down from the north, Carl Stokes walks in shirtsleeves down nicely edged sidewalks on the far West Side, through a neighborhood of identical thirty-year-old 1,400-square-foot houses with two-car garages, surrounded by camera crews he pretends aren't there, shaking hands with anyone he happens upon, asking about their troubles and what the city can do to help. Except for a blue sedan full of his public information officers, trailing about a block behind, he may be the only black man for a mile in any direction. Housewives see the camera crews and come to their picture windows. A few venture outside and shake the mayor's hand. Stokes imagines they are touching a black man for the first time in their lives. Were he alone, unaccompanied by white folks with familiar logos on their cameras, these women would call the police.

Behind the blue sedan are three more cars, one apiece from each TV station.

A starved-looking woman with dark eyebrows and a blond wig ventures down her driveway, stomps her foot, and asks why he thought colored people ought to get their streets cleared first? "People around *here* have jobs to go to in the mornings," she says, "unlike those people in some other places I could mention."

Stokes looks her in the eye. During the winter's first snowstorm, the white supervisor, since fired, had tried to make Stokes look bad by sending crews only to the black wards. Stokes explains that there was never any such policy. Mistakes were made. He asks if the streets got cleared adequately after that first storm. The woman takes her hands off her hips. "Better," she says, "but only because we complained."

"Terrific," Stokes says. "You keep letting us know when we screw up, ma'am, and we'll keep doing our best to respond."

Soon the procession reaches a senior citizens center, a place that smells like mildew and freezer-burned ice cream. Stokes hears things about thieved union pensions and federal programs beyond his authority, but he keeps lis-

[502]

tening. The cameras pan across the peeling paint on the walls, the Dutch ovens positioned to catch the dripping water. Stokes explains how the public-private partnership he's calling "CLEVELAND: NOW!" will provide funds to fix this place up. He stresses the recreation centers the funds will build for their children and grandchildren. What they really want to hear, he knows, is that those centers will give black kids something better to do than rob them. Carl Stokes speaks with a warm, calm voice.

For three grueling days, he's talked to every sort of person in every kind of neighborhood. He's taken camera crews to places they'll only go if some-one's been killed or something is on fire. When he presented CLEVELAND: NOW! to a closed-door session of council, a crude outline of it was leaked to the *Press* and *PD,* which ignored any good the program might do and specu-lated that the city income tax might be raised. This program can't be en-trusted to them. It's too big, too revolutionary: a ten-year, $1.5 billion plan to reimagine Cleveland. It has to be presented on TV, directly to the people. Stokes got the TV stations to agree to film this, pay for it, and air it simulta-neously. This show will be edited tonight and air tomorrow.

He's been mayor for five months and can't remember the last time he's had more than four hours' sleep. He can't remember the last time he had a long conversation with his wife that didn't involve a complaint. He can't re-member the last time he played catch with Carl Jr.

All that's left to film is Stokes's intro. The director wants to film it in Stokes's office. As they drive downtown, Stokes rides with the director and tries to convince him otherwise.

"My office sends the wrong message," Stokes says. "This whole thing takes the matter to the street. What about there?"

They're near the West Side Market, and the director says that's a great idea and on the two-way radio tells the other cars to pull over. It's an open-air meat and produce market, an inner-city haven for the ethnics.

"No," Stokes says. He's pointing beyond the market, toward the Guardians of Traffic. "I meant the bridge."

"The wind is too much," the director says. It's midday, which also makes the lighting tricky. The logistics are too tough all the way around.

"Give it a try," Stokes says. He doesn't have to walk all the way. He'll start partway up it.

A patrol car is summoned. It drives, hazards blinking (the siren or the lights would show up on film), slowly ahead of one of the TV cars.

On cue Stokes heads across the Lorain-Carnegie Bridge. Twice the director has him start over because the soundman says there's too much wind. The soundman tries yet another filter. Stokes puts on a windbreaker to address the matter of his fluttering necktie.

"After the tragic assassination of Martin Luther King Jr.," Stokes says, walking, "almost every city in America broke out in riots, in frustration. Except Cleveland." He keeps his head steady, eye on the viewfinder. Another camera shoots him from across the bridge. The third is positioned at the far end. This bridge is longer than he'd thought. He's never had any cause to walk it before.

"The night of the assassination, the streets were full of angry people. Priests, rabbis, pastors, and preachers went out into the night to restore calm. Professional football players and baseball players went out into the night to restore calm. Television personalities went out into the night to restore calm. Businessmen and -women went out into the night to restore calm. Ordinary Clevelanders of all races, colors, and creeds went out into the night to restore calm. We talked to one another. And, my friends, peace reigned."

The bridge has more of an incline, too, than he'd thought. The rails are lower than he would have imagined. Far below, the river looks like bubbling tar. *Fall in the Cuyahoga*, goes the joke, *and you won't drown, you'll decompose*. From up here the river doesn't smell.

"As I walked the streets of this city that terrible night," Stokes says, breathing a little hard now, "I was so proud to be your mayor. Deeply proud. Our darkest nights were behind us. A new day was dawning. I knew we could work together, as we've never worked together before. We have an opportunity," he says, "unique in the history of this great city."

He is near the crest of the bridge. A gust of wind nearly knocks him into the street, but Stokes, an athletic, graceful man, rights himself so quickly it's barely noticeable. The director waves at him to proceed, and Stokes keeps walking toward the other side.

But moments later, as he heads downhill, the director waves him off. "The footage is usable," he shouts, "but the audio's never going to work; they've tried everything." They'll have to reshoot him saying all this back in his office. "It *looks* great, though," he says, "you walking."

In silence, Stokes finishes crossing the bridge. Right after the town meeting he convened in the wake of Martin's death, two old white women rushed up to Carl Stokes, embraced him with their parchment-skinned arms, and thanked him for saving their city. Stokes looks beyond the slum of Central Market, to the spire of Terminal Tower, where the Indians flag waves. He glances back at the distance he's covered, at the cars following him, at the gawkers honking their horns, at the empty place at the crest of the bridge. He is the mayor of Cleveland. Anything is possible. Everything is possible. When he reaches the other side, the cameraman, who happens to be white, sets down his gear and applauds.

⁓

BROTHER FINISHED SCHOOL yet again and went to the wizard for a more permanent job. The wizard waved his hand.[16] Suddenly Brother was a constable in charge of those who sold strong drink. During the travels this task required, he met and married a woman named Shirley, with whom he'd spend the rest of the next two years. Soon after that, he met and married another woman named Shirley, with whom he'd spend the decade or so after that.

Billy became a man of law. He married a woman with whom he'd spend the rest of his days.

Brother grew tired of the journeys his trade required, wearier yet of the weaponry and epithets hurled at those who attempt to control rogue tavern keepers. So he obeyed the rule of threes and again went to the wizard. The wizard sighed and again waved his hand. Brother became an officer of the court, helping criminals adapt from life in the dungeon to life in the realm. He saw how the laws of his land were applied; every day he swam in a river of injustice, filth, and bigotry. A lowly officer of the court made little difference in people's lives, Brother realized. Only a great leader could do that. One day the wife of a man Brother was assigned to help summoned him in a panic to her dwelling; rats had attacked her baby. By the time Brother arrived, the screaming baby's nose and upper lip had been gnawed off. As he rushed the baby to seek what care there was to give, Brother vowed to become that great leader.

First, he followed Billy's footsteps and became a man of law. Though Billy was happy for this, he knew that when they hung out their shingle reading Billy & Brother[17] these days of law were for Brother numbered—a stepping-stone in his quest.

Billy helped his brother become that leader. What no one could have guessed, and what Billy himself had never imagined or desired, was that Billy would become a greater leader still.

The legend of Billy and Brother is that they were opposites. Billy would choose a single difficult path and remain content trying to walk it well.

---

[16] He made one telephone call.
[17] Stokes & Stokes, with offices on St. Clair Avenue, in Glenville.

Brother was restless for new challenges. Billy married one woman. Brother married three, each younger than the last. Brother was acute, Billy was chronic. Brother was a story, Billy was a novel. Brother led, Billy governed. Brother was a shooting star, Billy was a comet.

A mirror image is an opposite, too. Narcissus fell in love with himself in fact but his opposite in truth. Any good legend that chronicles opposites features people ultimately more alike than different.

Cleave. To sever and to join.

When either Billy or Brother was asked how he came to be so different from his brother, he'd laugh and tell you that's a myth.

∽

THIS IS HOW it ends.

Eight o'clock on a Wednesday morning in July. About a hundred squabbling black people assemble in council chambers, the only room in City Hall big enough. The young wear dashikis, blue jeans, kente cloth, tie-dye, but also more suits than one might guess. Most of the older ones wear dark suits, but there are some in coveralls, in bright sport coats, in sport shirts. The younger women wear pants; the older wear dresses. This meeting wasn't even called until five hours ago. Almost everyone Stokes's people called to invite was already awake. Everyone they called is here. A select few of the quieter people here were in Glenville the night before.

Carl Stokes enters. His people lock the door behind him. His latest reports are that three of the dead are white Cleveland cops, three are kids who fell in with Fred Evans, and the seventh was a bystander. On the police radio in Stokes's office, he's heard angry men argue that they should leave the whole mess in Glenville for the nigger mayor. *They're nigger friends of his. Let our great nigger peacemaker and his junglebunny friends go in there and fucking fix it.* The voices, angry as they are, can be heard to laugh.

For a long time Stokes sits in a chair off to the side, sipping one cup of coffee after another, letting other people do the talking. He tries only to listen. The discussion quickly breaks down into a shouting match over whether or not to pull the white police from the scene. Most of the older, wealthier people say no. Most of the younger, louder people demand otherwise.

No one in the room has had much sleep, but Stokes has had none at all. Last night he came straight from the airport. He'd been gone a week, meeting with people in Washington, speaking to groups in New York. When he left, as far as he knew Fred Evans was just some punk hustler who ran the Jomo F. Kenyatta Giftshop, a chapter of something called the Black Nation-

[506]

alist Organization of New Libya, and a playground program. The only thing scary about his end-of-the-world astrology and predictions of revolution (half his rap was lifted from that movie *Battle of Algiers*) was that Evans seemed on the verge of believing his own bullshit. While Stokes was gone, black cops warned their superiors that Evans had changed his name from Fred to Ahmed and was stockpiling tommy guns. The warnings were ignored. Last night Evans declared war on the police and issued a death sentence on the race-traitor Carl Stokes. Stokes had swallowed hard and summoned the National Guard.

Now, in council chambers, some of the quiet ones are predicting that even though Evans and everyone in the JFK House surrendered an hour ago and the house itself was shot up so badly it's rubble now, the cop killing may resume again tonight. No one seems to know how many other people in Glenville are followers of Evans's. The only way to make it stop is to present no more white targets. Hotheads or no, they're not going to shoot at brothers.

A black councilwoman points out that for as long as there have been blacks on the force, white mayors confronted with racial incidents in white neighborhoods—in Little Italy, say—have *routinely* ordered that black cops be kept from the scene.

Late that morning a consensus emerges.

At about noon Stokes finds himself giving the order. No white cops. The National Guard will stay at the perimeter of the situation. For twenty-four hours black cops and black leaders will patrol Glenville.

To Stokes's surprise, the police accept the order. All day the racial slurs on the police band get worse and more frequent. Somehow he can't stop listening.

Wednesday night he wants to go to the scene, but his family and the cops on his security detail beg him not to. In Glenville there are problems with looting, but that's it. No one is shot. The strategy seems to have worked.

Thursday morning Stokes lifts the ban.

At dusk that night, riding in the passenger seat of a gray unmarked police car that a toddler could tab as an unmarked police car, Stokes arrives at the perimeter of the scene. At dinner he'd told his wife he'd forgotten something at the Hall. Not even all the cops on the police detail assigned to his house know he's here. There are no reporters here to watch. There's a tail car, though, identical to the lead car, only with two detectives in it.

The cars pull up to a National Guard checkpoint. It's nearly dark, but as far as the eye can see no lights come on: no streetlights, lit signs, no houselights, not even the glow of a TV. They're parked next to a four-story apartment building. The windows on the first floor are smashed. Every other window is curtained or covered with floor rugs. A helmeted young man with a machine gun approaches the car.

Stokes's driver, a plainclothes black cop, rolls down the window, extends his arm, and displays his badge. He'd taken it out blocks and blocks from here. This is no place for a black man to be reaching inside his suit coat. "I have with me his Honor, the mayor." With a very slow jerk of the head, the cop indicates Stokes.

The young man bends down. He is a boy. He has *freckles*. "That so?" he says. He sticks the machine gun through the window. Stokes, who handled machine guns in the army, in occupied Germany, sees that the safety is off. If the gun went off now, it would pulverize the cop's left shoulder. "Good to meet you, sir."

An older soldier approaches, a lieutenant. The boy shoulders his weapon and comes to attention. "It's the mayor, sir."

The lieutenant asks Stokes if he has any identification. Stokes would have been no more startled if he'd been carded trying to buy beer. He's tempted to ask the lieutenant if he subscribes to *Time* magazine. Instead he asks for permission to reach for his wallet.

The lieutenant happens to be black. His head is practically shaved. In the *Guard*.

"If you don't mind me asking," Stokes asks, "what do you do as a civilian?"

He hands Stokes's driver's license back. "I'm a medical student, sir," he says, which is when Stokes realizes this man is just back from Vietnam.

A Jeep roars up. The lieutenant tells Stokes and his driver to step out. The men in the tail car get out, too, and raise their hands. Around them must be twenty guardsmen with guns. The lieutenant gives a signal, and the guns are lowered. The lieutenant tells Stokes he cannot drive into the area but motions to the Jeep. In back is a blond guardsman manning the floor-mounted machine gun. Stokes's driver climbs in and sits on the wheel well. Stokes gets in the passenger seat. The lieutenant drives.

Other than soldiers, there's no one on the streets. A curfew—Stokes gave the order for this himself—allows cops to arrest anyone out after nine. All these shabby little up-down duplexes, all with the windows covered and looking deserted. At regular intervals they pass cannon, half-tracks, and other armed Jeeps. Always, the machine guns are trained on them.

Not far from the law office he'd once shared with his brother, Stokes's guts heave. Before them is a *tank*—not a half-track, a huge olive-green *tank*, on the streets of the city of Cleveland. Its turret swivels toward the mayor. For a moment Stokes is sure he's going to lose it. His eyes water from the strain. When he closes them, they cannot help but spill. The wind cools his face, and he keeps his eyes closed for a long time. The lieutenant asks if he is OK. The mayor shakes his head no. But then he opens his eyes and asks to see more.

༄

THE SHOOTING WAS over. Peace was restored. The Guard receded.[18] Those responsible were tried and briskly sent to death row. None of that was enough to save you.

You survived it when the news broke that Fred Evans bought his cop-killing guns with a grant from CLEVELAND: NOW! It helped that the story wasn't true: his playground program got six thousand bucks from a group that was funded by a group that was funded by CLEVELAND: NOW![19] You might have survived Glenville, too. But whitey didn't love you. Whitey saw you as someone who'd go out in the streets and keep the bad Negroes from kicking off the revolution. Truth be told, you believed it yourself. Tragic flaw, Brother.

Back when you were a hero, your enemies feared you. Glenville sunk you because after that you were just a man. For many, just a black man. For more than a few, just a nigger.

The people who ran the police department never forgave you. The fire department joined ranks. The newspapers never liked you. Everyone who thought their vote for you came with complimentary bulletproof insurance from the wrath of angry Negroes began to look for a house in the suburbs. Or a job in another state. Soon you'd join them.

The hero died, but you lived: a boy who'd learned his political skills in a pool hall and the power of compromise from a churchgoing, goal-oriented hooker. For three more mortal years you served as mayor. Because of you, your brother became a congressman—by accident, really. You turned the

---

[18] The next time these guardsmen will be so deployed, they'll stop shy of Cleveland, in the very white college town exurb of Kent.

[19] The CIA, in the interest of peace, gives a lot more money to characters a lot more dangerous than Evans. The United Way could have given six grand to the Jomo F. Kenyatta Youth Program and survived. CLEVELAND: NOW! was three months old and not the CIA or the United Way.

organization that elected you into a political machine that reelected you. You made the decision not to seek a third term the day an angry mob stormed up 110th Street toward your house, and the security detail ordered you and your family to turn off all the lights and get down on the floor and don't move, then broke out the tear gas.

You gave your machine to your brother and sought a new challenge.

You became, of all things, a TV anchorman. You moved to *New York*, of all places. From behind an anchor desk there, you kept a straight face when you reported that your successor as mayor, Ralph Perk, had declined an invitation to the White House because it was his wife's regular bowling night. You kept a straight face when you reported that, at a trade show in Cleveland, in an unfortunate but probably overdue incident, Perk's shel-lacked hair got too close to some sparklers and caught on fire. Bert Porter's arrest for embezzlement was local news, not worth reporting in New York; you enjoyed that one unchecked.

But *New York?* Go to New York, you get what you get. Among what you got were poor ratings, a younger, blonder wife (#3 in a series), and restless.

You came home. You served as chief counsel to one of those unions that, years before, wouldn't talk to you. You got restless. Your brother watched out for you, and you became a muny court judge. You got restless. You acci-dentally stole a screwdriver and got caught, and six months later accidentally stole a bag of dog food and got arrested. You were not a kleptomaniac. There were perfectly logical explanations. You were acquitted.

Meanwhile, your brother kept your machine together, dispensing jobs and wielding influence. He became one of the longest-serving African Amer-ican congressmen in history, and perhaps the most powerful. You woke up one day and were the ambassador to the Seychelles Islands. The Seychelles Is-lands are almost nine thousand miles from Cleveland.

You would not call those last twenty-five years anticlimactic or sad. You were misunderstood. You lived an extraordinary life in an extraordinary city in extraordinary times.

You died. Everyone loved you. People fell over themselves to say how much you'd meant to Cleveland. If you'd lived to see some of the people who said and wrote that, you'd have laughed very hard.

For the record, Carl Stokes was the first African American to be elected mayor in a major city where white people were the majority. And also the last. For eight unremarkable months in an otherwise remarkable life, he served as an American hero.

— 25 —

EARLY ONE SUNDAY morning in the spring of 1969, the first day of the year he'd been able to put the top down on his obligatory red sports car (American; a Mustang), looking to kill some time and in Bay Village anyway, David Zielinsky tried to find the Sheppard murder house. All these years and (except for countless photos and on TV) he'd never seen it. He knew it was right on the lake, and he figured he'd know it when he saw it. It had been sold soon after Sheppard won his second trial, but as far as David knew, it was still there. He drove Lake Road from one green, shaded end of Bay Village to the other, looking around each bend for that familiar Dutch Colonial house. The other cars on the street were dark sedans. The people in them wore church clothes. Truth be told, it wasn't quite warm enough to have the top down, especially this close to the lake. David turned his heater up a notch.

On the second pass he found it and pulled over on the berm to stare. Part of why he'd missed it was that the new owners had planted ugly, fast-growing shrubs to screen the house from the street, but, equally, he'd missed it because it was so much smaller than he'd imagined like a scale model of the image of it he'd carried in his head all these years. The house had been gray but had been painted blue recently. A pile of silver, disassembled scaffolding lay in the driveway, between a station wagon and the closed garage. Next to the garage door was a Big Wheel and yellow plastic Crazy Car—children's toys: children's vehicles. The decals on each had not yet faded or begun to peel. David had sold battered versions of each of these (they'd been Brad's) in a garage sale last year.

From behind the house came a short, dark-haired young man in a beard, green sunglasses, and a suit, followed by three small children. David's pulse quickened; he put his car in gear and would have sped off except that—of *course*—cars were coming. A line of them. The oldest child—a boy about Brad's age, probably a schoolmate of his—looked David's way and shouted something. The father palmed the boy's head and turned him toward the open door of the station wagon. The father kept his head down. Finally, David was able to pull away; his tires bit the pavement and squealed. He winced. He glanced in the rearview, behind him, and then at himself. "Ghoulish motherfucker," he muttered. David felt like he should take another shower. He wondered how long it took that poor bastard to go from being pissed off at people to ignoring them.

David pulled out the scrap of paper with the directions to Dr. Lamb's on it. The paper was from one of the notepads he'd had printed up for his run at county commissioner. He could not, in two lifetimes, need to jot enough notes to use them up.

David knew the house was not on the lake, and as he drove, a mean and petty part of himself was happy about that, and rooting for the house to be medium-sized and ordinary. But he was getting close now, and the houses and the lots were getting larger.

Maybe the house was never gray. It occurred to him that he'd never seen a color photograph of it. Really, what they should do is make that Sheppard murder house a museum. And not just to the murder. Where better for the Twentieth-Century Museum of Cleveland?

David shook his head and sipped from a Styrofoam cup of cold and bitter coffee. What *they* should do? That's how saps think. Once, David Zielinsky was *they*. He had power and big hopes. He was on Walter Cronkite and on *Huntley-Brinkley*, in *Time* and in *Life*. He'd been interviewed by reporters from France. Where did it get him? Now what was he? A thirty-five-year-old washout, alone, thirty pounds overweight, full of self-pity and consequential self-loathing, driving a newly washed car down leafy streets on a Sunday morning, one step short of becoming a peeping tom.

◌◌

It was a Sunday morning, but Anne O'Connor had been up since dawn, sitting in her back room, trying to work on her book. About all she'd done was drink coffee, smoke, play the new Aretha Franklin record loud enough to blow one speaker, and stare out at the lake. At about nine the phone rang and she jumped. Too *much* coffee. "John!" she said.

"Excuse me?" It was Len Petocek. Her news director.

"Sorry," Anne said. "My brother's about to . . . well, his wife's about to have a baby."

"That's nice," he said. "Look, are you busy today?"

"Very," she said, which was a lie. Was he about to ask her out? There had always been vibes there, stronger lately. She tried to ignore this.

"Doing what?" he asked. "If I may ask."

"Just busy," she said. "What do you want?"

"I'm thinking of making all the on-air talent have listed telephone num-

[512]

bers. It'd be good PR for the station, I think. All you people would be approachable and real and in the book."

Or maybe he was going to fire her. "You called me to tell me this?"

"No," he said. "I called to tell you Dorothy Fuldheim's deathly ill, and—"

"Oh no!" Anne said. Though the woman must be, what, seventy?

"It's not that," he said. "Jesus, you're a ghoul. She's just got some bug that's going around. She was supposed to give the commencement speech at Baldwin-Wallace today, and the people there apparently had their hearts set on a women's lib angle this year and so they called me and asked me to ask you to pinch-hit." He told her how much this would pay. It wasn't much. "I'll expect my usual 10 percent," he joked.

"I don't really want to do it," she said. "I'm busy all day." She was trying to write a novel. After Kenneth had seen part of it and called it "promising" (no one else had seen word one), she put herself on a strict schedule, twenty pages every weekend.

"I already told them you would," Petocek said. "If you want to cancel, you'll have to call them yourself." He gave her a name and a number.

⁀

EVEN FROM THE base of a long driveway, David could hear the noise. *Teddy.* David smiled. Near the house the drive became circular, the kind that allowed you to pull up in front of the house, as if you were disgorging passengers from a carriage. In the lawn in the middle of the oval was a fountain with a marble lamb in it. The fountain wasn't on; David hoped it was broken. Behind it, the house was a flat-roofed monstrosity of modern architecture, a sprawling, gray-sided split-level—three staggered, boxy levels actually, buttressed by carportlike patios and finished off with metal-pipe railings. The house was a Frank Lloyd Wright homage gone wrong.

The noise was coming from the right box of the house: the wail of a Jimi Hendrix record and Teddy's game attempt to play note for note along.

David rang the bell. No one answered. Who could hear it over that noise? Inside, Precious trotted into view and barked. David rang the bell again.

Finally, Irene came to the door, dressed in a white tennis outfit. "Kids!" she yelled over the music. "Your father's here."

"How can they hear you?" David said. The dog kept barking.

"What?"

She motioned for him to come in. "Kids!"

"I said, how can they hear you?" David had his mouth an inch from

Irene's ear. She was using a different shampoo. Her hair was long and straight, a Twiggy cut that was both dated and too young for her.

"It's a phase, I hope," Irene said.

Suddenly Teddy stopped playing. A moment later so did the Hendrix record. At Christmas—the first since Irene left him, and, because of a lengthy out-of-town trial, the last time he'd seen the kids—David had spent more than he could afford. But now, hearing that wall of sound brought to bear upon Dr. and Mrs. Lamb, the cost of the amp seemed a small price to pay.

"This is an amazing house," David said.

"Thanks." Irene sounded sincerely happy for his approval. "It still needs some things. We have plans."

Precious stopped barking, and David knelt down to pet her. Docile as ever, she rolled over. She was never really his dog anyway.

"I saw the article in the *PD*," Irene said. "Betty must be excited. Tell her congratulations for me, won't you?"

"I will," David said. He pointed at the skirt of Irene's tennis dress, and stood. "Since when did you take up tennis?"

"Turns out I have natural ability," Irene said. She rolled her eyes, like a girl. "That's what the pro at the club says. He gets paid to say that. I'm awful, but it's fun." Her pendulous breasts were somehow raised high and pressed youthfully against the tennis dress. It reminded David of her in her nurse's outfit, a long time ago. "I'll go see what's keeping them."

The house had no entry hall; David stood in a big room with a twenty-foot ceiling, a fireplace, a sunken conversation pit, a black plastic-cased Japanese TV on a glass end table, and a harvest-gold pair of rocking, reclining love seats. Other than a low Danish-style coffee table in front of one love seat, nothing—other than the dog, Irene, and the kids—used to be David's.

"Hi, Dad," Teddy said. His voice had deepened into something alien.

"Don't sneak up on me like that."

Teddy had pimples all over his face and wire-rimmed glasses that seemed designed to deemphasize the thick lenses but had the opposite effect. His black hair was parted in the middle and more shaggy than long. He did not look like the person who'd been playing that music. He was wearing church clothes. He'd been playing that music in his church clothes.

Teddy made the first move toward a hug. It went on long enough to embarrass them both.

"Well, anyway," Teddy said. He let out a breath. He'd been holding his breath. "I hope you're not in a hurry. It takes a nuclear warhead to get Liz out of the damn bathroom." Teddy plopped himself slouchily across a love seat. He kept one foot on the floor, to rock himself.

David was the only one who still called her Lizard. He let that *damn* go. "And Brad?"

Teddy jerked his thumb toward the sliding-glass door to the back patio. Across it, David could see Nolan Lamb. He was in tennis clothes, too: white shorts and a red alligator shirt the color of David's car. He looked like a tennis player, one of the hairy Australian types. He was pretending to do something in the garden.

"I don't see him," David said.

Teddy yelled his brother's name. A closet door opened, and Brad stepped out. He was a stocky eight-year-old version of Mike Zielinsky, right down to the mohair sweater. He got down into a three-point stance and charged; David sidestepped him, but Brad caught enough of one leg to trip his father up and bring him down.

"Wow!" David said.

"He's already a pawn of the military-industrial complex," Teddy said, shaking his head.

David tousled Brad's hair. "How you doing, sport?"

"He doesn't talk, either," Teddy said.

"How long has that been going on?" David said.

"I do, too, talk, you mook!" Brad shouted.

"OK, he doesn't talk very *often*."

David laughed. "Do you even know what a *mook* is?"

"I don't hate you," Brad said. "Nolan says you'll probably think that."

"Why would I think that?" David glanced outside. Nolan averted his eyes and went back to his make-believe gardening.

"Why wouldn't he think that?" Teddy said.

David started to alibi yet again, as he thought he'd done adequately on the phone from Washington, about his job as counsel for one of the Teamsters locals and how, as a new guy, eager to make a good impression, he can hardly refuse when he's enlisted as part of the defense team for out-of-town trials.

Teddy let him go on and on. Finally he said, "His hating you has nothing to do with that."

"What then?"

"Brad's not that deep." Teddy rapped his own skull with his fist. "He's getting C's and D's in everything. I love him to pieces, but he's a little rockhead. Aren't you, Brad?"

"Yes," Brad said.

"Hey," David said.

"That's all I'm going to say for now," Brad said. He went over and turned on the TV and sat down cross-legged in front of it. The TV came on instantly.

"Nice TV," David said.

"Two nuclear bombs, maybe," Teddy said. "Probably we'll all die before she gets out."

"You're getting good on that guitar," David said.

"I'm in a band," Teddy said. "More like starting one up, I guess."

"Tell me about it," David said. "What's it called?"

"You wouldn't understand," Teddy said. "It's music you'd hate. We don't have a name."

"I liked what you were playing when I drove up," David said.

Teddy thanked him, then sat up and sang the first two lines of "Purple Haze." How was a skinny, reasonably clean-cut fourteen-year-old white boy from the West Side of Cleveland able to pull off such a perfect Hendrix impression?

"That's great. That's amazing."

Teddy frowned. "How would you know?"

"It's Jimi Hendrix." David didn't like most new pop music, but Hendrix had enough blues in him to be listenable. "I'm not a hundred years old, you know."

"It's just copying," Teddy said, shrugging. "I have a ways to go. We might call it 30,000 Sludge Worms Per Square Yard. The band."

From the left wing of the house came the sound of someone running down a hallway, and then Lizard emerged in a tie-dyed T-shirt and blue jeans. Her blond hair looked exactly the same as her mother's. Just in the time since Christmas, she'd started to develop.

"Oh lord," David said.

Lizard stopped. "Daddy!" she said. She sounded happy to see him, but she just stood there, across the room from him, at the bottom of a half-flight of stairs. Then she frowned. "*Yes*, this is what I'm wearing."

David shook his head. "That wasn't what...," he said. *Develop* was the word he used even in his head. He didn't want to think of any of the other words. This wasn't a thing he'd thought to think. Or maybe it was something he'd been too successful in ignoring. Maybe he should ask good old Nolan what *he* thought. "It doesn't matter," David said. "You look fine. You look terrific. Cool. Let's go. C'mon, Brad."

[516]

"Liz is a hippie," Brad said, his back to them, eyes still on Gumby and Pokey on the TV. "Whattaya gonna do, huh?"

"I thought you weren't talking," David said.

"He talks to her and about her, but that's about it," Teddy said. "He worships her."

"Shut up, loser," Lizard said. "C'mon, Brad." Brad turned off the TV, and they went.

❧

BROWN AND YELLOW hand-painted signs and brown and yellow balloons led to the parking lot beside the football field. Anne pulled her blue Corvette onto the grass. She could feel her tires sink slightly into the rain-softened ground. As kids in yellow vests and black flashlights directed her to the next desired space, she wondered if this was such a good idea. She wondered how muddy this would get if it rained, which was called for. It was eleven-thirty, half an hour later than they'd hoped she could be there, but an hour and a half before the festivities started.

Anne gathered up her purse and her note cards—which she'd been looking over and trying to tweak the whole time it took her to drive from one of Cleveland's northeasternmost suburbs to one of its southwesternmost—and hadn't gotten ten feet from her car before a campus cop rode up on a motorscooter, calling her name and waving his arms so wildly she was afraid he'd fall. "We can't have you parking here, Miss O'Connor. You'll get those nice shoes ruined." *Rooned*. West Side Cleveland. "We have VIP parking," he said, unduly proud. He turned the bike around and waved for her to follow him.

"This is fine, really," she said. "Is it far to walk?"

"People are waiting for you. A little nervous and all. I have my orders, ma'am."

She got back in her car. He showed her to a roped-off section of blacktop behind a small gray academic building, pulled the rope aside for her, waved her in, and refastened it. He pointed out where she needed to go and asked if she wanted him to escort her. "No need," she said. He blushed a little and said he'd recognized her immediately and that he'd been watching her since he was a kid and that if he might say so, she was more beautiful in person than on TV.

Since he was a *kid*. The campus cop, also a redhead, was balding. She'd thought he was about her age. Though she was bad at that, guessing ages.

Outside the threshold of a small lecture hall that had been set up as a hospitality suite, a skeleton-thin old man in a cap and gown was pacing and smoking.

[517]

"*There* you are!" He was some kind of assistant or associate dean.

"I had to get my thoughts together," she said. "My speech."

"Of *course* you did," he said, extending his arms to take her coat, then hustling her inside. "We are *so* deeply grateful, Miss O'Connor, that you could help us out on such short notice. We *know* what an imposition this must be. It's not you I was worrying about; it's our weather."

"It won't rain," Anne said. Her arm still hadn't been wrong yet. "Trust me."

"Those weathermen of yours," he said. "They just make things up, I think."

The hall looked new and was full of people, about half of whom were already in their caps and gowns. There were also several ministers of some kind. In the front of the lecture hall, pastries and luncheon meats were spread on the tablecloth-covered countertop that must ordinarily be used for science experiments. The deep little lab sink had been pressed into service as a wet bar. Lined up next to it were the makings for bloody marys. On a table along the wall were stacks of cups and saucers and a silver coffee urn half as big as an oil drum. The periodic table of the elements had been draped with a cloth banner reading, CONGRATULATIONS, PROUD MEMBERS OF THE CLASS OF '69. Anne pointed at it.

"'Proud members'?" she said, chuckling, "'of the Class of '69?'"

"Excuse me?"

Whoever made the banner had to have been going for the joke. "Nothing," Anne said. "I'm really flattered you thought of me," she said. "Late notice or not."

At this point in what was already a long morning, she was sincere. She'd done several high school commencements and had something of a stock speech for that, but this would be her first at a college.

The assistant or associate dean ushered her toward the food, asked if he could get her anything, and told her that there were people he wanted her to meet. What this was likely to mean, Anne knew, was the women who worked here and weren't secretaries. "I'd *love* a bloody mary," she said, "but what I need is some hot coffee and, if it's not an imposition," she said, pulling her note cards from her purse and waggling them, "someplace quiet I can go to think."

The man's gaunt face fell, but all he said was that he understood, of course. Of course. He took her through an open door in the front of the lecture hall, into a hallway flanked by office doors, at the end of which was a conference room. He flicked on a light. The seminar table was covered with overcoats and discarded newspapers.

"This will be fine," Anne said. "Just great. If I could just have a few minutes to gather my thoughts. Fifteen minutes, twenty at the very, very most."

He piled up the newspapers, said that someone from the bookstore would be by momentarily to fit her for her cap and gown, and closed the door behind him.

She wished she'd asked things about the school—undoubtedly this would have come up in chitchat. She hadn't thought it was a religious school, but it appeared to be. In addition to the ministers, there was a cross on the wall of the conference room. Probably not Catholic. She'd have known if it was Catholic. The school was private, but she'd have known if it was wealthy. Certainly she'd never known anyone who went here. What this meant, she thought, was that she should emphasize the stories about her father and how he grew up poor and was mayor and made Cleveland great. She'll talk, too, about her dead brother, who died to keep America free. She'll use that as a segue into this war, and then onto civil rights, equal rights for women, the crisis of air and water pollution, and the other challenges and responsibilities of the present and the future. She'll be diplomatic when it comes to the war and civil rights, issues that divide our country, but she won't duck the fact that she's against the former and for the latter. It was a campus crowd; possibly no one would boo.

She looked at the note cards spread across the table in front of her. Women's lib. That was apparently the main thing she'd been invited to talk about. She picked up the two cards that covered this topic. She was prepared to say that ours was still a world run by men, but that this was changing by the minute; that women still have to work twice as hard to get half as much credit, but, still, they *can* get the credit, and so stay true to your dreams and don't give up; that she firmly believed that the men and women of the Baldwin-Wallace Class of 1969 would live in a world where it would not be unusual to see female doctors and lawyers and judges, female artists and pilots and scientists and astronauts; female presidents of banks, museums, and universities. Today's graduates will, Anne was prepared to predict, live to see the inauguration of *America's* first woman president.

Anne growled, swept the cards off the table, and watched them flutter to the floor.

Commencement speaker? Who was she kidding? She was a fake. Everything she had was given to her by her father or because she was pretty. Those are the keys to making it in a man's world! She didn't have a husband or any children, and while all that was fine with her, absolutely fine, it was also not absolutely fine. A husband would be nice. She wasn't sure she wanted to die childless, but she was thirty-three and had to face facts. Maybe it was her destiny to be Patrick's kids' (and John's!) colorful, worldly auntie. *Dorothy Fuldheim,* now there's a woman who's not a barren fake: homely and poor, she ascended to the top of a profession she helped invent. *She* had a husband. *She* had a child. *She* earned everything she had. *She* was the person the Class of 1969 had voted to hear. *She* was the best of Cleveland.

Anne O'Connor was a rich girl, afraid that even the things she imagined she'd earned had in truth been handed to her. She loved her hometown the way one loves a loyal family pet during its arthritic, bad-smelling final years. She was someone who pretended to be bold and brazen, but isn't it true that she left New York and came back here not because she loved her family but because she was afraid?

She left the index cards on the floor and picked up a few sections of the paper. She began to leaf through it. Almost immediately, on the front of the city section, she saw the headline—"TAINTED LEGEND'S WIDOW FINISHES 4 DEGREES,/BECOMES B-W'S SALUTATORIAN, OLDEST GRAD"—and a head shot of Betty Lychak.

Turns out Anne did know someone who went here.

The story had almost everything, how the childless widow of an old Cleveland Untouchable-*cum*-Red-baiting private eye (and also the sister-in-law of convicted racketeer Michael "Mikey Z" Zielinsky and the aunt of former city councilman David Zielinsky, nationally known for the televised inspirational speech he'd made on behalf of Carl Stokes before the final debate of the 1967 election) had for almost thirty years been taking classes for the sake of taking classes. Technically, many of her credits had expired (including coursework transferred from Mundelein College in Chicago, where she first enrolled, in the 1930s), but the university president interceded to make sure she received every degree she'd earned: psychology, music, elementary education, and English. The president himself had come to her house and convinced her finally to apply for graduation. She was fifty-six, oldest in her class this year. She'd declined a full scholarship to any of several master's programs there and would, in the fall and with no scholarship support, start classes at the Cleveland-Marshall College of Law.

Someone knocked; Anne's heart lurched and she tossed away the newspaper, as if she'd been caught reading someone's diary. In walked the skeletal assistant or associate dean and a mousy young woman bearing a cap and gown. "Hope we didn't scare you," he said. He would have made an excellent undertaker. "Hope you're ready."

"Ready as I'll ever be," Anne said, and attributed the mess on the floor to a sudden gust of wind. The windows in the seminar room were closed. No one called her on it.

The story hadn't mentioned Betty's sister. Anne was sure Betty had no idea.

୭୭

ONCE, BETTY LYCHAK had been the wholesome-looking sister of a great beauty. Now, on her graduation day, she had the taut-muscled, bright-eyed look of a champion gardener; nearly every young woman in the room muttered behind her back that they hoped to look as good as that when *they* were fifty-six. For most of these women, of whatever age, it was already too late.

In the newly dedicated science lecture hall, a string trio set up in a corner and began to play obvious Bach pieces. Nearby, in her graduation gown, Betty posed for picture after picture: with classmates and their parents, with secretaries and administrators, with professors. Some of these were shot by a photographer the university hired to cover the day's proceedings, but most were thick-trunked amateurs brandishing Instamatics. One of the professors had been a classmate of Betty's in 1959, had gone off, done his doctoral work, been hired by his alma mater, and taught Betty's final class there— Civil War history, an elective. The official photographer took a picture of him handing back her final blue book examination. He'd written the "A" in Magic Marker, so large a person could have seen it from across the room.

Across the room Anne O'Connor, also in a black graduation robe, was surrounded by well-wishers of her own.

Betty and Anne made eye contact. Anne waved. Betty nodded. There was nothing anyone watching could read into that except that they knew each other, which the assistant or associate dean did note and which Anne confirmed. "That's marvelous!" the man said. "As the Vienna quack said, there are no coincidences."

"So you're a psychology professor?"

He was. "*Wa-a-a-ait*," he said. "I remember now. You were the one who did the story on Mr. Lychak. *I* saw that. The whole nasty business with the Red scare. I'm afraid we may have a bit of a situation on our hands here. You and Mrs. Lychak, that is."

"I don't think so," Anne said. "That was a long time ago. Years ago."

What a relief! Everyone agreed that Betty Lychak was an inspiration to women everywhere. "Not just women!" someone said, and everyone agreed with that, too.

Eventually Anne excused herself. With a rustling of black sateen, she slide-stepped across a row of folded-up seats to where Betty stood. Betty met her glance and Anne waved. It was a very long row.

"So," Anne said, "I hear we'll be sharing a podium. It's an honor for me. Congratulations, Mrs. Lychak." She extended her hand.

Betty hesitated, as women sometimes did with handshakes, then clasped Anne's hand and shook it. Betty was a woman with a warm hand and a firm grip.

"Anne O'Connor," Anne said. She pursed her lips. Betty let go. "Perhaps you don't remember me? It's been, what, fifteen years?"

"Of course I remember. My goodness, this must be awkward for you. Dear."

Anne flipped back a hank of her rich red hair. The thicket of people around them seemed to find in themselves a sudden need to cross the room in search of food, drink, or other people.

"Someone told me you'd been asked to step in," Betty said. "I'm sure it's difficult, coming up with a speech on such short notice."

"I owe you an apology," Anne said. "I know that. I'm sorry."

Betty shook her head. "You don't owe me anything. I understand that you had a job to do and did it. Those were confusing times."

Anne frowned. "Which? When I did the story, or when Mr. Lychak... you know. Named names."

Betty took a deep breath. "When you're my age," she said, "you'll realize that they're all confusing times."

"I realize it now, believe me."

"Do you?"

Next to them, the three students in the chamber trio kept their eyes on their sheet music.

"Maybe I don't," Anne said. "You're the one with four degrees."

Betty didn't say anything.

"I'm sorry," Anne said. "We both know this... difficulty... we both know there's more to it than—"

"They've divorced," Betty said. "Are you satisfied?"

"Excuse me?"

[522]

"They've divorced."

Neither woman seemed to see the need to spell out the antecedent. The chamber trio began to play louder.

Anne held up a peace sign. "It's ancient history, Mrs. Lychak. All of it. I only came over to congratulate you, all right? I haven't seen—"

"I didn't say you had."

"There's another subject, actually, that I wanted to talk to you about. This isn't the time, I know. But—."

Betty kept looking past Anne, as if she were expecting someone. "What are you suggesting? Lunch? Tea? A few rounds of polo?"

Anne laughed, reached out, and touched Betty on the elbow. "Sure," she said. "I've always liked you, Mrs. Lychak. Any time that's good for you, anywhere that's convenient. Just call me at the station."

"And what station would that be, dear?"

"I should let you go," Anne said. *And, anyway, it's a few* chukkers *of polo.* "It's your day."

She turned around and ran smack into David Zielinsky's daughter. The girl stumbled. Anne reached for her, steadied her.

"Watch where you're going, lady," said Brad, David's youngest. The morose-looking oldest, Teddy, wrapped his great-aunt in a bear hug.

The girl, Elizabeth, regarded Anne O'Connor. Her gamine eyes were as impassive as a monk's. "I know you," the girl said.

"You do?"

The girl was thirteen years old. On her right hand was an old-fashioned sapphire ring, obviously some kind of heirloom. "You're on TV," she said.

"Oh," Anne said. "That wasn't what—" She stammered and reached out as if to touch the girl's hair, and stopped herself. "I really should go."

"Yes," Betty said.

By then David Zielinsky, limping a little worse than ever, had caught up to his family. Anne's eyes grew wide, but she lowered her head, walked right past him, and disappeared into the increasingly robed crowd.

Betty gave David an arched-eyebrows look that said she'd explain later.

David hugged his aunt, a hug that looked awfully stiff given the joyous occasion, and took his Polaroid Land camera from around his neck and directed his reluctant children into happy poses. The crowd was sagging back toward Betty.

"Where's Dorothy Fuldheim?" David asked. Ever since that commentary all those years ago, Fuldheim was a hero to the Zielinsky family.

"She's not coming," Betty said. "She's ill."

"You're kidding. Nothing serious, I hope," David said. "How old is she, about seventy?"

At the lab sink now, Anne O'Connor accepted a bloody mary.

Bystanders and classmates came up to Betty and asked if these adorable children were her grandkids, and for a while Betty corrected them until finally Lizard just said, "Yes, we are."

Betty leaned toward David's ear. "So much like your mother," she whispered. "Headstrong."

David nodded. He couldn't keep his eyes off Anne O'Connor. She looked like a surprised version of her younger self. Rumor had it, she'd had plastic surgery. David doubted that. Anne had always been vibrant and beautiful. It was just that he hadn't seen her in person for years. He kept looking at her now but couldn't seem to catch her eye. He had no idea what he'd do if he did.

Brad told Lizard it was time to strap on the old feed bag, and she went with him to get some food. Teddy had pulled out a paperback copy of *Catch-22* from one of the wide side pockets of his shabby suit coat and sat in one of the lecture hall seats to read.

"And," Betty whispered, "the spitting image of her."

David's daughter was not the only person there in blue jeans and tie-dye, but she was among the few. "In costume maybe," he said. "So tell me what *that* was all about."

"What was what all about?"

A young man with hair so long it covered his face, a fellow member of the class of '69, thrust the *PD* story toward Betty. She thanked him. He said, no, he wasn't giving her an extra copy; he wanted her to sign it. She thanked him again and obliged.

"What's she doing here?" David persisted. Meaning Anne, of course.

"My thoughts exactly," Betty said.

⁊

An hour later, in a cafeteria with windows facing the football field, the faculty and honored guests assembled for the procession. Severe-looking women in plain dresses tugged at hoods and adjusted caps like a cadre of grim den mothers. Outside, the families were in place in the bleachers, the band played "Pomp and Circumstance," and, led by Betty Lychak and by the young woman who beat her out for valedictorian, the students had begun to file toward their seats.

In her right hand, Anne palmed her small stack of index cards. It was cold in this room, but, lined up behind the university president, its chaplain, and several assistant or associate deans, Anne was sweating. She'd just gotten off the phone with John: Doreen was fine; nothing had changed; the baby wasn't even due until Wednesday. Anne hadn't written down the jokes she'd planned to start with. Suddenly, she was blank. Something about being the first alternate for Miss America. Her head hurt. *Maybe I have brain cancer.*

From the back of the room, a cheer went up. A chorus of laughter and applause.

In strode Dorothy Fuldheim.

Surrounded by people, she was too small for Anne to see, until, finally, the skeleton-faced assistant or associate dean elbowed through like the prow of a ship. Fuldheim followed, dressed in a cream-colored high-necked taffeta evening dress encrusted with what Anne assumed to be costume jewelry. There was even a golden brooch the size of an apple and the shape of a pineapple. Her face was pale, but then again her face was always pale.

"I wouldn't dream of upstaging you," Dorothy said. "Especially after you were so good to drop everything and—"

"Don't give it a second thought," Anne said, removing her cap and looking for someone to take it. "It's you they're coming to see."

"Bah," Fuldheim said. "People come to graduations to see a loved one shake hands and take a diploma. I could stand up there stark naked and set myself on fire and a year later no one would remember anything but the pose their child struck as he crossed the stage."

Anne could have lived a happy lifetime without thinking about Dorothy Fuldheim naked. "I'm just glad you're feeling better."

"I'm not feeling all that much better," Fuldheim said, "but I'm still here. You're sure, now, this is all right with you?"

Anne told her not to be ridiculous.

Fuldheim whispered to her that of course she'd split the honorarium with her.

That tiny, symbolic-seeming honorarium! But just as Anne was about to again tell Dorothy Fuldheim not to be ridiculous, she caught herself and took split-second stock of how ridiculous things already were. "That's nice of you," Anne said. It was small recompense for a bollixed writing day. She did not bother to whisper. "You can mail it to me at the station."

This did not throw Dorothy Fuldheim. "I'll have my driver drop it off," she said. "Will tomorrow be good enough?"

This did not throw Anne O'Connor. "That's the question we ask our-selves every night," she said, "isn't it?"

This did not throw Dorothy Fuldheim. "You'll outgrow that," she said, "when you realize it's enough that tomorrow comes at all."

Uncle, Anne thought. "Break a leg," she said.

The assistant or associate dean hustled Dorothy Fuldheim to the head of the line. She soldiered indomitably forward. No one suggested she wear a mortarboard or a tam. No one made an effort to drape her shiny gown with a black one.

∽

As she drove to her brother's house (John and Doreen would be home from mass by now), Anne couldn't stop thinking about how and whether to tell Betty about her sister's murder. Lost in thought, she drove too fast even for her, forgot about the speed trap on Cedar Hill, had to talk her way out of a ticket. The cop went back to his patrol car and sat there for a really long time, and came back and instead of a warning gave her a ticket and instruc-tions for paying it. Speechless, Anne listened and nodded. She had talked her way out of at least a dozen tickets, but this one was her first: the end of a thirty-three-year streak of being protected by her father's power and her own beauty and fame. She pulled out into traffic.

What she really couldn't stop thinking about, she finally admitted to her-self, was the look on David's daughter's face. And the way it reminded Anne of that same girl, years ago, running hatless through the snow.

That wasn't true, either.

She'd been thinking about David off and on since she was at the City Club for the fourth Stokes-Taft debate and saw him give that speech. *I grew up as a racist, a bigot, and did not know or care.* Carl Stokes had looked up at him startled, and David seemed to have lost his place in his notes. The room grew quiet in a way that gave Anne a sick feeling. David hadn't lost his place. It was a calculated pause. He launched into a story about going to see Satchel Paige pitch for the first time in a Cleveland uniform, a story rich with cigar smoke, peanut shells, and optimism, a story about being a minority himself for the first time and how it scared him and made him see the world with new eyes, a story about how a boy who grew up where he grew up came to be a man who believed what he believed because he could not root for Cleveland's great Negro heroes—Paige and Doby, Motley and Brown—and conspire against Cleveland's Negroes. He was on fire with passion, pounding on the lectern, in much better shape than he was when she saw him today. He had the whole City Club practically holding its breath. He still wore off-the-rack suits. His everyman shabbiness made him look so vulnerable, anyone would have wanted to hug him and tell him everything was all right.

Once, she had loved him. Then, she'd moved entirely on. Then this happened.

He threw everything behind Carl Stokes. Stokes won. David lost. David lost nobly and was briefly famous for it. He'd been drubbed in his council election by a Republican realtor who'd never even held office in her garden club. Most of Stokes's appointments went to black people, and in a newspaper story about that, David did not complain about being passed over. He said he was weighing other options. The next year David was drubbed even worse trying to run for county commissioner. Off and on, vandals would spray-paint *nigger-lover* on his house or car. In a newspaper story about that, David wouldn't comment. He was gallantly silent.

First at John and Doreen's brick house in University Heights and then at the house where Anne grew up (she still can't bring herself to think of it as Patrick and Ibby's), she made her dutiful-auntie rounds. She did not say word one about her day so far. She touched Doreen's grotesque belly, right against the tight tiger-striped skin, and felt for the baby's kicks, and played peekaboo with their two-year-old Jenny, and endured John's tiresome complaints about John Carroll's decision to go coed. Then, with Patrick and Ibby's girls, over the adenoidal drone of Monkees records, she played Barbies, Twister, and Mystery Date. She did not stay for dinner. She said she had work to do. No one in her family knew she was writing a novel. In her car she decided that she'd call David when she got home. But it occurred to her that, given his situation and the kind of crank calls he must have gotten, his number was no doubt unlisted. And, really, what would she say? When she got home, she made herself a pot of coffee and sat down to write. The words just came.

⁓

THE PART OF the speech that wound up on TV the most is this, the end:

"Once, the late, great Thomas J. O'Connor [in magazines and newspapers outside Cleveland, it was explained in brackets that O'Connor was Cleveland's first Catholic mayor] looked me in the eye and said, 'Kid, strategy gets you elected, politics keeps you there, but they're just tools. What matters isn't how you use them, but why.' For me, *this* is why: this moment in our city's history. This is a moment bigger than strategy, bigger than politics, bigger than ourselves. [Here, David looks right at Carl Stokes. This is where the network sound bite begins.] I did not vote for John F. Kennedy because he was white, as I am, or Catholic, as I am. I voted for him because he represented a new America. I will not vote for Carl Stokes because he is black. I will not vote for Carl Stokes in spite of the fact that he is black. I will vote for him, as you should, because he represents a new Cleveland, and a hope for a new and *better* America."

This is followed by one final banged fist and a standing ovation. Then Carl Stokes stands up, and he and David Zielinsky enjoy a manly embrace.

∽

DAVID TOOK EVERYONE out for dinner at Mama Isabelle's on Pearl Road and joined Betty in drinking a little too much wine, then drove his shivering kids (he kept the Mustang's top down) to the home of the surgeon Irene left him for, kissed them good-bye (on top of the head for Teddy, the same only feather-light for Lizard; Brad flinched, and David planted a kiss on his ear), slipped them each twenty bucks, and drove home. *Home.* Hah. It was a freshly painted five-room lakeview apartment in a Gold Coast tower in Lakewood. He'd bought it from his father for a dollar. All that was in the master bedroom were unpacked boxes, unpacked suitcases, and a new waterbed. The other bedroom was empty. The kitchen table had been in David's garage. The faux suede sofa and love seat in the living room were covered in a garish nautical print: housewarming presents from his father, delivered along with a note that said *I never liked Eileen anyway. Joke. Chin up, Michael J. Zielinsky.* David hadn't been sure which was the joke, botching Irene's name, getting a personal note his father had signed using his whole first name and middle initial, or the sofas themselves. Which were surprisingly comfortable. The only thing in the place that was 100 percent set up was his stereo and—alphabetized, categorized, and shelved—his records. Last night, unable to sleep, he'd stayed up listening to new reissues of very old Louis Armstrong sides and counting his records. David had 862 45s, 1,391 LPs. He did not count his 78s; too depressing. He'd transferred much of that music onto reel-to-reel tapes, for permanence, but he hadn't gotten around to recording it all. And now he no longer had a turntable that would play 78s. (It was in Teddy's room now, in a big house belonging to a hairy man named Nolan Lamb. It was inconceivable to David that he'd ever loved Irene, but still: how could a person fuck someone named Nolan Lamb?) Though they remained uncounted, his 78s, too, were alphabetized and shelved.

David turned on the hall light and the TV, volume off, then opened another bottle of wine and threaded a reel-to-reel tape onto the machine. He hated the overhead lights; tomorrow, he vowed, he'd buy lamps.

The tape held some of his oldest 78s. The Moondog House music.

He turned the volume up loud enough so he knew it would piss someone off, and he opened the door to his little balcony, and as those saxophones honked and grown men got ecstatic over prospective hucklebuckery, David Zielinsky hopped up and down, facing the wind, looking out over the bubbling ooze of Lake Erie. Every song was about sex and/or drinking. He drank the wine right from the bottle.

He hated himself. He'd been gone for five months and had called his kids every other week long distance and didn't feel like a creep about his self-absorption and that time apart until today. He was a big phony. He was a sellout whose new job involved any number of legitimate union concerns (for which David, despite everything, was a sincere advocate), but it also had him lobbying and cutting deals and working as the dignity-item co-counsel on cases in areas of the law he understood only well enough to be dangerous. The job took him too many places and showed him too many things. David had been a two-term city councilman and had not thought himself naive in the ways of the world, but the interconnectedness of the Feds, the cops, the Mob, and the unions made his head swim. Every day he'd get more new signals on who was playing both sides of what. Every day was an exercise in figuring out who might be providing unlikely protection for whom, and when it would all end. His father had avoided prison on charges of selling thousands of dollars of advertising to nonexistent or undistributed union newsletters by becoming an informant for the FBI, only he quite possibly already was one (David didn't want to know). Danny Greene, supposedly a friend of his father's, had been ousted from the Longshoremen and found a way to keep himself out of prison and only two months ago tried to throw a bomb at a bar where Mike and some people he knew were having lunch, only the bomb hit the frame of the car window and bounced back into the car. Greene jumped out and the car blew sky-high. No one was hurt. Greene's story to the cops was that someone threw a bomb at *him*. Into the open window of a moving car in Cleveland in March. It hardly even made the papers, and people in Washington put a halt to the investigation and that was that. Mike's theory was that Danny was informing to different Feds than Mike was. David finished his wine, reared back, and, using his legs, the way his uncle had always yelled at him to do on long throws, heaved the bottle as far as he could. It cleared the parking lot and landed in a clump of sparkleberry bushes. His shoulder and knee hurt like hell, just from that one throw.

Then he went back inside and turned the music down to a reasonable level. Someone was banging on his door, but David didn't answer it or say anything. Instead, he sat cross-legged on the floor, hunched over his phone, staring at it, rocking back and forth like an autistic. Before long, the music stopped and the tape slapped against the take-up reel. The wine was gone. David switched off the tape deck, picked up the phone, and hung it up. He picked up the phone and dialed three numbers and hung up. He growled. He was thirty-five years old. He hated himself. In the dark now, bathed in the flickering death-pallor-blue light of his TV, David took a deep breath and dialed.

The number had been disconnected. How long had it been since he'd called her there? Years.

He didn't allow himself to pause. He called the operator. There was no Anne O'Connor at the address he mentioned. There was an A. C. O'Connor on West 124th; an Ann O'Connor, no *E*, on West 105th; an Anne O'Connor in Parma. There was also an A. O'Connor in Bratenahl whose number was unlisted. For no good reason, he asked for the Parma number. He dialed it. The voice that answered was an old lady's. "I'm sorry," David said, "I have the wrong number."

"I'm not her," the voice said. "Lord love a duck, that station doesn't even come in good."

— 26 —

IT TOOK ANNE three more weeks to get so disgusted with herself that she broke down and looked to see if David really was in the book. One Monday—after yet another Sunday's writing had been thrown off, this time by the late but uneventful birth of John and Doreen's ten-pound son Thomas—Anne got to work and, even before she got herself a cup of coffee, she looked. He wasn't in the book. At that point, though, she was committed. She called City Hall and was kept on hold so long that she had to yell for one of the interns to get her some coffee. Just as she was yelling, a different voice came on. Anne apologized, and the voice gave her an office number that may or may not still be current. A body in motion tends to stay in motion; Anne called the number before she had the chance to think better of it.

"Law office." David answered his own phone.

"This has to stop," Anne blurted.

"Who *is* this?" David said.

She was caught short.

"Joke," he said. "I thought it did stop. I sure was under that impression."

They caught up. Anne had friends—most of them—that she could not see for a month and the conversation would be stilted. Phil Weintraub, for example, visited from Atlanta last month, and they'd had a lunch with more awkward pauses than sentences. Anne hadn't had a conversation with David in almost four years, and *that* had been sort of an argument, yet when she'd seen him at that fiasco in Berea she knew she had to call, and when she did they talked like they'd seen each other last night over a few beers. Boilermakers, even, in some West Side bar with sawdust on the floor and Dean Martin on the jukebox. David was still that same idealistic, patriotic boy, the one who first gave her a vision of a life other than the one she'd been raised to lead, who fed her tips on the Sheppard case, who was just devious enough to be a worthy foil, who was her married lover back in days of yore, when that was a thrilling taboo and seemed like a safeguard for her career. Anne wondered if it was possible for the opposite ends of any decade in history ever to be more opposite than the poles of the 1960s.

She and David had been talking for about twenty minutes when Anne heard the theme music for the noon news and looked up at the monitor on her wall. Sure enough: there was the noon news. It hadn't been twenty minutes. It had been two hours.

"OK, look, I need to go," she said. Not because of the news, per se. But she was too busy to toss two hours away like that. Also her head was pounding, and she needed more coffee. Her arm hurt, too, bad enough for a pill.

"I should go, too," David said, but then he stammered quite a lot and eked out some long observation about how the Palace Theater was closing next month.

"Not a movie," Anne said, presuming that what he'd meant was a movie. To hear David give that speech and now to hear him fall into incoherence trying to ask her out, after all these years! She had to stifle a laugh. She had no idea why this made her so happy. She hadn't had much sleep. "I want to beat you at something else."

David didn't know what she meant.

"I beat you at Ping-Pong, then I beat you at golf."

"You didn't beat me at Ping-Pong. I beat you."

"You're going senile, mister."

"Another sport, huh? So we can break our 1–1 tie, see who takes two out of three?"

Anne was quite certain she'd beaten him at Ping-Pong. They quibbled about this for a while before Anne suggested tennis and David said no, anything but tennis, and Anne told him to suggest something, and—she should have guessed—he chose bowling.

"I've never bowled," she said. "But fine."

Without having to stop to think about it, he suggested an alley on her side of town. Friday would work fine because it's not a league night. He gave her directions. He knew too much about bowling. She wanted to renege but of course couldn't. She was going to have to find time to get a lesson or something. How hard could it be?

"I really do have to go," she said.

"Oh, and loser pays," David said. "This isn't a date."

"Who said it was?" she said. Only after she hung up did it occur to her she'd just made a date—or whatever it was—on a weeknight, a night she was supposed to anchor the news.

She did the math. She'd known him for seventeen years. More than half her life.

YELLOW I-BEAM poles had been newly driven into the treelawn beside the curb cuts, and thick, ropy chains connected the poles, blocking the entrance. Two white sedans with security company logos on their doors were parked dead center in the otherwise empty parking lot, 69'd so the men inside could talk. Seven o'clock on a Friday night in June, and the biggest bowling alley in Cuyahoga and its six contiguous counties was dark. It wasn't even ten years old. No signs had been posted to explain, not even—at least that David could see—one that said CLOSED. Idling at the curb was a hard-topped blue Corvette with its hazards on. David saw Anne behind the wheel. He waved, made a U-turn, pulled up behind her, and got out.

"I don't know what to say," David said, bending over to talk to her the way a friendly cop would. "I had no idea this place had closed."

"Nice car," Anne said. "You're a convertible man again."

David did not have his top down. "Want to go somewhere else?"

"You're the kegler."

He shook his head. "Not really," he said.

"On the phone it sounded like you had a map of Cleveland's bowling alleys in your head."

"No," he said. "Just this one. My dad used to own a little piece of it, before they . . . well, before he decided to sell it off."

"Good timing on your father's part, it would seem," she said.

On the seat next to her was a new-looking bowling ball case. He pointed. "Thought you said you'd never bowled."

"It's my sister-in-law's," she said. "The one who just had the baby. John's wife."

"You know," David said. "I finally read that book."

"What book?"

"*The Great Gatsby,*" he said. "It always bugged me why John called you Daisy."

"You're kidding," she said. "You just read that?"

"I'm ignorant," he said. "A hapless product of the public schools. Shoot me."

"That's not what I meant. C'mon."

"I know. I'm kidding. I should have read it ages ago. I meant to. You look terrific, by the way."

She had on a white-and-yellow sundress. Her auburn hair was pulled back and clipped with a plain silver barrette.

"I thought this wasn't a date," she said, "but thank you."

"It's not," he said.

"I didn't use up a day of vacation to go bowling," she said, "for nothing."

One of the rent-a-cop units drove over and told them that the place was closed. David said that they could see that; did he know when that happened or why?

"Just this week and none of my business," said the rent-a-cop.

"Well, do you know another bowling alley nearby?"

The man rattled off a list of names and addresses, and David and Anne thanked him.

"I don't know where any of those places are," David said.

"When's the last time you went to Euclid Beach Park?" Anne asked. "It's only a few miles from here." She stuck her arm out the window and pointed north. "They have those little bowling machines in the arcade. What do you call those? The ones with the bowling balls the size of shot puts?"

"Bowling machines," David said. "I was at Euclid Beach last year, for the Steer Roast with Hubert Humphrey. If that's what you want to do, fine."

"I haven't been there since I was a kid," Anne said. "I want to go before they close."

Euclid Beach Park was closing forever at the end of the season. David wouldn't have minded setting the match to the place himself. Or operating the bulldozer or the wrecking ball. However the place went down, good riddance.

"Bowling machines, huh?" David said. "This sort of ruins the loser-pays arrangement."

"True," she said. "But there's nothing more dutch than pay-as-you-go. It still won't be a date, I promise."

"You sure I can't interest you in a little Skee-Ball instead?"

She laughed. *Christ,* did she have a great, silvery laugh. He followed her there. He told himself he'd follow her anywhere. Though he wasn't kidding about the Skee-Ball. He had a gift for Skee-Ball: rolling the ball up the ramp with just enough speed and backspin to hop up toward the high-point circles, bite, and go right down the hole. Once he won a pink panda the size of a wing chair playing Skee-Ball. He gave it to Irene, and now, like so much else, it was gone. Sold for pocket change at a garage sale. Probably in a landfill by now.

ᔕᑎ

OUTSIDE THE SURPRISE House at Euclid Beach Park, Laughing Sal, that motorized mannequin, still rocked back and forth in her glassed-in portico.

Already, before the park even closed, this chipped and faded clownish night-mare looked like a piece of equipment you'd see in a museum of American kitsch. Tinny speakers failed to disguise her famously orgasmic cackle.

Anne already regretted suggesting they come here. The park still had three months of life in it, but there was a dazed, rapacious look to everyone there that made her think of the joyless opportunists who stand in line at 6 A.M. waiting for estate sales to open. Or the ghouls who steal Scrooge's bed curtains during the Ghost of Christmas Future part.

"Look around," David whispered. "What don't you see?"

"Anyone having fun," she said.

"You're not having fun?"

"I'm talking about other people." Despite herself, she grinned. "No, I'm sorry. I'm having fun. I am. This is so odd, being out in public like this, and not worrying about . . ." She shrugged, and David reached over and gave her shoulder an avuncular squeeze.

They went straight to the arcade. She didn't get asked for her first autograph until they were finally standing still, before the Bowl-O-Matic.

David bowled the way he made love. It took him forever to get ready to roll. He spent a lot of time taking deep breaths, squinting, and shifting his weight. He was able to laugh at his quirks right after but couldn't stop doing them. Despite all this, he performed surprisingly well. "It takes me a long time to concentrate," he said. "When I don't do it, I—"

"Forget it," Anne said, rolling yet another strike over those wire loops that made the pins, attached at the top, swing violently backward and thump out of sight. "Do what you have to."

It turned out he was good at this, but she was better. She waited until after she'd beaten him three straight games, each by fifteen or fewer pins, before she declined the ten-dollar side bet and told him there was one of these games in her favorite bar in college and also in the game room her brother Patrick had made out of the carriage house where Anne once lived.

By this time in the evening she'd signed about twenty autographs.

"So," she said. "Skee-Ball?"

"Does your brother have one of those, too?"

"Aw," she said. "You're cute when you pout."

"Why did you say you didn't see other people having fun?"

"I just didn't, OK?"

"It was the wrong answer, though. To my question. That wasn't what I was driving at."

She said she gave up.

"Blacks," he said, sotto voce. "The NAACP has had one kind of suit or another going against this place for, I don't know. Forever. All the crap you read in the paper about how sad it is this place is going under and how it represents the end of an era, what do you think the folks who wrote those letters are really sore about?"

"Aw, c'mon," she said. "You're taking this a little far, don't you think?"

"You never read stories about the NAACP suits, do you? Or see stories. Why don't *you* do a story about it?"

"A little late now. In three months the Euclid Beach Park menace will be no more."

"Laugh if you want," he said. "But this place is so racist, it's sick. And what's even more sick is that all those years I came here as a kid, I never even noticed it."

"I'm sorry. I shouldn't joke about it," she said. "Hey, look! There's some." She pointed at a black family in line for the Flying Turns.

"Shh!" David said.

She laughed. "I'm pretty sure they know they're black."

"The worst thing is, this place is closing, but that's not why it's closing. You should do a story on all the wrangling over the rezoning of this place. The amount of money that's going to change hands in City Hall over this would just blow your mind, believe me."

"No more shop talk," she said. "Want to go?"

It was well after nine but still not dark. Tomorrow would be the longest day of the year.

They wound up back at her house, drinking wine on her back porch. He kissed her good-night on the threshold of her house, and she grabbed him by the front of his shirt and told him not to be ridiculous. It was 1969.

As with conversation, things settled back in as if they'd never been apart. They spent the night alternately making love and taking separate barefoot trips to the bathroom and to the refrigerator and talking and laughing and marveling aloud about what a ridiculous species we're members of. Late in all this, they even managed in the dark to have a stilted conversation about plastic surgery. It came up when David mentioned how much he wanted that tattoo removed, the one of his ex-wife's name. Anne confessed that she'd had a small procedure done. David told her he never would have guessed. Anne said nothing; she just kissed him. He rubbed her back. They drifted off into what little sleep they'd get.

Early the next morning (*very* early; clearly he remained a morning person), he snuck out while she was still sleeping. She woke up as his car pulled away. She got out of bed, pulled on a T-shirt, and let the dog out. She found a Frisbee and walked barefoot out into her dewy yard. It wasn't even seven o'clock, but the sun was bearing down hard. In this light the lake looked almost blue.

Babe was a Frisbee maniac. Ibby had trained her well. The dog gave the Frisbee back without even tugging.

The difference, Anne thought, between David and any other man she might be with is that if anyone else left like that, she'd either be upset or not give a damn. With David, she knew what he was doing. He didn't have to say or even leave a note. She kept playing Frisbee until he got back from the store.

"Ready for your farm-boy breakfast?" he asked. It was like he was never gone.

She heaved the Frisbee, and on a dead sprint Babe leaped and caught it.

"I always wanted a dog that could do that," he said.

"Those are nice sunglasses," she said. They were green-lensed, old-fashioned, prescription. He always did look great in a convertible with the sun on his face. "You *know* I can't eat all that," she said, pointing at the grocery sacks swollen with milk, bacon, eggs, butter, doughnuts, orange juice, potatoes, syrup, onions, green peppers, ketchup, and pancake mix. "And I won't."

"I know," he said.

And she knew that he knew that she knew with metaphysical certitude that she'd eat it. He'd never been to this house, but she knew that he knew she wouldn't have anything to eat here. She knew he wouldn't have even stopped in the kitchen to look. He knew, and he was right.

"Oh, I do have plenty of orange juice," she said, just as he was going into the house.

He turned around to look at her, over the top of his sunglasses.

"It's pretty old, though," she said. "I wouldn't drink it if I were you."

∞

"LET ME GET this straight," Mike Zielinsky said. It was the next day, a Saturday. He and David were at lunch at Corky & Lenny's, in a strip mall in University Heights; it was a glorified deli with dark, dark wood and red velvet upholstery. "First, you cancel out on me for the game, which is fine, even though I asked for these fuckin' tickets special from guys I don't like to ask too much from, but OK. Ah-ah-ah-ah!" He held up his hands. "Let me finish. Then *you* want my tickets—instead of just buyin' cheap seats and slippin' a tenner to the usher like a normal person. What for? So you can take some broad to a ballgame to see the worst fuckin' team in baseball play some team that got made up out of thin air. What are they called?"

The name was right on the tickets, which sat on the table between them. "The Seattle Pilots," David said.

"The Seattle Pilots. Like there's a woman alive who's gonna be impressed by that, but, hey. I say fine. A-OK by me."

Of the twenty-odd people in Corky & Lenny's, about half are staring and about half are regulars and have seen Mike Zielinsky's act before.

"Instead of making you come all the way out to my place to come pick the tickets up, I think, nah, I'll save the boy a drive and meet him halfway, so I invite you to lunch, my treat, and on top of *everything* I do for you, the first fucking thing you do is waltz in here and ask me for *another* favor?"

David shrugged, and he could not help but grin. He loved his father, he really did. The favor was of course *not* the first thing David did when he got there. What he did first was to slip the waitress his BankAmericard and convince her to run the card through the cruncher and let David sign a blank charge slip, all while Mike was out feeding his parking meter because David lied and said he saw a cop giving tickets (the judge Mike faced for the most recent racketeering charges had said so much as a traffic ticket and the probation would be yanked). David told the waitress to give herself 20 percent when the time came and to please not bring the check within ten feet of the table. (These weren't the most elaborate means he'd gone to pick up a check with his father; this was standard.) The second thing was to ask his father about the bowling alley closing, the answer to which was predictably elliptical. ("Brunswick, the company that builds lanes? They loan money to fucking anybody. What the fuck did any of *us* know about running a bowling alley? Huh? Tell you what, though, you want a line of work where people steal from you, go into the bowling alley business.") David's question about a boat he could borrow on Sunday was (ignoring the exchange of pleasantries and the ordering of cold adult beverages) at best the third thing.

"What I want you to help me understand," Mike said, "is how it can be that the first fucking thing you say to me is, 'Dad, do you have a boat?'— which you know I do not—and then you sit there and expect me to *find* one for you?"

"That's not what I said. Not *find* one," David said. He'd mentioned two people Mike knew who had boats. All David wanted was that he'd ask those guys, on David's behalf. "And I did say thank you for the tickets. Anyway, all of it's spur of the moment. I admit it's crazy."

Slowly, Mike's face was transformed from scowl to wide grin. He reached across the vinyl-covered two-top and gave his son a slow, soft pat on the cheek. "It's good to know people, huh?"

David handed him one of his business cards, which had the number of the answering service. "You can leave a message there anytime."

"I have this," his father said. But he pocketed it anyway.

David knew the kinds of things that went on with his father, and he knew the lengths to which his father had gone to protect David from the specifics. He was an easy man to love, if you let yourself. "If I can have the boat all day," David said, "I could take the kids in the afternoon, and you, too, maybe. She has to work in the afternoon."

"So, all right. You've told me everything but the important part. Who is she?"

David told his father to sit still, which was not among Mike's strengths, and he told him.

Mike banged the table with both palms. "A-*ha!* I *knew* it," he said. "Sometimes with people, it's just like that!"

"Like what?"

"With your mother and me, it was like that. We were meant to be together. Whenever we were with anybody else, it wasn't so good. It hasn't been so good." Mike, for his part, seemed to be involved with someone new every six months. "Everybody's got that one true love."

"Could be," David said. He didn't believe that. At all. But there he was, after one night with Anne O'Connor and six years apart from her, and he had that feeling again. Ridiculous. Illogical. Hard to explain, except to anyone who's served time as a human being.

❧

ANNE WROTE ALL afternoon, like a maniac she wrote (fourteen pages!), and it made her a half hour late. As she hurried down the slope of West Third toward the stadium, she looked at her watch to see if she was later than she'd feared. She had to be; there was hardly anyone around. The people must already be inside. She crossed the bridge over the railroad gulch, the only person headed that way. Her watch said half past six, though. David must have had the starting time wrong.

He was pacing in front of the Tower A ticket window, dressed in an obviously new denim jacket and a much-weathered Indians cap. A small line of people stood waiting to buy tickets.

"How much have we missed?"

David shrugged. "Batting practice."

She remembered him saying once that the true fan comes in time for batting practice. Her brother John, a fellow purist, felt the same way. Anne liked baseball but didn't understand why anyone would want to watch anyone practice anything. "We didn't miss any of the game?"

He handed her a ticket. "No. Why do you say that?"

"Where is everybody?"

David laughed. "How long since you've been to a Tribe game?"

It had, it's true, been a season or three. "I'm not sure." She did know that the Indians were awful this year, that they'd been in last place since opening day and were mired there now.

It was a team whose only stars were Sudden Sam McDowell, a big hard-throwing left-hander who might have been the biggest drunk in the history of baseball, and Tony Horton, the intense young sweet-swinging, haunted-looking first baseman, who never smiled even when he homered and who, the following year, would have a nervous breakdown in the middle of a doubleheader, attempt suicide, and quit baseball forever.

David bought a scorecard. He'd brought a pencil with him. The lines for a dog and a beer couldn't get much shorter, but she told David she liked to go at least look at the field first, before she bought anything or did anything else: just make a beeline for the green field. "Great," he said.

They went straight through the nearest tunnel. "Oh my lord," Anne said. "My god."

"This is what last place looks like."

Cleveland Stadium was a sea of empty red and blue seats. Anne had never been here for anything with this few people. She'd seen games on TV and seen the empty seats, but in person it looked a lot worse. "I had no idea," she said, "that Clevelanders had become such a bunch of fickle front-runners."

The field itself was a mess, too, with brown, trampled spots still visible from some rock concert.

"It's not as bad as it looks," David said. "I'd guess there's twelve thousand or so."

"That's pretty bad for a Saturday night game, though, isn't it, even this year."

"I've been here when it's worse."

They made their way toward the field and down the lowest walkway up the first-base line and to their seats. Front row.

"You're kidding." She looked at her ticket. "*These* are ours?"

"Great, aren't they?" he said. "I mean, I know there's plenty of seats," he said, indicating with a wave the sixty thousand empty ones. "But these you sort of have to know someone to get."

These were the exact same seats her father had once had.

"Or," she said, "you could just bribe an usher to let you stay here."

They made small talk. After a while David brought up his kids and mentioned that he'd gotten his ex-wife to let him see them every Sunday afternoon. Anne wanted to tread easy around that subject, and so she just let him talk, which he did, filling out his scorecard with the names and numbers of the starting lineups and not looking at her.

She looked at the visiting team, then at her ticket stub, then back at the unfamiliar blue-and-gold team, and then at David's scorecard. "Seattle?" she said. "Is this an exhibition game?"

"They're an expansion team," David said. "The Seattle Pilots." He shook his head sadly. "Even they have a better record than we do."

Underneath several coats of paint on the seat next to her were the initials SFO. It could be anyone, she thought. She hadn't remembered that from those days. But there was a lot she hadn't remembered. Her novel was about that, a little. Kenneth had told her not to talk about what her novel was about, but Steven was in there; she couldn't pretend otherwise.

They rose for the playing of our national anthem.

"So, is *this* a date?" she asked.

He put his hat right over his heart; it was just adorable. "Yes," he said. "Of course."

"Because we arrived separately," she said. "Can it be a date if it's separate cars?"

He wouldn't answer her until the national anthem was over. They didn't even have anyone performing it. It was just some recording; an instrumental. That's how bad it had gotten.

"Well, we're here," he said, putting his hat back on. "Things don't have to be classified, I guess. They can just *be*." He rolled his eyes. "Listen to me," he said. "My daughter is a hippie, and now I am. It's contagious. Hippies."

The game began.

Anne had never learned to keep score. David taught her. After a couple innings she took over, lost in its intricacies: drawing the little diamonds, indicating every throw and catch, fair or foul, with an elegantly simple code. It was at once visual, narrative, and mathematical.

She was missing a good deal of what was going on only a few feet away from her. Passed balls, hit batsmen, errors, wild pitches: everything. Cleveland was getting destroyed.

"This is why people love sports," she said.

"What do you mean?" David asked. It was late in the game, but the sun hung tough on an unnaturally orange horizon. Two days a person should always get to the ballpark: the last day of the season, and the longest day of the year.

She ran her hand over his scorecard. "It's so clean," she said. "So knowable. Things add up. Outcomes are clear."

"If your life was really like that," he said, "it would bore you silly."

"I'm not talking about life as opposed to sports," she said. "Damn it. I'm just talking about sports."

He broke up laughing, and so did she. He leaned right over and kissed her, hard by the first-base line.

⌒

LATE SUNDAY MORNING, as a surprise, he came to pick her up in a borrowed boat—a clunky, newish eighteen-foot Starcraft with orange Naugahyde upholstery and a cramped below-deck cabin. He stopped near the base of an especially eroded cliff. Pine trees and elms with exposed roots looked only one stiff gust of wind away from plunging into the green-gray phosphate froth of Lake Erie. Exposed shale flaked off in pieces the size of pie tins.

David, an inexperienced boater despite being an honorably discharged veteran of the United States Navy, had hugged the shore all the way from the Lakewood Marina. He'd also had a hard time finding the place and was uncertain if the ramshackle dock and stairs near which he'd dropped anchor were hers. He'd never been on that dock or down those stairs, but he'd stood briefly at the edge of her cliff and looked down, and he'd been inside her house. The wooded edge of the cliff above him did look right. The gingerbready white crest of the house that was visible from here was almost certainly her house. He wasn't sure, though; nothing looked quite the same from the water side of things. He killed the engine and sat in the boat for a long time before he summoned the nerve to sound the horn. The bleat it made sounded like the amplified torture of a house cat. David had expected a foghorn—or at least something with a lot more bass.

In her back room, in a cloud of cigarette smoke, seated at a hulking mahogany desk with a leather-insert top (she'd bought it at an antique store because it reminded her of one her father had in his law office, which could have been hers for the asking if she'd asked at the right time), vibrating from the pot of coffee she'd drunk to compensate for the sleep she'd forsaken, Anne O'Connor hunched over a brand-new IBM Selectric, typing and concurrently revising the pages she'd written longhand the afternoon before. The pages were about her hero playing the cornet in a club in Greenwich Village. She was playing a Bix Beiderbecke record full blast through her remaining speaker. It was a good enough stereo to drown out the sound of the horn from the lake below. Also, the lake had not yet claimed enough of her big backyard for her to be all that close to the edge of the cliff.

She had been out late with David the night before. She'd left his apartment with all its shiny, pleasant lamps very early this morning. The idea that a few hours later he might be at the base of her cliff in a boat, beginning to sweat, would never have occurred to her unbidden. It was a Sunday. She had work to do.

David honked the horn again.

Anne kept writing.

Finally, he undid a length of nylon rope from one of the cleats, balanced himself unsteadily on the side of the boat, and jumped to the dock. His bad leg plunged straight through a rotted board, and the rest of him fell forward. He screamed—more a scream of surprise than pain. The other boards held, and the board he'd smashed hadn't provided much more resistance than wet cardboard would have. His leg was soaked from the knee down. He'd worn canvas sneakers and blue jeans, and the jeans had protected him from splinters. He wasn't hurt. A thirty-five-year-old man can't look forward to many more bad falls that lucky.

Anne didn't hear him scream, either. She had recently arrived at the conclusion that every single word she'd written yesterday was a steaming load of monkey shit. (That said, the novel will turn out fairly well. Her old friend Alton Herrick, a book editor in New York, will recommend that the book be published. He will be overruled. The book will have many other close calls. Alton will tell Anne she should move to New York, that living there is good for a writer's career.) She typed faster and pounded the keys harder, trying to keep herself from outthinking herself.

The wood on the stairs was fairly new, but some of the posts wobbled as David climbed up, his sneaker squishing warmly with each step. At the top he sat down to take his socks off. He found himself out of breath.

What she did hear was Babe's barking. Anne, in reflex, told the dog *no*. But the barking seemed deeper and more savage than what Babe would direct at squirrels or stray cats. Anne stood and ground her cigarette in the blue china ashtray. (The ashtray was shaped like a stylized tidal wave and bigger around than a gravy-boat platter. Big, ostentatious ashtrays, suitable for many party guests to use simultaneously, were about to go the way of the dodo.) Her brothers were always half seriously nagging her about the dangers of living way out here alone. The worst part about being killed by an intruder would be to prove them right. The second-worst part of that was the image of her mother in a wheelchair, watching the second of her four children get buried, head rocking, quite probably too far gone to know what was happening, but you never know what's going on deep inside her head, not for sure.

Something was in the untended brush at the back of the lot. A deer, probably. The dog bared its teeth and bounded from one rear window to another. Anne opened the bottom drawer of that desk. Next to a modest, carefully rationed cache of pain pills was the gun with which her naked father had chased her bra-clad mother, a gun that was, unbeknownst to Anne, a gift of prudent obeisance from Eliot Ness. Babe's zeal scared the hell out of Anne; there had been deer in the yard before, and the dog never barked like this. Anne slipped her hand around the handle of the Smith & Wesson. It was a heavy, marvelous thing, this gun. It begged anyone who held it to lift it, aim it, and fire. Anne had never fired it.

Anne could see a shape. A human shape. A large man. She raised the window screen. She flicked off the safety. She squeezed the trigger.

At the same split second David mistook Beiderbecke for Louis Armstrong, Anne fired a warning shot.

A split second after she fired it, she saw that the man was David.

David frowned and looked around and behind him, but he didn't flinch, and he proceeded with his limping shamble toward the back of the house.

The bullet splashed harmlessly into the lake.

Anne threw the gun back into the drawer and slammed it shut. She ran outside to intercept him so he wouldn't smell the cordite. Like Anne, the dog had never seen an unexpected person emerge from the lakeside, but now Babe, too, ran toward David with an intensity not unlike happiness.

"Did I hear a *gunshot*?" David said, incredulous.

Well, of *course* he heard it. How could he not hear it? "My neighbor has a backfiring antique car he takes out for a drive every Sunday," she said. "You never know when he's going to take it out or when or if it's going to backfire, so you can never prepare yourself for it or get used to it, and even after living here all this time every time it happens it practically gives me a heart attack. It's really a nuisance, and I should probably talk to him about it, but I haven't been able to bring myself to do it because he's such a nice man otherwise." Adrenaline and coffee were making her talk very fast. Adrenaline and coffee were making her heart beat so hard it hurt. The upper chambers of her heart seemed to bang off the underside of her left collarbone. Usually she loved things that made her heart race.

"Oh," David said.

"Long time, no see." She had never fired a gun in her life. She'd kept that revolver loaded in her desk drawer since she'd moved here, and all that time she'd evaded the idle temptation to take it out in the backyard and blast away at tin cans the way decent folk in the movies learned to shoot. The gun hadn't kicked as much as she'd imagined it would.

"Four and a half hours," he said. "It was all I could stand."

It was hard to tell how sarcastic he was being.

"What'd you do to your leg?" she asked. "How did you get here?"

"In a boat. I broke a board on your dock, I'm sorry. I'll pay to fix it."

"A boat? You're full of surprises," she said. The dog loved David. Aren't you supposed to trust a man who appeals to your pets?

"It's borrowed," he said. "I'm not interrupting anything, am I?" David bobbed his head around, a gesture that, Anne imagined, was meant to be an approximation of looking for other lovers hidden somewhere on the property.

"You scared the fuck out of me," Anne said. "You know that, right?"

"I remember when you used to be bad at swearing," David said.

"You met me half a lifetime ago," she said. "I used to be a lot of things." *Like effortlessly pretty.* The small lines a woman her age should have were absent, and her features were lifted just enough that she always looked slightly startled and one degree happier than she really was. It had been a minor procedure, as those things go, but now every time she looked into a mirror, she saw something false. "I had you pegged for a lot of things, Councilman, but backdoor man wasn't one of them."

Neither was *pest*. Neither was *needy*. Before, when they sort of lived together, the limits he honored were part of what she'd loved. That, and the fact that neither he nor she ever felt the obligation to break down and declare their love to one another all the sloppy time.

"I'm not sure I want to be pegged as anything." *Councilman.* Was that supposed to be as mean as it felt?

"You're too old for that," she said. "That's what young people worry about, their infinite possibilities, et cetera."

"'Et cetera'?"

"Everybody gets pegged as something," she said.

"You don't have to like it," he said. The back of his terry cloth shirt was sweated through. He sweat a lot more now than when he was younger. Hair had begun to disappear from his head and sprout coarsely from his back and ears.

"Who said I like it?" she asked. "Who said anyone did?"

"I *am* interrupting something," he said. "This was really stupid. I'm sorry. I should go."

Anne's heart wouldn't slow down.

"I'm making a fool of myself," he said. "All these years, and then I come on too strong."

She watched him scratch Babe behind the ears.

"All right," he said. "I'm a jerk. I'm sorry. I should go. I'll go."

Anne couldn't believe she'd been so jittery and preoccupied that she'd just grabbed that gun and fired it, warning shot or no.

"You can bail me out here anytime," he said.

She laughed. "So why *did* you come here? In your...in a borrowed boat?"

❧

THE FIRST TIME he had seen Anne O'Connor she was lying across the prow of a speedboat, rocketing north, under a blue sky and across this same lake when the water was something a person still might swim in. She was a vision.

The first time she had seen David Zielinsky, he was playing Ping-Pong defensively with that tough pug uncle. The sight of him seemed to trigger the right music on the jukebox. He was a vulnerable, unaffected young man who knew where to drop a shot.

❧

THE PLAN WAS to go to Kelley's Island.

When they got to the bottom of her stairs, the knot he'd tied to the dock had slipped loose and the unmoored boat—happily, still tied to its anchor—had drifted about thirty feet out into the lake. The water was hardly inviting.

"So," Anne said.

"So," David said.

But what choice really did he have but to strip off his jeans (he had his swimming trunks underneath; he'd brought a change of clothes, including clean white underpants, along with an optimistic six condoms in a vinyl tote of the kind airlines used to give away) and wade out after the boat? What choice did Anne have but to genially mock him for his chivalry?

David sunk down in the muck, to the middle of his calves. David's son Teddy had gotten the idea for the name of his band from an article he'd read in school that said the bottom of Lake Erie, near the Cleveland shore, was carpeted with thirty thousand sludge worms per square yard. David did not know this. Knowing what was causing the tickly, squirmy feeling he had as he trudged through the warm mire and drew near the boat would not have made the experience any more pleasant. Better to think of it as the heebie-jeebies.

"Just pull it over here," Anne said.

David shook his head. He did not want to wade back to the dock. He climbed up into the boat and tried to wash off his tarry legs in the part of the lake that was water. On the floor of the boat was a rusty red gas can with an oily rag knotted to the spout. David used it.

"You know," Anne said, "I *was* kind of in the middle of something." She studied the rotted, broken board and wondered if she could get her brothers out here to work on this, just for fun. "If you're going to primp all day I'm going back up."

David started the engine and nosed the boat to the dock, and Anne jumped on board, and they headed west.

"Don't hug the shore," Anne said. "It's nicer out farther." Meaning *cleaner.* "And it's a lot faster, too."

"I don't really know the way," David said.

"Then what did you lure me out here for?"

"I didn't *lure* you," he said. "You didn't have to come. I just don't know any other way other than to follow the land to Port Clinton and cut over from there."

If she were honest with herself, she'd have to admit she'd been happy for the distraction. She imagined that Coleridge was in fact happy to see the visitor who interrupted "Kubla Khan," that they'd broken out the scotch and the opium and begun to tell lies like men, and afterward Coleridge could never finish the poem and managed to place the blame on someone else and to make the poem famous for being a fragment.

Also, she told herself, this was romantic. The surprise. The boat.

"I'll navigate," she said. "Unless you want me to drive."

"Drive, if you want," he said.

Most men would say this with an edge in their voice, but David was flatly sincere, and Anne took the controls and swerved the boat due north and opened its sluggish engine up, full throttle. It was not a windy day and it was not a fast boat, but there was still enough chop and enough horsepower to make the boat buck, to make Anne laugh like hell and David hold on tight.

Romantic. Right. And that was aside from the gun she'd trained on him and fired, and the rush she'd gotten from dodging the biggest mistake of her life and having everyone survive to tell the tale.

∾

ALL THERE WAS to getting to Kelley's was to go out a few miles, turn west, and after about an hour watch the horizon for the Perry Monument. Aim toward the monument, and before you get there, Kelley's will emerge on the right.

David began to adjust to the speed and the boat bucking on the waves and reached over and ran his hand over Anne's thigh.

He had to be kidding. She was pretty sore and would really, really rather not.

He kept it up and proceeded to her shoulders, and she had to admit that the most attractive part of a new love affair—or even a resumed one—was this: this decadent, hungerless gluttony. She knew it would come to this; she just hadn't until now known she'd known.

Anne throttled down. She was also a sucker for a back rub from a gentle, long-fingered man. "You've got to be kidding," she said.

"About what?" he said.

"Don't be like that," she said. "I'd much rather you be direct, and honest."

In David's experience, women say this but don't want this. Anne included.

"It's just romantic," he said. "The sun, the wind in your hair, all alone like this."

There were other boats in sight—bass boats, ore carriers, even a stray sailboat—but none close enough to see the people on board.

"All alone?" Anne asked, pointing.

"There's a cabin," David said.

She rolled her eyes, but as she did there was just the trace of a smile.

David dropped anchor.

∾

"IT HAPPENS," ANNE said, because that is what *Cosmopolitan* said a woman should always say. "It's normal. It happens to everybody."

According to what David had read in *Playboy,* this was true. *Playboy*

[548]

said that at such unhappy moments, any good woman would say what Anne just said. *Playboy* also recommended that servile, carnal gratitude be paid a woman who had the tact and kindness to state this fact at such an opportune time, and David knelt before her and did his best.

His best wasn't good enough. Anne reclined on the beach towel-covered foldout couch and watched David's head lurch energetically between her legs. She couldn't concentrate. She thought about everything else: the book and that it probably needed more sex. If she'd fed the dog. If the station would renew her contract, and if that's what she wanted. Her ratings, since the surgery, had steadily risen, but much of the credit had gone to her new co-anchor, the man. When she got back to shore, she really should go see John and Doreen and fat baby Thomas. God, what a fat baby he was!

She should, she knew, fake an orgasm and get on with her day.

She took a deep breath expressly for that purpose, when along with the intake of breath came a vision of that woman in the blond wig, or whoever it was that left the blond wig on the boat on which her father died.

That was it. That was all she could take. She knew it was wrong, but she had no choice but to reach down and give David a tap on the shoulder, to curl her fingers under his damp armpits and tug him gently upward.

It was David who had said that the mystery *is* the fact.

She held him. She pulled him tight to her and kissed him when he started to talk and shushed him when even the kiss failed and held him tighter yet.

The woman in the wig. Who was she and where was she now?

Who was the closeted homosexual drag queen in the Indians' locker room who in a moment of unguarded exuberance used his lipstick to write WE'RE IN on top of Vic Wertz's head? Why did Alan Freed destroy himself? Why couldn't Carl Stokes save Cleveland? If Dorothy Fuldheim is so great, why didn't she leave? Why, when Anne had been so self-righteously certain that Sam Sheppard had killed his wife, hadn't she recognized Louie Seltzer's earnest horse sense as the banality of evil?

Did Dr. Sam kill Marilyn?

Whatever happened to the man who walked out of the 79er Cafe?

What made Anne think she'd solved the mystery of David's mother? Yes, *probably* Gigi Madison had been killed by the man for whom she'd left David's father, after she'd left *that* man for another man, who'd been murdered by god knows whom. The bigger mystery might be why David's father hadn't joined the carnage. Anne thought she knew what happened, and she'd thought it would be better if David's aunt knew, too, but she realized that David's uncle hadn't told her, or that he had, or that there was nothing to tell. It was all so confusing it made Anne's head pound. All she could be grateful for was that she'd never broadcast any part of the story.

It was a mystery to Anne, now, why she'd presumed she should tell Betty.

Anne had never thought there was any mystery at all to her brother Steven's story, that David had dragged Steven's name into things just because he was so furious she'd been investigating his mother's death. Steven's story was straightforward. He was perfect. He was martyred for the love of God and country, and in the process unwittingly and innocently killed his family, too. But when she'd tried to write a novel about this, thinking that the story was so tragic and inevitable it would tell itself, she realized no story told itself. Stories are unruly. All a story can hope to be is a great unraveling of accepted truth. The mystery *is* the fact.

She had been crying for a long time now, and David was good enough not to say a thing about it, to withstand the temptation to say he'd never seen this side of her, the greater temptation to ask what was wrong. He'd never seen her cry. Why she was crying now was, for David (and also for Anne, really), another mystery. He held her as tightly as she held him.

֍

THEY TURN BACK, and on the way back they do not talk much and David drives the boat and again, because it is the only way he knows, he hugs the shore.

He draws near Cleveland, and he sees his apartment building. "Hey," he says, pointing, "there's my apartment building."

Anne O'Connor is dressed and has draped a towel around her like a shawl. She sits on the back bench seat of the borrowed boat, hugging her knees. She nods.

They pass Whiskey Island, its sparkling gray dune-mountains of stockpiled rock salt, its abandoned shacks. David waves at the lighthouse keeper, only it's the idea of the lighthouse keeper he's waving at, because that's abandoned, too.

They are near the mouth of the Cuyahoga River now, with Cleveland Stadium looming over them, and the water grows dark, nearly black. An oil barge slides toward them, as smoothly and slowly as if it were being excreted by a gigantic beast with a fatty diet.

"Have you ever sailed up the river?" David asks.

Anne shakes her head no.

"I never have, either," David says. "I don't know anyone who has," David says. "It's right here all the time, underneath us. But . . ." He stops himself. Last November Cleveland voters overwhelmingly approved a $100 million bond issue to clean up the river and the lake. "I was just curious. How bad it was. What's upriver. It's stupid. Forget it."

Anne looks up. He doesn't deserve this, to be made to feel like this. He didn't do anything wrong, really. He is overeager and excessively romantic. He is mildly crippled and limited in his imagination. Other than that, he's a good man.

"No," she says. "Do it. Let's go upriver as far as we can."

"Are you serious?"

"Deadly," she says. The river's about eighty miles long. Anne is prepared to take it all the way. Probably it's not navigable all the way, though, really, she hasn't the first notion whether the town called Cuyahoga Falls, which is way down almost to Akron, took its name from an actual waterfall, or whether there were locks there, or whether the name was merely poetic and/or prescient.

David turns the boat into the black-and-blue ooze of what—in the time of Moses Cleaveland, in the time of the unimpressed Charles Dickens, and even in the time of the births of David Zielinsky and, more than two years later, Anne O'Connor—had once been a current. Along either side of the river are boarded-up warehouses, overgrown train tracks, half-dissembled aqueducts, and the rusted hulks of inoperative Huletts. Gas bubbles erupt at the water's surface, like some kind of grim cocktail.

Anne leans over the rail and looks at the blackening hull of the boat. Possibly, this would wash off. She was afraid to say anything, afraid David would take even a complaint about the smell as a girlishly manipulative way to get him to turn around and go back.

At Collision Bend, bobbing on the starboard side, floating, are four dented once-white refrigerators. Just beyond the bend is a half-submerged stack of iron girders, slathered in what looks like axle grease. They pass through an oil slick, with fumes of visible orange and blue, and the driveshaft of the engine groans as the propeller labors to chop its way through the puddinglike ooze. The slick keeps going, around one bend and another, underneath railroad bridges low enough to make a person feel he is walking underneath a ladder. The slick subsides, yielding to water more chocolate in color. Soon they round yet another bend and come across a culvert big enough around to drive the boat into; from it, a torrent of thick greenish-brown liquid surges into the river. A month ago the Big Creek interceptor main ruptured. This had been in the newspapers (buried), but not on TV—*in* the news, but not *on* the news—and neither David nor Anne connect that culvert with the story they'd only skimmed in the first place. Every day since the main broke, twenty-five million gallons a day of untreated sewage have joined the usual effluent of filthy runoff and motor oil dumped by a city of industrious shade-tree mechanics into their nearest storm sewer to surge out of this culvert like a viscous, malodorous cataract. Some things it's better not to know.

They have not seen another moving boat since that oil barge. It is a Sunday. The steel mills, which they're now approaching, no longer run all day and all night and on weekends. It's not that kind of city anymore, and not that kind of country, either. Words from David and Anne's childhood—*war, recession, price controls, inflation*—have floated into view as surely as those gas bubbles.

David and Anne keep winding down the crooked river, past the steel mills, past the house on the ridge overlooking the west bank that David once called home and does not now point out, through a canyon of tank farms, through the heaps and piles that, from this angle, David is convinced anew are the true skyline of Cleveland.

They do not say much, because, in the face of this, there is not much to say. Also they are each trying not to breathe. Anne is breathing through that beach towel.

As they get farther upriver, farther into the Cuyahoga Valley, the water starts to go from brown to pine green, and the smell goes from sulfurous to bearable, and David asks Anne how far she wants to go.

"It's up to you."

"Because I think I've seen enough," he says. "Every inch we go is another inch we have to see again."

"Maybe just a little farther," she says.

What she wants to say is that she wants to keep going until they get to that little ski resort, the one where she shattered her arm. She's never told him that she shattered her arm. They have that bond, she thinks: her arm, his leg. There is world enough and time. Isn't there? She can tell him about her arm. She can tell him about her novel. She can let go, give over, breathe, relax, move on. Many things are possible.

He pulls back on the throttle. "I really think I've seen enough. My god. I don't know what I expected, but my god. Dead fish, maybe."

"There aren't any fish," she says. "Anymore. Even the trash fish have been gone for years. There aren't even any sludge worms or higher parasites. They're all gone. Dead. We had a story on it last week. The river's down to what some scientist called 'opportunistic microbes.'"

"Opportunistic microbes," David repeats. That's what Teddy ought to call his band. The Opportunistic Microbes. "Christ."

"We can go back, I suppose," Anne says. "It's OK."

She really only said that to be accommodating: the long arm of deb class come back to haunt her. Being a man, he takes her at face value when it suits him, and so turns the boat around and heads back toward the lake.

For the second time today they are stopping shy of their destination, first his, then hers. They've had bad sex. After all that, what is there to do but go home?

"I was just thinking," he says.

"There's your first mistake," she says. She actually winks at him and instantly would give anything to have been able to take that back. Who winks?

"When you said you hadn't been to Euclid Beach Park since you were a kid," he says. "Weren't you there for that Democratic Steer Roast, the JFK one?"

On the north horizon is a cloud of black smoke.

"Yes," she says.

"I saw you," he says.

"You *saw* me? Why didn't you say anything?"

"I saw you from pretty far away. You were up on a platform or something. I wasn't sure it was you."

"It was I," she said.

For a split second he thought she was correcting his grammar. "Well," he says, "you said you hadn't been there since you were a kid."

What is he talking about? "I *was* a kid," she says.

The return trip never feels as long as the journey out. The heaps and the piles and, higher, the echo-skyline of Terminal Tower and its dwarf brethren is drawing closer. The cloud of smoke couldn't possibly be more opaque, any more black. Anyone's first guess would have been a tire fire.

"You were what, twenty-four years old?"

"You don't think twenty-four is a kid?"

"No, do you? You do. Twenty-four is a kid? By the time my uncle was twenty-four, he'd already brought down Al Capone. By the time my parents were twenty-four, they'd had me and screwed up their lives and in the case of my mother, may she rest in peace, died. And in the case of myself—"

"Right," she says. "I get it." She is not David. She wants to believe the best is yet to come. She likes to believe she has not settled for anything. She is not sure she believes this, but she doesn't like to think about that.

They round the next hopelessly kinked bend, and without warning a plague-caliber cloud of acrid white smoke, driven their way by gathering lake-effect wind, rolls into them, like the smoke that comes out of an oven full of blazing meat, and they're coughing, choking, startled. The smoke is thick. Particles of the black smoke that had surrounded the white now harden or incinerate or undergo some other kind of unholy alchemy and start slowly to fall, like flakes of black snow through the white haze.

Together, they look up through watering eyes and, about a quarter mile away as the crow flies, but still two or three as the Cuyahoga tumbles and turns, they see it: *bam,* a wall of orange flame, reaching up about sixty horrible feet from what must be a building on the shore.

Anne screams and reaches over and yanks the throttle down.

"It's the river," she says.

The wind picks up, and they can feel the heat on their faces now.

The river.

The wind bears the sound of sirens.

The flames loom above them, still safely distant, though Anne gives David a look and he gets out of the way and she backs up the boat about a hundred yards to the previous bend. She nods to David and he takes a rope and tries to tie the boat to the dock of a vacant shipbuilding factory. This time, hardened by fear into clarity, he stops to recall what he'd been taught in the navy, and the knot is a beauty. That's when he looks down at the hull of the boat and realizes what a mess he's made.

Anne gets out of the boat, too, and for no reason in particular they join hands as they run down the well-built unused dock to the cement of the shore.

The flames are brighter now, and taller, and the sirens louder. Through the smoke they can see a coast guard fireboat pumper—about the size and the shape of a tug, a craft designed to put out fires on flaming boats—attempt to use water cannons to put out the river itself.

David Zielinsky is thirty-five years old and has spent his adult life talking for a living. Anne O'Connor, who is thirty-three, does not need to make a living, but has made quite a good one, and she's made it talking. And now they stand on a desiccated shore of a dead river, holding hands, and between them, they cannot think of a word to say.

The flames rise. The fireboat seems to catch on fire itself. The flames reach a railroad bridge that's every bit of sixty feet six inches above the river. It's hard to say who is squeezing the other's hand harder, David or Anne. They do not move. Soon, they can smell creosote from the burning bridge.

David turns to Anne and finally thinks of a thing to say.

"I love you," he says. His voice cracks as he says it, like a fool kid's. It is the first time either of them has said this to the other.

"You *what?*" she says. She turns to him, frowning. "You *love* me?"

He shrugs. She doesn't say anything more, and neither does he. The fire is being fought, but the flames do not seem to diminish, and the clouds of smoke get thicker, and the ashy black flakes keep falling. Heat presses down on their bodies worse than if they were standing next to a bonfire. They do not stop holding hands. The tears in their eyes could certainly be blamed on the smoke. Time stops, and they watch their river burn.

EPILOGUE

෨෭

Vincit Qui Patitur

August 1969

NOT EVEN IN a sports arena: a sweltering high school gymnasium that smells like varnish and fresh popcorn. No spotlights, either, just the gym's chicken-wire–covered fixtures overhead. The wrestling ring—a rented boxing ring, in fact—has been set up in the middle of a basketball court. It's surrounded by metal folding chairs. The wooden bleachers are pulled out. People trickle in. The vulgar. The curious. The disbelieving. The press-credentialed. The drunk. Several of us belong in more than one of these categories. We are lovers of spectacle and violence, of kitsch and mystery. When it comes to someone else's abyss, we are shameless voyeurs. A surprising number of us are women.

The gym is half empty when the first match starts. Even the biggest fans of the wrestling shows that air on grainy UHF television haven't heard of these guys. For the first several matches, the wrestlers come out in pairs and quartets. They fake their corny accents (Russian; southern; Boston Brahmin; both kinds of Indian). They choreograph moves they've stolen from Gorgeous George, Gorilla Monsoon, or Bobo Brazile; conk each other over the head with spit buckets and folding chairs. They produce various concealed weapons (barbed wire; billy club; pop bottle). None of it gets much of a rise out of us. Things proceed like this for over an hour. Only a few more people arrive. Attendance would have to be considered a disappointment. Finally, without warning, the lights go out. Moments later they're back on, and inside the ring is a fat man, 300 pounds if he's an ounce, rampaging around the ring, shouting *amateur* this, *amateur* that. The ringside announcer introduces the fat man, who wrestles under the name of Wild Bill. Now *this* is the match we've come to see!

In a corner of the gym, two security guards pull open the door to the boys' locker room. Out comes Dr. Sam Sheppard, pumped up and naked to the waist, his buzzed head bowed. He is snarling.

Some of us boo! Some of us cheer! Some of us labor under the delusion of professional objectivity. Some also laugh. We're not sure if Dr. Sam is or is not in on the joke. We have no idea if Dr. Sam is supposed to be the hero or the villain. Like everything else about him, we stand on the periphery, morbidly fascinated and utterly puzzled.

The second act of American lives is a freak show.

Several more security guards (moonlighting coaches from the high school) push through the crowd. Sheppard falls in behind them. When he raises his head, it's not to look at us but at Wild Bill. "*Amateur*, huh?" Sheppard yells, pointing. "I'll show *you* what an amateur can do! Ten years in prison for a crime I didn't commit, you don't think that teaches a fellow to fight? You don't think I've had to whip men a lot more dangerous than the likes of *you*? I'll show you, you dumb ox!" He reaches the ring, grabs the ropes, climbs up. "I'll kill you!"

The match hasn't even started yet, but Wild Bill and Dr. Sam rush each other. The referee (George Strickland, a wrestler himself, who met Sheppard at a health club and suggested all this) manages to separate them, warn them, tell them he expects a fair match.

He'll kill him? What can Sam Sheppard be thinking? What we wouldn't give to be inside that man's head!

∽

AGAIN THE CUYAHOGA River burned, and again it was scarcely noticed outside Cleveland. The local TV stations all had spectacular footage of a firefighting tugboat that itself almost caught fire, but none of the national newscasts chose to air it. The *PD* and the *Press* both covered the fire amply. Photos made it out on the wire services and were used in newspapers all over the country, though rarely on the front page. There was Vietnam news. There was the impending trip to the moon. Riots, protest marches, sit-ins.

The Cuyahoga became a national laughingstock a month after it actually burned, and all because of another body of water: a tidal pool on Chappaquiddick Island. Near the pool was a bridge that a car driven by JFK's younger brother failed to negotiate. The car plunged into the brackish water. In the passenger seat was a young woman to whom the slain president's brother was not married. The brother, himself a U.S. senator, was able to swim away.

Marilyn Sheppard was murdered on the Fourth of July.

The week man first walked on the moon, Mary Jo Kopechne drowned.

It took a few days for the inevitable scandal to mount and to push the moon walk off the front page. But it happened. The issue of *Time* with Senator Kennedy on the cover (wearing a neck brace; in his first photos after his wife was murdered, Sam Sheppard, too, wore a neck brace) was among the best-selling issues in the formerly Cleveland-based magazine's history.

By chance, that same issue contained the debut of a new section: Environment. It was teased on the inside cover with a letter from the publisher and a picture of the Cuyahoga River with someone's slime-covered hand in the foreground. Inside, the story was about how polluted America's lakes and rivers had become, but it singled out Lake Erie and the Cuyahoga—even though in the case of both (unlike some other lakes and rivers we could name), cleanup measures had already begun. The story used a big photograph of the river burning.

Millions of people picked up that issue of *Time*. When they put the magazine down, they began making Cleveland jokes.

Here's a good one: What's the difference between Cleveland and the *Titanic*?

Cleveland has a better orchestra.

We've heard 'em all, but the hits just keep on comin'. Hey, hey, hey, play, *go-o-o-o-o!*

⌒⌒

DR. SAM SHEPPARD stands on a turnbuckle, breathing hard and flexing his muscles, posing, glowering, looming over the fallen Wild Bill. The big fat bejeweled gold ring Dr. Sam wears on his right hand glints in the light, even in this dull light.

We are cheering now, though some of us are still booing.

What is he thinking, above us, surrounded by us, up on that turnbuckle?

Is he thinking about those ten years in prison? Ten years in prison for a murder he either did or did not commit. (Probably not, but we can't be sure. None of us really are. The only one who knows for sure is Dr. Sam, and who knows what he's thinking?) Ten years of hard time, of being a model prisoner, of being drawn into fights worse than this one, of the daily brawny vigilance it took not to become some other convicted felon's girlfriend?

Is he thinking about Ariane? Goebbels's sister-in-law? She left him last year. The divorce will be final next month. Is he thinking about all the things she accused him of doing? The pill popping? Drinking two fifths of booze a day? Carrying guns, knives, even a hatchet? Savage bouts of irrational jealousy? Of riding his motorcycle in the snow? Of putting his convertible's top down on subzero days? Of threatening her? Beating her? *Did* he do those things?

Is Dr. Sam thinking about his son, Chip, in college now? Is he thinking about Chip's dorm room, where, after Ariane left him, he lived for a while? Is he thinking about Chip's girlfriend, that sweet young thing? Is he sorry about the time he fucked her?

If only we could get inside Dr. Sam's head!

Wild Bill stirs. He bellows like a steer with a gut wound.

Is Dr. Sam thinking, *My god, look what I've come to?* Making a sort-of living as a professional wrestler, after the malpractice suits that—after ten years in prison, ten years of metaphorical rust on his scalpel—now, in retrospect, seem inevitable? Over the course of a career, almost every doctor has a patient die who perhaps should not have. Almost every doctor gets hit with a lawsuit or three. But his were front-page national news, from New York to Los Angeles. His, effectively, ended his career.

Or is he thinking about high school, when, in a gym in Cleveland Heights a lot like this one, he was young, blond, strong, handsome, earnest, unmysterious, and admired, dressed in a yellow-and-black singlet, wrestling for the varsity? Marilyn was in the bleachers, watching him, adoring him. His life stretched out before him, a vista of limitless happy possibility.

Wild Bill stands. Staggers. Dr. Sam leaps from the turnbuckle, sails through the dank air, and tackles the 300-pound pro. Then he reaches down and picks him up, slinging him over his shoulder like a jumbo-sized sack of dog food. Dr. Sam spins around once, twice, three times, then slams Wild Bill to the canvas.

Dr. Sam is forty-five years old, but none of us would want to meet up with this guy in a dark alley.

"Amateur, huh?" Dr. Sam taunts, standing over Wild Bill. "Fight me, fatso!"

How can anyone truly fake such rage?

Sheppard turns his back on Wild Bill and begins to bow to the crowd. He circles the ring and bows, again and again and again. Suddenly there is no cheering, no booing. We are stunned silent. We can't *imagine* how this man's story could get any more strange.

(This is a failure of imagination. Next month, after his divorce is final, Sam Sheppard will tour the armories, roller rinks, and third-rate sports arenas of the American South, losing night after night, his role of villain more clearly defined. At the end of each evening, he and George Strickland join forces and wrestle together, tag-team partners in a steel-cage death match. They never die. Every other night they win. Strickland's twenty-year-old daughter goes on the tour along with her father. She and Sheppard fall in love. At the end of the tour, she hops on the back of Sam Sheppard's motorcycle and they ride south, into Mexico. They return a week later and claim to be married. They move into a spare bedroom at George Strickland's house on the outskirts of Columbus, Ohio. In April, in the wee small hours of the morning, Sam Sheppard wakes up shivering, on fire with a fever, speaking in tongues. Among the few coherent things he shouts is Marilyn's name. He gets up and goes to look for his medical bag. He finds it, but before he can take anything, he collapses onto the cold linoleum of the kitchen floor. Age at time of death: forty-six. Call it natural causes.)

Behind Dr. Sam (who is still bowing), Wild Bill stirs. Wild Bill again rises to his feet. He shakes out the cobwebs. Some of us scream. We try to warn Dr. Sam, but he is oblivious.

Wild Bill grabs Dr. Sam's shoulders from behind and slams him to the canvas. "Amateurs shouldn't wrestle professionals!" he shouts.

Dr. Sam pops right back up, like a muscle-bound blowup toy, and feints with his right fist, as if he's going to throw a punch to his opponent's fat gut. That would be illegal! But before any of us can even get the *boo* out of our throats, Wild Bill flinches, Dr. Sam stops the punch, and—*bam!*—thrusts his thumb into the man's gaping mouth, grabs his chin, and squeezes. *Squeezes!* The fat man shrieks, then slumps to the canvas. He is out cold.

Of *course!* The mandibular nerve! Sam Sheppard is, or was, a doctor.

We should have seen it coming. What a great gimmick! We cheer! Some of us despite ourselves, but we do cheer.

The match took eight minutes: forever, if you're a pro, if this is your life.

George Strickland raises Dr. Sam's right arm in triumph. Again, his ring catches the light. Inscribed on its side are the words *vincit qui patitur*. He who endures conquers. We cheer until we taste blood, until his hand curls into something like a fist, until every man, woman, and child in that gymnasium shivers, and feels wrongfully accused.

The end.